⚜ FOR THE ⚜
BLOODY
MARQUESA!

THE CONFLICTS: BOOK II

ZACHARY T. SELLERS

For the Bloody Marquesa!
© Copyright 2023 | Zachary T. Sellers

Cover Art © Micah Epstein
Cover Designer: James T. Egan of Bookfly Design
Map Illustrator: Tracy Porter aka Pixeleidown
Art Content: Doan Trang
Editor and Formatter: Kristin Campbell @ C&D Editing

Identifiers: LCCN: 2023914294 | ISBN 979-8-9857045-6-3 (Hardback); ISBN 979-8-
9857045-7-0 (Paperback); ISBN 979-8-9857045-8-7 (Ebook)

Contents

BOOKS BY
ZACHARY T. SELLERS

THE CONFLICTS

THE NEW HARTLAND CIVIL WAR
1109 N.F. (E.Y.) –

For the Prince! For the Queen!

DESRYOL WARS OF
REUNIFICATION
1109 N.F. (E.Y.) –

For the Bloody Marquesa!

Acknowledgements

Welcome to my second book in my three-book opener to my fantasy series. As readers of my first book know, the root stories of my fantasy world go all the way back to 2006 and have grown over time. This story and storyline can be considered the youngest of the three openers and developed outside of my original story that I drafted in high school. It's also gone through the most changes of any storyline to date that, while some names sprinkled here and there are the same, it is mostly a completely different direction.

Still, there are people to thank. First again are my parents, Clark and Pam Sellers, for their continued support. My father, as well, continues to be my unofficial beta reader.

I also wish to thank my returning beta readers for this book: Nita Fowler, Donald Gooch, Brett Roberts, Kirsten Simmons, Forrest Stobaugh, and Elizabeth Talkington. Thank you all again for taking the time to read this book, which has a different tone and new characters from my first book, and providing me with more honest feedback.

Kristin Campbell at C&D Editing once again did an excellent job as being my books' editor and formator. She continues to edit my work with the professionalism and care I have come to expect and admire from her.

I wish to recognize the returning artists who brought their talents into this book. Doan Trang created the illustrations for each character's chapters and Tracey Porter, aka Pixeleiderdown, created the map yet again to bring another setting of my world to life. Master cover artist, Micah Epstein, created yet another masterpiece for this book's cover art. Lastly, James T. Egan of Bookfly

Design brought all the pieces together to make a great design for the overall cover.

Thank you to everyone on this list and your individual contributions. And thank you, dear readers, as well, and I hope you all enjoy.

Dedication

To my old friend, Morgan Cook.

Map

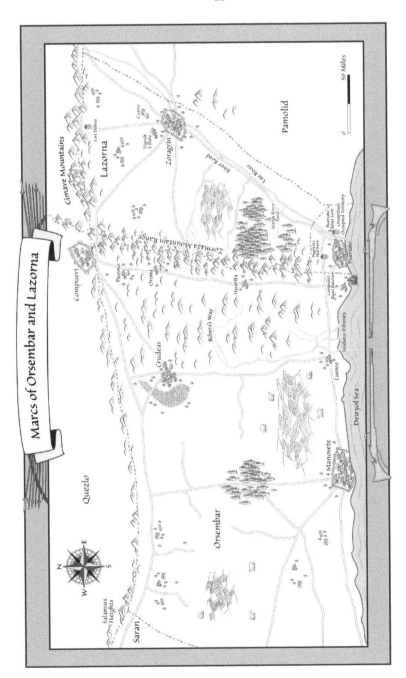

Marcs of Orsembar and Lazorna

Prologue

11th of Aster, 1016 N.F. (w.y.)

Dama Recha Mandas pressed her face into her hands but had no more tears left to shed. Her cheeks stung and clammily stuck to her palms. When she pulled them away, her skin peeled apart, and she blinked to adjust to the room's poor lighting.

She sat huddled in a corner, unable to leave yet desperate to avoid glancing at the body laid out in the center of the room. A stubborn holdout in her heart anchored her to her chair, hoping that merely refusing to accept the truth would change it.

It didn't. He was still there.

Dark drapes covered the windows of the small, square room. Besides the few chairs along the back wall around Recha, a lone, ornamental table sat in the center, with four, lilac-scented candles standing at its corners. The observation room was meant to be a place where fallen Heroes of the Campaigns were presented for the marqués's visual, to be honored before the corpses were sent to their families.

Recha hated this room. It was frivolous and served no meaning but for her uncle to say some practiced words of sacrifice and glory the dead had performed for the marc before going back to his senseless game. Him and all the other marquéses and marquesas.

A fluttering shadow caught her eye. One of the drapes wasn't fully shut, sending a beam of white sunlight cutting through the center of the room. Her eyes followed it, back to her beloved's face.

Why are there birds still flying? she lamented. *Why did the Westerly Sun rise today?*

She weakly pushed herself to her feet and shuffled over to the body. Death mired Sebastian's handsome face. His coppery skin was gray, and his angular features were sunken in. Someone had shaved his face and slicked back his dark hair, revealing the fresh nicks and cuts he'd received in battle. His other wounds were all stitched up and covered up by the fine suit and purple burial cloths he was laid out in.

Recha snickered despite herself. He looked ridiculous.

You hated purple, she recalled, looking him over and shaking her head. *Just as much as you hated shaving.*

He'd been trying to grow a beard over the last few years. Instead, all he could manage was a rugged, scruffy look. Fortunately for him, it had worked in his favor. He'd teased her with how prickly it was when they would share kisses and in their most intimate moments. Those moments now, like him, were all gone.

Recha's face contorted. Her heart thundered in her chest, signaling another bout of grief. Yet, instead of tears, something else erupted deep within her, something she had held in during the honor's procession.

"Why?" she hissed, the dam within her breaking. She leapt at the table, cupping Sebastian's cold face in her hands. "Why? Why? *Why!*" Her wail reverberated in the small room. She squeezed his face, as if the force of her demanding cry would breathe life back into him long enough to answer her. "You didn't have the men," she said, her tight grip making his head vibrate. "You didn't have the supplies. The intelligence on the enemy. A strategy. Your *Companions*! Nothing! *Why!*" Recha pressed her face into his chest, her shoulders sporadically rising and falling from her haggard breaths. Tears amazingly sprung from her eyes and stained his clothes.

His scent barely remained. In its place was alcohol and clove to keep the smell of decay at bay. But Recha didn't care.

"Why?" She rubbed her face against his chest. "It makes no sense."

"Betrayal."

Recha hissed and jumped up from the table, whipping her head around at the still, haunting voice. She brushed her dark bronze hair out of face, composing herself while facing the man looming silently in the doorway.

"What are you doing here?" she asked cautiously.

Harquis Escri took a careful, measured step into the room with his fingertips pressed together in front of his waist. He neither paused nor looked about the room. He couldn't. The flickering candlelight danced in his eyes' white pupils. His long, bald head drew one's gaze to his pointing, hooked nose and distant expression. Despite being blind—for the most part—his thin mustache and beard were neatly trimmed to points, as well.

"My Master sent me," he replied. His drawn-out steps finally led him before Sebastian's body, where he stopped.

A chill ran up Recha's spine, and she risked a glance at the medallion hanging from the man's shoulders and across the center of his chest—the Pink Eye of the Viden de Verda. She had found the cult laughable as a youth. Their symbol itself seemed preposterous. She couldn't believe anyone could find an eye emblazoned in pink intimidating. Even against the red of Harquis's doublet and brass buttons, the emblem stood out.

Then she had met Harquis, and his *Master*. People calling them Seers of Truth was not hyperbole.

"Why?" Recha asked guardedly.

"He foresaw calamity," Harquis replied.

"He?" She snickered. "Don't you mean *it*? Of course, given your master's vessel, shouldn't you say *she*?"

Harquis's expression remained placid, ignoring the jab. "My Master saw disaster. One which requires my attention to possibly correct."

"Your attention?" Recha arched a thin eyebrow, but as the white void of his eyes bored into her, her eyes began to widen. She stood in silence, feeling as if the man stared into down into her core.

Until Harquis slowly bowed his head and turned, looking up and down Sebastian's body.

"He is Scorched," he announced.

Recha took a shaky step back, frantically looking between the cultist and her dead beloved. The hairs on the back of her neck stood on end.

"Don't play games with me, Seer of Betrayal," she hissed.

"I never lie about what I see," Harquis replied, calmly raising his head. "This man, all the men he saved"—his head twitched toward her—"you . . .. The Blue Flame has Scorched you all. And it walks these very castle halls."

The pounding of Recha's heart drowned all sound from her ears. Most called the cultists tricksters, promising to reveal truths to the downtrodden and desperate. Many doubted they had any strange, mystical powers. The Church of the Savior, the historical church of Lazorna and the other marcs of Desryol held this cult of truth, which claimed its Master granted their followers the knowledge to see through the lies of this world and mystical powers to its most devote, as either dangerous, nonsense, or a pathetic nuisance.

Harquis was different.

If he claimed to see blue flames engulfing someone, that meant betrayal burned in their hearts, whether it be betraying an oath or a person. Those who were betrayed, he called Scorched, because they appeared as burnt corpses to him.

"Who?" she said aloud, but more as a thought.

Many had been jealous of Sebastian after his successful effort in last year's campaign. He and his Companions had made a daring strike into Pamolid, the marc to their east. They had defeated a larger army in detail, had seized lands further south along the Sea of Desryol, and had widened Lazorna's grip of the Laz River. A rarity in these days when most commanding officers would cower, negotiate, and sell out their own men to save their social positions rather than face a greater force in battle. His men had proclaimed him the Hero of Laz, and that had made him enemies from barons, marshals, and other calleroses.

But which of them . . .? Who could have considered Borbin would attack Puerlato? She knew any of them could have conspired to bring her beloved low, but none of them could have planned Orsembar's sudden attack. It was also *inconceivable* any of them would have schemed to sacrifice an entire city in the process, too.

"The Blue Flames command these very castle walls," Harquis said in a hush.

Recha sprang her head up. Harquis had stalked around the table without a sound and now stood before her. Shadows covered his face, out of reach of the candlelight.

His assertion sent her mind spinning, and she remembered the procession. She had sat alone, away from everyone, and Cornelos, one of the Companions, had approached her.

"A day," he had said. *"Orders were delayed by a day. If we'd gotten them sooner, Hiraldo would have reached Puerlato in time."*

The words had meant nothing to her at the time. Nothing spoken during the procession had meant anything to her. She had still been reeling with the fact that Sebastian laid dead on that table.

But Harquis's presence, the delay in orders, and her question of who was in position to betray her beloved, those pieces fell neatly into place.

"My uncle," she said softly, barely a whisper.

Harquis stiffly nodded.

"You've seen him?"

Another stiff nod.

Recha turned away. The white beam slicing between the space in the drapes made her squint.

Why, Uncle? She breathed heavily through her nose, her pulse quickening. *Why? Campaign is upon us. Lazorna needs every man! Why? Sebastian was a hero—*

She sniffed sharply, every muscle in her body tensing. The answer was obvious, and she couldn't believe she hadn't seen it. More had been jealous of Sebastian's distinction and success than she had realized.

"Savior *forsake* him!" she hissed.

Her hands balled into fists, digging her fingernails into her palms until she felt a piercing sting. She growled, and her breathing quickened. Everything within her screamed, demanding someone pay. Demanding someone bleed.

"My Master stands with you," Harquis whispered behind her, "if we can reach an accord."

My Companions will stand with me, as well, Recha thought. *And they're all here now. With their contingents.*

She grabbed the drapes, taking deep, calming breaths. However, her mind was already made up.

"Very well," she said, pulling the drapes closed. "What is this accord?"

~~~

The smell of roasting meat wafted down the castle's corridors from the banquet hall. Boisterous laughter bounced off the close, stone hallways. They, and the long, checkered red and black rug, muffled Recha's slipper heels while she straightened her hair and violet veil over her face on her way to the feast.

Just a simple excuse, she assured herself while making sure her hair covered her mangled left ear. A deformity of childbirth. The nurse had been too eager in pulling her from her mother, leaving her left ear misshapen and the cartilage curling in the wrong direction. Sebastian had always assured her it took nothing away from her, but she had always retorted that it was impossible for a woman to consciously forget about it. Thus, she always made sure her hair was long enough to cover it.

Uncle's not going to care if I'm late, she told herself, straightening the square neckline of her black dress and loosening the red lace embroidery around its edges from digging into her collarbone and making her itch. *Not as if my advice is particularly welcomed.* She sniffed disdainfully.

She turned the corner, and the soldiers standing guard by the banquet hall's open archway snapped their halberds against their shiny breastplates. The candlelight reflected off the ridges of their capped helms. She gave them a passing glance before grimacing at the campaign feast.

5

The banquet hall's three open firepits cast crimson shadows dancing on the stretched, vaulted, stone ceiling. A large carcass was divided between the pits, mounted on spits. The marbled flesh puckered and sizzled, despite the dining was apparently mostly over. The gentlemen at the two long tables down the sides of the hall were mostly conversing with each other instead of gorging themselves.

They slaughtered a torago? Recha gritted her teeth at the large ribcage divided among the three pits; the largest in the center pit half the length of a man. Most of the meat had been carved off the center ribs, while few above the smaller ones were left roasting untouched.

Toragos were large beasts, twice the size of bulls, which swam and fed in and around the rivers and inlets of the Sea of Desryol. They used to be numerous, but centuries of hunting had nearly wiped them out. Now, they were delicacies of the marcs, their meat belonging only to the marquéses and marquesas.

What a waste, she thought at seeing the meager size of the attendees. Half of the long tables sat empty, so most of the meat would go uneaten. The deberes spent on this show of vanity would never be recovered.

"Ah!" her uncle's nasally voice cut over the den. "Recha, my dear. You grace us with your presence."

Her uncle, Si Don Berlito Agrin, Marqués of Lazorna, motioned her forward from his table that sat elevated at the back of the hall. His feasting table—like his guest tables—was noticeably empty, with only his son, Don Credo, stuffing his chubby face beside him and an empty chair to his left.

"Forgive me, Si Don," Recha said, pressing her right hand to her heart and bowing her head while pulling her skirts to the side with her left hand. "I wasn't hungry and didn't wish my lack of appetite to sour the mood of your feast."

"Of course," her uncle said. "Lazorna mourns the loss of a promising calleros this day. Are you certain you wish to attend? None here would fault you if you didn't wish to."

"No, dear Uncle. There will be time to mourn later." Recha rose, her veil covering her glare. "I am *very* interested in our plans for this year's campaign."

"Very well then." Her uncle sounded disappointed, unsurprisingly. Women didn't generally attend campaign feasts. Baronesses and the calleroses's wives viewed them with as little regard as tavern backrooms where they husbands could drink, eat, belch, and play games before coming home. That was all the campaigns were to them and their husbands—a game.

Despite being the largest landholders in Lazorna, barons were more a hinderance to campaign efforts than anything else. If they weren't demanding commanding positions in the army, they were complaining about their roles, their expenses, their calleroses, their supplies, or the ever-existent complaints over taxes.

The calleroses, men-at-arms trained from birth to fight and represent the barons and marc in the campaigns and command the ranks, were a mixed group. Some viewed their station as a means of service for their families. Few embraced their station, becoming true soldiers and leaders of men, like her Sebastian. Far too many shared their barons' views that campaigns were games, serving to gain more favor with their barons while the barons served to gain more favor with the marqués. Too many of those happened to be here tonight.

Recha walked behind the left-side long table, not sparing a glance for the men sitting there or across the room. She could feel their eyes on her, though.

I know what you're thinking. She took advantage of her veil and bit her lip to keep from snarling. *Sebastian's dead. Making me an available woman. As if any of you could take his place.*

She stepped up onto the dais to her uncle's table with servants scurrying about, readying her place. One poor fellow ran all the way around to slice a flank of meat, while others fixed the rest of her plate with bread, cheeses, and carrots, and poured her wine—Crudeas violet, she deduced from the liquid's dark purple, nearly black color.

While she waited, her uncle's banner hanging on the back wall caught her eye. It was slanted. One of the nails had come loose, and a frayed, yellow cord threatened to pull it out. The gold design was supposed to be a flower on a white field. The stem was too wide, though, and from how it curved up into the swirls, which were supposed to be its petals, Recha thought it resembled smoke bellowing out of those new cast iron pots that had sprung up a few years ago. Bombards, the calleroses called them. New toys for sieges.

If only we could besiege an enemy instead of being besieged ourselves.

A servant cleared his throat, holding her chair out and waiting.

"Thank you," Recha replied softly before smoothing her skirts and sitting.

"Are you sure you are well?" her uncle asked.

A man of middling years, the sides of his head were turning gray while the tips of his thin mustache were as oily as ever. His dark eyes watched her over his pointed nose, and his concern seemed genuine. However, his smile was strained. Forced. He reached for his wine and drank, revealing a small trail of sweat running down the side of his face.

Recha watched him out of the corner of her eye. Her uncle had once been a stalwart marqués, according to Sebastian's father, Baltazar Vigodt. Yet, his once marshal frame had gone soft long ago, and now threatened to go to fat.

Unlike his son, Credo, who was sprinting toward obesity as fast as he could. His marigold doublet stretched over his round frame. His undershirt and the folds of his belly stuck out under the garment's strained edges as he sat, still gobbling down slices of meat.

Recha picked at the meat on her plate. It was cooked all the way through and tough to pierce with her fork, narrowly burnt.

More waste.

The scraping of wood against stone made her look up.

"Si Don!" Marshal Migel Lluch, the eldest of the three marshals at the head of the right-side table, stood with his wine goblet raised. "My barons! My fellow calleroses! Before we proceed with our plans for this year's campaign, I wish to offer a toast. To fallen comrades! May they march with us in the battles to come."

Several of the other calleroses stood, but the rest merely raised their goblets, including the other marshals and barons.

Marshal Lluch's hazel eyes gleamed at her from over his goblet while he drank. He had led the relief force, which had become a bulwark against the Orsembar advance, saving the remainder of Sebastian's force from being taken prisoner and recovering his body.

He means Sebastian, she surmised, *but won't say his name. Or maybe . . .?*

She again glanced at her uncle, who sipped his wine.

Recha stood up, drawing most of the eyes in the room, and raised her cup. "To fallen comrades," she repeated to Marshal Lluch. "And lost heroes."

Marshal Lluch nodded to her, and Recha tilted her head back and drank.

The sweetness of grape and the spike of alcohol rushed down her throat, but instead of sipping, she took steady gulp after gulp until she gasped after the cup was drained. Her cheeks flushed warmly, and her head spun briefly as she took deep breaths to calm herself. A buzzing tingle ran through her body, and she remained standing to let it pass. When she straightened her head, she looked out to see all the men in the room gawking at her.

What? Never seen a bereaved lover drink before?

She turned her cup upside down and slammed it onto the table. The crack of wood against wood bounced against the stone walls as she sat, leaving the ringing in everyone's ears.

"Dare I say, cousin," Credo said, mulling over his own wine cup, "you should go easy on the furniture, as well as the wine. Such fine things should be appreciated." He chuckled, wobbling his pudgy cheeks, and drained his cup with a loud, slurping gulp.

"I won't be appreciating them for a while," she retorted, leaning forward to make sure everyone heard what she said next. "I swear, wine will not touch my lips again until Puerlato is reclaimed and Cal Sebastian Vigodt is avenged!"

A few of the calleroses clapped their cups on the table. Otherwise, the rest remained quiet, save for a couple extra grunts.

Credo snickered. "Rather bold, don't you think, Recha?"

"If you hadn't noticed, dear *cousin*, we've been invaded!" Recha shot back. "Now *is* the time to be bold. This year's campaign hasn't even started, and we're *already* on the back foot."

"Agreed," her uncle said, standing and putting himself between them. "My barons and calleroses, as you are all aware, for the past two months, we've assembled our army and campaign supplies in and around Estribac. I'm sure many of you believed I planned to strike into Quezlo this year . . . but those plans have changed."

We better be marching to push them out of Puerlato.

"For a year, I've been in negotiations with Marqués Borbin in an allied push against Compuert," her uncle said, pulling out a folded parchment from his doublet. "Borbin's betrayal has changed everything and, instead, I have proposed an alliance with Marqués Dion. Just last week, he signed the agreement. This year, we campaign with Quezlo *against* Orsembar!"

Recha sat, taken aback like the rest of the room. Alliances were common during the campaigns. Too common. They were made, shifted, and broken each passing year. They often broke down during campaigns from either both sides not fully trusting the other or fearing betrayals if victory was achieved. They hardly brought the gains the allied parties hoped for in the beginning. They also took time to build.

But this one did have promise.

If Quezlo strikes from Compuert, like usual, any reinforcements Borbin can send to Puerlato will be needed to blunt them. Recha contemplated while biting the inside of her cheek. *We could push them out!*

It was feasible, although she doubted they would gain much. Probably just retake what they had lost. They would have to march quickly before the Orsembar forces surrounding Puerlato could entrench—

"Marshal Ismun Mola," her uncle said, pointing at the marshal at the end of the right-side table.

The middle-aged man rose, straightened his back, and snapped a salute—clapping his heels together coupled with a sharp nod and his hands to his side. While he probably thought he was smiling pridefully, his smile was crooked and made his wide eyes bulge and his large ears more prominent. The pair of reading spectacles hanging off his waistcoat made him appear more like a clerk than calleros.

"You will take command of the army," her uncle ordered. "In a fortnight, you will march through Estribac and join the Quezlo army. With our combined forces, we drive into the very heartland of Orsembar and claim as much as possible before Marqués Borbin can react!" He barked a laugh. "We might just reach the gates of Manosete before he even realizes!" He sat back down and smugly watched the reactions.

That's . . . Recha's mind raced from his implications, *ridiculous!*

"Have the divisions of conquered lands been decided yet?" Baron Ristal asked.

"Or the supply requirements?" Baron Ibarra added, both men practically speaking over each other to be first.

Of course, Recha chided, *Ristal's only concern is what he can gain, and Ibarra's is what he has to pay.* Both barons held lands around Zoragrin, Lazorna's capital and her uncle's main backers.

"All in good time," her uncle assured, chuckling. "We first need to conquer to divide. The supply requirements are as usual for this season."

Baron Ristal sat back and nursed his wine, but Baron Ibarra was pleased enough.

Happy your campaign taxes aren't going up, are you? Recha wanted to yell. *That's pointless compared to what we all could be—*

"What about the Orsembian forces in Puerlato?" Baron Puig asked. The soft-spoken man sat with his elbows on the table, holding his hands as if to catch his head should he fall forward. From the hollowed-eyed look and bags under his close-set eyes, the baron appeared to be on the verge of collapse. "They were marching into my lands when Marshal Lluch stopped them and nearly overran my estate. How are we going to stop them without the rest of the army if they come again?"

Recha watched her uncle out of the corner of her eye again. Goosebumps ran down her arms. This was it. The crucial answer that would tell her everything.

"I understand your concerns, Baron Puig," her uncle replied. "Having one's home invaded to such an extent is not one any of us should relish."

The barons shifted, notably avoiding glancing at the empty place left for Baron Gordon of Puerlato. He hadn't made the retreat with Sebastian.

Likely eating in a feast with his Orsembian conquers, I'd imagine. Recha balled her fists in her lap to prevent them from shaking. *That's what barons do— run from the opposing side until they can't. And then join them.*

"But I am confident," her uncle continued, "with Marshal Lluch's forces holding the line and our combined armies attacking Orsembar from their northeast, the Orsembian forces will not advance any further. In fact, I'm *certain* Borbin will withdraw as many troops as he can from Puerlato to throw against our advance. He won't risk those lands, his greatest achievement, being taken away from him. So, never fear, Baron Puig. Within in two weeks, the Orsembians will be withdrawing from your lands, probably entirely, I assure you." Her uncle took up his goblet again and held it out to Puig before confidently drinking.

Puig cupped his face in his hands and rubbed his eyes, making his tangled combover wobble precariously. Despite another baron clasping his shoulder, little could help Puig's exhausted attitude.

There was no help for Marshal Lluch, either. The seasoned marshal sat deflated in his chair, arms folded in his lap and head hung. The image of a military man given orders resembling a death warrant.

"That's . . . *ridiculous*," Recha hissed under her breath.

Her uncle's sip turned into a slurp. He arched an eyebrow briefly over the rim of his goblet before his eyes went wide and he snorted. "What?" he coughed, wiping the stray droplets of wine off his face. "What was that?"

Recha inwardly cursed herself for her tactless outburst, but there was no hiding her feelings now.

"Your plan, Uncle," she replied, keeping her voice calm yet firm. "It's based on too many assumptions and . . . too hopeful to be realistic. Did you even change your campaign plans after Puerlato fell?"

Her uncle sighed. "Recha, we all know you think yourself as a campaign planner, given your . . . early upbringing. But this year's plan is complex. There're more concerning matters involved this year. Matters more experienced minds have looked over and given their blessing."

"Yours? Or Marqués Dion's?"

Recha's uncle was stubborn. On past campaigns, he had refused to allow changes to tactics and strategies to answer circumstances on the ground or to break the conventions of the Rules of Campaign, even when Lazorna would have benefited. She doubted Marqués Dion cared for Lazorna's sudden change in fortunes, either.

Her uncle slammed his cup on the table. "There is no call for such accusations! Especially when we're on the cusp of such a grand enterprise."

Credo snorted. "She's just upset we're not sending everyone to avenge her precious *hero*."

Recha glared at her cousin through her veil. His sweaty face flushed brightly, and still, he continued to drink. Instead of snapping at him, she turned her ire back on her uncle.

"Your *grand enterprise* is dead," she hissed, "and wouldn't have been grand if it succeeded. How long do you think it'll take the Orsembian army to hear you've counterattacked? Two weeks? *Three*? They'll have Zoragrin under siege by then and won't even *care*!"

"Now you're just being hysterical," Credo chided, rolling his eyes. "Honestly, Recha, so much fuss over a man who wasn't even your husband."

Recha slapped the table and leapt to her feet, toppling over her chair. "He should have *been*!"

Her outburst rang through the hall. Everything went eerily quiet, save the wood popping in the firepits and her haggard breathing.

Sebastian had asked her uncle for her hand when he'd been declared Hero of the Laz, but her uncle had refused, claiming he was still a calleros and needed more honors to marry the niece of a marqués. Recha held her suspicions that the denial was based more on her uncle indecisively clinging to use her in a possible marriage-alliance that would undoubtedly be as ridiculous as his campaign plans. Lazorna's weak position and obscurity among the neighboring marcs had likely saved her from that nightmarish battle.

"Recha"—her uncle glowered up at her—"you're letting your emotions get the better of you."

"As if you haven't, Uncle," she hissed back.

He slowly rose to his feet and attempted to loom over her, despite being the same height as her. A servant rushed to drag his chair back.

"Watch your tone," he growled, "or this will be the last campaign feast you'll ever attend."

"There won't be another campaign feast," Recha retorted. "The Orsembian army will smash our defenses before our army attacks."

"*Enough!*"

Recha yelled over him. "They'll be at our gates before the end of the month!"

"Get out!" Her uncle pointed toward the exit.

"By the time our army claims a *foot* of Orsembian soil, Lazorna will have *fallen!*" Recha screamed.

Slap!

Her veil obscuring her sight, Recha hadn't seen him rear back until her uncle had slapped her across the face. Her head snapped around. The force of the blow ripped her veil off and sent it flying over the table. She reeled, turning with the blow, and fell against the table. She slammed her hands against the tabletop, barely catching herself in time to stop from falling on the remaining food.

"Dama Recha Mandas," her uncle said in an official sounding tone, "you are no longer welcomed at my campaign feasts. Now and forever! Now get out and clean yourself up."

Recha heard him flop back into his chair with a sigh, but she remained bent over the table. She caught sight of her veil, resting on the edge of the nearest firepit. A lick of flame caught it. She dug her fingernails into the table's wood and watched the silk flare and quickly burn.

"You killed him," she said coldly.

Her uncle sighed. "Do *not* make call the guards to escort you out."

Recha peered through her eyelashes without raising her head. "What guards?"

"Guards!" her uncle yelled. "Come in here!"

Seconds passed in silence. No response.

As more moments passed, the barons and calleroses turned, one by one, in their seats and toward the exit.

"*Guards!*" her uncle called again.

Recha straightened and smoothed out her dress. While she did, she reached into the small pouch sewn into the side.

Her uncle sat up, staring perplexed at the end of the feast hall. He turned to his right, clutching the arms of his chair, and said, "Where are my guards?"

"You don't need guards anymore," Recha said coldly.

Her uncle wheeled around.

Recha pulled out a hand pistol from an inner fold in her dress and pressed the barrel into the center of her uncle's forehead. It was a small weapon—two hands long—and light. The polished wood incased in silver handle perfectly curved into her palm.

Sebastian had commissioned a special pair made from weapons merchant after his triumphant campaign. He'd shown her how to clean it, how to load it, and how to shoot it. She wrapped her finger around the trigger.

"Recha?" her uncle gasped. His eyes were trembling, and sweat poured down his face. His back bowed, but his chair's armrests prevented him from pulling away. "What are—"

"Do you take me for a fool, Uncle?" she asked. "It takes more than a couple of weeks to correspond with Quezlo. You must have been talking with Marqués Dion for months to have an accord in hand now. And, all the while, you were making promises to Marqués Borbin. *Marqués Borbin*, who's notorious for making brutal examples! You sent Sebastian to command our border against a man like that with *nothing*! And then you *abandoned* him!" She cocked the fascinating locking mechanism with a swift pull of her thumb. "I swore Sebastian would be avenged against *everyone* who betrayed him. Remember?"

"*Recha—*"

Pow!

The pistol's trigger was a gentle squeeze. The burning, sulfuric smoke of the powder made Recha's nose wrinkle and eyes water. She stared, numb at the sight of a small, black hole in the center of her uncle's forehead. A small trail of blood slowly oozed out, and he jerked.

Her uncle's eyes rolled inward. His mouth gaped as a long hiss escaped his throat, and he fell back in his seat to dangle in the corner where the armrest connected to the chair's back.

Visibly shook, Credo stared, wide-eyed and horrified, at his father's contorted appearance.

"*Ah!*" Behind her, Baron Ristal wheezed as a servant repeatedly stabbed him in the back.

Baron Ibarra's terrified scream at his fellow baron's butchery sounded much too feminine and was silenced when another servant slashed his throat.

"To arms!" Marshal Ismun roared.

His head was caved in by a hammer before he was an inch out of his seat. The calleros beside him barely had time to turn before Harquis's backhanded swing cracked the side of his skull, too, and sent the man sprawling on the floor.

The feasting hall erupted into a den of slaughter and haunting howls. Knife-wielding servants, revealing themselves as Viden in disguise, mercilessly fell on every calleros loyal to her uncle, Baron Ristal, and Baron Ibarra, slicing and stabbing them like the hunks of meat they had eaten for supper. The rest were hoisted from their chairs with knives at their throats and dragged to the center of the room in front of the marqués's table.

Recha numbly watched. There was no surge of joy. No delighted glee. No satisfaction by watching her uncle's petty rabble slaughtered like cattle. Nor horror or revulsion from seeing throats slit and bellies stabbed or listening to the dying men plead for their lives. Everything felt muted, as if she watched and listened through thick, paned glass.

"Why?"

The hairs on the back of Recha's neck stood up at the whimper. Turning her neck stiffly, she looked to see Credo cradling his father's head, tears running down his flushed, round cheeks.

"Why?" Credo cried up at her. "We're family. Why—"

The spike end of a hammer smashed the round top of his cranium, cracking his head like a melon. Like his father before him, Credo spasmed and jerked, his mouth gaping while his eyes rolled inward. He fell backward, but his bulk made his chair crack under the weight and spilled him out onto the floor, spilling the gore from his head wound.

"Family does not betray family," Harquis said, stepping around her uncle's chair. Blood dripped from the hammer at his side. Although blind, he was able to wield it. His empty eyes stared back at her, cold and blank from the death he and his cult members had wrought.

There's no turning back now, Recha told herself at the sound of marching footfalls from the hallway outside.

Despite the hopeful looks that the remaining barons and calleroses made over their shoulders, those looks fell when they saw the soldiers storming into the room, wearing Vigodt velvet and red. Cornelos, Hiraldo, and Sevesco, her beloved's Companions, led at their head. Their appearance meant one thing.

Zoragrin was taken.

"Dama," a gruff voice said. "Dama Mandas."

Recha shook her head.

The remaining barons sat on their knees, their shoulders hunched, and their heads bowed. It was Marshal Lluch who had spoken, standing behind them with two cult members holding him by the arms.

Recha's forearm ached. All through the slaughter, she had kept her pistol leveled ever since pulling the trigger, and now her raised arm was on the verge of trembling. She dropped her arm to her side and pulled strands of hair out of her face, collecting herself.

"You may speak, Marshal Lluch," she said, her voice soft, almost to the point of cracking.

"May I ask the meaning of this? Do you know what you've done?"

She stared back into the aged marshal's steely gaze. It was resolute, as if accepting his fate.

He thinks I plan on murdering them all.

"I know exactly what I've done, Marshal," she replied, sliding her pistol back into her dress pouch but keeping her hand shoved inside so no one would notice it shaking. "I've taken revenge on one of the men responsible for Sebastian Vigodt's death."

Recha gave her uncle one final look. Blood still ran from the small hole in his forehead, across his face, dripped off his cheek, and onto the floor.

"And now," she addressed the remaining barons and calleroses, "I will take responsibility for my uncle's death. From this night, as my uncle's closest living relative, *I* am Marquesa of Lazorna! And I swear I will have the rest of my vengeance. On the Orsembians. On Marqués Borbin! On this Era of Campaigns! I will see it *all* torn down and over. Once and for all!"

Her Companions led the soldiers in a boisterous cheer, but the barons and their calleroses remained stone silent. She knew the claim sounded too bold, one that all the other marqués and marquesas had discarded nearly a century ago. Recha intended to keep it. She also knew actions carried more weight than rousing speeches.

"Now, Marshal Lluch"—she waved for a servant to pick up her chair so she could sit—"how long would you need to march the entire army south?"

~~~

The patter of rain falling against a distant window, coupled with the lounge's soft cushion, made it harder and harder for Recha to keep her eyes open.

15

Her body yearned for sleep. Her muscles throbbed and ached from continuous strain, longing to relax. Her head dipped from the lack of strength to keep it up.

Every time her eyes closed though, she saw her uncle and Credo staring back at her. Her uncle demanding. Credo pleading. Both haunting.

You deserved it! she screamed inwardly while her eyelids fluttered. *You sent Sebastian to die!*

Neither spoke. Instead, blood ran down their faces, and they turned pale.

Why? Recha growled, throwing her head back. *Why am I questioning myself now?*

She wiped her brow and flung sweat and stray strands of hair out of her face. She squeezed her eyes shut and tried to sit up, to keep her focus. The weariness came back faster this time, and her shoulders slumped.

A log cracked in the small fireplace. Recha watched the flames dance on the charred wood, casting shadows through the iron bars across the plush white carpet. They made her eyelids flutter again, and she had to look away.

The small room was lavishly furnished with black varnished furniture, a siting table, and several cushioned armchairs. The firelight barely caught the streaking rain on the small window. The world outside was as dark and foreboding as the one behind her closed eyes.

"*Taking a life is . . . strange,*" Sebastian had said to her while describing a Bravados he had answered on his first campaign. "*I had to win. But the Bravados is different from the heat of battle. You circle each other. Measure one another. Think it out. Waiting for the right moment to . . . You're different afterward. You feel it . . . somewhere. I still see his face—*"

Recha had kissed him then to make him stop. That had been a night of many firsts, and she had resolved to herself that he would never sound haunted like that again. She had made sure he would turn to her should it ever return. He had never answered a challenge during the Bravados again, though.

Now Sebastian was gone, and *she* had taken a life.

Who am I going to turn to?

A soft knock on the door made her blink, and she felt the tears running down her face. Recha hurriedly wiped them away and collected herself before the door opened.

"La Dama Mandas," a warm, motherly voice said. "Welcome to Cuevo. May Truth be your guide."

"Evening, Vastura," Recha said, refusing to be lulled by the woman's motherly aura and held the silver box she carried tightly.

Vastura was another high-ranking cultist, like Harquis. However, if Harquis was a hammer, Vastura was a gentle caress. A homely woman in her mid-forties, lines marked her round face from her permanent soft smile, and gray dusted her auburn hair to match the marble tint of her robes. Yet, just as Harquis, her eyes were milky white, and a pink eye medallion hung on her chest.

"Is your master ready to receive me?" Recha asked. She lightly tapped the silver box in her lap, knowing the cult master desired its contents.

"Naturally, the Master saw you coming," Vastura joked with a humble chuckle. "Follow me, please."

Recha didn't laugh. Not at the joke or the irony of the blind woman leading her. Despite her exhaustion, only a true believer or desperate fool would be at ease in the headquarters of the Viden de Verda. The small estate covered over ten acres north of Zoragrin, and the seven-story mansion was older than the establishment of Lazorna. The true origins of the cult and its master, though, was beyond Recha's guessing.

Yet, this wasn't the main mansion.

Vastura led Recha through the dark, tight spaces of the small house in the center of the mansion's gardens. Despite the lavish decor on the inside, it might as well have been a cottage compared to its surroundings.

Recha wrapped her arms around herself and held her silver box tightly. The house was silent and still, disturbed only by her and Vastura's footsteps. No servants. No guards. No fellow cultists walking around, chanting in robes. Just their lonely footfalls.

Vastura led her farther in, through a small door, and then down a tight corridor. Recha had been here only a couple of times before and still found the path unsettling. This time, however, she was on a mission.

Vastura opened another door that arched at the top. The smell of rain mixed with dozens of floral bouquets drifted in.

"The Master will *see* you now," Vastura said.

Recha hesitantly entered the small room, illuminated by a few lamps flickering in the corners. The chamber felt more like a prison cell than a bedchamber. No pictures hung on the bland, plaster walls. It had no windows. No books. Merely a bed with a chest at its foot, a rocking chair nestled in the corner, and a dresser off to the right.

A lump formed in the back of her throat when her eyes settled on the woman in a white nightgown standing in front of the dressing mirror.

"Elegida?" Recha called, tightly pressing the box to her chest.

The woman's eyes opened, and violent pink pupils stared back at her.

"The child wishes to sleep," the woman said in an unsettlingly deep tone.

She flickered a glance behind Recha. "You may go. The marquesa and I have much to discuss."

Vastura had remained outside the entire time and, without a word, pushed the door shut.

The woman turned, and Recha swallowed. She couldn't get passed seeing her own face staring back at her, and yet not. The same supple nose. The same thin eyebrows. The same dimpled cheeks when they smiled. Yet Elegida's skin was paler, less coppery, and blended toward pink. A white streak ran down the center part of her dark hair, and her left ear wasn't twisted or mangled.

Recha still reeled from the five-year-old shock of learning she had a twin sister, but more so that she'd been given over to the cult. She had learned she still had direct family, only to be given another blow by learning their appearance and blood were all they shared.

The mind—this *being*—which stood before her now *was not* her sister.

"I'm glad to see you were successful, Recha," the being said. "You are much more capable than your uncle"—her eyes flickered to the silver box and twinkled, her grin growing broader—"and you uphold your agreements better, too." She reached out for the box.

Recha hesitated, that hungry grin giving her pause.

Is that what I look like? she wondered. *Did I look like that when I—*

She choked back her revulsion and handed over the box.

"I keep my word," she said, "Verdas."

Verdas yanked the box away possessively, attempting a comforting smile. "Please, Recha, there's no need for animosity between us. You may call me Master if you wish."

"I am not one of your followers, spirit," Recha said sternly to Verdas' back as it took the box over to the dresser. "We're partners in this."

"Yes, yes." Verdas gave her a dismissive wave before setting the box down then gently, almost reverently, opening the lid. A violet, near-ebony glow exuded from inside.

Recha watched Verdas' face in the mirror. Its eyes went wide, cheeks twitching, and mouth agape. In an instant, it went from longing, to relieved, to pained, before closing the box back.

"Just a mere shard," Verdas said, hanging her head and leaning against the dresser. "I thought it would be larger."

"That's the Lazorna relic," Recha assured. "As promised."

"I wasn't claiming you'd not held up your part." Verdas raised its head. Those pink irises gazed back dismissively and bored. "I was only hoping it'd been bigger." It slid the box back against the mirror and straightened, pulling its hair back and frowning. As it did, the eye medallion it wore became visible, pulled back from fussing with its hair. This one, however, had a pink crystal fashioned as its pupil, sparkling against her chest. "About our continued arrangement" —Verdas tied its hair in a top knot—"I trust you understand the benefits. To us both."

"For your premonitions, I grant your . . . followers privileges," Recha said, folding her arms. "In return, you lend some of them to me to ensure the loyalty of the nobles."

Verdas sat back against the dresser and rolled its eyes. "Why do mortals always explain our agreements with disdain? I am Truth, Recha. I cannot lie."

"I've come to learn many things can be true at the same time. Beneficial *and* harmful at the same time."

Verdas hummed appreciatively. "You're much smarter than a few others I've dealt with. Yes, you'll do."

"Do what?" Recha snapped. The idea of being another one of this being's pawns didn't sit well with her. She had her own goals, her own visions. She would not allow this *thing* to believe she was her puppet, like her sister.

She stepped closer to loom over the other woman. "Since you claim to be truthful with me, I'll be truthful with you. *I* am Marquesa of Lazorna, and *I* will govern it from now on. We are partners in some endeavors, but in the end, you will serve me."

"Done posturing?" Verdas raised an eyebrow. The corners of its lips twitched as if it were about to burst out laughing. "Good. I trust you've diverted from your uncle's doomed course."

"If you're asking if I've ordered the entire army south against the Orsembians, then yes."

Verdas sighed. "Good. Then you have rescued your people from destruction. I told your uncle two years ago that if he went through with his plan to court with Borbin, he'd be thrown down by a hero and his lands pierced by a white sword. He laughed and thought I was making riddles, but the farther I look, the cloudier the picture."

Recha's body tensed until every muscle ached. Her skin crawled, and her fingernails dug into her arms. All the while, her eyebrows went higher and higher.

Hero? echoed in her mind. *Did she . . .? Did she tell my uncle . . .? Did she make him . . .?*

Recha leaped at her, grabbing it by the nightgown and ripping the silk as she pulled her to its feet. "Did you poison my uncle against Sebastian!" she screamed.

To her surprise, Verdas pulled back, startled. Recha had actually caught the spirit off guard. It only lasted a moment, though, before Verdas shook her head.

"My dear mortal," Verdas said, taking her by the wrists, "it wasn't your beloved I saw being your uncle's downfall."

Recha frowned. Her passion slowly ebbed, and she began turning over the rest of what Verdas had said.

Me? she thought at first. *Am I . . .? No. I'm no hero. Heroes don't kill their own family, even if they have the right. Then what—*

It struck her like a bolt. *White sword. White Sword.*

"*Ribera!*" Recha said in a hush. "Marshal Fuert Ribera is in Puerlato?"

Verdas nodded, smugly confident. "He is."

Recha let go and backed away, shaking, until she met the bed and sat down with a flop.

The White Sword is in Puerlato! She ran her fingers through her hair and rested her elbows on her knees. *Sebastian, you never had a chance.*

Marshal Fuert Ribera was Orsembar's most renowned marshal, with the long-earned moniker of the Hero of the White Sword because of the white sword on his banners. Ten years prior, he had led a campaign, conquering a quarter of Quezlo. He was also undefeated in the field. Reasons that slowly made Marqués Borbin call on him less and less.

Until now.

"We can't retake Puerlato," Recha said, shaking her head in despair. "Not from him. If he gets even one opening . . . even after what I've done . . . we'll still *lose!*"

Verdas calmingly shushed her. "Don't worry; you'll hold. I've seen it."

"But there's no way we'll retake Puerlato!" Recha dug her nails into her scalp, fighting the urge to scream and break something. Anything!

"You don't need Puerlato, silly Marquesa." Verdas stepped in front of her. "You just need to hold your defenses. And afterward, put a pause on these silly campaigns."

Recha frowned, thinking hard on the implications. Pausing the campaigns wasn't a bad idea, but it would hurt her reputation and the marc, if they didn't retake Puerlato.

But what if we could?

"And then?" she asked.

"Wait," Verdas replied. Its hand gently slid under Recha's chin and lifted her head up to see it grinning down at her. "And build."

Chapter 1

Necrem Oso swung his hammer down.

Ping! Ping! Ping! Metal sang on metal. Sparks flew and impurities drifted into the air, crumbling to dust.

Necrem drew a sharp breath through the nose hole of his leather face mask as one of those impurities landed on his thick left forearm. The sting of near-molten metal burning his flesh was an old acquaintance but bit the same as the first day he had felt it. He wiggled his arm, keeping a firm grip of the tongs holding the sheet of metal he was fashioning, and shook off the debris.

He shifted his footing and got in another angle before raising his hammer again.

Ping! Ping! Ping!

No debris touched him this time, and he sighed, listening to the metal sing. It was the most comforting sound he knew. It was loud and sharp, but solid and true. The sound of a lump of earth being fashioned into something more. Something useful.

So long as it wasn't a weapon.

Necrem raised his hammer again. His biceps tightened and bulged, and he was forced to pause. When hammering metal, a blacksmith must stay relaxed and not pound away believing it would take shape if he hit it enough times. A blacksmith's motions had to be practiced, methodical, almost fluid. It was something he had learned from his papa.

"*It isn't your arm that does the work,*" he would say. "*It's the hammer. Let it do the work for you.*" So, whenever Necrem felt his arm stiffen up after working for a while, he knew it was time for a break.

The new plowshare was coming along well. He still had to weld the thicker blade portion onto the moldboard and chisel, but all in good time. Good metal work couldn't be rushed.

He set the steel off to the side then laid his hammer and tongs down on the anvil. His shoulders were suddenly incredibly stiff without a hammer in his hands. He always lost himself whenever he hammered and worked on a piece, and now his body's senses were returning, demanding he stand up.

He clasped his knees with his broad, callused hands and pushed himself to his feet. Instantly, his body began to stretch. He grunted from his knees popping. Then a series of creaks and knocks ran up his spine, making him throw his arms in the air behind his head. He clenched his jaw on instinct while a groan escaped between his teeth. He couldn't risk his jaw opening wide or risk one of old his facial scars tearing and bleeding.

When the stretch finally subsided, he sighed contently and scratched his side under his leather apron. All was well for now. All was as it should be.

"That was a *big* one!"

Necrem whipped his head around then down at grinning girl bouncing on her heels in the opening of his forge.

"Just needed a good stretch," Necrem said, rubbing his right bicep. "Steel working men like your papa need them every now and then, Bayona."

Bayona rolled her baby-blue eyes. The glaring suns' light formed a halo around her shoulder-length, light brown hair.

"A man's here asking for you," she said.

"A customer?" he asked, arching an eyebrow while rolling his shoulder.

"Mmm . . .." Bayona's cute face scrunched to the side while she thought. "I don't think so. He didn't bring anything needing fixing. He said something about collecting something, but I've never seen him before."

That gave Necrem pause. Despite her age, Bayona had taken to staying up front for respective customers while he worked in the back. It gave her an opportunity to practice her spelling and learn what things were. Necrem wanted her to know how things worked, despite that she was a girl.

Collecting something? Necrem turned the child's phrase over in his head. *Collecting something . . .. A collector—*

A chill ran up his spine, and his cheeks started to twitch, irritating and pulling his scars. He glanced at the glaring light around Bayona for assurance on the time.

It's too soon for the campaign tax. So, why? Necrem clenched and unclenched his broad fists in a nervous tick while every crazy reason played out in his head.

"Should I bring him or say you're busy?" Bayona asked, breaking Necrem out of his worrying spiral.

He sighed. "No. I'll see what he wants. You can take a break from watching the front."

"Yay!" Bayona clapped and hopped, flopping her gray dress's skirts up and down.

Necrem instinctively smirked while taking off his leather apron, but a stinging tug on his cheek made him relax his face. His work mask must have dried his face out, meaning his scars were that much likely to bleed if he wasn't careful.

I'll need to apply extra salve on them tonight.

Bayona was still waiting for him when he pulled back the rolling door to his forge. She was grinning with hands behind her back, as if she had a secret.

"What?" he grunted, walking past her and onto the yard's crunchy gravel. He squinted against the bright day, the mixture of white and yellow shining up from the loose dirt and down from the slat rooftops.

"Mama's having a good day," she replied cheerfully.

"Oh?" Necrem looked down at her skipping along beside him, now tall enough to almost reach his waist. She was growing fast and already as tall as children five years older than her. He always teased her whenever she asked for seconds, telling her she was growing up to be a giant like him just to see her cute pout. She might not like the idea, but that was how Necrem *knew* she was his daughter.

"Mmhmm." Bayona nodded. "She got out of bed, ate breakfast by the window, and even brushed her hair. Do you think she'll want to come downstairs today?"

Necrem frowned and, shielding his eyes with his hand, looked up. His family's home and combined blacksmith shop was a long building with a storefront in the center that divided a single-floor dwelling to the left and a two-story dwelling to the right. Even with his eyes shaded, Necrem squinted against the blazing light reflecting off the roof slates to catch a glimpse of the second-story window.

Eulalia wasn't there. He hadn't expected her to be.

But if she's having a good day, maybe I'll see her today.

23

A sudden, stabbing pain shot through his left eye, and he had to look away. He rubbed his eyes and stifled a curse so Bayona wouldn't hear. The suns had finally gotten too bright.

Eight days. He growled and blinked to get the sunspots out of his vision. *Savior cursed Exchange.*

The Easterly and Westerly Sun both hung in the sky at their respective ends, illuminating the world in dazzling white and yellow while they traded it. At the end of each year, the suns came together to pass the world between them. People simply called it the Exchange, a continuous eight-day period without any night until the world was handed over to the other sun. Last night had only lasted for two hours and, after the exchange was all set and done, it would be a few more nights before everything became right again. Until then, there was nothing else people could do but wait and try not to go blind or insane.

When his vision finally cleared, Necrem glanced down and saw Bayona squinting up at him. "Mind your eyes," he said comfortingly, patting her head. "Go find some shade while I see to the man up front."

"Yes, sir!" Bayona said cheerfully then ran inside the house.

Necrem watched her go and bore the twinges of his cheeks to allow himself a small smile. After everything he and his wife had endured, it amazed him how lucky they were to be blessed with a happy child.

The inside of the house smelled of wood and steel, almost like his forge, except without the acrid smell of sulfur and burning coals. Necrem's papa had always said a worthy forge should smell like burning wax and sweat. Necrem had never had any wax, but he knew sweat. Fortunately, the cool of his house smelled sweeter than that.

His heavy foots steps thumped down the hallway, and he lowered his head to step into the shopfront.

The well-dressed man behind the rough counter took a step back in surprise. His eyebrows went up as he traced just how tall Necrem was. Necrem was used to it. After all, a man nearly seven feet tall was not something everyone saw every day, and he was sure his mask covering half his face made him appear more intimidating. Necrem hunched his broad shoulders and hoped that help.

"Good Exchange, sir," he said, stomping up to the counter. "I'm Necrem Oso. My daughter said you, wished to speak with me?"

"Ah . . ." the gentleman, much younger than Necrem realized seeing him up close, opened his mouth to speak but said nothing. He stood out with his nice clothes and light complexion in Necrem's small shopfront with its beaten-up counter and iron and steel tools displayed on the few cabinet shelves.

Definitely from the city, Necrem surmised, but he wasn't their usual tax collector.

24

Sweat glistened off his brow and dripped on his cream jacket's high collar. His shaking hand slipped into his vest pocket, but his fingers fumbled around as if he'd forgotten what he was reaching for.

"You're *Necrem Oso*?" the man squeaked.

"Yes," Necrem grunted.

The man swallowed. "I'm—" His voice cracked, and he cleared his throat. "I'm Sir Luca Quindo of Si Don's Impuesto. I've recently been assigned to this district and been going around introducing myself." Sir Luca grinned, probably thinking he was being polite and nonthreatening.

Necrem didn't care. He was a tax collector. They never brought good news or came around just to chat. His only telling feature was that he was early.

"Just get on with whatever you're here for," he said, hanging his head.

Sir Luca flinched. The corners of his strained, upturned lips twitched as he gently pulled out a folded piece of paper from his inner vest pocket. "Campaign season is upon us," he said, unfolding the paper. "And Si Don Borbin has decreed the marc must make additional preparations—"

"How much is the tax this year?" Necrem set his shoulders. He already expected them to be high. They were always taxed higher for Easterly Year campaigns than Westerly Years. Longer time to stay at war demanded more money.

"One-hundred and fifty deberes per household," Sir Luca replied.

Necrem threw his head up. "That's *twice* as much as last year!"

Sir Luca stepped back, holding his wide-brim hat up as if to protect himself. "It's just for this year!" the tax collector said, sounding a little desperate. "And there are other services and methods of payment that can go to the campaign effort. Especially for a blacksmith like yourself—"

"I'm not a member of the Union," Necrem said gruffly.

Sir Luca's mouth opened and closed, but nothing came out. His brow furled, confused, clearly not having expected that. Nearly every blacksmith belonged to the Union of Forgers who assigned blacksmiths to armies on campaign, adjusting their fee for services and exemptions from taxes.

Except Necrem wasn't a member anymore.

He folded his arms and shoved the past away. *A hundred and fifty deberes*, he calculated. *I might have enough saved and with these next two jobs to cover it. I'm going to have to work over night, though, to—*

"Also," Sir Luca added, "the tax is due at the end of the Exchange."

Necrem's eyes went wide. "Seven days!" he gasped. "That's impossible."

Sir Luca raised his hands even higher. "That's the decree! I'm merely doing my duty. If you're not part of the Union, there are other ways to contributed to the campaign effort. A big man such as yourself could . . ." Sir Luca's suggestion died on his lips.

It wasn't until Necrem felt his cheeks stinging that he realized he was glowering down at the man.

He softened his expression and turned away. "I'll find the money."

"Oh?"

Necrem looked back over his shoulder, and Sir Luca swallowed and nodded.

"Very well then," Sir Luca said, putting his hat on while backtracking toward the door. "The Impuesto will be expecting you."

As he opened the door, Necrem noticed only two soldiers waiting in the shade, rapiers on their hips and dressed in the bright orange uniforms of Marqués Borbin, but no armor.

"Sir Luca," he called.

The tax collector paused and glanced over his shoulder. "Yes?"

"Best you get more guards," Necrem warned. "Most here in the slums aren't going to take too kindly to your news."

Sir Luca nervously laughed but then stopped. He swallowed and left with a nod.

Necrem stood there a while after he'd left. The daunting task of getting twice the usual tax two weeks early kept pounding him over and over like a hammer. The slams threatened to break him rather than mold. There was no other way around it. There wasn't enough time to finish his current jobs in time. Considering the amount of the tax, he wondered if his customers could pay him *and* the tax both.

Damn the Marqués, he cursed, squeezing his arms with his thick fingers. *Probably planning another glory hunting campaign.*

That was what higher campaign taxes usually meant, like the campaign three years ago when Orsembar had conquered Puerlato from the Lazornians. Yet, what could men like Necrem do but pay?

He glanced around the shop at the hammers, horseshoes, cutting knives, and nails, all wares he'd forged to sell to people. Most, though, came to him for individual needs, and he would help them if they couldn't pay it all at once. That was how people in the slums had to live. They had to look out for each other because no one else was going to.

He grunted and began to walk back through the house, heading back to his forge to think.

"They say there's going to be a big campaign this year!"

Necrem stopped. That was a child's voice, but a boy's voice.

"Oh really?" Bayona asked, sounding inquisitive.

"Yeah!" the excited boy replied. "The recruiters are coming around already. Banging drums and claiming they're giving each man who joins up five deberes that day!"

Bayona cooed. "People could buy five of Papa's hammers for that!"

Necrem snickered. Children didn't know what they were talking about, and Bayona was thinking people were going to spend the money on his work.

Why is a boy talking to Bayona?

The sudden fatherly instinct demanded to know who the boy was. He walked into the bottom floor of his wife and daughter's side of the house and found Bayona sitting on her knees by the open window. The kitchen was clean, and iron pots and skillets were stacked in the lower cabinets Necrem had built for her once she had become insistent on taking care of Eulalia, despite her age.

A young, freckle-faced boy outside stood up straight when Necrem walked in and caught them. Audaz was a local boy, one of a local group Necrem had seen running around the streets.

"Good Exchange, Sir Oso," the thirteen-year-old lad said. He stood straight and tense as a board. He puffed his cheeks, probably thinking he was grinning, but it made his face pinch up. A small breeze rustled his dark brown hair.

"Good Exchange," Necrem grunted. He didn't say any more and just waited.

For each passing moment, Audaz's puffed cheeks grew redder, and beads of sweat began forming on his forehead.

"You should be careful not to stay too long outdoors during the Exchange," Necrem warned. "Not good for you to get all this sun."

Audaz passed a nervous glanced between Bayona and Necrem. "I . . ." he nervously started. "I guess I better go home them. Talk to you later, Bayona?"

"Later!" Bayona said happily.

Audaz gave a final nod then slowly walked away. A few seconds later, Necrem heard running footfalls crunching the street's gravel.

"A new friend of yours?" he asked Bayona.

Bayona shrugged. "Audaz just stopped by while I was cleaning to say hello. He and his friends run around here a lot." She grinned up at him.

All Necrem could do was shake his head. Bayona looked older because she was taller. Necrem was surprised it had taken so long to get the boys' attention. Then again, there was probably a different reason Bayona had a hard time making friends. One he was inadvertently responsible for.

"What was he saying?" he asked.

"Nothing much," Bayona replied. "He'd just said hello, bragging about how much his brother was getting for joining the campaign. It sounded like good money!"

Necrem's brow furled at hearing her speak like that.

He lowered himself down to one knee. Even then, he had to hunch his back to get eye level with her. Bayona's grin slipped away, replaced by a worried frown.

He gently rubbed her shoulder with his massive palm and stroked her cheek with his thumb. "No, Bayona," he said as comforting as he could grumble. "Nothing good ever comes from the campaigns. Nothing."

Chapter 2

Recha methodically read each line of the proposal and tried not to bite her left pinky's fingernail. She had chipped it somehow, and her subconscious craved a distraction from reading the overly long fifteen-page document.

It was only eight pages last year, she recalled. *Marqués Dion's either pushing his luck or . . . worried.*

Recha and her delegation sat with a delegation from Quezlo in the Velvet Room of her new mansion in Zoragrin. She called it the Velvet Room because of the plush, velvet carpet, and with its open space and large window, it was the ideal choice for her official negotiations with other marcs. Provided they were friendly.

She wore a velvet dress to match the room with a flock, white bodice, and high lace collar. The long sleeves and collar didn't bother her so much, but with her hair done up in a bun, covering her left ear, she had to endure sweating while she read.

Recha's eyebrow twitched at the next line item she read.

> *The Marc of Quezlo pledges that should the Marc of Orsembar invade the Marc of Quezlo's staunch ally, the Marc of Lazorna, Quezlo will marshal an army of fifteen thousand troops to send to its staunch ally's aid.*

She glanced over the thick parchment at the man sipping tea on the opposite side of the table. Quezlo's somber ambassador, Baron Perde Westendor, tediously drank his tea, holding the cup precisely so not to dampen the points of his long mustache or smash the oiled tip of a beard on his chin. His unassuming and quiet nature was one Recha had come to respect in the years after becoming marquesa. The unassuming baron might be a little vain about his looks, considering no amount of combing or oil was going to bring his fleeing hair back, but at least he behaved respectfully toward her.

However, that didn't make him any less shrewd.

She looked down at the following line items, turning through three more pages for the clause that required Lazorna to provide twenty thousand or more troops should Orsembar invade Quezlo or some other near impossible stipulation. She didn't find it.

That must be a mistake. Dion wouldn't pledge support for nothing.

The lack of requirement for Lazorna wasn't the only thing that Recha found out of character. She supposed she wouldn't find some inkling of an answer unless she started probing.

Let the negotiations commence then.

"Your marqués's proposal is very extensive, Baron Perde," Recha said, holding up the pages and putting on a diplomatic face. "He must really be trying to put my counselors to shame." Her two-page proposal was simple—lower trade tariffs, provided both marcs agreed not to campaign against each other this year. She had hoped that would make these negotiations go faster.

"Not at all, La Dama, not at all," Baron Perde protested. His crisp speech cut off every constant and made the tips of his mustache twitch as he set his teacup in its saucer. "Si Don Dion assured me himself that he wished to further our relationship with you. *Especially* since you have been our best neighbor these past three years."

Recha snickered. Not just from how obvious the comment was, but also Perde's smile made his mustache frame his cheeks and looked to be reaching for his ears. "Yes, well"—she cleared her throat and tried not to stare—"considering our other neighbors, that isn't too difficult."

Perde laughed, and the rest of the Quezlo delegation joined him.

Recha chuckled along … for diplomacy's sake. They were allies, after all.

Although, Perde did have more people with him than she did. He had his secretary shadowing him, but also his staff of no more than fifteen other people just standing around in the back. Beside him sat five counselors, each one reading a copy and going over every line item in Recha's proposal. Every now and then, one would scratch a word out or scribble a note to one of their colleagues down the table.

In contrast, Recha had brought one counselor. Esquire Valto Onofrio sat back in his chair with his head propped against it. His pursed lips made his weathered, pox scars stand out on the left side of his face. The old counselor was a former, long-sitting judge, well into his retirement years, yet he remained in Recha's service.

He wouldn't admit it, but Recha knew it was because he found retirement boring. His wife, Golina, had told her so. The elderly woman sat beside her husband, pen in hand to interpret whatever Valto told her.

The counselor frowned at his copy of Marqués Dion's offer, flipping through page after page and squinting through his thick spectacles, making his bushy eyebrows shake. Finally, he looked up at Recha, perplexed.

"It is illogical that there be such a volume of gratuitous guarantees without demands in return."

Recha glanced at Golina.

"Not enough tit for tat," the esquire's wife interpreted.

Valto was an impressive jurist; however, his mind had thought in terms of jurisprudence for so many years that he had difficulties speaking normally. Fortunately for everyone, the Savior had guided the perfect woman to sit at his side to do that for him.

"Too much pledging and not enough requiring something from us?" Recha added.

Valto grunted in the affirmative and dropped his copy on the table.

"Ambassador Perde," Recha started, "your terms are very generous this year, but"—she leaned forward and picked at the edges of proposal in front of her—"I'm afraid I can't accept them."

The small conversation that had broken out between Perde's staff in the back fell silent. His counselors stopped what they were doing. One paused writing mid-sentence. Another rapidly blinked at her. Another looked up at her dumbfounded.

They weren't expecting that.

Perde, to his credit, remained placid. "Is there something wrong with them, La Dama? Surely you don't feel Si Don left anything out?"

"Well"—she flipped through proposal for show—"he didn't mention anything about a decrease in tariffs?"

"A minor thing," Perde scoffed. "Something the counselors can write in."

"It doesn't mention further de-escalation on our borders."

"We're allies!" Perde cheerfully waved. "We barely station a garrison on our small border with you."

Recha's face hardened. "There's nothing about further release of Lazornian *sioneroses*."

The room grew still. Perde's smile slipped, and his staff and counselors nervously turned inward.

"Forgive me, La Dama"—Perde's voice was stern and strained—"but I'm afraid I do not have the authority to discuss this matter. Si Don Dion gives you his word he is having every roll check for any *sioneros* hailing from Lazorna. But it's going to take more time and a matter he's reserved to speak with you about it personally."

Sioneroses were prisoners of war. Traditionally, they were taken directly by the victorious marc in the aftermath of battles. However, a bartering practice had grown between the marcs, a form of payment so the barons wouldn't have to give up their wealth, or the calleroses wouldn't have to sell their skills to the larger force. They would sell their men off instead, especially to avoid battle with a large army. Some soldiers were traded and never seen again. Many formed free workforces for the larger marcs and barons. Serfs essentially.

The vilest of betrayals.

Recha had torn that entire system down in Lazorna, along with a great many other changes. She granted all the *sioneroses* a choice—go home or stay and work as free men. Many went home. Others stayed. That was easy. It took more . . . force to deal with some of the barons who objected. Getting her own people back from the other marcs required something more, even from her self-proclaimed allies. She wasn't in a position for such action.

Yet.

"Very well," she said, turning back to their proposal.

The tension slowly evaporated from the room, staff softly exhaling and shoulders slumping.

"Besides what I mentioned"—she held up their proposal—"these are exceptionally good terms of peaceful alliance, as you said, Ambassador. What concerns me—and my counselor agrees with me—is that this proposal mentions you using your military . . . a *lot* to aid us."

"Again, we are your allies," Perde said, picking up his tea again. "Right?" He took a small sip but noticeably avoided gazing over its rim at her.

Recha wasn't going to be deterred. There was something here. Another purpose for this alliance, and Quezlo was using everything, down to a written treaty, toward it. She was concerned by it all aiming toward her and Lazorna, too.

"Right," she agreed. "But if I must say, you're being *very* loud about it."

Perde snorted, shooting some tea back into the cup and hurriedly jerked away, fumbling not to drop the delicate porcelain. His secretary hastily brought a handkerchief and dabbed his nose and face, careful to avoid his mustache and chin-beard.

"*Loud*?" Perde coughed, waving his secretary away. "We're being too *loud* about our alliance?" He looked to his counselors, and they shook their heads and shrugged, confused. One snickered.

"Allow me to be blunt, Ambassador," Recha said, dropping the proposal to straighten and put on a regal display. "Do you, or Si Don Dion, believe Orsembar plans to campaign against Lazorna this year? The amount of aid and number of pledged soldiers certainly suggests it."

Perde's lips formed a tight line. His eyes danced across the tabletop momentarily before he waved for his secretary. He whispered something and, moments later, the secretary began shuffling the staff behind them out. The counselors remained.

"As a gentleman and honest ally," Perde said in a serious tone after the extra staff was gone, "I must respect your bluntness, La Dama, and return it. Si Don Dion *does* suspect Orsembar will campaign against you this year. Borbin is planning something."

"So soon?" Recha inquired. "After arranging his son's marriage to Si Don Narios's daughter?"

Si Don Narios was the Marqués of Saran, the marc bordering Orsembar and Quezlo to the west and equal in size to them both. Borbin had campaigned against Saran the previous season and came out with a forced marriage between Si Don Narios's daughter and Borbin's son.

Perde nodded. "Five thousand Saran troops escorted Dama Emilia into Orsembar two months ago. They never left. Si Don Narios's forces appear to be gathering close to our southwestern border, *but*"—he held up a finger—"my marqués suspects Borbin plans to use the additional support he has from his new in-laws to strike against you."

It was possible; Recha could concede that. Their stalemate with Orsembar over Puerlato had left Borbin as frustrated as she was about the situation.

But there's a much more obvious possibility.

"Has Si Don Dion considered Orsembar and Saran uniting to invade Quezlo?"

Perde jerked back and snickered. He chuckled, and his counselors joined him. "They could try, but both would have to invade through well-defended positions. Historically *defended* positions! Every time Saran has campaigned against us, we've forced them back on the Salamus Heights. And for Orsembar, Borbin will never take Compuert. Not even the White Sword could!"

Recha kept calm the best she could while Perde and his counselors laughed. She balled her fists in her lap. She was sure he didn't mean it as a slight that their city could hold off the White Sword but hers fell. The memory of the hero who slew her beloved Sebastian always threatened to make her temper flare.

She flipped through the proposal to the back page with the signature lines. "Well, if you are so confident." She dipped her quill in the ink and went to sign then paused. "Are you certain you don't want an added provision that Lazorna must provide troops to you? You know . . . just in case."

Perde waved her concerns away. "That won't be necessary, La Dama. Si Don Dion knows the lengths you are taking to keep your marc out of the campaigns. He doesn't wish to put too much of a strain on his now peaceful neighbor."

Not much of a strain as you think.

"As you wish," she said aloud and signed her name.

Nor as peaceful.

She slid the proposal back to him, and Perde eagerly took up his quill.

As he signed, Recha got another thought. "If you want, for good measure, we could add a couple lines about the tariffs," she proposed. "Just to keep up appearances that this is more than a military alliance."

"Let the counselors add that in," Perde agreed without looking up.

"I do admire your confidence." Recha leaned forward. "Tell me, ambassador, what *really* makes Dion so certain Borbin will campaign against me?"

Perde glanced up, his eyebrows arched as if it were obvious. "The Rules of Campaign, La Dama. The easiest fight to win is the one everyone chooses."

Recha hoped her grin wasn't too predatory. She was doing her best holding back a chuckle.

Those Rules are about to change, she inwardly growled. *And we're not so easy as everyone may think.*

~~~

"Where did you get so many *fine* vintages?"

Recha wiped the edges of her mouth with her napkin and smirked at the strutting fool doubled over perusing her wine selection. She smoothed out her sleek, silk skirts before hiking her feet up under her and stretched out across her lounge. She fluffed out her wavy hair and made sure her square neckline didn't reveal too much before posing and propping her head up by leaning against the lounge's single cushioned arm.

"You'd be amazed what you can get when don't go on campaign, Don Cristal," she replied. "Merchants love shipping their wares down roads with no armies marching up them."

Cristal snorted, sliding a dark green bottle from the shelf. He tossed back his foppish, thick dark hair from his face so he could read the label. His handsome, square jaw stuck out as he ran his finger along the words, checking the providence and bottling date. His bright yellow jacket made him seem even taller because of its flaring tails.

"Please, La Dama, call me . . . Cris," he said, taking his eyes away from the bottle and spotting her pose. Those light green eyes traveled along her frame, and a grin slowly spread across his face.

"I'm not so sure about that," Recha replied. She picked at her dress skirts but allowed herself a small smile at how she took the man's power of speech away. "We haven't known each other for *that* long. And this was supposed to be a small luncheon to go over this upcoming campaign season."

Cristal was the ambassador of Pamolid, the marc to the east, and a nephew of Marqués Hyles. They had met over two years ago, shortly after Recha's coup at a diplomatic reception in Pamolid. She found him amicable, mostly because Recha picked up on a special family trait that seemed to run through the entire Hyles male line.

They all had uncontrollable wandering eyes for women. All it had taken was one dance with young Cristal, and he had become adamant with his uncle to make him his ambassador.

"Why should that be a problem?" Cristal asked. He rushed around the lounge meant for him and came to kneel beside hers, bottle in hand. "We have good food, good wine, and a terrific view." He gestured out toward Zoragrin, laid out before them from Recha's upper-story patio.

The shining lights of the suns reflected off the slated rooftops of the city below and spread across the Laz River. The river's slow current made the soft waves dazzle like emeralds in the green water. Thanks to her patio's covering, they were able to eat outside and enjoy such a view for a time before the Exchange became unbearable.

"And all the time in the world," Cristal whispered, "to get to know each other better."

Recha gave him a sly look. He grinned back, almost crookedly. It dimpled his cheek and made the small mole on the right side of his jaw stand out.

Well, at least he does have his own charms, she mused. *Poor boy doesn't have any brains, though.*

"Sorry, dear Cristal," she said, "but this isn't a luncheon where we both get to lounge about and enjoy the view before the temperature drops. We have *actual* matters to discuss."

Cristal sighed and rolled his eyes and head dramatically. "Fine. Can I at least pour for you?" He held out the bottle toward her cup, but Recha hastily reached over and covered it.

"None for me." She shook her head. "But you may drink as much as you want."

"You're not being fun." Cristal pouted to be cute or charming, but it was easy for Recha to hold her ground. She had no interest nor felt any temptation. She was playing with him, and not the game he thought they were playing.

"All right, all right," he said getting to feet and walking around her lounge. "Just let me know when you get bored and—"

Recha closely watched him, expecting him to try something. The instant he moved like he was about to sit on the edge of her lounge, she shot her feet out, risking showing too much ankle to deny him a seat.

"Ah-ah." She wagged a finger at him then pointed at the lounge opposite her. "You have your own."

"You are such a *tease*," Cristal said through gritted teeth. "I adore it."

"You may adore it from over there."

Finally, Cristal retreated to his seat. He causally poured the sparkling blue vintage in his glass and fell back into the lounge's pillows with a sigh.

Recha had constructed her patio for this purpose alone. The best view her mansion could offer, covered by elements of thick golden canvas, stocked with the best wines she could purchase, and all the comforts. It provided the perfect atmosphere for dealing with diplomats and nobility like Cristal. Once they were relaxed and entertained, they were much easier to deal with.

Even if she had to endure banter and advances from a few who had no chance of receiving her affections.

Cristal sipped his wine then let out a long, content sigh. He propped his foot on the small table, clattering the silverware and remains of their luncheon, and leaned his head back.

"Comfortable?" Recha asked, arching an eyebrow at his foot.

"Very," Cristal replied without looking open.

"Well, don't get too comfortable." She leaned across and smacked his foot off her table. "We still need to talk about your proposal."

Cristal suddenly perked up, wine dripping from his lips and running down his chin, and his eyebrows leaped up.

"My dear Recha!" he exclaimed. "I've been waiting, *hoping*, for the moment to tell you how I feel!"

Savior, help me not to throw this boy off the patio! she prayed, struggling not to roll her eyes. Her sentiments about his age were a little unforgiving. Cristal was only a year younger than her, but his behavior, like a love-sick teenager, was especially taxing on her nerves.

"Not *that* kind of proposal, Cristal," she replied with a pointed look. "I meant mine and your uncle's proposals for this campaign season."

Cristal deflated and fell back in a huff. "Why so boorish? You're the marquesa of an entire marc! You have all the food, money, *this*! Why can't we enjoy it? It's not nearly as fun at home." He pouted again and sipped his wine.

Cristal failed to realize the reason he led such a luxurious life as ambassador to her marc was because, *one*, she allowed it; and secondly, his uncle didn't have much interest in Lazorna presently. He bordered larger marcs to his north and south, and Recha was eager to keep him distracted.

As for Cristal himself, not a weekend went by without Recha receiving word of him attending a party where he would become a little too wild. He was enjoying his youth. Sowing wild oats. Being completely incompetent in his official duties, as she had hoped. The added headache of not getting the official business with him done quickly was becoming the glaring price.

"Work before play, Ambassador," she said comfortingly. "It's a rule you learn if you get to rule a marc. If we get it finished quickly, I promise some after-luncheon entertainment you'll find *very* fun." She winked at him teasingly, and his grin split his face.

"Very well then!" Cristal set his glass down and cupped his fingers in his lap. "I sent your proposal to my uncle two weeks ago, but I'm afraid I haven't heard back yet."

"What?" Recha blinked rapidly.

Cristal threw his hands up. "Uncle left before the proposal reached him. He traveled east, but my so-called *counselors* won't tell me where. It's like they don't trust me sometimes."

I wonder why, Recha mused. Although, hearing his uncle was looking east was encouraging.

If it was true; if his uncle's counselors didn't trust him, it was also possible his uncle no longer trusted Cristal, either. He could be using Cristal's loose tongue to lull her in a false sense of security before blindsiding her while she worried about the other marcs.

Recha shook her head. *Hyles isn't that clever.*

She still needed more, though.

Turning back to Cristal, she smiled softly. She reached over and began meticulously dropping sugar cubes into her teacup. Her pose and dress's square neckline teased the undisciplined Cristal.

"But can I take your word, though, that we'll still have peace this campaign season?" she asked. "I'd *hate* to lose all the good will we've built up." She poured her tea and tried not laugh as Cristal blushed. He had some natural charm, sure, but still … love-sick, teenaged mindset.

"Ah . . ." he coughed, but his eyes kept wandering. "No. No! My uncle would never campaign against you! I swear, if he does, I'd protest to my mother and have him stop."

Oh, that means a lot.

"So, can I assume we'll still have peace?"

"Absolutely!" Cristal's wandering-eye-blood was winning, almost turning into a leer.

Recha sat up before the desire to slap him became too overwhelming and took up her cup. "Excellent! Just have your counselors send over a temporary proposal, and I'll sign it."

"Sure!" Cristal raised his wine glass, as if expecting a toast.

Recha sipped her tea to hide her disappointment. She wanted to get all these proposals settled, but it appeared she would need something more to make sure Pamolid didn't surprise her this year.

"Didn't you promise some after-luncheon entertainment?" Cristal teased after draining his wine.

"So, I did," she replied. Recha set her teacup down and clapped her hands.

A trio of musicians walked out onto the patio, carrying drums, a flute, and a clarinet. They were followed by a trio of women with blazing red hair and matching dresses, carrying a train of their flowing skirts in hand. They wore sashes wrapped diagonally across their bodies with jingling coins hanging down the sashes' hems. Their high heels knocked against her patio boards. One woman carried a fan while another clicked finger cymbals together that she wore on her index finger and thumb.

"Trio Bailer!" Cristal exclaimed, excitedly bouncing on the edge of his seat.

Recha gave him a smiling nod.

The Trio Bailer was a tradition dance performed by three women during which one selects a man to join. The man selected was supposed to be heralded as the Lord of Dance for the night, and the dance was usually only held for special events—birthdays, celebrations, and parties—but not weddings.

Being the lone man on the patio, as soon as the musicians started playing, the dancer not carrying anything held out her hand for Cristal to join them while her companions swirled around them. The poor boy was so eager that he didn't even spare Recha a second glance before he was spinning and laughing with the dancer in his arms. He wasn't half-bad, either.

Recha lounged back and let them have their fun, her mind turning over what Cristal had said. *I might need extra insurance against Marqués Hyles.* To her amusement, such a plan quickly formulated while watching Cristal laugh, being passed from one dancer to another.

~~~

Bars of light sliced through the repurposed observation room in Zoragrin Castle, striking mounted crystals to light up the sparce surroundings.

Recha sat with her back straight and fingers laced in her lap. Her wide-open sleeves hung from her sides like drapes. That kept her from messing with the white ribbons lacing her dress instead of buttons. The sleek, black silk of her dress glittered from the reflected crystal light. Once again, she made sure not to show her discomfort from the sweat of a high collar and her hair pulled back from her face, bound in a braid against the back of her neck.

Her eyelids fluttered, and her head felt heavy, longing to droop. Longing for rest.

She breathed heavily through her nose and forced her eyes open. She couldn't rest now. She couldn't show any weakness. Not with the odious man opposite her.

The hook-nosed Orsembian, Ambassador Valen Irujo, sniffed sharply at the parchment in his hands. Despite his thin eyebrows arched like arrowheads, his ebony eyes were bored. His placid expression was starting to skew to the right side of his narrow face, threatening to purse his lips.

This isn't that complicated! Recha wanted to scream. *It's the same proposal as last year.*

And simple. A guaranteed peace for this year's campaign season or a promised five-year peace if Orsembar relinquishes its dominion of Puerlato and return it to Lazorna. No mentions of tariffs. No requirement neither harassed the other's trade at the mouth of the Laz River. No exchange of *sioneroses*.

Valen was intentionally dragging it out. He'd been the same way three years ago. He had forcibly taken over Orsembar's campaign after the White Sword hadn't defeated Recha's army fast enough to Borbin's satisfaction. Once he had taken over, he had overextended Orsembar's line, and Recha's army had been able to take advantage of it, pushing them back and holding their defenses. Campaign season had been over for every other marc before Valen had entertained talks.

Valen turned the proposal over, as if he expected her to have something written on the back, and then held it up, unimpressed.

"Is this *it*?" he asked, annoyed. "You made me wait for *days* just to hand me the same piece of paper you handed me last year!" He slammed the proposal on the small table, a mere stool, between them.

Recha remained unfazed, but her ears twitched at her guards' shuffling feet behind her. Because they moved, Valen's two calleroses behind him shifted, as well, hands sliding toward their rapiers while setting their feet. Recha ignored the posturing and Valen's dismissive grimace as he folded his arms.

"You brought me the same proposal, as well, Ambassador," she calmly replied with a flickering glance down at his proposal. "This doesn't seem to be any more important to you or Si Don Borbin."

Borbin's proposal was a simple counter. He promised lasting peace if Recha relinquished Lazorna's claim to Puerlato and the surrounding land.

"Si Don's proposal is genuine," Valen said. "A show of respect for your dogged pursuit of peace and diplomacy in this time of such strife and hardship. Especially for a . . . young marquesa such as yourself."

You mean inexperienced, Recha knew. She was also sure he and Borbin obviously thought her desire for peace trumped everything else, but something in their proposal didn't read truly genuine.

She had given the proposal over to Esquire Valto to look at last year, and he had dismissed it in an instant. The promise of a lasting peace meant nothing because lasting had no definition. Lasting could mean an hour, a day, a year, or nothing. The entire proposal merely wanted her to relinquish Puerlato on paper.

"A more proper show of respect would be returning the city you stole from my marc," she said.

Valen's left nostril twitched, failing to hide his sneer. "That which is conquered during campaign cannot be seen as stolen, by the Rules of Campaign."

That's possibly the most ridiculous thing I've ever heard.

Although, in Valen's case, he would cling to the Rules. They favored him, and he was a campaigning baron; a baron who went on campaigns personally to lead their calleroses and filled their own pockets along the way.

It suddenly struck Recha that he might have another reason to be annoyed about being made to wait for this meeting.

"Are you in a hurry, Ambassador?" she asked, noticing his leg twitching. "In need to be somewhere else, perhaps?"

"Anything to leave this decrepit, old castle would be appreciated, La Dama," Valen replied.

"That's understandable." Recha smiled, enjoying Valen's discomfort of being the only ambassador not permitted to attend her at her mansion. She reserved this room specifically to meet with any ambassador from Orsembar. The room in the old castle where Sebastian's body had been laid out on display. A symbolic reminder to Valen what his marqués took from her.

"But really, Ambassador," she said, "you seem very upset about a simple matter such as this."

Valen exhaled loudly. "If I may be blunt, with all your talks of wanting peace with my marqués, Si Don Borbin finds your plots with Quezlo against him . . . *distasteful*."

"Oh?" Recha tilted her head and blinked coyly. "Really?"

Valen wasn't amused. "You talk of peace, yet instead of proving you can defend your land yourself, you connive for Marqués Dion to fight for you instead. Do you have no pride to fight your own battles?"

"I'm plenty capable of fighting my own battles, Ambassador. I mean"—she shrugged—"you should know."

Valen glowered at that. "Says the woman who had another marc promise her fifteen thousand troops."

Perde! You couldn't keep our agreement confidential until after the Exchange!

Recha kept calm. Quezlo's proposal was more a show of force for Borbin's benefit. Perde had said as much. Still, more decorum would have been nice.

"What about the five thousand Saran troops still in Orsembar?" she retorted. "Your ally has already sent you soldiers, but you want to complain about mine supporting me if I'm attacked? Rather hypocritical, don't you think?"

Valen drew himself up. "Those troops are garrisoned for the Dama Emilia's protection."

"Protection against whom?" she asked dryly, arching an eyebrow. "Her own husband? Or her husband's father?"

Valen stared at her blankly. "This is getting us nowhere."

"Agreed. Should we finish this then?" Recha tossed away his proposal. "I'm not agreeing to relinquish Puerlato, and neither are you. Shall we just agree to peace this year, like last year? You'll get to take your leave sooner."

Valen grimaced at his marqués's proposal thrown on the floor and back to hers. With furious determination, he took up his quill to strike lines through the second line item on her proposal, almost ripping the parchment.

"This," he hissed, signing his name, "has been a complete *waste* of time."

"Most campaigns are," she quipped back.

Valen gave her a dark look, slapped the quill down on the stool, then rose to his feet. "I trust this concludes our business?"

No, not until—

Recha cut off the thought so not to risk losing control.

"To another successful negotiation. I'll have an official copy sent to your lodgings to take to Si Don Borbin."

Valen turned on his heels and stalked toward the exit, not waiting to witness her signature. Recha motioned to the guards behind her, and they trailed after him and his escort to make sure he didn't get lost. She signed her name and wondered if Valen's signature was as dishonest as hers.

Chapter 3

The gentle rocking of the carriage lulled Recha into a restless half-sleep. The curtains were drawn and provided the darkness she craved, but the suns' combined lights pierced every crack they could, casting thin streaks of light randomly throughout the cab. The carriage rolled around a bend in the road, and one of those rays shined across her eyelids. She groaned in protest and rolled her head away. Her loosely hanging hair pulled against the cab's cushioned seat, and another streak of light was waiting to shine into her face.

"*Gah!*" she exclaimed in frustration and threw her head up. "Why couldn't we have *nailed* the curtains down?"

Cornelos Narvae grunted, blinking at her over the rim of his spectacles hanging off the bridge of his nose. He was in the middle of shuffling a pile of reports in his lap, somehow reading through them in the dim light.

"I think that'd be a security risk," he replied dryly.

Recha shook her head. "It was only a joke, Cornelos. Don't be so serious."

Cornelos glanced at the curtains then back at her with the same cautious look. "That's my job."

Recha smirked at her personal secretary. He was the most organized-minded member of her Companions and someone she could trust absolutely. She also preferred having a calleros as her secretary over a common civil servant. It brought additional prestige and sent a message that anyone who wanted to reach her would have to get through her calleroses first. After all, after three years, Lazorna's transformation was complete. All calleroses now swore their allegiances and service to the marc. No shared loyalties divided among the barons.

Meaning they all served her now.

"We have twenty guards riding with us," she pointed out. "*And* it's the Exchange. I think we can relax on worrying about security risks."

"Not considering where we're going," Cornelos argued.

Recha allowed herself an immature pout and flopped her head back against the seat. "Fine." Her eyes drifted closed again, but her temples started to throb, and she was forced to rub them.

"Should I order the coachman to turn around?" Cornelos asked over shuffling his papers.

"Why would you do that?" Recha slid her fingers from her temples down to rub her eyes.

"You're tired. You need to rest before the Exchange gets to you."

Recha sighed and dropped her arm to flop against the seat next to her. "I'll rest after this. I have too many questions and need to get some insight into them if I'm ever to sleep again."

"You could wait for Sevesco." There was a twinge of hope in Cornelos's suggestion. Perhaps a prayer she would agree to turn from her destination. "There's still time for him to return. He's likely gathering the last of the reports from his espis. They might have your answers."

Sevesco was another one of her Companions and the man she had put in charge of rebuilding Lazorna's intelligence network. She couldn't call them professional espis—spies. That would be too laughable. A minor setback for Recha's coup was that many outside sources of information had been severed, leaving her scrambling to get reliable news afterward.

People hailing from other marcs were usually assumed to be espis or informants of some nature. Visiting nobility were generally seen as the most obvious and potential double agents, depending on the outcome of campaigns.

Giving the responsibility of rebuilding Lazorna's intelligence network to Sevesco was the best she could do. Like Cornelos, he was the only person she trusted to do the job and do it well. Still, she couldn't wait.

"No," she replied, sitting up. "It's possible Sevesco might bring some insight, but it's just as possible he'll only report what we already know. I *need* definitive answers. Borbin's up to something, and unless I have *something* suggesting what, I'm going to be spinning around in my own head."

Cornelos frowned. "Sleep could help with that."

"As if I'm going to get any sleep." Recha folded her arms and shook her head, tossing her hair over her shoulders. "If it's not worrying about Borbin, it's worrying about the barons and their complaints about taxes, or where troops should be stationed, or disputes between the church and the cult. Can any of these people get along for *two minutes*?"

Cornelos stared at her, unmoved. "You are the one who took over the marc."

Recha set her jaw. "I'm not going to get any sympathy from you, am I?"

"None." Cornelos pushed his spectacles further up his nose. "That's also part of my job. And since you can't rest and refuse to take my advice to turn around, this would be a good time to go through the reports I have for you." He patted the side of his stack of papers, making sure they were all neat and orderly in his lap.

Recha groaned and slouched, looking at them.

Always something else, she lamented. *This must be the reason Uncle made up such a horrible campaign plan. He wasn't incompetent; he just wanted Borbin to put him out of his misery.*

She was on the verge of giggling at her joke when the memory of her uncle dead, his head bleeding from a small hole, sprung into her mind. Those flashes had lessened over the years, but they were still there. Bad memories waiting just below the surface until something stirred them. Only finding serious distractions made them go back to the abyss.

"Fine," she surrendered. "But only the serious ones. I have enough to worry about than small things with easy fixes."

"I expected as much," Cornelos said, lifting the first sheet of paper higher to read it in the dim light. "That's why I've been sorting them."

Smart aleck. Recha huffed and turned her head at him predicting what she would want.

"Madre Leticia has requested to speak with you—"

"What has the Viden done *now*?" Recha snapped.

Madre Leticia was head of the Church of the Savor for Lazorna, a religion spanning back farther than the founding of Desryol and the exploration of the continent. The fracturing of the country soon led to the fracturing of the church, each denomination trying to stay in the good graces of the marc they lived in. Their involvement within the state and people's daily lives depended much on the ruler of each marc.

Recha found Madre Leticia a practical woman. She didn't condone Recha seizing power, nor did she condemn it, either. The madre's focus tended on church affairs and spoke highly on Recha not campaigning for the last three years.

It was Recha's involvement with the Viden de Verda that had put the most strain on their relationship. There was no denying the cult had official state backing, and that rubbed many of the church's devoted the wrong way. It also didn't help if individual cult members got into arguments with the church, either.

"Nothing," Cornelos replied.

Recha blinked. "Oh."

"No philosophical debate turned argument turned brawl this time, I'm afraid." Cornelos slid the request into the stack. "The madre wants to discuss when your personal chapel will be finished in your mansion so she can assign a deaconess."

Recha winced. She didn't have any plans to build her own personal chapel. It was much better to go to church with everyone and be seen. She figured Cornelos was letting his faith guide him again. He was the most devote of her and her companions, after all.

"Well, I hope the next request is more important than that," she grumbled. "Otherwise, I'm going back to napping."

"Baron Puig has submitted a complaint." Cornelos swallowed. "*Again.*"

Recha threw her head back and barked a laugh. She kicked up her feet, spreading her skirts about her as she turned sideways in her seat and laid her legs across it. She left her shoes discarded on the floor.

"Let me guess"—she wrapped her arms around her knees—"he's either complaining about the troops garrisoned on his land or he's heard about Orsembar moving their troops in Puerlato."

"*Both*, actually." Cornelos smirked and held up two sheets of paper. "He complained about the first two weeks ago, and a week later, he's alarmed that Orsembian troops are marching out of Puerlato in force."

Recha laughed again then stopped, leaning back against side of the carriage. *Borbin's moving troops out of Puerlato, is he?*

There was less light where she held her head. She closed her eyes and reveled in the uninterrupted darkness.

"Puig is lucky he's not devious or incompetent. I'd send the Viden to interrogate him if I didn't have to worry about his concerns after this year."

The carriage grew quiet. She began to drift with the rocking of the carriage and soft creaking of the wheels turning on their axles in her ears.

"Are you sure it wouldn't be prudent to . . . wait another year?" Cornelos asked.

Recha opened one eye and found him hunched, head drooped with his lips pressed in a thin line.

"Cornelos, are you well?"

"I'm fine." He didn't sound fine. Almost regretful. "It's just . . . peace these last few years has been fairly good for us. There was some discontent at first, but the people are happier. Maybe if we hold the peace for just a little longer, our position will be even better. Next year's campaign season will be shorter with the Westerly Year. A much better time for a surprise strike, don't you think?"

Recha stared back at Cornelos, holding his gaze while the silence dragged out. She understood his reasoning. She had promised to end the cycle of campaigns, an end to the year after year of leveeing armies in the prospect of fighting for little to no gains. Peace was good. It was letting her people actually live. A hint of how life could be. How life *should* be.

Recha also knew the realities beyond their borders. The other marcs were willing to let her play in a corner alone for now, but that could snap at any moment. That peaceful life everyone enjoyed for past three years hung over a knife's edge. An illusion that could be shattered at any time. She preferred to shatter it on her own terms, if she could. Or rather, her old oath, harboring and building inside her all these years, demanded it.

"No," she finally replied. "Borbin is moving, and I plan to strike before he can. We can't wait any longer." She laid her head back.

My vengeance can't wait any longer.

"Very well," Cornelos conceded, his serious, official tone returning. "In that case, Hiraldo is requesting you observe a field exercise after the Exchange."

"Oh? Is he wanting to show off this *new* formation he's invented?"

Hiraldo was the last of her Companions and devoted to reorganizing her armies. He excelled, with a keen eye for tactics. When they were all younger, he had always been coming up with new, sometimes crazy and impossible ways of organizing a battle. This time of peace had allowed him to experiment with those ideas, and Recha allowed them. To a point.

"Yes," Cornelos hesitantly replied.

Recha's eyebrow twitched at that, and after he failed to say more, she asked, "Did he ask for anything else?"

"He's also hoping you'll approve another . . . purchase he made after you've seen the exercise."

Recha jerked away and clenched her eyes shut. Her fists tightened into balls, pulling on her skirts. She clenched her jaw and bit back her urge to scream.

Hiraldo! He had a habit of buying—or rather, promising *she* would pay—for the army without asking permission or thinking about where the money had to come from. Fortunately for him, some of his ideas were brilliant and competent. *It had better be worth it.*

She took a long, deep breath, calming down but refusing to open her eyes again as she leaned her head back.

"No more reports," she groaned. "I'll deal with them later. Just wake me up when we get to Cuevo."

~~~

"Welcome, La Dama Mandas."

Recha squinted from under the rim of her parasol, groggy from the little sleep she'd been able to squeeze out. She didn't bother smoothing out the wrinkles on her dress. After all, Harquis couldn't see them.

The Seer of Betrayals waited alone at the bottom steps of the Cuevo estate, the headquarters of the Viden de Verda. The five-story wings of the sprawling estate flanked her on both sides, built out of brick and granite. Gravel crunched behind her as her coachman and guards retreated to the shelter of the estate's stables to get out of the suns. The suns didn't faze Harquis, however. The cultist stood unhooded in the glare, almost basking in it. The rays danced off the pink eye medallion on his chest.

"We are honored," Harquis continued, "for your visit at this late hour."

"Who can ever tell the hour during the Exchange?" Recha grumbled. "Is your master available?"

"The Master is always available for those seeking truth." Harquis's frown hardened. "However, during the Exchange, he prefers . . . solitude."

Cornelos leaned in close beside her, shifting gravel under his feet. "They're taking this divine heraldry a bit too seriously, aren't they?" he whispered.

Recha bit the inside of her cheek. Her partnership with the Viden was always going to be a tenuous one, even from her own Companions. Cornelos didn't believe an ounce in the cult's beliefs, only their results. She hadn't told any of them the truth about the cult's master, or whom the spirit possessed. Some truths were best left unknown.

"It's urgent I speak with your master," she insisted. "Things are happening very quickly. And if your master still cherishes our partnership and doesn't want to see it wasted, *he* will see me."

Not he. It! she resisted the urge to hiss, being mindful of Cornelos.

Harquis's frown turned bored, and his head turned between her and Cornelos. His milky, glossy eyes barely moved, but Recha felt a chill run up her arms, certain he was looking for something.

"Very well," he finally said. "We can always ask." Harquis turned on his heels and carefully walked up the granite steps, each footfall carefully measured.

Recha followed, Cornelos cautiously on her heels with one hand resting on his rapier.

Harquis led them to a large, white oak door with a large eye carved into it. Its silver knob sparkled in the sunlight.

The cultist grabbed a gold cord hanging beside the door and tugged three times.

Recha listened, but she heard nothing. Moments later, a heavy bolt sprung from within the door with a *thud*, and the door creaked inward. Harquis didn't step inside until the creaking stopped and the door stood agape.

The scent of hibiscus struck Recha instantly once inside. The estate was lavish. White linen drapes hung over every window, and a crystal chandelier hung above the foyer, dazzling the honey-colored walls and interior granite pillars with light.

They were led farther into the estate, ignoring the marble staircases to the higher floors. Their footfalls and shoe heels echoed on the polished stone tiles.

Despite this being the cult's headquarters, the estate was eerily quiet and empty. There were no servants going about their duties. No wandering initiate walking the corridors or groups of cloaked figures standing about, whispering, arguing, or chanting. Cuevo had been like this every time Recha visited. If she didn't know better, she would have thought the cult was farce.

Unfortunately, she did know better.

Farther in, the corridors got tighter, and the walls changed from stone to wood paneling. Windows disappeared, and their path was illuminated by lamps hanging from the walls, each one spaced to the point a small shadow formed between the yellowish glows.

Recha knew where they were going, having walked this path several times. She glanced over her shoulder, worried about Cornelos.

He stepped lightly on the balls on his feet. His jaw set, he twitched and watched each passing door, as if expecting assailants to burst out of them at any second. His hand still rested on his rapier, and his spectacles were tucked neatly into the right breast pocket of his dark jacket, its buttons neatly buttoned up the jacket's left breast.

"Relax," she gently whispered to ease him. "Don't let them frighten you."

"It's not me I'm frightened for," Cornelos whispered back, still checking the doors.

Recha allowed a small smile. After Sebastian had died, her other three Companions seemed to have put aside their grief to try to comfort her. They had all been friends since childhood, having grown up together, but it had become something more now. Cornelos had been the most tentative, almost making himself available at her beck and call.

"It's fine, Cornelos. They won't dare harm us. The Viden need us more than we need them." She smiled broadly at that, hoping it would reassure him.

Cornelos stood a little straighter and merely glanced at a few passing doors, but his shoulders remained tense, and he stepped lightly.

They rounded a bend, and sitting in front of a small, arched door was Vastura, back straight and hands folded in her lap. Her head slowly turned toward them as they approached. Her glossy eyes passed over them and back to Harquis.

"Seer," Vastura greeted him.

"Seer," Harquis greeted back. "How is the Master?"

"The Master is communing with the Exchange."

Communing with the Exchange? Recha arched an eyebrow. *Is she putting on an act of sounding mysterious for us?*

Cornelos made a sound, like catching himself from clearing his throat. Recha gave him look, and he apologetically winced.

"Is the Master beyond our reach then?" Harquis angled his head oddly.

Vastura pursed her lips and turned to Recha. "Maybe for us. Probably not for her. Should the Master be inclined."

Harquis hummed and turned around. "You shall go with Seer Vastura, La Dama. Your guard shall remain."

"I am La Dama's secretary!" Cornelos snapped, stepping protectively in front of Recha before she could react. "Where she goes, I go."

Harquis drew himself up, and Vastura glowered at Cornelos, as much as that was possible for a blind woman.

"*Cornelos!*" Recha hissed, intervening before he stepped too far over the line.

Cornelos stepped back, flustered.

"Stay here!" she hissed again, glaring at him to convey she would suffer no arguments. "I'll be fine."

Cornelos dropped his head bashfully and moved aside. "Apologies, La Dama," he whispered.

"We'll talk about this later," she whispered back, walking up to Vastura.

The female seer unlocked the small door, and Recha shielded herself with her parasol before the sunlight spilled into the corridor. She followed her new guide outside, leaving Cornelos and Harquis to glower at each other after the door closed.

Spilling out before her was the garden maze in the center of the estate. The thick hedges were pocketed with dozens of different varieties of flowers, predominately with purple petals. Purple mats and small flowers that acted like weeds clung to the sides of hedges, while various clovers, dusters, and thistles cropped up underneath them, poking up in patches to catch the light.

Vastura led Recha down a stone path that hugged the walls of the estate before turning sharply into the maze. Recha knew the way, of course. She had memorized it after walking it a few times. It led to a small cottage in the center of the maze.

Despite this grand estate and all the rooms and comfort it offered, they housed the most important person in a small, single-story house—her sister.

She took a deep breath to steady her aching heart. *I can't change that now*, she reminded herself. *But maybe someday ...*

Vastura turned left off the path instead of turning right.

Recha pulled up short, staring after the woman then back the way she knew was right. "Shouldn't we have turned to the right?" she called, hoping she didn't alarm the seer with the fact that she knew the way on her own.

Vastura stopped. "Come," she said from over her shoulder. "The Master is this way."

Recha swallowed, glancing at the long purple mats sticking out from hedges, like fingers drooping over the path. Steeling herself, she set her parasol at an angle and marched after the cultist, pushing the small bulb heads out of her way.

One bother dealt with, another soon emerged. With her parasol protecting her from the suns, her head was showered by pollen from the ends of the parasol brushing the hedges. The dazzling sunslight messed with her sense of direction. Recha soon didn't know where she was or how to get back. She twirled her head around to recall her route. Her eyebrow twitched as she tried to map it out in her head, to no avail.

This could be bad. I might—

Recha pulled up short. An angelic, child-like humming floated down between the hedgerows, making her ears perk up.

"Elegida?" she gasped. Her heart pounded in her chest, and she sprung forward, pushing around Vastura without thinking of propriety. "*Elegida!*"

No reply came, but the humming continued, drawing her heart ever forward. She failed to realize she wasn't holding her parasol until she was standing at the end of the path where the hedge rows opened to create a circular enclosure.

Elegida sat on a wooden bench in the center of the enclosure, swaying back and forth. She tried to swing her feet, but her legs were too long, and her heels scraped against the grass underneath. A halo shined off her pristine, white robes, reflecting the Exchange's light. Her head bobbed at an angle as she swayed, bathing in the suns.

Recha hiked up her skirts and strode out onto the grass. She hadn't had time to change after her meeting with Ambassador Valen, and the black silk starkly stood out compared to her sister. She noticed Elegida's eyes were closed as she got closer.

Please, she prayed. *Please don't let this be a trick.*

"El . . . Elegida?" she said hesitantly.

Elegida's humming cut short. Her eyes snapped open, milky white orbs without the ability to focus.

"Recha?" she called, her voice was soft and high-pitched, like a child. "Recha, is that you?" Her eyes rolled upward, as if trying to remember how to see. Her head bobbed back and forth, turning her ears from side to side—the hallmark of a person who had learned to see with their ears. She reached out, fingers spread wide, as if groping in the dark. An excited smile split her face. "Did you come to play with me today?" Elegida bounced on the bench, giggling, and stretched even further.

In that moment, Recha forgot why she had come. Her questions. Her uncertainty. Even her exhaustion. She took her sister's hands and fell beside her on the bench.

"I'm here!" she replied. "I'm here!"

"Yay!" Elegida exclaimed and happily laughed. Their fingers intertwined as she started swinging their arms up and down. "Recha's back!"

At first, Recha didn't know what to do, but she quickly laughed and followed along. This was how her sister was now whenever her body wasn't being possessed by that spirit. Elegida's body had grown, but her mind and personality hadn't.

The sisters had been separated after their mother had died of consumption when they were both two years old. Now they were twenty-three, but Elegida spoke and behaved as if she were nine.

Recha's vision grew blurry, and her cheeks wobbled while staring into that happy, laughing face, so like and unlike her own. She couldn't help it. Elegida was her sister.

Her grip tightened, and she pulled Elegida into an embrace, causing her sister to grunt cutely. Recha wrapped her arms around her, gradually squeezing, and pressed her face into hair. The scent of sweet apples was nearly overwhelming as she held her.

It didn't last but a few seconds before Elegida began squirming. "Re . . . Recha?" she gagged, fidgeting from side to side. "You're . . . choking me."

"No, I'm not," Recha retorted and squeezed a tad tighter.

Elegida made an exaggerated choking sound and waved her arms. "I can't breathe! I can't breathe! You're so big! Recha's . . . crushing . . . me. *Gah.*" Elegida fell limp, pressing her full weight into Recha, forcing her to hold her up.

Recha tried to keep her balance but ended up laughing instead at how childish it all was. She finally had to let her go. And the instant she felt her chance, Elegida pulled away and began taking deep, overdone breaths.

"It was only a hug, Elegida," Recha said, wiping the tears from her eyes.

"You were trying to *crush* me again." Elegida pouted. She suddenly winced and rubbed her cheek. "*Ew!* There's something wet on my face!"

Recha blinked and realized some of her tears must have rubbed off. She wiped them away so Elegida wouldn't have to fumble around. "It's fine," she assured her. "All better now."

Elegida petulantly turned her face away, groaning as if annoyed.

"*Aw,*" Recha cooed. "Are you mad at me now?" She lightly pulled Elegida's hair back and over her ear, which immediately made her shake her head.

"Stop picking on me!" Elegida puffed her cheeks out, pretending to look upset, even though she didn't know how.

"But I like picking on you." Recha scooted closer and messed with her hair some more, running her fingers through it and trying to straighten it despite Elegida's attempts to shake and fluff it out. "I don't get to see you that much, so I got to take every opportunity."

Elegida flung her hair more fiercely. After spitting strands out of her mouth several times, Recha changed tactics and goosed her sister under her arms.

Elegida squealed and bounced in her seat, nearly sliding out off if Recha hadn't grabbed her.

"No!" Elegida cried and laughed. "No fair!"

Recha wrapped her arms around her and held her close. She rocked her and set her chin on Elegida's shoulder. "I've missed you."

Elegida cradled Recha's arms instead of struggling and snuggled back against her. "I missed you, too."

Recha's chest tightened. She wanted to drag this moment out, to keep her embrace for as long as the Exchange made it feel like time stood still. She wasn't alone. Not everyone had been taken from her. She held her family in her arms, and she never wanted to let go.

"Hey," she whispered, "do you think they'd let you leave? Maybe for a short trip?"

"I don't know," Elegida replied. "They've never taken me anywhere before."

"Not the cultists. What if *I* took you somewhere? To the place I gre—am living now." Recha swallowed, catching herself at the last moment. Elegida's mind was not the only thing stuck as a child; her perception of Recha was still that same-age twin she knew when they'd been separated.

"I don't know," Elegida repeated. "Is it nice?"

"Mmhmm." Recha let her sit up and rubbed her shoulders. "It's not as big as this place, but there are plenty of good people who'd love to meet you. There's a big yard to run in and big beds to jump on."

Elegida giggled. "Vastura doesn't like it when I jump on the bed."

Recha giggled back. "You can jump on as many beds as you like. Oh! And someone special makes the best cakes in the world. Fluffy and sweet. You'd just love them."

"Cake!" Elegida burst into a gaping smile. "I *love*—"

Her breath caught, allowing a mere strangled whimper to escape her throat. Elegida's body tensed and started trembling. Her face remained frozen in her wide smile, yet the edges of her lips twitched, and her eyes began to widen.

A brilliant and violent pink light burst from the crystal in the center of her eye medallion, and Recha knew instantly what that meant.

It's coming!

She seized Elegida's shoulders. "I'm still here, Elegida! Your big sister won't ever abandon you! I'll always—"

Pink liquid squirted into Elegida's irises, swirling like water flowing into milk, until all the white was replaced by the same violent pink. Tension left Elegida's body, and her face relaxed to an emotionless frown. Her eyes fluttered closed, and her shoulders rose and fell as she took several deep breaths. Her eyes slowly reopened . . ..

But the person was no longer the same.

"Recha," Verdas said with a voice more mature and eerily like Recha's own, "why do you disturb me?"

Recha pulled away reluctantly and clutched her trembling hands in her lap to regain her composure. Her sister was gone. Ripped away to wherever the spirit suppressed her consciousness when it took control. She was no longer talking to family but a dubious ally.

She straightened her shoulders and back and took a deep breath. "I didn't mean to disturb you," she replied. "Things are moving, and I thought you'd want to know."

Verdas snickered. "You mean now that the time has come, you have doubts. Maybe some worries that you just couldn't answer. So, you came running to me."

Recha squeezed her hands together and remained calm. *Don't slap it,* she told herself. *I still need its help. Besides, that's Elegida's face I'd be hitting.*

"Can you answer them?" she asked.

Verdas smirked and stood. It ran its fingers through its hair before sighing, turning its face to bathe in the suns.

"I long for this time." Verdas stretched out its hands up at the sky, fingers sprawled out as if to cradle the suns. "You have no idea how *blessed* you are, mortal. Of the sacrifices this world required. This time is for every being to reflect and be grateful."

Recha squinted at her. Her brow furled more and more until she was finally forced to shut her eyes and turn away.

53

"I've made sacrifices, too," she replied, shielding her eyes with her hand. She rose and walked around to look Verdas in the face and to keep the suns out of hers. "But I cannot sacrifice any more time. I call upon our bargain, Verdas. I need your . . . insight."

Verdas lowered its arms but kept its head tilted back. Its eyes opened and glanced at Recha warily and annoyed. "Very well. Tell me everything."

Recha did. She left nothing out. It wouldn't have benefited her if she had. Verdas would naturally know if it wasn't given the whole truth. Recha told her about each meeting with all three ambassadors, their agreements, and her expectations and concerns from each of the marquéses. By the time she was finished, Verdas had sat back down again. Its legs neatly crossed and crookedly smiling as if everything was obvious.

Do I look that smug when I know everything?

Recha shoved the question away to focus on the present. "Well? Borbin is planning something. That much is obvious. If he attacks us now, though, all our waiting and building could be for nothing."

"Patience is never without its rewards and costs," Verdas replied. "And your deduction is correct that your foe is moving. However, I'm afraid you have all assumed a non-truth."

"Which is . . .?" Recha folded her arms.

"You say these 'Rules of Campaigns' dictate that the easiest prize will be the one taken. However, the oldest rules of war, created long before your people's existence in this world, is that war is all about deception.

"Everyone believes you are in a weak position." Verdas held out its right hand. "And, in response, your own allies believe they can use your land as a grinding stone to weaken your foe. But, in so doing, they don't make you the *easiest* prize. They have altered their own arithmetic."

Verdas held up its left hand. "That leaves the other possibility. A people who can be assailed from two sides at once and offer up a much larger and . . . easier prize."

Recha didn't need a moment to decipher the spirit's needlessly cryptic response. "Quezlo!" she said. "You agree Borbin and Narios plan to pincer Quezlo from two directions."

Verdas smugly shrugged. "The truth is quite simple when one takes mortal ego and worry away. You should really consider spending more time here, Recha. It'll broaden your mind."

Recha was deep in thought on the implications to hear Verdas's offer. She replied with a grunt and set to pacing back and forth, skirts raking the grass as the thought of troop deployments and supplies racked her brain.

"So, now *is* the time to strike," she finally said, stopping to glance at Verdas.

Verdas's half-smile melted away, leaving her with an emotionless visage. "If you don't strike now, your vengeance is lost forever, Recha Mandas."

The cold, nearly prophetic tone of the spirit's voice struck Recha to her core, stopping her in her tracks. Everything within her screamed she had to move. No more waiting. No more stalling. The urge to storm off, find Cornelos, and begin ordering all troops to assemble nearly made her grab her skirts and dash away.

The heavy need to figure out all the logistics stopped her, however.

She began pacing again.

"We have the men," Recha mumbled, her neck craned downward, eyes glued to the grass out of the suns' reach. "Hiraldo's seen to that. The barons will have to be informed. Then there's Don Cristal to deal with before we even attack." She rubbed the back of her neck then stopped. "I'll have to have a field marshal!"

That was another issue. Her coup and subsequent restructuring of Lazorna's military hadn't sat well with every calleros. After halting the Orsembian advance, many older calleroses, those who would have been in line for senior officers, had chosen instead to go into retirement, free of their barons' campaign obligations. Several others had joined disgruntled barons in fermenting decent and near rebellions. She'd been forced to purge those elements.

Afterward, Lazorna's armies had gone through a period of reform and restructuring. She had basically given them to Hiraldo and a generation of junior calleroses to experiment with what worked and what didn't. Now, the time was upon her, and of the few marshals still serving, she hesitated to consider giving— or rather sharing—command of the armies with any of them.

Chuckling snapped her out of descending spiral. Verdas was grinning at her again.

"You're letting your mortal worry deny you of the truth again," the spirit said. "There is only one you need to consider. Only one you *know* you need. No matter how much he claims he can't, he most certainly wants to."

Recha tensed. "Papa?"

Verdas nodded.

Recha frowned. "Baltazar Vigodt is retired, as he's been so fond of telling me for past three years."

"Convince him otherwise," Verdas encouraged. "A truth about mortal vengeance—it doesn't just burn in the hearts of grieving lovers, but in the hearts of grieving fathers, as well."

Chapter 4

"Sorry, but I don't need any," Gael grunted out, shifting boxes around his storefront. The middle-aged cobbler hefted a box of bootheels and hauled it the back of the storefront, sweat staining the back of his shirt.

Necrem wrung the wide brim of his hat while he stood in the middle of the emptying cobbler store. The windows were boarded to block out the suns and keep some of the heat in. They certainly kept in the heavy scent of tanned leather and wood. The few shelves were empty, no samples of shoes or boots to catch a needy or working man's eye.

He's going with the army this season, Necrem surmised. Armies always needed more camp workers than they did soldiers—cooks, cobblers, laundry washers, doctors.

Blacksmiths.

It took a host of other people simply to get the fighting men to the fight. If they ever fought at all.

"I'm sorry, Necrem," Gael said, walking back in and raking his wet, stringy hair out of his face as he squinted at Necrem, "but no, I don't need any more nails." He walked over to his stool in the far-left corner and picked up a board with sheets of paper tacked to it. He flipped over a few of the sheets and squinted again.

"Are you sure you have enough?" Necrem asked half-heartedly. "Campaigns can be . . . hard to plan for. You can never be too certain you have everything." He choked back the bile he felt from repeatedly having to asking. He was thankful his black cloth mask hid his discomfort. It felt too much like begging than trying to sell his wares. Asking people to buy his work had always been difficult for him. Everything was so much easier when people came to him to fix things or make something new for them.

He had to do this, though. He was running out of time.

"I'm pretty sure," Gael replied, flopping the pages back over. He sat the board on his knees, and then his face lit up like he had a thought. "Now, if you had a shipment of hides, or knew someone selling hides, that would be something I could use."

Necrem shook his head. "I only have metal."

"I'm sorry then, Necrem, but I really can't help." Gael sighed and looked Necrem up and down, slumped in his stool. "It's this year's campaign tax, isn't it?"

Necrem grunted.

"The tax nearly got me, too." Gael folded his arms. "If I hadn't shown that collector my permit as an army cobbler for this season, I'm sure he'd have turned my name over to the press gangs. But you—"

"Thanks for your time, Gael," Necrem said, turning for the door and putting his hat on. "Hope I wasn't a bother."

"No bother, Necrem. No bother at all."

Necrem opened the door, flooding the room with blinding Exchange light. He angled his hat's wide brim to shield his eyes.

He was barely able to make out twenty feet in front of him.

"You're a friend of Daved's, aren't you?" Gael called when Necrem was halfway out the door. "Surely he can help you."

Necrem's grip tightened on the doorlatch until the wood gave a protesting creak.

No, he told himself, closing the door. *A man shouldn't go begging to his friend.*

31st of Manas, 1018 N.F. (w.y.) ~ 1st of Petrarium, 1019 N.F (e.y.)

Necrem huddled in the narrow shadow of the building's eave. He held his arms tight across his chest while the steam of his breath spilled around the edges his mask like mist. He shivered.

The Exchange must be halfway over.

He wasn't certain how many days had passed. It could have been four, could have been five. The constant light was disorienting, and Necrem couldn't trust counting the number of times he had slept.

The sudden cold was the only true measure of time. It defied all logic with both suns bearing down on the world, but the world grew colder halfway through the Exchange. Necrem had heard tale of water *freezing* under the suns in the far north. The cool air dried out his skin, and his facial scars pulled and shriveled tightly on his cheeks, threating the exposed portions of his gums.

When it got warm again, though, that announced the Exchange was ending. *I'm running out of time.*

"What do you want?" the squat, stockyard manager demanded. Sunslight reflected off his bald scalp, tanned deeply, like leather. The two, gray tuffs of hair above his lip failed to pass for a mustache and looked more like hairs growing out his bulbous nose. Especially from how he was scowling up at Necrem with his fists on his hips.

"Good Exchange," Necrem grumbled, reaching for his hat.

"Savior damn the Exchange!" the manager snapped. "What do you want?"

Necrem pulled back, keeping his face muscles as still as possible. Even frowning threatened to split a scar, causing it to bleed.

He took his hat off to be respectful. "I'm looking to sell nails and horseshoes for the campaign stock," he replied. "I was hoping you were still buying."

"What would I do with them?" The manager spat off to the side. His right eyebrow twitched.

"For the campaign," Necrem stated pointedly, thinking it obvious. "For wagon repairs and replacement for the horses." He gestured out in the yard. Half of it was full of wagons, both loaded and unload, lined up in columns and waiting to be hitched up. The corrals for the horses and cattle, though, were empty. They had already been moved to barns and stables to be kept out of the suns. Necrem knew the campaign would call for hundreds of horses and even more heads of cattle for the army.

"That's a waste of space," the manager said dismissively.

"What?" Necrem grunted.

"Have you never been on campaign before? If a horse throws a shoe, then one of the armies' blacksmiths just makes another one. And if a wagon breaks down, they just leave it. No one's got space to haul around a bunch of nails and horseshoes, and I'm not going to waste any deberes, either. You just get out of here and stop wasting my damn time! Idiot!" The manager grabbed the latch of his door and slammed it shut. A faint *click* followed as he locked it.

Necrem stood there, staring at the door. He balled his fists until his hat's leather bit into his palm, ground his teeth together, and his cheeks started to sting.

He breathed heavily through his nose, puffing out wisps through his mask. His vision suddenly blurred, and he gasped, snapping his eyes shut.

Don't get mad, Necrem urged himself. *Don't get mad!*

His arms trembled, but after a few deep breaths, he finally calmed down. He took a deep breath and put his hat on.

Home. Necrem shoved his broad hands into his pockets and walked out of the yard with his shoulders slumped.

2nd ~ 3rd of Petrarium, 1019 N.F (e.y.)

"Didn't mean to bother you," Necrem said as another door slammed into his face. His shoulders fell, and he sighed heavily.

He walked off the steps and back into the street, the gravel crunching under his feet. He headed to the next squat, clay plaster house, yet he found little strength or willpower to knock on the door when he got to its steps. This was too much. Too desperate. Even for him. So, he kept walking.

No one needs any nails. No one needs any horseshoes. No one needs a new skillet. Necrem's head hung lower, the wide brim of his hat providing blessed shade for his whole face. *No one needs anything.*

The small line of sweat running from his hairline down his jaw made everything worse. Warmth was returning quickly. Soon, the Westerly Sun would fade back, and the Easterly Sun would become dominate in the sky. Night would return, and everyone would get back to their lives.

And the tax collector will come back to collect.

Lifting his head up, Necrem's world was still an unsettling glare. Most of the houses he passed were clay plaster and shingled houses, sturdy and closely built together. The slums were quiet, as if everyone had boarded up their homes and buried themselves underneath to get out of the suns.

Farther down the street, Necrem just barely made out Manosete's high stone walls, sticking out in stark contrast to the pitiful dwellings outside them. Beyond that loomed the Hand of the West—a towering structure of marble, granite, and black obsidian, each clashing design built together to resemble a hand stretching up into the sky with five towers branching off it.

Legend told it was built on the site where the founding head of the Desryol family, the family who had led humanity west, died. It was said he died with his hand stretched out toward the suns because his only desire was to go ever westward, as for as he could. Yet, here he died, and the Desryol commemorated the spot with a gaunt monstrosity at the center of their kingdom.

The story was stupid. Necrem knew any story the nobility made up was stupid, but that one was a special kind of stupid. Nobles might be morbid, but they weren't *that* morbid.

Sweat slipped under his mask, and the salt seeped into a scar and stunned his face.

Actually, some are. Necrem squinted, though he could see the Hand of the West trying to grasp the Easterly Sun. *Starting to see things. Might as well head—*

A woman's soft crying made him stop. Peering from under his hat's brim, he saw a door ajar three houses down. He turned on his heels, away from the house, but the crying got louder.

Just walk away, he told himself. *Nothing good will come of it. I can't help anybody.*

The crying persisted.

Gritting his teeth, Necrem turned back and headed toward the house. The Exchange could be a dangerous time. The constant sunlight did strange things to people, turning those usually calm and gentle into raving animals from the delirium. It was especially hard to get help if anything went terribly wrong, too, because everyone was hunkered down until the Exchange was over.

Necrem cautiously walked up the steps then hesitantly knocked on the door. Despite trying to be gentle, his knuckles pushed the door farther in, its hinges creaking.

"Hello?" he called. "Is everyone all right?"

"Who's that?" a stern man's voice demanded.

Necrem took off his hat and stopped at the threshold, abiding the rules of hospitality and not entering unless he was asked.

The door creaked open wider to reveal a small common room filled with clutter, shelves with knickknacks and old family heirlooms, an empty fireplace with an iron hook to hold kettles and pots over the fire, and a pair of worn rocking chairs.

In the corner sat a man and, presumably, his wife at a table. The homely woman's face was buried in her hands. Her sweat-soaked shawl threatened to come loose and spill her hair out.

The man grimaced at Necrem. Although his face was weathered and in need of a shave, he didn't look no older than Necrem. He sat with his right leg stretched out, unnaturally straight, under the table. He held up his walking cane as if pondering whether to throw it or use it as a club.

"I beg your pardon!" Necrem said, throwing up his hands. "I heard crying and thought something might be wrong."

"There's plenty wrong!" the man spat. "But nothing you can do about it. And if you're one of those Exchange house robbers I've heard about; just so you know, I was once in the Marqués's own First Company, you hear!" The man held his cane higher above his head and waved it about, but he stayed seated.

"Hush, Rego!" the woman snapped. "You were not! Put that stick down before you make things worse."

The woman sniffed and rubbed her eyes before turning to Necrem. "Forgive us, but there is nothing you can do … unless you can bring our son back." She hung her head, and tears dripped onto the table.

Her husband, Rego, begrudgingly did as she said and lowered his cane.

Necrem felt the urge to say his condolences to whatever had happened and leave, but he felt suddenly awkward standing in their doorway. His feet were so stiff he couldn't move.

"Has something happened?" he asked. "Do you need a doctor?"

"Doctors are no help," Rego replied. "They ain't got no cure for tax collectors and their press gangs."

Necrem perked up. "Press gangs?"

"Aye," Rego said. "Tax collector came in, bold as he pleased, and demanded the campaign tax early. Gave him every last damned deber we had, and it still wasn't enough." The man sneered. "So, his men took our eldest."

The woman burst out crying again. Her face slapped down into her palms, and her shawl came loose, spilling her dark hair about her shoulders.

"Jeorjio's only fifteen!" she cried. "Only *fifteen*!"

As the man consoled his wife, rubbing her shoulders and keeping a tough expression, Necrem felt cold.

They're demanding the tax already! Necrem shivered. *And they're taking men.*

The image of the tax collector coming back to his forge while he was away, with only Bayona and Eulalia there, made his blood turn cold. He took one step back without thinking, but then he remembered the open door and crying couple beyond. He reached back for the door latch and gave them one final look.

"I'm sorry," he said then pulled the door closed.

He stuffed his hat back on his head and strode off down the steps in a single bound. He turned directly for home, his long legs carrying him several blocks before he slowed to a stop.

I still don't have the money.

If the tax collectors were already resulting to bringing men along to press young boys into the Marqués's army, it was unthinkable they would let a big, non-Union member blacksmith who couldn't pay off. He needed deberes. And it didn't matter how he got them.

Swallowing whatever pride he had left, Necrem walked to the end of the street and turned right instead of left. Gravel crunched under his boots as he determinedly marched with his fists clenched tight to keep his nerve. And go beg to a friend.

~~~

Sanjaro's Butcher Shop was still open. People had to eat, even during the Exchange. Butcher Lane was a wide side street skirting the northern corner of Manosete's outer wall. Despite being part of the outer slums, these were the best houses and shops outside the city. Several even had two stories and brick foundations that could easily pass for inner city lodgings.

Sanjaro's shop was a large, two-story, brick building with a clay shingled roof. A sign in the glass window read, *"No fresh poultry until after Exchange. Only smoked red meat available."*

Necrem raised an eyebrow. The poultry, he understood, but not the red meat.

It's between summers and campaign's about to start. How does he have any red meat left?

Although, if Sanjaro did have red meat to sell, maybe he was able to help.

Necrem ducked his head and stepped inside. A long, wooden counter divided the shopfront. The counter bore a smooth, polished shine from years of cleaning, chopping, and preparing meats. To his right were a couple of tables and chairs that looked inviting to his worn feet, but he didn't want to sit and risk collapsing one. Being indoors, he suddenly felt tired.

Necrem's nose flared, and he breathed deeply to suck in the spicy, heavy scent of smoking meat drifting through the shop from somewhere in the back. His mouth watered, and he pressed a hand to his belly to stop it from rumbling.

When was the last time I ate? he wondered, but then he shook the thought away. He had more urgent things to take care of than food.

"Sanjaro!" he called out, walking through the empty shopfront.

Farther back lead deeper inside the shop and then to the stairs to the upper floor where the butcher lived. Necrem rarely visited these days. It was hard for him to admit, but even his oldest remaining friend reminded him of what he had lost ten years ago. Out of respect for the rules of hospitality, he remained up at the front.

"Sanjaro!" he yelled again.

A thud came from upstairs, followed soon after by angry, muffled voices. Necrem tracked the sounds of footsteps on the ceiling and listened to them coming down the stairs in the back.

"Sorry," a man said groggily. "We're closed! Must've forgotten to lock the—"

Sanjaro Daved stopped in the doorway at the back of the shop with one arm up in the air, trying to slide into his robe sleeve. The robe itself hung open, revealing the man's undergarments and portly belly. His once angular face had gone soft, and his cheeks pudgy, but his hook nose was still as prominent. The tuffs of his dark hair stuck out in every direction around his bald crown.

He stood, mouth agape, eyes blinking in the doorframe.

"Hello, Sanjaro," Necrem said. "It's been . . . a long time."

Sanjaro squinted then gawked. "Necrem?" His face split in a wide smile. "Necrem Oso! My friend!" Sanjaro wrapped his robe around him, fumbling as he tied it and almost tripped as he rushed into the storefront. He rushed up to Necrem with his arms outstretched. They clasped arms together instead of embracing because of Sanjaro's average height.

They stood there a moment. Necrem felt slightly awkward from Sanjaro's happy greeting. Sanjaro's hands trembled and gripped Necrem's arms while he beamed up at him.

"It's so good to see you!" Sanjaro said. He let go and urged him toward a table. "Come sit down! Sit down!"

Necrem stomped over and collapsed in a chair. He stretched his weary feet out and stifled a sigh.

Sanjaro took the seat opposite him. "How long has it been? Six? Seven years?"

"Six years," Necrem replied. He folded his hands atop the table and rubbed his knuckles. Part of him felt ashamed for being here, knowing what he had come to ask for.

"Six years." Sanjaro shook his head. "How is Eulalia? Is she doing better?"

"She . . ." Necrem swallowed, not wanting to tell the truth. "She has her good days."

Sanjaro snickered. "So does my Annette."

"Sanjaro!" a woman yelled from upstairs, as if summoned. "Who's down there?"

Sanjaro rolled his eyes and turned back to yell down the hall, "Necrem Oso, dear! You remember! My old friend, the blacksmith!"

"Doesn't he know how late it truly is?" Annette sounded annoyed and not at all happy. "Tell him we're closed!"

Sanjaro laughed halfheartedly while light footfalls marked Annette's retreat upstairs.

Necrem wasn't surprised. He hardly remembered Sanjaro's wife, except that she didn't like him much. He had either forgotten the reason why or never knew it to start with.

"Please, forgive her," Sanjaro asked. "She's just a little exhausted from the Exchange."

"This Exchange has felt longer than usual," Necrem agreed, his shoulders slumped.

"You look worn out. Like a cut off the flank that's been sitting out too long and beaten." Sanjaro tilted his head then slowly grinned. "I bet Bayona's been running you ragged, hasn't she? She and every other kid must be going crazy being cooped up like this."

Necrem lowered his gaze, thinking about his little miracle back home. "She's actually taking the Exchange very well. She's getting to where she's taking care of us more and more."

But what kind of childhood is that? he wondered begrudgingly. *She should be out playing with the rest of the children rather than playing maid to a couple broken parents beyond mending.*

Necrem raised his head. The thought was sudden. Unexpected. He didn't know where it had come from. Then he suddenly realized Sanjaro had said something.

"What was that?" he asked.

"How old is Bayona now?" Sanjaro repeated, slouching back in his chair.

"Ten."

"*Ten!*" Sanjaro whistled, shaking his head. "How tall is she?"

Necrem snorted. "Almost reaches my hip."

Sanjaro chuckled. "She's going to be tall then. Just like her papa."

Necrem turned his head slightly, not wanting to appear embarrassed. Yet, even sitting hunched over the table, he felt his chest swell.

Sanjaro cleared his throat. "So then, what brings you around? Want to surprise Eulalia with a smoked ham, or a fat frier? I hope Bayona is learning to be a good cook because, as I remember"—he laughed—"you weren't."

"No," Necrem replied quickly, shaking his head. "No, it's . . . it's not that." He sat there, working his mouth, but the words just wouldn't form. He rubbed his hands together and squeezed sweat through his rough calluses. "I need . . . help." Necrem took a big breath, as if even asking took a lot out of him.

"Well, sure," Sanjaro said. "What help do you need?"

Necrem raised his head, but his teeth clenched. He was grateful for his mask; otherwise, he would look like he was snarling. His scars began to sting again. The last vestiges of his pride tightened his throat, desperate for him not to say. But he did.

"I can't pay the campaign tax," he finally admitted, hissing through his teeth.

"Oh." Sanjaro's smile faded, and he sat up.

Necrem turned away, unable to keep looking at his friend but also unable hold in his frustration. "They've *doubled* this year's tax! I thought I could finish my latest order and scrape enough together to pay it. But after working"—he paused to add up the time, but the numbers refused to sum, and he shook his head—"at least more than a day and night, it didn't matter. The tax collectors got to the farmer, too, and he couldn't pay me.

"I've been going around, trying to get anyone to buy my steel. Nails to cobblers. Nails and horseshoes to the stockyard. Tools to workmen. Skillets to any woman who'd open their door! No *one* needs to buy anything! No one . . . wants my steel." Necrem's chin felt damp, and he sucked in, realizing drool had leaked through his exposed gums. He wiped his chin and rubbed his hand on his pants.

"Do you remember when I repaired Baron Emousia's sword?" he asked.

"Our second campaign," Sanjaro replied, nodding.

"Our second campaign. Third year as a member of the Union. *One* year out of my apprenticeship. I worked on that blade all night. Practically made it new. Remember what that baron said?"

Sanjaro snorted. "You used it for a sales pitch for years. 'Finest steel I've ever held,' he said. If I'm not mistaken?"

"You're not." It curdled Necrem's guts hearing it now. Partly because he'd been complimented by a baron who probably wouldn't give a deber for his value as a man. Worse, another part of him still felt a sliver of pride hearing it again.

"And now no one wants my steel." He hung his head. "No one wants my iron. Press gangs are already out with the tax collectors. If they're conscripting boys, what do you think they'll do with me? What'll happen to Bayona and Eulalia if I can't pay and they take me?"

That was Necrem's greatest fear. It shook him to his core. There were always stories of wives and undefended children set upon by anyone, from wandering strangers to corrupt guardsmen. He had long put them off as rumors. People scaring themselves into believing them. But the worst fear of all was him being taken away and not coming back.

Who would look after them? He trembled. *Who would look after a sick, poor blacksmith's widow and child?*

The mental image of Bayona and Eulalia on the streets, turned into the beggars, made him gasp. He pounded his fists on the table to force the image away and, unfortunately, startled Sanjaro.

Sanjaro straightened his robe and sat forward, leaning against the table. His brow furled. "Necrem, have you *not* paid your taxes yet?"

"No," Necrem replied. "The tax collector said it was due at the end of the Exchange. But I saw a family today who had to pay today and couldn't. The collector had a press gang with him, and they *took* their oldest son. If they're demanding payment early, they're probably already heading to my forge."

They could be waiting for me right now, he thought, rolling over the possibilities in his mind. *Waiting in front of my door or in the store. Or in the kitchen. They better not upset Eulalia. She was having a bad day when I left. They better leave—*

The room had gone quiet.

Necrem glanced at Sanjaro, finding him frowning with his chin pressed into his chest. He was working his mouth and grimacing, as if chewing on a bad piece of gristle. His brow contorted, and he looked away quickly when he noticed Necrem looking at him.

"What's wrong?" Necrem asked.

"Necrem," Sanjaro grunted then worked his mouth, as if finding words difficult. "Everyone . . . everyone around here had to pay their taxes on the first day of the Exchange. I . . . can't give you any money. I don't have a single deber."

Necrem felt numb. *You mean . . . it's all for nothing?*

He fell back in his chair, the wood creaking against his weight. His arms felt heavy and slid off the table to hang by his sides.

"They came by here the first hour after both suns were high," Sanjaro explained. "I'd decided I wasn't going to sell off meat to the stockyards, so the greedy bastards charged me triple. *Triple!*"

For nothing, Necrem thought again. His head drooped, and he felt a mounting, dull pressure growing beyond the periphery on the sides of his head. His scalp tingled.

"They don't care," Sanjaro continued, "that every year we have less and less food for everyone or people can't afford to buy much. They want support for their campaign efforts, or your taxes go up. Simple as that."

Nothing.

"Simple as them not caring," Necrem said lowly, clenching his fists into tight balls. "Because they never cared."

"Necrem?" Sanjaro said nervously.

Necrem didn't look at him. "But why should they? They take our wares, our food, our crafts, even blood. And for what? For *what*?"

His arms came up like hammers and, just like hammers, he dropped them with all his might, slamming them on the table with a crack. Splinters flew into the air, and the table folded like brittle, thin steel.

"*Nothing!*" he bellowed, lumbering to his feet.

His head was pounding, his cheeks were stinging, and he didn't care. His vision blurred. The only thing he wanted was to pound something. Anything!

"Necrem!" Sanjaro cried, his voice muffled, as if far away. "Necrem, *please*—"

Something tugged on his sleeve, and Necrem batted it away like an annoying fly. His blurred vision fixed on a long counter of smooth, polished wood. Breathing heavily through his drooling teeth, he lumbered up, raised his arms, and slammed them down on it. The counter held, only creaking where the tabled folded. The pounding in his head went undeterred, and he raised his fists again, slamming them down.

Nothing! Necrem screamed inwardly as he repeatedly beat the counter. *There's nothing I can do! Nothing I can ever do! Nothing matters!*

A woman screamed.

The terrified screech pierced through the fog.

Necrem gasped. His arms hung in the air. His fists and forearms stung. His face burned intensely while his mask clung to him. A damp, warm tingling ran across his face where the hem of the fabric touched his skin.

The counter in front of him bowed downward. It was cracked in multiple places but still intact. It looked like someone had taken a mallet to it and bashed it, hoping to fold it together.

Did I . . .?

Sobbing from off to the side sent a chill down his spine. Necrem tensely turned, his neck stiff, as if his whole body was desperate not to move.

Annette, Sanjaro's homely wife, cradled her husband's head while he laid sprawled out on the ground. Sanjaro's breathing was labored, his face twisted in pain from a gash running across his forehead where he had struck the doorframe.

Annette's spooled brown hair had come undone and spilled down across half her face. She looked up at Necrem, her visible, tear-filled glare on him, mixed with pain, hate, and terror.

"What have you *done*?" she screamed, her mouth gaping and gnashing her teeth. "Monster!"

"No!" Necrem gasped, not sure what to else to say. "No, I couldn't have—"

Did I do it again?

He reeled, trying desperately to recall the last few moments, but it was all a red blur.

That terrible red blur.

The shop's front door burst open.

"What goes on here?"

Necrem turned and went still. Soldiers filled the doorway. An officer, by his clean clothes, polished breastplate and helmet, and decorative sword on his hip, stomped into the shop. Two of his men followed behind, while the rest stood outside.

The officer took in the scene with a glance before turning his nose up at Necrem, his hand casually resting on his sword's scabbard. "Is this all your doing?"

Necrem swallowed. "I ... don't ..." He shook his head, knowing it probably was, but he couldn't remember. He couldn't believe it.

"He did this!" Annette shouted, pointing at Necrem while hugging her husband close. "He came asking for money, and when my husband refused, he did *this*! He's a monster!"

Necrem winced. The motion made his face sting and burn even more. Something dripped out from under his mask. The officer watched it all the way to the floor.

Necrem looked down and spotted drops of blood between his feet. He had ripped open his scars again.

"You're coming with us," the officer said coldly. "If you don't come quietly, we'll take you by force. You may be big, but I assure you we have enough steel."

Necrem worked his mouth, searching for the words to make this all right. But there were none. There was no one to save Necrem and his. There never was.

"I'll come," he replied, defeated.

Necrem didn't look back when they led him out. He just hung his head in shame, knowing he had probably just lost everything.

Chapter 5

Recha casually slapped her riding crop against her thigh in time with the drumbeats and footfalls of the marching columns of infantry parading in front of her.

Tap!

Tap!

Rap! Rap! Rap!

Try as she might to remain stoic and commanding, she grinned broadly as the first column of pikemen paraded before her. They marched in lock step. Their fourteen-foot-long poles stretched high and straight in the air. The Easterly Sun's rays gleamed off their pikes' spearheads, their polished pot helmets, and their breastplates.

Recha always found it stirring to watch armies on parade. She couldn't be exactly sure why. Whether it be the sight of any entire army marching as one, the sheer awe and inspiration of fighting men moving in formation, the intimidating sight they created, or simply her womanly fancies to witness fighting men on display, the demonstration impressed her, nonetheless.

Savior take it, Hiraldo, she inwardly chided. *I was wanting to storm in and demand you explain for why you needed more money. But you beat me to it!*

She had departed for Fort Debres the day after the Exchange had ended. A mere three hours of relative darkness was hardly enough for a peaceful sleep, but it was the last time she'd been in a bed. The importance of this visit had been too great to put off for longer.

However, before she could ride in and take charge, Hiraldo had an escort waiting for her a day's ride from the fort. They had escorted her right up to the parade stand inside the fort to witness her First Army parade for her inspection.

"I'm please your impressed, La Dama," Hiraldo said. The second member of her Companions stood beside her right, beaming proudly at his troops. "I promised you wouldn't be disappointed!"

Hiraldo Galvez stood tall with a military baring, broad in the chest and narrowed waist. He was the only one of her Companions to match her beloved Sebastian in military prowess. He had forgotten to shave that morning, black specks of stubble bristling his square jaw and cheeks. His hazel eyes danced up and down each passing line of men, hunting for a single soldier out of step.

"I can't help but notice," Cornelos said, standing on Recha's left, "but the entire army appears to be dressed in purple. Is that the reason you requested more funds, Hiraldo? Testing your idea of providing all enlisted soldiers with uniforms?"

The soldiers were dressed in purple jackets under their armor, leaving only their sleeves visible, and black trousers. Hiraldo was dressed the same, with his violet, high collar jacket and black buttons running at an angle down his right side and black trousers matching his soldiers.

"Dyeing cloth doesn't cost *that* much, Cornelos," Hiraldo replied dryly. "Besides, all the men march and stand better dressed in our La Dama's colors."

Recha bit the inside of her check. The flattery and seeing an entire army dressed in her colors added to the awe-inspiring sight. However, she couldn't let it sway her from overseeing everything.

Incidentally, she had chosen a violet riding dress with black leggings and trousers underneath her divided skirts. Her hair was spun up on the left side of her head, covering her ear and providing a resting place for the black bonnet with a white honey blossom facing upward toward the sun.

"I thought of wearing armor myself," she said, raising her riding crop to a column of swordsmen marching by with their rapiers on their shoulders and their round shields at their sides. "A decorative breastplate or such."

"I thankfully talked her out of it," Cornelos chimed.

Hiraldo grunted in approval. "Soldiers can always see through a commander trying too hard to appear formidable."

"Are you say *I'm* not formidable, Commandant Galvez?" Recha slid her gaze around, fixing him with a stern, sideways glance, and slapped her skirts with her riding crop.

Hiraldo swallowed and folded his hands behind his back at attention. "Of course not, La Dama! I apologize. I meant no disrespect."

Recha's cheeks warmed. She hadn't meant to give the appearance of berating him in front of his men. "No need for apologies, Hiraldo. Stand easy."

A stillness fell over the trio as more companies marched by. At the head of each marched the company's capitán, drummer, and bannerman. The capitáns were mostly younger calleroses, enlisted into her new armies after having been freed from serving their families' old barons. They raised their swords in salute as they passed her, and their bannermen likewise lowered her banner.

She'd had Lazorna's banner changed after her coup. The deep violet cloth fluttered with the bannerman's movements, swaying the black bars at the top and bottom of the banner, separated from the violet cloth by red straps. A red *I*, symbolizing the First Army, was emblazoned in the center of the banter with their company number and pike below it.

She held up her riding crop to them as a return salute.

"Hoorah, Mandas!" they shouted. "Huzzah!"

Recha shivered. Every strand of her hair stood on end. She grinned broader and waved.

"Huzzah!" they shouted again.

"*Hoorah!*" the company that followed shouted.

Regaining her composure, Recha glanced at her two Companions. Hiraldo stood stoically, chest out and back straight, imitating a perfect statue. Cornelos wore a half-smile with his hands clasped behind his back but stood just as tall.

"I didn't mean to be harsh to either of you," she said. "But I do prefer both of you keeping the other in line rather than teasing me." Recha gave them both a smirk.

"We only meant you don't need armor to impress the army," Cornelos said.

"Your reputation alone succeeds in that," Hiraldo added.

"Oh?" Recha tapped her riding crop against her thigh again. "And what reputation would that be?"

"Your reputation for promoting competent, confident, and loyal officers," Hiraldo replied.

Cornelos grunted in agreement.

Recha clutched her riding crop in both hands. *And for . . . killing*—being the most honest, yet not so damning term—*my uncle, his family, and anyone else in my way of taking over Lazorna.* She left the thought unspoken so as not to dour the mood.

Another company marched in front of them, and Recha's jaw dropped. Row after row of men marched by carrying muskets on their shoulders. They wore the same breastplates, and their clothes were the same color as the other columns. However, they wore wide-brimmed hats with their right sides pinned to cap of the hat and leather straps running diagonally across their breastplates with several dangling appendages hanging from them.

What surprised her most was the number of them. A company of two hundred musketeers marched by, followed by another column of sword-and-shield-men, then another company of musketeers after that. The column's bannerman waved a violet standard with their company number and emblazoned musket.

"Hiraldo," Recha said, rubbing her jawline with her riding crop while adding up the number of muskets in her head, "do I have to *ask* what you're requesting more funds for?"

Muskets were a relatively new addition to the battlefield. Several marcs had started employing the powder and shot weapons some thirty years ago. There were many types, designs, and sizes and no one had a uniform method of deploying them, unlike crossbows. The development of bombards proved more and more powder weapons were being developed, despite most marcs' and officers' unwillingness to use them effectively. Another holdback by the Rules of Campaign.

They had one thing in common, too—muskets were expensive.

"No," Hiraldo replied. "But I assure you, Recha, they're worth every deber. They'll make up for our armies' smaller numbers and aid us in reaching our campaign's objective when the time comes. That's why I made advance promises to try to requisition as many as I could."

"I'll hold them to that." Recha pressed her lips together and studied another column of pikemen. She put her riding crop under her arm and folded her arms. "And you."

"I guarantee they will perform their duty. As will I."

"As will we all," Cornelos added.

Mounted calleros thundered by. Their leading officer raised his rapier to her while the riders behind him dipped their lances. Recha nodded to them, but her mind was still considering the implications of having so many muskets and Hiraldo purchasing more.

How many did he buy? she thought, suddenly fearing the bill.

"I will need a demonstration," she said.

"Everything is prepared," Hiraldo promised.

"Of *everything*!"

"Yes, La Dama. The officers have their orders, and the men will be ready. But there is someone who wants the speak with you first. He's the merchant who's providing us with our firearms."

Recha pursed her lips. *Wanting a promissory note, no doubt.*

"After the parade," she said then grinned as another column of pikemen marched by cheering. "I'm enjoying this."

~~~

After the parade, Hiraldo offered her an inspection of the *entire* army. Fort Deber was a sprawling fortification, nestled in the shadow of Cimave Mountains. The high, snow-covered peaks offered the perfect boundary for Lazorna's northern border and the perfect place to recruit, train, and build her new armies. Away from the inquisitive eyes of the neighboring marcs.

However, Recha couldn't have hundreds of men stand around just for her to look at while passing by. They had already done that on parade.

One unit is just as good as the whole army, she supposed while walking down a row of pikemen with her hands clutching her riding crop behind her back, inspecting their ranks.

"Did you replace all our spear-and-shield-men with pikemen?" Recha asked Hiraldo. "Or did you take their spears away in favor of swords?"

"An innovation of both," Hiraldo replied. "It's something we noticed during the Pamolid Campaign. Spear-and-shield formation was meant to close in on the enemy while blocking arrows. But in Pamolid, we didn't encounter a single troop of archers. Crossbows, yes; but archers, no." He snickered. "Sebastian almost ordered the entire column to abandon the shields to get them to march faster, but we convinced him otherwise."

"It would have been a waste of metal and marc resources," Cornelos concurred.

"Pikemen *are* better," Hiraldo continued. "The pikes give them longer reach and better protection against cavalry. And with less weight to carry, they can march and deploy faster on the battlefield. So long as they keep their formations tight."

Recha brought her hands in front of her and tapped the riding crop against her palm. She was trying to envision how the squares of pikes would move and fight, but she was still uncertain. Theory was one thing, but nothing compared to seeing an army fight in a real battle.

"Ah!" Hiraldo's raised voice brought her back to the inspection. "This is the special group I wanted you to see." He stepped up beside her and ushered her toward a company of swordsmen.

"Company!" its capitán, standing three paces in front of his men, shouted. "Attention! Present swords!"

As one, the company raised their sword before their faces, their blades dividing their faces while their round shields hung at their sides.

Recha raised her riding crop to them then stopped, squinting at their company standard in the center of their front rank. They were her colors, and as the rest underneath the First Army's *I* in its center was their company number, *1*, with an emblazon sword beside it. However, beneath them were the words sewn in red, *"Puerlato Marching Home."*

"Puerlato," Recha said under her breath and turned to Hiraldo.

Hiraldo nodded and stepped up to the company's officer. "At ease, Capitán. You may remove your helmet."

The capitán sheathed his sword, loosened his chin strap, then slid his helmet off. Dark hair, parted down the center of the man's scalp, spilled out over the sides of his head, down to his ears. The middle-aged man's prominent nose was bent slightly out of shape from numerous breaks. His mustache was thick and bushy, along with the rectangular strip of hair that ran horizontally down the center of his chin.

"La Dama," Hiraldo said, "may I present Capitán Alon Queve, First Sword Company of the First Army."

Recha's eyes widened, recognizing the name. "You were with the rearguard retreating from Puerlato."

Capitán Queve's face darkened. "A dark night that was, La Dama," he said. His voice was higher than Recha had expected.

She could only imagine—fleeing one's home while it was being overrun, witnessing an enemy claiming it, and stalling their advance long enough to allow the fortunate few to escape. She did know the loss, though.

"Were you there when"—her throat clenched, but she swallowed and forced it open—"when Commandant Sebastian Vigodt fell?" Her uncle had promoted Sebastian the day before he had given him the ill-fated command. Recha had glowed with pride that day. It made her want to vomit thinking about it, even now.

"Yes, La Dama," Capitán Queve replied. "I was on the line trying to hold an orderly retreat on the road when it happened."

"Do you recall how it happened?"

"Pardon, La Dama," Cornelos interjected and tried to move between her and the capitán, "but are sure you—"

Recha slapped her riding crop into Cornelos's chest without a glance and pressed against him until he moved back. She stepped closer to the capitán to make sure Hiraldo didn't get the same idea.

For the past three years, she had scraped for any shred of information, any witness to tell her how Sebastian had died. She had a few pieces, but her heart still craved for the entire story.

"Do you recall how the commandant died, Capitán?"

Capitán Queve took a deep breath and set his shoulders. "The commandant was rallying us to withdraw in good order and hold our formation. The commandant insisted on riding with us at the rear, wanting to be the last in the column. But it was raining, and the road churned with mud. Before we knew it, three Orsembian calleroses came charging out of the dark.

"The commandant held his ground. You'd have been proud of him, La Dama. He charged them alone, one sword against three. Swords flashed and clashed like thunder and lightning, they did. He slew two before we could reach them. The third, though . . . got lucky. His sword struck the commandant under his arm and plate.

"We sprinted to the commandant's aid, but it was too late." Capitán Queve hung his head. His gloved fingers tightened and squeaked while holding his helmet. "Forgive us, La Dama. We couldn't do more. The commandant fought nobly until the end."

Recha's eyes drifted closed. Her nostrils flared as she went over the events in her head. She could smell the rain and hear its pattering on the armor. The pattering gave way to pounding hoof beats, and then steel slicing against steel. Men yelling and crying in pain. Sebastian being the last to cry out.

"Very noble," she agreed, nodding. "Almost romantic." She slowly opened her eyes. Then she slapped her riding crop in her palm and twisted her grip around it, making the leather squeal.

Capitán Queve's mustache started to quiver. His lips pressed tightly together, and lines of sweat ran down his forehead.

"How did he *actually* die, Capitán?" she whispered coldly.

Capitán Queve's face scrunched, as if a sword were thrust under his arm. "It wasn't three calleroses," he said. "They were regular soldiers. We didn't know who they were in the rain and dark. Even the commandant thought they were stragglers, wandering around like they were. He rushed out to them, trying to get them to join the line.

"He was pulled out of the saddle before any of us knew it. Before we could rush in and help, an Orsembian had his boot on the commandant's back and speared him."

Recha's stomach pitched and rolled. She pressed her fists and riding crop against her belly to hold in the urge to scream.

No! She didn't want to scream. She wanted to rage! Her teeth cracked together, barely holding her desire to cry out until her voice echoed to the highest peaks of the Cimave Mountains!

"*Recha!*" Cornelos whispered worriedly.

Recha breathed in sharply.

Capitán Queve's face was drenched with sweat. The tips of his mustache were starting to droop. Hiraldo had precariously distanced himself, as well. Even the soldiers stood straighter and more apprehensive.

Oh no! Recha felt her cheeks warm. *Don't tell me I grinned!*

She took a deep breath to regain her composure. "We will make them pay, Capitán," she said. "You have my word." She turned to the men and raised her voice.

"Soon, men of Puerlato! You will all be marching home!"

Capitán Queve snapped his heels together and raised his fist in the air. "Huzzah, La Dama Mandas!"

"Huzzah!" the company shouted, raising their swords in the air. "Mandas! Hoorah!"

The chorus of over a hundred men shouting her name stirred Recha's blood. Her whole body flashed, and her hair stood on end, unable to contain the rush. A grin split her face and, caught up in the moment, she raised her riding crop in the air like a sword.

"Huzzah, Puerlato!" Recha yelled. "Huzzah!"

The infectious cheering spread to the other companies and echoed through the fort by men in the barracks or on duty. It took a while to die down, but Recha didn't want the feeling, the rush, to leave her.

"Do you approve, La Dama?" Hiraldo asked when it finally did.

"What?" Recha gasped, nearly out of breath. She nodded and regained her composure again. "Yes. Yes! I approve. This is all splendid."

Her gaze tracked across the pikemen, the swordsmen, and finally landed on the musketeers. The final company for her to inspect and one she wanted a more thorough demonstration of.

"Dismiss all the companies save for the musketeers, Hiraldo," she ordered. "Tell their officers their men are given an extra ration of wine for their excellent performance!"

The officers didn't have to relay the message. The men at the front heard and raised a cheer that rippled through the ranks like fire. It took the officers minutes to get them back in order to dismiss them. When they were, the men kicked up clouds of dust that swirled in the yard as they lumbered and dispersed toward the armories and their barracks.

Recha waved the dust out of her face. She turned away then paused seeing Cornelos standing rigidly with his hands behind his back. His head was hung, and his cheeks were sucked in.

"Did I handle that badly?" she asked softly.

"It's not my place to say," Cornelos replied.

Recha gave him a dry look and poked him with her riding crop. "Cornelos. Don't hide things from me."

"You shouldn't . . ." Cornelos shook his head and bit his bottom lip. "You shouldn't hurt yourself, Recha. Sebastian wouldn't have wanted that. He wouldn't want you haunted with the images of how he died."

Recha stepped in front of him to ensure he couldn't look away from her and gave him a stern look. "I've been haunted by his loss since I saw his body laid out in Zoragrin, Cornelos. Knowing how he died doesn't add to my loss. It only furthers my resolve to see it answered for. Understand?"

Cornelos raised his head but remained tense. "Yes, La Dama."

That could have sounded more convincing. It was probably the best he could do though.

Recha left it be to turn back to Hiraldo's musketeers.

"Recha?" Cornelos whispered. His brow was furled, and his eyes shifted.

"Yes?" Recha raised an eyebrow, unsure what he was about to say.

"How did you know the first story was a lie?"

"Because it was romantic." She chuckled. "Like Papa told us growing up— no one dies romantically on a battlefield."

Cornelos's mouth fell open. They had all grown up together under Baltazar Vigodt's tutelage. Some were actual lessons, while others were just sayings or random thoughts that stuck with her. The man knew how to phrase a sharp remark.

But I also looked at Sebastian's body, Recha lamented. After her coup, she had to know where the killing blow had been struck and discovered the massive wound in his back. She knew it didn't come from a sword.

"Let's leave that rest, shall we?" she said, turning on her heels. "I still need a demonstration of—"

Recha's voice caught, and she squinted in the noon-day's glare.

"Cornelos." She pointed her riding crop at a man walking across the yard from one of the buildings. "What's that?"

The man's light tan wardrobe stood out starkly in the sea of dark violet. His doublet was unbuttoned and open at the collar, exposing his white shirt underneath. His trousers were merely shin length, leaving his tall socks and buckle shoes at the mercy of the dust. He fanned himself with his round, crowned hat instead of doing the sensible thing of wearing it and protecting his pale skin from the Easterly Sun.

The man's pale skin stood out the most. He lacked the look of a soldier entirely. His cheeks were flushed and puffed. His light brown hair stuck to his glistening, sweaty forehead. He coughed violently while walking through a thick cloud of dust.

"Looks like a lost, sweaty man," Cornelos replied.

Recha sniffed sharply. "You're a *big* help."

"That is my duty as your secretary, La Dama."

"Shut up."

The stranger staggered by and gave the musketeers a respectful nod. He brightened when he saw Hiraldo returning from dismissing the other companies.

"Commandant Galvez!" the man shouted with an accent that drew out his vowels. He rushed Hiraldo with a broad smile and threw his hand up to clasp Hiraldo's in a vigorous shake. "I hope you don't mind me joining the proceedings. It was terribly hot in your office and to open a window only invited dust and flies."

"Not at all, Sir Averitt," Hiraldo said. "We were just about to see a demonstration of your firearms."

"You *were*?" Sir Averitt's eyebrows leaped into his drenched hairline. "What fortuitous timing! Splendid! *Splendid*!"

Recha frowned and tilted her head. *Fortuitous timing? Splendid? Who talks like that? Either this Sir Averitt's putting on strange airs or he comes from a stranger place.*

"But first," Hiraldo said, motioning to Recha, "allow me the pleasure of introducing you to La Dama Recha Mandas, Marquesa of Lazorna."

Sir Averitt's emerald eyes widened and sparkled, drinking her in with one absorbing look. His eyes were closer set than what Recha originally thought and, despite his happy expression, she got the impression they just weighed her.

Sir Averitt stepped closer and made a flourishing bow, sweeping his hat out to the side. "It is an honor to finally meet you at last, Your Ladyship," he said while rising. "Permit me to introduce myself. I am Lord Basil Averitt, humble agent and representative of the Wesson Manufacturing and Shipping Company."

"Pleased to meet you, Lord Averitt," Recha said, nodding and formally pulling the left side of her divided skirts. "I trust you and your company are the ones I have to thank for supplying my marc's army?" *And the undoubtedly massive bill I haven't even seen!* She flashed Hiraldo knowing a look.

"It is indeed." Sir Averitt obliviously smiled. "I can't express how thrilled my company is to service you. What you are doing here is visionary. Absolutely visionary! But please call me Mr. Averitt, if you wish. I'm still getting accustomed to having a title. Oh!" His eyes went wide. "I would be Sir Averitt here, wouldn't I? Forgive me, I'm still getting used to being an agent abroad." He chuckled bashfully and rubbed the back of his head.

Recha shared a look with Cornelos, eyebrows arched. *Definitely a merchant. Too talkative, though, for an arms supplier.*

"You don't say," she said. "Well, thank you for the service, Sir Averitt. Commandant Galvez was about to perform this visionary demonstration for us."

"So I heard! May I join you? I prefer to be on hand in case my company's clients have any questions or needs." Sir Averitt's eagerness shined through his sweaty visage. He appeared on the brink of jumping up and down in excitement.

Recha's first instinct was to decline his offer and have Cornelos see to the merchant. His personality wasn't the most taxing she had met, and she held no animosity toward his profession. Merchants, simply by their nature, always had more things to sell and, most of the time, very *tempting* things. The best way Recha knew how to handle the temptation was to keep at a distance, from both hers *and* the marc's pocketbooks.

But his company is the one supplying my army, she mulled. *And I've not paid them yet.* One thing the campaigns had taught everybody was that arms merchants didn't need a reason to sell to your enemies. Therefore, it was best to avoid giving them a reason to sell to your enemies and *not* you.

"Not at all, Sir Averitt," she replied, smiling diplomatically. "Please, join us."

"Thank you, Marquesa." Sir Averitt bowed. "Thank you."

"La Dama," Cornelos said pointedly.

"Huh?" Sir Averitt stared obliviously.

"The proper way to address her is La Dama Mandas," Cornelos sternly informed him.

"Oh! Yes! I beg your pardon again, La Dama Mandas." Sir Averitt apologetically bowed his head repeatedly.

"No offense taken, Sir Averitt," Recha said. "You're still learning, yes? Let's observe this presentation the commandant has prepared for us."

"Thank you, La Dama," Sir Averitt said, putting on his floppy hat. "I'd be delighted."

When his back was turned, Recha gave Hiraldo a narrow-eyed look, hoping to convey his demonstration better be worth it even more now. Hiraldo, for his part, took it all in stride.

"Capitán Urban!" Hiraldo yelled. "March your company to the firing grounds to perform exercises for La Dama! We will join you."

"Yes, sir!" Capitán Urban replied, snapping his heels together.

"The firing grounds is a new addition to the fort," Hiraldo explained while Capitán Urban repeated his orders and got his company of musketeers on the move. "The old archery range wasn't big enough and too close to the stables."

"You didn't shoot any horses, did you?" Cornelos asked.

"No," Hiraldo replied without a hint of catching the joke. "The noise spooked them."

"It does take time for animals to grow accustomed to powder combustion," Sir Averitt added, shaking his head. "It took me a while myself."

"I guess this is your way of telling me we're walking," Recha said to Hiraldo.

Hiraldo's brow furled, but before he could reply, Recha gave him a soft smile and set off after the marching company, giving her uptight Companion a tap on the arm.

The company wasn't hard to follow, leaving a large trail of dust in their wake, and the taps of their drum easily cut through the bustling returning to the fort.

Most common folk bore the impression that forts were places were men put on armor and weapons and stood around, waiting for orders. In truth, forts were more akin to small cities where most of the men held the same job.

"I must say, La Dama," Sir Averitt said, squeezing between her and Cornelos as they walked. "This is a very impressive fortification. The buildings all look new and evenly spaced. Did you recently build it?"

"Hiraldo can tell you more about that," Recha replied.

"The fort itself is over fifty years old," Hiraldo continued. "Upon taking up my post as commandant, it was obvious work was needed to make it equipped to house and train the kind of army Lazorna needed. We tore down nearly every building and redesigned it." He threw his hands out and waved them down the street, pointing at numbers above the doors of the three-story square buildings lining the dirt pact street. "Every barrack is now laid out in formation with every squad, every company, and every regiment. The men eat, train, and sleep together as a unit."

Children laughing caught Recha's ear. A group of children were playing in the shade between buildings. Four of the children eagerly kicked a balled to the next person, determined not to be caught with it by the time their fifth member stopped counting.

"Only officers and those men with certain qualifications can move and live with their families here," Hiraldo said, nodding at the children and the smaller, single-story houses on the other side of the street.

"Very efficient," Sir Averitt said thoughtfully.

The hairs on the back of Recha's neck stood up at the merchant's tone. *He's not fascinated by it. He's impressed. And storing it for memory.*

"Have you seen many forts in . . .?" Recha pretended to think. "Where do you come from, Sir Averitt?"

"Hmm?" Sir Averitt blinked then smiled. "Oh! Forgive me, La Dama. I'm currently based out of Crescent Bay of New Hartland. Although, my heart will always belong to Tradon."

"And that, too, is in New Hartland?"

Sir Averitt chuckled. "Of course, La Dama! Tradon is the greatest city of commerce in the kingdom. If not all the world, even!"

"Oh." His pride of his home aside, Recha didn't have much knowledge of foreign places. They were so far away, removed from the struggles she and the rest of Lazorna faced each year.

We might as well be as distant as the suns.

"And are there any forts in your country?" she asked.

"Forts. Castles. But all antique and ancient compared to what you've built here," Sir Averitt replied.

"Must be nice to live somewhere not constantly at war." Recha frowned. "Maybe someday, we can have the same here."

Sir Averitt's mouth hung slightly open. His eyes danced for a moment, searching for something to say. Blessedly, he closed his mouth.

Awkwardness settled over them. Dirt and gravel crunched under their feet. The drum tapping ahead of them had stopped moments before and allowed the noises of the fort to fill the void. Men laughed somewhere close. Distant shouting in unison of pikemen drilling. Metal clanged against metal in what could have been any number of things happening in the fort.

The barracks and houses fell away, but the lane continued. The company of musketeers slowly came into view, still in formation, standing ready in the center of a wide, cleared-out space.

The firing range was a level, dirt pact field with round bales of hay and mannequins in armor along the back stretch of it. In the far corner stood several storehouses, evenly spaced and far away from everything else.

"Did you replace all my crossbowmen?" Recha asked Hiraldo.

"No," Hiraldo replied. "The Third Army and what makes up the Fourth still have crossbowmen."

"Do you *intend* to replace all my crossbowmen?"

Hiraldo hesitated. "Depends."

"Don't make me ask," she said with a sigh.

Hiraldo's skills were a blessing and a curse. He excelled at organizing an army. He had promised her two new professional and trained armies after she had put him in charge of reorganizing Lazorna's armies from scratch. He had given her three and a half. To do so, Recha had given him a free hand and hadn't forced him to ask her permission to make major changes.

Maybe I should have.

"It depends on how the new techniques work in the field," Hiraldo explained, "how many more muskets we can be supplied with, and . . . whether you approve or not, La Dama."

Recha stopped.

Hiraldo licked his lips nervously, looking over the musketeers but clearly avoiding her.

Or maybe I didn't have to.

"Present your demonstration, Commandant," she said.

"Capitán Urban!" Hiraldo yelled, marching out onto the range. "Present your front rank on the firing line!"

"Sir!" Captain Urban saluted. "Front rank, light matches and form on the firing line!"

The first rank of musketeers, ten men, stepped forward and filed by the company's drummer holding a small lantern. As each man passed, he lit a long cord and followed around to form a line in front of the mannequins.

"La Dama," Hiraldo said, beckoning her beside the line with Captain Urban.

Recha hesitated for a moment. Firearms could be tricky things.

"It's perfectly safe," Sir Averitt said. "I assure you, La Dama, my company's firearms are the finest in the world!"

You don't have to over sell it. Recha bit the inside of her cheek. *I've already bought them, for Savior's sake.*

The line of musketeers did make an intimidating sight looking down their line from the small haze of smoke lingering in their faces from their burning cords.

"Carry on, Capitán," Hiraldo ordered.

"Muskets!" Capitán Urban yelled. "Charge pans!"

As one, the musketeers flipped open their powder pans on the right side of their muskets' locks, blew on them, uncorked their lowest hanging bottles on their leather bandoliers, and then put powder in the pans before closing them.

"Load muskets!"

The musketeers set the butt of their muskets on the ground, uncorked their highest hanging bottles, carefully poured powder down their musket barrels, took a led ball from a pouch on their hips, then rammed the ball down with a stick from the underside of the musket.

"Prime match!"

The musketeers hosted their muskets under their arms, keeping their barrels up in the air at an angle. Each of them blew on their cords. The tips glowed red as they set them in a curved, metal device on the right side of the musket's lock.

"Present!"

The musketeers brought their muskets up, pressing the butts into their shoulders while looking down the barrels. Recha spotted the closest musketeer flip his musket's powder pan with a flip of a finger.

"Fire!"

As one, the musketeers pulled their muskets' levers. The matches fell into the pans. Sparks burst into air.

Pow!

Ten small cracks formed one eruption.

Recha winced from a slight ringing in her right ear, her left protected by her hair bun. Her nose wrinkled at the smell of sulfur and smoke. The whitish-gray cloud hovered over the musketeers' faces before catching the breeze and wafting away.

That was nearly thirty seconds, she reflected. *It takes me a couple of minutes to load Sebastian's pistol.*

"Shoulder arms!"

The musketeers put their muskets on their shoulders and waited.

"Care to see the results?" Hiraldo offered, motioning toward the mannequins.

"Of course!" Recha replied eagerly. She moved before any of them, her divided skirts slapping against her legs as she rushed to the targets.

The mannequins were simple posts with a cross board for arms and a ball for a head. Their breastplates and helmets were standard for her army, although these had makeshift slabs and squares of metal nailed into them, presumably from repeated repairs. Several of the ten used for firing practice had punched in holes from where the lead balls found their marks. They were scattered and uniform, though. A few were in the belly. Some on the left side. Only two had hit near center or close to where the heart would have been. One was untouched, while another's helmet laid a few paces behind the mannequin.

"Not very accurate," Recha said, walking down the line of targets, haphazardly slapping her riding crop against her leg.

"Accuracy won't be what's important," Hiraldo said. "Let me show you." He crouched and began scratching out rectangles and squares in the dirt with a stick he found. "The formation is simple. A company of pikemen will form the center of every line." He pointed at the center and biggest rectangles. "Between and among them"—he pointed at the two smaller squares of the rectangle—"will be a company of musketeers—fifty men each. And encompassing them will be a company of swords." Hiraldo gestured at the three long, thin rectangles surrounding the other three. "A hundred swords and shields to ward of skirmishers that get too close, plug up holes until the pikemen can reform or withdraw, and take care of the rout."

Hiraldo's eyes grew more intense as he looked down at his drawings. "Each formation is to work as one down the line. As they advance, the musketeers will rotate their volleys, each rank firing and the next stepping up to fire after them. Once the lines close, the pikemen will crash into whatever remains of the enemy's frontline. Their distance and weight will shatter any unorganized formation. And the swords"—he stabbed his stick into the dirt—"will rout any remaining resistance." He looked up at her and caught her grinning.

Recha could see it now. She glanced back at the holes in the mannequins and could see volleys tearing into the Orsembar ranks. The pikemen's long spearheads crashing into the poor souls who remained, unable to even reach their attackers. Then the swordsmen afterward, finishing off any foolish enough not to give up their fallen standards.

"We don't have enough muskets for the Third and Fourth Armies, do we?" she asked, running a finger around a hole in the closest mannequin's plate.

"We do, but . . ." Hiraldo stood, tossing the stick away.

"Your remaining shipment of arms are on my company's ship in the Desryol Sea," Sir Averitt said. "We're happy to deliver, La Dama, but we'll need a larger port to unload our cargo."

"Sir Averitt and his company have been sending us arms through small shipments up the Laz River for a couple of years, in small shipping boats under Borbin's nose," Hiraldo said. "But now—"

"Time is of the essence," Recha agreed. She slapped her riding crop against her skirts and turned to face them. "Commandant Galvez!"

Hiraldo snapped to attention.

"I am promoting you to general and overall commander of the First Army," she ordered. "I want this army marching south within the week. The other armies will receive their orders to join you there."

Hiraldo drew himself up. His chest stretched and stuck out a little further. "It will be done, La Dama."

"Good. And give Cornelos a list of recommendations for generals of the other armies before we leave today."

Hiraldo nodded.

Recha left them to sort that out and sauntered over to Sir Averitt. "And Sir Averitt"—she slid her arm through his, ignoring his sweat, and began leading him off the firing range—"I believe *General* Galvez made a few contracts as my representative to your company."

"Yes, La Dama," Sir Averitt replied, nervously glancing at her arm and tensing at her touch. "I didn't want to mention them as soon as we met, but there are a few outstanding contracts in need of—"

"I'll sign them." Recha waved her riding crop nonchalantly. "And, as for our current delivery problem, I think I may have several solutions. But I'd like to discuss matters first with my field marshal, the man who's going to command all my armies. Would you mind returning to Zoragrin with me when I leave?"

"I'd be honored, La Dama. But I must send word to my company's contact in Puerlato in a few days to make the arrangements."

"I'll make it happen."

"Excellent!"

"Excellent!" Recha chuckled.

She raised her riding crop to the musketeer company as they passed. "Perfect marks, musketeers! Huzzah!"

"Huzzah!" the company cheered back, raising their muskets in the air.

Recha grinned from ear-to-ear, listening to her men cheer but hearing and envisioning their musket volleys in her head.

Chapter 6

Necrem soaked his mask in a small bowl of water that he held. He sat extremely still, not risking a needlessly twitch a single time. The small bunk bed was fragile and creaked simply by him breathing. The frame barely contained him, forcing his legs to hang off the foot of the bed at his knees when he laid down.

He had broken one bed already, and the guards warned him he wouldn't get another if this one collapsed, too. Sleeping on the floor of the musky, damp cell gave Necrem chills. As did the rats. The fat, black balls of fur scuttled about on the cell blocks. One never saw them in the gloom until they squeaked when someone nearly stepped on them. He didn't want to lose his last bed and sleep on the floor with them. Not with the scars on his face still healing after splitting open.

The only blessed thing the cramp, cool cell offered was the dark. After endless hours of sunlight, Necrem had welcomed it at first. Now, however, it was starting to drain him just like the suns constantly beating down on him.

How many days has it been? he wondered. *The Exchange is bound to be over by now.*

He shuddered, knowing what that meant, and squeezed his eyes shut.

Savior, he prayed, *please let Eulalia and Bayona be all right.* His big hands trembled holding the bowl. *Please! They can do whatever they want with me, but let my family be all right.*

Bang!

Necrem jumped from the slam of wood against metal. His grip slipped, and the bowl fell between his hands, crashing on the stone floor and sending water everywhere.

"Necrem Oso!" a guard shouted.

Necrem gasped in panic from a key turning his cell's iron lock.

My mask!

He fell to his knees, heedless of the water soaking his pants while he groped in the dark for his mask. His fingertips found the drenched cord just as the guards pushed the cell door in and flooded the room with lantern light. He slapped the mask to his face and squinted against the light, barely making out two figures. He ignored how heavy with water the mask was. Having it on was all that mattered.

"Get up, Oso," one of the guards ordered. "The commandant wants to speak with you."

Necrem grunted, pushing off his knees and rising to his feet. The top of his head lightly grazed the cell's ceiling, and he stooped. His knees bent and wobbled in protest. Everything about the cramped space gave him the feeling the walls were closing in on him. A chance to get out of it, even *briefly*, was a welcome.

The guards jumped back, flanking either side of him and keeping plenty of distance. The one with the lantern raised his club next to his face while his partner readied his spear.

Necrem stood there and waited. He knew any sudden move could set the guards off, and any assurances or promises that he meant no harm would fall on deaf ears. So, he waited, with his head hung and hands folded in front of him until they were satisfied.

"This way, big man," the guard with the lantern said, motioning with the lantern to follow.

Necrem did. Quietly. There was no use asking questions or starting anything the guards might take as trouble.

The squat, two-story jailhouse was quiet, but Necrem knew it was full. A few of the inmates stared out of the small, barred windows of their cell doors. The haunted sights of the lantern light flickered against the pale whites of their wide eyes following his every step.

The guards led him down a tight, twisting staircase. Necrem had to pull in his shoulders and hunch his back to squeeze between the walls' clay bricks.

The room they brought him to was smaller. He ducked his head to enter the windowless, square room lit by candles mounted on the walls that cast shadows off the legs of the square, battered table and two chairs in the middle of the room.

"Sit!" the guard with the lantern ordered, setting the lantern down on the end of the table and pointing at a chair with his club.

Necrem drew the chair out and eased down into it. The immediate groans and creaks of the wood proved his suspicions right. *People in jail don't need anything but flimsy furniture.*

A boisterous, almost mocking laugh broke the enforced quiet. A tall shadow spilled in through the doorway and cut across the table.

"Wait out here," a too pleased voice instructed before the man outside stooped under the door.

"Sir Necrem Oso!" the man said, taking a big draw of his thick cigar between his teeth and snorting out light-blue smoke. "I am Commandant Forell. It's my privilege to meet you."

Necrem cautiously watched him, unsure of how to respond to that.

The commandant strolled into the room with an easy-going stride. Beyond the doorway, Necrem could tell he was middle-aged by the gray sprinkling his beard and thinning hair. He was tall, but not muscular. He had the beginnings of a pot belly showing by the curve in the front of his dark, velvet suit.

Commandant Forell pulled back his chair, scraping its legs across the floor, and flopped down in it.

Necrem sat up a little straighter, expecting to see it collapse and send the man sprawling onto the floor, but the chair sadly held.

"Yes, sir, Sir Oso!" Commandant Forell took another drag of his cigar, careless of the ashes sprinkling on his suit. He leaned forward over the table, smiling with a twinkle in his eyes. "Gives us a change from having to deal with pickpockets and drunks, the regular dregs you see out there. It really means something to have a known *killer* in one of my cells."

Necrem threw his head up. His blood ran cold, and goosebumps ran down his arms. "*Sanjaro!*" he gasped. "Is Sanjaro well?"

"Sanjaro?" Forell's thick eyebrows scrunched together, and he took his cigar out of his teeth and turned toward the guards. "Who's Sanjaro?"

"The man the prisoner assaulted," the guard with the club replied.

"Oh!" Forell dismissively waved, flinging ashes and smoke in the air. "No. He's fine. If he wasn't, this would be a *whole* different conversation." Forell made an exaggerated face, stretching lips out and tightening his neck until all his veins stuck out. It was there and gone in an instant. The commandant chuckled and chewed on the end of his cigar some more.

Necrem snorted from the cigar's heavy, rotten scent bleeding through his mask's nose hole. He coughed, swallowing his impulse to gag, and shifted in his chair.

"No," Forell said, propping his elbows on the table, "it's a real honor. You know we get all kinds of troublemakers brought in here this time of year— thieves, tax avoiders, conscription dodgers, extortionists . . ." The commandant's eyes flickered, and Necrem stared back at him. The bluish haze of cigar smoke lingered between them as silence settled around the room.

Necrem kept his breathing calm, his shoulders slouched. He didn't want to appear threatening or hint he might have been riled. He kept quiet, voicing no denial. It wouldn't do him any good.

He just stared back.

Forell finally blinked and shrugged. "But nope"—he rolled his cigar between his fingers— "we don't get many killers here. Si Don's Cubiertas get to have fun with them."

Only if someone important is involved. Necrem bit his tongue to keep the snide remark back.

The Cubiertas were the Marqués's special police. They only took interest in crimes happening to or around important people. Yet, should a man be stabbed in the back alley of the slums, Necrem knew not even the guards around him would come around asking questions. They wouldn't come around to bury the body.

"Excuse me, Commandant," Necrem said wearily, lowering his head to appear he meant no disrespect, "but what does—"

"*Ah!*" The commandant pointed at him. "Don't spoil it. It's hardly ever I get to talk with a better class of people. Especially those I can reminisce with." He chuckled and took another drag on his cigar, filling the room with even more blue smoke and stench.

"Reminisce?" Necrem blinked, both from his eyes watering from the smoke and confusion. *What does reminisce mean?*

"Yes!" Forell laughed. "I was on campaign ten years back, same as you. Although I was a sergeant then with a company of foot at the time, but I was there all the same." Forell grinned crookedly and leaned forward, his breath as horrible as his cigar. "I knew a guy that said he saw what's under that mask. He said it was a *gruesome* sight. Probably the most eloquent thing he ever said." The commandant threw his head back and laughed. It rang sharply in Necrem's ears.

He squinted and squeezed his hands together under the table. There was something grating about the man's laugh. Something mocking.

Necrem knew what his face looked like now. It was terrifying. It was the whole reason he had to wear a mask to even step out of his bedroom! As horrible as he looked, though, it was nothing compared to what Eulalia had suffered.

Still, he kept quiet.

"But, at least you got to keep your head, eh?" Forell smirked.

Necrem shifted uncomfortably and wrapped his arms around himself, gripping his elbows. "What's going to happen now?" *Please, don't take my family's home,* he prayed. *And please! Anything but the* sioneros *reserve.*

He'd been dreading that the most ever since his arrest. It was the marqués's special punishment, which everyone—from the barons on down—were eager to oblige. Instead of sacrificing their soldiers, the marqués had created a force labor pool of criminals made to work until traded to other marcs as *sioneros*.

However, the marqués hadn't been forced to trade any *sioneros* to another marc for several years now. That didn't stem the rumors flowing through the slums that the *sioneros* reserve was still being filled with men. The implications were clear—men were being forced to work and imprisoned just in case. Necrem would never see his family again if that was his sentence.

"You didn't have to go and ruin it," Forell complained. He sighed and leaned back in his chair. The fragile wood creaked, but the commandant ignored it and chewed on the end of his cigar. "You were arrested, having assaulted a man after demanding he give you money and was destroying his shop. Do you deny it?"

"I didn't demand money," Necrem replied. "I was asking for help."

"And when he refused, you hit him and began rampaging through his shop."

"No!" Necrem shook his head. "I didn't hit—"

"Then, why were you trying to tear up his shop?"

"I didn't mean to!"

"But you were!" Forell pointed his cigar at him. "You were found destroying a man's shop and him bloody on the ground. Do you deny it?"

Necrem dug his fingernails into his elbows, scratching his skin. His teeth ground together, and his face muscles went taut, against his best effort. His scars began to pull, stinging his cheeks. For a second, red bled into the sides of his vision.

No! he gasped, driving it away. *I need to . . . stay calm. Tempered. Nothing I say will help, anyway.*

He took in a few more deep breaths. Air whistled and hissed through the gaps exposing his teeth.

"I was only asking for help to pay the tax," he replied, hanging his head.

"I was wondering when we'd get to that," Forell said. "Come in, Impuesto."

Necrem looked up to see Sir Luca step into the room. The young tax collector glared sharply down his nose at him, a far cry from the timid, shaking man who stood in Necrem's shopfront days ago.

"That's him," Sir Luca said, pointing at him.

"Of *course* it's him," Forell barked. "There's no mistaking Sir Oso here with anybody else." He laughed at the man, enjoying his little joke alone.

Sir Luca blinked down at the commandant. "I thought you wanted me to identify the tax dodger?"

"Huh?" Forell frowned up at Sir Luca. Then his eyes went wide. "Oh! Yes, yes. Got to keep all the formalities. Go on then."

"This man refused to pay the campaign tax," Sir Luca said.

Liar! Necrem bit his tongue and gripped his elbows tighter.

"And as I was leaving," Sir Luca continued, "he said I should 'have more guards with me next time.'"

Forell snorted another cloud of cigar smoke. "Is that true?"

"I was told the tax was due at the end of the Exchange," Necrem replied as calmly as he forcibly could. "Then, seeing how few guards Sir Luca had protecting him, I thought it well to warn him he need more protection in the slums. The Impuesto isn't well liked, especially the lying ones."

The room fell silent, and everyone stared at him. The guards shuffled on their feet, sharing confused and unsure glances at each other, Necrem, and their commandant. They were likely expecting more curses and threats, easy excuses to put him in his place.

Sir Luca's face went white with a shine of sweat glistening in the candlelight. His eyes were wide and blank, stunned.

Forell's jaw dropped, making his face longer. His lips barely held on to the end of his cigar, just a nub hanging from his mouth, threating to fall into his lap. He snatched it before it slipped and slammed it on the table. Everyone jumped, but the commandant let out a throaty laugh.

"You still have stones of iron under that mask, don't you?" Forell laughed some more and pounded his fist on the table.

Necrem hunched back in his chair. *None of this is funny.*

Forell threw his head back. "Oh yes, this is much more fun than the usual rabble they bring me." He drummed his fingers on the table. "But you know, Sir Oso, I'm going to have to take Sir Luca's word over yours."

Necrem never doubted that. He nodded with a grunt.

"And with this assault and extortion issue, things don't look good for you."

Necrem nodded again.

"Usually"—Forell leaned back and folded his arms—"the order would be to make an example out of you—a public lashing or sending you to the reserve to show the rest of the rabble what happens when they make trouble not paying the campaign tax. But *you* are already an example, aren't you?"

Necrem's grip was so tight his biceps stretched the sleeves of his shirt. His forearms pressed into him, threatening to fold him over. His back ached from being hunched.

"*However!*" Forell threw his hands up with a broad, near gleeful grin. "This season, Si Don has great plans, as great as ten years ago. And me and every other poor commandant have a certain quota to reach. Kind of like our tax collector here. Only, instead of deberes, I require men." He stood up and leaned over the table, hoovering over him. "I can make all these charges *and* the taxes go away, if you join Si Don's army."

Necrem stared blankly up at the commandant. "Conscription," he grumbled. His throat swelled at getting the word out.

"Think of it as *enlisting*." Forell shrugged.

Memories flooded him of old army camps. The pounding and hurried shaping of metal. Constant demands for more repairs, more armor, more weapons. Men and women working in the camps, mingling and avoiding the soldiers. The cries of wounded and dying men.

Three darker memories came to the forefront. A woman wailing in torturous agony. A man bellowing demands for justice. Both were cut off by boisterous, uncaring laughter.

Red began to seep into the corners of his eyes.

"I . . . can't," Necrem hissed, trembling.

"Then you'll be sent to the *sioneros* reserve," Sir Luca said.

The tax collector was smirking now. A glance between him and Forell told Necrem all he needed to know.

They planned this.

The red began to grow. He sucked air through his mask, trying to keep calm, but his breathing became labored. His chair creaked from his shaking.

"Think of your family," Forell said.

The red instantly vanished.

Forell sniffed and rolled the cigar stub between his fingers. "Enlisting may sound bad—you'll be away all season, may have to fight—*but* it is better than the reserve. You'll probably never see them again then." The commandant's low chuckle echoed menacingly in Necrem's ears.

I can't go on campaign! he inwardly reeled. *I can't be a soldier. Not with . . .. Who's going to take care of Eulalia and Bayona?*

The looks on Forell's and Luca's faces showed they didn't care about his concerns. They had quotas to fill, and they were going to fill them. It was just like smithing on campaign. The sergeants gave you quotas of repairs to meet, and the smith had to meet them or not get their commission.

"Can I . . . see my family before I go?" Necrem asked. He swallowed his pride and gave Forell a pleading look. "I need to tell them and make sure they're taken care of before I go."

"Absolutely not," Sir Luca said coldly, shaking his head.

Forell raised a hand, a deep frown on his face. "Is your wife the same . . . from ten years ago?"

Necrem swallowed and nodded.

Forell studied him, rolling his cigar stub between his fingers. "You can see them," he said, flicking his cigar away.

"Commandant!" Sir Luca protested. "You can't do that! He'll run."

"No, he won't." Forell rubbed his nose. "But you'll stay here a couple more days. We have to deliver our recruits in four days. I'll give you parole for a day to settle your business. If you don't show up on the fourth day or try to run, we'll hunt you down and send you to the reserve. You got that, killer?" Forell smirked crookedly.

"Yes, sir," Necrem replied.

"Return Sir Oso to his cell," Forell ordered the guards. "He's tired and got a lot of things to think about."

Necrem followed the guards out the same way they had led him in, with his shoulders hunched, his stride slow, and movement unthreatening. This time, however, Commandant Forell's mocking laughter haunted him each step of the way, blessedly cut off only by his cell door slamming shut behind him.

Chapter 7

12th of Petrarium, 1019 N.F (e.y.)

Recha traced the crudely carved letters etched in the back of a worn, marble statue of a woman pouring a pitcher in the center of a fountain. No water flowed through it, though. It had clogged years ago and been left neglected.

S. y R. was dug into the center of the woman's back.

Forever was scribbled underneath.

A mild breeze rustled the leaves of the trees surrounding the fountain and rippled through Recha's hair and skirt that she held up above the ankle-deep water. She still remembered the day Sebastian had waded into the fountain—working then—took out his dagger, and carved those words.

They were both thirteen years old. Sebastian had wanted to show her something after his fencing lessons. He had led her to the ground's cottage behind her now and showed her a tree nearby with the same carving dug into the bark.

That was the first time Sebastian had said he loved her. She had laughed.

Recha smiled, remembering it. He had tried so hard to be suave and romantic. She couldn't help but laugh at how awkward and cliché it had felt instead. Something out of a romance tale told to make young girls giggle.

"Are you just trying to kiss me to tell your friends, Sebastian Vigodt?" she had teased with her hands on her hips. *"The bark will grow back, you know."*

Recha had eavesdropped on Sebastian and his comrades' fencing lessons for years, entertaining herself by watching them try to best each other and trade insults. Recently, before then, some of those insults had turned into who had kissed how many girls and who.

Instead of denying it or making a joke, Sebastian had charged off, straight into the fountain, and chipped away at the marble with his dagger until he'd completed the same carving.

"Stone won't grow back!" he had declared. *"I'll love you forever, just like this will be here forever."*

Maybe it was because she was young or something in the way he'd said it, but Recha's heart had drummed at that.

She'd been lost in the haze of youthful emotion until she'd blinked and realized Sebastian had been leaning in to kiss her. She might not have caught him in time but for him being sheepish about it.

She had playfully pushed him back, and he'd lost his footing in the fountain's slippery surface. Recha had gasped and cupped her face, watching him flounder in the knee-deep water. When Sebastian had come up, spitting water, completely drenched, her face had burned, darkening red, and she'd run away.

She had giggled as she had, too.

Despite it being immature, Recha giggled now as she remembered it . . . until her finger traced over the final *R* of *forever*. Then her giggles died.

Her arm suddenly felt heavy, and she let it fall, lightly scraping the coarse stone with her fingernail.

It can't last forever if we're apart, she solemnly thought.

"Morning, La Dama Mandas."

Recha turned at the humble voice, the algae coating the fountain's floor squeezing between her toes and the water rippling and splashing.

Inez, Baltazar Vigodt's home secretary, stood patiently behind her with his hands folded in front of him. The middle-aged footman was aging gracefully. His once dark hair was now ashen gray but still thick and neatly parted. A couple of age spots had grown on the right side of his angler face, beside his dark eye. His left was covered with a patch.

"Good morning, Inez," Recha greeted back. She gingerly walked through the fountain and eased one foot after the other over and out of the pool, careful not to slip. Her white dress would be ruined by the oily, black-green water. "I was"—she paused, kicking algae off the bottom of her feet on the soft grass—"remembering a precious memory."

Inez's eye flickered at the statue. "I understand, La Dama. Sira Vigodt wished to know if you slept well. She's preparing lunch on the veranda."

The moment Recha had arrived, Mama Vigodt had been shocked by her fatigued appearance. She'd remarked that Recha had bags under her eyes that made her look *twice* her age, which was the last thing Recha had wanted to hear after being gone for so long. Mama Vigodt had insisted she get rest right away with no hope of Recha persuading her otherwise. There was only one place, though, she had wanted to stay.

She smiled thoughtfully. "Tell Mama I slept very well and thank her for letting me use the ground's cottage." She gave the humble dwelling behind Inez a reverent, longing look.

The small cottage was nestled between a grove of trees. It had once been meant for a gardener and his family but had been rundown and abandoned for years while she was growing up. Sebastian had taken it as a special project to make it livable again between campaigns.

At first, Recha had thought it was his romantic streak running away with him again. Yet, as he had fixed the slated roof, put up new walls inside, and cleared the weeds and shrubs away from around its rock walls, it had become clear it meant much more than that to him. It had been a way of gaining some independence from his father's shadow as he had turned it into a little place where Recha and him could get away from everyone.

The outside might have been fit for a servant, but the inside was fit for a baron. She had fallen asleep the moment she had crawled into bed last night and had only awoken an hour ago.

"Where's Papa?" she asked, rubbing her feet on the grass a little more before slipping on her slippers.

"The marshal is playing jedraz with young Sir Santio in the back gardens, La Dama," Inez replied.

"I hope he's playing fair for Santio's sake." Recha gave Inez a sly smile and started toward the back lawn of the estate. "It's no fun playing against someone who could beat you in five turns if he wanted."

"The marshal would never do that," Inez said defensively.

Recha stopped and raised an eyebrow over her shoulder back at Inez.

Inez held her gaze briefly. He coughed into his hand and started toward the Vigodt estate. "I'll let Sira Vigodt know you'll join them for lunch," he said in passing.

"Thank you, Inez." Recha chuckled, grinning at Inez's hastily retreat toward the main house.

She took a longer path around the house. The Vigodt Estate was modest for a retired marshal. The two-story, brick and mortar house stood out, surrounded by fields of wheat and corn, with the only trees standing in groves within the estate's five-acre square.

She took a small, deeply worn path through thick ferns and grass to the back of the house. She stepped lightly and took care not to get her dress's skirt and open sleeves hung on the briers. It was a modest dress but did cling to her figure in places and could be mistaken for a nightgown because of its lack of multiple layers of skirts. It was cool and didn't make her sweat!

Despite her heritage, her power, and her mansion in Zoragrin, to her, the Vigodt Estate was home, and she was going to relax for the few precious moments she had left.

The worn path turned to rock under Recha's feet, leading her up a hillside, and finally out of the briers. What Inez called the back lawn was really a cleared training yard. She had spent hours watching Sebastian and his Companions exercise here from the second-story windows in the house when she was supposed to be studying her etiquette.

Weather-worn posts were all that remained from those days, still standing in a line down the back of the lawn, tarnished black from the suns. They were covered in nicks, cuts, and punctures from Sebastian and his Companions practicing the sword, although the boards that held up makeshift shields had fallen off. The rest of the training grounds had been taken over by grass.

Recha snickered at yellowing blades under her feet. *Mama Vigodt finally got her back lawn back.*

"Are you sure you want to move there?" a low, hoarse voice asked. "You still have to look out for my calleros over here."

Recha had let nostalgia distract her again and had failed to notice the two people sitting at a small table several feet away.

Baltazar Vigodt sat lounging in a rocking chair with his back to her. His light, cream-colored shirt caught the Easterly Sun's rays just enough to give him a small halo. The back of his hair was pulled back and bound in a small tail to keep it from curling around the back of his neck. Despite being streaked with gray and he in his upper fifties, Baltazar's hair was still thick and mostly black.

Poor Santio, however, wasn't lounging in his chair. The six-year-old boy's fingers firmly gripped his jedraz piece. His hand trembled with indecision on whether he wanted to let go or not. His cheeks were puffed out and rosy, as if he were pouting, while his hazel eyes danced back and forth across the jedraz board.

Sensing they were both distracted, Recha bit her bottom lip, clutched her skirt to keep it from rustling, and stalked forward on the balls of her feet.

"Remember, Santio," Baltazar said, "once you've taken your hand off, you're committed. An officer can't snatch his men away once they're gone."

Just—Recha took another step, getting ever closer to Baltazar—*a little*—another step, slowly bringing her foot down on the brittle grass—*closer.*

Santio blew out his puffed cheeks loudly and finally committed to leaving his piece where it was. When he looked up, his eyes flickered at her, and he sniffed sharply.

Recha stopped in her tracks, her heart pounding in her ears. Her body went so stiff that a firm breeze could have toppled her over.

"Good morning, Recha," Baltazar said without glancing back. He started rocking in his chair. "You slept late today."

Recha exhaled. "Morning, Papa."

She slapped her hands against her sides, pouting. "Is he playing fair, Santio?"

"*No!*" the boy replied, folding his arms and sitting back in a huff. "Grandpa's put his calleros in the middle of the board and *won't* move it."

"Well, you must make me!" Baltazar laughed, reaching across the board. "You can't expect your opponent to move just because you *want* them to. As in war and jedraz, you want your opponent to move"—his calloused fingers wrapped around one of his lightly lacquered espi pieces—a man clutching a roll of parchment in one hand and dagger in the other—and slid it diagonally across the board to take Santio's piece that he had just put down—a charcoal-colored espi—"make them."

"*Ah!*" Santio grunted, gaping and making the cutest expression of a child getting his toys taken away from him. Which he was.

Both he and Recha tracked Baltazar's hand that added the taken espi to the rest of his conquests. Baltazar had captured over half of Santio's pieces while Baltazar was barely missing a quarter. Only two of Santio's soldiers—the frontline pieces—were left, and on opposite sides of the board, leaving the entire center for his grandfather to move.

He dominated that space with a single calleros, a lacquered man on horseback, right in the center facing down Santio's marshal, the tallest charcoal piece, a man with a scepter in his hands. A marshal could be placed in three locations on the board—center back or one of the squares beside it—and he couldn't be moved once set. A player had to defend his marshal and capture the opponent's marshal to win.

"You're not making it fun for him, are you?" Recha commented, pursing her lips.

Baltazar chuckled. "Being patronized is never fun, either." He lifted his head and gave her a knowing smile. She felt his dark eyes take her in at one glance, deep pools which, even relaxed, demanded respect under his commanding brow. He had let his mustache grow out, thick and curling, but kept the rest of his weathered face clean shaven.

"Nor is never winning," Recha retorted.

"But being allowed to win, isn't winning." Baltazar shook his head. "That's not how the game is played. Your move, Santio."

The boy was grimacing at the board and his scattered, remaining pieces. He sat hunched with his arms wrapped around him like he had a stomachache. His eyes constantly danced from one piece to another, but Recha followed his line of sight and saw he was mostly studying his grandfather's pieces.

Uh-oh, she thought, *he's defensive now. After losing so many pieces, he's too worried about losing the rest. He's afraid. And going to lose.*

Baltazar, however, rocked back in his chair; calm, gentle rocks. He laid his head back and waited, patiently watching his grandson.

Recha suddenly got an idea and grinned. "How about we even the odds?" she asked.

Baltazar shot her a glance. Then his eyes narrowed. "On your toes, Santio. Recha's evil look is upon us."

Santio sat up and tilted his head, curious.

"Why do you always—" Recha put her hands on her hips and shook her head. He was trying to get into her head now. "What's the matter? Not up for a challenge in your old age?"

Santio gasped. His mouth flew open in silent laughter with the edges of his lips curling, and he eyed his grandfather.

Baltazar remained cool and relaxed, his rocking speed unfazed. "Age has nothing to do with it. State your challenge."

"Take a look at the board," Recha replied, pursing her lips in a half-smirk. "Take a good, long look."

Baltazar took a long, unblinking look at the eight-by-eight square board in front of him. Recha figured he probably knew where all the pieces were, but she wanted to be sporting. Of the sixteen pieces he had started out with, Baltazar still had eleven, including all his important pieces, save one calleros.

Poor Santio only had eight left, with only his hero piece—the second tallest piece shaped like a man with broadsword—in position to defend his exposed marshal. The boy was in a bad predicament.

While Baltazar was studying the board, Recha causally moved behind him. "Think you've got a good look, Papa?" she asked, winking at Santio.

The boy giggled.

"I think I have," Baltazar replied.

"All right." Recha reached over his head and put her hands over his eyes. "See how good you are now."

Baltazar stiffened momentarily, but then relaxed.

"Aunt Recha!" Santio cried, concerned.

"No, no." Baltazar waved. "It's all right. I'm up for this kind of challenge. The fog of war is no stranger to me. *But*"—he raised a finger—"if I'm to play like this, then Recha, you can't tell Santio where to move. *He's* the marshal, and he must be responsible for his own moves. And if I win, I get to say I defeated both of you."

Recha felt his rough cheeks push against her hands. He was smiling.

She gave Santio a confident look. "We can best him."

"Yeah!" the boy agreed with a determined nod and looked back to his pieces eagerly.

A little too eagerly.

Santio took his remaining calleros and advanced it three spaces up and one to the right, directly between two of Baltazar's soldiers. In two more moves, he would be able to threaten Baltazar's calleros in the middle of the board, or his espi.

Baltazar reached out and hovered his hand above his pieces, barely grazing them with his palm. Recha made sure her hands covered his eyes, preventing him from peeking from under them.

Baltazar's hand paused over Santio's calleros then took the soldier to its left, moving it up one.

He's going to bring out his other calleros, Recha surmised, planning future moves. *Santio needs to bring his bulwarks out.*

The bulwarks were the two pieces at the ends of the board, carved men with polearms. They could move horizontally up and down the board. They could be perfect defenders for Santio's center. Unfortunately, Recha couldn't tell the boy that, per her agreement.

She snorted frustratingly when Santio moved his calleros again, moving predictably two right and down one, obviously threatening Baltazar's espi.

A little too obvious.

Papa will move it. Even with me blinding him, he'll—

Baltazar reached out but didn't feel the board. He went right to the soldier he moved last turn and advanced it up another square.

Recha stared at the board, her mouth slightly gaped and her brow furled.

What's he doing? She racked her brain with moves, following the path of the soldier and checking to see if it left a gap for another move. But it didn't. The only thing he can move out was his other calleros, and he could have done with his last move.

Something nudged her in the back of her mind. *I'm missing something. I know I—*

Santio picked up his calleros again with a big grin on his face and took Baltazar's espi. Then Recha finally saw it as the boy slammed his conquered piece down on his side of the table.

"Santio!" she gasped.

"Ah!" Baltazar barked, holding up a finger. "You gave your word."

Recha closed her mouth and painfully grimaced at Santio. The young boy looked between her and his grandfather, puzzled.

Baltazar reached out and took his calleros in the center of the board. He pulled it back two and over one, taking Santio's remaining calleros.

"Finish," he declared.

Santio sat up and gaped at the board. His head bobbed and weaved, checking every angle. The boy slowly realized what Recha had seen and deflated in his chair.

Sometime earlier in the game, Baltazar had moved his hero to stand in front of his marshal, hidden behind the calleros. The calleros out of the way, the hero now stared down Santio's marshal, and Santio had no defenders to block.

Santio's hero was now *blocked* by the little soldier Baltazar had spent two turns moving forward. Unable to move his marshal and with no pieces to block with, Baltazar would capture Santio's marshal next turn.

The game was over. Santio had lost. *They* had lost.

Recha sighed and took her hands away. She walked around the table again, shaking her head. "How did you do that?" she asked, more astonished that, in all these years, he still had ways to impress her rather than him winning.

"I was challenged," Baltazar replied, interlocking his fingers together on his chest. He held his head high, pridefully, but his smile was soft, humble. "And I answered."

Recha shook her head.

"I want a rematch!" Santio shouted. He hit the table, rattling the wooden pieces.

"I'm afraid someone else is looking for you," Baltazar replied. He pointed toward the house where a plainly dressed young woman, a few years older than Recha, was stepping out.

Julieta walked out onto the lawn, tussling her dark hair in a struggle to tie it behind her head. Her apron was stained with a mixture of grease and orange spots from sauces, undoubtedly from helping her mama in kitchen to prepare lunch. Despite having this large house and servants, the one thing Mama Vigodt would not surrender was her dominion over the kitchen.

"Mama!" Santio yelled. The boy hopped out of his chair and ran to his mother.

Julieta smiled wide and knelt, arms outstretched.

Recha caught a quick glance that reminded her of Sebastian, seeing the way her lips curled and angled her cheeks when Julieta smile. Recha's chest tightened, watching mother and son embrace.

That could have been—

She stopped the thought in its tracks. It was selfish and ungrateful to the family who had taken her in when she had been young and unwanted. Still, it hurt too much.

She took a deep breath and put on a strong face.

"Morning, Julieta!" she called.

Julieta's head jerked up from hugging Santio. Her smile barely slipped, but her lips twitched, as if being forced. The scornful, warning look she flashed her was unmistakable.

"Morning, Recha," Julieta dryly replied then quickly turned away to her father. "Mama says lunch is about ready, Papa."

Baltazar nodded. "I shan't keep her waiting." He remained seated, however.

Julieta passed a glance between him and Recha. She took Santio by the hand and led the boy away, but not without giving Recha one last warning look from over her shoulder.

"She *still* doesn't like me." Recha sighed and slipped into Santio's vacant seat.

Baltazar grunted. "It's not that. She's just being protective of her papa."

"What's she got to be protective about?" Recha pouted teasingly. "You're my papa, too."

Baltazar smiled warmly but turned his head away. "Guill Mandas was your papa. I was just the looked-over marshal who wouldn't stand for his late comrade's children to be picked apart and thrown away."

Recha caught the light flickering in Baltazar's eyes, small trembles in his eyelids. The struggle still raged within him between the side of him who loved her being part of his family and the loyalty he held for his old comrade. Recha had never met her birth father. He had died on campaign against Quezlo.

"Would . . . they be proud of me?" she asked the question long held inside, now tumbling out.

"Hm?" Baltazar blinked.

"My parents," Recha said then winced. "My *birth* parents. Would they'd have understood what I've done?" She opened her eyes reluctantly, expecting a brutally honest response.

Baltazar licked his lips. His gaze drifted to the board, the ground, the house, all avoiding looking directly at her. He took a deep breath, expanding his chest, and sat up straighter. "Guill would have . . . had reservations. He was the most dutiful and honorable calleros I ever fought beside." He snickered. "The only thing he ever pursued without asking permission was your mother."

Recha's cheeks warmed. He had never talked about her parents' relationship in that way before. As for Recha's birth mother, she was barely a memory, more a foggy image.

"Would she have approved?" she asked.

Baltazar finally looked at her, his gaze piercing. "Yes."

Recha straightened. Few talked about her mother after her death and Recha and her sister had been split apart. Most just referred to Recha's resemblance to her and that her beauty had been inherited from her, yet none had said they were her friend. Even growing up, Baltazar had never spoken of her like this.

"Marita Agrin was a passionate woman," he said reverently. "Much like you. I remember when your grandfather tried to marry her off to the Zurit family. She was sixteen and marched into that banquet hall with everybody laughing and drinking, a piece of parchment balled in her fist. She stormed right up to Marqués Zurit and screamed, 'I'll *never* marry your wuss of a son!' Then she"—Baltazar broke into a laugh—"spat right in his face and lunged for him before anyone knew it. The marriage proposal was halfway down his throat before five calleroses could tear her away. Screaming and cussing all the way out of the hall." He threw his head back and laughed. "I'd never seen the like."

Recha leaned forward, propping her elbows on the table and her chin resting in her cupped hands, captivated, grinning from ear-to-ear.

Why didn't I hear more stories like this growing up?

"Were you one of the ones who pulled her away?" she asked eagerly.

"No." Baltazar shook his head. "I had just completed my training, but I knew which battles to avoid even then." He chuckled, showing teeth. "Your father, though, he was the first one to jump in and got kicked in the . . ." He caught his words and looked away not too subtly to cough and clear his throat. "Well, let's just say he was doubled over and wasn't one of those who dragged her away. But he may have fallen in love that day."

Recha bit her lower lip, imagining it. The first time her parents had met being one where her mother had made a scene and kicked her father before they had even known each other. It slightly reminded her of pushing Sebastian in the fountain, although they had known each other for years. It seemed she and her mother had a knack for embarrassing the men they loved.

"Like mama, like daughter," she mused under her breath.

Baltazar hummed in agreement, his ears still sharp in his old age. "She would have understood your reasoning for what you did. But she may not have cared for the marc as well as you. She railed for campaigns against Quezlo for years after Guill died. To the point of almost . . . No, it was absolutely reckless. But she wanted revenge, no matter the threat from the other marcs."

Recha jerked, feeling slapped out of her warm imagining. Baltazar stared back at her, his eyes hard once again.

"I take it"—she straightened, folding her hands in her lap and assuming a calm, almost calm demeanor—"that was a subtle warning to me, as well?"

"You've done a lot of good these past few years, Recha." Baltazar shifted, resting his hands on the arms of his rocking chair and sitting up for a more commanding presence. "Your parents may have understood your reasons for taking the marc from your uncle, but some of your actions afterward . . ." He let the comment hang, unfinished.

Recha held firm. "I've had to make difficult decisions like any marquesa."

"You ordered columns of men to attack when you should have held your positions and wear down the enemy first," Baltazar retorted.

"I stopped the Orsembian advance." Recha still remembered those sleepless nights, marching back and forth, fighting over fifty miles of ground, barely making a difference, and being forced to dig in at a ford along the Márga River.

"You've executed many," Baltazar said accusingly. "Barons, judges, calleroses, old civil servants. Some are *still* under house arrest."

"They were plotting a rebellion." Recha stopped from spitting at the memory. Not three months after throwing back the Orsembians, several barons, marshals, and their calleros had conspired their own coup in response to her initial declarations of restructuring the marc's armies, releasing all *sioneroses*, and making it clear there would be no more seasonal campaigns. "If Sevesco's espis hadn't caught it in time, they could have torn this marc apart. They were betraying Lazorna. For *that*, they faced justice!"

"You've sent the Viden de Verda to drag people from their homes!" Baltazar's words were so sharp he nearly spat. "You've allowed that superstitious *cult* free reign to ruin people's lives. For what? Some perverse sense of *truth*?"

"They're a necessary evil."

"Why? Tell me *why*."

"I *can't*!" Recha bit her tongue.

She knew he hated the cult. Many did. However, she could never tell him about the bargain she had struck or whom she had struck it with. Baltazar didn't believed in the strange powers of some of the cultist. She didn't know how to explain to him that a spirit possessed her sister to command the cult. He didn't even know Elegida was still alive.

"I have blood on my hands, Papa," she said, shaking her head. "I don't deny I took the marc out of revenge. I killed my uncle, my cousin, their closest friends, all out of revenge. They betrayed the man I loved—your son—and their campaign plans would have betrayed us all. So, I killed them.

"Then I ordered men to die in battle. All leaders do. There was no getting around that. Then I killed to keep my power. Those barons and marshals who were left had to know I would suffer no betrayal, even if it was merely talk. And I've let a cult whom, I admit, I do not trust, kill in my name. I have done a lot of bad.

"And look what we've gotten." Recha's calm demeanor cracked with a pleading look. "*Three* years of peace. My carriage is accosted by people every time I ride through Zoragrin, men take off their hats, women have raised up their children to me and cried, 'Savior bless the Marquesa.'

"I *saved* Lazorna!" She breathed deeply and drew all the strength she could to straighten her poise. "I am the marquesa, and I will bear the responsibility for the good and the bad. Every past and future decision I make is mine, and I will bear the responsibility for all of them. Even those things the great Baltazar Vigodt disapproves of, I'll bear those, too."

Baltazar sat like a statue. Unwavering. Undaunted. Not a single blink. He stared back as if the embodiment of an impartial judging, weighing her words on scales only he could see.

"For that," he said, his face softening and his eyes moistening, "your parents *would* have been proud. Their little Recha, Savior of Lazorna. Many marqués can find an excuse for what they must do for the marc. It's the hallmark of a worthy one to accept the responsibilities of their decisions."

Recha's body, stiff from sitting so straight, trembled, on the verge of collapse. She clasped her hands together to calm down, but her palms slipped and rubbed against each other's clammy embrace. Her vision clouded, and tears escaped the corners of her eyes. She had to close them to hold in the rest.

Something inside her very core shook. She didn't care what other people thought of her. She hadn't been able to afford to worry in the beginning, just so long as they got the message that *she* was in power, and *she* was not to be betrayed was enough. Then she turned her attention to governing and preparing and lost track of people's thoughts altogether, save for the other marquéses she had to deal with.

Yet, those few words, that small, comforting acknowledgment, were the most meaningful things she had heard in years.

Recha sniffed, regaining her courage. "It can't last, Papa," she said, wiping away the stray tears. "Borbin is planning something big this season. If he succeeds, even by a half-measure, he might become too powerful for us to do anything against."

"You plan to campaign," Baltazar said, frowning deeply, his lips disappearing under his mustache's thick curls.

"Plans have already been set in motion." She sniffed, clearing her head, then began turning the lacquered marshal in circles with her thumb and index finger. "Hiraldo is moving the First Army to our southern staging grounds, and I've sent appointments, raising generals for the Second and Third Army to mobilize. The Fourth Army is not at full strength but is already in the south."

"Armies?" Baltazar raised an eyebrow.

"Yes." Recha grinned, excited to finally tell him. "Armies. Model armies. None of those barons-funded, conscript armies with a handful of calleros who ride off whenever they want. Model armies just like you made when you carved through Pamolid, Marshal Vigodt, the Half-Conquering Hero!"

She trembled, nearly giddy. His campaign record was second to none in Lazorna. Probably second to none in all Desryol, save maybe the White Sword. He would never boast or brag about it, but when she was a child, his old comrades had come around to tell war stories. She would be right next to Sebastian, sitting on the floor, mesmerized by every detail.

Baltazar snorted. "That title was partly an insult. I should've gone farther, but—"

"But my uncle stopped you, I know." Recha leaned forward, not letting his dour comment stop her. "But he's gone now. So are the barons who complained you didn't give them their fair due. And the calleroses you denied permission to galivant about and punished when they tried to protest by abandoning the campaign.

"My armies have been recruited and trained to fight as units for years. Look"—she wiped away the remaining lacquer soldier pieces from the board—"no more common soldiers. But columns of pikes." She picked up the lacquer bulwark pieces and slammed them down in the middle of the board. "Each full-strength army ten thousand strong, mostly of pikemen for the frontlines. Between them and behind, swords-and-shields to route and plug gaps. And between them, musketeers."

Baltazar perked up, his eyes slightly widened.

Recha nodded, knowing he was seeing it. "That's right, Papa. I have musketeers. Hiraldo has a tactic that could change the way war *itself* is fought."

Everything she saw at Fort Debres came spilling out. The pikemen tightly marching in step and forming a wall of a spear points with a five-foot reach advantage against common spearmen. The swordsmen were each drilled by calleroses and taught the art of the duel and how to fight together with interlocked shields. And the volleys of the musketeers. She shook the table, clutching it and laughing at their rate of revolving fire.

Through it all, Baltazar remained stoic.

"Well?" she asked, wheezing, her shoulders falling up and down. "Aren't you going to say something?"

Baltazar glanced at the makeshift formation of pieces on the board with a mulling frown then up at her. "You're too excited."

"Huh?" Her grin slipped, and she blinked rapidly.

"You're too excited. Too eager. You say your strength is thirty thousand men—"

"Thirty-six thousand," Recha corrected. "Hiraldo wasn't able to recruit enough men to bring the Fourth Army to full strength, but we have an additional six thousand mobilizing, as well."

"Thirty-six thousand." Baltazar shrugged. "And Borbin can field how many? Twice, maybe three times that number? This new tactic of Hiraldo's sounds impressive, Recha—it really does—but if you put too much faith in it and become overconfident, they can still be overwhelmed. You said so yourself—you don't have *all* your armies fully armed."

She bit her lower lip at the cold reality being dumped on her expectations and hopes. Still, she knew they couldn't let those problems and odds stop them. It was strike now or never.

"That's why I need *you*, Papa. I need a field marshal who can command multiple armies at once, either marching together or apart. One who'll work with me and not be afraid of me. One who'll help me find a way to take Puerlato, get the rest of our armies' weapons, and—"

"Forget Puerlato."

Recha stared at him disbelievingly, her words caught in her throat. "*What*?"

Baltazar's nostrils flared as he deeply exhaled. He picked up his calleros piece and put it back in the middle of the board. "Why did I move this here?" he asked.

"To claim the center of the board," she replied, shrugging, but Baltazar slowly shook his head. "To threaten Santio by being able to strike out any direction."

Baltazar kept shaking his head.

"To . . . to . . ." She frowned, turning back toward the board. Taking a moment to clear her head, she cursed herself for forgetting the game so easily.

I must have let the excitement get to me. She chafed at the thought.

"It was a diversion," she answered.

Baltazar nodded. "The calleros itself never mattered. So long as Santio was focused on it, he'd never see the real threat right behind it."

He leaned forward and tapped the calleros piece. "Puerlato is the calleros. It's only a danger if it were being used as a staging ground for an offensive, but *you* are the one attacking. Its only real purpose then is to delay you, a diversion from the real threat." He pulled back to tap his hero and marshal pieces down the row. "Borbin's field army."

Recha soaked it all in then narrowed her gaze at him. "You've been thinking about this. You were planning to say yes all along."

"Old skills never die," he replied, reaching over the table to pick up one of her bulwarks and put it two squares in front of his calleros. "What you need to do is this." He took the rest of her pieces, pushed them all the way across the board, then several rows up, facing the rest of his pieces.

"Puerlato cannot move," he said. "Break every defense outside the city, then surround it with a small, dug-in force to keep it bottled up under siege. Then, with your smaller, faster armies, march into Orsembar.

"*Speed* is the key." He looked from the board, his dark eyes so intense Recha fought the impulse to shrink back. "That's how I marched through Pamolid. I structured my armies to move fast, faster than the Pamolidians could react. Our armies will have to be *twice* as discipline than them, but it could be done."

Recha's eyebrows leapt upward. "You said *our*! That means you're saying *yes*, right?" Her breathing quickened. She quivered and tingled from the bottom of her soles to her scalp. The excitement threatened to overwhelm her, and she didn't care.

Baltazar sat back and laced his fingers on his chest again. "If I do take command, I have conditions."

Can't you just say yes!

She ran her fingers through her hair, lightly brushing against her misshapen ear. "And they are . . .?"

"If I take command, *I* will command the armies. I know it's pointless to quibble about you coming along or not, but regardless, I give the armies their orders. I will not look over my shoulder or have the other officers look over theirs for your approval each time an order is given."

She swallowed at his harsh tone. But having him agree to campaigning with the armies was a win she could take.

"Agreed."

"I will have my own staff—"

Recha snickered. "Done."

"—whom *I* pick." Baltazar's tone remained harsh, fully embracing his commanding role again.

"Of course you'll have your own staff, Papa," she said with a wave. "I'll have Cornelos send you a list of candidates to—"

"I want Tonio Olguer as my marshal of horse," he interjected, "Manel Feli as my marshal of logistics, Josef Bisal as my marshal of scouts, and . . . Ramon Narvae as marshal second."

Recha's excitement died little by little with each name. She clutched the table to stop her trembling but only shook the table and softly rattled the pieces. She knew each name well. They were all connected with the conspiracy to usurp her.

"Traitors," she hissed, her voice ragged. "Each and every one, *traitors*."

"Comrades," Baltazar retorted, unshaken. "Loyal friends I can depend upon."

"But I *can't!*" She sprung to her feet, hitting the table and spilling pieces onto the ground. "Olguer, Feli, Bisal, all three were running messages for the conspirators. Narvae was one of the marshals arrested with them! I only spared him because he was a friend of yours." And because he was Cornelos's uncle, although their relationship was strained now because of the conspiracy.

"They are men of honor." Baltazar's voice was cold as he slowly stood from his chair, staring her down with his military bearing, gut sucked in and chest out. "When you took the marc, you killed your family, your blood. Despite your reasons, and me staying out of it, their honor couldn't let your actions go unanswered. But they have paid for their disobedience and honorably obeyed their house arrest since."

She shook her head. "But they're not loyal."

"They're loyal to *me!*" Baltazar gritted his teeth, a mere flash before regaining his composure. "And I am loyal to you. They will follow their honor, and in their loyalty to me, they *will* be loyal to you."

Recha set her jaw. Betrayal was betrayal, regardless of the reasons. She needed people who were competent but also loyal. However, she also needed Baltazar Vigodt. There was no other marshal capable enough, no one she trusted enough, to command the armies.

"I'll issue the appointments in the morning," she said begrudgingly. "But they will all be your responsibility. If one of them acts to betray me, I will see it as an act by all of them."

Baltazar mulled it over, his mustache shifting over his twisting lips. "As it should be. They'll be officers under my command, after all."

"Done." She took a deep breath and sighed. "Anything else?" *Savior, I hope not.*

"Keep the Viden de Verda out of my way."

Recha froze. Harquis and his truth seekers were going to accompany her armies, per her agreement with Verdas, but she hadn't told anyone those details.

Not even Cornelos. There was no point in lying to Baltazar about that now, though.

"They won't interfere with you," she agreed. "Or your orders and staff."

"Then"—he reached his hand out—"in the name of Sebastian Vigodt, my beloved son, I am yours to command, La Dama Mandas."

Recha stared at his hand, her stomach fluttering and her heart threatening to burst from her chest. She tried to calm her breathing, to no avail.

"In the name of Sebastian Vigodt"—she took his hand, clasping his rough calluses—"my beloved, I couldn't be prouder to accept."

He squeezed her hand firmly, holding it in place as if to seal a pact. Recha squeezed back while also fighting to keep her vision from becoming blurry again. Her cheeks began to hurt from her grin threatening to tear a facial muscle.

Borbin, we're coming to make you pay.

She was already mulling over what their victory would look like when Baltazar took his hand back.

"Oh, and one more thing," he mumbled softly while walking around the table and spilled pieces. "You get to be the one to tell Mama Vigodt."

Her mouth dropped open, speechless at the daunting task, but Baltazar was already walking toward the side of the house, chuckling, before she realized.

"*Papa!*" she yelped, rushing after him and knocking over her chair in the process.

Even at the end, after getting everything she wanted, he had pulled one last trick she hadn't seen coming.

Chapter 8

"*Why!*"

A wooden plate slammed into the wall a few feet from Necrem's head. Flakes of crumbs leftover from his wife's dinner scattered in every direction. A few sprinkled on his face. He remained perfectly still on his stool with his hands on his knees, sitting but a foot inside his wife's bedroom.

She hasn't had it this bad in years, he lamented.

Eulalia sat curled up in her bed, rocking with her arms wrapped around her legs. Her wrinkled, oversized nightshift covered her from neck to feet. Her honey-brown hair splayed down her back, easily reaching her waist, and the tips curled up on the lumpy mattress. There were more grays since he had seen her last, and she was missing more hairs around the split of the natural, central part of her hair above her forehead. Most of her face was shielded behind her knees, but her wild, hollowed eyes shifted nervously, intentionally avoiding him.

"Why were you gone?" she mumbled.

"I was . . ." He failed to find the words to gently explain. The days in solitude hadn't been enough for him to come up with a way of saying it without the sting. "I was trying to pay the tax. I failed."

Eulalia groaned and buried her head deeper into her knees.

"What's the tax?" Bayona asked.

His little miracle sat between him and her mother, kneeling on the wood floor while laying an arm on the side of the bed. There were bags under the girl's eyes, smudges on her face, and her hair needed combing. She looked how he felt—exhausted.

Poor thing must have gone nights without sleep taking care of Eulalia. He held in a proud smile, but his freshly salved scars were still pulled taut. *Our brave, little girl.*

He sniffed sharply through his nose, air whistling through his clean mask's air holes, and cleared his throat. "A tax is money we have pay to the marqués because . . . because . . ." Again, he searched for a way to explain something, and again, words failed him.

His brow furled, puzzled. *How do you explain taxes to a ten-year-old?*

He shook his head, giving up in less than a second. "Because the marqués says so."

"Why?" Bayona asked, blinking blankly at him with her head tilted. "Did he order something?"

"No." He chuckled, and then it hit him. "Well, yes. He ordered us to pay, and we must pay."

"Why?"

"Because he's the marqués, and he says so." Necrem's shoulders went tight, fearing he was about to descend into a never-ending loop.

"Why?"

He started to say something but stopped and shook his head. "I don't know. I've been wondering that for—"

"We must sell *everything* we can!" Eulalia screamed, throwing her head back.

Bayona squeaked and leapt back from the bed.

A jolt ran up Necrem's spine and nearly sent him tumbling off his stool.

Eulalia wheezed through her exposed teeth. Her cheeks, once flush and sun-kissed, were now as hollow as her eyes, sunken in to outline her cheekbones. Her pale lips were brittle and chapped from burying her face in the linen cloth of her sheets and nightshift. A twisted bent in the bridge of her nose and a thin scar curving around her neck ruined her once delicate features. Her own scars from ten years ago.

"Sell . . ." She pointed at the old dresser against the wall facing the foot of the bed. Her finger trembled when she saw the tall, oval-shaped mirror was gone.

She's forgotten again. Necrem swallowed, knowing what was coming. They had sold the valuable glass years ago.

"Sell—" Eulalia made a choking sound when she didn't see her grandmother's silver tea set on the small, round table by the window overlooking the street, barely marred by the Easterly Sun's evening rays.

Sold that three years ago for Borbin's last great campaign. He remembered her screaming then, too, but only out of refusal to part with it. *The next thing she'll look for will be . . .*

Eulalia scrambled to the far side of the bed, toward a small drawer doubling as lampstand. She flung open the three drawers, tossing each away then skidding across the floor when she didn't find what she was looking for.

You won't find it, dear, he wanted to tell her.

His chest was taut. His heart wept seeing her like this again. But there was nothing he could say to remind her this had all happened before, and now they truly had nothing left.

He glanced to his side and found Bayona standing in the corner of the room. Her little hands covered her mouth while she watched her mother intently. Her legs shook. This was the first time Eulalia had had a spell like this that she could remember.

A hard thump snapped Necrem's attention back to his upset wife. After rummaging through the last drawer, she'd just dropped it. Her arm hung limp over the bed, and her long hair draped over her face.

"Gone," she wept. "All gone."

"We sold the locket to buy the house, Eulalia," he reminded her. "Nine years ago."

The locket had belonged to her mother, and it was solid gold. That, with all the deberes Necrem had, had been enough to make sure they never had a landlord. His family owning their house and forge meant more to Necrem at the time than anything else, the only security he could give them.

Eulalia wheezed and sniffled. Her head bobbed, and her shoulders were quivering. "What are we going to do? What do we have left—" She threw her head back, gasping and flinging her hair everywhere. She wheeled about, rolling and twisting the bedsheet around her, her face a mask of terror. "They're *not* going to take my house!" she screamed.

Necrem wasn't bothered by the screams. They echoed through his mind and memory daily. And, after ten years, he had forgotten what life was without them. He could only look at his wife with pity and wait for her to catch her breath. A little bit of calm before the next hammer fell.

"They're not going to take our house," he said as calmly as he could. "I've . . . agreed to another way."

Eulalia's heavy breathing slowed. Her eyes narrowed at him, as if remembering he was there, and then she slowly, defensively recoiled.

"What way?" she asked, her voice thick with suspicion. "Going to give them more *pots* and *pans*?"

Necrem didn't feel the sting from her words. He knew this wasn't her. This wasn't her fault. It was the trauma's fault. It was his fault.

"Me," he replied solemnly. "The marqués wants men more than money this year. So, I gave them me. I have to go back tonight and enlist in the army tomorrow."

With each word he spoke, Eulalia's face grew whiter and whiter. Her arms creeped up her body, crisscrossed until her hands cupped her shoulders. She pulled back against the bed's headboard, drew her legs up in front of her, and then shielded her face with her hair. By the end, Necrem could only hear her deep breathing, growing faster and faster, and see her shoulders rising and falling.

"You're *leaving*, Papa?" Bayona asked.

His little miracle's fear appeared gone, yet she remained in the corner with her arms wrapped around her. She stared at him, pleadingly. Her eyes welled up, on the verge of tears. It was evident by her wrinkled brow and pouting lips that she didn't understand.

Necrem's scars twinged from seeing her like that. Not only was his wife distraught, but seeing his daughter like that, as well . . . both looked so similar. The thought of his daughter suffering something to make her like his wife twisted his guts, and a shiver ran down his spine.

Be strong, he told himself, swallowing and sitting straighter. *I must be strong, tempered to the finest degree.*

"Only for a little while," he lied. There was no telling how long a campaign would last, or if he would come back from it. "But I'll be back. Your papa will always come back, Bayona."

He tried his best to sound confident and comforting. Even with the mask, he tried to smile.

Bayona's pouting lips and chin trembled. Tears leaked from the corner of her eyes and ran down her cheeks. She sniffed from the runny snot oozing from her nose.

"Aw, it's fine, Little Miracle," Necrem said. He stood from his stool and stepped toward her. "It's—"

"*Ah!*" Eulalia's ear-piecing shriek ripped through the room.

Bayona cried out in terror at her mother's sudden outburst. Necrem reeled, slamming his back to wall, eyes wide with shock, realizing his mistake all too late. He had stepped into her room.

This is one of Eulalia's bad days!

"*No!*" Eulalia screamed. "I'm not going! *No!* Get out!"

She kicked her feet furiously in the air, sending the bedsheet sailing into the air and off the bed. While she kicked, she buried her face in her hands. Her fingernails visibly dug into her scalp.

"What's wrong with her?" Bayona cried. The terrified girl huddled in the corner, crying harder than before. "What's wrong with Mama?"

Necrem winced, desperate to think of some way to calm this situation down. "She's just—"

"I won't go back!" Eulalia cried, slamming the back of her head against the headboard, rattling the wall with hard knocks against the wood. Her fingernails clawed down her face. "Never! Never! *Never!*"

She continued to slam her head against the headboard, and Bayona screamed.

She's going to crack her skull!

Necrem sprung onto the bed, not caring that coming into Eulalia's room could make her grow worse. He didn't know how much worse she could get after going so far.

She screeched incoherently when she saw him coming and flailed her legs, kicking and scrambling, trying to get off the bed, but she got caught up in her long nightgown.

Necrem threw his arms around her, pinning her arms under his to stop her from clawing herself, and then he held her tight, which only made her thrash harder.

"Let me *go*!" Eulalia grabbed his forearms, fingernails biting into his flesh. She wiggled and squirmed, trying to make him let go or slip out from under his arms, but he held. She growled, gargling as if she was drooling, and flailed her head, shaking her hair everywhere. The musky scent of oil and sweat filled his nostrils from her being in bed all day and not bathing.

Fearing he might lose his grip, Necrem fell on his side, dragging her down with him, and held her against the bed.

"*No!*" Panic filled Eulalia's voice, and she frantically but uselessly kicked his legs. "Not again! Not again!"

She threw her head back, catching Necrem by surprise and slamming into his face. His vision flashed, and he didn't see her throwing her head back again. His nose crunched from the impact. Seconds later, he tasted iron from warm blood oozing from it.

He held. He gripped his forearms, refusing to let go, even when his muscles pulsed and grew numb.

"I'm not going to hurt you!" he bellowed. His scars stung and burned from his mouth stretching wide. "I'd never hurt you, Eulalia!"

Eulalia cried and shook her head. "No, no, no."

"I'd never hurt you, Eulalia. I'd never hurt you."

It became a chant, him repeatedly swearing never to hurt her, and her repeatedly refusing to hear him. Bayona sobbed in the background, unable to understand what was going on, horrified by all the screams.

Necrem lost track of time. Calming Eulalia down was all that mattered. He repeatedly promised her that she wouldn't be hurt, she continuously refused to believe it, and Bayona softly whimpered. By the time he realized Eulalia had stopped struggling, the Easterly Sun was no longer shining through the window, and she was reduced to sobbing into the mattress.

He cautiously relaxed his grip. She pulled away once he let go, curling into the fetal position.

"It'll be all right, Eulalia," he said softly. "I'll make sure you and Bayona are taken care of. Nothing's going to happen to you." He gently touched the back of her head, checking she wasn't injured after hitting her head against the headboard and trying to be comforting. She gasped and recoiled, pulling more into herself, and he jerked his hand away.

"Please go," she begged. "Please . . . please go."

Necrem knew there was nothing more he could do. He crawled away and sat hunched on the side of the bed. He stared down at his shaking hands, at every crease, crack, callus, and line crisscrossing his big palms and thick fingers.

What am I supposed to do? He wanted to cry. He wanted to yell, demand to the Savior that question that had haunted him for the past ten years but kept inside instead. *What am I supposed to* do?

He didn't know how to help his wife. He had seen what had happened to her, but her pain was immeasurable to him. He had thought she would heal with time and had done the best he could to give her some comfort in this world with the meager things he could provide. He had never been able to comfort her himself, though.

What am I supposed to do? How can a man comfort his wife when she can't bare the touch of him?

He balled his shaky hands into fists. From there, his whole body shook, vibrating the bed. Gritting his teeth, he let out a long, frustrated sigh. There was nothing for it, nothing he could do now. He was out of time and knew he needed to see to things he could do before having to leave.

He raised his head, meeting Bayona's eyes. His little girl's face was red, her eyelids raw from crying and rubbing them. She sat slumped on the floor and, like her mother, her arms wrapped around her legs.

"It's all right, Bayona," he said. "Mama . . . Mama's just having . . . a *very* bad day."

"Is . . .?" Bayona sniffed and wiped her nose on her sleeve. "Is she all right?"

No, he wanted to say. *She'll never be well.*

"She just needs rest," he lied. "Then she'll have good day tomorrow."

"You sure?" Bayona sat up, still at the wonderous age of clutching every grain of hope that was promised without question.

Necrem nodded. "I'm sure."

She sniffed and wiped her nose on her sleeve again. "But what about you?"

He chuckled and wished he could smile for her. "You let Papa worry about Papa. Let me pack some things"—he pushed off his knees and groaned, rising off the bed—"and then we'll go see if . . . an old friend can be forgiving."

~~~

"Where are we going?" Bayona asked. Her small hand squeezed his pinky and ring fingers.

"I can't just leave you and your mama alone for who-knows-how-long," Necrem explained for the hundredth time. "We're going to see an old friend of Papa's and see if he can forgive me and look in on both of you."

The slums were quiet tonight, save for a baying dog a couple streets over and a couple arguing with their window open two houses back. No one was out on streets, not even to sit out on the front steps to enjoy the cool night air. Anyone caught out at night this time of year risked being suspected as a thief, or worse. Such suspicion was all the press gangs needed to conscript a poor soul into the marqués's army.

Unfortunately for Necrem, his fate was already sealed.

"Why does he need to forgive you, Papa?" Bayona asked.

He winced. This was the one time he wished she wouldn't be curious. "You know how sometimes you argue with the other kids and get angry?"

"Yeah."

"And sometimes you might get angry enough you feel like you want to push them or something?" In ten years, Necrem had found this the hardest part of parenting—trying to explain something he believed simple simpler.

"Yeah."

He swallowed, wetting his throat and renewing his courage. It took courage to admit to your child that you had made a mistake. They never forgot it. "Well, Papa and Sanjaro, my friend, got into an argument, and Papa . . . pushed him."

"*Papa!*" Bayona squeaked, squeezing his fingers. "Was he hurt?"

"I think so."

"Was he real mad at you?"

He shook his head. "I . . . don't know. I had to leave before I could say I was sorry."

They walked down the street in silence for another block with only the crunching gravel and sounds of bugs in the distance to keep the quiet from being maddening. He looked down at her, but only saw the top of her head in the dim light.

With everything she's seen tonight, what could she be thinking now? he wondered. *Her papa suddenly has a temper and must leave, and her mama's going crazier than usual and hurting herself. How is any kid supposed to—*

"But you're sorry now, right?" Bayona asked. "And we're on our way to tell him that, right?"

"Yes," Necrem replied, unsure why she was asking.

"Then everything will be all right. That's what you're supposed to do when you fight with your friends. You say sorry and everything is all better, right?" She grinned up at him, swinging her free arm like she hadn't a care in the world and had it all figured out.

Necrem smiled softly under his mask, not feeling any stings or pulls from his scars after the amount of salve he had rubbed on them before leaving home.

He rubbed his thumb against her small hand. "Right, Little Miracle," he said. "You're so right."

She giggled and pulled on his hand, trying to swing it with her arms. He let her, of course, making sure it didn't throw her off balance while they walked.

He marveled at her resilience after everything she had seen and yet remained so innocent. Finding something to be cheerful about, even if it was the simple logic of a child.

I hope she remains cheerful, Necrem prayed, hefting his heavy-laden bag on his shoulder. *Savior, please let her be as cheerful for as long as she can.*

He feared she would be too scared after what she had seen her mama go through to come with him. He had taken his time packing the things he knew he would need and the things he could afford to lose. He'd changed his boots, putting on his best pair and putting his work pair in the bag. He'd stuffed the insides of his boots with a couple of extra pairs of socks and filled his pockets with spare masks.

The rest of his spare clothes were in his bag, along with his stock of salve for his scars. He had holstered his small sewing kit in the hem of his pants, having no room in his pockets and didn't want to risk it getting stolen when his bag was eventually ransacked. The tin case was riding his hip bone, though, and starting to hurt.

When he'd been ready, Bayona had wanted to go with him, her face still red and chapped from crying and rubbing it. He couldn't tell her no. In fact, he needed her to come. He felt lousy doing it, but Necrem hoped Sanjaro would be forgiving enough to hear the plight of his family and show some pity.

They round the corner to Sanjaro's butcher shop. The street was as quiet as the rest. Now that the nights had returned, there was little light showing the way.

Rumor had it the marqués and several well-off quarters in Manosete were putting up streetlamps to light up the night. Here in the slums, though, light either came from lamps in windows or the stars in the sky. Tonight, there were little of both.

Necrem slouched his shoulders when they finally reached Sanjaro's shop. He figured the shop would be closed, but there were no lights on the second floor, either.

"Oh no," he said gruffly.

"What's wrong, Papa?" Bayona asked, tugging his hand.

He grunted. "They're asleep."

"Does that mean we have to come back tomorrow?" There was cheerfulness in her voice, a sly, happy hope that hinted she thought he could get to stay longer.

Unfortunately, he knew that couldn't happen. "No. It means we're going to have to wake them up." *Again.*

The previous events haunted Necrem enough; he didn't want a repeat. He got a bad feeling he had done this before, though, as he led Bayona to the shop door and began to knock loudly.

No answer came. No movement or light from above.

He knocked again, louder this time, rapping his knuckles against the wood panels and making them sing out over the quiet street.

"Stop that!" an angry woman's voice shouted.

Necrem groaned. Annette was the last person he wanted to ask for help, and after last time, he was sure he was the last person she wanted see again.

"Who's down there?" Annette demanded.

Candlelight flickered overhead. Risking a glance upward, Necrem saw he and Bayona were shielded by the building and couldn't be seen. Instead of risking being turned away from his friend's wife, he knocked again, harder and more determined.

A frustrated growl came from above, and the candlelight disappeared.

He kept knocking. He had to talk to Sanjaro. He didn't know how much time he had left, but he had to see his family cared for, even if he returned to jail at daybreak.

Finally, lamps were lit in the shop. Necrem stopped knocking and was stepping back when the door flung open.

"Who the—" Annette's words violently cut off. She snarled the moment she made him out in the candlelight. "How *dare* you come back? Get out of here before I call the guards again!"

She tried to slam the door, but Necrem caught it with his foot, grunting from the hard edge digging into the leather and hitting him.

"I need to talk to Sanjaro," he begged.

"We have nothing to say to a beast like you," Annette spat. She kicked his foot, but when he didn't budge, she pulled back the door and slammed it again.

He growled, holding back a curse from the door's corner smashing the side of his foot, and braced his shoulder, catching another slam before it hit. That made Annette more frantic.

"*Help!*" Annette screamed. "Our home's being invaded! Help!"

A cold sweat ran down Necrem's back. Here and there, lights came on in the other houses. If the guards were called on him a second time, they might send him to the *sioneros* reserve.

"Sanjaro!" he bellowed. "Sanjaro, please! My family needs you. Eulalia and Bayona, they need you!"

Annette slung the door again, and Necrem's shoulder gave out. His arm stung from the impact's hard *smack*. His footing slipped, and he stumbled away from the door. In the next instant, the door slammed shut.

He stood there a moment, rubbing his shoulder and staring at the door. He couldn't look down. After everything that had happened tonight, he didn't want to see the look of disappointment or fear on his little miracle's face.

She called me a beast. In front of Bayona. He shuddered. *How do I explain that?* He hung his head, suddenly feeling exhausted on his feet. *Maybe I should just take her home and . . . and . . .*

He couldn't think of anything after that. There wasn't anything after that. No one else to turn to he could trust or ask for help. He would have to leave them. Alone. With nobody to help them.

A still, small knock echoed through the night.

Necrem opened his eyes and saw Bayona up by the door, knocking.

"Hello?" she called. Her knocks were soft compared to his. "Hello? Papa said he has a friend here? He says he's really sorry for pushing him, and he didn't mean it."

Bayona kept knocking. Still, soft, persistent knocks. She kept apologizing for him, too, over and over, saying he was really sorry. Necrem thought he heard other voices, too, but when he looked around, no one had come out to see what was going on, though several lights were still on.

"Hello—"

The door slowly opened and, in the crack, stood Sanjaro, once again struggling to close his nightgown. Necrem was immediately drawn to the wrap of bandages around his head and looked away, his heart heavy by a sudden strike of guilt.

"Hello," Bayona said. "Are you my papa's friend?"

Necrem glanced out of the side of his vision. Sanjaro frowned at him with a hurt look on his face.

"I . . . was," Sanjaro replied.

"Oh." Bayona rocked on her heels, clearly not sure how to respond to that immediately. "Well, he's *really* sorry for shoving you. He didn't mean it. Do you think you can forgive him?"

Necrem grimaced, his scars pulling and pressing against each other as he stood there and watched his little girl apologize for him. Even though she was doing it without realizing it, it still stung to listen to.

He looked up and caught Sanjaro looking down at her, his frown softening somewhat.

"No . . ." Sanjaro said, sighing. "No, I guess he didn't mean it. Did they treat you badly, Necrem?"

"Not as bad as they could have," he replied.

Sanjaro weakly nodded and looked back inside his house. "Well, if . . . if everything is all right—"

"I'm going away, Sanjaro," he blurted out. "I don't know how long I'll be, but . . ."

Sanjaro's face went white, and his jaw dropped. "Are they sending you to the reserve?"

Necrem shook his head. "Just conscription."

"Oh." There was a hint of relief in Sanjaro's voice, and he licked his lips. "But do they know who you are?"

"They know. I think they knew all along."

Sanjaro's shoulders slumped, and his frown returned, more out of pity now. "I'm sorry, Necrem. If there was only something that could be done."

"I don't think anything could have been done. I think they had something like this planned from the start. The marqués wants men, and none of the press gangs care where they get them this season. I just have one thing to ask of you."

"What?"

Necrem patted Bayona on the shoulder, and she grinned up at him. He looked back down at her with furled brows. "Look after Bayona and Eulalia for me, please. You're the only one I can ask. The only friend that . . . knows."

Sanjaro's face hardened. His chin wobbled slightly, and his eyes glistened. "I can do that. It's the least I can do."

Necrem gave him a nod of thanks then turned toward the hardest part of the night. Bayona was still grinning up at him, probably thinking two friends had made up and everything was going to better in her innocent, child logic.

He knelt and took her by the shoulder. His pulse quickened. He knew what he had to say but, again, couldn't find the words. Rather, he couldn't speak the words. She had heard him tell Eulalia he was going, but now he had to make sure she understood.

He swallowed and squeezed her shoulder, drawing up the last bit of courage before it failed him.

"Papa's got to go now," he finally said. "You'll stay with Sanjaro tonight. He'll take you home tomorrow and make sure Mama's all right."

Bayona's grin faded into confusion. She blinked and tilted her head. "We're not going home?"

Necrem shook his head. "If we go home, I might not be able to leave. Then the soldiers will come and . . . take me away forever."

Bayona gaped in horror. "They can't do that! That's not right! That's not—"

He pulled her in for a tight hug. Her small body trembled against his. She buried her face in his chest, filling his nostrils with the mixed scents of soap, iron, leather, and cooked bacon from her hair.

"It's not right," he agreed. "But I have to go. Look after your mama like you always have. Sanjaro will look in on you to make sure you have everything. Just take care of yourself and your mama, and everything will be well." He gave her a tight hug, his shaking arm matching her shudders.

"But what about you?" She sniffed, rubbing her face and likely snot onto his shirt.

He briefly closed his eyes, forcing the tears back to prevent the last thing she might ever see of her papa was him crying. She still loved and cared about him, even after everything. That's all he needed.

"Don't you worry, Bayona," he replied, patting her back. "Your papa's a steel-working man. I've hammered steel into shape for nights on end until my arms almost fell off. I can go march around the country and back no problem.

"You just got to remember, Bayona"—he pulled her away to look her in the eye—"we're steel-working people. We're stronger than steel. That means we can endure anything. And we don't cry. Right?"

Her face was red again, her eyes puffy, and snot glistened on her nose. She sniffed loudly and tried to make tough face, but it looked like she was pouting.

"Right." She nodded.

Necrem's vision began to blur, and he knew his time was up. He ran a finger across her cheeks, wiping her tears, before straightening her hair. "Your papa loves you, Bayona. Always remember that."

He tilted her head forward so she wouldn't see him lift his mask. With his partially misshapen, partially missing lips, he kissed her on the top of her head. Then he rose and walked away, taking long, determined strides down the street before she had picked her head back up.

"Papa!" she cried. "Don't go! *Papa*!"

The last screech struck him to his core. The dam of frustration, strength, and pain broke, and he began to cry. The salt from his tears ran into his scars, between his exposed gums, and into his mouth. They disturbed the salve, making his face sting.

When he returned to the jail, the guards outside recoiled at his red, swollen face in the morning sun.

Chapter 9

"Filth!" the grizzled capitán spat. "All of you. I've never been saddled with a more pitiful excuse of conscripts in all my years. You!" He pointed at a man down the line. "Stand up straight.

"You!" He pointed at another. "Spit out what you're chewing! You're in Si Don's army now, not pissing around in whatever gutter they dragged you out of."

Necrem shifted his weight, struggling to keep his shoulders from slumping and his eyes open. He wanted to find some place out of the Easterly Sun and sit. He wouldn't need a bed or to lay down. After the previous night and being marched over ten miles north of Manosete, he could sleep anywhere.

Please don't take long. His back and legs ached, and his breathing flared every now and then if his focus slipped, both from exhaustion and nerves. *You hate us, and we don't like you. But we'll do as you say, or we're punished. Or worse.*

He'd heard these kinds of speeches before, back when he was a union member, but he never thought he would be one of the poor souls to be on the receiving end of one. He blessedly stood in the center of the ranks of two hundred smelly, raggedy men. Their ages varied from middle-aged, like him, to boys who hadn't had their first shave yet. All of them were tired, and most were scared, especially the younger lads.

Necrem spotted one off to his right, shaking and drenched in sweat. He sweated, too. He wasn't in the frontlines, yet he stood head and shoulders above most of the other men. Knowing his luck, he expected to be noticed at any time.

"I am Capitán Gonzel." The capitán put his gauntleted fists on his hips, the metal striking against the sides of his breastplate. He grimaced at the men up front, making his pockmarks stand out under his patchy, gray beard. From standing on his small stool, he could stare down the men up there and gaze back on the ranks, right at Necrem.

"Capitán Fidal Gonzel," he continued. "But just Capitán to the likes of you. I don't need to know a single one of your slum-scum names. If I even hear *one* of your names, that means you must be a problem." His eyes narrowed, glaring at them. "And I won't hesitate to rid my company of a problem. Do I make myself clear?"

Men shuffled about, nervously glancing at one another and shrugging. Necrem just stared back.

He means the sioneros *reserve.*

He worked his jaw and felt a prick his right cheek. His dried-out scars were chaffing against his mask from not having fresh salve applied to them since last night. He had to be careful. One false move could crack a scar open and start bleeding.

"*Well?*" the man left of the capitán, holding a halberd, roared. "Answer the capitán when he speaks to you, filth! Say *aye!*"

"Aye," Necrem said, not risking tearing a scar while everyone else yelled.

"Louder!" the man demanded.

"Aye!"

The man sneered at them, missing several teeth. He looked no better than the men he sneered at. His scraggly beard gave him a look of a man freshly conscripted himself, despite his polished breastplate over his clean clothes and the shiny helm on his head. He could easily have been a soldier who had spent his pay on a freshly made kit, but Necrem doubted it.

He remembered men like him from when he'd been a union smith. Men like that would rather spend their pay on liquor or women, not their arms. They spent other people's money for that.

"It's just as you say, Capitán," the soldier said, shaking his head at the officer. "Pitiful. But me and the boys will straighten them up."

"See to it, Master Sergeant," Capitán Gonzel replied. "This is Master Sergeant Raul, and he and his fellow sergeants are going to make sure whenever I say *run*, you scum *sprint*! Split 'em up, Master Sergeant. Be on the lookout for"—he scanned the ranks and, for a second, Necrem felt his eyes settle on him—"troublemakers."

"Aye, Capitán!" Raul saluted, slamming his fist to his heart.

Capitán Gonzel stepped down from his stool and wandered off into camp without another word, leaving them in the care of the master sergeant.

Necrem suspected Raul's treatment wouldn't be any kinder than the capitán's.

"All right, lads," Raul said, rocking on his heels with an unnerving grin, "me and the other sergeants are going to split you up into families now. Wherever we say to go, go. If you don't, we'll give you a kick in the ass to make you go."

"You," someone said in the back.

"You!" another yelled over to Necrem's left, just out of sight.

Nine men in armor, like the master sergeant's, and who'd been watching from afar, descended upon them, taking men out at random and ordering, sometimes pushing, men out into smaller groups. The one closest to Necrem, though, was the master sergeant himself, and he kept an eye on him. While the other sergeants went about their work with disinterest, Raul stalked between the ranks with a gleam in his eye.

Raul pushed through one rank, stopping in front of the shivering lad Necrem had spotted earlier. He looked the boy up and down, the uneasy smile never wavering.

"You," the master sergeant said, grabbing the boy by the shirt, "over there." He pointed with his halberd toward the right, close to the corner of the ranks, where no one had been directed to yet, and flung the boy out of line.

The boy yelped, stumbled, and barely caught himself in time before crashing into the dirt. Raul laughed as the boy picked himself up and walked, hunched over, to where he'd been ordered.

The master sergeant stalked away and, despite feeling bad for the young man, Necrem breathed a deep sigh of relief. Along with several others around him.

The selection and division continued. Necrem baked under the hot Easterly Sun, waiting for something worse to happen. His sweat-soaked shirt stuck to his body. His dry breath whistled through his mask. A couple of sergeants did walk by, looking at the other men, taking the man to his right, but never giving him a glance.

His attention wandered the longer he was ignored.

The army camp stretched for miles around. The sloping hills were covered with canvas from erected tents and flapping banners. He could never keep straight which banner belonged to which baron, company, or individual calleros. To him, they were all nobles and paid for most of his smithing work while traveling with the armies. Doing his work and being paid was all that had mattered to him back then.

He tilted his head. Through the growls of the sergeants picking men nearby and the hundreds of shouts, orders, and yells in camp, he thought he heard the faint *pings* of metal against metal, hammer against hot steel. He formed a fist, feeling the worn handle, the weight of the head, then the drop.

"Oh no," Master Sergeant Raul growled, snapping Necrem out of his daze.

He heard boots crunching and the heavy thump of a halberd handle slamming into the ground. He couldn't turn his head to see, but he felt a closer presence right behind him.

"Maeso Corri." The master sergeant spat. "You thieving rat. Couldn't keep your greasy fingers out of other people's pockets this time either, eh?"

"I did try, Sergeant," a snarky voice replied. "Forgive me, Master Sergeant. The higher rank suits you—it really does. But, you know, sometimes life after campaign can be hard for humble men like me."

"*Humble*?" Raul snickered. "Since when have you *ever* been humble, Maeso?"

"Since I was three, sir. Honest."

"You've never been honest a day in your life." There was small scuffle before a short man with thin, patchy hair came scrambling around Necrem, flailing his arms to keep balance. "Get over there with my group and behave, if you know what's good for you."

The short man, Maeso, turned and bobbed his head, keeping his back hunched and his hands folded together. The thin line of a mustache on his upper lip and narrow nose certainly gave him a rat appearance. He was missing some teeth, and Necrem barely got a glimpse of his eyes before he scurried off. The other sergeants laughed, but then, one by one, fell silent.

The hairs on the back of Necrem's neck stood up. That presence still lurked behind him. He saw the master sergeant's shadow out of the corner of his eye, just standing there.

Then he moved.

He slowly stalked around, walking with his halberd *thumping* on the ground with each step. The master sergeant stopped in front of him and looked him up and down.

"All right, big bastard," Raul growled. "How much trouble are we going to get from you?"

"None, sir," he replied.

Raul squinted at him. "What was that? Speak up, big man! Am I going to get any trouble from you?"

"No, sir," he said louder.

"That's no, *Master Sergeant*, giant!" Raul stomped his halberd in the dirt. "You're in Si Don's army now, and I'm going to put you in your place right now.

I know your kind. If you crack any skulls or throw any weight around without me telling you first, I'll have you broken down to size. You understand me?"

"Yes, Master Sergeant!" Necrem made sure to be a little louder but tried not to push it.

He knew Raul was just asserting his rank and was showing the other men he wasn't scared of Necrem's size. It didn't matter to him. He simply had to do what he was told and do his best to get back home, alive.

"Louder!" Raul snapped.

"Yes! *Master Sergeant!*"

A ripping sting raced across his right cheek. Something warm slowly trickled down, and the familiar taste of iron and salt seeped between his exposed teeth.

That was a stitch! He forced his breathing to still. *My face is too dry.*

Raul growled and shook his head. "I still can't hear a damn word you're saying. Take that stupid mask off."

The veins in Necrem's neck tensed. It was as if the eyes of everyone in camp were upon him. "Sir . . . I can't—"

"Take off that *damn* mask!" The master sergeant slammed his halberd into the ground again. "That's an *order!*"

Necrem briefly thought to explain what he was hiding, why it was best no one saw his face. The determination in Raul's face, his disgusted sneer, and uncaring eyes, however, told him instantly that wouldn't work.

"Fine." He reached around the back of his head, slowly as not to frighten anyone. "You want to see?"

He untied the leather band, careful not to pull his hair. The stiff leather caught on his prickly, dry skin and peeled off his right cheek from the bleeding stich. The hot air instantly struck his face. Grains of dust blew between the open cuts in his cheeks, embedding themselves in his exposed teeth.

Raul's sneer drained from his face, along with the blood from his face. He gaped up at Necrem, all his bluster and authority evaporating as he stared.

A growing murmur spread through the onlookers. Men shuffled around in their groups to get a look at him, only to recoil at the sight, cussing and touching their own faces in some fashion.

Necrem didn't blame them. His face was crisscrossed, gouged, and carved from one ear, following his jawline and along his cheekbone, under his nose, and to his other ear. Some cuts were shallow, but the deeper ones sliced into the muscle, and the stitching had barely helped them heal because patches of skin had been carved off his face.

Part of his lips were also missing, combined with the multiple slashes, and his teeth and gums were exposed in several places. He knew several of them were brown, too. The missing skin and frenzied nature of the cuts meant he had to continually sew some of his scars back up to hold his face together, allowing them to heal the best they could as his skin pulled taut across his face over the years. They also needed fresh salve applied regularly to keep the skin and scars moist and clean.

His face resembled a living corpse's—hanging flesh, exposed muscle, gums, and teeth—but all alive and constantly healing, reopening, and bleeding again.

With his mask off, saliva began pooling at the edges of his exposed teeth and dripped down his chin. Blood from the ripped stitch ran down and left a warm streak curving under his jaw, finally dripping onto his shirt.

"What . . .?" Raul stammered, shaking in his armor. "By the Savior, what the . . .?"

"Punishment," Necrem hissed and whistled through the open sides of his face. The whistling continued from his breathing, and he switched to breathing through his nose. "Can I put my mask back on now, Master Sergeant?"

"Yes!" Raul couldn't speak fast enough. "Never take the frickin' thing off again. Get over there with the others. I'll make sure you don't cause trouble for the capitán personally." He waved him away then went back to sorting through the remaining conscripts.

Necrem begrudgingly put his mask back on. Not that he cared what everyone else thought, but the blood already staining the inside of the mask. His stitching needed to be redone, and the rest of his scars needing salve. He wanted to treat his face away from prying eyes. He suspected the master sergeant wasn't done with them.

After tying on his mask, he picked up the bag by his feet and trudged off to his assigned group. Most of the men had already been divided up and, at quick glance, he could see they were being split up in groups of twenty. Some of the sergeants were already berating their chosen men.

People watched him.

Before, he had just been a tall curiosity because of his mask. Now he was a walking horror. The men who the master sergeant had selected stepped away from him, giving him space and not meeting his eyes as he walked to the back of the group. A quick count told him there wasn't a full twenty yet.

He set his bag between two tents, squatted, and then pulled out a tin of salve.

"How'd that happen, you wonder?" someone whispered behind him.

Necrem untied his mask and put it away in his bag before popping the can's lid off. The heavy musk of the fatty, cream-colored contents hit his nostrils, and he held back a gag. He'd been gagging for over nine years, but it was the only thing to soothe his tattered face.

"Pissed off the *wrong* people," someone whispered back.

You're not wrong there.

He dipped the tips of his fingers into the thick, slimy salve, coating them, and then brought them to his face. The salve seeped into every crack and line on his face. Some rolled into his exposed mouth, and he heaved at its overwhelming salty, oily taste. It made his eyes water.

It took another dip to salve all his scars. He wiped the blood off his cheek and neck before covering the right side of his face. He hissed and clamped his teeth together the moment the salty salve touched his ripped stitch. He gently tapped the stitch, feeling the tear.

I'll have to pull the entire stitch. He didn't look forward to that. He was still terrible at stitching, despite his years of practice.

Necrem salved the rest of his face, bearing the musky smell under his nose and the oily taste on his hacked lips, and then he put the salve away. He breathed easy after fishing a clean mask from his pocket and tied it on. This mask—made of cloth—pressed down on his slickened skin and formed a seal, but also let him breathe.

After putting his things away, he stood up to find everyone still watching him. Unsurprisingly, they shied away from him, not risking looking him in the eye. Yet, he could already pick out smaller groups forming among them.

The younger men stood apart from the older, those who had seen a campaign stood together with their arms folded, and the raggedy, nefarious types were huddled together, whispering as if already conniving a pecking order and planning to steal everyone's possessions.

Seeing them, Necrem picked up his bag and held it close.

"You look better with the mask," Maeso said, crookedly grinning from the middle of the raggedy bunch.

The band of thieves surrounding him hushed, and everyone passed cautious glances between the two men.

They're expecting me to growl or say something menacing.

Everyone expected that out of Necrem. To average folk, a man as big as him had to be mean or intimidating. It was just an image that came naturally to them.

He shrugged. "I never had looks."

They all blinked at him.

First, there was a snicker. Then a chuckle. Finally, the thieves broke down laughing, and the veterans smirked.

"All right! Shut up!" Master Sergeant Raul ordered, hauling in his last pick by the collar.

The man didn't fit in with any of the three forming groups. His wavy hair reached below his shoulders. His clothes were unstained and not those of a working man from the slums. His dark, high-collar jacket was clean, his trousers only had a layer of dust, and he wore shoes instead of boots.

"Please, sir," the man begged, "there must be some mistake."

"The only mistake you keep making is not *shutting* your trap!" The master sergeant sneered in the man's face before tossing him in with the rest.

The man fell into one of the veterans, who in turn tossed him aside into another. That repeated while the fancy man flailed aimlessly, like a spark dancing in the air until he finally flailed out and fell into the dirt, much to the thieves' amusement, them pointing and laughing at him.

"Shut up, *filth*!" Raul snapped. "You're all in Si Don's army now and, for better or worse, get to serve for the honor of his son, Don Givanzo. You better start acting like it and follow orders fast, or you're all going to start off with a flogging!"

That returned everyone's sour mood and silenced the laughing.

"Good." The master sergeant smirked. "Now, take a good look around. This is your family for the rest of the campaign. While we'll march with the entire company, you will eat, train, fight, and sleep with the men around you. And you're all responsible for each other.

"If any man is caught stealing, him and five more of you will be flogged." Raul stalked in among them, glaring warningly at the thieves when he mentioned stealing. "If any man is caught slouching on their training, him and five more of you will be flogged. If any man can't keep his weapons and armor clean, him and five more of you will be flogged. If any man is caught mistreating camp followers, he may be hanged, but five more of you *will* be flogged. And, if any one of you tries to desert"—Raul stopped in front of Necrem and sneered up at him—"*all* of you will be . . . punished."

The master sergeant let the threat hang in the air while the other men stared at him.

Necrem just hung his head. *Deserters are hanged. There's no reason to—*

He spotted the young lads trembling. The sweaty one's face was pale.

He's just scaring everybody.

"Do I make myself clear?" Raul asked, looking back over the rest.

"Yes, sir," several mumbled and nodded, including Necrem.

"Yes *what*?" Raul spat. "I can't hear you, filth!"

"Yes, Master Sergeant!" they all said louder.

Raul grunted and strolled through them.

Necrem reeled back to avoid the master sergeant's halberd that he swung carelessly on his shoulder.

"From now on, you're all part of my personal squad. Which means you do whatever I say before everyone else does. And if any man doesn't do it fast enough, well . . . are any of you smart enough to know what happens?"

They remained quiet. A mutual feeling on not being stupid enough to—

"He gets a flogging along with five others," Maeso replied. "Right, Master Sergeant?"

"Good to see you still remember, Maeso." Raul chuckled. "Maybe the lesson will stick this year."

"Truer words were never spoken, Master Sergeant." Maeso rolled his shoulders.

There were a few nervous chuckles from his shabby band, but no one else found it funny.

"All right then." Raul cleared his throat. "On to—"

Drumming started from somewhere deeper in the camp. Raul and the other sergeants stopped their beratement and listened. More drums followed. Then a bugle call. Then another. The lads shared confused looks, but Necrem and the veterans knew what they meant.

The army's been ordered to move.

Glancing over his shoulder, he spied camp followers already rushing into the tents, hurrying to pack. He remembered doing the same when he had followed the armies. It was the hardest and worst job to do—loading all his tools and equipment as fast as he could so as not to be left behind.

"Sounds like Don Givanzo is eager to start the season," Raul said then grinned at the young lads. "Here's your first lesson, boys. In Si Don's army, you run. *Everywhere*. Get moving! All of you *move*! Move!"

The other sergeants echoed their master sergeant, and Necrem and the rest of his conscripted company were soon sent dashing through the camp.

He threw his bag over his shoulder, holding it tightly while wincing with every footfall. He wasn't sure where they were leading him, but he was *certain* his knees were going to hate every step of the way.

Chapter 10

Recha laughed and clapped at the most ridiculous sight she had seen in years. A middle-aged man danced on top of a table, dressed in a skirt with two bailer dancers. It was anyone's guess where the man had gotten the skirt to put over his clothes, but he and everyone else at Don Cristal's party were flushed with wine. He could have gotten it from a lady guest, and no one would have known for sure.

The man's cheeks and across the dome of his head's bald crown were red, nearly purple. He kicked his feet from side to side and shimmied the skirt with the dancers. The hair he had left hung off the sides of his head and slung about as he tried to imitate the dancers.

The women laughed and kept trying to give him pointers on how to kick his feet out, exposing their black lace, hose-covered legs, much to the other partygoers' thrill, and kept from getting tangled up in his borrowed skirt.

The man tried, but he, too, was getting distracted by the women and wobbled drunkenly. The table lurched to one side.

The women cried, flailing their arms to keep their balance, and the partygoers went silent momentarily, eagerly leaning in to watch. As for the drunken man, he kept trying to dance.

The table swayed to one side, and the partygoers swayed with it. Then it swayed the other way, and the women cried, struggling even more.

"Watch out!" someone cried happily. "It's going to—"

Crack!

A table leg snapped.

The women jumped off to either side of the table where a couple of gentlemen just so happened to be waiting to catch them. As for the poor man, he yelped when his footing disappeared and dropped along with the collapsing table.

The partygoers roared with laughter, pointing at the man and raising their wine cups. The bailer dancers easily forgot about him and instead danced with their rescuers.

"Recha!"

She turned away from the chaotic scene and found Don Cristal wading through his guest toward her, his arm around his own bailer dancer's waist. His flush face matched his guests, and his hair was wild and tossed, as if he'd been rolling around on the floor.

Or perhaps a bed.

Recha raised an eyebrow at his unlaced linen shirt, half-untucked in his trousers. He was also missing a boot but seemed obliviously happy to hop along.

She put on her coy smile she used only for him. She knew she could mentally dance around him, and he wouldn't be able to keep up in his current state, but she couldn't afford to make mistakes now. Not to anyone.

"Lovely party, Don Cristal," she greeted him. "I must say your farewell celebrations grow more elaborate every year."

"Thank you, Recha!" Cristal yelled loud enough to make her blink. "Your attendance always brightens up the room!" He laughed and wobbled, slowly looking her up and down, before frowning at her. "Why Recha, you aren't dressed to suitably enjoy the celebrations! Much too formal."

True. She was the most modestly dressed person in the room, perhaps the entire Pamolid embassy. Her dark blue, linen dress was meant more for the falls months, but she also found a use for it on nightly outings like this. The collar wasn't too high and buttoned up just under her neck. No lace to make her neck itch or get in her hands' way. The skirts were simple, elegant, but not voluminous. The perfect night dress to slip in and out places.

Such as here.

She wanted to slip in and out of here as fast as she could. There was another place she had to visit before finally getting some sleep. She only came to make sure one little concern was taken care of.

"I know, Cris dear," she said, giving him a pretend pout and taking him by his free hand. "I know. But, unfortunately, Madre Leticia has been insistent that she speak with me. If I don't go to chapel tonight, I fear she'll hold services on my front step next Savior's Day."

Savior's Day was the church's largest religious holiday and held a festival and revival all week long, celebrating the Savior's teachings and leading humanity out of Oblivion. Services were held throughout the city, and Madre Leticia had threatened to hold one on her doorstep several times in the past.

"You can go to chapel anytime." Cristal waved dismissively. "When do you get to enjoy a celebration like *this*!" He made a grand gesture at the mayhem around them.

Cristal had instituted a tradition after becoming the Pamolid ambassador of throwing a lavish party every year before departing ahead of campaign season starting. This party had started two days ago while Recha was abroad, and she feared she wouldn't be able to step in and make sure her plans for this year came to fruition.

Upon arriving, she instantly knew there was nothing to fret about. Cristal had gone out of his way to make this farewell party the most lavish yet. There were musicians of every kind, fluteplayers, drummers, violinists, guitarists, along with singers scattered about in nearly every room of the three-story embassy. Each tone and style clashed with the others, and the musicians, being drunk themselves, did nothing to improve their key.

Then, of course, there were the dancers. Not only had Cristal hired troops of bailer dancers, but there were women dressed from lavish gowns of long silk trains to women barely dressed at all.

Perhaps that's where the drunk, dancing man had gotten his skirt.

Despite after going on for three days, people still came and went. Recha knew many of them, mostly sons of neighboring barons close to Zoragrin and sons of the city's wealthy. Then, of course, was the entire embassy staff, which themselves were mostly young sons of Pamolid nobility. After Cristal had taken up his post, he'd quickly started filling it with all his friends from back home after telling them about the wonderful time he was having, much to Recha's intention.

Now, all those young men were heavily drunk, laughing and dancing without a care in the world. Just as she wanted.

"It is a marvelous party, Cristal," she said, smiling broadly.

Despite being flushed with wine, Cristal grew a shade redder. "Then you must stay. I know! A glass of wine. No! A *bottle*! Yes! A bottle is just what we need."

"No—" Recha interjected, reaching out to grab him, but it was too late. He was already off and swirling into the crowd of partygoers in search of his magic bottle.

She sighed and dropped her arm. *He never will take my oath of sobriety seriously.*

Regardless, he did leave her with the perfect opportunity to speak with the one person she truly came to see.

"Aren't you going a little too far, Silvaja?" she asked, arching an eyebrow at the conspicuously quiet woman.

"Hmm?" the shapely, auburn-haired bailer dancer, who had drifted a little to the side after Cristal had unceremoniously abandoned her upon greeting Recha, hummed. "Begging your pardon, La Dama, but this is Don Cristal's party. I'm just looking after my girls." She gestured at the other bailer dancers, dancing and laughing with guests throughout the room.

She was a few years older than Recha, and most of the other bailer girls, but still well in her prime. No wrinkles marred her supple lips, around her dark eyes, or the forehead of her round face. Her olive skin tone also gave her a mature look compared the paler-skinned bailer dancers.

She also wasn't fully what she appeared.

"You can lower your guise for a moment, Silvaja," Recha said, glancing about the room to make sure they weren't being watched. "You've taken Sevesco's tips to heart of never breaking character, but I'm afraid I don't have time for a discreet update. Besides, if anyone asks, you can just say you were looking after the Don's important guest as his"—she shot her a glance, particularly at Silvaja's state of dress—"lady?"

Silvaja wrapped an arm around herself, propping her hip to the side. Her dress matched the other bailer dancers—red silk with white layered skirts underneath and a sewn-in sash of gold bangles running around her hips. The descending neckline showed the curve of her bosom while only cords and lace, tied in a knot behind her neck, kept the dress up. There were no sleeves, exposing her shoulders and the top of her back. She also wore long, red, silk gloves that reached past her elbows.

However, there were several things out of place. The laces running up the side of Silvaja's dress were crooked and sloppily done up on both sides. An underskirt was missing—there should have been three layers, but hers only had two. Silvaja's right glove had fallen and clumped up below her elbow while the left was still snuggly covering her to her forearm. Not to mention her dress's blouse hung a little too low, hinting at a little too much cleavage, as if the binding cords hadn't been done properly. Things a man, especially in a drunken party like this, wouldn't think twice about, but Recha knew more.

"Whatever do you mean?" Silvaja asked, looking away with her lips pursed, bemused.

"You know what I mean," Recha replied, stepping a little closer. "Did he force you?"

"No, La Dama," Silvaja snickered. "There was no forcing."

Recha rolled her tongue along her teeth, trying to keep her expression placid and not show her disapproval. "When I gave you this assignment, I asked you *not* to get involved with anyone here, especially Cristal himself. Do I need to worry?"

Please don't make me worry. She liked Silvaja. More importantly, Sevesco liked Silvaja.

He had met her two years ago, sneaking out of Orsembar. His covert dealings had still been new then, and Marqués Borbin's espies had been after him. At great personal risk, Silvaja and her traveling bailer troop had given him shelter and helped him back home under Borbin's nose. In return for their help, Sevesco had turned around and began teaching her his craft of being espi. If Silvaja had turned, her betrayal would not only be against Sevesco, but Recha and Lazorna, also.

Silvaja held her gaze, her smile never wavering, as if she didn't know if Recha was serious or not. Then she threw her head back and laughed, shaking her hair everywhere.

"Have no fear," she said. "There's nothing to worry about. You see"—she took a step closer, almost talking into Recha's ear—"some of the girls ventured down into the wine cellar to prepare tonight's *special* vintage when Don Cristal became insistent on making sure there was enough wine to keep his party going. *Very* insistent. Nothing simple could distract him." Silvaja sniffed and folded her arms, taking a careful glance around the room before continuing. "I couldn't let him walk in on the girls. And, considering his age, his position, and him already being drunk, there was really . . . only one thing I could use to make him forget about the wine."

Recha bit the inside of her cheek and lightly rubbed her hands together, folded neatly in front of her. She felt a twinge of guilt for doubting her, but even more guilt for what Silvaja had done for the sake of her assignment.

"I'm sorry to have put you in that position," she said. "When I gave you and your troop this assignment, I promised it wouldn't be that kind of work."

Silvaja smirked. "I wasn't forced, either by him or you. I'm a grown woman, and I can take care of myself. Just ask Sevesco." She winked and grinned, making Recha not want to consider what that implied. "Besides"—she looked through the crowd, as if searching for someone, and shrugged—"it was kind of fun."

Recha's cheeks warm. *Time to change the subject.*

She cleared her throat. "Is everything ready?"

"Mmhmm," Silvaja hummed, nodding. "Our special vintage should take effect in the next hour or so."

"Excellent." Recha crookedly smiled, straining to hide her thrill from her scheme working so well. She bounced her gaze back and forth across the room, watching as the dignitaries and embassy staff toasted each other or drank straight from bottles.

Years of toying and bantering with Cristal were paying dividends now. In her plans to strike back against Borbin, Pamolid was the uncertain factor she had to be wary of. It wouldn't do her or Lazorna any good to finally strike against Orsembar just to have Pamolid march in and crush them from behind. However, after building a smooth relationship with Cristal, and him sending word back to his uncle that neither she nor Lazorna were threats, now she only needed to ensure that Marqués Hyles didn't learn of her attack against Borbin for as long as possible.

That was where Silvaja and her troop of bailer dancers came in. Recha's little gift to Cristal after their negotiations to distract the young man from her opened the path to introducing him to Silvaja tonight. Cristal, ever eager to have his fun, had played right into her hands.

She wanted to laugh. She wanted to hop up and down and clap her hands at seeing such a scheme work out in front of her eyes. Best of all, she didn't even need Sevesco's devious mind to think it up.

I wonder if I should worry about that? Recha was enjoying herself too much to worry.

"I do have one concern, La Dama," Silvaja said.

Recha raised an eyebrow at her, not wanting her inner moment spoiled. The other woman didn't seem to notice.

"We seem to have caught more fish in our net than we thought." Silvaja gestured at the sons of the local barons and wealthy Zoragrinits. "They've been drinking our wine, too, and are probably going to be just as sick. Any suggestions what we should do with them?"

Silvaja's special vintage was wine poisoned with lemon bean extract, a yellow bean with a citrus scent that's nearly impossible to eat unless specially prepared.

In just an hour, most of the guests in this room will be falling over, suddenly becoming weak and vomiting, Recha imagined, reminding herself of the poison's effect. *After that, they will be in for days of fever, headaches, and . . . diarrhea.* Then she quickly thought of some of her barons' sons being caught in that, as well. And how to use it.

"Keep them here with the rest," she replied. "And keep to schedule. Once guests start getting sick, send word to Esquire Valto. He already has orders prepared to declare an outbreak of bellum fever and put this place under guard. That should leave Don Cristal and everyone else in your and your girls' nursing hands." She grinned. *And keep Marqués Hyles in the dark.*

Silvaja grinned back. "Yes, La Dama."

"Having sons of my own barons also fall sick will make the sudden illness more believable," Recha added. "You might be able to distract Cristal for most of campaign season." *And keep some barons from thinking twice with their sons under guard.* She could never be too careful with them or their loyalties.

"I can keep him distracted," Silvaja promised, swaying to the music. "Me and the girls will nurse them so well they may stay the *whole* season." She giggled.

Recha nodded. "Then I'll leave them in your capable hands. Please give Cristal my regrets, but I'm afraid, after visiting his party this year, I am in *desperate* need to go to chapel."

"I promise to console him. Have a good night, La Dama." Silvaja bent her knees instead of nodding.

"And to you, Silvaja."

The bailer troop leader turned and swayed into the crowd, slipping around guest after guest, in search of her query, like a hunter.

Maybe I should worry for Cristal? Recha mused.

She shook her and made her way downstairs, to Cornelos waiting for her outside.

~~~

Recha draped the thin linen shawl over her head and let the ends fall over her shoulders. The fabric's light blue color contrasted with her dress's dark blue, but she didn't mind. This was a late-night visit to chapel for personal reasons, not her stately visit on Deliverance Day.

The chapel of Zoragrin was a modest, two-story house of worship, barely able to fit a quarter of the city's devoted population for services. It was humbled by the Grand Temple in Manosete and the First Mission in Prizaje, but it suited Recha fine.

She preferred the close, personal interaction with a small church than the pomp of a large one. At least, that was the feeling she got when dealing with clergy from the Church of the Savior.

After becoming marquesa, she'd had long conversations with both Madre Leticia and traveling deacons from other marcs and the Grand Temple. Her sudden rise, the methods she had used, and her deal with the Viden de Verda were things she had treaded carefully with them. In many ways, she still did.

As she stepped into the sanctuary, Cornelos stepped away from her and knelt against the back row prayer pew. The pews had no seats. The church's services were a mix of standing and kneeling to pray.

Recha softly smiled over her shoulder at him. While Cornelos folded his hands on top of the pew, she saw his eyes remained open, watchful.

Devoted as ever, she mused, finding it flattering he could hold his duty as her secretary at the same height as his devotion to his faith.

He wasn't the only one praying tonight. The lantern light showed people kneeling and praying throughout the sanctuary, most of them women.

The sanctuary was lit by cast iron lanterns mounted along the wall. While, to an outsider, they gave the chapel a rustic appearance, the lanterns were in fact iconography of the church. It was believed the Savior himself went into the old world with only a lantern to find wayward people, trapped in the blackness of the oncoming Oblivion and delivered them to safety.

"Blessed Savior," an elder woman kneeling on the end of a row to Recha's left mumbled. "Please be with my Antin. He hasn't written in two weeks, and the army's mail is so slow. Please, Savior, let everything be all right."

"Dear Savior," a woman in her mid-thirties, holding a baby girl to her right shoulder and clutching a few-year-old, gaping boy to her left side, prayed. "Please watch over Izan. He was ordered to leave so suddenly. Please guide him home whenever he is done."

They're all family members of my soldiers, Recha realized as she walked down the center aisle and listened.

They were mothers, wives, lovers, sisters, praying softly but aloud. Here and there also knelt a father beside a mother, mostly older men past their prime. They remained stoically silent with their heads bowed but eyes open, praying along and listening to their wives.

It was the practice of the church. Women would pray aloud for their families, like the women who cried out in the darkness for the Savior to come with his guiding lantern to lead them to salvation. The men would remain silent with their eyes open, like the men who looked for the Savior's lantern coming at the call of their wives.

Recha softly smiled, remembering joking to Sebastian when they were younger that the wives kept the practice because they mostly prayed about how much they wanted their husbands to do better, and the husbands would have to listen. When he had gone on campaign, though, she had come here, too, praying for him. Especially that last time.

Her smile faded, listening to the prayers. *Forgive me, ladies,* Recha steeled herself, *but I'm about to send them to war.*

At the front of the chapel stood a deaconess in a pristine white linen dress, long sleeves, and high collar, with no embroidery of any kind. She stood with her head bowed and hands folded in front of her. A white shawl draped over her head and hung like a shroud, obscuring her face.

Behind her was a modest altar, more a wooden railing, separating the sanctuary from the madre's podium on the right and the choir loft on the left, both empty and casting long shadows from the lantern lights.

Recha thought she was being quiet and the soft, mingled prayers behind her would mute the sound of her footsteps, but the deaconess's head perked up once she was close.

The deaconess was younger than she'd expected, just a few years older than herself. She had kind brown eyes and matching her hair that softened with her dimpled smile.

"May the Savior guide you," the deaconess said.

"May the Savior guide you," Recha repeated, stepping close but keeping her own face hidden by her shawl.

"What troubles you?" the deaconess asked. "May I pray with you?" She reached out her hands, palms up, as if asking for a bundle to be placed in them.

Recha shook her head. "Pardon me, Deaconess, but my time is short. Can you please find Madre Leticia and"—she raised her head so the deaconess could see her face—"tell her Recha Mandas is here?"

The deaconess's eyes widened, recognizing her. She folded her hands back in front of her and replied, "Yes, La Dama. Please wait." She nodded respectfully before stepping away. She didn't rush, but her pace was light and quick.

That left Recha alone at the front of the sanctuary with everyone praying able to stare at her. Feeling a little self-conscious, she folded her hands in front of her, like the deaconess had, and wandered off to the side.

Most probably weren't paying attention to her, but being she was trying to move in anonymity, she found it best to avoid drawing attention to herself. She ran her gaze down the entire, vacant front row and spied the end was in a shadow between two lanterns. The perfect place to wait.

No one wants to kneel on the front row, even when services aren't *being held.* She snickered.

She arranged her skirts before easing herself down on the pew's kneeling brace, a long plank of wood extending out from the base of the pew, polished from centuries of knees and fabrics rubbing against it.

As she waited, the women behind her kept praying, and as some would finally take their leave, more would wonder in to replace them.

I can keep my troop movements from my enemies and allies, Recha reflected. *But not from my troops' families.*

She knew a lot of wives and lovers would probably also make up the baggage trains and camp followers of her armies. They were a staple to any army and, according to Papa, they did a lot of the work around camp that most marshals failed to consider.

Something began to eat at Recha while her wait dragged on, listening to their prayers, their worries and fears. She wasn't devoutly religious. She believed, but she missed service more than she attended. She had prayed and attended regularly when Sebastian had gone to campaign and wasn't allowed to go with him.

However, the women of Zoragrin's endless stream of prayers made her tense. It was the way they were praying, as if they expected something terrible to happen and wanted them to return home. No prayers for strength or courage. No prayers for steadfastness or boldness.

No prayers for . . . victory.

Recha folded her hands in front of her and, gazing at the flames flickering the lanterns above the choir loft, she prayed, "Savior, guide my soldiers. May they have strength that will not break. May they have courage that will not yield. May they hold fast to their duties and their strike be the first to end these horrible campaigns. May they march and not grow weary. May they always be singing and moving forward. Guide them—guide *us*—to victory!"

"Recha?"

She sharply looked up, finding Madre Leticia frowning down at her with concern.

The madre was a homely woman. She wore the same pristine white dress as her deaconesses. Her head dress, part hat and part shawl, set her station apart from the other clergy members. The shawl wrapped around her head, covering her hair and neck, leaving only her face exposed. The hat was a round cap that sat atop her head.

Her sharp, dark eyes looked Recha up and down. Her thin unibrow wrinkled when she gazed back at her face.

Recha realized she'd been grinning while she prayed. She cleared her throat then quickly collected herself before rising to her feet, standing a head taller than the madre.

"Madre," she said, straightening her shawl then respectfully nodding. "Thank you for seeing me at this late hour."

"Not at all, La Dama," Madre Leticia replied softly, keeping her voice down, and returned her nod. "I understand you have been very busy of late, and I am grateful for your time. May you join me?" She motioned toward the rear of the sanctuary, at a door behind the choir loft.

She wants to talk in private, too, Recha perceived. *This might be more serious than me missing services.*

"Yes, Madre," she replied.

As she followed behind, another realization hit her, but she waited until they were safely alone in the choir room before speaking.

The choir room was more of a waiting room where the deaconesses gathered before services each morning to walk out together and fill the loft. Two long, wooden benches ran down the length of the walls, and the lamps in the corners reflected off white plaster, filling the room with light.

When Recha heard the door close, she finally said, "You know I have assembled the armies, don't you, Madre?"

Madre Leticia folded her hands in front of her then glided to the center of the bench on the right side of the room to sit before answering, "The number of prayers we have had for the past week have been little else than prayers of loved ones of men called to service. We all heard the declarations at the beginning of the Exchange and believed our cherished peace from the campaigns would continue. Were they lies, Recha?"

Recha's diplomatic senses stirred. She put on her best calm, placid expression before smoothing out her skirts and sitting down directly opposite the madre. She crossed her legs, placing her hands on her knees and sitting straight back with her head up. If the madre wished to talk of matters of the marc, then she would be handled like any other diplomat.

"They were not lies," she replied. "No declarations of war were exchanged during my talks with the other marquéses' ambassadors."

Madre Leticia frowned. "Do you expect one of the other marquéses of breaking their word?"

"No, Madre." She closed her eyes, taking a deep breath before reopening them. "I intend to break mine."

The madre sat up straighter. Her eyes widened, her pupils trembling as she stared.

"Yes, Madre," Recha continued. "Lazorna is returning to war."

Madre Laticia's frown deepened. "That is most unfortunate. These past three years have been a boon to the people. Not just our partitioners here in Zoragrin, but all over Lazorna. Deacons have begun singing your praises, as well, even beyond the surrounding marcs, as a shining example that these campaigns could end if only the marquéses just *stopped* fighting."

Deacons, men of the church, traveled between chapel to chapel, spreading guidance to the villages and distant hamlets between the cities and towns. They also brought news and messages of the outside world. Recha knew they spread word of how she governed her marc, both good and bad, and tried to use it to her advantage.

She twitched from a sudden chill and barely caught it before it made her shake. *If the families of my soldiers here in Zoragrin are praying, the families of my soldiers from the towns and villages are probably praying, too. Madre Laticia may not be the only one of the church who has figured out I'm mustering my armies.*

Her mind tumbled over the multiple variables and timetables she had in her head, wondering if one small comment, one observation from a traveling deacon, could make it to the wrong person and ruin them all.

"Recha?" Madre Laticia called. "Does that give you second thoughts?"

Recha lifted her head, unaware her gaze had drifted down to her hands while she had thought. Madre Laticia sat leaning forward, curiosity and hope sparkling in her eyes, but drained when she saw Recha's serious expression.

"Sorry, Madre," she replied, "but you and I both know that's not how the world works. And if the deacons are spreading news about me, they must also be spreading news about the other marquéses. Including Borbin. Tell me"—she leaned forward—"have they brought you news that he's planning something grand this year?"

Madre Laticia's expression hardened. "Forgive me, La Dama, but you know the church stands neutral in the affairs between the marcs. We will not be espis."

"I beg your pardon, Madre." Fearing she might be getting too close to a line, Recha conceded and leaned back. "I meant no offense. But you requested to speak with me before I decided to marshal the armies. Shall we discuss that matter?"

Please let it be something mundane.

Madre Laticia's expression remained unchanged, bordering on a scowl. "It's the Viden."

Shit! Recha's right eyebrow twitched. *What have those truth zealots done now?*

"There was an incident in Clova," Madre Laticia continued, "a couple months back, between a deacon and a group of Viden . . . *priests.*" Her mouth twisted, as if wanting to spit. "While the deacon assured me that he did not start the argument, his faith could not allow the Viden's challenge to a theological debate go unanswered."

Faith? Or pride? Recha held in her internal quip, but her eyebrow refused to stop twitching, and she had to squeeze her hands together to stop herself from rubbing it.

Arguments between the church and the Viden weren't common. If they were theological in nature, Recha found the Viden generally began them, questioning deacons' beliefs and the retelling of the Savior's missions through Oblivion. Most arguments the deacons and deaconesses began with the Viden involved them coming upon a cultist inciting and convincing people not to attend chapel. There had been a couple instances of deacons rousing a mob to drive cultists out of towns for such offenses.

"The argument drew the attention of the townsfolk, and I'm afraid a fight did break out," Madre Laticia said, drawing in a deep, calming breath. "I only wanted to ask, when you have fully investigated the matter, please don't punish the local townspeople too harshly."

Recha pulled back, blinking in confusion from the odd request. "I'm afraid I haven't heard of these events, Madre. And I promise to have them investigated, but why would I punish the townspeople?"

"Because they rose to violence against the Viden," Madre Laticia replied matter-of-factly. "I know you are a devote follower of the Savior, La Dama, and blessed are you for being so. However, it is known the Viden do act as part of the marc, and such acts against them could be looked at as acts against you."

The madre was no fool. Despite her firm stance in the church's neutrality, she was adept at political maneuvering, having dealt with Recha's uncle when he'd been marqués. Recha's relationship with the Viden and their master further complicated matters and once again seemed to be coming back to bite her.

I don't have time to deal with this right now. The last thing I need is a religious war in the middle of Lazorna before we've gone to war.

"I can assure you, Madre, it will not come to that," she replied.

The madre remained back straight and hardened, so Recha decided to change her approach. With a deep sigh, she rose from her seat then moved across the room to sit beside Madre Laticia. Her shawl slipped and fell, hanging lopsided from around her neck.

"As I said," she continued, dropping her formality and sitting a little slumped with her fingers lacing and unlacing on her legs, "I haven't even *heard* of this before you told me. But if there's been any local investigation, I'll let that be the end of it. Neither the townspeople nor your deacon need fear any punishment from me."

Madre Laticia studied her for a moment. "And the Viden?"

Recha snickered. "Leave them to me. I'll send a letter to their master to rein in their more . . . enthusiastic members. Along with a reminder that such acts could risk our relationship. Trust me, Madre; their master can't risk that."

Neither can I. For Elegida's sake.

She maintained her soft smile for the madre's sake. "That should put the Viden on notice and keep something like what happened in Clova from happening again."

Besides, we're all about to be a lot busier soon.

Madre Laticia's expression shifted from hard, to skeptical, to worried in a matter of seconds. "Be careful, Recha," she finally said with motherly caution in her voice. "This *relationship* you have with the Viden is most worrisome. Like a child who wants to keep a *mellcresa* chick as a pet—the more you feed it, the larger it will grow, until you can no longer control it."

Recha pursed her lips at the analogy. Besides horses and dogs, she had little love for animals, especially man-sized predators. She had once considered ordering hunts to decrease their numbers as dangers to the marc's livestock after dealing with numerous complaints from farmers every year about the beasts but was persuaded against it.

Sebastian would have kept one, if he'd have found one, she mused. *He would've made a special banner and everything for it—*

She shook her head and returned to the matter at hand. "I appreciate the concern, Madre. And trust me; I know very well the Viden are to be handled carefully. I assure you, my arrangement with them is a means to an end, not something that's going to last forever. Once our goals are reached, then our relationship will be over."

And once I free Elegida from that spirit, then the entire cult will be through.

"And what goals are those?" Madre Laticia inquired.

Recha gave her a sly smile. "Now, Madre, you know I can't involve you in matters of the marc. Just know they do have certain skills that they put to my service, as payment for my allowing them to operate in my marc."

"And do you intend to employ their . . . *skills* on campaign, too?" Madre Laticia worked her jaw, as if she was chewing on something tough.

Recha stifled a frustrated sigh and felt her right eyebrow twitch again. "Perhaps. But if I do, they won't be doing any recruiting for their cult. If you're worried about any deacons traveling with the armies being accosted by them, let me assure you"—she fixed the madre with a firm glare and her tone hardened— "that *won't* happen."

Madre Laticia stared back at her, and Recha held her gaze. They had always had a pleasant relationship, but Recha's ascension as marquesa had changed that. There was always a hesitance with these talks, a distance between them. While Recha was the marquesa, she had also murdered her closest blood relatives to become it.

Others in the churches would have, and many did, condone her actions. Madre Laticia probably felt she had to tread carefully. Recha felt the same, as well, for the past three years. She wouldn't have been able to handle the barons, reinvent the armies, or maintain the peace with the other marcs if the deaconess across the marcs preached against her. Lazorna would have been too fragile, and it all would have come crumbling down.

Recha took it upon herself to always find time to answer Madre Laticia's request for an audience and come to her to prevent that.

The madre finally nodded. "Then I shall leave these matters in your hands, La Dama. I shall instruct the deacons there are sons of Lazorna who will be in need of guidance soon."

Recha respectfully lowered her head. "Thank you, Madre. I will send word to my field marshal to have the camp provosts prepare places for them."

She waited for Madre Laticia to stand first, not wanting to appear eager to rush off. Upon leaving the choir room, they found the number of practitioners had decreased during their little chat. The younger wives with small children especially. There were a few older women here and there, still praying. Cornelos still waited in the back.

The sight of a deacon, kneeling with his head bowed in one corner of the front row, where Recha had waited, caught Madre Laticia's attention, and she veered toward him.

"Deacon?" the madre called. "Is everything all right?"

The deacon's dark, curly hair clung tightly to his scalp, as if he'd been traveling for days without rest, revealing a growing bald spot on the back of his head. His white travel suit was stained with dirt, almost turning brown. He lifted his head, blinking as if deep in meditation. Thick bags hung under his piercing green eyes, and a day's old stubble of a beard covered his face, giving him an older appearance. He looked around, head bobbing as if trying to remember where he was, before finally gazing up at the madre.

"Pardon me if I worried you, Madre," he said in a baritone voice that was almost captivating. "It seems I let the rigors of my travels steal into my devotions with the Savior."

"Then, by all means, Deacon, you may retire to our parsonage for your rest," Madre Laticia implored. "It would certainly give you a chance to wash off the dust of the road." She folded her hands in front of her and pointedly looked at the small layer of dirt surrounding him.

"Thank you, Madre." The deacon bowed. "But there are still things I need to pray to the Savior about. *Urgent* things." He shot a glance behind the madre.

Right at Recha.

She stood as straight and quiet as she could, gripping her hands so they wouldn't shake. Her throat felt tight from holding in the urge to yell, and her cheeks hurt from stopping a compulsive grin.

What is he thinking—

She suddenly caught his hint and stepped between them.

"I also need to offer a few more prayers, Madre," she said, much to Madre Laticia's surprise at her sudden intervention, but Recha didn't give her a chance to talk. "Perhaps I could pray beside the deacon? That way, both our prayers are given, and the deacon has someone to keep him awake?"

Madre Laticia frowned, her eyes flickering between the two of them, unsure of what to do. Finally, she shrugged. "Very well. Be sure to get plenty of rest afterward, Deacon. A great many souls are about to need your guidance."

"Yes, Madre," the deacon replied with a respectful bow.

"And you, dear," the madre cupped Recha's hands and pressed warmly, "may the Savior guide you and protect you."

Recha gave her a warm smile. "Same to you, Madre."

Madre Laticia gave her hands one final squeeze before turning away. Recha watched her go then knelt beside the deacon.

She glanced over her shoulder, making *sure* the madre was truly walking away before starting to pray, "Blessed Savior, give us guidance in these troubled times. Give us the strength needed to do what we must. And please give *Sevesco* a good reason why he's dressed like a deacon." She shot the false deacon a sideways glance, not daring to turn her head to keep up the ruse they were praying, and glared.

Sevesco merely smirked. "Do you think I fooled her?"

"For about the next ten minutes while she checks with her deaconesses on whether another deacon was supposed to arrive," she hissed but remained facing forward. "*Where* have you been? You're weeks overdue. I haven't received any reports, and I've been forced to make decisions on assumptions."

"I've been moving constantly," Sevesco replied. "Orsembar is becoming a frenzy. Not a day went by that I wasn't checking up with one contact or another, but Borbin has amassed an enormous army. Barely a single baron has been left out or calleros not called up."

"Are you sure?" Recha inched little closer. "Do you have confirmation and not just rumors?"

"Recha, you wound me." Sevesco snickered then, in a flash, was serious again. "I've seen it personally. When I left it a couple of weeks ago, it was over eighty thousand strong, and still, they were bringing in more levees. I've placed a few trusted espis among their camp followers to allow us to track its movements. That's where I picked up this outfit." He wiped more dust off the front of his shirt and jacket.

Eighty thousand! Recha turned the number over in her head and tried to imagine it. *And still growing. That could be big enough to attack Quezlo and turn a portion around to hit us. Or both.*

"Did you get an idea of its organization or leadership?" she asked. "Who's Borbin's commanding marshal?"

Sevesco shrugged. "That's something I left espis to find out. Every baron had their own miniature camp, and from what I gathered, the rank and file don't know who's ultimately in charge, except Borbin himself. The marqués himself had his own personal camp, but I couldn't get anywhere near it." He snickered. "Serves me right for the Baroness Liamena affair."

Recha glowered at him again for reminding her of *that* debacle. Baroness Liamena was one of Borbin's most doted mistresses, but last year, he had begun giving his affections to another. Sevesco tried to sway her to being a confidant for him. Instead, the baroness had tried to trap him to return to Borbin's favor. He narrowly avoided Borbin's espis, with the aid a certain troop of traveling bailer dancers.

Unfortunately, it made his identity known, and Recha couldn't send him as an open diplomat or long undercover missions anymore. Her eyebrow started to twitch again.

"Yes, it does," she said sternly.

Sevesco glanced at her, and his smirk disappeared.

"Did you gather any information on where Borbin intends to attack?" she asked.

"Quezlo," he replied without hesitation.

Recha felt a rush run through her body, making her hair stand on end and her scalp tingle. "Are you certain? Do you have maps? Communications?"

Sevesco shook his head. "Confirmation from other sources. Reports have comandantes amassing food stores and putting guards on all the granaries from Huarita to Orona and Pisemo."

"The highway to Compuert," she said.

It was a highway on the western side of the Balaur Mountain Range that served as a bulwark between Lazorna and Orsembar and guarded the marc's western flank. The highway lead toward Quezlo's own bulwark, the fortress city of Compuert, the city that held off the White Sword. However, simply because towns were stocking up on food before campaign season began was nothing new.

I need more.

"How can you be *sure* if all you have are deductions?" she inquired. "Food stored at Huarita can easily be convoyed to armies attacking us. Do you have any word about what's happening in Puerlato?"

"Nothing is happening in Puerlato." Sevesco lifted his head, smiling and snickering. "I traveled through there on my way here. The garrison is too relaxed, barely checking anybody entering or leaving the city. The port authority is still prickly, but they're more concerned about ships paying for berth than their cargos. And there're no preparations to house and feed a large army. Even if Borbin divides his forces evenly, Puerlato wouldn't be able to accommodate them."

"What about feeding them from sea then?" Recha pressured him. "Any word of Borbin's fleet?"

"Still anchored in Manosete. Espis there report they aren't being provisioned this year." Sevesco grunted and reached down to rub his knees. "Think we've prayed long enough that we can take this outside?"

"*No*," Recha replied sharply. "I'll have it all right here. Where is Borbin's army now? Still gathering men?"

"Nope." Sevesco hunched over to rub his knees more and shift his weight. "Marched over a week ago. I left just before they started marching. The vanguard should be near Huarita by now."

Recha broke the guise and rounded on him. "Why didn't you tell me this *first*?"

Sevesco straightened back up but didn't shy away from her. Instead, he gave her a bland look, as if she were overreacting. "Because I knew you'd react like *this*. You may have leapt up and ran out before I told you the rest."

Recha fumed, breathing heavily through her nose. "*Sevesco*, you've left me without word for four weeks and now are telling me our enemy's army is marching within striking distance of us. How am I supposed to *react*?" She kept her voice down but growled just the same.

"I didn't keep you in the dark, Recha," Sevesco replied, holding his ground. "I made sure my deductions were right before returning. If Borbin had sent a single detachment toward Puerlato or Lazorna, I *would* have sent word before now." His lips curled into a bemused smile. "But he didn't. Not a *single* additional soldier has been sent to Puerlato."

Recha held his gaze then sat back and thought about his report. It was confirmation on what they had suspected—Borbin planning something big and campaigning against Quezlo instead of finishing off Lazorna. Her ally was about to have a rude awaking, but Recha's immediate thought was how that fit with her plans.

The size aside, if Borbin's grand plan this season is to throw everything he can muster against Compuert, he might not be able to turn around and send help for Puerlato. Or a detachment big enough to block our path.

She began to tremble. Her eyes widened, envisioning an open road stretched out before her.

Right into Orsembar's heartland.

Sevesco chuckled. "You're grinning."

His comment pulled her back to the present, and Recha hastily composed herself. "After we've gone our separate ways, clean yourself up and out of those clothes and go to the Pamolid embassy. Make sure Silvaja's assignment is still on schedule."

"Ah!" Sevesco brightened, sitting up straight with a bemused twinkle in his eye. "Silvaja. It'd be good to see her again!"

Recha resisted the urge to elbow him. "She's *working*. It's important her mission is a success. If she doesn't need any help, then get some rest before reporting to me tomorrow. We'll head to the First Army's camp together."

"Oh, excellent!" He sounded even more thrilled at that. "It's been a while since I traveled with people who know my real name. Cornelos will be with us, I presume?"

Recha frowned. "Of course. Why?" She squinted at him suspiciously. "What'd you do this time?"

"Nothing much." Sevesco shrugged, reaching into his pocket and pulling out a watch on a long, silver chain. "I just didn't know if it would be more fun to give this back before I left or tomorrow morning. He saw the deacon-white suit and didn't even realize it was me." He beamed a proud, crooked grin.

Recha recognized the watch instantly as Cornelos's. Sevesco had a long-standing habit of teasing, pickpocketing, and performing antics on him. He always said it was to keep their youngest companion on his toes, but Recha suspected it was more because he got more of a rise out of Cornelos than any of the others.

She snatched the watch out of the air and glared at his pout. "You make a terrible deacon."

Sevesco nodded in agreement but without a hint of shame. "True, but that's what makes me good at my job."

Recha rolled her eyes, but also sensed their time was up. She glanced over her shoulder and saw a deaconess pacing in the back of the sanctuary.

"Time to go," she said. "Check with Silvaja, and then report to my mansion in the morning."

"Right," he grunted, the charm replaced with seriousness as his deacon persona emerged. "May the Savior guide you, La Dama." He stifled a groan as he used the pew to pull himself to his feet.

Recha suddenly thought of something and gripped his hand that was stilling holding onto the pew before he could pull away. "And Deacon, *don't* drink the wine." She smiled up at him, hoping he caught the hint.

Sevesco arched an eyebrow then nodded and pulled away.

Recha watched him head to the front of the sanctuary, to another door that led further in. She was sure he would make his own way out, leaving her the front. She had to use the pew to pull herself up, too, her knees stiff and aching from kneeling so long. She took tentative steps at first, stretching out joints before finally being able to walk normally again.

When she got the back of the sanctuary, she found Cornelos in a frantic state, turning out all his pockets as if he had lost something.

"Here," she said.

To his surprise, when Cornelos looked up, he gaped at his pocket watch dangling in front of him.

"*You* have it?" he asked, confused, taking the watch from the air. "When did . . .? How—"

"Doesn't matter." Recha shook her head. "Come, we still have work to do tonight." She turned on her heels and headed for the exit.

Cornelos gasped behind her, probably from rising too quickly. Recha couldn't help herself from allowing a small grin.

Cornelos rushed behind her, his boots thumping against the chapel's wood floor. "*Still* have work? What else is there to do?"

"We need to send out messengers," she replied as they stepped out into the night. "To all the marshals and generals of the armies, especially Papa. Puerlato marches home. *Now!*"

Chapter 11

Necrem stabbed his spear into the straw-stuffed sackcloth tied to a post that represented a man. All around him, men of his squad yelled as they made their thrusts, stabbing their training posts.

Not him.

He had split his facial scars two times in as many days from all their forced exercises. He wrenched his six-foot-long weapon back, careless of whether the spearhead pulled out too much straw on the way out.

Like his hammering, Necrem fell into a rhythm with these drills. Step up in the line. Take his stance and level his spear. Wait for the command. Then thrust. Over and over again. It took less effort and thought than forging. He didn't have to watch the fire's heat, how hot the metal was, or how hard his hammer struck. Just thrust and pull back without deciding to ram the sharp metal head into the post.

"Rest!" Master Sergeant Raul yelled.

Necrem and the rest of his squad stepped away from the posts, followed behind multiple *thumps* from resting the butts of their spears on the ground.

He hissed through the holes in his leather mask. The humid air did little to relieve his irritated scars and skin rubbing against the sweat-soaked fabric, making it stick to his face.

He winced from his breastplate pinching his sides. He had taken too big a breath again. The plate was meant for a smaller man, as was everything when it came to Necrem. It reached only his abdomen, not reaching his waist, leaving the bottom of his belly exposed. It was also tight. He felt pressed between two walls with his slippery, sweaty shirt and puffy jacket to keep him from being crushed with little to help him breathe. He tried to suck more air through his nose holes, but his sides expanded, and the plate got too tight.

I need air!

Sweat dripped into his eyes, and he started to pant. He reached for the strap on the side of his plate.

"Shoulder spears!" Master Sergeant Raul yelled.

No! Necrem growled, following the command with the rest of his company, and shouldered his spear. His breathing quickened. *I need to breathe! Just let us rest!*

"Company will run!" Raul mercilessly ordered.

Groans rippled through the company to be met with the ridicule from the other sergeants.

"That's an extra mile, *filth*!" Raul snapped. "After that, rack your spears, clean your kits, and report to the camp kitchens. Move!"

Necrem desperately shoved his exhaustion down and followed the man in front of him. The company had to form blocks of squads to run together, but his plate denied him any time to catch his breath while it did.

"Quick run!" Raul shouted.

One by one, the lines in front of Necrem started moving.

His limbs felt heavy when he moved with his line. He grunted from the aching protest of his knees. They throbbed and begged for him to stop, his size and age finally catching up to him. His feet squished inside his boots as if they were filled with water, although they were likely filled with sweat, adding more weight for him to lift.

"Battles are all about running!" a company sergeant yelled as he sprinted up the line but didn't carry a spear like the rest of them. "You run to form up, you run into position, and you run as you charge! An army that doesn't run dies! No slacking!"

Necrem lowered his head and did his best to bull through everything—the frustration, the aches and pains, the sweat. All around him, men grunted and panted. Their spears knocking against their shoulders and plates, filling the air along with the sound of their rumbling boots.

He fell into a rhythm again. Just one foot in front of the other. Head straight, staring over the head of the man in front of him and down the line ahead. Looking for the end of the road, panting and struggling with every step.

~~~

Necrem clung to his spear, leaning against it as he struggled through the main camp, hunched and doubled over, toward his company's tents. His boots made loud, wet squishes with every step. His feet burned. A biting sting pierced the side of left foot, just where the inside curve met his boot.

I'm going to have another blister in the morning. He had already dealt with several, and the camp doctor was already complaining about the number of injured feet he was having to deal with. He kept moving despite the pain in his feet and creaking of his knees. He wasn't welcomed here.

"Walk it off, levy!" the fifth calleros, wearing Baron Cayeton's bronze, yelled at him. "We'll make a soldier out of you yet!"

Laughter followed him, but Necrem kept moving without looking back.

Their army camped against a tributary to the Desryol Sea, north of Luente, a town with the only bridge across the tributary's largest creek, the Ruela. Their camp was twice as large as the town, and no one from the conscripted companies, Necrem's included, were allowed near it.

Conscripted companies made up the bulk of the camp, close to seven thousand men, all crammed together to sleep and eat between the daily routine of being marched out to train and exercise. Surrounding them, pinning them against the tributary, were the multiple companies of barons assigned to escort Don Givanzo Borbin, the marqués's son. A couple of those companies were from Saran.

A sour smell in the air told Necrem he was coming up on his company's tents. The large tents of the calleroses and their chosen men fell away, revealing the smaller, squat tents of conscripts. Long spear racks divided the two camps with provost guards in shining plates, red jackets, and halberds, watching everyone who passed between the camps.

Necrem knew the routine without the guards having to order it. He was already making his way toward the nearest rack with an open slot before the first guard stepped to block his entry. No conscript was allowed to bring their spears with them into their camp. The master sergeant had made it clear that was another flogging offense.

He put his spear on the rack and braced himself against his knees. He squeezed and rubbed the throbbing joints. Without his makeshift walking cane, the rest of his trip was going to be the most painful.

He stood as straight his could, but he still limped. His right leg felt heavier than his left, requiring more effort to pick his foot up. The shooting pain from the knee nearly caused him to drag it behind him. He winced at every second step from the bouncing torture of his blistering left foot and near collapse of his right leg.

"Step lively, soldier," a provost guard ordered. "If you don't clean your kit up in time, you won't eat."

Necrem nodded and limped by.

I'm too exhausted to eat. The only thing he wanted was to strip out of the ill-fitting armor and wet clothes then collapse in his tent. His stomach, however, suddenly growled.

"And get that breastplate strap fixed!" another guard shouted after him. "If you've neglected Si Don's arms, it will come out of your pay or off your back."

Necrem grunted. He hardly noticed the small, scraping *taps* of the strap clasp on the side of his plate. He vaguely remembered wrenching the clasp loose so he could breathe during the run. Now, he didn't care.

The Easterly Sun's descending rays reflected off the tops of his company's tents, ten rows of twenty-five, all divided by squad and sergeant. Being in the master sergeant's squad, Necrem's tent was on the main lane through the tents, but all the way in the back, near the alarm lines by the woods.

"Hurry up, Jandr!" Maeso yelled. "We're starving." He and six others waited impatiently outside a tent, arms folded and somewhat cleaned up after their day's training.

The conscripted thieves in their squad had formed their own little cadre, as Necrem saw them, with Maeso as their leader. They did everything together and grouped with one another outside of training, for alibis when the master sergeant came around asking about things being stolen around camp and protection from other cadres of thieves in camp.

Necrem hobbled over to the far side of the lane to avoid them.

"Getting old, big man?" one of them called after him when he was almost past them.

He didn't stop. He might be big, but there were more of them, and he was in no shape for any amount of trouble.

"Hey! I'm talking to—"

"Leave him alone," Maeso warned. "Man with a face like that ain't going to be intimidated by you. Probably doesn't have any—Jandr! Finally, we can eat!"

Necrem glanced over his shoulder and watched Maeso wrap his arm around the shoulders of a man leaving the tent. The lead thief pulled the man along as his cadre formed around them, laughing toward the camp kitchens.

With a small sigh of relief, Necrem continued to his tent.

The air around his tent was the cleanest in camp. The scent of weapon oil and unwashed bodies was stronger farther down the rows. Horse manure and the latrine pits were on the far side of camp, and the only comforting smell of smoke and coals burning over heated iron clung around the southside of camp, around the smiths. Here, the smell of wood and running water greeted him.

Necrem finally unclasped his remaining armor's straps then hastily pulled the plate over his head. He gasped in relief, finally free of the suffocating metal corset. He breathed deeply, his chest expanding and pushing his damp jacket out.

He poked his head inside, carelessly hefted his plate off to the side, and checked his bedroll. It still lay flat, undisturbed. Clenching his teeth, he knelt and rolled it over, revealing his stash of possessions spread out underneath. A quick glance and count told him everything was there.

Well, everything that remained. As expected, his second pair of boots had disappeared the first week, followed by a couple of shirts and a pair of socks. Sacrifices to the camp thieves. They had even stolen a can of salve one day, but it showed back up the next, laying discarded in his tent as if someone had tossed it inside.

He fetched a can of salve, a fresh mask, his sewing kit in case he needed it, another pair of socks, and a cloth before rolling the bedroll back over his meager possessions then lumbering back outside.

He struggled with each step, feet dragging on the dry, dusty ground, as he rounded around his tent and dropped out of sight beside it with a gasping sigh. His legs jerked and spasmed, and his whole body quivered from the relief of finally being off his feet.

The urge to lean back was overwhelming, but all that was behind him was his tent's canvas and his weight would bring it down. He settled for laying his stuff in his lap then curled his feet toward him.

His boots were stubborn, like always. He figured, after sweating so much, they would slide right off. Instead, they clung tightly to his shins. He wrenched and pulled, teeth gritting together as he dragged the leather down bit by bit until, finally, it slipped off.

Sweat poured out like stall water, and Necrem turned his head, nose wrinkling from the sour corn smell. He set the boot aside and did the same to his other boot. This time, he pulled his sock off along with the boot.

He shivered as the cool blast of air his foot. He peeled the other sock off and found his other foot in the same state. Both were pale and pink. Their undersides were wrinkled like prunes and soft from soaking in sweat all day. He checked his left foot. As he feared, he found an oval blister on the side of his heel.

With nothing else to do about his feet, he stretched out his legs and set them out to dry in the grass.

Now I know why all those soldiers were in such a bad mood back in the day, he inwardly groaned. *They were bone-tired, and their feet hurt.* His own feet were pulsing, as if blood was finally flowing to them again.

He sat there for a while, listening to his own breathing and the distant trickle of water from the nearest creek. His hands laid in his lap. He knew he should take his mask off, but his body felt relieved not to be moving.

Finally, forcing his exhausted limbs to move, he reached up and untied his mask. The leather had to be slowly peeled off his face, hanging and snagging on every inch of skin. Necrem forced his eyes closed, concentrating only on making sure he got the mask off while also not ripping a scar open or snapping a stitch.

The dry air blew across his face and into the holes in his cheeks, sending his skin crawling. He instinctively closed his mouth the best he could, but two cuts on the sides of his face could never be closed. The muscles flexed, but the missing flesh wasn't there. It took him a minute to get used to the sensation of breathing from the sides of his face.

He didn't want to keep his face uncovered for long, but just like his feet, it needed air. This was the best time of day, being alone with no one to disturb.

At least no scar ripped today.

That was the worst thing that could happen. Not only would he bleed for the rest of the day and the mask needed to be heavily washed, but he would have to stitch it up at night. He hoarded a small, broken piece of mirror with his positions but didn't want anyone to know he had it. Glass was valuable in camp and, without it, he would have to see a camp doctor for stitching. Having his face on display for everyone in camp to see was something he desperately meant to avoid.

His head lulled back as he grew accustomed to breathing the open air. A warm breeze blew along the tree line and gently swept over him, seeping through his damp clothes, tickling his wrinkly feet, and brushing across his face.

Leaves rustled overhead. Through half-lidded eyes, Necrem tilted his head up to watch the trees sway. The pines' prickly leaves were dry, brownish-orange colors cascaded across their limbs. The limbs pulled with the wind then snapped back, making a waving motion.

The waves of brown pine needles remind him of hair; long, flowing brown hair.

I wonder if Eulalia had a good day.

His thoughts naturally drifted to his family in times like these and late at night, but the near paralyzing fear of being away from them no longer haunted his every second thought. He figured it was the constant training. Being worked until he couldn't move or until his feet were covered in blisters certainly drained him to the point that all he could do was collapse, exhausted, each night.

He snickered, thinking on what Bayona would say if she saw her papa now. *Maybe she'd laugh and call me old.*

His snickers became chuckles, his shoulders rising and falling, until he felt a scar tug. He caught himself smiling and relaxed. He then sighed and picked the cloth up from his lap.

"She wouldn't be wrong," he mumbled under his breath before wiping his face.

It would have been better if it were wet, but the nearest water barrel was by the spear racks, and he was in no condition to hobble back up there. He dabbed his cheeks with the cloth, avoiding drying them out while also checking for blood. There was none.

Satisfied he had cleaned his scars the best he could, he discarded the cloth back to his lap then grabbed the can of salve. He was just dipping his fingers into the fatty goo when his ears twitched from the sound of hurrying footsteps.

"Get him into his tent, boys," a familiar, gravelly voice instructed. "The doc said to keep him out of the sun and let him rest."

Necrem shuffled over deeper into his tent's meager shadow to remain out of sight. He began applying the salve to his face while also keeping a watchful eye out for the approaching people. Long shadows soon crested the sloping lane between the tents, heading for the other end of the lane.

Hezet Amort, an older veteran and the mediator of the squad, appeared first, still dressed in his stained training clothes, and carrying a heavy bucket. He came to a halt beside the tent opposite Necrem's then spun around, sending water sloshing over the lip of the bucket as he pulled open the tent flap.

"Come on; hurry," the veteran ordered. His sun-red face glowered with concern. The fuzz of a beard on his chin trembled.

Grunting announced the arrival of two struggling youths, Ezro and Leondro, carrying their third and youngest squad member, Stefan. Like the thieves, the youngest members of their squad had joined together, but more out of necessity, having little in common with the other squad members and feeling threatened by some.

Necrem barely got a minute to see what they were up to, but he caught how Stefan looked to be in a bad way. His jacket and undershirt had been stripped off, leaving the boy's sweaty body out in the sun. His head bobbed, and his mouth hung open while he was carried, as if he couldn't keep his head up, and his eyes were half-closed.

"Make sure he drinks plenty of water," Hezet ordered after the other two boys hauled Stefan inside. He set the water bucket inside the tent then pulled back. "Ezro, do you think you can watch over him yourself?"

"Yes, sir," Ezro replied, confused.

"Why?" Leondro asked.

Hezet waved him out. "One of you needs to get food for him and your squad mates. Stefan needs water for now, but later, he'll need food."

"You want me to get food and bring it back?" Leondro asked hesitantly. "Why me?"

Hezet put his hands on his hips. He was a taller man, compared to the average person, built like a soldier with gray sprinkled through his dark hair. He looked down into the young lads' tent but, while firm, his voice lacked any bite.

"Because you're the biggest, Leondro. You stand a good chance of getting more food and not getting into any trouble." He spoke like a father pushing his son out into the world. "Now, crawl out of there and bring back some food before the kitchens close."

Leondro groaned but crawled out from the tent and set off, rather reluctantly, toward the camp kitchens.

"Make sure he drinks," Hezet instructed Ezro. "Drink some yourself. You lads have been putting in some hard days. You should be proud."

A mumble came from inside the tent, too low for Necrem to catch.

He watched as Hezet leaned down again, looking more directly into the tent.

"You did good, Ezro," the veteran praised warmly. "You saw your squad member was in trouble and stopped to help. You have the heart of a soldier. Don't let anyone else tell you differently."

"Thank you, sir," Ezro said.

Hezet shook his head. "You don't have to call me sir. Just get some rest and make sure you both drink." He pulled the tent flap back and moved to leave, but then he stopped and turned his head, staring right at Necrem.

"Oso?" the veteran called.

Necrem realized he had edged out a little closer to watch what was going on, exposing himself. He shied away again, turning his head especially, not wanting his scars to be seen, and went back to salving those he had left untouched.

Approaching footsteps told Hezet wasn't deterred so easily.

"Oso? Are you—?" He hissed sharply. "Your *feet*!"

"I've had worse," Necrem said, keeping his face turned while applying salve to the scars on the right side. He also kept his hand blocking that side of his face from view.

"You need to see a camp doctor," Hezet advised.

Necrem flinched at the sound of bootheels grinding dirt underneath them, expecting Hezet to move closer. Yet, when he glanced back, he found Hezet was standing with his back toward him, his hands on his hips, as if attempting to block Necrem from view.

He's . . . being respectful? he pondered, studying the man. Most in Necrem's squad gave him his space. Sure, one of the thieves might say a snide remark and a veteran would give him a passing nod. Beyond that, they all gave him a wide berth. Even Master Sergeant Raul barely spoke to him.

He's odd for a conscript.

"It was a good thing you did," he said, going back to doctoring his face. "Helping those lads."

"They helped themselves mostly," Hezet replied. "Poor Stefan collapsed from the heat and probably would have gotten trampled if Ezro hadn't hauled him out of the column. I only got involved when a sergeant was yelling at him and Leondro . . ." He paused. "Almost finished with your face?"

Necrem grunted while applying the last, flayed ends of his lips with his salve.

"Good. I'll be back." He hastily stepped away before Necrem could say anything.

Necrem frowned, pressing the freshly salved portions of his lips together and felt them stick. He listened at the retreating footsteps, and then faintly caught a tent's flaps being thrown open.

What's he up to?

He turned his attention back to his lap. The can was half-empty, and he had already used up one. *I'm going to have find a way to make more.*

He screwed on the cap then exchanged the can for the clean mask laying in his lap. It was leather, like the previous one, but shallow, parallel cracks were forming across it. If he wasn't careful or kept on repeatedly washing them, his leather masks would all split and tear, leaving him with only the cloth ones.

I may need to see if I can get more masks made, too, he thought while tying the mask on.

That brought up another problem. He didn't have any money. The sergeants had been promising their first payday was coming, but they hadn't said when. They were conscript companies though—men mostly pressed into service from jailcells. It was doubtful the marqués or his son were in any hurry to pay them.

"Have your feet started bleeding?" Hezet asked, suddenly returning. He was unrolling a bundle of cloth strips as he knelt in front of Necrem's feet, frowning at them.

"I'm fine," Necrem replied, pulling his legs back and staring at the man. He felt more confident now with his face covered.

Hezet frowned back. "You ever *seen* an infected blister before, or what they can do to a foot?"

"I've had blisters before." Necrem had pulled consecutive nights forging rush orders and had suffered blisters on his hand. He had worked through them before. He could do it now.

"Had any marching before?" Hezet folded his arms. "They burst and bleed. Before long, they're infected, and you're not taken to a camp doc. They carry you to a surgeon. And there's only one thing they'll do for you then."

Necrem held his stare. He didn't find many common men intimidating and most were intimidated of him because of his size.

Hezet, however, didn't back down. He set his square jaw, sporting its own scar on the right side of his face that jaggedly snaked down under his chin. His face was weathered, like leather, and his nose was bent to the left from old breaks. He kept his head up and back straight with a commanding air about him.

"Why do you care?" Necrem finally asked.

Hezet tilted his head. "We're soldiers. And you're in my squad."

"That's it?" Necrem stared at him. "We're forced to be in this miserable shithole together, and that's enough for you be everyone's den mother?" He turned his head, more out of how harsh his words came out than worry he had angered the other man.

It just didn't make sense to him. He had watched fights break out between the men while they weren't exercising and the provost guards letting them happen. The arguments. The stealing. There was no comradery to be found in a place like this. Necrem hadn't expected to find any, either.

"Forced or not, we are *still* soldiers together," Hezet replied.

Necrem looked back. Hezet remained with his arms folded, but held his head a little bit higher, his jaw jutted out a little more. A gleam from his eyes caught the fading Easterly Sun's rays, as proudly seeing something on the horizon. It was as baffling as everything else.

"You know we're all here just to march around and look intimidating, right?" Necrem leaned forward and lowered his voice, unable to hold his tongue. "They *don't* care about us. From the sergeants, to the capitáns, the barons, and the marqués *himself*! They will use us, abandon us, or sell us in an instant. There's no *point* to any of this."

He glanced down to his blistered and cracked feet. A dull sting pulsed on the side of his heel. Their color had returned, but now his soles were brittle and flaky. He looked over the pile of knickknacks in his lap, and it hit him that this had become a daily, monotonous routine.

Forced awake each morning, rush through a bland, sometimes undercooked breakfast, be marched and drilled until the sun was almost down, and limp back here to tend to his scars and change his mask. And for what?

When he forged, he would fall into a rhythm of smelting, watching, and hammering, sometimes losing himself to it. He created something when he forged.

Nothing will be created from this.

"They may not care about us," Hezet admitted, "but that does not mean we don't have to look out for each other."

Necrem lifted his head, seeing the veteran still held firm.

"And there may come a time," Hezet continued, "after the calleros prance about and have their Bravados, and the marshals talk, that we're not ordered to stand around and look intimidating. When that day comes, the only people we'll be able to count on will be our squad mates around us. And I prefer mine caring about me instead of not giving a damn if the worst should happen.

"Now, are you going to let me bandage your foot and get you to a doctor so they won't have to cut it off later, or do you want to sit here and mope?"

The two men stared at each other, neither one finding the other intimidating. Necrem blinked first and looked back down at his foot.

That blister's not going to get any better tonight . . . And I'm going to be drilled tomorrow, too . . .

With defeated reluctance, he stuck his injured foot out.

Hezet seized his foot without a hint of hesitation and unrolled the bundle of cloth.

Necrem hissed through his teeth as the coarse fabric was wrapped tightly over his blister and under his heel. "Tying it a little *tight*, aren't you?"

"It needs to be tight," Hezet replied, tying off a knot in the cloth on the top of Necrem's foot that almost threatened to cut off his blood circulation. "That way, it doesn't rub. The camp doc will probably make it just as tight if they put something on it."

"Do I have to go?" Necrem sourly looked down at his bandaged foot, hoping it would just be enough so he wouldn't have to get up.

"No," Hezet replied. "Not if you're fine with risking your foot being cut off."

Necrem glowered at him. "You really *enjoy* hanging that over my head."

Hezet shrugged. "In my experience, threat of loss of limb is a very good motivator for soldiers. Savior knows it's kept me alive a few times."

Necrem growled and began collecting his things.

"Need help?" Hezet offered.

"I got them." Necrem shielded his possessions with his arm and snatched up his boots beside him, not wanting to risk dropping anything.

He struggled to roll aside to stand up. He could barely get a leg under him. The muscles along the back of his legs twinged and ached, as if threatening to snap should he force them. Instead, he was left with no choice but to hobble on his knees around his tent toward the flaps.

"You sure you don't need help?" Hezet offered again.

Yet again, Necrem growled and shook his head. He didn't want the other man to see inside his tent. He might have offered to help him, but one good deed and grand words didn't mean Necrem could trust him. They were still conscripts, after all.

He put his things back under his bedroll and made sure it looked undisturbed before limping back outside the tent. He sat down in front of the closed flaps and struggled through his protesting leg muscles and tender feet to force his boots back on.

Although his feet had dried, the inside of his boots were still moist. The clammy leather stuck to his skin, pulling on his leg hairs. The boots had also shrunk from the moisture, making putting them back on that much more difficult.

Then came the hardest thing of all—standing back up.

His legs visibly shook. His knees burned, refusing any weight he tried to put on them. He tossed and turned, bracing himself on his right arm, and then his left, trying every angle to push himself to his feet. But his tired body refused, and he crumbled under his own weight, grunting as he fell back to the ground.

He groaned and looked up at Hezet just standing there, watching him with his arms folded again.

Necrem let out a raspy sigh and held out his hand. "Fine. I need help for this."

Hezet simply nodded then stomped up and took his hand. Necrem put his right hand under him and pushed while Hezet pulled. Even still, they struggled to pick him off the ground.

"*Damn*, you're heavy!" Hezet swore, snarling and sweating. He pulled Necrem with a surprising vice grip and grabbed his arm with his other hand.

"*You're* the one who wouldn't leave me alone," Necrem growled, but they eventually made progress and he rose to his feet.

He wobbled and braced against his knees. He sucked air through his mask's holes while sweat dripped from his brow to the dry dirt between his feet. The shaking in his legs continued and crept up his body.

"I figured"—Hezet gulped down air, taking deep breaths before standing up straight—"a man as big as you, this would be something you're used to."

"I'm a smith," Necrem coughed out, "not a soldier." Taking a deep breath, he pushed of his knees and straightened.

Hezet stood there, looking taken aback. "Now there's a story."

"You don't want to know it." Necrem shook his head and limped toward the other side of camp, with Hezet silently taking up beside him.

The wrapped cloth prevented the blister on his heel from rubbing, but Necrem regretted not putting a sock on his other foot. His boots were still clinging to his feet, and he feared another blister was forming on his exposed right foot while he climbed up the small rise and into the heart of camp.

Hezet trailed him, silently.

He wasn't the only thing that was quiet. The whole camp was somberly hushed. They passed tent after tent but didn't find anyone.

Where is everyone? Necrem glanced between every tent, feeling an anxious itch sprout between his shoulder blades.

A quick look over his shoulder, and he spotted Hezet frowning and looking around, too. They were heading toward the camp kitchens to get to the doctors. They should be hearing the dull rumble of hundreds of men eating, mingling, and bustling. Instead, there was nothing.

"You men!"

Necrem and Hezet both stopped. A few provost guards suddenly stepped out between the tents ahead, halberds resting on their shoulders.

The lead guard pointed at them. "Why are you loitering there?"

Necrem's shoulders fell. Provost guards stopping men at random couldn't mean anything good.

"My squad mate and I are heading to the camp docs, sir," Hezet replied, stepping up. "His feet are badly blistered and need tending to."

Necrem stifled the impulse groan. He didn't like his business being announced so loudly, even if it was something as minor as this.

"The doctors are busy," the provost guard retorted. "All soldiers were ordered to gather at the punishment grounds thirty minutes ago."

Necrem and Hezet shared a look. The punishment grounds were a cleared patch of dirt between the camp kitchens and doctor tents. The provost marshal and other officers deemed it fitting to have men whipped in front of the others while they ate.

"Step to!" the provost guard shouted.

Necrem did his best, limping the rest of the way to the other side of camp, now with the provost guards following, making sure he and Hezet went.

They found the rest of the camp there waiting. The lines of tables sat with food bowls, plates, cups, and food still sitting on them. The smell of roasting meat hung in the air, and small columns of smoke still rose behind the kitchen wagons in long, trailing wisps.

The mass of men wasn't arranged by their companies, and the fact there were more than one ordered to watch meant this was no ordinary punishment. Normally, only the company with a squad being punished had to be forced to witness it. Everyone else just got to hear it happening if they wanted to eat.

"Please!" someone shrieked. "I didn't steal anything. I *swear* it!"

Necrem stopped. A cold sweat broke out on his forehead, and he briefly didn't feel any ache or pain in his entire body.

A man swung from the lynch pole, a ten-foot-tall post with an arm attached to a winch where a man could be hoisted by the neck to hang. The hanging man's eyes bugged out, and his tongue swelled in the open air as his face turned blue. His feet kicked, but his hands were bound behind his back.

The man who had begged was squirming in the hands of three provost guards at the foot of the post, hands bound behind his back, waiting his turn. Tears streamed across his reddened face. His bare feet kicked up a cloud of dust, but the guards held him.

"You still deserted," one of the guards sneered, slapping him across the face. *Crack! Crack! Crack! Crack! Crack!*

Necrem's head snapped around. Being taller than everyone had its advantages, but that also meant he could see the gruesome sight plainly.

Five more men hung from their wrists on the whipping stumps, four-foot-tall posts with chains to shackle men's wrists while they were stripped to the waist and whipped. None of the men were standing, and their backs were bloody shreds. More men were held behind them in chains by provost guards, awaiting their turn.

"What is *this*?" Hezet gasped. While not as tall as Necrem, he could still see what was going on. His face was as white as canvas.

"Didn't you hear?" a man next to him asked, elbowing him. "They caught those deserters who they said ransacked one of the Don's wagons a few nights back."

Hezet swallowed. "Deserters are hanged. But what's all *this*?" He gestured at the men being whipped.

"Baron Ignaso ordered the entire squad to be punished because the deserters robbed from the Don," the man replied. "Because there were only four deserters, though, the Baron ordered an additional man out of the squad be hanged and the rest whipped."

The man nodded toward another man behind the lynch post, and Necrem saw a younger man, probably in his early twenties, visibly shaking and weeping while a deacon of the Savior prayed with him. The deacon stood out in his white suit, stained with travel dust, wide-brimmed hat, and crooked walking cane with an unlit lantern hanging from it.

"There's no saving him," Necrem grumbled reflectively under his breath.

He spotted two bodies laid out just off to the side of the lynching post. The first executions.

Crack! Slap! Smack! Crack! Crack!

166

"These are done," an officer ordered, looking over the men being whipped. "Unchain them and bring out the next five."

The five provost guards, who had the task of whipping, took a break, gasping and resting their hands on their knees. Their long, black whips smeared blood across their pants and dripped gore from their tongs. More guards unlocked the chains on the men slouching against the posts and dragged them off to the side.

Necrem watched them. They were dragging them off to the round green tents of the camp doctors. The tents where he'd been heading.

"This isn't right," Hezet said.

Necrem turned and found the man shaking his head, his arms folded across his chest and muscles tense, threatening to rip the sleeves. His jaw was set, and his eyes blazed.

"This isn't *just*," Hezet hissed, bringing a few nervous looks from the men around him.

By their looks, Necrem cautiously glanced around. All the provost guards seemed to be stalking around them. They weren't alone, though. He picked out calleroses in their decorative armor and weapons, along with their individual guards in armor, carrying spears. The show of force was obvious.

"This is a message," Necrem whispered to him, keeping his voice low. "Keep our hands off our better's things or suffer."

"Their decimating an entire squad," Hezet growled.

"Because they don't matter to them." Necrem hung his head. "They never did."

The squeal of iron scraping against iron cut through the air, and the winch began to spin. The third lynched man plummeted to the ground with a *thud* and laid in a heap, not getting up. Curses and growls came next with the clanking and jingling of chains as five more men were dragged and locked, hunched over the whipping posts.

The whips cracked again, and this time screams and shrieks followed. Guards untied the noose around the third man and dragged the corpse away to join the first two. Then they hauled out the fourth man, still kicking the dirt in vain.

"Please!" the man cried. "*Mercy!*"

Necrem hung his head, not wanting to watch them wrap the noose around the poor man's neck.

"There's no mercy in this world," he mumbled under his breath before he turned away and began to limp and lumber toward the doctor tents slowly so he wouldn't draw attention.

"Where're you going?" Hezet whispered before he got two steps.

"To get in line for a doctor," Necrem answered from over his shoulder. "I fear it's going to be a long wait." He pressed on, ignoring the pleas of mercy as they turned to choking while the winch was cranked.

Chapter 12

7th of Andril, 1019 N.F (e.y.)

Recha gazed out into the night, vigorously searching for any flicker of light. She tapped her riding crop against her leg.

Did it have to be this cloudy and mirky?

An inky blackness covered the expanse before her. A rolling mist had settled between the lower hills below, with an overcast rolling in from the Desryol Sea, blocking out the stars. Being several hours from dawn, the light from fires, whether they be from torches, lanterns, or open braziers, gave the only hints to where things were. The added difficulty was keeping straight what light belonged where. And to whom.

"You shouldn't wander away, La Dama," Cornelos chastised, coming up behind her. His armor grated against each other, and his rapier tapped against his tassets on his thighs.

"Why?" Recha smirked. "Think I'll be mistaken for an enemy soldier?"

Cornelos stepped beside her. "That's not funny."

"Just some battle humor," she said, tapping his breastplate with her riding crop. "I heard it takes the edge off."

Cornelos frowned at her in response.

Recha sensed another worried speech from her dutiful secretary and rolled her eyes. "Speak, Cornelos. Get it out now before we go to the war council."

Cornelos looked around, checking to see if anyone was near, then stepped closer. "With all due respect, Recha, this is a battlefield. As commandant de marquesa, I need to know where you are to make sure you have the proper guard."

Now that the campaign had begun, Recha had commissioned Cornelos an officer's rank to go along with his station. He would command her personal guard while also screening her correspondence from Zoragrin and other civil matters. She believed it prudent to ensure the others wouldn't think less of him, but he was taking the commission with his usual zeal to duty.

It was starting to grate.

He followed her more intently than before and was the only high-ranking officer she had seen wearing armor over his uniform. Although it was just the breastplate, pauldrons, braces on his forearms, and tassets on his thighs, it was noticeable.

"Cornelos," she said, rounding on him. She cast an intent stare at him to reflect off the light of the campfire behind her. "*Relax*! I'm perfectly safe in my own army's camp." She snickered. "Well, in *one* of my armies' camps."

Cornelos's frown darkened, unamused. "You can't be sure of that. Even with our rushed deployment, we're drawing hundreds of camp followers. Any one of them could be an *assassin*. Or an opportunist."

"I'm not some baroness who's come to see her husband off and believes an army camp is a *picnic*!" Recha snapped, but instantly regretted it.

She looked away, thinking over what he had said and found it reasonable. In her eagerness to begin the campaign and see the battle preparations, she had let protocol slip. She was accustomed to it after three years of ruling Lazorna her way.

"That was uncalled for," she apologized. "Follow your duties, protect me, but please, Cornelos, don't *coddle* me."

Thum!

Recha snapped around. In the distance, off to her far right, she faintly made out the last remaining percussion of a bombard rising in the air—a small fire, dancing and withering in an instant. The smoke and burned powder disappeared into the night and melted into the surrounding mist.

Boom!

A thunderous crash of stone, iron, and dirt shot out through the night, killing any sense of tranquility. Recha couldn't see where the bombard impacted, but she made out the distant lights flickering in a loose square in the sky.

"The First Army is testing their range," she surmised.

"Hiraldo guarantees those new bombards will breach the fort's walls in a day, if not hours," Cornelos said.

Between Puerlato and the road winding into Orsembar was an old hill fort, centuries old and decades unfit for current military innovations. Their strategy for Puerlato aside, the logistics of the fort left them with one option.

It had to be taken. And quickly.

Recha and Baltazar knew their armies couldn't be held up on a siege of a minor fort, a mere pitstop on the road, no matter how prologued it was. One day wasted on it might be too long.

Thum!

Another bombard fired. This time, she caught the sight of the barrel flare, lighting up the small hill the First Army's artillery had set up on and could make out the five bombards and shapes of people before the fire flared out.

How impressive would it be if they all fired at the same time? Recha danced from foot to foot. *Or when the Second Army brings theirs?*

"Let's get to the war council," she said, turning on her heels, "before Papa sends people looking for me, too."

Two armored guards were waiting for them between two of the picket tents. Recha spotted the red strips on their violet uniforms under their breastplates, marking them as her guard. Cornelos probably had brought them with him.

She casually flicked the ends of her divided riding skirts with her riding crop, and they fell in beside her without a word.

The camp of the Third Army was bustling, despite it being hours from dawn. Stockades and ditches were being dug around the perimeter, provost guards were directing where different companies were to be stationed, and tents were going up.

It made things rather chaotic.

One of her guards jumped in front of her, his arm spread wide as a small group of horsemen thundered through a wide lane between the tents.

"You would think we were under attack," she said over her shoulder, breathing deeply.

"Would have been safer back in your tent," Cornelos teased.

Recha warningly glared at him. He held his hands behind his back and pretended to look up at the stars that weren't visible.

"Don't be smug." She turned back and found the guard still standing protectively in front of her, waiting. "Go on."

Deeper in, the camp became more organized. Being the first thing mapped out by the provost marshal, most of the tents were up and filled with sleeping men, snoring. Recha's party passed through a lingering haze of smoke from dying and smoldering campfires, making her cough and her eyes water. She waved the wisps out of her face.

Well, it's not the worst thing I could have smelled or walked into. The idea of latrine pits was the one aspect of campaign life she planned to make every effort to avoid. Because she was the marquesa.

The lanes of tents widened, and the tents themselves grew larger the deeper in they went. In the center was a large, octagon-shaped tent from its multiple posts. Its black and violet striped canvas absorbed the lantern light trying to escape, barely casting shadows of tent's occupants inside. It was raised on a wooden deck, surrounded by provost guards, and stood apart from the other tents.

While anyone would think it was her tent, it was the field marshal's command tent.

Recha had followed Baltazar's lead on having a more conservative tent, comparable to the other marshals, but still a little bigger for her womanly needs and, again, because she was the marquesa.

"Wait!" she said, suddenly stopping in the middle of the open ground between the other tents and the command tent. She put her riding crop under her arm and went to straightening her clothes.

"What's wrong?" Cornelos asked, sharing puzzled looks with the guards.

"Making sure my clothes are straight and hair is right," she replied.

The checkered velvet and black riding dress was appropriate for her station and let her travel more freely. She straightened her jacket and ran her fingers over its lower buttons still done up. Then she made sure her white chemisette was properly tucked in under the jacket, leaving the gold embroidery on the garment's front exposed.

Her guards casually looked away while she looked to her divided skirts, but in limited light, she couldn't tell if they were badly stained with dust or not. As she ran her fingers through her hair, keeping her misshapen ear properly covered, she spied Cornelos biting his lip, as if trying not to smirk.

"Hush," she said.

Cornelos gaped at her. "I didn't say *anything*."

"Mmhmm," she hummed, finishing her preparations. "I'm ready now." Recha strolled through her flabbergasted guard, leaving them to step lively to catch up to her before she reached the command tent's step.

"Halt!" one of the tent guards near the entrance ordered. He and his companion stepped out, gripping their halberds defensively, ready to lower them. "State your name and business!"

"La Dama Recha Mandas," she replied, stepping up onto the deck and into the light of the deck's brazier, "your marquesa."

Both guards snapped to attention, slapping their halberds against their breastplates. Recha smiled at that. One of them moved to open the tent flap to announce her. She, however, turned back to Cornelos and her guard.

"Have the guard stand with these men, Commandant," she ordered. "I'll only need you to accompany me."

I can't have more personal guards than Papa, she thought, considering her tact. *Not in front of his—my—other senior staff. It's probably muggy with everyone else in there, anyway.*

"As you command, La Dama," Cornelos replied.

Recha nodded as he set about relaying her order then turned back to enter.

The guard slammed the butt of his halberd on the deck before opening the tent flap and yelling, "La Dama Recha Mandas!"

Laughter from within was suddenly cut off as the tent flap was pulled back. Recha flinched from being bathed in the orange light spilling out from within. She blinked rapidly, adjusting her sight.

"Thank you," she said to the guard then ducked inside.

The grating sound of multiple wooden legs scraping against the floor greeted her. The command staff rose to their feet around a large, white maple table, shaped like an octagon in the center of the tent. It was littered with maps, scattered rolls of messages, piles of dispatches, quartermaster lists, and provost camp reports. A few cups of water and small glasses of liquor were spread about, as well.

"Good morning, gentlemen," Recha greeted them as she strolled to the open seat by the tent flap to the left of Hiraldo and directly opposite of Baltazar. "I trust I didn't keep you waiting long. I had to see if I could make out Puerlato. Unfortunately, it's too cloudy tonight."

"Not at all, La Dama." Marshal Josef Bisal laughed. "We were just trading old campaign stories." He was two chairs to her left, standing tall in his new uniform. His broad shoulders kept the starched collar of the jacket flared out, but he failed to suck in his gut, ruining his posture. His sandy-brown hair hung from its natural part in the center of his head down to his ears, needing a trim. The crook in the bridge of his hooked nose stood out in the candlelight by the near comical grin he wore, which was missing a tooth.

Recha kept her smile as placid as possible. Having one of Baltazar's staff picks speak so candidly to her was strange after she had placed him and his family under house arrest for a year. She'd expected him and the others to be sourly apprehensive at seeing her.

Baltazar cleared his throat, frowning at Bisal. "What my marshal of scouts meant to say is we serve at your pleasure, La Dama."

Recha gave him a respectful nod. "Thank you, Field Marshal. Let us get on with the business, then. To your seats, gentlemen."

As the generals and marshals took their seats, a servant from off to the side came up and pulled her chair out. The walls of the tent were lined with servants and staff officers standing or sitting off to the side. Recha spied Sevesco siting in a corner and took the mental note of his uniform jacket being half-open.

I'm going to scold him about that later. She sat and placed her riding crop on the table.

"With your permission, La Dama," Baltazar said, "may I give a report on where things stand?" He was a far cry from the retired, stately grandfather she'd met with several weeks ago. His uniform naturally fit him, as if no other clothing was worthy. His face was clean shaven, revealing the aged, stern wrinkles on his hard cheeks. The mustache remained, but trimmed and barely curled over his upper lip. His hair was slicked back, and he showed no sign of weariness, despite the early hour. Even while sitting, Baltazar was at attention.

"By all means," Recha replied.

"Upon the arrival of the Third Army, we now have twenty thousand troops at the outskirts of Puerlato." Baltazar flipped through a couple of dispatches. "Commandant Leyva's latest dispatches put the Fourth Army a day and a half from us and has met no resistance while marching down the west side of the Laz River.

"The latest dispatch from General Priet confirms the Second Army has engaged the enemy at the old river fort on the east bank of the Laz. The general couldn't give an estimate of the enemy's strength there, but he expressed his confidence of taking the fort and the east bank either today or tomorrow."

"The sooner, the better," Marshal Manel Feli commented, tapping his finger on the table. "We may need the Second Army's bombards to support the First's if that old hill fort's defenses are stronger than they appear." Baltazar's marshal of logistics both grimaced and squinted at an open ledger book. His close-set eyes made his spectacles balance precariously on the bridge of his nose. His uniform looked ill-fitting, as if a size too big on his thin frame.

"The First's bombards will breach the fort's walls by noon tomorrow," Hiraldo promised, folding his arms. His chair squeaked from his shifting weight.

"Oh, oh, oh," Marshal Ramon Narvae chuckled, spinning the tin thimble cup with his fingers on the table. "That's quite the boast. You're putting a lot of faith into those metal tubes."

Recha had been avoiding glancing at the man sitting to Baltazar's right. She had hoped she could look each man in the eye, see them in her uniform, and trust they were loyal. Loyal to Baltazar if nothing else. Ramon Narvae, however, was still hard to accept, and his manners made it even harder.

The years of house arrest had not been kind, either. He looked worn out and sat slumped back in his chair. The crown of his head was now bald, and the hair around it was all gray. A black eyepatch stood out, covering his right eye, and a thin scar ran from his temple to his cheek.

He slammed his cup on the table. His remaining eye shot a glance across the table at Hiraldo. The lamp light caught his cold, icy look of contempt. He shifted his shoulders and appeared a little nervous, as if avoiding something.

Or someone.

Papa, why did you have to pick him? Recha squeezed her riding crop until her knuckles went white. Baltazar might have promised all his old comrades would be steadfast, but she was *not* impressed with his choice as marshal second.

"I assure you, Marshal Narvae," Hiraldo said, "my army's gunners *will* demolish the fort's defenses, and we *will* take that fort tomorrow. The marshal may not be aware of this, but we have proven and tested many things while he has been out of service."

Recha's eyebrows shot up, snapping around at Hiraldo.

He was the levelheaded member of her companions, never jumping into anything impulsively or quick to anger. Now he sat there, glaring at Narvae with his chin in the air, as if answering a challenge. His pride, or rather his pride in his army, was on full display.

Recha held back a smirk. *Well done, Hiraldo.*

Then she remembered where she was and whom he had said that to. Her impulse to smirk drained away. She glanced about the table, and then the rest of the tent. Everyone sat or stood on edge. Every adjutant was up, standing stiffly on the balls of their feet. The adjutants of the command staff watched those of Hiraldo and General Ros, general of the Third Army sitting to Recha's right, and vice versa.

Those at the table sat a little stiffer, glancing back and forth between Hiraldo and Ramon. Except Baltazar, who sat with his head hung and arms on the table.

Recha caught the faint vibrations of his mustache, and then she looked down to find his hands balled into white-knuckled fists.

"You"—Narvae growled, sneering at Hiraldo and moving to stand—"stuck up, insubordinate, son of a—"

"*Enough!*" Baltazar yelled, slamming his fists on the table. His head snapped around and bore down on Narvae, halting the other man halfway out of his chair.

The two men held each other's gaze and only heightened the tension in the tent.

This must stop! Recha's mind raced. *If it doesn't, my army will fall apart right when we're about to begin.*

She swallowed, recognizing she was the only person in the room who could do that and prepared herself. She took a couple of deep breaths to calm herself before putting on a calming appearance for everyone.

"Indeed," she said as firmly yet serenely as she could. "With your permission, Field Marshal, before this meeting can continue, I believe there are things that need to be discussed first. Things *I* need to discuss with the officers at this table. May I have the floor?"

Baltazar and Narvae stared at each other for a moment longer before he blew out a deep sigh from his nose. "The floor is yours, La Dama," he said, turning around, with Narvae settling back in his chair.

"Thank you. First"—she gave Hiraldo a stern stare—"General Galvez, apologize to Marshal Narvae. Your pride for your men is understandable, but it is still unbecoming of a junior officer to insult a superior. No matter how surprisingly tactfully."

The color in Hiraldo's face drained. Maybe he had gotten carried away with his pride or let Narvae's dislike for Recha cloud his judgment. It didn't matter.

"My apologies, Marshal Narvae," he said, lowering his head. "I meant no offense."

Narvae sat hunched over the table with his hands folded in front of him. He worked his jaw, dancing his one good eye between Hiraldo and Recha for a moment, before glancing at Baltazar, who was scowling at him. "I accept your apology, General," Narvae finally said.

A ripple of slumping shoulders rolled across the tent, accompanied by deep, deflating breaths. Narvae began to sit back—

"*Stay*, Marshal Narvae," Recha snapped. "All of you, stay in the light. I want to see your faces."

She glanced about the table. Narvae remained leaned forward on his arms, hunched low enough Recha could see him rolling his shoulders. Baltazar's scowl had soften some, but his deep frown pulled his mustache's curls down. Meanwhile, Marshal Bisal's head gently wobbled, as if he were on a horse, with a half-grin that made Recha worry he was slightly simple. By contrast, Marshal Feli took his spectacles off, put them in his breast pocket, and then sat straight, as if expecting a scolding.

Recha's generals, Hiraldo and General Ros, both turned to her. Ros was a middle-aged man and the oldest general in her service. His long face and uniform still showed signs of his long march. His mustache and tuff of hair on his chin were bristly, and he needed a shave. His eyelids drooped, and bags were forming under his dark eyes.

Recha locked eyes with was Marshal Tonio Olguer last. Baltazar's choice as marshal of horse had been oddly quiet. He sat rubbing his broad knuckles with light sheen of sweat on his face. The stout man had gained weight in his years of house arrest but was more darkly tanned than the rest. He had spent his days in forced retirement as a horse trader, breeding and examining horses from his estate.

"I know some of you might hold some animosity for me," she began, "maybe even hatred"—she shot a look at Narvae—"but I'm not sorry for what I did, or the things I have done."

A collection of grunts sounded around the table, but Recha ignored them.

"I will *not* suffer betrayal." Her voice became stern and harsh. "Of *any* kind. If I did not make myself clear three years ago, I will do anything to keep Lazorna from the futile, petty squabbles the rest of the marcs indulge in. And I must be honest; when I heard the four of you were involved in that conspiracy, my first instinct was to have you all executed with the other conspirators." She looked into the eyes of each of her marshals.

The marshals' faces each went white. Bisal's smile was finally gone, Olguer was sweating more profusely, and Feli shifted uncomfortably. Narvae, though, stared back at her, unflinching.

"But I couldn't," she admitted, working moisture into her mouth. "I couldn't . . . and lose the love and respect of the most respectable man I've ever known." Recha turned to Baltazar, still sitting stoically with his back straight and arms folded. His hard mask didn't crack, but the light reflected a twinkle in his eyes. "Nonetheless, I couldn't have any of you avoid punishment. Having you all stripped of commissions and placed under house arrest was the most lenient punishment I could have granted each of you. Making each of you destitute would have been paramount to execution; therefore, house arrest it was."

She turned back to each of them. "I don't expect *any* of you to like me or obey my every whim. I have called you back to service because you are the only men Field Marshal Vigodt will serve with. He has *personally* vouched for each of you. And as I said before, I hold him with the highest respect. His word is all I need to know each of you are loyal soldiers of Lazorna and will strive to do your duties to best of your abilities."

Recha leaned forward against the table, hardening her expression one more time. "But if any of you cannot forgive or stomach serving me, then speak now. I will dismiss each man that says they can't and allow them to leave here without facing any punishment, their house arrest ended, their liberty unrestricted."

A tense quiet settled over the tent. A gust of wind sent ripples across the canvas ceiling and tugged on the tent flap. It also carried the distant, muffled thunders of the First Army's bombards. It sounded like they were all firing now.

"Well"—Bisal coughed loudly, startling several people, Recha included— "I'm good with that. Let bygones be bygones, eh?" His chuckle sounded forced, perhaps nervous, but nonetheless accepted.

Olguer grunted approvingly next, nodding his head. He still dripped sweat on his uniform collar, but at least color was returning to his cheeks.

Recha nodded back.

"La Dama," Feli said humbly, "after hearing your reasons and choice, I am honored to return to your service and the service of Lazorna. You have my pledge. I shall follow my duties to the letter."

You don't have to overdo it, Marshal, she wanted to say, but let it be.

That left only Narvae.

The old calleros sat there, staring at her. He remained motionless, ignoring everyone else in the tent turning toward him, Baltazar included.

"Is that it then?" he said finally. "A long-winded explanation, a sob story of making *hard* choices, and an offer to let things be is all it takes for the rest of you to forget what she's done? What she's been doing?"

"Oh, come now, Ramon," Bisal protested.

"*Don't* 'come now, Ramon' me!" Narvae snapped, slamming a fist on the table before pointing at her. "You've killed a lot of good men. Some of them were conniving, scheming barons, I grant you, but how can you sit there and justify having calleros—good, experienced officers—executed just because their sworn barons spoke ill of you one night over wine and brandy?"

Recha's eyebrow twitched, and try as she might, she couldn't hide the growl in her voice. "How can you justify sitting with some of those same, conniving, scheming barons against the marquesa who pledged to avenge the death of the son of your sworn friend?" She expected him to blanch at that, but Narvae didn't flinch.

"Young Sebastian's death, as tragic as it was, was a casualty of campaign and can happen to any of us. What you did, La Dama, amounted to *purging* anyone you saw as your rivals without allowing a lot of good men to prove themselves."

The tension Recha had wished to dispel was quickly returning. Baltazar himself sat uneased on the edge of his chair, watching her intently.

She squeezed her riding crop again until she heard the leather squeak against her palm. *He still has his brazen pension for saying the unspoken out loud.*

These men were Baltazar's oldest companions and had visited his estate many times in her youth. Narvae and Bisal were always in competition to retell all the old war stories in full detail, many unsuitable for children. Narvae, however, was always blunt about his commanding officers and barons, especially when their political agenda went against military strategy.

"I did purge my political rivals," she admitted, pushing herself to her feet, scooting her chair back and making its legs grind against the floor. "But *only* after they conspired to betray me. I took no chances with the calleroses too closely sworn to them, either. It's irrelevant if that shocks your sensibilities of honor, Cal Narvae, but if any of those conspiracies had succeeded, or if their calleroses felt it their duty to carry them out, they would have done the same thing to me, everyone who supported me"—she gestured to Cornelos behind her—"and probably anyone they believed to support me." She shot a glance at Baltazar.

Narvae gazed behind her at Cornelos. The faint creak of wood hinted at her secretary-now-commandant shifting his weight.

Steady, Cornelos, she prayed. *Don't let him intimidate you.*

She couldn't imagine his feelings on this. Upon his request, he had been with the troops who had gone to arrest the conspirators. He'd taken his uncle into custody personally. He was the one who had taken Narvae's eye and left him with that scar. In the years afterward, Cornelos had avoided talking about him and that night.

"We all have to choose sides," Narvae said through gritted teeth, as if strained to admit it.

"That we do," Recha agreed. "The only thing that matters is what side you choose now, Ramon Narvae. Again, you don't have to like me. You can go on hating me. I ask you, though, to look at what I offer each of you. A new, model army, with no interference from barons making demands on the march. No calleros wanting to make grandstands and challenges. A professional command. And I also wish to remind you that you are here at the personal request of Field Marshal Vigodt."

Narvae folded his hands, flexing and relaxing his entwined fingers while pursing his lips. For the first time, the harsh look in his eye faded, replaced by a thoughtful one.

"What about you, La Dama?" He flashed a look up at her. "What's your role in this campaign to be?"

Recha allowed herself a small smile, more out of seeing a way to give someone else the chance the lead the conversation. "I believe Field Marshal Vigodt can explain that better than me," she said while sitting back down. "Field Marshal, if you please?"

"The La Dama and I have agreed that all military strategy and decision be run through this staff," Baltazar said, seemingly happy to take back over and have everyone's returned attention. "Everything is to go through proper command channels without having to receive La Dama's approval first."

179

"No going above anyone's head," Narvae simplified, shooting a glance at Hiraldo before turning back to Baltazar.

"Exactly." Baltazar nodded.

Narvae shifted in his chair, appearing more interested. "Still, if I'm allowed to ask again, what is La Dama's role going to be?"

"To oversee the campaign's political needs," Recha interjected. "Communications from Zoragrin, dealing with local barons, and any negotiations with enemy commanders who invoke the Rules of Campaign. The boring things I'm sure you'd find tedious."

Narvae drummed his fingers on the tabletop, but his thoughtful expression remained.

"But I'm sure we can trust you to share everything important with us, correct, La Dama?" Feli requested. Being marshal of logistics, it was natural for him to ask a question like that.

"Of course," Recha affirmed.

That settled, the waiting quiet returned, broken only by Narvae soft, drumming fingertips. However, the tension wasn't as suffocating as before.

"What say you, Ramon?" Baltazar asked. "Satisfied or not?"

Narvae jutted his jaw out, passed another glance between Baltazar and Recha, before snorting deeply. "I'll serve," he replied finally. "For you, Baltazar."

The men gave each other an understanding nod, and Recha had to accept it.

"Then let's continue discussing our strategy," she said, trying to get the meeting back on course. "Field Marshal, if you please?"

Baltazar moved a few papers out of the way to reveal a map of the surrounding area. "Some of you may believe," he began, "we are making a lightning strike to retake Puerlato before the Orsembians can send a relief force. However, the recapture of Puerlato is not the main objection of this campaign." He pulled out another map showing the greater interior of Orsembar. "The goal of this campaign is to march into Orsembar and break Marqués Borbin."

The heart of Orsembar, Recha mentally added while everyone at the table leaned forward to look at the map and all the adjutants passed hasty whispers amongst themselves. *It would have sounded better to say, "the heart of Orsembar."*

"By our initial reports, Marqués Borbin has taken personal command of his army this season and has marched it against Quezlo." Baltazar ran his finger along the map, tracing the Compuert Road and stopping at Compuert. "We believe the Orsembian army's vanguard should have reached Compuert a few days ago and begun siege preparations."

"Believe?" Narvae inquired, raising an eyebrow. "Are we not sure?"

Baltazar folded his hands together. "Our information is based on Capitán Viezo's informants." He turned, and the rest of the table followed his gaze, to look back in the corner at Sevesco, who was snoozing. He had moved an empty chair beside him, that an adjutant must have abandoned, and braced his arm on the top of the back of the chair with his cheek pressed against his fist.

"Capitán *Viezo!*" Baltazar roared.

Sevesco snorted, jerking awake. "Time to go?" he grunted and half-stood. He blinked rapidly, clearing the sleep from his eyes, then paused when he found everyone in the tent staring at him. "Guess not."

Sevesco! Recha gritted her teeth to stop the impulse to scream at him. Instead, she folded her arms, leaned back in her chair, and crossed her legs to prevent the impulse to throw something at him. There were enough clashing egos under this tent without him causing trouble.

"Good morning, Capitán," Baltazar said dryly. "Glad you can join us. Do you want someone to bring you a coffee, or can you stay awake long enough to give us your report?"

Sevesco brightened. "If you're offering—"

His snide remark died in his throat, and his face made a sudden pinched expression, like a child who had pressed their parent too far. Recha couldn't see Baltazar's face, but she was *certain* his glare could curdle milk.

"I can give any report you wish," Sevesco said before hastily adding, "sir."

Baltazar continued to stare at him.

A new tension fell over the tent, though not like last time when everyone felt the meeting was going to disintegrate into shouting and blows. This was the tense, strained silence of a commanding officer bearing down on a junior, waiting for something, expecting something, and Recha knew Baltazar wasn't going to continue until he got it. She could see Sevesco faintly sweating even from across the tent.

Sevesco finally broke, rising to his feet while buttoning up his uniform jacket. Once done, he stood at attention with his head up and hands behind his back. "Capitán Viezo reporting, sir!" he shouted, though unenthusiastically.

"Better," Baltazar said before glancing back to his map. "Capitán, can you confirm Borbin's army has reached Compuert?"

"Their vanguard should have, sir," Sevesco replied. "The latest reports I've received said the Orsembian main army should have marched out of Orona a few days ago. Their baggage train, though, is probably still stretched between there and Huarita."

"That's a long baggage train," Narvae grumbled, squinting at the line marking the road between the cities. "It'll take days to get food to their vanguard. How large is Borbin's army?"

"The vanguard was supplied food from Pisemo," Sevesco replied. "As for the Orsembian army"—he shrugged—"last count had it around eight-five thousand."

Everyone under the tent jerked awake at that number. Even Bisal gaped.

"Well!" Narvae sat back, throwing his hands up. "With an army that big, what in damnation are we supposed to do? Last I counted we had . . . what? Thirty-five? Thirty-six thousand troops? With the numbers Borbin has, he can dispatch a quarter of them to block us while we're stuck here retaking Puerlato, and *still* take Compuert."

"Which is why," Baltazar said, looking toward Recha, "La Dama and I agree that we will not remain here to besiege Puerlato."

The flow of everyone's attention returned to her, and Recha got the hint Baltazar wanted her to take over.

"The field marshal and I went over the intelligence reports and formed a plan," she began. "Once the First Army takes the hill fort and the Second Army breaks the fort at the river mouth, the Fourth Army will remain here and hold Puerlato under siege with the First and Second Armies' bombards to keep the city's port closed."

She caught Hiraldo frowning at her mentioning losing his army's field guns, but she pressed on.

"The Third Army, General Ros, will march into Orsembar tomorrow, immediately after we are certain the road is clear, and secure . . ." She reached over the table but was just short. "Pass the map, if you please, Field Marshal."

Baltazar spun the map around then sent it gliding over the tabletop with a flick of his finger. Recha caught it before the parchment could slide under her arm and set it down in front of General Ros.

"Once you march into Orsembar, send your vanguard to secure this cove," she instructed, pointing to a spot on the map.

Ros sat up, intently staring at the map, studying the route and surroundings. It was a cove on the Desryol Sea, five miles west of Puerlato and ten miles south of the Compuert Road Junction.

The general's brow furled. "Forgive me, if this is being presumptuous, La Dama, but shouldn't the junction be our primary target to secure?"

"In normal circumstances, yes," Recha replied. "But what should be anchored in that cove is much more important than a road junction. A ship, carrying enough muskets, ball, and powder to outfit your army and the needs of the Second, should be there. We need those weapons."

General Ros sat up straighter, and his eyebrows shot up the moment he heard that. "Indeed! But are we sure the ship is there?"

"We arranged it nearly a month ago." Recha smiled assuredly. "And Capitán Viezo should—" She glanced and found Sevesco, still standing, only his head had fallen back with his mouth gaping.

"*Sevesco!*" she hissed.

Sevesco threw his head up, snorting, blinking, and grunting all at the same time. "Hmm?"

"The *ship!*" she demanded. "Is it in the cove?"

"Yeah"—Sevesco stifled a yawn before correcting himself—"I mean, yes, La Dama. An informant confirmed it when I arrived to camp this evening."

"Good."

At least we know his informants are working, she thought, turning back to General Ros.

"So, at dawn—or as soon as General Galvez guarantees the road is open—march the Third Army to the cove, secure it, and bring those weapons ashore as fast as possible."

"Yes, La Dama," General Ros affirmed.

"Speed will be vital," Baltazar interjected and commandingly looked about the occupants at the table. "Not just in retrieving those weapons, but in every step of this campaign."

"Naturally, we're going to need speed." Narvae snickered, as if stating the obvious. "We're going to need to get up to Compuert before Borbin knows it and bite him in the ass while he's focused on those walls."

"Just like old times." Bisal chuckled, rocking in his chair.

That brought about a few more people chuckling in agreement.

Except Baltazar.

"We're not going to attempt a pincer maneuver. Borbin's army is too large. Even while focused on Compuert, he could pull half his army around and overwhelm us."

"What about the Quezlians?" Narvae asked. "Don't we have an alliance with them?"

"Not with the terms of our agreement this year," Recha piped up. "Quezlo agreed to come to our aid if Borbin invaded us. They didn't agree to fight with us if we sent troops in response to Borbin attacking them."

Their agreement was only enforceable to make Lazorna a charnel house in case Borbin tried to march through us to get to them, she mentally added. *If we win this, I'll have to talk to Marqués Dion about more mutually beneficial agreements.*

"Besides," she added, grinning, "why share the spoils?"

That brought more chuckles. The tension from earlier seemed to have disappeared, and Recha was grateful for it.

"And, by spoils," Feli said, pointedly staring down his nose at a map, "I can't help but notice the road to Manosete is open. If not Compuert, do you mean to march in and seize Manosete while Borbin's away?"

Baltazar shook his head. "We still don't have the numbers, nor the supplies to perform two sieges at the same time and have a reserve to hold off whatever relief force Borbin will eventually send. The plan instead is we march into the heartland of Orsembar and cause enough chaos and confusion that Borbin has no choice but to march his army away to stop us."

"The barons will be in an uproar," Recha added. "Once they hear rumors and news of us marching on their lightly defended estates while they're away fighting for Borbin's ambition, they'll demand protection."

"And an army that size will have to break up to pursue us," Baltazar concluded. "That is when we strike. With our model armies, more mobile and able to work independently, we can draw these smaller units into individual battles, on ground of our choosing."

"Crush them in detail," Narvae said, his eye twinkling now that he saw the plan. A faint hint of a smile played on his lips as the old calleros grasped the strategy.

Defeating an army in detail was a tactic a smaller army could use to spread out a larger army and defeat the spread-out segments, one by one. Baltazar had convinced her it wise to use such a strategy here, and the same tactic Sebastian had deployed that had earned him his own fame. Like father, like son. All that mattered here was getting inside Orsembar and luring Borbin's army away to be defeated piecemeal.

"Marching into Orsembar does present a problem, though," Marshal Feli said, his frown making his close-set eyes squint. "Our supply lines will be stretched thin the deeper we go. If the enemy claims the Compuert Road Junction, we'll be cut off from Lazorna."

"Each army will have to live off the land," Baltazar conceded, rubbing his hands together. "Every town, village, and estate we come across will have to be taken for supplies."

"Especially the estates," Recha added. "It's vital for our plan that the barons make trouble for Borbin, and having their homes threatened will do just that."

That came out a little harsh, she thought, noticing some of the adjutants shifting on their feet nervously. *But this is war.*

"As you've pointed out, Marshal Feli, there's only one counteroffensive Borbin can take that will ruin our entire plan." Baltazar stared right at her. "If he hears what we're doing and, instead of marching to stop us, he moves to relieve Puerlato, this entire campaign is over. If he moves at full force toward Puerlato and takes the Compuert Road Junction, then no matter what any of our armies are doing or engaged in, I *will* order a retreat to Lazorna. Whether we all make it in time is irrelevant.

"If I receive word of such a move, I will have no choice but to order the retreat. If we get cut off completely from Lazorna, we are doomed. And if we allow Borbin to relieve Puerlato with his numbers and us still inside Orsembar, Lazorna is doomed."

He sat up straight and folded his arms. "Do you understand, La Dama?"

Recha swallowed, looking at the map. She understood the strategy. It was just like the jedraz game. They weren't taking the distraction with Puerlato and marching into Orsembar to strike at Borbin's heart. However, their plan was bold and risky. If Borbin deciphered it, he could, in turn, answer their maneuver in kind.

But this is my only chance, she told herself. *If I don't strike now, I never will.*

"I understand, Field Marshal." She stared back at Baltazar, holding his gaze. His stern, commanding expression never wavered, as if he wished to drive the point he would do as he said to her with his eyes alone.

"Very well," Baltazar finally said. "Then the last order of business for tonight are some orders of transfers. While I agree the Fourth Army should be left to hold Puerlato, I wish to move some companies in and out of it. General Galvez, I understand you have several companies formed entirely of Puerlato natives, correct?"

"Correct, Field Marshal," Hiraldo replied. "They are some of the First Army's finest."

"Very good." Baltazar had fished a pair of spectacles and was already writing orders. "I want them all transferred to the Fourth Army. The Fourth Army is, in turn, to transfer the necessary companies to fill the spots left open in the First."

Blood drained out of Hiraldo's face. "May I ask why, Field Marshal?"

"For morale, General," Recha interjected, touching his elbow. "The men of Puerlato want their city freed. It would harm their morale to order them to invade Orsembar while leaving their home in enemy hands. Therefore, those companies will hold the city under siege, using the field guns to stop any ships from providing provisions while starving, or *waiting*, the defenders out. The least amount of damage as possible. We all want to bring Puerlato back into the fold, not destroy it in the process."

The men around the table nodded at that, most of the adjutants joined concurring.

Hiraldo frowned stubbornly, like a boy being told it was best for his favorite dog to be taken away and knew it had to be done. "Yes, La Dama." He finally nodded. "My army, though, is deploying for battle, Field Marshal. With your permission, I request all transfers wait until after we've secured the fort."

"Granted," Baltazar said without even looking up from writing. "The fort will be the perfect transfer point, anyway."

The tent fell into silence again, save for Baltazar's pen scratching. Feet shifted. Boards softly yawned. Or that might have been one of the adjutants; Recha wasn't quite sure.

She glanced and found Sevesco lightly sleeping again, this time with his arms wrapped around himself.

She ran through her mental lists and found it running low. She wasn't sure if there was anything left to . . . to . . .

Her eyelids started to droop. Her head started to feel a little heavy. The soft scratches of the pen seemed to echo louder and louder. Sound seemed to muffle. The tent was getting darker. Or maybe it was just her vision? Recha couldn't tell. Only, she felt very . . . relaxed.

"Halt!" the tent guard outside shouted. "Halt!"

Recha threw her head up at the sound of pounding boots on wood. She squinted and blinked rapidly as her eyes readjusted.

"Let me through!" a young man demanded. "I swam the Savior damned Laz to bring this dispatch!"

A cacophony of grunts, muttered curses, scraping armor, weapons, and boots burst into the tent as two of the guards struggled to hold on to a determined soldier, desperate to force his way in. Everyone who could reached for their swords, except for Recha, who looked around to see what was going on, and Baltazar, who calmly rose to his feet.

"What is the meaning of *this*?" Baltazar demanded sternly but kept his firm voice low, accompanied by a glare that could set wood aflame.

The scuffling men broke apart and snapped to attention. The soldier in the center, the one who the guards were struggling with, was drenched from head to toe. His uniform was soaked through and clung to his body, same for his curly brown hair sticking to his forehead. A pool was quickly forming where he stood.

"Sir!" the soldier shouted, quick to be the first to respond. "I come bearing an urgent dispatch from General Priet of the Second Army, sir!"

"Then deliver it, soldier!" Baltazar ordered.

"Sir!" the soldier hastily saluted before digging through his leather dispatch sack hanging from his shoulder and on his waist. As he pulled out a parchment, his eyes met Recha's, and he gasped, "La Dama!"

Recha softly smiled.

The soldier held out the dispatch to her, his hand shaking from the wet.

Recha took the message without thinking and began to open it. Only when she had, did she see who the message was said to go to, written on top of the dispatch. She stopped, glancing out of the corner of her eye to see her command staff, Baltazar especially frowning.

Oops. She took a deep breath and looked up at the soldier. "Who were you ordered to deliver this to?" she asked.

The soldier swallowed then confusedly replied, "To Marshal Feli of the field marshal's staff, La Dama."

"Then follow your orders, soldier," she said, handing the dispatch back to him, "and deliver it."

The soldier lowered his head and hastily took back the note.

As he strode around the table to properly deliver his message, Recha caught a faint, approving smile from Baltazar.

She nodded back. *I just promised them to respect the chain of command and almost broke it because I'm drowsy. If I don't get sleep soon, there's no telling what I'm going to do.* She fought the urge to rub the corners of her eyes while also fighting to keep them open.

"The fort at the river mouth has fallen!" Feli announced, siting straight and alert while reading the message. "General Priet reports the defenders tried to evacuate after the first few volleys of their bombards. During the retreat, members of the thirtieth company of sword and thirty-second company of pike stormed and seized the gates. General Priet reports close to two hundred and fifty riders escaped, heading toward Puerlato. He has calleros in pursuit, but he cannot be sure if they can stop them in time."

"Send dispatches to Commandant Leyva immediately!" Baltazar ordered, sending every adjutant in the tent into a frenzy, rushing the table for a surface to write on. "He is to change the course of his march and proceed down the Laz to ensure the Second Army's crossing and send every mounted company he has toward Puerlato from his position to cut off the fort defenders.

"General Galvez, General Ros, which of your companies of horse are most rested?"

Hiraldo and Ros shared a look before Ros answered first.

"My companies are still resting from their march, Field Marshal, but their horses should have gotten enough rest by now."

"Some of my companies are standing by," Hiraldo replied, "in case there is a sally from Puerlato or those in the hill fort try to retreat."

In all the flurry of activity, Recha slunk in her chair. The meeting was apparently over, and Baltazar was showing how fast he could take over his duties.

He passed a quick look between the two generals, as if weighing them, before finally saying, "Rouse your men, General Ros. I want three companies of horse blocking the road from the river mouth fort to Puerlato within the hour. General Galvez, keep yours in position. The men at the river fort have nowhere to go but Puerlato, and we also cannot allow one man from the hill fort to slip into Orsembar."

"Yes, sir!" both generals replied then turned to their own adjutants.

Recha folded her hands in her lap and just watched the activity. *Is there really nothing for me to do? Maybe I shouldn't have been so agreeable to be cut out of everything.*

"Recha," Baltazar's fatherly voice called through the upheaval. He was holding two pieces of paper in both hands, looking at her over the spectacles on the bridge of his nose. "Go get some sleep. We got it handled here."

Recha slumped. *Did making him field marshal make him a mind reader, too?* However, she was too tired to argue.

She pushed off the table to her feet. "Happy hunting, gentlemen," she wished the generals.

Each of her staff paused what they were doing to rise and wish her goodnight. Cornelos cleared a path for her, and the guards held open the tent flaps.

Recha's body felt heavy, and each step she took felt like she was walking on water. Then the night wind brushed against her cheek, it's cool touch sending a chill down her spine and making her start awake before she tripped off the edge of tent's support deck.

"Thank. The. *Savior!*" Sevesco yawned, stretching his arms high into the air. "I thought that'd never *end.*"

Recha groggily arched an eyebrow at seeing him, glanced over her shoulder back at the tent, then looked back to make sure she was seeing him right. "How did you get out here?" she asked.

"Hmm?" Sevesco grunted. He looked over his shoulder with half-lidded eyes. "Oh. I snuck out the moment all of'—he waved back at the command tent—"*that* started."

You snuck away? She put her hands on her hips, more to keep herself standing. *Why am I not surprised?*

"Shouldn't you be in there helping? Or . . . checking in on your espis?"

"Ah!" Sevesco waved a finger in the air then spun on his heels around in front of her. "I should check for more reports. In my tent. Excellent idea. But first, just to let you know"—he lowered his voice—"Silvaja's party was a complete success. Lots of happy guests, and everyone on the list did *not* leave." He gave her a wink.

I'm too tired for subtlety and subterfuge, Recha thought, getting his meaning, but her legs were starting to wobble.

"That's nice," she replied sleepily.

Sevesco grinned. "There he is!" He pulled back, waving at Cornelos, who was walking up beside Recha. "The most gallant commandant in the whole army."

"Does that make you the most unlikely capitán in the army then?" Cornelos retorted, glowering at him.

Recha had told him about Sevesco's prank, and he was still not amused.

Sevesco shrugged. "I'd rather not have a rank, but *someone* insisted."

"Baltazar?" Recha guessed.

"Nope." Sevesco shook his head. "Feli. Said he wanted information vetted by an officer to be sure it's genuine. Bisal didn't care one way or another. I knew I always liked him best."

Recha grimaced. Baltazar had given her the recommendation of giving Sevesco an officer rank. She had assumed it was to make sure all her companions had a place in the army.

I should make sure I ask for reasons for recommendations for now on.

"Now, if you two will excuse me," Sevesco said, "I'm going to my tent and stay there until they pull it down around me."

"Don't pickpocket the wrong person on your way," Cornelos warned.

Sevesco snorted, shaking his head. "Cornelos, Cornelos. I'm too tired to pick anyone's pocket. But seriously"—he dug into his trouser pocket, pulled out some folded papers, then tossed them at Cornelos, making him jerk and fumble to catch them—"you shouldn't carry such important things around. A list of Recha's guards? Such a list shouldn't be put to paper."

"*You!*" Cornelos yelled, but Sevesco was already scurrying off between the tents, leaving Cornelos fuming, breathing deeply through his nose. He mumbled angrily under his breath as he stuffed the papers into his pocket.

Recha shook her head. "You know he only does that because he enjoys picking on you, right?"

Cornelos about-faced, his face red, grimacing no doubt from yelling even more. He hung his head, deflating, and sighed. "May I escort you to your tent, La Dama?" he offered.

"Oh, by the Savior, *yes!*" Recha accepted, deflating a little herself. As groggy as she felt, she wasn't sure she could remember where her tent was.

When Cornelos set off, Recha hopped off the command tent deck after him. She barely realized the guard she had left outside the command tent had joined them until she lazily glanced over her shoulder and found them following behind.

Her tent was slightly smaller than the command tent, several tents down and surrounded by more guards. Recha struggled to keep her head up and barely acknowledged them when they snapped to attention when they approach.

"Make sure I don't oversleep," she instructed Cornelos as he held open her tent flap for her. Her commanding air, though, was broken when she yawned loudly.

"Yes, La Dama." Cornelos chuckled, his broad smile plainly lit by a nearby campfire.

"I'm serious," she said, giving him a stern look. Though, again, she wobbled on her feet.

"I promise to wake you if anything happens," Cornelos assured her.

Accepting that, and desperately wanting to get off her feet, Recha gave him a dismissive wave and slipped into her dark tent.

The servants hadn't left a light lit, but luckily, there was nothing in her way. All her trunks were still stacked to one side while her bunk was straight back in the rear of the tent.

She stumbled through the tent, pawing at her clothes, trying to loosen them to take them off, but not having the strength or willpower. Finally, she flopped down on her bunk and stretched out, sighing. After a few deep breaths in time with the bombards' distant reports, her eyes drifted closed, and she went fast asleep.

Chapter 13

The Easterly Sun's blazing noonday rays stung Recha's eyes, making her tilt her head to shade her face with the brim of her silver hat.

That also limited her vision to the carnage before her.

"Clear a path!" the calleros at the head of her escort ordered. "Make way for the marquesa!"

Soldiers of the First Army scrambled out of the way of the galloping squadron of calleros in their full, varnished black-plate armor riding up the steeping slope toward the hill fort. Their closed visors gave them quite an intimidating appearance with their round eye holes with curved slots arching downward from them like makeshift corners of eyes that followed the bridge of a metal nose.

Recha rode in their center with six members of her guard, one carrying her personal violet banner. Save for her hat, she hadn't changed since last night. She'd been awoken an hour ago and, between having to decide to eat or change clothes, she had chosen to eat.

She was regretting that choice now.

She put on a strong face and tried not to grimace at the sight of her soldiers limping, leaning on fellow soldiers, or being carried on stretchers to the camp doctors and surgeons who had set up their stations on the slope of the hill after the fort had been taken. The smell of bile and blood mixed with the heavy scents of smoke and dust lingering in the air.

How many did we lose from taking one measly, old fort?

Recha raised her head to avoid the sights of men gripping wounded legs and hastily bandaged heads. Trails of gray smoke still rose from inside the fort. It was thickest still on the north side.

Cornelos had informed her that the wall had come down right at dawn. That was when the battle for the breach had begun. From the reports, it sounded like the defenders had fought in earnest from the start.

Recha ground her teeth together. *And he let me sleep right through it! I must remember to give him extra work, or have Papa assign him to latrine digging, or . . . or*—she grunted from her right hip having fallen asleep, forcing her to shift her weight—*or make him ride* sidesaddle *for a couple of days.*

The old fort of weathered stone stood a couple stories tall, a monument to centuries long forgotten. The ancient royal crest of Desryol—a shield depicting a hand and forearm that should have been black, reaching up to grasp a blazing sun out of reach—was still carved on the turrets of the fort's castle gate.

The crest of a long-dead bloodline wasn't important.

Recha's chest swelled at the sight of hers fluttering in the wind on the turrets themselves, alongside the banners of the First and Fourth Army, the latter having arrived to take up the siege of the city a couple of hours ago.

The fort's gate stood open. Squads of pikemen stood guard on both sides, as if an honor guard to the wounded lumbering and being carried out to the doctors below.

"Make way!" the calleros capitán, marked by the red feather sticking out on the back of his helmet, bellowed. "Clear the gate for the marquesa!"

The pikemen snapped to attention, stamping their feet and pounding the butt of their pikes into the ground as one. Men rushed to clear the gateway for the calleroses.

Recha casually raised her riding crop to the pikemen before instinctively ducking her head to pass under the portcullis. She didn't want to risk one of those iron points snagging her hat and ripping her hair back. She had pinned the hat to her hair, bundled up and propped to the side to forgo brushing after rolling over it during her sleep.

Riding into the fort was like riding into the past. The wide, square curtain walls surrounded a centuries-old keep, five stories of brown stone. The bailey yard was a mixture of ordered chaos and a charnel house.

"Any wounded who can walk need to make their way to camp doctors outside the fort," an officer from a sword regiment, distinguished by the shield strapped to his back, ordered to a group of men helping the wounded. "The rest of you, break up into teams and carry the wounded who can't walk. We need this yard cleared!"

"Easy with clearing those rock!" a sergeant bellowed at another group of men, most of them camp workers because they weren't in uniform, clearing rubble in the breached north wall. "We need this breach cleared but don't bring the rest of the wall down! Careful where you step, too! What's left of some poor bastards are under there."

Recha watched one man stumble back. His face was struck pale from picking up a stone and finding the squished remains of an enemy soldier who hadn't been quick enough to avoid the bombards blasting through the wall.

"What did I just say?" the sergeant snapped.

A woman's scream tore Recha's attention away from those cleaning up the pieces of men and stone.

"Where do you think you're hiding?" a soldier snapped, dragging a woman out from the side door of the keep by under her arm. Her white apron was stained with blood, her brown dress torn in several places, including her right sleeve, and her face was gray from stains of smoke with only streaks from tears offering to wash them off.

"All prisoners belong by the stables," the solder, another swordsman, ordered. "That includes *you*!"

"No!" the woman screamed. "Mercy! *Please*! I don't want to be taken as *sioneros*!"

The soldier carried out his duty, dragging the begging woman, a fort servant who most likely worked in the kitchens, out of sight with stern conviction.

The woman's pleas pinged Recha's heart.

"Capitán!" she called. Upon entering, she and her escort had simply waited while Recha surveyed the damage.

The capitán wheeled his horse around, lifting his visor open in salute. "Yes, La Dama?"

"Go after that soldier," she ordered. "Remind him, and whoever's in charge of overseeing the prisoners, that all prisoners are to be treated with respect unless so ordered. Tell them the marquesa herself will be very *displeased* if she hears of any mistreatment. *Especially* to the women. We are a professional army. And our reputation begins here. Tell them, if the I hear of any man tarnishing that, she will oversee their discipline *personally*."

"By your command, La Dama!" the capitán replied. He slammed his visor down and gestured to a few of his fellow calleroses, tearing away half her escort as they left.

"And tell them that comes straight from the marquesa *herself*!" Recha added, pushing up in her saddle to yell it louder.

She didn't hear a reply, probably because the helmet muffled it, or the thumping horse hooves did. Either way, she sat back, smiling, satisfied in giving an order and seeing it carried out. True, her agreement with Baltazar meant she couldn't interfere with the chain of command, but she would be *forsaken* if she saw her army abusing people in front of her and must ask someone else to make it stop. She didn't have to ask. She could command that!

"Huzzah!" someone shouted to her left. "La Dama Mandas!"

Recha turned and saw Capitán Alon Queve exiting the southeast corner turret with two fellow swordsmen following him.

She beamed a smile at him. "Huzzah, Capitán Queve!" She raised her riding crop to him. "I trust the battle went well for you and your company?"

Queve stopped a couple of paces away, stamping his feet together. The two following him did likewise. He held one hand on his sword hilt while carrying his helmet underneath his left arm. His breastplate couldn't conceal the fact that he was puffing his chest out, although it did make the dark smear of dried blood that raked diagonally across it stand out more.

His hair was matted from dried sweat, and his cheeks were a little sunken in. He looked tired and yet still alert, either from the last remaining adrenaline from the battle or inner discipline.

"It was hard fought, La Dama," he reported. "But the First Swords upheld the honor of Lazorna and Puerlato with distinction."

"That's excellent to hear!" Recha couldn't help but crookedly smile at his boast, a proudful, soldier's boast.

"Thank you, La Dama!" Queve gave a sharp nod, lowering his chin to his breast then snapping it back, like a bow without bending. "Also, General Galvez's compliments. He wishes for you to join him and Commandant Leyva in the southeast turret's observation room."

Recha glanced up at the turret but couldn't see anything through the turret's slit windows. She shifted her divided skirts so they wouldn't get caught when she dismounted. Holding the reins in her right hand, she moved her left leg over the pommel simultaneously while sliding her right foot from its stirrup. Once she was sitting completely sideways, she simply hopped off before any of her guard had dismounted to offer to help her.

She straightened her skirts then handed her horse's reins to her nearest calleros. "Take our horses and wait with the others," she ordered.

"Yes, La Dama," the calleros replied, taking her reins.

They took the reins of her guard, as well, and Recha waited for them to ride past before heading toward the capitán. Her guard fell in behind her while Queve led them to the turret door.

The yard was covered in weeds and patches of sand. Her heels dug into the loose dirt with every step, threatening to trip her.

She was relieved to reach the turret door but paused at the threshold. "You two remain here," she ordered two of her guard, keeping her voice low. "Members of the Viden should be arriving soon. Escort them to me when they do."

The guards nodded and took up positions beside the door.

"Capitán!" Recha called, alerting him on the staircase that she had paused. She rushed to catch up, past his fellows, to walk up the steps beside him. "You mentioned the battle was hard fought," she said, using the rickety railing to steady her up the stair's steep incline. "Were you referring to the enemy or your company's losses?"

"The First Swords fought well," Queve assured her. "The men stayed together, storming over the breach's rubble. None broke off to fight alone, kept each other covered when they could, and kept up the pressure to widen the breach and get more companies through. All in all, our losses were manageable."

Despite his positive report, Recha noted some strain in his voice and his furled brow, as if he was holding something back. She was about to ask him more when a potent, acidic scent struck her, making her wince. She put her hand over her nose then took the final step to the third-floor landing and stopped.

The room, which must have been for the soldiers to relax in between patrolling the walls, was in complete upheaval. Every piece of furniture was overturned in a makeshift barricade. It was as rickety as the stairs from apparently being made in haste, and musket-ball holes peppered the wooden tabletops, backs of chairs, and marked some of the back wall with black spots. The stinging smell of burned powder still hung in the air, along with the faint scent of blood, because of the turret's small slit window.

"It was getting the musketeers on the walls that finally broke them," Queve said from beside her. "Once they started volleying from above, the defenders broke." The capitán's sternness remained, and his former pride was replaced with what Recha thought sounded like regret.

"Is everything truly all right, Capitán?" she asked in concern. "You don't have to remain stoic in front of me because of your rank or because I'm the marquesa. If there is something wrong, I would prefer to be told."

Queve drew himself up again, pressing his lips tightly together, as if to keep quiet, but Recha fixed him with an intense, unblinking stare.

"It's nothing serious, La Dama," he replied, relaxing. "Some of the men . . . During the battle, it was dark, and most of the men were trying to stay alive while pressing the attack. Afterward, though, some of the men admitted they weren't sure how hard to press." His frown deepened. "They couldn't be certain if the defenders they were fighting were Orsembians or men of Puerlato."

Recha softened her stern expression. She glanced at the swordsmen with Queve. Although they gave nothing away, she was sure they probably held the same lingering thoughts. They'd been sent to attack their own people.

It was easy to see the possibility. With the city being under Orsembian control for three years and she having all but relinquished claim over it by pursuing peace, those left in the city might have found it natural to serve and defend it alongside the Orsembian garrison.

And now the Puerlato soldiers in my army are wondering if the carnage here is going to spill over into the city itself, she thought. *The very home they're trying to liberate.*

Recha stepped up and took Queve by the arm, squeezing it comfortingly. "I promised you and your men—all of you—will be marching home," she said. "I further add now that I will not turn your homes into slaughterhouses. You'll learn it all in time."

Queve stood a little taller, though the serious frown remained, a soldier's frown who knew nothing was a guarantee in war. "Thank you, La Dama," he said anyway.

"Let's join the general and commandant." She pivoted sideways, like she was leading him now. "Shall we?"

"Of course, La Dama!" Queve snapped to attention, as if suddenly remembering something he had forgotten. He raised his arm, ushering her further. "This way."

They continued in silence. The stomping of heavy boots and creaking wood from another poor staircase the only thing breaking it until they reached the switchback.

"I wish I could move the bombards up more," a man's voice, a young man by its tenor, who Recha didn't recognize, said. "But that's the only spot we can cover the seaport and defend properly."

"That will leave the eastern part uncovered," Hiraldo said in warning. "If the bombards on that side of the city can't fully cover that area, then you might be leaving a corridor for ships to sail in and out of."

Recha and her escort walked up the landing and found Hiraldo standing with his hands behind his back next to another man, presumably Commandant Leyva, who was bent over and looking through a long spyglass propped up on the windowsill. Unlike their soldiers, both men were dressed in their uniforms, which were both equally disheveled from being worn all night.

Queve stomped forward then snapped to attention, the stomps reverberating against the observation room's wooden floors and wooden vaulted ceiling.

"Begging your pardons, sirs!" he announced loudly. "La Dama Mandas has arrived, sirs!"

Hiraldo turned smoothly on his heels. Deep bags hung under his eyes from being awake all night. It was a wonder he was still standing. Meanwhile, Commandant Leyva leapt around, startled and mouth agape.

Recha kept her expression as placid as possible to hide any surprise.

Leyva was young. Reaching as tall as Hiraldo's shoulders, his curly auburn hair and bright brown eyes gave her the impression of a young man fresh off a farm. He even had *freckles* on his cheeks, for Savior's sake, and not a hint of stubble after forcing a night march. Unlike Hiraldo.

"Good morning, La Dama," Hiraldo somberly greeted her with a respectful nod. "Sleep well?"

"It's past noon, General," she replied, approaching them. "And yes, I slept well. Thank you for asking, but I'm afraid I slept too long. I missed too much, and now I'm rushing everywhere to get caught up."

When she stopped in front of them, she glanced at Leyva, expecting a greeting or comment from him. However, he remained silent. Recha watched a trail of sweat run down his face before shooting a glance at Hiraldo.

Hiraldo simply stared back, forcing her to stare harder at him.

Is he so tired he can't introduce the commandant to one of my own armies? She considered ordering to rest, but unfortunately couldn't. They all still had work to do.

"Hiraldo," she said calmly. "Aren't you going to introduce me to your fellow officer?"

Hiraldo took a deep breath, blinking rapidly. "Yes! La Dama, may I introduce"—he gestured to Leyva—"Commandant Leyva, Commandant of the Fourth Army."

Leyva sharply nodded, pressing his chin against his chest before snapping his head back up, like Queve earlier.

"Welcome to Puerlato, Commandant," she said. "My compliments on your swiftness getting here. Was your forced march successful?"

"Yes, La Dama!" Leyva shouted unnecessarily, making Recha wince and her ears ring. "Very successful, La Dama!"

Recha stepped back, rubbing her right ear and working her jaw. "At ease, Commandant"—she waved at him—"at ease. It's too soon after waking for people to be shouting."

Leyva's face went pale. He hung his head then folded his hands behind his back. "Apologies, La Dama," he mumbled.

Recha gave him a small smile but, still rubbing her ear, it probably wasn't as comforting as she thought. "How go the siege preparations?" she asked, wanting to change the subject to dispel the awkwardness.

"Preparations go as schedule," Leyva replied, suddenly perking up. "The general and I were observing the bombards' emplacements just when you arrived."

"Really?" Recha arched an eyebrow then glanced at the spyglass. "May I see?"

"Certainly!" Leyva jumped, excitedly clearing a path to the spyglass.

Recha crookedly smiled, stepping up to the window. His reaction reminded her of a child wanting to show off something they had done to a parent.

The spyglass was mounted on a small tripod, wooden legs fastened to a brass mount for the spyglass to be set in, pointed southward. The windows for this room were long and narrow, probably to give the archers a wide range of fire around and below the corner turret while the slanted ceiling proved protection for arching return fire.

Recha bent over to peer through the glass, and she grinned.

Gone was the morning mist. Now the tall walls of Puerlato stood out bright and clear, along with the top of the city's white belltower. The outlying buildings outside the walls, the surrounding farm fields, and hills around the port city stretched out clear in every detail. Beyond them was the deep blue of the Desryol Sea. She could faintly spy the light-green traces of water from the Laz River mingling with the sea water behind the city.

She easily picked out the hill she'd overheard Hiraldo and Leyva discussing when she had entered. Her banner flew over a hill outside the east side of the city, near the sea. She turned the spyglass, first to the right and then the left, learning how to adjust it until she could see men digging emplacements and trenches around the hill. Already, the bombards of the First Army had been moved up the hill after last night's work.

The glint of metal drew her attention away, making her angle the glass to watch a squad of pikemen march around the perimeter of the hill.

"Has the city garrison tried to fight us for the hill?" she asked. There didn't look like there had been a battle yet—no bodies lying around or being moved like what she had ridden by into the fort but wanted to be sure.

"No," Leyva replied. "They seem content to watch us and keep their gates closed."

"They probably don't want to risk opening the gates," Hiraldo said groggily. "Especially knowing there are a couple companies of calleros stationed around those fields."

Recha glanced up from the spyglass and found the tall man leaning with his back against the long, thin seal, partially against the stone and partially against the wood. His arms were folded, and his head slightly drooped.

"How would they know for certain that we have calleros stationed around fields?" she asked. They were there to be a defensive screen to allow the Fourth Army to set up their positions for the coming siege, meet any counterattack from the city's garrison, and give the other armies time to mobilize. They weren't supposed to expose their own positions.

Hiraldo gave her a reprehensive sideways glance, watching her for a moment.

I've missed something, Recha realized.

"What's happened?"

Hiraldo turned around slowly then bent down to squint out the window, looking for something before he reangled the spyglass. "Some of the defenders of this fort tried to flee during the battle. There's another exit near the stables. Our calleroses had to give away their positions to stop them from reaching the city, and they made a fight out of it."

Recha peered through the spyglass again and grimaced. The riders had gotten down the hill and into a field below, beyond a grove of trees and wagon track. Dead horses lay scattered in the field on their sides with a flock of *alca-viotos*—razorbill gulls—squawking over them.

One large gull had ripped open the stomach of a horse. The tips of its folded, leather wings pointed into the air, along with its long, rigid tail, providing the finely-haired scavenger balance while perched on top of its meal. The beast's bill, with its upward curve and jagged, interlocking, scissor shape, more suited for snatching fish from the surface of the water, now dug and pulled red flesh from the horse's belly.

Recha's stomach rolled, forcing her to look away. She hid behind her hand for a moment so the men wouldn't see her stifling a gag. She cleared her throat to collect herself.

"Were any captured?" she asked.

"Yes," Hiraldo replied. "The commandant of the fort, several capitáns, a couple of adjutants, and a sergeant were the highest ranked. Those who died were mostly their guard, but once they fell, the officers surrendered quick enough. The commandant is the nephew of some Orsembian baron. Sir . . ." He grunted then frowned and squeezed his eyes shut. After a moment, he gave up and shook his head. "I can't remember."

Recha shrugged. "Doesn't matter. They must have gotten spooked, like their compatriots at the river fort, once our bombards opened up." She smirked at the rest of her soldiers, hoping they would join her. "Instead of facing us, they fled as soon as their walls collapsed." She smiled wider, but no one joined her.

"They fled before we breached the walls," Hiraldo added.

Recha blinked rapidly up at him. "What?"

"They fled the fort as our bombards were finding their range."

Recha frowned, turning it over in her head and trying to find a reason for that. "The fort commanders fled *before* the fight? But Capitán Queve was kind enough to report to me the defenders put up a desperate defense until the muskets started firing."

"I'm afraid we don't have a solid answer yet," Hiraldo replied gruffly. "If I was to guess, from the looks of it, it seems like they abandoned their post. Their former commandant, though, has already declared he wishes to speak with you . . . under the Rules of Campaign."

Recha's pondering frown drained away. "Did he?" Her voice sounded cold, even to her own ears.

Hurrying footsteps drew her attention to the stairwell as one of her guards, whom she had left below, rushed up. He slid to a halt the moment he hit the landing, and everyone stared at him. He came to attention smooth enough, breathing heavily.

"La Dama," he panted, "I come to report"—he took a deep breath—"the Viden have arrived. Their leader—a blind priest—is requesting to . . . see you."

Harquis.

His arrival wasn't surprising. In fact, Recha had planned on him being the one Verdas would send. Now that he was here, he could be of use.

"I believe we can settle the question of the fleeing commanders, General," she said, folding her arms. "I saw a soldier dragging a woman to the back of the fort when I arrived, something about all the prisoners were to be gathered there. Is this true?"

"Yes," Hiraldo replied.

"Out in the open?" she inquired further.

"Yes."

Recha harrumphed. "Then let's have a look at them. From on the wall." She turned to the door she assumed led out to the wall.

"Escort the Viden up to join us," she ordered her guard before looking over her shoulder at the rest. "And someone bring up those fleeing commanders. *All* of them. If they want an audience with me"—she grinned—"I suppose I shall oblige them."

~~~

Recha clasped the brim of her hat against the sporadic gusts of wind as she studied the pitiful sight below her. Of the seven-hundred-man garrison, less than two hundred and thirty remained, and it was debatable how many of them would last the week.

They sat huddled in a great mass by the stables, no uniforms or insignias to mark where they had come from or what company they were in. Their clothes were ripped and torn. Many of their sleeves had been stripped off to use for makeshift bandages and slings for their arms and legs. Every face was smeared with soot and dirt, with blood accompanying many. They sat hunched over with heads bowed between their legs.

Defeated.

Just away from them, huddled the fort's servants, women, young men, and some children. Each clasped another as if a gale threatened to swoop in and snatch them away. Every now and then, Recha would catch a glimpse of one of them or a soldier glance up at her then quickly snap away.

They think I'm selecting which ones would make the best sioneroses.

She grimaced to hold in the bile it brought to her throat. She forced herself to look away and spotted one of her guards leading Harquis toward her.

The blind cultist walked with his usual, deliberate pace; his fingertips pressed together in front of him. Gone were the robes. He wore a bright red, high-collar uniform jacket with the pink eye emblazoned across his chest and brass buttons running down the front. Upon the belt of his black trousers hung a war hammer, the head and curved, reversed spike perfect for cracking skulls. He led two other cultists behind him. They, however, only wore black jackets, but that only made the pink eye stand out more and, like their leader, carried war hammers on their belts.

Recha gently elbowed Hiraldo beside her, making him grunt, raise his hung head, and open his eyes. He had taken the reprieve while they waited to nap, but their reprieve was over.

"Look," she whispered, gesturing toward the cultists, "the Viden have come to war with us."

Hiraldo squinted at the sight. "Will they be of any use?"

"For what I plan on using them for," Recha replied, smirking coldly, "yes."

She took several deep breaths then straightened, preparing herself.

Plans or no, Harquis was still unsettling. His milky eyes peered toward her as if he could still see. His expression was placid, making him completely unreadable.

Just behave, she prayed, mentally preparing what she wanted to say. *Stand here, look menacing . . . and don't do anything unless—*

Harquis suddenly stopped mid-step. A deep scowl broke his blank expression as his head slowly turned off to the side, casting downward, as if he were peering into the yard below. Recha tracked his glossy eyes. He was staring at the prisoners.

He noticed them? The hair on the back of Recha's neck stood up, sending a creeping crawl across her scalp.

When she turned back, her guard was looking back at the cultist, frowning with trepidation.

Recha slipped away from Hiraldo and waved the guard away. While his underlings watched her closely, Harquis didn't move as she approached him, stopping only a breath away.

"What do you see?" she whispered.

"Scorched," the cultist growled. "They are a mound of gray, like piles of ash."

Recha's heart began to beat faster. Her breathing quickened. Her mind spun as if a piece of a puzzle she didn't know was missing had suddenly fallen into her hands. The fort's commanders fleeing before the walls fell didn't match the remaining garrison's desperate defense. *Unless they believed it wouldn't be desperate.*

She pressed her lips tightly together to prevent a snarl.

"How many?" she asked, lowly fuming.

Harquis turned his pale eyes upon her and replied, "All of them."

Recha's cheeks started to warm. She ran her hand along the left side of her dress's waist, feeling her small pistol's outline nestled in its special inner pouch, loaded and primed.

"General Galvez!" She snapped around. "Where is—"

Leyva and Queve were leading five well-dressed men from the southwestern turret toward her. The air of nobility hung around them, each walking with their heads in the air, unabashed and unashamed of the travesty that had befallen their post. Rather, what they let happen.

I don't know that for certain, Recha reminded herself.

She got a better look of the lead prisoner behind Queve. He walked with a swagger. His forest green doublet hung open with the slanted, overlapping folds flapping as he walked, clicking the brass buttons together and revealing his white shirt underneath. He was almost Hiraldo's height, but not as broad shouldered. The wind ruffled his curly brown hair and the lace around his doublet's collar sleeves. His crooked smirk made his pointed, square chin jut off to the side. He also saw her and none-too-subtly ran his dark eyes up and down.

Recha patted her secret pouch in her waistline again. *But I'll find out.*

She rejoined Hiraldo, with Harquis and his fellow cultists trailing behind.

"La Dama," Leyva greeted with a sharp head bow before gesturing to the swaggering man behind him, "may I present Sir Pel Mazo, commandant of this fortress.

"Commandant"—Leyva gestured toward her—"Her Excellency, La Dama Recha Mandas, Marquesa of Lazorna."

"A pleasure to make your acquaintance, La Dama," Pel said, bowing with his right hand to his heart. His tone was as brash as his smirk. "I offer my sincerest apologies. If I had known I would be presenting myself to you, I would have requested to surrender my sword to you." He held out his hand to her expectedly.

Recha arched an eyebrow and left it untouched. Instead, she folded her hands behind her back. "You surrendered in battle, Commandant," she replied. "Your sword properly belongs to the commander who defeated you—General Galvez." She gestured with a curt nod at Hiraldo beside her.

Pel coughed, although he quickly recovered, retaining his smirk. He rose from his bow, dropping his hand away. "Please, La Dama, let's dispense with military ranks and speak as the nobility we are. People of quality, such as us, shouldn't be held to such rigid orders as guardsmen."

He ignored the hard looks her soldiers gave him, but Recha wasn't surprised. *The smug fool thinks I view my soldiers the same way he views his*, she mused, seeing an opening.

"Then, do I take it that you wish me to address you as a noble of Orsembar?" she asked. "You and the rest of your staff?" She tilted her head to peer over his shoulder. The rest of the prisoners were perking up, smiles blossoming on their faces as they gave each other encouraging nods. Except one young man in the back. He was looking down at prisoners with a pained grimace on his face.

Recha turned her attention back to Pel, finding him beaming.

"Absolutely!" he replied excitedly. He let out a small laugh and rocked on his heels as if he were about to jump for joy. "I cannot express how honored we are to *finally* speak with someone as clearly cultured and refined as yourself, La Dama." He took a step closer and lowered his voice. "We have been citing the Rules to every officer we've met. Forgive me for saying so, but several of them need to be reminded of the *proper* ways of doing things."

Despite his closeness, his arrogance, and mildly sour breath, Recha struggled not to grin. He had taken the bait.

"General"—she lifted her head up at Hiraldo, who stood stiffly beside her—"you heard him. Sir Mazo wishes to be treated as nobility instead of military officers. That makes them mine."

A light sheen of sweat formed on Hiraldo's face. His feet shifted under him, grinding his heels against the rock. "The prisoners are yours, La Dama," he said, stepping back hastily.

Recha grinned at that. *Now I don't have to worry about what Papa might say. This isn't a military matter anymore.*

A loud *clap* snapped her out of her musings.

"Excellent!" Pel exclaimed, rubbing his hands together and still far too happy for Recha's liking. "Shall we retire and discuss terms, La Dama? Preferably someplace out of the wind with drink." He turned on his heels and joined his fellows, laughing together as if they were at a banquet.

"Actually, Sir Mazo," Recha called back, stepping up to the parapet and gazing out at Puerlato, "I thought we might talk here for a moment. I'm getting used to the view." She let out a small laugh as a light gust tugged on her hat, making her angle her head slightly so as not to lose it.

Her poise must have been alluring to her prisoners because their laughter had stopped, and they were all staring at her.

"It's been so long since I've seen Puerlato. Tell me, who commands the garrison?"

"Why, surely La Dama jests." Pel ran his hands through his hair in a futile attempt to straighten it then buttoned his jacket before stepping up to join her. "My sworn sovereign, Si Don Borbin, bestowed Puerlato to the illustrious Baron Ejarque three years ago. Are you in need of an introduction?" Pel's eyes widened and twinkled. "Or maybe someone to act as a go-between for negotiations?"

"Negotiations?" Recha snickered at his attempt at charm. "What negotiations?"

Pel blinked rapidly. "Why, to come to an understanding before this nasty business grows out of hand," he replied, as if stating the obvious. "Your army performed a marvelous demonstration last night, La Dama, but surely your calleroses have warned you that attacking Puerlato is a hopeless cause."

"Oh really?" Recha feigned ignorance. "Is Baron Ejarque's defenses really that strong?"

Pel scoffed and shrugged. "The garrison is strong enough to answer *any* challenge." His condescending tone made Recha want to rip his tongue out. "Baron Ejarque's calleroses will answer *any* duel and win. Heed my words, La Dama, there is no chance of besting them in such a Bravados."

"Oh." Recha pretended to pout and think.

That was an element of the Rules of Campaign. Before battles were drawn up, calleroses of each side were given a couple of days to challenge each other in front of both armies. To the victor went whatever spoil the calleroses determined on their own. It was meant be a boon to the morale of the victor's side and a blow to the loser's. All while their marquéses bargained with each other out of sight. A waste of time and blood.

"Then perhaps we'll just skip formal challenges"—Recha shrugged—"and just attack."

Pel gawked at her. "You can't . . ." he stuttered, as if too flabbergasted to complete his thoughts. "With the *deepest* respect, La Dama, you *know* you can't do that."

"Why not?"

"Because the Rules—"

"Or, how about we just besiege the city until this Baron Ejarque comes out to fight or gives up?" Recha smiled, enjoying Pel's face growing paler and paler as she teased.

"La Dama"—Pel coughed then turned a growl into a struggling laugh—"please. We realize you haven't been on campaign for three years, but still"—he smiled, but his cheeks were tense, the corners of his lips twitching—"this is not how things are done."

Recha let the silence hang in the air. The satisfaction of his once boisterous attitude struggling to remain intact was too delicious to end prematurely.

"You're right," she relented.

Pel and the rest of his fellow Orsembians sighed, but she wasn't done.

"I am a little rusty on the Rules. Tell me"—she took a step closer to him and lowered her voice—"which part of the Rules allows for a commander to abandon his post and his soldiers just as a battle starts?"

Pel blankly stared at her. "What?"

"That's what General Galvez reported to me." Recha gestured toward the dead horses, still being fought over by the *alca-viotos* in the fields. "He said that's where my calleroses caught you, fleeing the fort just when the first bombards struck the walls. The battle hadn't even begun then. Which part of the Rules is that?"

Pel snickered then drew himself up, his smug air returning. "La Dama, the Rules don't mention things like that, or care. They understand that the noblest among us must look out for what's best in all situations."

"And it was best that all of you leave your soldiers behind while you fled?"

"Of course! Look at this place." Pel gestured at the inner fort with his chin. "This crumbling-down, pile of rocks is hardly fit for people such as we."

A couple of Pel's fellows grunted and nodded in agreement.

"But what about your men?" Recha gestured to the prisoners below. Many had noticed their conversation. Grim-covered and bloodied faces gazed up at them with bleak expressions and slumped shoulders.

"What about them?" Pel scoffed.

"They fought bravely for you." She watched him intently from under the brim of her hat, wanting to catch every moment of his next reaction. "Surely that must mean something."

Pel simply shrugged. "They fulfilled their purpose. They are soldiers after— Ah!" He held up a finger, that beaming light returning to his eyes. "If you're wondering if they can be included in our negotiations, I assure you, La Dama, any number of them would make excellent *sioneroses*."

Recha jerked her head up, making the bold Orsembian step back. The excitement left his eyes as his brow furled and cheeks twitched in a mixture of confusion and surprise. His reaction made Reach realize her smile had slipped and she now glared at him.

She turned away, hiding her face under the brim of her hat to collect herself. Everything inside of her wanted to order her guards to drag these wastrels out of her sight and give them to Sevesco for questioning. Yet, when she caught sight of Harquis, his face a blazing red, on the verge of becoming purple, from his deep scowl and his white eyes fixed on Pel behind her, she got another urge.

"One more question, sir," she said, tilting her head to watch him out of the corner of her eye. He had gone to whisper to his fellow prisoners, each of them sharing the same confusion as he had moments before. "My soldiers reported your men fought bravely after you departed. Even after the breach fell to my pikes and swords, and the gates were thrown open, they didn't surrender until we raked them with musket shot. I find it baffling why you would leave when you had such brave soldiers."

"La Dama," Pel began with a sigh, as if suddenly tired, "while your comments about our soldiers are very flattering, it still doesn't change the fact that this position was just . . . impossible to hold." He shrugged then stepped forward a few paces. "The Rules are clear that, in such times, we of quality should look after ourselves, for the good of our marcs. The soldiers did their duty, fighting so long as they could. And if we had reached Puerlato, I would have sent reinforcements as I promised, but"—he shrugged—"that was doubtful."

Recha gripped her waistline, squeezing her hidden pistol, her fingernails dragging against her dress's fabric. "You promised your men reinforcements?"

"Yes." Pel hesitantly chuckled. "But—"

"But you didn't have faith in your men to hold out," she finished for him. "You weren't planning on coming back with reinforcements. You just left. *All* of you did. And left your men with false hope to give you more time."

"Now, La Dama, please." Pel waved her accusations away. The corners of his cheeks were twitching again, the smile clearly strained. "The Rules clearly allow—"

"The Rules of Campaign are *dead*," Recha stated coldly, turning her head to glare at him. "And what you did to your men was abandonment. You betrayed them!"

"Now really, La Dama!" Pel loudly protested. "This has gone on quite far—"

Crunch!

The crunch of a flat, metal head splintering the side of the Orsembian noble's skull was as sickening as it was satisfying.

The conceited sir had been fixated on only those he believed his equals, so he hadn't noticed the cultist's calm approach until Harquis had struck, swinging his hammer across Pel's face and sending him spinning off the wall and falling into the fort's yard below. The body landed with a *splat*, followed by the women prisoners screaming and surrendered soldiers breaking out into shocked shouting.

"How dare you?" one of Pel's fellows bellowed, storming up to Harquis.

Before anyone could react, Harquis reversed his grip and brought the spike end of his hammer down on the man, embedding it into the man's forehead. The man's jaw instantly went slack as his eyes rolled up and blood poured from his caved-in cranium.

He's going to kill them all! Recha realized.

"Stop him!" she ordered, pointing at the deranged cultist.

Queve's men leaped, grabbing Harquis by the arms then dragging him against the parapet. His guard stepped to come to their leader's aid, but Recha's guards blocked them.

"Take those men away!" Recha ordered to the rest of her guard. "Take them to camp then wake up Capitán Sevesco. Tell him I want everything they know about Puerlato's garrison, and if they don't talk, give them to the Viden."

The remaining nobles were still in shock as her guards ushered them away. Their world being torn away in seconds left them too stunned to cope with the one Recha was replacing it with.

But they'll learn.

She rounded on Harquis, the cultist growling at the soldiers holding him. However, his gaze followed the imprisoned commanders.

She grabbed him by the chin and forced him to face her. "Only *I* tell you when to kill!" she hissed. "And who! Act on your own accord like that again, and I will send you back to your master and our arrangement will be over. I will not have you behaving like a madman in my army." She squeezed his face, digging her fingernails into his skin. "Do you *understand*?"

Harquis's milky eyes bore into her skull as he grimaced back. Recha, though, just kept squeezing.

"As you wish, La Dama," he finally said. "I will await your command. But you of all people should know those wreathed in the blue flames can never be trusted again."

"I said nothing about trusting them." She pulled her hand away, scratching his face. "I just said I decide on when you get to execute them."

Harquis's grimace drained away, and his arms relaxed. However, the soldiers holding him tensed, their eyes flickered nervously between them.

"Return to camp," she ordered Harquis, "and take your men with you. You've spoiled enough of my plans for today."

The cultists left as chillingly calm as they had arrived, her soldiers giving them a wide berth. Recha wanted to rip her hat off and pull her hair out but settled on rubbing her palms together. She couldn't go into a rage in front of her soldiers, not after their first victory.

She stepped around the body of the dead Orsembian and noticed Hiraldo frowning at her with his arms folded.

"What?" she asked, a little harsher than necessary.

"Was that necessary?" he asked.

"They had given up their military privileges, Hiraldo," she reminded him. "As per my agreement with Baltazar, they were mine. And I can do with them as I wish."

"And what about their men?" He nodded down at the yard below. "Whom do they belong to? Should we divide them up, too?"

Recha frowned up at him then looked about and found the remaining men around her—Leyva, Queve and his men, even her remaining guards—either refused to meet her eye or were shuffling their feet.

"Follow me," she ordered then stormed through them, taking purpose-driven strides across the wall.

She kept her pace down the turret, taking the steps two at a time without a care for how unstable they were. Not waiting for her guard to catch up, she threw open the door herself, slamming it against the stone, then charged out into the yard.

Every eye fixed upon her, the prisoners and her soldiers. She passed the frightened fort servants without a glance, heading to stand in front of the soldiers, with their dead, former commandant behind her.

Every man was on his feet. The bleak expressions were gone, replaced with wide-eyed trepidation. The second she met one of their eyes, they would quickly look away. Recha waited for the rest of her entourage to join her before putting her fists on her hips and addressing them.

"*I* am La Dama Recha Mandas! Marquesa of Lazorna!" Her voice reverberated around the yard and off the stones.

A rumbling murmur rolled through the crowd but quickly died down.

"And in my name, I promise each and every one of you"—she ran her eyes over them—"that none of you will be *sioneros*."

Some of the prisoners stood straighter while other watched her suspiciously. The weeping women suddenly cut off, and they looked up from their huddled mass.

"All of you who are Puerlato born, step forward!" she ordered.

There was some hesitancy at first. Men passed nervous glances among themselves. A few shook their heads to one another. One man began walking forward for another to grab him by the arm.

Then one stepped out. Then another. The man whose arm had been grabbed pulled away to join his brethren. Many of the keep workers joined them, including most of the women.

Once Recha was satisfied those of Puerlato had identified themselves, she turned to Queve. The capitán and his men were watching her intently. Their rigid postures gave her the image of a rope about to snap.

"We have come to bring Puerlato back into Lazorna," she said loud enough for all of them to hear, "not to make war against its inhabitants. We are all Lazornians! You are all my people." She smiled as comforting as she could, but the people stared at her, flabbergasted and amazed.

"Capitán Queve"—she gestured toward those who had stepped forward—"they are in your custody now. I'm sure, Puerlato born yourself, there is no other man here more deserving to see them quartered and looked after."

Queve stood off to the side. His quivering chin, twitching lips, and glistening eyes cracked the stoic figure he was trying desperately to maintain.

He snatched off his helmet, wet hair sticking up in every direction. "As you command!" he replied, his voice cracking. "La Dama!" He gave her a sharp nod before turning toward his people.

"My fellow Puerlatoians! Well fought!" He gave them a sharp bow, too, and then a broad smile split his face. "What say you to drinks?"

The Puerlato prisoners looked at each other then back at Queve.

The other two swordsmen stepped up beside their capitán, their helmets off and smiles to rival their commanders. More of the First Swords who had gathered in the yard when Recha had begun addressing the prisoners began to laugh.

"Aye!" one prisoner yelled.

Another followed. Then a chorus, followed by more laughter. Queve gestured them away, wrapping his arm around the shoulders of one man as they began exchanging street addresses of where they used to live in the city.

"Bless you!" one of the women praised Recha as she walked by, tears of fear turning to tears of joy. "Savior bless you!"

Recha simply nodded and let the woman dash off with rest.

Her heart thundered in her chest, forcing her to breathe deeply to calm the tingling fire spreading through every nerve in her body. The elation of using her authority to do one act of kindness threatened to overwhelm her.

However, she couldn't let it. She still had work to do.

"As for the remaining workers of the fort!" she yelled, moving on. There was only a handful left—men, probably laborers who had come looking for work. "Once we know for certain who you are and what you did, you will be free to go. You can stay and find work in the camps or move on."

A few mumbled thanks came along with some nods, but the guards made them remain.

Recha turned her attention to the soldiers remaining. A quarter of their number had been from Puerlato, leaving many sulking, longingly to be in their number.

"Soldiers of Orsembar! The Marc of Lazorna is now at war with yours. As prisoners of war, you will remain here until our campaign is over. Commandant Leyva"—she waved for him, and Leyva stepped up beside her—"of the Lazorna Fourth Army will be in command of Puerlato's siege.

"Commandant, you will receive orders to use these men as laborers." She gave him a commanding look. "Treat them fairly."

"Yes, La Dama," Leyva replied with a sharp nod.

"Work well, soldiers of Orsembar," she told the prisoners. "And as I promised, once this campaign is over, you will all be free to go home."

The prisoners looked at her somberly now. They were still uneasy, many thinking about what she had said and done, but none of them said anything.

"I leave them to you, Commandant," Recha said, setting off again, this time not as fast.

She strolled around the keep. Queve and the First Swords had already led the former Puerlato prisoners away, their laughs still echoing in the distance. There were less people clearing stones from the breach now and, out of curiosity, Recha began to scale the few remaining rocks to stand on it.

"La Dama!" Hiraldo called, rushing after her. "Where are you—"

"Go get some rest, Hiraldo," she said from over her shoulder. "You're about to fall over. You can make your report to Baltazar later, but"—she shrugged—"he'll probably agree I saved him a lot of time deciding what to do with those prisoners, even if he grumbles about me skirting the line."

She glanced over her shoulder. Her Companion stared up at her, reaching out but wobbling on his feet. She gave him a soft smile, folding her hands behind her back.

"Go on. You've done enough for one night and day. It's the Third Army's turn."

She looked out through the breach, down at the long column of men below. Companies of pike, swords, and musketeers followed a twisting road around the hill and into a valley westward, marching lockstep to drums.

Recha followed them with her gaze and grinned.

The way into Orsembar was open.

Chapter 14

"I tell you, gentlemen," Maeso cheerfully said, "*now* is the best time to be in the army." The head thief sat between two of his cadre at one of the tables. His plate sat empty in front of him while he propositioned a few other soldiers across the table.

"True," the thief continued, "the past month was torture, all that endless running and marching, and spear jabbing"—he waved his hands in front of him dramatically—"but now is when camp life starts getting good. We're not being drilled as hard *or* as much"—he began counting on his fingers—"we're not being watched after every second of every day, and the best part . . . we are *finally* getting pay." The thief chuckled, elbowing both of his companions beside him to make them chuckle agreeingly with him.

The men across from him didn't join in, though. The man directly across from him was the former fop who begged Master Sergeant Raul he was there by mistake, named Joaq Estavan. He had gone through a bit of a transformation over the past month. He was now bulkier around his shoulders and arms. His wavy hair hung from his head down to his shoulders. He never paused eating his beans, bread, and nearly burned pork as Maeso talked.

To the left of him was a younger man who sat with his arms folded, listening to everything Maeso said. However, every now and then he would glance around, as if looking for a provost guard to wander by.

The last man was on older, balding veteran who watched the bigger men at the ends of the table—Maeso's bodyguards who he had recruited a couple weeks back.

As for Necrem, he watched and listened, sitting on a stool several feet away from the tables, holding a bowl of minced meat stew. He hoped the small, bobbing brown pieces in his bowl were pork, like Joaq's nearly burnt meat, but one could never be certain with what the camp cooks put in their pots unless you watched them. However, he couldn't afford to be choosy. He'd been eating meals like this for ten years now. They were the only kind he could eat.

He sat between a stall and tent, facing the stall with his back to the tent. From out of the corner of his eye, he could watch the tables and kept his ears sharp for approaching footsteps.

Eating had become an added torment to his new routine. Wearing a mask already got everyone's attention, and after his company had learned what was under it, word had spread and more people wanted to see.

He was forced to eat after mostly everyone was done and out of the way, so fewer would notice him. He kept a mask on but slightly lifted and folded in half over his nose, allowing him to lift a spoonful of soup to his mouth and snap his head back to swallow as much of the contents as possible.

He had to be quick, keeping his tongue flat to make sure none of the liquid sloshed between the open cuts in his cheeks and leak out. The technique barely gave him a second to taste the food, but the contents hinted at being salty and watery. Necrem took it for it being a blessing that he couldn't taste the soup fully and settled for it filling his growling belly.

"This is the perfect time for men such as yourselves to branch out into every available opportunity," Maeso said, pointing at each man across from him.

Joaq kept on eating, while the other two remained silent.

Finally, the nervous man to Joaq's left grunted, "What?"

Maeso dropped his arms on the table, rattling the plates and knives. He mumbled something to his cadres beside him, too low for Necrem to hear, but it made the cadres chuckle.

The nervous man's face grew red, and he slammed his hands on the table, leaping to his feet. "I'm not so stupid to get mixed up with the likes of you!" he growled then stormed away.

Necrem watched him leave then looked back to the table just in time to catch Maeso waving the men at the end to sit back down.

They're either going to get themselves hung or flogged, he thought, throwing his head back to swallow another spoonful of soup.

"Well, one prospect gone," Maeso said, his cheerful demeanor sounding slightly strained. "What about—"

"I'm too old for this," the veteran groaned out, shaking his head as he departed.

Maeso was left gawking, but he quickly recovered, smiling at Joaq across from him. "I guess that leaves you, Joaq," the head thief said, folding his arms. "You interested in making camp life a little more interesting? Maybe a little more *profitable*? Or are you too busy shoving food in your mouth?"

Joaq finished his bread, chewing slowly, as if savoring each bite. He sat back then fished out a cloth from the inside of jacket to dab the corners of his mouth, glancing from side to side at the other departing men.

"Why don't you . . . give it up, Maeso?" he retorted before taking a sip from his cup. "If those other two could spot a setup, whether they knew it or not, what makes you think I can't?"

Necrem paused. His spoon dangled halfway to his mouth.

Maeso, as well, sat agape for a second before blinking rapidly. "Come again?"

"There are more ways to steal, my friend," Joaq replied, smirking. "And in more than one circle. But, considering where we all are, I would advise you to keep it small. Anything that requires scapegoats is too big right now." He got up from the table, collected his things, then slightly bent over the table toward Maeso. "Please don't get us all killed."

Still smirking and holding his head up high, he left the table, heading for one of the stalls near Necrem to put his plate and cup away.

Maeso scowled after him. "You know, Joaq," he called, "you might be too smart for your own good!"

Joaq shrugged. "That's been said of me before," he retorted back from over his shoulder. Then he gave Necrem an acknowledging nod as he passed by.

Disgruntled, Maeso gathered up his cadre and left the tables, his two burly bodyguards trailing behind them. Maeso and his three fellows huddled together, whispering and shaking their heads as they left.

Necrem trailed them from out of the corner of his eye, gently swirling his soup with his spoon. He only realized he was holding his breath after they were out of sight and sighed deeply.

"That lot's going to get us all in trouble," he grumbled, turning back to his soup.

"Hopefully, we march out of here before that."

Necrem jumped, his wooden spoon clattering against his bowl as he spun around to find Joaq standing over his shoulder. Remembering his mask was up, he scrambled to unfold it and pull it over the rest of his face.

"You shouldn't take chances," he warned.

"Sorry, Oso," Joaq apologized. "Didn't mean to sneak up on you."

"No, not that," Necrem said, finishing straightening his mask then looked back over his shoulder at the fop. "You should've just said no and left like the other guys. You said too much, and now Maeso may remember that."

"I just wanted the petty scoundrel to leave me alone." Joaq strolled around in front of him and folded his arms. "I'm finally not being made to run around and march in circles from sunup to sundown, I don't want my blissful freedom taken up by whatever schemes him and his ilk are plotting."

Necrem squinted up at the fop. Despite the long hair and changes to his physique, the man still shaved his face every day and meticulously made sure the thin line of hair across his upper lip was perfect. No one in the squad knew where he found the time, but several just joked it was for some camp woman, maybe more.

The way he talked and preened himself gave Necrem another idea, however.

"You're related to a baron family, aren't you?"

Joaq shook his head. "No. Guess again."

Necrem studied him some more. This had been the most he had spoken with the man. Besides the few passing greetings in the mornings, there had been no time for conversation. No talking had been allowed during drills and afterward, and Necrem preferred to be by himself.

Still, he was certain his suspicions were right by the familiar way Joaq spoke and handled himself.

"You're either lying or grew up as one," Necrem said, which made Joaq grunt. "You've also never lived in an army camp before." He turned back to his soup, stirring it before remembering he had covered his face again. He flashed a grimace from not being able to eat in peace, but that pulled on his scars, and he quickly relaxed his face.

The dry grass crackled under Joaq's shoes as he squatted in front of him. His pointed jaw jutted to the side while he squinted at Necrem's face, studying him over his pointed nose. "You must have an interesting story of how you got here yourself," he said, rubbing his thin fingers. "I was a painter. I made portraits for ladies while their husbands went off to campaign. And then painted their husbands in their armor so they could have matching pictures to hang on their mantles and exhibit in their parties.

"To be a great painter"—he wagged a finger—"you need to portray your clients as beautiful as possible and remember your place. Just because you're invited to parties and everyone loves your art, doesn't mean you can make love with a baroness's daughter."

Necrem stared at the man. His confusion over why he was talking to him had soured. "You're lying again," he said. "You'd have been executed if you had done that."

"If mother baroness's men had caught me." Joaq snickered with a shrug. "It's just my luck a conscription squad caught me trying to sneak out of Manosete and took me for a vagrant."

"Rather unlucky," Necrem grunted. He turned back to his soup and waited, wondering if he stared long enough at it, the fop would take the hint or get bored.

"How did you end up here?" Joaq asked instead.

A low groan caught in Necrem's throat. "Couldn't pay the campaign tax."

Joaq frowned, disappointed. "That's rather boring. I'd have thought it would have to do with those scars. No offense."

Necrem squeezed the bowl tighter until the wood gave a small, creaking protest. The soup rippled from his trembling grip, the small bits of meat bobbing under and out of the liquid repeatedly. The frustration boiled into his ears as he stared downward.

"It's always my scars," he grumbled. "Everyone just wants to know about these *damn* scars. As if it matters. As if *any* of this matters. The taxes, the drills, the punishment, the *waiting*, the whole damn . . ." Necrem bit his tongue then took a deep breath through his nose.

He didn't think such a small conversation with a happenstance question would get him riled. Shockingly to him, though, his heart pounded in his chest, drumming in his ears. His hands were wet from some of the soup sloshing out on them. He used the moment to wipe his hands on his trousers to calm down.

"Sorry," he said, glancing hesitantly back at Joaq.

The former painter was staring at him more intently now, as if he found him fascinating, like some of Necrem's metal work he used to do, back when his craftsmanship shined.

"You're a bit of a radical," Joaq whispered, amused, "aren't you?"

Necrem furled his brow. "I'm a blacksmith," he replied, not knowing what a radical was. Saying what he was, though, made him think of home, and his expression softened. "Who's homesick."

Joaq snickered.

"Oso!"

The sound of Master Sergeant Raul's voice sent Joaq leaping to his feet. Necrem, however, couldn't move that fast. He pushed off his legs with a groan, his knees popping as he struggled to stand. They were starting to do that more frequently, along with his back aching and his shoulders constantly needing a stretch from being constantly tense. He just wasn't sure if it was from the demanding exercise or his age.

Master Sergeant Raul marched through the tables toward him, with three provost guards trailing him and Necrem's breastplate in hand.

Necrem rolled his shoulders. A sudden knot formed in the center of his back.

"What is this?" Raul demanded, holding up the breastplate in Necrem's face.

"My . . . breastplate, sir," Necrem hesitantly replied, certain it was a trick question, but not sure what the trick was.

Raul grimaced up at him. "*This* is Si Don's breastplate, Oso," he growled. "The marqués himself graciously bestowed upon you, a fighting man in his army, *and* under the direct command of our illustrious Capitán Gonzel, a worthy plate to keep you alive in his service." He shoved the breastplate further into Necrem's face, the metal brushing against his mask. "Look what you've *done* to it!"

Necrem pulled his head back, squinting at the worn metal. "I've kept it clean, sir." That was about all he could do with it.

"The *strap*, you big oaf!" Raul growled. "You've nearly ripped it off!"

The master sergeant turned the plate, revealing the inside strap on the left side dangling precariously at an angle. The metal clasps that were supposed to hold it in place were bent outward, preventing the leather strap from being fastened tightly.

Necrem flashed a grimace before catching it, to not pull his scars. "It was too tight."

"*Too* tight?" Raul gave the provost guards, who had formed a circle around Necrem and Joaq, an exaggerated look. "Did you hear that? He didn't like how it fitted him, so he defaced Si Don's armor."

The provost guards shuffled closer, their eyes hard set on him while their fists tightly gripped their halberds.

This is bad, Necrem realized.

Raul pressed the breastplate into Necrem's chest. "I warned all of you," he said lowly, "what happens to soldiers who don't take care of their kits."

Necrem glanced at the lashing posts. There hadn't been a punishment demonstration since that entire squad had been decimated. The sight of twenty men being lashed and five others hanged in quick succession had been enough for everyone to mind their manners and tread lightly. Or not get caught. An evening shower had washed the blood away from the ground, but the stains still soaked the posts like lacquer.

"I can fix it," he said.

"Oh?" Raul grunted, arching an eyebrow. "Saved some pay, have you? I'm not sure it will be enough, though."

Necrem had barely spent any of his pay that they had finally started getting a couple of weeks ago, and he only spent some deberes on more salve from the camp doctors. He was sure he had enough. If he didn't, there was another way.

"I'm a smith," he said firmly. "I can fix it."

He held Raul's stare. The mean bastard of a master sergeant's small smile turned to a sour scowl once it became clear Necrem wasn't going to take it back after a few minutes.

"All right, Oso." Raul flung the breastplate into Necrem's hands, making him spill his soup. The bowl and spoon tumbled to the ground, splashing the lukewarm contents down the inside of his trouser legs. "You have until morning inspection. If that strap is still wrenched out of place by then, you and four"—he shot a look at Joaq, sweating quietly off to the side—"others will receive a flogging. Am I clear, soldier?"

Necrem clutched the breastplate. His broad fingers squeezed the metal until he thought he felt it give under his thumbs. His scars started to sting, but he didn't relax his face this time.

"Yes, sir," he replied, his low voice masking the growl in the back of his throat.

"Until morning then." Raul turned on his heels then sauntered away, the provost guards slowly behind him.

Joaq exhaled deeply and slumped his shoulders once the master sergeant was out of sight. He gave Necrem a sympathetic frown. "Sorry about that, Oso," he said. "Do you need any help or—"

"No," Necrem snapped. The undeserved harshness made him wince, sending a biting pain across his left cheek that finally forced him to relax. "I said I can fix it."

He turned away, heading for the southern end of camp and leaving his discarded soup bowl on the ground.

To fix the plate meant he had to go to the one place he had desperately been trying to avoid.

The camp smiths.

~~~

Ringing hammers filled the afternoon air. The familiar, acrid scent of heated earth blended with the musky odor of molten metal and coal smoke hung over the lane of smith tents. A camp this size required dozens of smiths, each making repairs to armor, weapons, wagons, and any other need the army required on any given day.

As Necrem strolled down the lane, looking over the smiths with his breastplate hung over one shoulder, today's need was obvious.

Their shoeing a lot of horses, he noted. He had yet to pass a smith not hammering out a new horseshoe out of a furnace or nailing one into the hoof of a waiting horse.

Besides the smiths and their apprentices, the lane was filled with the horse handlers, each bearing the crest of some baron or calleros on their jackets and wearing odd, floppy hats that tilted to one side of their heads.

The sight of so many horses being shoed at once brought an old instinct Necrem had learned from when he'd been allowed to take his forge on campaign.

The army's preparing to move soon.

He pulled up short as a horse handler led a horse into the beaten lane. The bronze-colored animal snorted in his face as it passed, lightly pulling at its reins.

Finding a smith to fix his breastplate was going to be harder with all these handlers demanding their horses be shoed.

Each smith held a membership with the union, which guaranteed its members places in the campaign's camps, assigned each smith to a camp, and guaranteed a percentage rate for the work the camp needed. That was on top of the individual tasks each smith picked up doing the day-to-day jobs the camp needed. Unless a smith wasn't union member, they weren't permitted on campaign.

The system allowed smiths to work together to ensure each camp was provided a smith and allow the smiths to compete for the small tasks while giving each of them a share of the larger whole. Most of the smiths were preoccupied with the big task of shoeing the army's horses, meaning they were all getting a commission rate.

Necrem knew this meant the small fix to his breastplate was a job most of them either wouldn't have time for or wouldn't want to take over the larger commission of shoeing the calleroses' horses.

Not them. He turned away from a large tent where ten smiths were hammering out shoes, and their apprentices were nailing them on horses as fast as they could. A shingle hung on the stall in front of tent that read, "*Ambrose and Sons Smithing.*"

Too busy.

He walked past one tent where the smith was laughing with a couple calleros while his apprentices were doing the work.

Too vain.

On and on he went, finding some reason not to stop and ask for help. Either they were too busy, there wasn't enough help, or just something about the smith felt off.

The sound of hammers pounding out metal was the most soothing sound Necrem had heard in over a month. He paused every five or so paces to listen to them ring. The smiths unknowingly produced a harmony together that made him want to stand still and listen. Their beat echoed in his head, drawing images of home.

A horse cried and shouts ran out from one stall. The handlers scrambled as a stubborn stud took a disliking to one of the smith apprentices trying to nail a shoe in. It also drove Necrem out of his daydream and sent him back on his search.

He finally wandered down to the end, near the edge of camp. The calleros and their handlers had thinned out several tents back. Most of the smiths here were looking after the horses that drove the wagons for the army's supplies and some for the camp followers. However, Necrem found himself making the same excuses and reasons not to stop for help as before.

Why do I need to ask anyone else for help? he grumbled to himself, his arm trembling from holding up the breastplate. *I'm a smith, too! I can fix this as good as any of them.*

He hung his head, standing in the middle of the lane. His pride threatened to choke him, but it was too big to swallow.

I'm a smith, too.

A high-pitched yelp, followed by metal clanging together and spilling across the ground, brought him out of his self-aggravation.

"Careful, boy!" a crotchety, elderly smith barked at a young lad, barely in his teens, picking himself up from the ground with a box of rectangular, metal plates spilled out on the ground around him. "I don't need any of those!"

"Sorry, *vaectro*!" the boy apologetically replied, hastily bowing his head multiple times, flailing his shaggy, dark hair. He hastily threw himself on the ground and began gathering up the scattered plates.

Necrem's eyebrows drooped, and he frowned at the leather collar around the boy's neck, marking him as *sioneros*.

A former camp follower, he deduced. *Whatever side he was on must have had a terrible campaign.*

Most *sioneros* were former soldiers. The marquéses, the barons, the marshals, they all played the same game. If a battle would be too expensive or costly, the losing side would give land, deberes and, lastly, men to the victor. However, some victors got greedy, and it wasn't so uncommon for the victors to demand a portion of the loser's camp followers, as well.

Necrem had heard stories of camp followers becoming traded as *sioneros* back in the slums outside of Manosete for years, and those had been growing. For the boy struggling to pick up the heavy box of metal, there was no telling how long he'd been one, either.

"Don't be so sorry," the old smith grunted, returning to hammering out a horseshoe on his anvil horn with a crooked wince on his face, as if he was regretful. "Just pay attention next time. And stoke the furnace. Can't have that blowing out."

"Yes, *vaectro!*" the boy replied, rushing farther back into the stall.

"And don't call me *that!*" the smith yelled after him. "Call me boss or whatever, but don't call me your owner." The marquéses had come up with the term *vaectro* for the people they divided up the *sioneroses* to.

The smith raised his hammer, and metal sang as he rounded out the horseshoe more.

The whoosh of the bellows making the small fire in the iron furnace made Necrem look over the smith's stall. It was smaller than the ones he had passed and more open. A canopy of tent stretched out over the furnace with a hole for the exhaust flue.

While the old smith hammered away on his horseshoes, another, larger anvil sat off to the side with tools on a wooden rack behind it.

"Are you lost?" the old smith asked.

Necrem jerked, realizing he had stepped up to smith's stall while looking over the familiar surroundings.

"I'm looking for a smith," he replied, shrugging and making the breastplate's straps rap against the metal.

"So am I." The smith spat out of the side of his mouth between two missing teeth. He was scrawny for a smith, but his bare, spindly arms were all muscle and sinew. "But my fool son had to go marry a camp woman a few days ago, leaving me with a skittish boy and my lonesome. Best you go find another smith." He picked up his hammer and gave the horseshoe another whack.

Necrem took a step back to walk away, but the horseshoe caught his attention. "You've let it set too long," he commented. "If you put it back in the furnace, it'll be easier."

"Blasted kid," the smith grumbled. He sniffed then rubbed his broad nose, wiping the snot away on his leather apron. "If he hadn't've—"

The smith jerked his head, giving Necrem a hard squint. "What do you know of pounding steel?"

Instead of simply answering, Necrem asked, "Why are you making horseshoes with no horses to shoe?"

Unlike the stalls he had passed, and some around them, there was no handler holding a horse for the smith to shoe. It didn't make sense for him to be making horseshoes without a customer.

"Keeping up with demand," the smith begrudgingly replied. "Some of the smiths were running out of shoes, so those of us that were free started chipping

221

in, making the shoes to get the Don's horses ready, and we still get our commission." He leaned forward. "That's what we smiths do. In the union, we look out for our own."

Necrem snickered despite himself. "Too bad someone couldn't have thought ahead and brought extra horseshoes before the campaign."

"If only." The smith shrugged.

Yeah, Necrem tried to not to glower, but the thought persisted. *If only.*

He held up his breastplate, showing the bent clasp on the side. "I need this fixed before morning. The master sergeant said they'll flog me if I don't."

The smith frowned at the clasp then traded glances with his horseshoes and Necrem. "Sorry, friend," he finally said, "but you picked the worst day to get repairs. We're all busy."

Campaign commission over individual jobs. It was a simple rule for smiths to remember which jobs took priority over others.

Necrem hefted the breastplate in his hands. Normally, he would have let that be the end of it. Yet the sight of an entire squad being flogged still hung in his mind—the screams, the wails, the sight of the men's backs shredded. He already had his face to constantly doctor. He didn't need his back ripped up, as well.

The lone anvil and untended tools seemed to call out to him.

"I can do it myself," he said. "How much to borrow the use of your furnace and those tools for an afternoon?" He looked over his breastplate, spotting various dents and remembering it was small on him. It could use some extra work to fit better. "Maybe for tonight, as well?"

The smith arched a thin, gray eyebrow at him. "You think yourself a smith, Broad Shoulders? Just because you're big doesn't mean you know how to work a forge. There's more to shaping metal than frickin' pounding it."

"I am a smith." Necrem drew himself up, straightening his back to its fullest and sticking his chest out.

The older man's crooked grin slid off his face as his eyes trailed him upward.

"And for ten silver deberes, I can prove it." It was all the money he had, all the pay he was able to save between paying the doctors to make more salve for him and a little extra salt that did nothing for the watery soup or gruel he ate.

He fished into his pockets, picking one deber here, another two there. He took off his right boot to drop out two. In camp, one can never be too careful with their money. Once he had all ten, palm-sized coins, he slammed them on the tabletop of the stall.

The old man sat up on his bench, rubbing his scraggly chin while glancing between the deberes and his unfinished horseshoe. "You going to break my tools?" he finally asked.

"No, sir," Necrem promised. "I'm never clumsy with tools, especially another smith's."

The smith scratched under his chin. "They aren't mine. They're my fool son's." His scratching grew more frantic, and he reached back to scratch the back of his head, grimacing. "Fine! Fix your plate or beat it into scrap. Just stay out of my way and don't touch anything else."

Necrem nodded, flung his breastplate back over his shoulder, then hunched over as he lumbered under the stall's low canopy. "Can't have a non-union smith working on union commissions," he mumbled under his breath.

"What was that?" the smith asked while walking around to the furnace.

"Nothing." Necrem tossed the breastplate over the anvil, separating the front plate from back to hang it by the shoulder strap as he pulled up a stool to look over the armor. He'd been wearing the cuirass for over a month, but despite all his inner grumblings over it not fitting right, this was the first time he looked at it like a smith to do something about it.

The wrenched strap twisted at an angle to the side was obvious and would have been a simple fix.

Take the leather strap out, Necrem mentally went through the steps. *Pull out the rivets holding the clasp, then straighten the clasp out before putting it all back together again.*

He reflectively grimaced then relaxed his face. *That would just make it too tight again.*

He thought some more, taking in the entire piece as he searched for a way to fix both problems.

Why have straps clasped under the arms? A simple belt around the waist would be just as good. Better to get in and out of.

He turned to the tools beside him, bouncing his eyes at the different hammers until he found one with prongs on the back of the head. With hammer in hand, he turned the plate over on its side and began taking out all the clasps, starting with the wrenched one, making a pile of metal and leather under the anvil.

That done, he opened the cuirass over his head and slid it on. Necrem poked his head out from the top of the breastplate, bent his chin down as low as he could, and tried to assess the situation. There was room, but the plate was hitting his broad chest and sticking out at an angle.

The chest plate needs more curve, he mentally noted. He fished around to feel where the back plate was. It, too, was at an angle, but not by much. He glanced at the leather straps holding the pieces together. *The shoulder straps need to be longer, too.*

223

He pulled the breastplate off then set to work again, unfastening the shoulder straps to take the cuirass apart.

"You sure you need to be doing that?" the old smith asked.

Necrem paused, halfway through wrenching out the last strap. "Hmm?"

"You're taking it apart," the old man said, pointing at the breastplate. He stood by the furnace with a pair of tongs, holding a horseshoe in the burning coals. "Certain you can put it back together again?"

"If you got to fix something"—Necrem grunted while wrenching the last strap off—"fix it right. There's more that needs fixing than a clasp." He set the back plate beside the sawhorse holding the anvil, tossed the shoulder straps underneath, then went back to studying the front plate.

"If you say so," the old smith said, shaking his head.

Necrem ignored him. Rather, he was drawn back into his own world. He would get lost for hours on end while working in his forge back home. It made those long, all-night jobs easier just to go into his head and focus solely on the work, the feel of his hammer on the metal, eyes watching every strike to make sure it was exact and didn't go too far or break something.

Until Bayona would eventually come bouncing into the forge to fetch him and bring him out of it.

He shoved the memories of his family away. Otherwise, he would never be able to focus.

I need to take the faulds off first.

He eyed the overlapping, horizontal pieces of metal hanging off the bottom of the chest plate like a metal apron. They were supposed to protect his waist and thighs, but his height and the cruisers being too small for him prevented that.

The faulds were another sign of how old the plate was. The calleros weren't wearing them anymore and were starting to favor brigandine armor over full armor suits. For Necrem and his company of forced conscripts, however, old armor was better than nothing.

He wrenched the faulds off their rivets, laying them across the anvil's horn for later. He exchanged his hammers for one more suited to hammering metal then took his chest plate over to the furnace.

The old man had gone back to hammering out his horseshoes, leaving the furnace to him. Necrem set the plate into the coals, making sure the chest had plenty of contact with the heat, then worked the bellows. He could have let the boy do it, but Necrem was too used to doing his work himself.

Time slowed to a crawl in his mind. Working the bellows, heating the metal, hammering out the plate on the anvil, watching its shape, it all ran together. The rings of his hammer blended with the hammers of the other smiths with the hissing of boiling water from hot metal being quenched adding to it.

As he hammered the chest plate, rounding it out more, he beat out the random dents in the metal. He had to repeatedly pause, letting it cool in the air, and estimate his progress. As he did, he concluded he needed to beat down the metal around the shoulders, to the point they were almost flat. It would let the cuirass fit lower on his body and protect his belly and lower sides better.

I'll have to do something different for the shoulder straps. The older straps wouldn't be long enough now.

He hammered out the edges of the plate to keep them from digging into his sides, and finally, after several hours, the front plate finally fit him. His heart thundered in his chest, making it swell against the plate, and his hair stood on end. He hadn't felt the familiar rush of pride in his work in months.

It felt *amazing*!

The feeling drove him on. He wanted to work more. The feeling of a hammer in his hands. The ringing and pings of metal against metal. The sticky embrace of sweat clung to his body as he remeasured and reattached the faulds to the bottom of the front plate, leaving a groove for a belt.

The back plate needed some dents hammered out, the plate around the shoulders stretched out like the front, and the edges around the waist widened. Reattaching the rivets and clasps on the shoulders took time, having him hunched over the anvil, tapping away with a smaller hammer to fasten them to the armor. The shoulder straps came last.

After looking over the leather he had, he knew what he needed but didn't have them.

"Buckles," he mumbled under his breath.

Loud, metallic jingles made him jerk his head up. Two buckles were sliding around the inside of his plates he had left laying on top each other on the anvil.

"Wondering how long it would take you to figure you would need them," the old smith said, carrying his tools toward the back behind the furnace.

"But—"

"Just take 'em," the smith called back. "You're almost done, anyway."

The mixed feeling of pride with wanting to finish his work and the pride of not accepting a handout clashed together. His hands trembled around the leather straps he held. In the end, he went back to work, punching holes in the straps he needed, attaching them to the clasps on the plates, then finally fixing the buckles.

He stood up once both shoulder straps were buckled together then slowly put the cuirass on. For the first time, the breastplate finally fit him. It didn't feel like it was crushing him, and he could breathe. The edges weren't stabbing him and were, instead, neatly overlapped. His entire upper body was protected.

"I'll need to find a belt," he said under his breath.

"Try this one."

A thin, leather belt slapped against his chest then tumbled to the ground. Necrem held the plate against his chest as he bent down, groaning to pick the belt up. He looked up and found the smith smirking with his arms folded.

"I don't have any deberes for it," Necrem said, holding the belt back out.

The old smith spat into the dying coals of the furnace. "We look after our own."

Necrem squeezed the belt tightly, its buckle jingling in his shaking grasp. His face stung from going stiff, pulling his scars, but he couldn't get this body to relax. He stiffly wrapped the belt around his waist, fitting it in the groove he had fashioned for it, then buckled the belt taut.

He stood straight, feeling the plates fit around his body. The red embers of the coals reflected off the front's smooth, round surface.

"You do . . . *damn* good work," the smith said, admiring Necrem's restored breastplate. "You're wasting your talents as a soldier. Want to stick around? I know a few smiths in camp who have some say in the union. Someone like you could be a damn good partner to have." The smith cracked a crooked grin.

"Sorry," Necrem replied, hanging his head. "But that's . . . that can't happen."

The old smith grunted, confused.

Trumpets blared from the center of camp, followed swiftly by drums beating to assembly. Necrem looked out from under the tent and discovered the Easterly Sun had set, possibly hours ago, and he hadn't notice. Calleroses in armor thundered down the lane, heading toward town.

"They're breaking camp," Necrem said. He put the tools he used back on the rack. "Thank you for the use of your forge." He hunched his head to step out of the stall's tent.

"Wait!" the smith called after him. "What's your name?"

Necrem paused. Stalls were beginning to be broken down around him and people were rushing to tents. The provost guards would soon be around, directing the madness, and once they saw him in armor, they would order him to his company. That worried Necrem most, though, was having the old smith look up his name with the union.

We're about to march off to wherever, he told himself. *What more can be done to me?*

"Oso," he said loudly through his mask and over his shoulder. "Necrem Oso. I was a smith. Once. Thanks again."

He gave a wave then headed into camp, back to his scrambling company. His shoulders slumped lower and lower from the growing weight of leaving the bliss of the forge with each step.

Chapter 15

14th of Andril, 1019 N.F (e.y.)

"*Faster*, you sluggish dogs!" Capitán Gonzel yelled from his horse. "Don Givanzo wants a glorious victory to bring to his father, and you, my thieving company, are going to deliver it!"

Every step the capitán's horse took made the grizzled, old officer bounce in his saddle. His armor was decades old, the feather plume of his helmet had lost most of its color years ago, though both were scrubbed to a shine. The rotund chest plate made him look fatter than he was, and the cheek guards on his helmet did him little favors—squishing his face and scraggily beard out. He also rode with a fist propped on his hip while shouting at them, making him look more ridiculous.

We're not going to fight, Necrem thought sluggishly. His inner thoughts matched his body's exhaustion. *We're just going to stand around while the calleroses prance about, yell at each other, and the Don or whoever either makes the Lazornians go away or sell us out.*

Necrem knew their game. Ten years banned from the campaigns couldn't take away that knowledge.

Capitán Gonzel kicked his horse to gallop up to Master Sergeant Raul at the head of their company's column but yelled loud enough for those several rows back to hear. "Push them, Master Sergeant! Speed up those drums! The Don wants us at Puerlato three days ago! Flog any man who can't keep up! We're going to whip those Lazornian cowards and remind their sniveling little bitch of a marquesa of her place!"

"Yes, Capitán!" Raul barked, lifting his halberd up in the air. "Company, quick march!"

Necrem joined the men around him in a shared groan as the drummer sped up the pace of their taps. Fortunately for them, their groans were swallowed up under their stomping feet.

"I can't . . . keep . . . running and stopping," a soldier complained behind Necrem.

"Fall out and . . . see what happens," another growled.

"I hate young commanders," Maeso grumbled somewhere to Necrem's left. "They're always in a hurry for nothing." He suddenly burst into a coughing fit.

Necrem's legs burned within the first few quicken steps. His knees strained to keep the jogging pace, popping randomly and making him grit his teeth. He didn't know why, but the quick pace between leisurely marching and running was the worse. Either it was because he couldn't stretch his legs fully, keeping them tense and measured while also keeping pace with the men around him, or the growing demands from his burning lungs to stop, double over, and gasp for air.

"Keep . . . your head up, Oso," Hezet panted beside him. The seasoned veteran trudged along as if born into his worn armor. "You'll collapse if you don't get enough air."

Necrem hadn't realized his head was starting to hang. It wobbled as he raised it, and he suddenly felt woozy. The weight of his tight-fitting helmet bearing down on him made him want to look down again. His vision blurred for an instant, forcing him to suck in as much air as he could through his mask's holes, but it was never enough.

"I need to stop," he wheezed out. His sweaty grip on his spear started to slip, and he nearly stumbled trying not to fumble it.

Hezet suddenly seized his left arm, attempting to hold him under the arm, but Necrem's height prevented it. "Keep going, Blacksmith," he urged. "We can't have you getting flogged . . . and I need you to fix my armor for me."

Necrem snorted. When he had returned to his company the night before they had marched out, Raul had seen his refashioned armor and grilled him with questions, stopping short of accusing him of stealing another breastplate. If it hadn't been for the urgency of breaking camp and the capitán's arrival, Necrem was sure he would have gotten around to it and had him flogged, anyway.

For the rest of his squad, most minded their business, wanting to avoid the sergeants in case they came searching for examples to be flogged along with him. Hezet and the other veterans, though, had become especially interested in

Necrem's work once they were on the march, and Hezet hadn't been the first to joke or ask him to fix or make new armor for them.

This march was too tiring to think about forging, though, even if he could after they made camp.

The Easterly Sun bore down on them oppressively. The clouds of dust hung over the road and columns were choking. Men coughed and spat, but Necrem's mask protected him from it. His eyes teared up from little grits getting into the corners of his eyes and sweat running down his forehead from under his helmet.

Suddenly, the men in front of him pulled up and slowed down. The drumming tried to keep the pace, but the taps eventually lost their rhythm.

"What's going on?" someone coughed out then spat behind him.

Being a head taller than everyone, Necrem peered ahead. He squinted against the shimmering haze created by Easterly Sun's rays bouncing off the columns of helmets and spear points ahead of them.

"We ran into the back of another company," he replied. He could see Capitán Gonzel at the head of their column, yelling at the rear of the other, but they weren't speeding up. "The capitán's yelling at them"—he took a deep breath, his shoulders rising and falling—"but they don't seem to be in a hurry."

"Savior bless them," Hezet gasped, breathing heavily.

Approving grunts, gasps, and nods followed, but the hot, grueling march continued.

~~~

"First squad!" Raul yelled, waving his halberd in the air. "Make camp here!"

Necrem staggered down the shrub- and fern-covered slope of the ridge the Don, or whoever was driving the army, had decided to make camp, just a few miles from the Compuert Road Junction. He would have been willing to lay down on the side of the road and sleep for days, and he was sure most in his company would agree with him.

The Easterly Sun was fading fast below the horizon, its fading rays casting a red glow across the drifting clouds.

"You five!" Raul shouted, pointing at five men. "Make fires! The rest of you, bunk down, eat something, and rest. We got more marching to do tomorrow."

"You five!" He pointed at five others. Fortunately, Necrem wasn't among them. "Come with me. The capitán's tent needs setting up."

The unfortunate five stifled exhausted groans while stacking their spears together then piling their armor and belongings beside their weapons before trudging after the master sergeant. Necrem had been selected once for that duty and had discovered the capitán was a ruthless, unsatisfiable ass when it came to having his tent prepared.

In the last rays of sunlight, Necrem found a patch of ground beside some ferns without any rocks he could find with his boot, laid his spear and bag of meager possessions off to side, then unceremoniously sat down. He sighed loudly, slumping forward. His feet pulsed in his boots, but he didn't dare take them off, or his armor. He worried if he did, his aching body would fall apart.

"You need water," Hezet said.

Necrem raised his head lazily, finding the veteran fishing out his water bag from his pack, his spear probably mounted with the others.

"I'm too tired to eat or drink," he said, shaking his head before pulling his helmet off then tossing it aside on top of his bag. "I'm afraid"—he wipe his forehead and face on his sleeve to stop the long trails of sweat running into his eyes and making them sting—"I'll peel more of my face off if I take my mask off."

"If you don't, you'll pass out tomorrow," Hezet replied, holding the water skin down to him. "Or worse, you may not wake up in the morning."

Necrem swallowed, his mouth and throat suddenly unbearably dry. He flashed glances at the other members of his squad working or resting behind Hezet. "Can you . . . turn around, please?" he shyly asked, taking the water skin.

Hezet nodded then about-faced, folding his hands behind his back and blocking Necrem from the others.

Necrem set the water skin down between his legs then reached behind him. He untied his mask's knot then gently began to pull it away. It was one of his cloth masks. They let him breathe easier than the leather ones, which all had cracks in them now. The cloth didn't fall away but remained stubbornly stuck to his face.

He had to peel it, just as he feared.

Bit by bit, the sticky, sweat-drenched cloth came loose. Every crack, split, and dangling piece of scarred flesh either hung or clung to it. A stinging spike shot through his face with every snag, only to intensify by a burning sensation by his damp, deformed features finally feeling fresh air again after the long day's march.

By the time he had half the mask off, Necrem was doubled over on his side, biting his tongue and clenching his eyes and jaw so as not to yell. The mask at last came free but pulled some of his lower, dangling lip with it, making him yelp despite his best efforts. He crushed the mask in his fist then punched the ground in his last-ditch effort not to shout or growl, bottling his pain and anger deeper within himself.

"Is he well?" a young voice asked.

Necrem peered through tear-shot eyes to see one of the boys in the squad, Ezro, curiously glancing around Hezet. The evening light was fading fast, and although Necrem could only make out shapes of men moving in the distance, he shielded his face with his hand, anyway.

"He's fine, boy," Hezet replied, stepping more between them. "Go on about your duties. The master sergeant wants those fires made and won't take kindly if they're not started by the time he comes back."

Ezro shifted his feet. "Yes, sir," he replied before leaving solemnly.

Once the boy was gone, Hezet peered back at him from over his shoulder. "*Are* you well?"

Necrem kept his hand up, covering his face. Everything inside him screamed to get it salved and masked again. After the day's long, hot march, breathing the sweet air without any fabric was too good to cut short.

"I haven't been *well* for years." His exhausted reply was more honest than he would usually give. He chalked it up to being tired as he reached for the water skin.

He paused while twisting the skin's cork. He glanced at his own skin, laying under his kit, only to remember it was nothing more than a deflated bag. He had drained, or rather spilled it on himself, at noon when they had finally been allowed to rest.

His parched throat beckoned for water. He pulled the cork off with a loud *pop*, maneuvered the sloshing bag the best he could as he lifted it to his lips, then tilted his head back. The water rushed out faster than he had anticipated. He gulped down as much as he could, but half of it squirted out of the holes in his cheeks, raining down on his armor and running down his neck. Yet the soothing amount he did catch forced his eyes closed and made him drink more.

When he finally pulled the skin from his lips, the bag sagged limply in his hands, nearly three-quarters of its contents drained and half of that spilled across his face and the front and under his armor.

Hezet was watching him, frowning deeply from over his shoulder.

Necrem apologetically held the bag up to him while keeping his head and face down. "Sorry," he wheezed out, licking his sliced lips. "But thank you."

"Keep it," Hezet replied. "Tend to your needs. Then"—he gestured toward the nearest fire—"come eat with us. Don't lay down and go to sleep in your armor. Your back will be killing you tomorrow if you do."

"But . . ." Necrem threw his head up, but Hezet was already moving away, taking off his armor and joining the others.

More fires were sprouting up, filling the air with dense smoke from the shrub and fern leaves that had been used to start them, leaving the men scrambling for wood to keep them burning. The night's coming blackness was being beaten back across the ridge, up the slope, and across the road, outlining their stretched-out camp. The biggest fires came from the center where the Don and the rest of the commanders were likely camping, right on the road.

Necrem sat up on his knees then took his armor off. The new belt and work made it easy to slip on and off now. That done, he turned his back on the light to salve and cover his face out of anyone's prying eyes.

As he spread the oily, fat salve across his flaking scars, he spotted the calleroses' horses grazing down the ridge. Beyond them, dense trees sprouted where the ridge leveled off and were already claimed by the night. A cool breeze rushed up from them as Necrem tied on a fresh mask, making him shiver in his damp clothes.

Maybe sitting next to a fire for a little bit isn't such a bad idea, he reckoned, grunting from pushing himself to his feet. He turned to join the others, the cool breeze still at his back.

Somewhere down below, a horse neighed and snorted.

~~~

"What is a battle like?" young Stefan shyly asked.

The other men sitting around the small fire shifted their weight. A small lull hung over them and the rest of the squad around their respective fires. Some munched on whatever food was available; dried jerky mostly. Some smoked on long-stemmed pipes, adding the nauseous fumes to the curling wood smoke being pulled away by the lingering breeze. The rest just sat. The shared exhaustion of the march with the added bliss of just sitting and resting in peace had been too precious to break.

Until their youngest member dragged up the courage to ask the question that lingered in the backs of everyone's mind, Necrem's included.

"Depends," Hezet reliably replied. "Not every battle's the same." He nodded to the veteran sitting beside him, Enriq.

Enriq nodded back. "And not all of them can be considered battles, either." He chuckled, showing his crooked teeth and making his puckered scar that ran from the outside corner of his right eye down his cheek shake.

Stefan frowned. "What's that supposed to mean?" The lad shifted his legs around in front of him then wrapped his arms around his knees, pulling them closer.

"Just follow your orders, son," Enriq replied with a wave. "No matter what, just follow your orders."

"Besides"—Hezet ripped off a piece of jerky with his teeth and talked around chewing it—"there might not even be a battle."

"*Really?*" Joaq piped up, springing his hung head up and startling those around him who had believed he was asleep. "Because the capitán sounded very adamant that the Don is *eager* to send us to either a glorious victory or a glorious demise for days now."

Necrem joined in with the rest around the fire to stare at the downtrodden artist; some out of confusion, others just blankly. Necrem was more of the latter.

"See here," Hezet said to Stefan, "no matter what the capitán, or *others*"— he gave Joaq a hard, sideways look—"say, campaigns follow a rhythm. Once we reach Puerlato, the commanders will probably order us into formation and wait for the Lazornians to meet us. The Don and the barons will ride out to meet whoever is leading the Lazornians, they will parley, and then the Rules will be set."

"Got to give the calleroses each a chance to shine," Enriq snickered.

A few others listening in chuckled with him.

"It's tradition that the calleroses get an opportunity to duel the opposing side's calleroses," Hezet explained. "The Bravados. There will be jousting, dueling, name calling."

Enriq spat into the fire, making it hiss. "That's supposed to be our job."

"We duel, too?" Stefan asked.

Men around him laughed.

"*No*," Enriq teased. "We get to draw lots to see which lucky company gets to form up on the battle lines each day and cheer on our brave calleroses." He raised a water skin, as if to toast before taking a swig. "As if not one of those smug pricks wouldn't run us down if we got in their way."

"Here, here," someone else said at a neighboring fire.

Enriq clumsily raised the water skin to them.

"The idea," Hezet dryly said, "is to damage the other side's morale without risking us soldiers."

"Hmm." Enriq nodded. "Because our morale certainly can't be damaged any further."

More men laughed at that. Snide barks followed by pats on shoulders. Necrem lowly chuckled with them, watching the flames in the small fire dance.

"All that matters is size," he said.

The laughter around their fire died down. While the laughs lingered around the other fires nearby, the men all around turned to him.

"Thought you never been on campaign before, Oso," Enriq said, lifting an eyebrow inquisitively at him.

Necrem held his gaze over the flames. He rubbed his knuckles, part of him wishing he hadn't spoken. Yet again, the day's exhaustion had made it easy not to keep his tongue.

"Not from here," he replied, "but you can watch as a camp smith and still see how campaigns are led. The only thing that matters is how big we are compared to the Lazornians. If we're bigger, then the calleroses get to prance around and we cheer in the hot Easterly Sun. If not . . ."

The breeze picked *that* moment to stir again, making the campfire's flames wither and ripple, its chill biting into his back.

"Just hope we are." He clenched his broad hands together, his eyes drawn again to the fire.

Being a smith in those days had come with the benefit of knowing he would never be selected as a *sioneros*. He'd been too valuable. He had seen others who weren't, and on campaigns that fell on the losing end. Old memories of men scrambling through the camp, seeking for a way out, a place to hide, or a farewell kiss to an ill-thought-out marriage to a camp woman the night prior, before the provost guards hunted them down for delivery. Those memories were over a decade old, some even older, but one could never forget the sound of a man begging for his life, or to stay with their loved ones.

He stared deeper into the flames, and their dancing seemed to take shape. He saw Eulalia, young, beautiful, and whole, as she was always meant to be, holding out her hand to him. She held Bayona close to her, stroking her long hair as his little miracle buried her face into her mama.

"*Oso!*" Someone shook him by the shoulder.

Necrem blinked tears. His vision suddenly cleared, revealing he was reaching out toward the fire. His hand was shaking. His face burned under his mask from how tense he was, the fresh salve preventing his scars from pulling.

He pulled his hand away and folded his arms. He hunched his shoulders from everyone still staring at him. "Sorry."

"You all right?" Hezet asked.

Necrem shook his head and sighed out, "I'm tired." With that, he painstakingly struggled to his feet. The back of his legs trembled and stretched, desperate to pull him back down. The soles of his feet throbbed under the weight.

The others, thankfully, let him leave in peace, limping back to his belongings to get his bedroll laid out. He could still feel their stares on his back, though.

"*Anyway,*" Enriq said, picking up the conversation. "The only thing you younger lads need to worry about is the calleroses are going to expect us to shout curses at the other side while they fight. So, keep your mouths shut if you can't swear worth a damn; otherwise, the rest of us are going to make fun at you for the rest of the campaign."

More laughs followed behind him, but Necrem was too focused on getting to sleep. He took off his boots to dry them and his feet out. He would have to check for snakes in the morning, but it was better to march in dry boots for half of the day at least.

A horse snorted farther down the ridge.

He squinted out in the darkness but couldn't see them.

Horses don't like this anymore than we do.

He unrolled his bedroll, smoothed it out, making doubly sure there were no hidden rocks, and then lay down on his back. He stared up at the blinking stars, winking in and out between the roaming clouds. His chest rose and fell, his breathing hissed through his mask's holes. Within a few moments, his eyelids drifted closed into a dark, exhausted sleep.

~~~

Eruptions split through the darkness!

Sporadic cracks echoed through the night like distant thunder.

When Necrem jerked awake, only the stars glittered down at him from above.

"What's going—"

More distant eruptions cut off whoever was yelling.

Did that come from up the road?

Groggy, Necrem couldn't tell for sure. He braced his arms under him then pushed up. Every muscle from the back of his neck, across the back of his shoulders, down his lower back, and through his legs spasmed and stretched. A deep groan, almost a bellow, erupted from deep within his gut as he sat up.

"What the *shit* is going on?" someone yelled as more eruptions, this time north of them and over the road on the other side of camp, ripped through the night.

Necrem blinked and rubbed the sleep out of his eyes, but when he looked, he couldn't see anything clearly in the dark. The campfires were all dim, the ones around them were faintly, glowing coals, and the larger ones deeper into camp only illuminated the tents nearby. What he couldn't see, however, he could hear.

Screams and panicked cries drifted down the ridge, adding to the confusion of those around him.

"Something's wrong," Hezet stated.

"No shit," someone snapped back.

"Where're the sergeants?" another soldier nervously asked. "What do we do?"

Uncertain grumbles answered, followed by more distant screams. Men were starting to get up from their bedrolls, their shapes forming shadows in the small light. Some stood stretching and looking about in place while others wandered about aimlessly.

More screams echoed through the night. They sent chills through Necrem's heart and made him turn west, staring wide-eyed, desperate to make out anything. Those had been women screams.

The baggage train? he fumbled for reasons but always came back to one. *Are we . . . under attack?*

It didn't make sense. No one attacked at night. It was against the Rules. Yet, he could think of no other reason why people were screaming and yelling across the camp or for those eruptions.

He rolled over on his side for his boots—no matter what it was, he was going to need them—and started fumbling in the dark to slip them on. In his hurry, he didn't bother with socks or wrapping his heels to prevent any more blisters; he just fought with the tight leather to get them on.

A trumpet blared alarm into the night.

Three notes in, the sound sputtered out.

"That can't be good," someone, sounding like Maeso, said.

"Do you guys feel that?" someone, sounding like Enriq, asked.

Necrem paused, his right boot halfway on and his left still hanging off his toes. The men around him fell into a hush, ignoring the growing yells and another clap of eruptions, this time from up the road. He sat there for a moment, and then he felt it.

Under him.

The ground's . . . shaking?

"What are lazy bastards *doing*?" Master Sergeant Raul rushed out among them and leaped over the remains of a campfire, half-dressed and waving his halberd in the air. "Get up, men!" he roared. "The camp is—"

The neighs and screams of horses swallowed his order, and up and down the line of strung-out camps, men were swallowed under the horses' hooves.

Necrem barely missed a galloping nag riding up behind him. He rolled at the last minute to the side of the thick patch of ferns and brush to his left. He lay on his belly and wrapped his arms around his head to protect against the beasts storming around him. The cries of the horses hitting or brushing the thorns of the brush as they charged past couldn't be blocked out.

Nor could the terrified yells of men being trampled around him.

The horses were stampeded.

Necrem panted through his mask, every effort to calm down eluded him. *That means—*

"*Calleros!*"

Underneath the crashing hooves and men crying in pain, there were whoops and angry yells.

Necrem risked a look, unwrapping his head then peeking out to survey the carnage. Most of the horses had stampeded past and deeper into camp. Somehow, more fuel must have fallen or were tossed on the campfires because several were burning brighter now, although others were completely out farther down the line.

In those fires were horse riders, calleroses, riding up and down the line, either waving swords in the air or bearing lances down on fleeing silhouettes.

"Get up, you *cowards*!" Capitán Gonzel demanded.

Necrem rolled around. He didn't recall when or how the capitán had gotten to them through the stampede. He wore half his armor, missing his helmet, yet with sword in hand.

"Fight, you dogs!" The capitán kicked the man crawling on the ground in front of him.

The man yelped in a high-pitched voice and folded in on himself.

The capitán reached down, taking the man by the shirt and pulling him up, snarling at him. The firelight revealed young Stefan's terror-stricken face staring wide-eyed up at the old man.

"Get up or I will kill you my—"

Galloping hooves were their only warning. The capitán dropped Stefan and spun about.

The calleros charging out of the night slashed Gonzel across the face. The upward cut twisted the old capitán into an odd angle, and dark blood followed the blade into the air. Gonzel's body bounced off the side of the horse, sending him rolling over Stefan in a crashing heap. Young Stefan curled back in on himself, tightly wrapping his arms around his legs and screaming and sobbing into his lap.

Screaming like that could bring more calleroses on us!

Necrem caught the shapes of men leaping up from where they'd been hiding and scattering in every direction; some toward camp, others out into the darkness. Stefan, though, kept sobbing.

Help him. I should—

He began to crawl toward the boy when a wail came from his right. Master Sergeant Raul ran into the firelight, dragging his halberd along the ground to collapse beside Gonzel's body.

"Capitán?" Raul yelled, shaking Gonzel's body. He heaved and rolled the capitán over, the armor plates grinding against each other, and then he cradled the old officer's head. "*Capitán!*" His hand came away from the capitán's ruined face, trembling in the air.

Crawling closer to Stefan and keeping an eye out for more calleros charging through the night, Necrem saw Raul's face twist from fear, to horror, to soul crushing sorrow as he stared wide-eyed at his blood-soaked hand.

Now that he was closer, Necrem got a better look at Gonzel's wound. The calleros's sword had sliced through his left side of his face at an angle, catching and splitting a wide, bleeding gash in the side of his neck.

"*No!*" Raul wailed. "Why didn't you get up?"

Stefan hunkered lower, visibly shaking.

"Why didn't any of you fight?" Raul demanded, but more into the night than at Stefan.

"Whatever you say, Raul."

Maeso slinked into the light, crouching and stepping lightly on the balls of his feet. The thief yanked Raul's head back by his hair then slid a knife across the master sergeant's neck.

Raul dropped Gonzel's body to clutch his throat, gargling and coughing as his own blood poured between his fingers to mix with his fallen capitán's.

Maeso shoved Raul aside and began frisking his clothes before he was dead. *Once a thief, always a thief,* Necrem recited, unsure of what to do.

Part of him told him to crawl away. Desperate times like this made men like Maeso even more dangerous. The night was getting brighter, however, and when he looked toward the center of camp, he spotted the reason. Tents were being set on fire.

The enemy was inside the camp.

Got to get out of here.

He moved to crawl back the way he had come, but the sound of growling stopped him. He looked back to find Maeso had moved on to stripping Gonzel. The thief held the capitán's legs up then flung them aside in frustration. He looked around—

Then he spotted Stefan.

The thief looked the boy over then said, "I'm going to need your boots." Maeso reached down to grab Stefan, knife blade pointing downward.

Necrem acted before thinking, pushing himself to his feet and lunging forward. He ignored his popping knees and the rock his left heel had struck because his boot had been flung off when he'd rolled to avoid the stampeding horses. He charged, taking four great strides. His hands balled into fists. He swung just as Maeso's head jerked up.

Smack!

Necrem's right uppercut slammed into the thief's gaping mouth. He felt his jaw crunch against his knuckles. Maeso's head snapped back, his feet left the ground, and he went flying backward into the shadowy night. Necrem heard the crashing impact more than saw it. From the snapping of crisp branches and ground scraping, he figured the old thief was taking a tumble through some brush before rolling to a stop.

He stood there for a moment, breathing deep and hard through his mask. *Did I just do that?*

The feeling of hitting another man kept ran through his skin and his mind, the giving impact of flesh against flesh and the hard crack of bones underneath.

Unlike the singing of metal striking metal, the wet slaps and smacks of flesh against flesh were sickening.

Crying sniffles reminded him of where he was, and he looked down at his feet. Stefan was looking up at him, blurry-eyed and scared, still shaking.

Necrem knelt, taking him by the shoulder. "We need to get out of here."

"Wh-where?" Stefan stuttered.

Necrem grunted. *Where?*

He looked back to the main camp. The fires were getting bigger. The cracks of eruption had stopped, yet the yelling and screaming hadn't. Galloping hooves still drummed westward where most of the other companies had slept.

Baggage train!

He glanced over his shoulder. Eastward, down the road, the baggage train and camp followers' tents were still visible, but not on fire. Besides the one scream earlier, they didn't appear under attack.

"The camp followers," he told Stefan. "We make it there, and we might find a wagon to get out of here on. Or hide." A glint of metal caught his eye. He reached over Gonzel's and Raul's bodies to pull the master sergeant's halberd from under him.

"Really?" Stefan asked, nervously rolling to his knees then gazing toward the baggage train. "Do you think we can make it?"

Necrem looked back again. There was a lot of ground between them and the baggage train. A lot of dark, open ground were a calleros could ride them down.

"We might if—"

Tap!

Tap!

Rap! Rap! Rap!

Necrem spun around. Below them, lanterns lit columns of men marching in step up the slope of the ridge. The columns stretched out across their line, their drums and footsteps beating in time together, followed by the clattering of long poles and armor tapping together.

And those columns were coming closer.

More men from Necrem's company or squad suddenly rose from their hiding spots and dashed off toward the camp, some heading for the baggage train, as well.

"We can't stay here," he said, hoisting the lad up by the arm and setting them both off after their running squad mates.

~~~

"Someone's coming!" Stefan whispered, grabbing Necrem by the arm.

Necrem stumbled to a stop, holding the halberd out in front of him. It was heavier than the spear he'd been stabbing a post for over a month but better than nothing.

He could barely make out anything ten feet ahead of him between the shadowy tents and wagons.

Stefan pulled his arm then slipped behind a wagon. The boy's ears were sharper than his own and had already saved them from running into wandering groups stalking the baggage train several times.

Necrem followed his example and squatted down next him. His knees burned from how low he crouched but froze when he heard rushing footsteps heading their way.

"Hurry!"

Necrem peeked over the top of the wagon and spotted four men rushing down the lane.

Provost guards, he deduced by their armor and halberds.

One lagged behind the others, clutching his left shoulder while the arm dangled as he ran. His foot caught a tent peg, and he fell to the ground with a yelp.

"*Dammit!*" one of his fellows hissed, going back for him. "We got to keep moving."

"I can't," the downed guard whined, shaking his head.

The others had stopped and tentatively watched the other two.

"Where did they come from?"

"Who *cares*?" a guard watching snapped. "The wagons are lost, most of camp followers with them. If we get caught, the Lazornians will either kill or sell us."

"But if the Don learns we lost his wagons, he'll kill us anyway," the wounded guard cried, doubling over on his knees.

The Lazornians are here. Necrem dipped his head down, his scars pulling as his face tensed. *Maybe there's no way out of this.*

The Lazornian columns marched into their abandoned camp right when Necrem and Stefan reached the edge of the baggage train. They were making steady, methodical progress up the ridge, probing behind every bush and shrub. Hiding men screamed or begged when they were found, only to be silenced an instant later.

The wagon Necrem was hiding behind rocked, its wooden planks and gears knocking together. He jerked back.

Stefan crouched, frozen on his hands and knees, staring back at him from over his shoulder. He had crawled a few feet away and struck the wagon's wheel with his boot.

"What was that?" one of the provost guards asked in alarm.

Necrem stared at Stefan and pressed a finger against where his lips should be. Then he tentatively glanced over the top of the wagon, fearing the provost guards were bearing down on them.

Yells and battle cries suddenly shattered the quiet.

Necrem looked to see soldiers emerging from the shadows. The provost guard standing over his wounded comrade failed to lower his halberd when he turned and received a sword thrust through his neck. The swordsman's shield batted him aside while the other soldiers stormed in.

The other two guards lowered their halberds, but the Lazornians, nine in all, soon divided and surrounded them. Both guards lashed out with their halberds, thrusting and hacking, but their attacks bounced off the swordsmen's shields.

Three attacked the guard on the right, one turning the halberd away with his shield, then another stabbed the guard in the side. The guard's back arched, and his gasp was cut short by a sword being thrust into his neck. The three soldiers stabbed him once more when he crumbled into a heap, as if for good measure.

"I yield!" the guard on the left yelled, throwing his halberd away then falling to his knees, hands raised in the air. "Mercy, please!"

The Lazornians lowered their swords then looked to one of their number.

"Take him back with the others," the Lazornian officer ordered.

Two of the Lazornians took the surrendered guard under the arms and dragged him away. The rest turned their attention to the wounded guard still clutching his shoulder wound, on his knees.

"I . . . surrender," the guard begged.

The Lazornian officer knelt in front of the man then looked over his shoulder. "I'm sorry," he said, taking the man by his good shoulder. "But you're not going to make it."

"No! Pleas—*Gak!*"

Blood gurgled out of the guard's mouth from the officer thrusting a dagger into the top of his throat.

The hiss of someone's breath catching sent a jolt down Necrem's spine. He twisted aside and again discovered Stefan had moved, kneeling right beside him and watching the entire scene. Panicked, he grabbed the lad's head then ducked them down in case any of Lazornians had heard.

"Spread out," the Lazornian officer ordered. "You two, that way. You two, that way. Keep an eye out for anyone we missed. If you link up with another squad or our relief column, lead them to the wagons."

"Yes, sir!" the others replied then stomped off.

"You two with me," the officer said.

Necrem held Stefan's head down and listened to the footsteps. *Just walk away*, he prayed. *Just walk away.*

Miraculously, they did.

Necrem held Stefan's head down while the footsteps against the sandy ground split into three directions and got softer and softer.

"They're . . . everywhere," Stefan whimpered softly. He hung his head and teetered on wrapping his arms around his legs again. "There's no way out."

Necrem didn't know what to say. Stefan was likely right, but he knew if agreed, the boy would probably give up. If he did, there was no way Necrem would get him moving again.

Should we give up? he pondered. *They're taking prisoners if you surrender and aren't dying. We could—*

He would never see his family again. Those who surrendered would likely be taken as *sioneroses*.

"That's not going to happen," he said. He took Stefan by the shoulder and shook him. "We need to keep moving."

He looked to see if the way was clear, especially the way the Lazornians had come and taken the surviving provost guard. Light was growing from that direction, although it was too small and weak against the ominous glow of the main camp off to their right. However, the lights did provide good direction markers.

"North," he said. "Between the camps. We stay quiet and slip right between them." He slapped Stefan's shoulder then slipped out from behind the wagon. "Don't give up, boy. We can make it if we don't give up."

His words sounded like wishful thinking, almost pathetic, yet he'd been clinging to that wish for a month and refused to let go now.

~~~

Necrem gingerly walked on the balls of his feet, down a row of abandoned tents, holding his halberd out in front of him. Stefan walked beside him, arms wrapped around himself and shoulders hunched, nervously glancing between each tent and jumping at every sound.

"Do we have to go this way?" Stefan asked.

"Unless you want to crawl through that cactus and briar patch," Necrem tiredly replied. "I can't."

The baggage train camp's setup was in disarray, as if the provost had neglected or disregarded any need to outline it before letting the camp followers make camp. The tents were broken up in uneven lines with wagons and stalls mixed among them. They wrapped around rocks, briars, cactuses, and dried-out trees without any regard for connecting lanes.

Necrem and Stefan had come across a large patch of briars stretching out around cactuses and dead trees that was more of a wall than a patch, blocking their way across the road. That left them with the apprehensive choice of following the patch east toward the main camp and battle, or west to the wherever the Lazornians were holding the camp followers. Necrem had decided the westward route. There was no telling what was waiting for them toward the main camp.

He gripped his halberd tighter with each step now. Their hopes of the patch breaking up and finding a way through were growing smaller and smaller as the light ahead of them grew brighter.

"May . . . maybe," Stefan stuttered, "maybe we should go—"

Something crashed behind them.

Necrem spun around, narrowly missing Stefan with his halberd, making the lad stumble and fall between a couple of tents.

At first, Necrem couldn't see anything. Then he heard running footsteps heading for them.

"Halt!" someone yelled down the lane.

Necrem was about to take to his heels when a figure emerged from the gloom. He couldn't make out a face but could make out the man wasn't carrying the round shields of the Lazornians. Instead, the man was glancing behind him every two steps, carrying something stocky in his hands.

The man dug his heels into the road when he spotted Necrem, jerking his head back and flaring his wavy hair.

"Get of the *frickin'* way!" the man yelled, pointing whatever he held at Necrem.

Necrem recognized the voice. "Joaq?"

"Oso?" Joaq lowered what he was holding. "How did—"

"Halt!"

Joaq sprung forward, taking up a position beside him.

Necrem finally made out what the artist was holding—an odd weapon with a stock like a crossbow and long, widening brass tube on top of it.

Charging feet made Necrem look up to see three Lazornians rushing down the road, shields held in front of them and swords in their fists. They slowed to a cautious walk then fanned out across the road once they saw Necrem had joined Joaq. Necrem shot a glance where Stefan had fallen. The boy was still there, hunkered down as low as he could.

"Drop your weapons!" the Lazornian in the center ordered. The soldiers held their shields out with swords poised, leveled by their heads, sword tips pointing over their shields' round rims.

"Stay back!" Joaq warned, thrusting menacingly with his weapon. "Or I'll pull this lever."

"Where's your match?" one of the soldiers asked.

"My . . . match?" Joaq's shaking ran up his arm until his entire upper body was trembling.

"You don't even know how to use that." The soldier on the right stepped closer, shuffling past Stefan unawares. "Put it down."

"Same to you, big man," the soldier to the left ordered.

Necrem pointed the halberd toward him, making him stop his inching approach.

"You're going to get one good swing before we close in on you," the soldier warned, "and that'll be it."

"Surrender, and we'll show mercy," the soldier in the center said.

The recent scene of the provost guards being slaughtered flashed through Necrem's head. The speed, the efficiency, the . . . callousness. He doubted he would fare any better.

But then I'll . . . I'll never see them again. Eulalia's and Bayona's faces shoved the sight of the provost guards dying away, and he tightened his grip on the halberd's shaft.

"I can't," he replied through a heavy, exhausted breath. "I won't be taken away."

The soldiers each took their stances, their knees bent, preparing to spring while also getting lower. There was a bounce to them, their boots grinding the dirt under them.

"Here they come," Necrem said under his breath to Joaq, who grunted.

"No!" Stefan screamed, leaping from his hiding spot and wrapping his arms around the waist of the soldier on the right.

As the soldier struggled, hitting Stefan's back with his shield, and the others paused, Joaq raised his stolen weapon, squeezing around the stock.

Nothing happened.

"Oh," Joaq squeaked. He gave Necrem a look. "This thing *is* useless."

Roars and yells snapped their attention back. Despite the months of training to use a spear, Necrem's instincts to raise a hammer kicked in, and he raised the halberd to hit a perceived oncoming foe.

Instead, more men came running down the road. The Lazornians turned to face this new threat when men with spears slammed into their shields. Swords slashed and spear thrusts struck against shields, leaving Necrem and Joaq staring at the sudden shift.

A spear struck the soldier struggling with Stefan in the back just as the soldier hit the back of the boy's head with his sword pommel. Stefan went down in a heap while the man with the spear drove the soldier to the ground and held him there, struggling and kicking, until another man ran up and bashed the soldier's head in with a club.

The other Lazornians fared the same. The body of men rushing down the road separated them on impact. Several men with spears drove the one on the left between two tents, thrusting against his hacking sword until they backed him against the briar patch. The soldier cried out as he was impaled from the briars and spears.

The soldier in center was surrounded. He blocked with his shield and slashed desperately against the probing thrusts. One assailant rushed in, yelling with a club raised over his head. The soldier gutted him for his attempt, but his sword got caught. The rest rushed him, knocking his feet out from under him and killing him on the ground with raining spear thrusts.

Necrem felt someone nudge his elbow, ripping him from another slaughter-witnessing-stupor.

Joaq looked up at him, grinning and half-laughing.

"Oso?"

Necrem looked back. Hezet was walking up to him, looking between him and Joaq in surprise.

"You both made it out, too!" The veteran laughed, shouldering his spear and rushing up to clasp Joaq on the shoulder then Necrem.

"How . . .?" Necrem asked then looked back at the others. There were probably twenty men filling the road. He didn't recognize most. One was bending down to take the helmet off the soldier in the middle of the road.

"Luck." Hezet shrugged. "Like the rest of us."

"Any more of us make it out?" Joaq asked.

"I don't know." He shook his head.

"Take it easy, boy," one of the men said, helping Stefan up. The lad was rubbing the back of his head.

The rest of the men, in various stages of dress, mixed weapons and armor, began to gather around them.

"We need to keep moving," Hezet ordered then turned to Necrem. "Do either of you know what that is?" He gestured at the light ahead of them.

"That's where the Lazornians are keeping the camp followers," Necrem replied, looking back at the red glow down the road. His shoulders slumped, too heavy to keep them straight. "We . . . overheard a group of them say it when they captured a provost guard."

"Explains why this place is frickin' empty," someone mumbled.

"We were trying to find a way around it and the main camp, but"—Necrem shrugged at the briar patch—"ran into something we couldn't cross."

"Well, we can't go back that way," Hezet said, gesturing back at the main camp. "The army's finished."

"Then we keep going this way," Joaq suggested, pointing west down the road with the blunderbuss. "Maybe we can slip past—"

A woman screamed from down the road.

Everyone went still.

"Are they killing them?" someone in the back asked.

"They said they were taking prisoners," Stefan replied, rubbing his head.

Necrem twisted his grip around the halberd's handle again. The woman's scream echoed in his head, echoing back to another night long ago. The smell of blood and smoke in the dark of night. Men laughing, drunk on victory.

And a woman crying.

"Oso?" Hezet called after him.

Necrem's legs moved on their own, walking down the road, toward the screaming.

"Oso!"

Stefan was the first to reach him, followed by Hezet and the rest.

"What are we doing?" someone whispered.

"Where are we *going*?" another demanded.

Necrem had no answers, only an urge. The screams called to him. Screams ten years old echoing into the present. He walked past empty tents and wagons without a glance. He ignored the stinging of stepping on loose gravel, barbs, and rocks with his bare foot. His vision narrowed on the red glow of the wagons down the road that became clearer with each step.

Got to get to her, he told himself. *Got to save her.*

He would have walked into the light under his singular determination had it not been for Hezet and a couple others pulling him aside behind a tent.

"What are you *doing*, blacksmith?" Hezet hissed, shaking his shoulder. "You nearly strolled out there."

Necrem blinked his fuzzy vision clear then peered around the tent. The lights were coming from large bonfires, former campfires that had tent canvas and beams stacked into the flames. The bonfires surrounded a square of wagons patrolled by Lazornians. Shadows of people sitting and moving around inside the makeshift prison was all he could see of the camp followers.

A quick measure of how wide the wagons stretched and the light from the bonfires told him the light stretched for nearly half a mile. He couldn't see any way around. His shoulders slumped again, and the back of his legs ached with a chilling throb from finally sitting down. The halberd slipped through his fingers, gently landing in the dirt.

There's no way around. He rubbed forehead, rubbing sweat and dirt across his face. His staggered, deep breaths came out as sporadic hisses though his mask. *I'm sorry, Eulalia, Bayona. I'm tired.*

"Looks like a whole company," Hezet said, conferring to another soldier beside him.

"Who knows how many more are patrolling through the camp?" the other soldier said. "Think they got all the camp followers in there?"

"Probably all they can find," Hezet replied.

He glanced over at Necrem and gave him a worried look. "You all right, Oso?"

Necrem shook his head. "I'm . . . tired," he replied weakly.

Hezet's frown darkened. He opened his mouth to say something—

"Move along!"

Necrem sighed, figuring they'd been caught but too tired to be afraid. However, he caught guarded looks on Hezet and the others huddling around him then heard the distant footsteps off to the right.

"They found some more," the other veteran said.

"Some provost guards, too," Hezet added.

The lucky ones. Necrem hung his head, contemplating if they would be better off surrendering.

"Please, *no!*"

The sound of a woman crying, begging, made him raise his head.

"Don't put me in there."

Thump, thump. Necrem's heart began to beat faster. The shadow images cast by the bonfires burned the image of two men dragging a struggling woman by her arms across the tent canvas in front of him. *Thump, thump!*

"Just get in there!" one of the men snapped.

Necrem rolled back around, the feeling in his legs dulled to nothing. Everything around him shrunk and went numb. The smell of an army camp, the smell of canvas, horse, iron, and smoke blended in his nostrils. The red glow from campfires and the night's darkness between.

I've been here before, he felt.

Thump, thump.

He looked over the tent. A line of people, provost guards, men in their small cloths, women in their shifts, walked in a line between the soldiers ushering them through a gap in the wagons. The sight of a woman pulling against two of her captors snatched Necrem's attention.

"Let me go!" the woman futilely begged, digging her bare feet into the ground in vain as the soldiers pulled her along inch by inch. "*Please!*"

247

The woman, dressed in a long, white shift, flailed desperately. Her long hair waved back in the air like a ribbon.

Necrem's body seized.

Thump, thump! Thump, thump!

Her hair was honey brown.

Thump, thump! Thump, thump!

The plea echoed in his head, blocking everything out.

But the pitch in the voice changed. "*Please, no!*"

Thump, thump! Thump, thump!

Necrem's vision narrowed, the corners tinting red. His hands balled into fists, cracking and snapping his knuckles. His knees popped from slowly standing.

"Eulalia," he said under his breath.

His body began to move. His fatigue gone. The pleas for help and the hammering in his chest were all he could hear.

"Eulalia!" he said louder. His vision grew blurry with a red tint from the fires he stormed past, his footfalls speeding up.

"*Oso!*" someone, he didn't know who or from where, yelled.

The soldiers looked, surprise morphing with amusement on their snickering, blurry faces. Necrem knew those faces. He had known them for years!

And they had their hands on *her* again.

"*Eulalia!*" he bellowed.

Distance blurred, and one amused face twisted into surprise again as Necrem drove his fist into the man's nose, crunching bones under his knuckles. As the first man spun, tripped, then fell into a heap on the ground, Necrem was already moving to the other.

The man had thrown *her* to the ground and was now reaching for a sword at his hip. Necrem slammed both of his fists down on the man's shoulders, not hearing his cries of pain before grabbing his armor's shoulder straps. He spun the man like a doll then flung him.

Into one of the bonfires.

The man crashed through the fire, kicking and screaming as the burning tent canvas wrapped around him and he couldn't get out of it.

Necrem kept moving. Two more men were rushing him.

The other two.

Necrem roared, charging them with his fists up. One drew up wearily, looking between him and the man on fire. Necrem clotheslined him with his left forearm, throwing him to the ground before swinging at the other.

Something slashed his left forearm. He brushed the pain and the blade aside, got in close to grab the man by the shoulder, then slammed his fist into the man's gut. It was like striking iron. However, the blow doubled the man over, gasping.

It wasn't enough.

Necrem hit him again. And again. And *again*!

That iron stomach gave in on the last punch. The man coughed blood as Necrem pulled his head back by the rim of the helmet he wore then smashed the man's face in.

"That's the fourth," he growled, hunched and wheezing over the man's body.

His shoulders rose and fell. His fists clenched and relaxed, blood dripping from his right. Dull pains echoed on the edge of his feelings, just beyond the red in his sight, yet they were still easy to ignore.

An incoherent shout made him snap his head up. A line of men with round shields were closing in on him in a semi-circle. He couldn't hear what they way were saying. He already knew what they were saying.

"Of course," he hissed. "Calleroses always have their picked men with them." His teeth clamped together until they cracked. His face burned like it was on fire. Something hot ran down his cheeks and dripped off his jaw. His world began to shake. "Picked, *lying* men! And *laughing* provost guards!" He sucked in air to bellow, "*None of you will touch her*!"

He sprung and swung. He bore down on the man in front of him without a care, driving his fist into the round shield the man thought would protect him. Instead, the man tripped, tumbling backward from the blow.

Necrem didn't focus on him, though. He had no singular focus. He swung at them all, driving a hard right against the next man to the left, ramming an uppercut to the shield on the right. He spun and swung, fists pounding metal, ringing a familiar yet off-key tone to his ears.

His opponents hid behind their shields. With every punch, he drove one back just to turn around and hit another. They didn't punch, kick, or fight back; they hid behind their closing wall of steel.

"You think this will stop *me*!" Necrem yelled, punching a shield dead-center. "I *forged* these shields!" He punched another shield. "I pound metal day"—he slammed another shield then spun in the opposite direction—"after day"—his bloody knuckles left a print in the bend of another shield—"after *day*!"

One of the men staggered back from a blow, his shield half-raised.

Necrem bore down on the man with his fists raised above his head. "Hammer or fist, no sheet of metal is going to stand against a steel-working *man*—"

Gleaming steel pierced through his face.

The pounding in Necrem's head went quiet, and the red clouding his vision pulled back. Out of the corners of his eyes, he traced the sword's straight blade jabbed through the left side of his face at an upward angle and exiting his right side. He felt the blade's sharp edge against his teeth.

He followed the blade downward, to the trembling hand that held it, and finally to the wide-eyed man staring up at him.

"You're not . . . hurt?" the man swallowed then pulled his sword out.

The force jerked Necrem's head and made him drop his arms. He felt something peel from his face. Instinctively, he reached to wipe it but stopped as several lines of blood pooled in his palm. His fist closed around the pool, his vision blurring red again.

"Yes," he hissed, raising his head.

The man's face twisted, eyes wide, mouth silently agape, lips peeling back in horrified disgust. The others around him shifted, some scrambling back.

"I am!" Necrem yelled, seizing the man by the neck and arm. *"But you won't hurt her!"* He squeezed with all his might.

The man gasped and kicked, trying to lift his sword, but Necrem wrenched his arm back. The man's face shifted from white, to red, and finally blue. Necrem felt the man's veins press against his neck bones through his palms. As the man's eyes rolled back into his head, Necrem lifted him off his feet then flung him down, bones crunching on impact.

He roared at the other men surrounding him.

And his roar was answered.

Out of the night behind him came other men rushing those with the shields. As the fight broke out, more yells and hollers came from people behind some wagons he hadn't remembered. Chaotic fighting soon whirled around him.

What's going on? He reached for an answer. However, he couldn't find one. As if he couldn't remember. *Who are these people? Have they finally come? Sanjaro? Miguel?*

"You've all finally come!" he cheered with joy, thrusting his fist in the air. "Stand with me! Stand with me!" He laughed and cried.

A man backed into him, one in armor. Necrem backhanded him with his fist when the man glanced behind him. He came up on another man fighting with a camp follower with a club. He grabbed the man from behind, hoisted him in the air, then flung him aside.

Again and again, he would find one of those armored men, those *picked* men, get in close, and punch, bash, and throw them to the ground.

"They're running!" someone cheered.

More cheers followed.

Necrem was kneeling over one who hadn't gotten away. The man's face was a bloody ruin.

It's . . . over?

He looked around. Men were clapping each other on the back. Women were laughing and hugging each other or the closest man they could find.

The red tint pulled back from Necrem's vision, yet it remained cloudy. He struggled to his feet. His head pounded and swam. Every step was a struggle.

"What am I . . .?" he stuttered under his breath. Then it caught. "*Eulalia!*"

He dove forward through the cluster of men around him. His big palms pushing them aside as easy as leaves. He stumbled back to where he had left *her*, sitting on the ground, looking up at him, trembling and terrified.

But safe.

"Eulalia," he sighed out, collapsing on his knees before her. His arms wrapped around *her* and pulled *her* close to his chest. "You're safe now," he whispered, rubbing her shaking head to comfort *her* the best he could. "We'll go home, just like you wanted." His vision blurred until every shape became clouded shadows. Tears poured from his eyes, and his chin wobbled. "We'll build a house . . . and forge, and never . . . never again go on campaign. Never . . . again." He started to rock, gently back and forth, running his fingers through *her* hair, yet made sure not to hold *her* too tightly. "I promise . . . Eulalia," he cried. "I . . . promise."

He continued to cry and promise until the world went black.

Chapter 16

15th of Andril, 1019 N.F (e.y.)

Snap!

A shooting pain snatched Necrem from oblivion. He gasped, jerking awake to a sea of pains and aches coursing through his entire body. The one that had awoken him emanated from his right hand and up his arm.

He lifted his swimming head to look, but the glaring yellow rays of the Easterly Sun blinded him. He rolled his head away as he felt multiple hands take a hold of him by the arms, shoulders, and pushing against his chest.

"Easy," a soothing voice urged. "I barely got you bandaged up. Sit still and let me set these splints, then maybe I can do something about your face."

Necrem's head rolled back toward the voice. He struggled to blink his vision clear to see Doctor Maranon, a balding, stout man with a sharp beak of a nose, sternly studying Necrem's mangled right hand. Dried, brown bloodstains crusted its back. The first three knuckles were split open and black around the exposed bone. His middle finger still pulsed from the doctor pulling it back into place.

He reached to touch it, but someone held his left arm down.

"Careful, Oso," Joaq warned.

"Stefan," he called from over his shoulder, "get Hezet."

"Yes, sir!"

Necrem heard running feet, unable to get a glimpse of the lad before he ran off.

"You've lost a lot of blood, Oso," the artist said, frowning at him as sternly as the doctor with deep bags under his eyes. His oily hair clung to his face. "Don't push yourself."

"It's a miracle he's even *awake*," Maranon mumbled, wrapping a loose strip of cloth tightly around Necrem's hand, holding in his knuckles. Then the doctor wrapped two sticks around his middle finger. "All these cuts and broken bones. His foot. His *face*. The Savior must *really* walk with you."

That was Doctor Maranon's favorite phrase. Necrem had overheard him use it many times when doctoring up a nasty injury or ailment made from the person's own stupidity. He'd been one of a few camp doctors who knew how to make the salve for Necrem's face and the only one who would examine his face. Ultimately, he'd had to admit there was little he could do, save give Necrem his salve.

"Wha—" Necrem choked on his words. His face felt like it was splitting from ear to ear, bringing tears to his eyes and leaving a burning sensation after the initial ripping sting.

"Don't speak!" Maranon snapped. "I got most of the bleeding to stop, but I can't be sure until I get in there and stitch what I can. You'll pull the bandage away and start bleeding again if you try to talk and move your jaw."

As the burning subsided, Necrem felt a cloth pressed against his face. After years of wearing a mask, he hardly noticed the difference until he realized half his face and head were wrapped in cloth from below his eyes to under his jaw.

His dry throat was scratchy, and he tried to swallow. Coarse cloth rubbed against his tongue, and he gently explored his mouth to discover clumps of cloth stuck in the holes of his cheeks and between his teeth.

This feels . . . familiar.

Too familiar. Like the day his face had been slashed for—

Necrem seized, shaking violently and squeezing his eyes tightly to drive the memory away. It'd been years since it was that easy to recall, and he forced it back within himself.

"Whash . . ." he spoke softly without moving his jaw or lips. He couldn't pronounce things clearly, though. "Whash ... haffen?"

"Eh?" Joaq grunted, pulling back slightly. "What'd you say?"

"He shouldn't be *saying* anything!" Maranon snapped, pulling the cloth taut around Necrem's broken finger.

Necrem sniffed sharply at the stinging jolt running up his arm. Now more awake, he looked back over his body.

He sat propped up against a wagon wheel, the wheel's hub digging into his lower back and its wooden spokes rubbing against his shoulder blades. Besides the lower half of his face, both of his hands were bound in cloth with dried bloodstains across his knuckles. His left arm and right foot were also bound in makeshift bandages. His clothes were in tatters, multiple rips and cuts zigzagging across his trousers and shirt. His shirt was stained a dark brown that grew darker around his forearms the closer the sleeves got to his hands.

Those stains matched those on his bandages.

Blood. His hands began to shake, and he lifted his arms weakly to get a better look. *That's a lot . . . a lot of blood.*

His wounds were too small to bleed that much. That left another option.

He suddenly sucked in air, trying to remember, but his memory was mirky.

He jerked his head back up, making Joaq jump. The artist had inched away a few paces, the corners of his frown twitching as he sat on the balls of his feet, as if ready to spring up and run away.

"What . . . did . . . I do?" Necrem asked.

Joaq swallowed then glanced nervously at the doctor. Maranon was rummaging through a sackcloth bag, metal clinking together from him rolling things around. He kept flickering watchful looks up from his bag.

They're afraid of me. Necrem dropped his hands into his lap, too weak to keep them up and desperate to remember what had happened last night more than ever.

"Oso!"

Hezet was rushing over with a trail of men behind. All of them were in various stages of undress; some wore armor while some didn't, and they brandished weapons from spears and halberds to swords and clubs. They spread out, watching him intently.

Hezet knelt in front of him, frowning and looking him up and down. "How are you feeling, Blacksmith?" he asked.

Necrem met his eyes and asked forcefully, "What . . . did I . . . *do?*"

Hezet glanced at the men around them then shook his head. "The craziest, damnedest thing I've ever seen in my life."

Necrem's brow furled, and he confusingly looked around as the others began chuckling and nodding in agreement. "I—"

"You charged half a company by yourself, you crazy, big bastard!" One man laughed.

"With your fists!" Stefan added excitedly, holding his fists up.

"You swung at *everything.*" A man to his left imitated punches. "You punched in breastplates!"

"And dented shields!"

"Real fists of steel!"

The group broke into more agreeing nods and grumbles.

"The broken knuckles suggest otherwise," Maranon grumbled. The doctor had stopped pretending to be looking for something in his bag and instead sat back with his arms folded.

The men around them laughed harder.

Necrem slumped, soaking it all in. His fingers and palms stiffly resisted from being moved, his finger joints refusing to bend. Sporadic twinges from his biceps were becoming more noticeable.

He looked from his hands to the bloodstains on his clothes then back up at Hezet, who remained frowning at him rather than smiling and joking like the others.

"I . . . hurt people, didn't I?" he asked.

Hezet reservedly nodded.

Necrem pressed his eyes closed, squeezing tears out of the corners. Visions of men screaming as his fists slammed into their faces, their bodies being thrown aside or laying mangled on the ground, made him gasp then quickly open his eyes. A cold sweat broke out on his forehead, and he started to shake.

"Easy," Maranon urged, placing a tentative hand on Necrem's shoulder, trying to be comforting yet keeping his distance. "After the ordeal you've been through, you need to rest."

"You're afraid of me," Necrem said lowly, making Maranon flinch. He looked over the men around him again. "You're all afraid of me."

The men shifted their feet, their nervous smiles slipping away, and most avoided meeting his eyes.

"You were . . . pretty terrifying last night," Joaq admitted.

"Scared the *shit* out of everybody," someone else added.

"Poor Lia certainly was," another said.

Necrem froze. "Lia?"

"The woman you charged out to save," Hezet replied. "We thought you knew her or something until afterward. You"—he swallowed and look away—"kept calling her someone else."

The men went silent, letting Necrem reflect in peace.

Eulalia. The memories of last night were becoming clearer, and he swore he had seen her there, in the middle of that mayhem. *She was there! I saw—*

Eulalia's face shifted to a young woman he had never seen before, with dark brown hair, a freckled face, brown eyes slightly farther apart, and a supple mouth, quivering in silent terror.

Necrem's chest felt heavy, and he sucked more air in. *I didn't . . . I didn't mean to—*

A baby started crying a short distance away.

Over Hezet's shoulder, Necrem spied a large group of people, mostly women, kneeling around a deacon standing and holding his cane and lantern in the center of them. One by one, the women were coming up to offer their prayers to the group, while the others held either each other, their children, or themselves close.

Most of the men stood around the wagons, gazing out to something beyond the perimeter, and only a few of them had weapons.

"Are we—"

Tap!

Tap!

Rap! Rap! Rap!

Hezet leapt to his feet and joined the others looking over Necrem's head and beyond the wagons.

Necrem angled his head. The ground underneath him shook from hundreds of feet marching in step, filling the air with their footfalls.

"They're rotating companies again," someone said.

"What are they waiting on?" Stefan asked.

"Probably on the Don," Hezet replied, looking back over his shoulder.

Necrem joined the rest and followed the veteran's gaze. He made out calleroses in ornate armor and, at a quick count, no more than fifty men-at-arms, gathered around someone in the center on the other side of the circle. Their attention was focused beyond the perimeter of the wagons, as well.

Necrem's heart fell just seeing them. "Where'd they come from?"

"A few minutes after we carried you inside the circle—"

"Came charging in, barking orders to get the wagons moving," someone spat, cutting Hezet off. "As if we had any horses to hitch up."

"The Lazornians don't seem to be in a hurry to storm us, though," Hezet added. "For now, we wait."

"On them," Necrem said, gesturing toward the cluster of calleroses.

Hezet nodded.

Necrem sighed, glowering toward the calleroses and the Don hiding among them. *We're doomed.*

***

Tap! Tap! Tap!

Recha bounced in her saddle, in time with the drums, unable—and unwilling—to tear the grin from her face.

We won! She was nearly giddy and clenched her teeth together to stop from giggling. *We won! We won! We won!*

They had done more than win. Her armies had *obliterated* the first Orsembian army they had found.

Recha still reeled from the speed of the march, the rush of getting everyone into place, making sure they had the ship unloaded in time to get the Third Army on the move to attack with the First and Second. The most important thing of all was that, this time, she'd gotten to *watch*!

She had retired early the day before to guarantee she would be awake for every moment. Keeping still had been her greatest struggle as she'd watched from a far. From waiting while the advance companies of sword had slipped stealthily into the enemy's camp from the north and west, bouncing as calleroses had stampeded the enemy's own horses into their camp, gaping as the fires grew larger and larger, and shouting at the sight of her armies' pikemen marching on the camp from three sides.

It was all so . . . *glorious*!

"You're too excited," Baltazar whispered from his horse walking beside her. "You need to relax, or the thrill of victory will run away with you. Also"—he causally nodded at a line of prisoners under guard by a squad of her swordsmen—"you may give the impression you're . . . ruthless."

"*Really*?" she asked excitedly, turning her grin on him. She straightened in her saddle, holding her head up high. "Excellent!"

"*No*," Baltazar grumbled lowly yet sternly. "Not good. The men will think you're bloodthirsty."

"Huh?" Recha arched an eyebrow, her grin slipping. "Blood—" She winced, realizing she was speaking loudly, and lowered her voice. "*Bloodthirsty?*"

Baltazar stiffly nodded. "We're surveying an after action. We don't have the casualty lists yet, but it's best to proceed as if they are high until we are certain. A commander should put on a strong face for his, or her"—he shot her a glance out of the corner of his eye—"men at a time like this."

Recha surveyed past the side of the road and across the mangled ruin of the Orsembian camp. At every other foot laid the smoldering remains of a tent, dark patches marking the rows where men had bedded down to sleep last night. Some had died in those fires, others had died scrambling out at the alarm, and others still had died before the fires had even started.

Now squads of her swordsmen were picking over the last bits of remaining tents, searching for survivors, information, and spoils. Lines of soot covered the half-dressed, many bloodied, prisoners being escorted to the rear, for sorting later. Everywhere she and her escort passed, she spotted grim faces, rummaging about the corpse of the camp without any sense of emotion.

"The men are tired," Baltazar said, "but their blood's still up. *This* is the hardest time to maintain discipline. They've been killing all night and probably seen friends die, as well. If they see an officer or commander ride in afterward, smiling and bouncing as if this was a game to them, they will lose all respect for that officer. They won't believe you shared what they've been through, and instead will think you enjoyed the carnage, sending them to kill and die then come in afterward without a care.

"Such thoughts can make men break, even if they've won. Best to give them a grimace." Baltazar shifted in his saddle, rolling his shoulders while making a stern expression, fit for an unfeeling statue. "You can always save the smiles for parades."

Recha leaned back in her saddle, contemplating on his advice in silence. Her excitement finally drained from her to the point she could control it. Yet she couldn't let him get the last word in.

"But you never smiled at parades, either," she quipped.

"I did at one." Baltazar flashed a soft smile that disappeared as fast as it had appeared. His eyes went misty for a second but followed the smile just as quickly.

The look sparked a memory of Baltazar standing and smiling proudly the first time Sebastian had gone on campaign at the head of his own force. The campaign he had come back from, heralded as a hero.

We were all smiling that day.

Recha took a deep breath and followed her field marshal's example, although he probably grimaced better than her. He had more practice, and she didn't want to create more wrinkles. Instead, she settled for a serene, composed posture with her head raised.

Their pace was slow. The road had to be cleared of debris from tents strung across their path. Work parties were dragging burnt wagons and a few horse corpses away by ropes.

Recha had wanted to survey the battlefield immediately after the Easterly Sun had risen, but Baltazar, Cornelos, and all their staff had held her back. When reports had come in that the enemy's baggage train had resisted and their advanced force had pulled back, Baltazar still held her back until they had received the final report he'd been waiting on.

The enemy commander had slipped the trap and now hid behind a circle of wagons in the baggage train.

Another commandant who couldn't handle the rules being ripped out from under their feet, Recha mused. *Or maybe a baron, late to join Borbin's main army and couldn't stand in the face of real war, perhaps?* A smirk cracked her serene mask as the ruins of the army camp fell away and they rode into the baggage train.

Tap!
Tap!
Rap! Rap! Rap!

The drummers leading the column sped up their tempo, and the gleaming points of the pike companies surrounding the wagons came into view. When the company of pikemen leading them turned aside, taking her banner with them, Recha got a full view.

There're more people than I thought.

Over the heavy-laden wagons, she made out a mass of people in the center of the circle, mostly women and children around a white figure, a deacon. Men hunkered down behind the wagons, the heads of spears poking up here and there.

"One push, and they'll give," Marshal Narvae said from behind them.

Recha pulled her horse to a halt, her guard forming up in the gap between the companies of pikemen flanking them.

"There are children in there," she said from over her shoulder. "We can't be too ruthless, can we, Field Marsal?"

"Hmm," Baltazar hummed while surveying the circle.

Recha followed his gaze to the cluster of calleroses in armor and their men-at-arms spreading out behind the wagons facing them. They were probably the only true resistance they faced. Marshal Narvae was right; they wouldn't hold if pushed.

"Those wagons bear Borbin's crest," Baltazar said.

Recha shifted in her saddle to get a better look. The wagons were bigger than the others, covered in tightly-wrapped and tied-down yellow tarps. The tarps bore the flaming orange shield of Borbin with a gaping *mellcresa* skull baring down a grasping black hand.

The black hand symbolized the Tower of the West. The Borbin family's fascination with the large, twin-crested predators was common knowledge. The crest was to symbolize that the Borbins held the historic capital of the old kingdom and, by right, held themselves above the other marcs. All because of a coincidence of geography and luck.

"Borbin's supposed to be at Compuert," she said, pursing her lips. "*Please* don't tell me this was just a supply convoy."

"This isn't a supply convoy," Baltazar said. "This . . . They're sending someone."

The Orsembians rolled back one of the wagons wide enough for four men to stroll out, one at a time. Two of them were in armor; one in red and the other green.

Calleroses, Recha surmised.

The man walking between them stuck out in his bright yellow jacket and flashy orange trousers. The right leg was stuffed inside his boot, while the left stuck out. The other wore sparkling silver; a polished breastplate was his sole piece of armor, and a gold and silver patterned cape hung from his shoulders. They strutted with their hands visible and rapiers rocking on their hips.

"Cornelos," Recha called from over her shoulder, "bring in our guests."

"Yes, La Dama," Cornelos replied then guided his horse around her with a few of her guards trailing behind.

"They'll likely declare to parley under the Rules," Recha told Baltazar as Cornelos trotted out. "How do you suggest we proceed?"

"You didn't need to ask for my suggestions outside Puerlato," Baltazar replied lowly.

Recha frowned and lowered her voice again. "I thought I explained that already. Those officers were cowards. They abandoned their military ranks the moment they thought they could hide behind the Rules. The situation called for *immediate* action."

"But you summoned the Viden to join you there," Baltazar countered, shifting his gaze toward her. "That hints at planning. Not very immediate."

Recha tightened her grip on her reins, her hands starting to tremble. *Why here? Why now?*

Baltazar wasn't a man to fume or throw tantrums, despite not appreciating what she had done at the hill fort, regardless of Hiraldo's report. Instead, he had decided to punish her by focusing on the needs of the campaign and avoiding her invites to dine for the past few days before finally opening back up.

I didn't break our deal! Recha knew pleading and yelling would get her no sympathy. This wasn't the right place for it, anyway. Thinking fast, returning hoofbeats sounding Cornelos's return, she could find only one response.

"Our arrangement stands," she said firmly. "If they keep their ranks, they're yours. If they claim the Rules and wish to be treated as nobles, then they're mine, but I shan't make any demonstrations or permit any violence like at the fort."

Baltazar gave her a sharp nod as the guard in front of her opened a path for Cornelos to walk his horse through.

Recha gave Baltazar a flat stare, trying to convey her thoughts through her eyes. *We are going to talk about this later.*

She straightened in her saddle, rolling her shoulders and putting on a masking smile as Cornelos approached. He walked his horse calmly, yet the blood had drained from his face, and his eyes flickered over his shoulder the moment they met hers.

Oh, now what—

Recha's mouth fell open. Her heart raced at the sight of the man in silver being led toward her.

Givanzo Borbin!

The son of Marqués Borbin had grown a pointed beard on his chin in the five years she had last seen him. Some ladies had gossiped that they found him dashing with his high, angular cheekbones and curly black hair. His hawkish nose, however, reminded Recha of his father, and holding his head up with an assured, confident air did nothing to quell that feeling.

His son! Recha gripped her saddle horn, digging her nails into the leather to stop from shaking. *We've captured Borbin's son!*

She pressed her lips tightly together, her desire to grin nearly overwhelming. She peeked out of the corner of her eye, and Baltazar's stern expression gave her the strength to control her mask.

"La Dama," Cornelos said, wheeling his horse to the side to address both her and the captives, "may I present His Illustrious Don Givanzo Borbin, and his retinue."

Givanzo sharply sniffed, his amber eyes flashing a glare up at Cornelos before bowing with a flourish. He slid his left foot back, kept his left hand on his sword, held his right arm out, and bent from his hip while keeping his head up.

How many hours must he have practiced that?

"Well met, La Dama," Givanzo said, rising from his bow. "I must admit, it is quite the shock meeting you here. We expected you to be at Zoragrin."

Recha's right eyebrow twinged at his implication of her remaining in her capital while sending her armies on campaign. "That's amusing, Don Givanzo," she replied. "I expected you to be with your bride."

She met his narrow-eyed stare without wavering. While she didn't have to be rude, she didn't have to be overtly polite and diplomatic, either. If he was going to make snide remarks about her not belonging on campaign, then she was to return the touch about his recent betrothal.

They were so proud of it several months ago, proclaiming it repeatedly *to everyone*, she recalled. *Maybe I should ask if the honeymoon was worth it?*

Baltazar cleared his throat and pulled them both out of their staring battle.

Recha pulled back, finding him concerningly watching her. "Pardon me, Field Marshal," she apologized.

"Don Givanzo"—she gestured to Baltazar—"may I present Field Marshal Baltazar Vigodt, field commander of the armies of Lazorna."

Baltazar gave a snapping bow, a sharp nod of the head that made the back of Recha's neck hurt from watching.

"Ah!" Givanzo's eyes lit up, and he smiled, turning to Baltazar. "The renowned Half-Conquering Hero Vigodt. Well fought, sir, well fought! I must

261

say, the unorthodox methods from last night make so much more sense now. I am honored to meet you."

"I thank you for your praise, Don Givanzo," Baltazar replied, unmoved and sternly scowling, as if carved from stone in his saddle.

That's your second mistake, Givanzo, Recha counted. *Sassing me is one thing, but throwing out false praise to Papa will get you nowhere.* She began to speak—

"Since you were kind enough present your associate, La Dama," Givanzo interrupted, "allow me to introduce mine." He waved the gentleman without armor forward. "May I present—"

"Don Givanzo," Baltazar said, "we have more important things to discuss than exchanging more pleasantries. I must ask you for your sword."

The man Givanzo had been introducing, most likely a baron, flustered like a shocked woman, much too dramatic for Recha's taste. Givanzo, on the other hand, glared up at Baltazar. His left nostril flared.

"Pardon me, La Dama," Givanzo said, his tone dripping with contempt as he turned to Recha, "I am afraid your field marshal is suffering from being retired from the battlefield for so many years. *Please* remind the field marshal of his place and instruct him the Rules of Campaign *clearly* state each commander is to introduce each of their staff by their proper rank and privileges due them." Givanzo tugged on his cape, making it flare and ripple.

His accompanying baron harumphed in agreement, folding his arms across his chest. Their calleroses drew up beside them.

Their shock was understandable, blind followers of the Rules as they were. The Rules of Campaign outlined that, when opposing commanders met, they were to exchange pleasantries, listing their officers by rank and status before listing their terms to each other. The side with the greater prestige—rather, the larger force—would typically get to go first. This rule was meant to be followed both before and after battle. If battle was joined.

Terms were to be negotiated and settled before the surrendering commander offered their sword. It was all a formality, though. The commander typically had their weapon back within the hour, as both commanders shared drinks in the victor's command tent, while a portion of the loser's army was auctioned off like cattle.

But we're not following the Rules anymore. The corners of Recha's lips twitched, threatening to smirk at how ridiculously dramatic it all was, yet she kept her mask intact.

She watched Givanzo, waiting for more theatrics. Instead, he waited, silently staring at Baltazar with his nose in the air.

You arrogant ass. She surprised herself with the thought, but she could think of no better description. *You* actually *think I will reprimand my own field marshal, the man who raised me, because you're not getting to grandstand? Promise or no, I should have you stripped and flogged. I should—*

She twisted in her saddle, about to yell over her shoulder, when she caught sight of Baltazar. He held Givanzo's stare, looking down at the Don with contempt.

Recha softly smiled. *I should let Papa have you.*

"Field Marshal Vigodt doesn't need to be reminded of his place, Don Givanzo," she said, relaxing back in her saddle. "He's the field marshal of my armies and, as such, he has final say on all military decisions . . . including accepting the surrender of an enemy commander, such as yourself."

She nodded at Baltazar. *Get 'em, Papa!*

"Don Givanzo," Baltazar said, snatching the disgruntled don's attention from giving Recha an impertinent look, "surrender your sword. The same for the rest of you. Then I will give you my terms to deliver to the rest of your men."

Givanzo's face turned red. He snarled, both of his nostrils twitching, and he danced his glare between both her and Baltazar. "You . . . *dare!*" he hissed, pointing at Baltazar. "You forget your station, *Field Marshal!* You may have been called a hero once, but you're still lower than a baron and barely worthy of polishing my boots! You may claim victory today, but you did so in violations of all the Rules of Campaign! *All* of you violated the Rules!" He frantically pointed at everyone around him, including Recha in passing, before addressing Baltazar again. "And when my father learns of this—"

"Your father is two hundred miles away," Baltazar stated coldly, propping a hand on his hip while leaning forward on his saddle horn. "Lodged in a siege he can't easily pack up and march away from. And by the time he even hears a whiff of what *might* have happened here"—he shook his head slowly—"you'll still be as *hopeless* as you were last night when we caught you sleeping. Your swords . . . *now.*"

All around them, men drew their swords, the finality of Baltazar's words acting like a call to Recha's soldiers, including Cornelos.

Tingling chills ran over Recha's scalp, making her hair stand on end. *And he was urging* me *not be ruthless?*

"Have . . .?" Givanzo hissed. "Have you all gone *insane?*"

The calleroses around him shifted, trying to shield their don. Recha's guards stepped closer, leveling their swords' thin points a hairbreadth away from their necks, forcing them still.

"You're *violating* the Rules!" Givanzo yelled.

Recha rolled her eyes. "We're not following the Rules of Campaign," she said, giving him a flat stare. "From this point on, Lazorna is following the rules of war. Accept your defeat with dignity and perhaps the good field marshal will let me decide where you'll be sitting out this war. Eh, Field Marshal?" She raised an eyebrow at Baltazar, waiting to see if he would play along.

Baltazar mirrored her, arching an eyebrow of his own, before sitting back straight in his saddle. "Perhaps."

"What of my property?" Givanzo demanded. "What of my attendants?"

"All spoils of the camp will be sorted to use for our war effort," Baltazar replied bluntly. "I'm sure we can arrange for you to get your important personal effects returned."

Recha's ears twitched from hearing a throaty chuckle, likely from Narvae, behind her.

"As for your attendants," Baltazar continued, "they shall join the rest of your surviving army as prisoners of war."

The baron blanched at that. "You mean to take men of *our* station as *sioneroses*?"

"We are not taking *sioneroses*," Recha interjected, grimacing both at the implication and the whining, nasal octave in the baron's voice. "The prisoners of war will be sent to Puerlato, workers for the siege works. All your camp followers will be free to go once we're sure of who they are. Any *sioneroses* will also be freed.

"As for you, gentlemen, the commandant we left in charge of the siege has a special place for you all to stay. I promise, you'll all be quite comfortable"— she grinned broadly—"if you cooperate."

Commandant Leyva's last report had stated he was using the hill fort as both a lookout post and guard station for important prisoners. Sevesco had approved, commenting the keep was perfect for putting a few of the cowardly commanders to the question.

He's going to be as giddy as a boy getting new toys when he hears we've captured Borbin's son, she mused.

Givanzo snorted in contempt. "What a farce is that?" he snapped. "Do you honestly expect us to believe such nonsense? No Orsembian would accept them. They're the most unbelievable terms I've ever heard."

"Considering the terms you're used to, that's understandable," Recha dryly quipped. "Although, when those terms are typically selling your own people for your failures, I'm not sure you have standing to claim our terms are a farce."

Men around her chuckled and snickered.

Givanzo, however, glowered up at her. "You've already proven none of you can be trusted," he said, folding his arms. "I refuse your terms."

Recha shifted in her saddle then glanced at Baltazar.

"Seize them," the field marshal ordered.

Givanzo tried unsuccessfully to shrug off the hands grabbing him. The baron yelped from his arms being wrenched behind his back. The calleroses offered no resistance with rapier tips still at their throats. In moments, they were all stripped of their swords and their arms pulled behind their backs.

"I'm afraid they leave us no choice," Baltazar said to her. "If their commander doesn't surrender, then we're left to force them."

Recha frowned, something in the way he said that not sitting right. "Very well . . ." she replied warily. "But I would rather not with all the women and children."

"I understand, La Dama," Baltazar said. "But if their commander doesn't order them to surrender, I'm afraid, militarily, that leaves me with only one option." He frowned, pursing his lips up and making his mustache flare out.

Is he . . . putting on an act? The feeling wouldn't leave her. Recha was used to Baltazar commanding and knowing what he wanted and what needed to be done. Him beating around a bush felt wrong.

"If only there was a less ruthless option," Baltazar pined.

Recha reactively sat up, the suggestion sparking something in the back of her mind. The sight of the burnt camp, the carnage, the exhaustion of the soldiers, the sight of the camp followers huddled around a deacon, they all ran together. Over the images, Givanzo's words repeated, *"No Orsembian would accept them."*

Let's see about that.

"Cornelos," she said, "you and a few others accompany me." She guided her horse around Cornelos and between guards then headed toward the wagons.

"Accompany you where, La Dama?" Cornelos asked after her.

"To make another offer," she replied, grinning over her shoulder.

***

Necrem sucked through the holes in his cheeks. The blood trickling into his mouth made him drool and made it hard to breathe.

"Stop that," Maranon growled lowly.

The doctor hovered over his shoulder. Sweat dripped off his forehead as he pressed a cloth to Necrem's right cheek with one hand and struggled to stitch a bleeding scar. The entire right side of his face burned yet numbed the stings of the needle piercing and thread pulling his flesh. They blurred together with the aches and pains pulsing up and down his body.

His throat closed from the rising blood and drool filling his mouth, forcing him to cough and fling droplets of blood from his mouth. More blood rushed back down his throat. On reflex, he turned to the side and spat out as much as he could, blood and spit spewing everywhere. The heavy taste of copper and salt made him gag and dry heave.

"Can't you stay *still*?" Maranon snapped with a huff, his face growing red. His string hung down from Necrem's face from the half-finished stitch.

Necrem shook his head. "Won't do no good." He coughed, reaching up to press his hand on the cloth that Maranon had pressed against his cheek. "I need salve."

The salve kept his scars moist and stopped any rips and cuts from bleeding. His last supply, though, laid scattered on that desolate ridge.

"There is no more salve." Maranon dug into his bag and pulled out more bandages. "Maybe the doctors in Lazornian camp will have some." He cut the loose stitch from where it hung on Necrem's face before rewrapping his face with the fresh bandage.

"I doubt they'll spare it on me," Necrem lamented. "Or any of us."

He looked at the men standing guard near him, studying their frowning faces, their eyes dancing one direction then another, their huddled postures behind the wagons. Every now and then, one would glance over their shoulders at the calleroses on the opposite side of the circle. They had moved a wagon aside a while ago to let the Don strut out to bargain their lives away.

They're taking too long.

The doctor tugged the bandage tight, jerking Necrem's head to the side as he cut the wrap and pinned the ends to the rest of the bandage.

Necrem worked his jaw against the pressing bindings, making enough room to breathe. He sucked in air through his teeth to be certain air passed through the cloth. His head felt heavy from being wrapped up again, wobbling back and forth.

"I want to get up," he said.

Maranon snorted. "Not after all my work putting you back together," he said, putting away things in his bag then wiping his brow. "You're going to have to be carried out of here."

Not having the energy to argue, Necrem sat quietly and let the doctor collect the rest of his meager tools then leave to tend to someone else.

He pawed at the loose gravel with his left hand, seeing if he could move it. His right hand was bound stiffly to hold the broken knuckles and finger in place, but he found he could still grab with his left.

He pushed off the wagon wheel he'd been leaning against with a grunt. His tense muscles ached from bending and rolling to his side.

"Oso!" Joaq hissed. "The doctor said not to move."

"I want . . ." Necrem panted, kneeling on his bad leg while putting his right under him and clutching the wagon wheel with his left hand. "I want . . . to see."

Sweat ran down his back, and his arm muscles throbbed from merely rolling around. His shoulders rose and fell from his deep breaths. When he pushed up with his good leg, his knee almost buckled.

Someone grabbed him under his arm, a camp follower he didn't recognize. Joaq joined them and, between the three of them grunting and pulling, Necrem finally stumbled to his feet. He blinked sweat out of his eyes to see the hopeless sight.

Rank after rank of violet uniformed and armored Lazornians ringed them. The Easterly Sun sparkled off the pike heads from the companies of pikemen forming the bulk of the army surrounding them. Between the companies were squads of swordsmen, holding their round shields in front of them, surrounding columns of crossbowmen.

No, Necrem realized after squinting at the weapons the Lazornians were shouldering. *Those are guns.* They were like the hand-bombard Joaq had found last night, except their barrels were longer and their muzzles didn't flare out.

He had seen several versions of the strange weapon when he had previously worked on campaigns. He never forged the metal barrels or knew how they were made to aim small explosions. Merchants had claimed they would one day replace the crossbow, while the calleroses had laughed it off as he replaced their horseshoes or repaired their armor. The Lazornians, however, appeared to have made the merchants' prophecy come true.

He followed the ring of columns all the way around. The way south was completely blocked, and he spotted trails of dust being kicked up in the air from horse riders.

"There's no way out," he said.

Joaq frowned darkly. The other man hung his head below the wagon then shook it. He didn't even have a weapon. He was like several other camp followers who stood next to gaps between the wagons, attempting to give the appearance they could guard them when, in truth, they couldn't.

Necrem hung his head, too. *It was all for nothing.*

Last night's slog to get to rear of the camp, the hiding, the fighting, the . . . killing, and his injuries, all of that to end up in the same position. Except, now they were waiting to hear their lives had been traded for their commander's. For Borbin's son.

Selling us as sioneroses. Necrem's panting filled his ears, and his vision swam.

A shooting pain snapped him out of it. He jerked back to find he had squeezed the side of wagon until the rim split. His hand trembled from the overexertion on his injured knuckles.

Shouting sprung up behind him.

Necrem looked over his shoulder and watched calleroses waving at their men-at-arms and the nearest provost guards, calling them away from their gaps to form into lines.

"Think the negotiations are over?" Joaq asked.

Necrem glanced at him. The artist was leaning against the wagon with an eyebrow raised, looking far too at ease for Necrem's taste.

"Probably won't—"

The commotion on the other side of the circle grew. Men were raising themselves on their toes to peek over the larger wagons on that side.

Horse hooves clomping against the hard-packed earth drew his attention beyond the circle. They grew louder as someone rode toward the wagons. Then around them.

Another wagon down, Stefan gasped as he gawked through his gap. Necrem followed his gaze and witnessed a woman riding around the wagons with a trail of Lazornian calleroses at her back.

Her straight-back poise on the horse marked her as highborn. Her deep violet riding dress matched the uniforms of the soldiers at her back. Her silver blouse, catching the Easterly Sun's rays as easily as the pike heads, preserved her dignity while displaying her youthful, womanly figure. Her long, dark hair fell in curls off to the left side of her head, giving everyone a view of her face's delicate profile as she gazed into the wagon circle as she rode.

"Now *that* is a sight," Joaq said under his breath, almost in awe. The artist was on his feet, his full attention fixed on the woman. "If only I had paint and canvas."

"I don't think a painting's going to get us out of this," Necrem grumbled.

"Who cares?" Joaq shook his head. "It'd still be *marvelous*."

More people were on their feet, watching the woman riding by. The women around the deacon stopped praying and began standing up. Men who hadn't taken up places behind a wagon rushed to find one. The line of calleros men-at-arms came running around, huffing to keep pace, pushing other people out of the way.

The woman pulled up on her reins sharply then turned her horse to face them. The calleroses following her spread out, taking positions around her. Their swords conspicuously out, and their blades resting on their shoulders.

"I," the woman announced, "am La Dama Recha Mandas, Marquesa of Lazorna!"

A low murmur spread behind him yet quickly fell silent.

"At this very moment," the marquesa continued, "thirty thousand of Lazorna's finest have you surrounded. The rest of your army is either captured . . . or dead."

A child began to cry.

"Orsembians, Don Givanzo refused to accept my field marshal's terms of surrender, even though he wasn't in any position to refuse. For that, he has been seized as a prisoner of war."

The men behind him, the calleroses and men-at-arms especially, grumbled and whispered to themselves after hearing that.

They've taken him prisoner? Necrem shook his head. *Is this a joke or . . . a trap?*

"Orsembians!" the marquesa shouted louder, cutting off the growing voices behind him. "I make you this one offer. Every soldier is to come out and lay down their arms. You'll be taken as prisoners of war to complete the siege works around Puerlato. After they are finished, you will all be held until this campaign is finished. Then you will all be released to return to your homes."

Necrem jerked his head up. Men gasped around him.

They're . . . not taking us as sioneroses?

"Everyone else will be free once we are sure of who you are," the marquesa added. "No women will be harmed, no camp laborers taken as prisoners of war, and any *sioneros* will be freed. You have my word!"

A stunned silence held everyone behind the wagons. The promises likely ran through everyone's minds as loudly as they did Necrem's. This sounded too good, too . . . fair, to be believable.

She's going to free *the sioneroses?* Such a promise coming from a marquesa, or any noble, sounded dubious. In this situation, it sounded devious.

"She's lying."

Necrem looked over his shoulder at a calleros marching across the line of men-at-arms, holding his chin up in the air.

"She's trying to make us lower our guard!" the calleros yelled to everyone. "If she'll take the Don prisoner, then her word can't be trusted. Stand firm, men!"

"But she said she'll let us go free!" a woman yelled.

"What about our children?" a man, a camp worker at the wagons, demanded.

"Enough!" a noble in a linen shirt shouted, storming in from across the circle with a group of guards behind him. "We must stand firm! Don Givanzo refused them, then we can't accept *any* terms from that lying bitch!"

A hush fell over everyone. The noble had yelled loud enough that his voice echoed and, as one, they all nervously turned to look for a reaction by the marquesa.

Necrem felt a chill run down his spine. The marquesa sat rigid in her saddle. Her head tilted, slightly angling her glaring eyes blazing down her pointed nose. She sat there without blinking, and as the time slowed, her eyes narrowed further, focusing on the noble.

"He *really* shouldn't have done that," Joaq whispered under his breath.

Necrem peeked beside him from the corner of his eye. The artist was hunkered down behind the wagon again.

"I've seen *that* look before." Joaq nervously laughed then pressed his forehead against a wagon rail. "She's going to kill us."

Necrem's brow furled. "Are you all right?" he asked.

Joaq shook his head. "No."

"Orsembians!" the marquesa yelled, snapping everyone's attention back to her. Her glare had softened, but her face was an icy mask. "If you reject my offer, my field marshal will have no choice but to order the companies forward. They will not be able to tell which of you are soldiers and which are *not*. The shot from my musketeers will *not* be forgiving."

At mentioning them, the musketeers in the ring stepped forward. The first rank knelt with their musket butts propped up on the ground as they blew on their matches. The second ranks stepped up behind them, holding their muskets in front of them and blowing on their matches likewise.

"Take my offer, Orsembians," the marquesa said. "Surrender and live! Or die for nothing."

Necrem watched her face. From the distance, he couldn't see every detail, yet he studied how she held her head, keeping her posture straight and her hands in her lap. Her expression reminded him of polished metal. No smirk or expecting smile mired her steely resolve.

"What are we going to do?" a calleros whispered behind him. A couple of calleroses huddled around the baron, keeping their voices down but not quiet enough. "Spread out?"

"We don't have enough men to guard *every* opening between the wagons," the other calleros snapped.

"You want to keep fighting!"

Necrem's head jerked around at hearing Hezet's voice. He and a few other disheveled men, who had escaped last night's carnage on the ridge, were marching up to the calleroses, but they were stopped short when the baron's men-at-arms formed a line, blocking them. Hezet and the others marched right up to them, spear shafts locking against spear shafts as a shoving match broke out.

"Look around us!" the veteran yelled. "The Lazornians have the numbers. There's no sense in fighting."

"Get back to your posts!" the baron snapped, pointing at them. "These matters are above dregs like you."

"There're women and children here!" a camp worker pushing against one of the baron's men-at-arms shouted.

"What about my baby?" a woman cried.

"Enough!" the baron screamed, his face turning red and the veins in his neck bulging. "Don't any of you see it? Clearly, this Lazornian witch is trying to set us against other! We must stand firm! We can't let her treat us like this. Not after how she's treated the Don and violated the Rules. It's not proper!"

"Damn what's proper!" a soldier shouted. "And damn the Don, too!"

"How dare you?" A calleros drew his sword, but the soldier had already dived back into line with the rest beside Hezet.

Two lines were already forming, and the yelling was growing. The baron urged the people to stand firm and reject the marquesa's terms. The calleroses shouted orders, and Hezet and the others shouted back. Women began screaming and pleading with the men, while children started crying. The deacon waved his cane and lantern in the air, but whatever sermon he tried to give was lost in the chaos.

Necrem watched, unable to add anything to temper the inferno raging around him.

Joaq snickered beside him. "We're all going die"—the artist laughed then leaned against the wagon again—"because we couldn't just agree to walk out here."

Necrem's eyes were drawn to the lever locking the wagon wheels in place that Joaq was leaning beside. He nudged the wagon with his good hand. Boxes and chests rocked inside, tightly bound down, yet the wagon did budge. He looked back at the lever again, drawn to it. He braced himself against the wagon with his right hand, careful with his broken finger, then started limping down the wagon.

"Pardon me," he said to Joaq before nudging the smaller man away.

"Eh?" Joaq grunted as Necrem pulled him by the shoulder of the wagon. The artist gave him a disgruntled frown for that. "What are you doing?"

Necrem didn't answer. He reached up and grabbed the lever, pulling it down with a metallic *creak*. The wagon jostled more as he limped over to the front. The wagon hitch stuck out to the side fortunately and not under the wagon in front of it. The harness for the horses were likely in the wagon. However, the hitch pole was long and sturdy enough.

Necrem pushed against the wagon again, this time under driver's seat, testing its weight and listening to it rock.

It might move, he pondered then looked at his cut-up, bandaged body. *But can I move it?*

"Get back to your posts!" the calleroses yelled. "Get back to your posts! The Lazornians could come any second!"

271

The baron was no longer yelling or trying to convince anyone. He just stood there, red-faced and pointing at the wagons as the calleroses and the men-at-arms tried to bully obedience. They weren't getting it.

"I'm not dying here!" a soldier yelled.

"Any man who deserts will be cut down before he steps one foot out of the circle," a calleros threatened.

"What about the women and children?" another man demanded. "At least let them go!"

Necrem shook his head and reached down, picked the wagon hitch on his shoulder, then placed his hands on under the driver's seat.

"Oso?" Joaq hissed worriedly, looking back and forth from him to the calleroses. "What *are* you—"

Necrem groaned and pushed. Instantly, the strain of the weight pushed back against his aching arms, then across his shoulders, down his back, and ran through his legs. He tried to keep as much pressure off his left, standing only on his toes, yet the back of that leg spasmed as he put more weight into his shove.

Sweat broke out across his face. His knuckles popped the harder he shoved, forcing him to grit his teeth from the pain stabbing through his hands. His head dropped, and he dug both of his heels in, adding more biting pain from his injured foot.

"Come on!" he hissed under his haggard breath. "Come on!"

He leaned with his shoulder more, putting his entire back into it, and heaved.

A wooden *creak* split through the air!

The wagon wheels gave, and the wagon started moving backward.

Finally getting traction, Necrem angled the hitch to the left, forcing it to turn as he pushed it back. His face burned, and flashing spikes, like molten embers, ran down his entire body with every step. He closed his eyes and forced them away.

One more step, he told himself, wanting to get the hole as big as possible. *One more step!*

His left heel slipped. He grappled to keep a hold of the driver's seat, but his broken knuckles gave out. He fell to his knees with a grunt, only to gasp when the wagon hitch came down and slammed into his back.

"Oso!"

Panting and sucking air desperately through the bandages around his face, Necrem blinked through sweat-soaked eyes to look over his shoulder. There was a wagon-sized hole right in the circle, big enough for a group of people to walk through. Joaq, Stefan, and a few others stood in the gap, gawking at him.

"What is the meaning of this?" the baron roared, charging through them.

The gap became a struggle as Hezet and his men joined Joaq and the others for control of the space. Necrem took the chance to roll the wagon hitch off his back. Then, hand over broken hand, he groaned and gasped as he pulled himself to his feet again. This time, he held on to the wagon, his trembling legs threatening to tumble out from under him.

"Someone seize that traitor!" the baron ordered.

The struggle between the soldiers and men-at-arms paused, everyone following where the baron was pointing.

Right at Necrem.

Necrem momentarily locked eyes with the man then slumped his head toward Hezet and the others. "There's . . . nothing here . . . worth dying for," he said, his chest rising and falling from taking long, deep breaths.

A lull hung over the men in the gap. Some looked to each other. Some looked at their feet.

Someone tossed their spear away. "Steel Fist is right," he said.

Mumbling agreements followed, and another tossed their spear away.

Joaq and Stefan walked out of circle and tried to take Necrem under their arms. Stefan yelped when Necrem almost fell on top of the lad. More men rushed out, Hezet included, to catch them.

Necrem's breathing became more labored, his chest burning, demanding more air. He gasped and breathed as deeply as he could, turning his lungs into the bellows of a forge that refused to be sated.

"Where are you going?" the baron yelled after them. "Get back here!"

Nobody stopped or turned around. Out of the corner of his eye, Necrem spotted a trail of soldiers, provost guards, camp workers, and women and children walking around them. Lastly, he caught sight of some of the Don's and baron's men-at-arms and one of the calleroses throwing their weapons down and joining them.

As they walked through a hole the Lazornians made for them, Maranon came rushing up from behind. The doctor had his bag over his shoulder and looked Necrem over intensely as they hobbled along.

"You stubborn oaf," Maranon cursed, studying his face. "You ripped your stiches open. All of them!"

Necrem sucked in more air and tasted copper on his tongue again. "Sorry, Doctor," he said weakly. "Sorry."

Chapter 17

"No more!" Recha begged. "Please, just let me eat in peace!"

She bent over the table and planted her face against the tabletop, pressing her check against the rough parchment in front of her. She pursed her lips and puffed strands of hair that fell across her eyes, blocking her view of her plate sitting off to the side.

The sight of the golden, roasted flank and leg of a *pavaloro*, or brush-turkey as some called them, made her mouth water. The steaming cherry peppers and small, boiled field potatoes on the side added a spicy aroma to the broiled meat. Some swore the *pavaloro* tasted like chicken, if cooked right and wasn't fully grown yet.

Recha always thought they tasted a little gamey, yet she would much rather be eating it now than looking at it.

"You have to," Cornelos insisted dryly without a hint of sympathy. "You haven't looked at a single correspondence for three days. If they get any more piled up, rumors might start spreading that the campaign has taken a turn for the worse, or"—he reached under her and gently pulled the parchment she was laying on out from under her, tugging some of her hair in the process—"officials back in Zoragrin might start making decisions for themselves without bothering to send dispatches."

Recha winced at the stings in her scalp. She rolled her face over to squint up at him sitting beside her.

He continued to sort through the stack of rolled and folded envelopes and parchments in front of him, opening the envelopes with his knife one minute and plucking a small potato from his plate to eat the next.

You can see me. Recha stared at him harder, knowing she was in his field of vision.

Cornelos continued with his mundane tasks, in stubborn defiance of meeting her gaze.

A twinge began growing in the small of her back, and the table's edge dug into her chest. Recha focused the irritation into a soft growl and squinted her glare as tightly as she could up at her secretary.

Still, Cornelos ignored her.

The table's edge against her chest began to rub, and she finally blinked. She puffed more of her hair out of her face then sat up, stretching her shoulders back to pull the twinge out of her back.

"You're going to make some lucky woman a great wife one day, Cornelos," she quipped, reaching for her ink bottle and quill.

Cornelos grunted and suddenly jerked his hand back, tearing the envelope he was opening too forcefully with a loud *rip*.

Recha pressed her lips tightly together, unable to stop from smiling but stifling a giggle, finally getting a reaction from him. With him distracted from sliding another dispatch in front of her to sign, she reached across to her plate and daintily plucked a cherry pepper.

She nipped at the mild pepper, holding it to her lips, then looked at him. Cornelos was giving her a flat stare, yet his redden cheeks deliciously added to his embarrassment. Recha gave him a small smile and shrugged before returning to devouring her pepper.

"Aren't they cute?" Ramon Narvae chuckled from across the tent, breaking the mood.

Recha snapped around, sitting straight-backed in her chair. Cornelos's face darkened from red to a shade of violet, nearly matching his uniform.

Narvae snickered, a crooked smile on his lips and a twinkle in his eye as he rested his elbows on the table, fiddling a steel thimble dangling from his fingers. His own plate sat beside him, his meal half picked over, and his own stack of dispatches in front of him.

Recha set her jaw, and her smile slipped. The thin skin of the pepper split between her fingernails, and her tightening grip squeezed out its juices, making the skin between her nails tingle.

"No throwing food, please," Baltazar gruffly said, chewing on a pulled strip of *pavaloro* meat while simultaneously signing an order.

They mirror imaged each other too perfectly. Recha and Cornelos on one side of the square table, fit for six people, and Baltazar and Narvae on the other.

After all the excitement with the battle and final surrender of Don Givanzo's army, Recha had suddenly become famished and hoped to eat with Baltazar before the armies resumed their march.

Unfortunately for her, while Baltazar had accepted the idea, he, Cornelos, and Narvae seemed to have silently agreed and conspired to turn her relaxing noon meal into a working luncheon. Baltazar hadn't even asked for the dispatches. Narvae had simply produced them, along with a tall bottle of brandy—looted from the enemy camp, when she did not know—as if by magic. Not to be outdone by his uncle, Cornelos had rushed to get the dispatches he'd been hoarding, and thus her long, wonderful, pleasant meal plans had been shattered.

"We're not children anymore, Papa," Recha said, tossing the nibbled pepper back on her plate then cleaned her fingers on a napkin in her lap, although the faint idea of throwing it at Narvae lingered. "We've grown out of food wars."

Growing up in a house full of training calleroses, save for one other girl, there had been times where jabs traded over dinner had turned into chaotic food battles. They would break out when Mama Vigodt had left to see the kitchen was cleaned, of course.

Returning to her tasks as marquesa, she pulled over one of her dispatches, a request from Baroness Itzel asking permission to levee a tax to fix a dam.

Now's not a good time to raise new taxes, she contemplated, holding her quill over the parchment. *I already raised taxes to fund this campaign. That, plus the down payment for the weapons, Lazorna's treasury is on the brink as it is.*

She put quill to paper and held it there. *But if that dam isn't fixed and it effects the harvest, the people in that region will face taxes* and *food shortages.*

Her fingers trembled, pressing a blot onto the parchment as scales of maybes, short, and far off effects, swung back and forth in her mind like a pendulum. She bit the inside of her cheek, and with the last bit of ink remaining on the tip of her quill wrote, "*Granted.*" Then she signed her name.

I'll revoke it once the dam is fixed, she told herself, stuffing the reminder in the back of her mind with a thousand others as she set the signed dispatch in a small pile in the center of the table.

She frowned at Baltazar's pile, twice as big and symmetrically stacked, despite the dispatches being different sizes from slips of paper to torn sheets. Baltazar himself sipped his watered wine then bit a potato in half to chew while signing or denying two more dispatches without looking away from the messages.

Recha shook her head. *How does he do that?*

Cornelos slid another message in front her, another request, and she groaned down at it. It was two pages long and, at a quick glance, appeared to have an itemized list.

"Huarita has been secured," Narvae said, setting his thimble on the table as he held out a slip of a paper to Baltazar. "Two companies of horse from the Second Army. Should we rotate them out with companies of sword or pike from the Third?"

"No," Baltazar replied, shaking his head. "Send an order to General Priet that those companies are to hold Huarita and scout the road north. We need to keep our lines of communications open, but if Borbin does abandon the siege to suddenly march south at full force, I want whoever's stationed there to be able to move quickly. Better for us to be free to move than hold positions at our strength."

"Right," Narvae agreed. He tossed the message away then got another piece of paper out of his disorganized mess to start writing down Baltazar's orders.

Recha craned her head up, longingly wanting to get a better look at those kinds of dispatches.

Ah, she inwardly groaned, *that's so much more interesting.*

Cornelos nudged her elbow and whispered, "Recha."

"Hmm?" she hummed.

"You're pouting," he replied.

Her eyebrows shot up at him. "I am *not*."

"What was that?" Baltazar asked, his normal voice echoing in the tent after Recha and Cornelos kept their whispers low.

Old instincts kicked in, and they both went stiff and still, as if being caught saying things they shouldn't have, like when they were children.

"Nothing!" Recha replied, shaking her head, making Baltazar raise a confused eyebrow. "Just . . ." she frowned down at list of complaints, having still not read them, "everybody's complaints and requests seem to follow me everywhere."

"Duties of the marc," Baltazar chuckled. "That's why I strive to rise no higher than marshal. Giving marching orders is much more enjoyable." He pulled off a strip of pinkish-white flesh from his *pavaloro* breast then returned to his dispatches.

"Yeah," Narvae grunted sarcastically. He picked up his thimble of brandy and tossed it back in one gulp, growling deeply afterward. "*Much* more fun."

Recha's ear twitched from a stifled hiccup coming from beside her. She glanced to find Cornelos battling between swallowing the remains of his *pavaloro* and laughing, his lips contorted in a tightly pressed, amused smile. Swallowing finally won the day, and then he coughed and gasped for air, dropping the *pavaloro* leg bone to reach of this cup of watered wine.

"Don't choke yourself," she said. She waited for him to take a drink then catch his breath before smiling slyly. "You're not going to interrupt my lunch just to leave me with all of this." She waved her hand at their stack of messages.

"Apologies." Cornelos coughed again, nodding his head. "Yes, La Dama." He took another drink then picked up a message he'd been starting to read before he'd choked himself. His eyes were halfway down the page when his head jerked, and he put the message aside.

"What's *that*?" Recha asked.

"Nothing," Cornelos replied halfheartedly, busying himself by shuffling the messages he had yet to open but not looking too closely at them.

Recha gave him a flat stare. "*Cornelos.*"

He sighed. "It's Baron Escon hundredth request to join the army and be commissioned to the marshal staff or a general staff." Cornelos shook his head in annoyance. "He's begging for anything now."

Recha frowned. Baron Escon was likely one of many requesting to join the campaign.

Probably thinks we've gone back to following the Rules and wants a share of any spoils. Another thought struck her. *Or get away from his wife.*

It was no secret that the barons who chose to go on campaign congregated together through most of the marches, spending little to no time tending to their men and instead leaving that to the lower capitáns and officers.

Minds focused on spoils and seeing war as a game. She sniffed disdainfully.

"That's the field marshal's decision whether to take on more staff officers," he said, her interest gone.

"No baron is going to request a field marshal for a posting," Baltazar mumbled lowly yet loud enough to hear, without looking up.

"As if we need them," Narvae added boldly.

Recha sensed a lull in the tide of papers Cornelos had been sliding her way as everyone shared their mutual sentiments of the limited role the barons had in the army. She seized it by snatching the *pavaloro* leg from her plate and began to eat. She bounced her eyes from one man to another, looking to make sure their heads were down and their attentions distracted by their work as she ripped the flesh from the bone.

They probably wouldn't care, she chided herself, fearing the men would be somehow upset at her taking proper bites instead of small, ladylike ones. Mama

Vigodt's teachings still lingered, however. She had taken her role of guardian to make sure Recha grew up as a lady seriously, which made the worry linger.

So, she ate faster, stripping the leg to the bone within minutes, barely getting a taste of the meat, which was going lukewarm. Her throat clung on one swallow, and she gulped it down just in time to prevent choking herself.

A sharp knock on a support post by the tent flap made her start and toss the bone back on the plate.

"La Dama!" a guard outside called. "Field Marshal! General Galvez is requesting to enter. He claims it is urgent."

"Send him in!" Recha called back, wiping her lips with her napkin.

Baltazar had his head half-raised and mouth open to speak, but she had replied first. He shrugged and ate a potato as Hiraldo slipped through the tent flap, carrying a midsized, iron chest with both hands.

"Hiraldo!" Recha said happily. "You caught us having lunch. Care to join? I'm sure . . ."

Hiraldo wore a tense, hard frown. His eyes scanned their medium-sized tent, large enough for the table and servants, but they had sent the servants away once they had set the food down. He glanced behind him over his shoulder, waiting for the tent flap to close back.

"Is something wrong, General?" Baltazar asked, sitting up and keeping his voice low.

"Nothing . . . wrong," Hiraldo replied nervously. "But we might have a situation. May I?" He looked at Cornelos and gestured with his head at the table.

Cornelos sprang up to clear a spot on the table. Narvae helped a little, mostly moving his pile of papers and clutching his bottle of brandy before sitting back in his chair.

Hiraldo walked up to the table then gently placed the chest on the cleared spot, minimizing any thud. However, Recha tilted her head at a soft, clinking sound from within.

"We were going through the captured baggage train," Hiraldo began, "when one squad came running to report *this*." He flipped open the latch then opened the chest lid.

Recha's eyes went wide, and she slowly rose to her feet.

Faintly glowing back at her were gold coins, golden deberes, in disheveled sacks, packed too tightly to dissolve into a jumble.

"How—" Her throat was suddenly dry. She seized her coffee cup then took a quick swallow, the lukewarm roast making her wince and her nose wrinkle, but at least it brought moisture back to her mouth. "How many is that?" she asked with a cough.

"By a rough count"—Hiraldo paused, glancing down at the chest—"probably five hundred."

"Congratulations, General," Narvae said, snickering while he poured brandy in his thimble then raised it to him. "You captured the Don's secret horde. To your spoils!" He tossed the thimble back in one gulp, oblivious to Recha and Baltazar frowning disapprovingly.

"Forgive me, Marshal," Hiraldo said respectfully but also frowned, unamused and tensely nervous, "but I'm afraid this situation is much more serious.

"Recha . . ." The corners of his eyes and cheeks twitched. He leaned over the chest toward her and lowered his voice. "There are over *twenty* wagons full of these chests."

The world went deathly quiet.

They were in the middle of an army camp of three converged armies. A gentle breeze had rumpled the canvas of their tent countless times while they had eaten, yet now it had conspicuously died down.

Recha's body went stiff, draining the feeling out of her as her mind spun mythical numbers until they devolved into ridiculous figures. She grew to the point she couldn't feel the coffee cup she held with the tips of her fingers.

"Ah!" Narvae snapped, breaking the silence, and everyone out the mental trap of adding up impossible numbers.

The marshal sat up with his thimble and brandy bottle both held out away from him as he grimaced down into his lap. His right hand dripped with red brandy, staining his uniform sleeve. He had apparently been refiling his thimble when Hiraldo had revealed the truth of their capture, got lost in the same quandary as the rest of them, and overflowed the small container before realizing.

Recha quickly noticed everyone at the table were holding their cups and joined Baltazar and Cornelos, casually putting her cup back on the table as Narvae wiped his hands and lap with a napkin, cursing under his breath.

"Hiraldo," Baltazar said, his voice hard and low, all propriety of rank abandoned, "how many know about this and who is guarding those wagons?"

"Me, my staff, and the squad who opened this chest first," Hiraldo replied. "All are under orders not to talk to *anyone* about this. Because their capitán sent for me and they didn't help themselves, I posted the squad who found them on guard of the wagons. They're too heavy to move, but—"

"They don't need to move the wagons," Narvae said, shaking his head. "One wrong word and the whole camp will storm them!"

"Keep your voice *down*!" Recha hissed.

"We should hitch those wagons and send them to Zoragrin as soon as possible," Cornelos said. "Every minute they sit there is a risk to our armies' discipline and a loss to the marc."

"There are over twenty of them," Narvae snapped. "You know how much manpower they're going to need to haul and protect? Who are we going to assign to such a detail? I can't think of anyone trustworthy enough to handle it." He drew himself up and gingerly turned to Baltazar. "No offense, Baltazar."

Baltazar grunted back.

Recha pursed her lips. *No trust or worry of offending me, I guess.*

She took a deep breath, calming her nerves before she attempted to calm the situation. "Before we can decide what to do with it," she said, straightening her divided skirts before sitting back down, "we need to know just how much we have. Any ideas of how many of those chests fill up one wagon?"

"Chests are pretty heavy," Hiraldo replied, studying the chest and working his jaw as he figured in his head. "Couldn't do too much digging out in the open, but I suspect there are around twenty or so to a wagon. Anymore, and they'd make too heavy a load."

"A rough estimate—twenty chests to twenty wagons you've found so far," Narvae said, leaning back in his chair with his arms folded and head drooping. "Add around five hundred deberes per chest, that's . . . that's—"

"Two hundred thousand," Cornelos finished. "Minimum."

Narvae let out a whistle and turned to Baltazar. "Did we just seize the Orsembian treasury?"

Baltazar snorted. "Too poor to be the entire treasury of a marc." He flashed a look at Recha. "Hopefully."

Recha shared a look with Cornelos. Lazorna's finances were a recuring nightmare that she could never get straightened out. Even with the three years not dedicated to campaigning, the marc's treasury was still a mess. Returning to campaign and funding her armies had placed Lazorna on the verge of bankruptcy, and the bill to pay the merchants for the armies' weapons alone could be just the thing to tip it over the edge.

So long as they don't call in their notes all at once. She stared at gold. *Perhaps defeating this army was Savior sent.* Her shoulders slumped. *Still have no idea what to do with it, though.*

"Still doesn't explain why Borbin's son was hauling it around," Narvae said.

Studying the deberes, something struck Recha as peculiar.

"Those are Saran coins," she said. Each marc minted their own coinage, each one tried to have some pattern, design, or shape to make them distinct. The deberes in the chest were shaped into octagons, the mold Marqués Narios preferred.

Where'd they get so many Saran—

Recha burst out laughing, reverberating straight from her gut as she leaned over the table, scaring everyone else in the tent.

"That . . .. That's . . ." she tried to speak but breathing and laughing were both making it difficult. She took a big gulp of air to push the giggles down. "Givanzo got this from marrying Narios's daughter. We just captured the wedding *dowry!*"

Rumor had it that Borbin had nearly drained Saran dry forcing the marriage. Now it was staring her in the face that that rumor was probably true.

Narvae joined in on the laughter, followed by Hiraldo. Cornelos snickered, but Baltazar just shook his head, refusing to break the seriousness of their discussion.

"I still advise we send it to Zoragrin," Cornelos urged. "That's where it'll be safest, *and* we can put it to use."

"And which army should we send back with them as escort?" Narvae asked condescendingly.

The two locked glares at each other over the table.

"If I might ask," Hiraldo interjected, breaking the staring contest, "could the First Army requisition some of the gold as spoils? It was a company of sword from the First that originally secured the baggage train."

"Not for long," Narvae said. "They were forced out at the last moment. Besides, if you make an official requisition, then all the armies are going to know what's in those wagons."

Recha sighed, her humorous jollies over realizing where Givanzo could have gotten so much wealth squandered by the returning debate. She had to fight the urge to rub her temples.

Terrific. We were worried about the armies fighting over this, but now we *are starting to. I should just order it all . . .* She groaned, rethinking the thought before it fully formed. *But will just sending to Zoragrin really help much?*

"We could use this money to supplement the armies' supplies and payroll," Baltazar suggested. "The deberes are already loaded and separated. Divided among the armies splits up the load, puts them under guard, and into each's coffers without any requisitions. It will also eliminate the need to keep the communication lines open to pay the armies and keep them paid if they are cut."

Ever the general, thinking of the armies first. Recha leaned back in her chair and began pulling her hair, wrapping it tighter and tighter over her left shoulder. *But two hundred thousand deberes. I can't just let that much gold go to one—*

"With respect, Field Marshal," Cornelos said, "we can't just spend all of this in one place. The marc has many obligations right now. Some are being told to wait until the end of this campaign to be addressed, but this prize could do a lot of good. Least of all paying for several obligations the marc has taken on to fund this campaign."

"If you're thinking of paying off the merchants early, don't," Hiraldo said. "General Ros reported their ship was weighing anchor as they unloaded the last crate to us."

"We can still have funds ready to pay them when they call to collect their note," Cornelos retorted.

He turned enthusiastically to Recha. "We need their continued business. Especially for the future."

"We need to pay the armies for today," Narvae growled. "Or there's not going to be any future business."

"And paid soldiers stand better than those who haven't," Baltazar added. "Especially behind enemy lines." His hard-set jaw told Recha he had already made up his mind. "General Galvez, divide the wagons—"

"In half!" Recha said firmly.

The men snapped around toward her. However, Recha focused on only one.

Baltazar's jaw remained hard-set as he laced his fingers together in front of him on the table.

"Recha," he said, his tone commanding yet respectful, "these wagons were part of the enemy's baggage train, taken by the army, after battle. As with the other spoils of war gathered from this camp, this is an army matter, and I must ask you to respect my judgment in this."

Recha's fingers sliced through the strands of her hair. She held his eyes, unblinking. "Papa," she said, leaning toward him against the table, "I'm not overstepping our agreement. I agree that most spoils an army takes should go to supplementing that army. But this is too much money to ignore.

"Half of it can be divided among the three armies in Orsembar to supplement their payrolls. The other half should be sent back to Zoragrin—ten percent to supplement the Fourth Army, a quarter held in trust as a payment to the merchants, and the rest for the marc's treasury. The armies will be served for the present and the marc's needs, as well.

"Besides"—she shrugged, relaxing her shoulders and offering a soft smile—"weren't you the one who said the armies need to move fast? Getting paid is one thing, but I think that's too much gold for us to carry and still be able to move like we need to."

Baltazar concealed half his face behind his laced fingers, elbows propped on the table. The bushy tips of his mustache twitched randomly as his eyes went in and out of focus, possibly thinking over his stance and Recha's. At least, that's what she hoped.

Finally, he gave a sharp nod. "Very well," he said. "Carry on, General."

"Yes, sir," Hiraldo replied. "La Dama."

Recha began leaning back to enjoy her moment of persuasive triumph when she caught the glint of the gold coins again out of the corner of her eye as Hiraldo started to close the chest. A sudden urge gripped her.

"*Wait!*" she blurted out, startling everyone again. She sprang stiffly to her feet, hands folded in front of her, then walked around Cornelos to beside Hiraldo. "May I?"

Hiraldo confusedly frowned at her but stepped aside. The chest's lid creaked on its hinges, its weight dragging it down as Hiraldo let go.

Recha leaped to seize it and pull it open again. She stared down at the coins and grinned.

"Recha . . ." Baltazar said worriedly, "what are you—"

Recha dove her hands into the coins. The stacks in the middle of the chest crumbled in her grasp as she curled her fingers around the palm-sized, minted metal. She grabbed as many deberes as she could then pulled them out. She squeezed them in her grip, tighter and tighter until the cold gold slipped between her fingers and rained back into the chest with musical jingle.

She giggled, listening to it and the shivers that the feel of gold falling from her hands sent up her arms. Her hands balled into fists after the last deber fell, and she shook them excitedly.

"I've always wanted to do *that!*" she said with a laugh.

Cornelos sighed, hanging his head. Baltazar tried to hide a bemused smile under his mustache. Narvae smirked approvingly, full thimble halfway to his lips. Hiraldo simply waited patiently aside.

Recha bit her lower lip, wringing her fingers together from the urge to run them through the gold again. Instead, she slammed the chest lid shut, breathing a big sigh of relief in curing the temptation.

"You have your orders, General," she said.

She pressed against the side of the chest to push it across the table toward Hiraldo, but it didn't budge. She frowned, wrinkling her nose at not being able to move it, and sharply sniffed to move out of the way. She caught Cornelos trying to hide a small smile, angling his head just so she could barely see around the top of his head.

As punishment, she snatched a pepper off his plate then bit the tip off it.

Cornelos threw his head up and gaped at her.

"What?" she asked, shrugging. "You weren't eating it."

Hiraldo stepped in to retrieve the hefty chest. He made a step toward the tent flap, paused, then turned back. "One more thing. We're starting to go through the prisoners and are finding some are conscripted men. Me and the other generals were curious on our policy regarding them. Are all prisoners to be marched back to work on Puerlato's siege fortifications, or can we see if there are any of the conscripted men worthy enough to recruit?"

Recha stared. "Recruit—"

A bit of pepper stuck in her teeth, forcing her to pause and run her tongue along her teeth to get it out. "Recruit *Orsembians*?" she growled.

"We will suffer more casualties during this campaign," Hiraldo explained. "As much as the armies need to be paid, the problem of reinforcing and replacing losses might be even greater. If we can supplement our forces with Orsembians who were conscripted, or veterans campaigning for pay, that could solve that problem."

"Might be risky, though," Narvae said to Baltazar. "Orsembians in our ranks while we march through their homes."

Baltazar was stroking his mustache with his thumb and forefinger. "It's not like they haven't marched through them before," he said thoughtfully.

Recha's eyebrows leapt up. "You're not *actually* considering—"

A sharp knock came from the tent pole outside.

"Pardon, La Dama," a guard outside said. "A Capitán Viezo is requesting to speak with you."

"Now what, Sevesco?" she cursed under her breath, taking a frustrated bite out of the remaining pepper. She spun on her heels toward the tent flap then stopped.

"Hide that," she whispered to Hiraldo, pointing at the chest, then stomped out of the tent.

She threw the tent flap back and pursed her lips at the head of her espis standing off to the side, out of uniform and dressed like a laborer in dusty trousers and jacket over his long-sleeved shirt. He was watching Hiraldo's staff standing away from him, none meeting his eye, with a practiced smile and his hands behind his back.

Great! Recha ate the remaining bite of her pepper then tossed the stem away. *He knows they're hiding something.*

"Sevesco," she said warningly, snatching his attention. She approached him, keeping her voice low. "You're out of uniform."

"People are more willing to talk if they think you're a common labor instead of an officer," he replied cheerfully.

"Oh?" Recha raised an eyebrow. "And whom have you been talking to?"

Please don't say wagon drivers carrying loads of gold, she prayed. *Please don't say wagon drivers carrying loads of gold.*

"I've been doing some snooping around the prisoners and camp followers you just caught," Sevesco explained, keeping his voice just as low, "looking for tidbits of information that might not be in any reports we collected last night—

camp rumors and such. Turns out you caught some Sarans in the mix, but that's not important. I ran across one particular story about last night that caught my attention, though. It was about how we lost the baggage train that you narrowly threatened to massacre to get back."

"I was *not* going to—"

Recha bit her lip. Being called ruthless by Baltazar was one thing, but by Sevesco, too?

"Did you find out something important or not? If not, or if you just heard a funny story, Cornelos has more paperwork for me."

Sevesco shrugged. "Would someone the Orsembians are calling a Hero be important?"

~~~

Recha's jaw burned from clenching her teeth together to preserve her calm demeanor. Every now and then, she would roll her shoulders back in a constant battle against the urge to warily hunker among her guards as they escorted her deep into the camp's infirmary.

Cries of hungry or scared children reverberated in steady pulses, interrupted by the sudden wails of men. A vile stench hung in the air—a mixture of bile, vomit, blood, and manure. The rising wind cast the camp into a muted gray by sweeping rolling clouds overhead, completing the macabre scene.

I guess it was a good thing I didn't eat all my lunch. Recha kept her hands folded in front of her, pressed into her belly.

Most of the tents or people sitting out beside tents weren't injured. Most were the women and children they had captured along with the enemy's baggage train, being sorted, their backgrounds checked, and looked after for injuries.

Companies of her own soldiers were tending to them, guarding them while staff officers sorted them. Red, bloodshot eyes and hateful glares followed her as she walked behind Sevesco through the infirmary.

I did this to them. She squeezed her fingers tighter together until her fingernails dug into her knuckles. *I took your loved ones away.*

It hadn't escaped her that soldiers on campaign often formed relationships and even married camp followers. It was an old lesson Baltazar had warned her Companions against when growing up, although he hadn't known she was eavesdropping when he had.

"*They may say camp women make good wives, but not for calleroses or you four,*" he'd said. "*You four are going to be proper officers and gentlemen. Paragons of what it means to be calleros. Not embarrassments.*"

"How much farther?" she asked.

"Just up here," Sevesco assured her from over his shoulder. He causally walked down the lane between the hastily erected, open tents, taking long, determined strides. The path was clear from word spreading that Recha was making a surprise visit. Sevesco walked several paces in front of them, hands in his pocket, shoulders hunched, trying look inconspicuous.

If he dragged me out here for nothing—

A deep, howling yell jerked her from her thoughts.

Sevesco turned off to a completely erected tent. The lane abruptly cut off, and several paces away sat a group of disheveled men, sitting on the ground under guard. Many of them gave her startled looks, while others grimly listened and looked at the tent.

Orsembian soldiers. She tilted her head, her curiosity growing. Her guard, however, formed a line between them and her, sharing nods to the soldiers guarding the prisoners.

"He's in here," Sevesco said, grabbing the tent flap then disappearing inside.

Recha and one member of her guard followed and halted at the entrance, staring at the scene before them.

"Hold him down, for Savior's sake!" a man demanded the instant she entered.

Four men wrangled with an enormous man filling up two short, wooden tables. They struggled to tie ropes around the giant as he kicked and jerked underneath them. Another man—a doctor Recha assumed—dressed in undershirt, suspenders, and trousers, held the big man's head. A roll of bandages hung off the man's face, covering half of it.

"There is nothing we can do," another man, standing off to the side with his arms folded, said. "He's just going to bleed out with those wounds."

"No!" Harquis yelled, charging across the tent and glaring at the man. "You must save him!"

The hair on the back Recha's neck stood up. *Harquis!*

As if hearing her thoughts, the cultist rounded on her, his white eyes locked on her.

She jerked back at his contorted features, the veins sticking out of his neck and pulsing on his sweaty forehead. His cheeks and knuckles went white, clutching the shafts of her guards' halberds. The pink eye on his jacket was the only color that stood out about him.

Recha stared, mouth slightly ajar, unsure of what to do. "*What* is going on here?" she demanded.

"*Eulalia!*" the injured man roared, arching his back and sticking his chest up into the air. He held the pose for a few moments until finally giving way under the weight of the men on top of him.

The yell ripped through the tent, leaving her standing speechless. She had heard many cries on her way here, many outbursts of pain and loss. There was something in the timbre in that cry, a longing lost that cut into her chest and rang in harmony with something deep within her.

Harquis snapped around as everyone else gawked at her. "Marquesa!" he said, pointing at the man on the tables. "This man *must* be saved! I beseech you, order these men to do so."

Recha passed perplexed looks between the equally confused doctors. She passed a glance around the rest of the startled faces of the men holding the bigger man down until fixing on Sevesco, conspicuously in a corner of the tent.

"What is *he* doing here?" she asked him.

"He is *Scorched*, La Dama," Harquis said before Sevesco had a chance. "He *must* live!"

"He found us," Sevesco whispered, shrugging. "But the man on the table—or actually, tables—is the man the Orsembians are calling a hero."

Recha looked back at the injured man. The doctors' helpers finally got the man's legs tied down. He was missing his left boot and bleeding from kicking his feet, loosening the bandage. His clothes were cut and slashed with shallow bloodstains up his body, as if he had jumped into a whirlwind of razor blades.

"He's too far gone," the doctor off to the side said. "Begging your pardon, La Dama, but with all those wounds, especially his face"—he grimaced at the man—"he's going to bleed out in the hour."

"We can stop the bleeding!" the doctor holding the man's head said. "Once we've stopped it and sewed him up, we can treat his face. Most of them are old scars."

Recha slowly approached the table, listening to the doctors and taking in the man now that the helpers were securing the ropes and getting off him.

Have I . . . seen him before?

Her brow furled as she thought back. A man of his size should have stuck out, but she couldn't place him.

"It would be better if it was done quickly," the other doctor suggested. "He's a soldier; he'd understand."

The doctor holding the man's head leaped between him and the injured man. "What kind of doctor are you?" he spat, growling up at them. His spectacles hung from his nose. "He only has multiple lacerations, not a gut wound. By the Savior, are mercy killings in place of care what passes for doctoring among Lazornians?"

Recha snapped her head up. "You're an Orsembian?"

Her guard at the tent entrance shuffled his feet and took one step in before she raised a hand to him.

The doctor with the spectacles dropped his head and kept it low as he turned about. "Doctor Maranon, at your service, La Dama," he said. "Formally of Don

Givanzo's brigade, which is now . . . I am only here now to look after my patients."

"We allowed him to stay out of professional curtesy, La Dama," the last doctor said. "He knew the condition of the prisoners, but I'm afraid there's no calming this one down! He's having a bad reaction to the laudanum. Whatever delusion he's in, there's no getting him out."

Recha's attention was drawn to the loose bandages wrapped and hanging off the injured man's face. Blood stained them from ear to ear. A gurgling wheeze escaped his mouth, interrupted sporadically with a mild cough that blew the bandage from his mouth. The cloth clung to his cheeks as if they were hollow.

Her eyebrows shot up. *He's the man that moved the wagon!*

The memory flooded her of the lone Orsembian who had pushed back a wagon from the circle while others had argued. Cornelos had pointed at the gap, expecting orders, but she had waved him down to wait. They had been too far away to hear what the man had said after moving the wagon, but whatever it'd been had made them start walking out, avoiding a bloodbath.

The sight of the blood dripping on the table under him, though, made her frown.

"He doesn't look good," she said, shaking her head. She looked at Harquis, meeting his glossy stare, then to Sevesco, and finally to the doctors. "If he's not going to make it, I won't allow any more suf—"

The injured man's great hand seized hers. His rough calluses gently held her in a tight embrace.

Recha froze, staring down at the man. Everyone else froze, as well.

The injured man was tied and no longer struggling. He stared back at her. A dark pair of eyes focused and unfocused, as if seeing yet not seeing her with pooling tears dripping from their corners.

"It's . . . all right . . . Eulalia," the injured man finally said, his breathing slowing, calming. He ran his big thumb across the back of her hand. "I'll take care . . . of everything. We'll . . . go home . . . soon."

Recha flickered a glance down at her hand, to his caressing thumb. *Is he . . . trying to comfort me?*

"It's all right," she agreed, forcing her voice to be as calm as possible. "Everything is well."

The man let out a deep breath and nodded, drawing a collective sigh of relief from everyone else. His head's motion loosened the bandages hanging from his face. Like falling leaves, they peeled off his cheeks and drifted onto the floor.

Recha's stomach rolled. A soft gasp barely escaped her tightening throat, cutting her breath and leaving her mouth gaping. She stared at the most horrendous sight she had ever seen, and she couldn't look away.

The man's cheeks weren't hollow; they'd been carved out. Red-soaked bundles of cloth were pressed into holes where the sides of his mouth should have been. Slashes and zigzagging scars were etched around them. His mouth muscles were visible underneath the remaining skin, and pieces of his lips were missing, exposing his teeth.

What happened to his face? The thought screamed inside her head. Her body started to shake. He was an enemy soldier. Anything could have happened last night under the cover of darkness. *Did one of my soldiers . . . do that?*

She glared at Doctor Maranon. "His face," she demanded, "who did this to him?"

Maranon held his hands up. "Forgive me, La Dama," he plead, "but I don't know. He's had those scars for years. I asked about them back when I first treated him, but he would never say how or who—"

"Borbin," the injured man hissed, barely a whisper.

Everyone in the tent turned toward the injured man, his head lulling back against the table, rolling on the wood.

"It's the laudanum," the other doctor said. "The delirium's making him babble."

Recha shot a look at Harquis. His milky eyes bore back into hers.

"*Scorched,*" the cultist growled, "as deeply as you." He turned his head down at the injured man. "He's been burning for years."

"What's his name?" she asked.

"Necrem," Maranon replied, dabbing Necrem's weeping cheeks with a damp cloth. "Necrem Oso."

Recha licked her lips then took a deep breath to steady her nerves. She squeezed Necrem's hand and calmy asked, "Necrem? Who did this to you?"

The man's head shot up at hearing his name. His pupils were wider than before, less focused. The remains of his lips peeled back, exposing all of his teeth as he hissed, "*Marqués Borbin!*"

Interlude

2nd of Iohan, 1009 N.F (e.y.)

Sweat ran down Necrem's face in streams, dripping on the polished top of his four-hundred-pound anvil that he struggled to load in the back of his tool wagon. The mild, True Fall evening breeze offered the only relief, sweeping across his drenched back, his soaked shirt clinging to him as the Easterly Sun's rays clung to remain in the sky.

He set the anvil on the wagon's floorboards with a *thud* then took it by the horn to move it over to the side. Being one of the heaviest things to load, he made sure it was near the rear of the wagon where he could easily pull it out and not have to carry it too far.

He breathed a heavy sigh of relief once it was resting against the sideboards of the wagon's bed. He braced his aching arms against the wagon, muscles flexing on their own after lifting such a heavy load and hung his head to take deeper breaths.

"Just a few more tools," he told himself. "Then no more unloading until home."

"That sounds wonderful."

Necrem lifted his head, grinning through his exhaustion and the wet strands of hair clinging to his forehead at the vision walking up to him.

Eulalia had a playful bounce in her step and a rich smile that made his heartbeat faster. Her honey-brown hair swayed behind her with every step she took, matching the swaying of her tan skirts. Her sleeveless blouse exposed her sun-kissed arms.

She hadn't liked the clothes at first; however, the heat from the constant traveling and being outdoors soon changed her opinion on the garment.

Necrem noticed a light flush running across her delicate cheeks, framing her button nose, and then he saw the two cups she was carrying.

"Joining in the celebrations, are we?" he teased, leaning one hand against the tool wagon and putting the other on his hip. "I thought you didn't care much for campaigning?"

"Oh, I don't," Eulalia replied, shaking her head. She walked up to him, her head only coming up to his chest, and had to crane her neck back to look up at him. "But even a village girl like me can celebrate one coming to an end." She winked at him and held out a cup.

"Thank you!" Necrem said, perking up at seeing a drink being offered after such heavy work.

His fingers lightly brushed against hers as he took the cup, sending tingling sparks running through his still trembling arm. He caught a smoldering, mischievous look in her eye as she gave him the cup and wrapped her arm around her waist. They'd been married only a year now, and he never tired of catching the looks she gave him.

She's up to something. He watched her watching him over the rim of her cup as he raised his to his lips. *I wonder if I'm going to get any sleep tonight or—*

The sharp, acid burn hit his tongue instantly. The fruity scent of mango and grape shot up his nose, making him snort as he pulled the cup back.

"What—!" Necrem coughed and peered into the cup at the pale pink liquid sloshing inside. "I thought this was beer!"

Eulalia laughed into her cup, her voice a musical trill. She hugged herself harder as her shoulders rose and fell.

"It's lamila berry wine." She giggled. "They were selling it cheap in the camp market, so I thought I would bring some of the celebrations to you since I just *know* you're going to find some reason to avoid them."

"I—"

Necrem's words died on his lips at the sight of raised eyebrows and grin from over her cup. He turned his head away, forcing himself not to smile while feeling his cheeks heat up. She had an incredible knack of knowing just what to say to tease him. Often, he liked it, but he wasn't going let her know that.

"I wasn't going to avoid them," he grumbled, lifting his cup to his lips. "I just have a lot of stuff to take care of, is all." He took a small sip of the wine, sucking in his cheeks at how sharp it tasted.

He hardly drank anything stronger than malted beer. Too much liquor could make one's hands shake, and that wasn't good for a smith who needed to keep a good grip on his hammer and make sure his strokes were precise.

"*Sure* you do," Eulalia said, elbowing him in the gut. "Even though you put away most of our things yesterday." She glanced at the anvil in the back of his tool wagon. "Why did you unload it all this morning?"

Necrem frowned and looked over his tool wagon. Past the anvil was his bellow works and movable furnace with the stall stacked on top of them. The furnace wasn't the biggest, but it was usable and fitted onto one wagon with room and weight to spare. Closer to the front were several iron toolboxes full of hammers and materials. Tied on top of all of that was his wooden stall where he would sit in front of his workstation for calleroses and other soldiers to make their orders.

"Because it was all too heavy," he replied, "and the wagon would have been better if we had to abandon camp in a hurry."

"Abandon camp?" Eulalia blinked up at him, her teasing smile gone and replaced with a concerned frown. "Why would we abandon camp? Did you . . . expect something bad to happen?"

Necrem gave her a small smile before dropping his head. He ground the dusty earth with the toe of his boot. Sometimes it was easy to remember this was her first time on campaign. Other times, he was so swept up in being married that he forgot.

"You never know how a battle's going to turn out," he explained. "You never know if they're even going to happen. But when they do, it's best to prepare for the worst. If the army lost today"—he swallowed, searching for the most delicate words possible—"I wanted to make sure our faster wagon was ready." His chest tightened. *Not very manly to admit you were getting ready to run.*

He hesitantly lifted his head, expecting her to be shaking her head or frowning at him disappointedly. Instead, Eulalia stared unfocused into the wagon, her hand holding her cup by her fingertips at her side while her free hand fiddled with her golden, oval locket hanging around her neck.

The glint of steel in the locket's gold chain caught his eye, the makeshift clasp and link standing out like a dent in a breastplate. He pressed the forefinger on his left hand and thumb together. The smooth calluses on their tips still fit neatly together after nearly two and a half years from forging the small pieces of metal.

It had been his first attempt to smith jewelry and his sworn last. Despite meeting the most beautiful woman in all Desryol and winning his wager, he never wanted to work with something so delicate ever again.

"Necrem," Eulalia said softly, snapping him back to the present. She looked up at him, her eyes soft, deep pools he could get lost in. "You would have been leaving your forge."

"It would have slowed us down. Besides"—he shrugged—"if we build that smith shop we talked about—you know, one with rooms above it and a forge in the back or the side—we won't have to worry about going on campaigns or need a movable forge."

Eulalia licked her lips and glanced down at her feet for a moment. "But dear"—she stepped closer—"how were you expecting to have the deberes to pay for building our shop if you expected the army to lose? If we lost, would the Union have been able to pay us your commission?"

Necrem grunted. He rolled his eyes upward as he thought. The answer quickly came back to him, refreshened by the first time he had gone on campaign and the army had been assigned to lost. He hadn't had any commission that year, and narrowly was allowed safe passage with his tools and a small portion of funds he had collected on smaller jobs.

He broke out into a sweat again, knowing what he was in for.

He glanced down at Eulalia, finding her staring up at him, her eyes narrowed, her lips slightly pursed.

"I'm guessing they wouldn't, would they?" she asked.

Necrem swallowed, looking away from being unable to match her stare, and grumbled, "No."

"What was that?" Eulalia turned her head, angling her right ear up at him. She was grinning now, too, and her eyes twinkled with a teasing light.

"No," he replied louder with a begrudging sigh, "if the army loses, then there is no payment to the Union. We wouldn't get a commission."

"Mmhmm," Eulalia hummed, nodding her head. She set her cup down on the tool wagon then reached up to place her hand on his chest, ignoring his sweat. "Darling, I know this is my first time on campaign, and you probably have been through this situation before and probably did this very thing before—"

"*But . . .*" Necrem expected that to be the next thing she said. He closed his mouth quickly, though, when she gave him her narrow-eyed stare again.

"*But,*" she continued, "we can't afford to think like that anymore. We *need* that commission. Not just for the shop, but also for . . . you know." She looked down at her belly.

She wasn't showing yet, having only learned she was expecting a few months ago. After the initial shock, a mixture of panic, excitement, and nervousness, everything became about settling down after this season was over.

"I know," Necrem replied, setting his own cup on the wagon. "I was just looking out for the more important things. I can always replace a forge. Or anvil.

Or hammers." Feeling her hand still pressed against his chest, he reached with one hand around her waist to pull her closer. "But not you."

"*Aw*," Eulalia cooed with a wide grin. "That's sweet! But *no*." She pressed her hand into his chest, pushed against him, and pulled back from him. "You are too sweaty for that right now."

"So?" Necrem smiled, keeping his hand on her waist while she pulled away.

I could just pull her back, he mused. *But when do I ever get a chance to tease her?*

"I thought you wanted us to join in on the celebrations?"

"*Necrem Oso!*" Eulalia whispered heavily, feigning a gasp. Her jaw dropped, though the corners of her mouth remained curled and she batted her eyelashes up at him. She also shot her arm out, locking the elbow and stiffened it in place. "Whatever gave you the idea of celebrating like *that*?" She narrowed her eyes again. "Is this a campaign habit you haven't told me about?"

Necrem saw through the tease and didn't fall for the look this time. "No," he replied calmly, "of course not." He pulled her waist, her arm unable to remain stiff for long and gave way as he gently added more strength to bring her closer. "I just thought, if my wife wanted to celebrate by bringing me wine after working so hard, she would want a more . . . *private* celebration. Just the two of us." He leaned down toward her, his cheek muscles aching from smiling.

Eulalia bit her lip as he slowly pulled her closer, never moving her hand away. Her shoulders started trembling as deep giggles boiled up from her throat and made her grin back.

Suddenly, she added her other hand to his chest then pushed back, sliding out of his grasp.

"Nope." She giggled. "Still too sweaty." She snatched her cup of wine and hopped out of reach. "If you *behave*, though, and clean up tonight, then . . . maybe then." She batted her eyelashes at him again over the rim of her cup as she took a sip of wine. Her free hand reached back up to fiddle with her locket again.

Necrem slumped his shoulders. After going through all that teasing only to be teased some more, it was almost too much for any husband to bear.

"If I behave?" He propped an elbow against the wagon then leaned against it. "What about all those things you said this morning? That wasn't very respectful, wife behavior, cussing like—"

"*Ah*!" Eulalia pointed at him, eyes wide and cheeks flushed. "That was because you were being so loud. Mama always said, never wake up or make a lot of noise around an expecting mama early in the morning." She sharply nodded her head and sniffed as if that had come straight out of the Savior's gospel.

Necrem closed his eyes to hide rolling them. Eulalia had suddenly begun recalling a lot of her mama's sayings ever since learning she was expecting.

Being she was the second eldest in a household of seven, he suspected she had heard plenty of sayings growing up.

"Hello to the happy couple!"

Necrem snapped his eyes open and turned to see Sanjaro Daved strolling through the remnants of the camp's smithing lane. The plucky cattle trader walked with a swagger in his step with his hands stuffed in his trousers. The fading Easterly Sun's rays glistened off the coppery, suntanned angles of his face, framed by dark curls of hair that needed a cut. It was a common joke that he grew it long while driving cattle to the campaign camps to hide the growing bald spot on the top his head.

Necrem raised his hand, a halfhearted wave, before checking on Eulalia. Her blush was gone, along with her eyes' twinkle. She folded her arms around her waist, holding her cup at her side. Necrem spotted the slight dimple in her cheek from her biting the inside of it before she put on a friendly smile.

"Hello, Sanjaro!" she greeted back. "Got paid your commission, I see."

Sanjaro stumbled to a stop, blinking at her. "Yes," he replied. "How did—"

"You had a very satisfied look about you," Eulalia said. "Like a happy, plump *pavaloro*." She grinned at her usual joke about his hooked nose. "Men usually get that look after they've finished work or . . ." Her cheeks flushed again. She shot a quick look at Necrem then cleared her throat and hid behind her cup, taking a small sip.

"Well, you're right there!" Sanjaro laughed, grinning broadly enough to show all his teeth as he walked up to Necrem. "I guess married life has taught you both a lot of things. Eh, happy Papa?" He elbowed Necrem in the gut.

Necrem hardly felt it yet straightened up and cleared his throat, anyway.

"So, they're paying commissions already?" he asked, hoping to change the subject. Eulalia's pregnancy had reached the ears of his friends in camp and fellow smiths in the Union. He wasn't sure who had teased him more about it— Eulalia or his friends. Sanjaro was one of the worst offenders, too.

"For me, anyway," Sanjaro replied, shrugging. "I brought in the beef, now everyone who's alive gets to eat." He barked a laugh. "And since there probably won't be any more campaigning after what happened today, they were eager to get me paid off and sent on my way. The marqués and all the stuffed shirts have a *big* party planned for themselves tonight!" He popped up his collar, stuck his chest and jaw out, and made a gruff look, as if imitating a baron or someone important. Or, at least how Sanjaro viewed the important people, anyway.

"Are you sure?" Necrem asked. "The campaign's over?"

"*Oh* yes!" Sanjaro nodded, and his eyes widened dramatically. "After the thrashing Ribera gave them today"—he frowned deeply and shook his head—"there's not a Quezlo man alive not running to Compuert."

"That bad, huh?"

"That bad." Sanjaro's face darkened briefly until he shoved it aside with a smirk. "But I guess you wouldn't know, would you?"

Sanjaro tilted his head and said to Eulalia, "He never watches the duels or the battles."

"Nothing much to watch," Necrem said.

He never got a taste for watching the calleroses duel between the armies, the banter and name calling that went on between them, the betting camp workers made on them, or watching battles when they rarely happened. Most of it was noisy bluster, a lot of words meaning nothing, and the rest simply . . . morbid.

Especially if one never knew if their side would be victorious or not. Best in those cases to stay around his belongings, like he did today, and make sure everyone knew immediately he was a smith.

Smiths were exempt from being chosen or taken captive as *sioneroses*. He had learned his second-year apprenticing on campaign it was best to remain in the smithing corner of camp after a fellow apprentice had wandered to watch the duels and got chosen to be a *sioneros* instead.

Poor Nicol.

"You'll never have to worry about him wagering on calleroses, will you?" Sanjaro barked a laugh, obviously trying to lighten the mood, snapping Necrem out of the memory.

"He better not," Eulalia said. She was looking up at him, swirling the wine in her cup. "An expecting mama doesn't want to hear good money was thrown after bad."

Sanjaro chuckled deeply from his belly, a deep rumble.

Necrem frowned and flickered glances at them. "If you two are going to poke fun at me," he said dryly, "I'm going to finish loading." He brushed past Sanjaro, toward a crate of nails and horseshoes.

"*Loading*?" Sanjaro called after him. "Some of the others are waiting for us in the market. You can't sit around in your wagon after a day like this!"

"*Excuse* you?" Eulalia growled. "Are you telling me you've come to steal my husband?"

Necrem hefted up the heavy crate. The loose nails and horseshoes clattered and rolled around inside as he turned around to see Sanjaro holding his hands up against Eulalia glaring down on him with a fist on her hip.

"No," Sanjaro said, nervously smiling. "No. Not steal. Maybe borrow for the evening. We do this every season. The campaign is over, and everyone wants to celebrate, except Necrem, still toiling away somewhere." He chuckled hesitantly. "Just trying to get him out more, is all. With your permission, of course! I promise he won't be kept out all night."

Necrem walked around them to load the crate into the tool wagon with the rest, watching Eulalia out of the corner of his eye. She kept a fist on her hip, but her lips were pursed and her eyes shifted.

She had made frequent comments about him needing to converse more with his fellow smiths and others in the camp. Her papa owned a mill in her home village and knew every shopkeeper by name. She said it was good for his business if he made as many friends as he could. That, unfortunately, meant she wanted him to be more sociable.

They're going to start conspiring against me, Necrem sensed.

"Fine," Eulalia said, fulfilling his premonition. "But Necrem Oso!"

Necrem snapped his head up from tying down the crate.

"You better come back cleaned up and sober," Eulalia said pointedly. A soft smile mulled about her lips. "We weren't finished with our *earlier* talk."

Necrem grunted then cleared his throat, going back to finishing tying the crate down. "Yes, ma'am."

Eulalia walked up to the wagon then snatched his wine cup. "Don't be out too late, darling," she said, flashing a smile up at him.

She strolled away, by the tool wagon toward their covered wagon. It was a small, cramped traveling house with wheels, larger than the tool wagon, with steps on the back and small door. Inside was a bed, barely big enough for them both, and a place for their clothes, all covered by thick, tan canvas stretched across the wagon's ribs. Eulalia gave him a wave once she walked up the steps then disappeared inside.

Once she was gone, Necrem hesitantly glanced at Sanjaro, the cattle trader had his head overtly turned away and hands stuffed in his back pockets, making his chest stick out. Sanjaro was a few years married himself and had probably caught all Eulalia's little hints.

I'm probably going to hear about it a lot tonight.

"*Well*," Sanjaro said, suddenly throwing his arms in the air, stretching, "want to find the rest of the fellows? You got permission from the wife, so you might as well enjoy it." He flashed another broad grin up at him.

"Let me clean up first," he replied, stifling a groan. "I'll feel better once I get all this sweat off me."

Necrem locked up his tool wagon then headed toward his and Eulalia's wagon to fetch a change of clothes. Sanjaro barked a laugh and trotted after him.

~~~

298

"To the White Sword!" a boisterous group of drunk soldiers toasted for the tenth time. Wooden and metal cups clinked together as men laughed then guzzled their beer.

"Got to hand it to soldiers," Miguel said, shaking his head and sending his shaggy, reddish-brown hair waving. "They can drink all night, make the same loud toasts, and still be as stupidly happy as when they started."

"They're just happy to be alive," Sanjaro said, taking a swallow of beer to wash down his beans.

"And getting all the attention," Rodjael grumbled, carving a hunk out of the roasted chicken breast sitting out on the table. He sawed haphazardly as he sneered at the camp women flocking the countless soldier sitting at tables and crowding the market.

"*Aw*, don't be sad, Rodjael," Sanjaro joked, elbowing the man. "You'll find a wife someday." He glanced up then winked at Necrem standing at the head of the table, content with his mug of beer and letting the others eat.

"You should be thankful," a camp worker three seats down from Miguel said through chewing a piece of meat. "Since you steelworkers haven't been paid yet, those soldiers are saving you money!"

The men filling the table and around it roared in laughter, joining the multitudes of laughing, cheering, toasting, and swearing going on all around them. Some pounded their fists on the table, making their cups, plates, and knives bounce and rattle on the tabletop.

The long table consisted of not only smiths, but also groomers, carpenters, and a few general laborers who did any work they were ordered and paid to do.

Necrem kept his chuckles low, hidden behind his mug. *I shouldn't laugh*, he told himself. *I'm a steelworker, too . . . and married.*

The small of his back itched, and he checked over his shoulders for Eulalia. That would have been the perfect time for her to appear after getting bored from waiting on him to return, despite him having arrived with Sanjaro less than half an hour ago.

"At least we steelworkers are going to *have* money to spend," Rodjael snapped back, straightening and leaning back on the bench with his nose in the air. He was trying to make himself look taller. He competed with Sanjaro in being the shortest man at the table.

"*Oh!*" some of the men cooed.

"Bravo!" another smith barked.

The camp worker who had started all this worked his chin while staring at Rodjael with narrow, close-set eyes as everyone else turned to him, itching on the edge of their seats with grins on their faces and mugs in their fists for a response.

"Maybe some of us are so good we don't *have* to pay," he finally retorted.

The grinning faces around him slowly curdled, dissolving into frowns. Men blinked and glanced at each other. Someone coughed. Another snorted.

"She must be cheap," someone grumbled.

A few cracked hissing laughs between their teeth while their shoulders bounced.

"You better thank the Savior you weren't conscripted," Miguel said. "Retorts like that would get you flogged by a calleros."

"But if you see that mythical woman tonight, better check your trousers before you leave," another man across the table said. "She's bound to have taken something out of them."

The laborer flung a half-eaten roll at the man across the table, causing everyone to erupted with laughter again.

Necrem took a cautious step back. If this developed into a food war, he would rather be left out of it. *It would make a good excuse to leave.*

Unfortunately, men around the laborer slapped him on the back and, soon, the table was divided with numerous small conversations.

Necrem's shoulders fell at watching his chance for an easy departure slip away. *I wonder if it is too early to wish them a good evening.*

The multiple conversations added to the mass noise around him. People talked over one another until it sounded like everyone was yelling at each other. This, in combination with the continuing toasting and laughing happening across the market.

The venders selling wine, beer, roast chicken and beef, bread, and numerous other foods were forced to shout over the crowd, eagerly pushing to sell as much food and drink as they could. This was the night they had waited for all campaign, after all. The night when the soldiers had their pay, most of the camp was relaxed, and there would be no marching tomorrow. The cooks spared nothing, filling the air with smoke from their cooking pits and roasted meats, which they had to sell tonight or risked it spoiling.

All the noise left a dull ringing in Necrem's ears as he lazily gazed around at the huge crowd. Being head and shoulders taller than most had a certain advantage in a time like this, and everywhere he looked, he saw groups of people as far he could see in flickering lantern lights on the tables and mounted on posts.

Probably half the camp's here.

"What's wrong, Necrem?" Miguel asked. "Get embarrassed by the mentioning of camp women, or are you checking to make sure the new wife isn't around to get on to you?"

The other smiths around their end of the table snickered up at him. Sanjaro had his head down, shaking it as he picked at the leftovers on his plate. Necrem was sure he was smiling.

"No," he replied dryly. He stepped back up to the table, his own size making him lord over it without meaning to. "I don't have to worry about that. She knows I'm coming home tonight."

"Oh, listen to him!" Miguel pointed up at him with his thumb as he faced the smiths around him. Miguel himself didn't look like a smith at first glance. He was as thin as a post, spindly looking, with a thick beard on his oval-shaped face. His arms, though, were all sinew, and he could hammer and work the bellows for hours with the best. "Barely a year wed, and she's got him trained."

Necrem ignored the snickers and chuckles. "Don't worry, Miguel," he said, setting his mug on the table. "You'll find out one day."

Miguel grunted, and a few others groaned, frowning from wanting more.

"That's all we're going to get out of him," Sanjaro said, pointing at table knife up at him. "As big as he is, you're not going to get a big boast out of Necrem." He shook his head then stabbed the last bit of chicken left on his plate, picked it up to his mouth, and ate it.

"That's because you're out driving cattle when we're hammering on smith row," Miguel said, rolling his eyes at Sanjaro.

He crookedly tilted his head up at Necrem. "What is it that you yell at people?" He held up his hands dramatically. "'Baron Emousia himself said your steel is the finest he's held.' Yes, *that's* not boastful at all."

More snickers followed, and Necrem again ignored them. Instead, he folded his arms, his chest puffing out on reflex.

"Hard earned praise is not boasting," he replied. "It's the same pride you can take in a hard-earned deber."

People around the end of the table froze in place. A couple held their mugs to their lips without drinking while a few, Sanjaro included, paused mid-chew to glance up at him. Miguel simply sat there, randomly looking back and forth at Necrem and the men around him.

"You really can't make fun of this man, can you?" he finally said to Sanjaro, resulting in snickers from the rest as they went back to finishing their meals.

Sanjaro shrugged. "Not about his work." He finished chewing then swallowed. "Now, about him being a proudly expecting *papa*, though." He grinned up Necrem.

Several of the men knocked on the table with their mugs.

"Here's to you, Oso!" one shouted, raising his mug in the air before chugging it back.

"Here's to another giant steel hammerer, eh, boys!" Another laughed, making more raise their mugs in toasts.

Others joined them down the table, yet it was likely they didn't know why they were toasting again. They likely didn't care, either.

Necrem waved them down. "Thanks," he said humbly, his chest deflating as he battled against the urge to step away from the table.

The congratulations had been endless since Eulalia had found out she was expecting. It was his own fault, too. Caught up in the moment of excitement so great it had overthrown his common sense, he had rushed down smith row to tell everyone.

"Any plans for after the baby's born?" Miguel asked. "Still going to join the campaigns or planning on settling into place?"

Nearly everyone at the table turned at that. It was a decision that stared every worker in the face that one day they would all have to settle down and give up campaigning, no matter what job they filled for the camps.

Necrem shuffled his feet as more leaned forward, waiting and angling their ears to catch his response through the rambunctious noise surrounding them.

"Probably settle," he replied. "She hasn't said anything, but I don't think Eulalia's liked this at all. The constant moving and all."

She doesn't like the soldiers. Surrounded by so many, he kept that to himself. He remembered her telling him many times that the soldiers made her uneasy whenever she went to fetch something outside or near the edge of other sections of the camp. She would catch them watching her, especially the calleroses, when she visited the camp market, and she didn't appreciate it.

"I think this year's commission and the money we've saved will be enough for a shop and forge," he continued, smiling just thinking about it. "Eulalia's thinking we can build rooms on top of the shop to sleep and live in, like real city folk."

"Oh!" Miguel cooed. "She's even doing the thinking for him."

"Well, she won't have to think of how we can draw business," Necrem retorted. "Having a baron say I make the finest steel should make a great slogan, eh?" He slapped Miguel on the back of his shoulder, the smaller man swaying from the impact.

"And you said he wasn't boastful!" Miguel said to Sanjaro.

Again, Sanjaro shrugged and held his hands up. "I could have been wrong."

Necrem laughed with the rest of the table and reached down with his right hand to pat and shake Sanjaro by the shoulder.

"Maybe you can help pick out a good spot when we get back to Manosete," he said. "You have a shop there, too, don't you?"

"Aye," Sanjaro replied, his smile eroding from his lips, "but Annette doesn't like it. She wants to live further inside the city. I keep telling her it's better for a butcher shop to be outside the city, nearer the freshest stock." He shook his head and grimaced. "But she keeps looking. Now she might have good ideas for a location for you. She actually *likes* Eulalia."

Necrem frowned down at his friend. "What about me?"

Sanjaro nervously looked up and winced apologetically. "*Well . . .*"

Everyone around them erupted in laughter, some pointing at them.

"Don't take it too hard, Necrem," Miguel said. "She may not like him"—he gestured at Sanjaro—"that much by the way he's always eager to go on campaign."

"Hey!" Sanjaro yelled, throwing up his hands. "I love my wife very much, I'll have you know." He sat up tall in his seat, jutting his jaw out. His head bobbed, and his jaw began to tremble, unable to hold back a growing smile. "I just need a few months out of the year away before I go back home, is all."

The table shook from the laughter and mugs pounding against it, plates and knives rattling off the wood, that other conversations around them stopped to take in the rowdier spectacle.

Necrem doubled over laughing with them. Yet, mentioning being away brought back his sense of time.

"With that," he said once those near him had calmed down enough to hear, "I think it's time I head back."

"Oh no!" Sanjaro protested. "You got to stay longer. You've barely eaten anything."

Necrem shook his head. "I'm not hungry. Besides, you heard Eulalia; she wanted me to be back before it got too late and after I cleaned up. Well, I'm cleaned up, and it's not too late yet."

Sanjaro waved him off. "Fine! Off with you then. Leave the rest of the beer for us!" He picked up his cup then clicked it against Miguel's.

"Have a good evening," Necrem wished them, turning away.

"You, too, happy Papa!" Sanjaro yelled after him. "Don't keep her up too late!"

Necrem missed a step as he tried to slip around a couple of chatting, unarmed provost guards. The laughter of the table was swallowed up by the conversations around him, and instead of looking back, he snickered and went on his way.

~~~

The camp grew quieter the farther he strolled away from the market. He stuck to the main paths dividing the areas of camp into the remains of the smith row, following the lanterns hanging from posts that the provosts had lit. Some, though, had been neglected, most likely the same reason there were less campfires among the tents. Everyone was either in a hurry to celebrate and forgot them or didn't see the need to light them.

They couldn't have lit a few fires, he grumbled then shrugged it off. It did make his trek back to his wagons that more difficult. *Eulalia will understand. I had to take the long way around.*

He couldn't cut through and around the tents without any fires. He knew he would get lost after the first few steps between the tents, then probably trip on every tent anchor, rope, and post he could bang his foot against. The idea of tripping and crashing through the side or roof of a tent and finding Savior knew what or whom inside was enough to keep him on the lantern lit path.

A slight breeze rolled into camp, tugging and sending tent canvas flapping against their posts. It whipped up dust around him, forcing Necrem to stop as the small grains whirled up from the ground and into his face. His eyes watered and stung. He turned his back to the wind, hunching against it, then immediately pressed his face into his hands.

Dammit. He rubbed his eyes profusely. *When are we going to get some rain?*

This was the first campaign he had been on when it hadn't rained once. On the one hand, it was a blessing not having to deal with muddy roads and sudden downpours. He didn't have to worry about his wagons, especially his tool wagon, getting stuck in the mud. However, the lack of rain gripped everything in a drought. If it didn't rain soon, times could get rough in a couple months when False Winter began.

A distant yet high-pitched yell drifted on the wind.

Necrem jerked his head up, blinking tears out of his eyes and looking about. Everywhere he turned, he peered down between alleys of tents before the blackness of night swallowed the light.

I swore I heard something.

He frowned, rubbing his burly forearms, the hairs standing on end. He had rolled his shirtsleeves up to his elbow after he had washed and changed. He fiddled with the thought of rolling them back down, yet instead walked on.

Army camps were strange places. They were moving cities, driven to provide the mass body of men marching out to either fight or stand around at whims of their masters. For the workers in them, it mirrored working in the cities and villages they came from, yet with stricter rules. However, just like those cities and villages, one could find all sorts of people doing things, especially at night, that were better off avoiding.

Necrem quickened his pace.

He breathed a sigh of relief when he found the remains of his stall. He had left up the tarp that covered his workstation around his forge that provided shade from the sun while he worked. A barren space remained with everything already loaded.

I'll finish this up tomorrow. He rapped his knuckles on one of the posts then walked under the tarp, through it and to the back. He checked out his tool wagon. A quick glance in the dim light told him everything appeared to still be in there.

Another nightly breeze blew across his face the moment he stepped out from behind the wagon. His nose wrinkled at the heavy scent of pipe smoke. The musky weed made him flinch.

Someone's been—

He stopped short.

A man sat slouched forward on the steps of Necrem's wagon with his elbows propped on his legs and a short-stemmed pipe dangled from his mouth. The lanterns hanging off the back of the wagon cast a long shadow out from the man, obscuring his face.

Necrem could make out the man's tousled hair from the outline of light and lime green coming off his loose jacket on his shoulders.

A request? He stared at the man skeptically for a moment. *Now?*

The man's shadow tremored, shaking back and forth.

Necrem glanced at the lanterns rocking slightly and their candles flickering, probably from another gust of wind that hadn't reached him yet.

"Go away," the man said, his voice low from speaking around his pipe. "Nothing for you around here tonight. Best you go join the rest of them someplace else." He made a flimsy wave back toward the camp market.

Necrem jerked his head back. "This is *my* wagon," he replied.

The man snickered then took out his pipe. "Sure it is."

Necrem balled his fists at his side. As big as he was, he had learned when he was young to keep his temper tightly hammered down. An outburst, even a small one, could lead to someone easily getting hurt. There were some things not worth getting mad about and some people not worth it. Some people, though, no one was allowed to lose their temper with.

Now, glaring down at the man, he didn't care about any of that. He stomped into the light, taking full advantage of his size to step in front and lord over the man.

"Get off my wagon's steps," he growled.

He expected the man to shrink and slink away. Most men would when faced with someone of Necrem's size.

The man on the steps snickered instead, took a long drag on his pipe, the embers within flaring red, before he pulled back and blew smoke up at Necrem's face. "Go away," he said. "There's no room for you. Tonight's all booked up as it is."

The musky smoke made Necrem's eyes water, and he waved it away. He glowered down at the man, his jaw starting to ache from how tense he held it. "What—?"

A muffled cry made his hair stand on end. It lasted only for a brief second, cut off suddenly. However, Necrem jerked his head up to where it was coming from.

Inside his wagon.

The lanterns shifted again, their lights flickering and weaving. But there was no wind. One of the wagon's axles squeaked. The man on the wagon's steps swayed from side to side.

The wagon jostled from side to side.

Necrem could barely make out movement within the wagon from a dim, obscure light.

Eulalia was in there.

"*Eulalia!*" he gasped.

He sprung forward, grabbed the man by the shoulder, then flung him aside with enough effort to swing his arm.

"*Hey!*" the man yelped in surprise to find himself pulled off the step and tossed out of the way like a bundle of cloth. He rolled on the ground with a grunt. "You can't go in there!"

Necrem was already up the steps. He seized the door latch with both hands then jerked it back. The door flung open, nearly hitting him in the face from his hurry. Narrowly missing it, he ducked down into the wagon—

The smell hit him first. His foot was barely over the threshold, a mixture of human sweat, human breath, closed in, stale air, and a sour, musky odor instantly gagged him. His stomach heaved instantly, and gasping for air made it worse.

"Eul . . . alia . . ."

His eyes adjusted, snatching away his words as the silhouettes in the dim light of small lantern nestled in the far corner of the wagon took form. Two naked men were holding his wife down on the small pallet of a bed, barely fit for two, filling up most of the wagon bed. One held her arms above her head with his knees while also choking her with her locket chain. The other knelt on top of her, grunting while holding her legs.

Necrem's chest suddenly tightened. It was as if his entire body was being crushed from within. His gaze focused on Eulalia's face.

Her mouth gaped, hoarse gasping sounds barely escaped from her either trying to scream or trying to breathe. Blood trickled around the top of her lip and across her face from her nose, now slightly bent. Her wide eyes stared up at the wagon's canvas, unfocused and haunting, as if her sight and mind had fled into the heavens to escape the mutilation her body could not.

Necrem's hearing abandoned him. His view of his surroundings vanished. Everything was closing. He panted, yet he didn't know how. The crushing within him should have squeezed his lungs flat. His heart boomed in his ears.

Faster.

Faster!

Faster!

The world became red.

"Get out!" a muffled, annoyed voice demanded. A third man, half-undressed, who Necrem hadn't seen lounging between the door and the violation, lazily rose to his feet with an arm outstretched toward him. "She's busy tonight. Come back—"

Necrem seized the man's arms with both hands. He gripped the sweaty limb, squeezed with all his might, then wrenched the man off his feet. He felt the muscles, veins, and bones in his grip and twisted it as he pulled, dragging the man off his feet. He drowned out the man's shocked, agonizing cry under a raging bellow that issued from his gut.

He turned on his heels, hoisting the half-dressed man out of the wagon, and threw him on the other trying to come up behind him, crashing them down on top of each other in a heap. Without a second glance, he spun around then sprung into the wagon. The pounding of his boots against the floorboards exploded like thunder with his heart booms to his ears.

The man on top of Eulalia leaned up then turned his head back. The dim light caught his sweat-slick, disheveled brown hair, his frustrated expression, and narrow jaw opening to speak.

Necrem swung with his right with his dash of momentum. His fist struck the man on the side of his face. His broad knuckles connected with the man's jaw.

He felt something give.

A muffled crunch.

Then the man's head snapped completely around to the other side. *Crack!*

Teeth flew in the air as the man's body jerked, his grip releasing Eulalia's legs, and then his body flopped over to the side at an angle against the side of the wagon.

His compatriot stared, mouth agape, shaking in place at his supposed friend slumped aside unnaturally.

Necrem grabbed him by the shoulder. The man jerked up, mouth still agape, green eyes dancing between Necrem's face and raised fist. "Wait—"

"*Let her go!*" Necrem roared.

His arm dropped naturally, as if he held a hammer. Only, it was his fist that drove squarely into the man's face, snapping and flattening his nose instantly.

The man's head jerked back then rolled around like a newborn. And Necrem kept punching.

The wet smack of flesh against flesh, the crackle of bones splintering inside, and teeth popping out shoved his roaring heart from his ears. Blow after blow, he rained down, splitting the man's cheeks and blacking then reddening his eyes.

Something snapped and something rolled across the floorboards.

Necrem froze. He drifted his gaze down between his feet, his bloody fist hung in the air.

Eulalia's gold locket laid there. The chain broken.

He looked and saw her staring up at him, trembling violently. Her face was covered in the man's blood. Her pupils shrunk and widened. Shrunk and widened. Suddenly, she sucked in air and screamed!

The high-pitched wail cut through his body, shattering the heartbeats in his ears. Her body was covered with red marks, the early stages of bruises, around her belly and hips. She flailed on the ground. Her legs furiously kicked the man on top of her away. Her arms now free, she rolled over, wrapping herself up, gasping and crying to the verge her throat was hoarse in moments.

The sight of her bruised body, especially her belly, made Necrem shake. He glared back at the kneeling man he held by the shoulder, lifeless save for a ragged breath escaping his swollen lips.

"You *hit* her?" Necrem growled. His teeth ground together. His fingernails cut into his palm. "*You hit her!*"

He didn't count the blows. He kept punching, over and over. The man's ragged breathing stopped, but Necrem kept hitting until the man's face was a red mush.

"You giant piece of shit!" the half-dressed man yelled, scrambling back into the wagon and lunging for Necrem.

He grabbed around Necrem's arm then pulled himself up to knee him in the gut. Necrem grunted but was saved from losing his footing by bracing the back of his shoulders against the wagon's ceiling. He tossed the beaten man away then rounded on the other holding his arm.

They locked eyes. The other man flinched, his snarl slipping away to gape, fearful realization.

"*None* of you will touch her again!" Necrem yelled.

He bulled through the man, using the man's grip on his arm to charge him out of the wagon. The man's footing slipped on the steps. He gasped and yelped, almost sliding under Necrem's feet if he hadn't grabbed the man instead. Necrem lifted him up, carried him down the steps, then rammed in him into his tool wagon.

The man made a gargling gasp. His body shook and spasmed from his back slamming into the wagon and Necrem's shoulder crashing into his chest. His eyes rolled back in his head.

Necrem, still being carried by momentum, wrenched his arm free of the man then grabbed the man's head with both of his hands. His broad fingers nearly reaching all the way around the top of the man's head.

"*Never* again!" he snarled.

He smashed the man's head against tool wagon. The man's skull made a hard *thunk*, as if it were splitting like a melon. More hot blood slicked Necrem's fingers, letting the weight of the man's body pull him down into a pile on the ground.

"You won't touch her again!"

His shoulders rose and fell. His labored breathing made puffs of steam in the cooling night air. Aches from his legs, arms, and particularly his right hand were springing up in his mind. He suddenly felt like he was about to collapse or—

Necrem caught the flash of steel flash out of the corner of his eye.

He jerked back, yet the dagger's edge sliced across his left cheek. The stinging slice made him wince then snarl as his blood leaked down his face.

"You're quicker than I thought," the last man said, holding a dagger out in front of him in a strange stance. He coldly glared at Necrem with an expressionless look on his face—no sneer, snarl, or raging grimace. "Do you have any idea what you've *done*? Do you have any idea who we *are*?"

Necrem's fatigue vanished. His vision narrowed down to the remaining assailant. "You . . . *raped my wife*!"

"She wasn't your wife, you deluded fool," the man said. "She's a camp whore. No matter how many times she let you bed her, she was still a whore." He shook his head. "I should let them hang you, but let it never be said that Cal—"

Necrem sprang with a bellow. Each slur against Eulalia made the muffled drumming louder and louder in his head. It felt like it was about to explode.

The man slashed at him, trying to fend him off or back away. Necrem took a cut on the arm from batting the dagger away then grabbing the man's arm. He slammed into the man, throwing them both down on the ground.

Their struggle quickly became a grapple. Both men wrapped around each other, hitting and kicking. Necrem tried to keep a hold of the man's arm wielding the dagger; however, the blade did slice his forearms a couple times.

In one of their rolls, Necrem slammed his free fist into the man's gut, driving all the air out of him in a whooping gasp. His grip slackened, and Necrem knocked the dagger away then rolled them over, pressing his knee on the man's chest.

"You *hurt* her," he growled down at the man.

The man coughed. "I'm—"

Necrem wrapped his hands around the man's throat. Then squeezed.

The man's eyes instantly bugged out of his head. He gulped and choked, working his mouth to speak but unable to make a sound. He began to kick the ground and squirm. He hit Necrem's arms, making Necrem only squeeze tighter.

The man's face began to turn red in the dim lantern light. He swung his arms up at Necrem's face like a desperate child, yet he couldn't reach. His gaping mouth open and closed with a wet, sucking sound coming from within.

"You," Necrem hissed. His burning grimace made the sting from his cut cheek dig into his skull. *"Will. Never! Hurt her! Again!"*

The man's sucking gasps became gargled. Then hissed. His eyes rolled back. His body spasmed. Then arched. Finally, he collapsed and went still.

Necrem squeezed for a while longer. His arms shook, and that spread across the back of his shoulders and down his spine to the rest of his body. He exhaled deeply, sucking in air as if he'd been the one strangled. He let go the man's neck then pulled back.

His shoulders slumped. His arms were heavy. It reminded him of the exhaustion of working for several days straight without sleep.

Color returned to his vision.

The dead man's bulging eyes stared up at him, candlelight flickering in the wide, dilated pupils. Necrem stared back, struck as if seeing him for the first time. His shaking limbs drew his gaze down to his hands, sticky from a drying, lukewarm liquid covering them, blackening them in the night.

Blood? he realized. *Blood!*

He doubled over, hyperventilating, unable to get any air. Everything he did raced back to him. The nightmare played out in his mind as if watching a play.

How . . .? How could I—

The unfamiliar rage still echoed inside him. However, the memory of his wife flooded back to him.

"Eulalia!" he shouted, crawling off the man he had strangled. His weak, trembling legs forced him to crawl hand and foot to the wagon steps. *"Eulalia!"*

She remained huddled in the far back of the wagon, curled up with a blanket pulled tightly around her in several loops. From the doorway, Necrem saw her shaking and felt the floorboards vibrate under him.

"Eulalia!" he cried, scrambling toward her, over another dead body. When he drew near, he reached his hand out to touch her.

"No!" she wailed.

His pulled back. His ears rang.

When she stopped screaming, he looked back to find her staring at him, wide-eyed and terrified, not recognizing him.

"Eulalia," he called softly, pleadingly. "It's me. It's . . . Necrem." His cheeks throbbed, and his vision blurred. Tears suddenly streamed down his face. "No one's going to hurt you again. *No one*."

He held out a hand to her, but she again reeled back from him.

The tears poured more, stinging the slash on his cheek. Tears ran down Eulalia's cheeks, as well, yet she still didn't hint that she knew him.

"By the Savior!" someone gasped.

Necrem spun to see men standing outside the wagon. The dim light and his blurry vision obscured them into shapes. He could make out figures wandering around outside, hunched over the men he had killed, and others staring into the wagon. They were carrying long poles. Halberds.

Provost guards.

"This is Cal Suiro Pela," someone outside said.

"Seize him!" another roared angrily followed by men scrambling into the wagon.

"Wait," Necrem said, clumsily trying to turn around on his knees. "They—
"

A truncheon hit him on the side of his head. Then another struck him across his left shoulder. He threw his hands up to defend himself from the blows, but the hard, wooden sticks hit the bleeding gashes across his forearms, battering them away and forcing Necrem on his elbows and knees. Curses filled the wagon as they hammered his back.

Eulalia's screams were the last thing he heard as the last, hard blow struck the back of his head.

~~~

"Bring him out!"

The tent flap ripped back. The glaring morning sunlight shined through Necrem's eyelids. He jerked away then hissed from the burning sting on his cheek. Every muscle in his body teetered, threatening to cramp.

Six provost guards stomped into the tent where he was kneeling, took hold of chains wrapped around his shoulders and back, then dragged him out. He yelped from the feeling of falling forward and instinctively tried to put his hands out in front of him. The chains binding his arms behind his back held, and the grips of the provost guards were all that saved him.

"Stop struggling!" the provost guard beside his right shoulder demanded, snarling.

The crisp, morning air struck his face like a slap upon being dragged outside. He blinked furiously against the Easterly Sun's rays, desperate to get his eyes to focus and see where he was. All around, he could make out the grumblings of low voices, snickers, and yawns.

"Eulalia?" Necrem asked. "Where's Eulalia?"

"Shut up," another guard replied.

Suddenly, the guards let go.

Necrem's suspension disappeared, and the ground rose to meet him. His knees struck first, sending him tipping over and grinding his face into the dirt. His poor luck and lack of time to think about which side to land on resulted in the gash in his cheek sliding across the hard-packed soil. He let out a pained growl as the tiny grains buried themselves into his burning face.

"This is the man?" a man asked.

"Yes, Si Don!" a provost guard replied while the rest snapped their bootheels together. "We found him over the bodies of *four* of Your Excellency's noble calleroses, including Cal Suiro Pela!"

Anger growls and murmurs spread around him.

Necrem blinked the last bit of dust out of his right eye and peered off to the side. He was surrounded by well-dressed men, in fine, embroidered linen suits, fit for travel but more for show. Many carried swords on their hips with shiny, silver handguards, and some with jeweled hilts.

Barons. Or perhaps calleroses? They could also be other well-off gentlemen who were allowed to be with the highborn. One thing was certain— he couldn't spot a single working man among them.

There were also soldiers. In polished, sturdy breastplates and cap helmets, with long brims making a point at their front and plumes coming out of the tops. Their boots were clean, and their trousers were pressed.

"He's a beast, isn't he?" the first man said. "Raise him up so I can see him."

The guards grabbed his chains then pulled him back to sit on his knees. His legs slid underneath him because of the chain binding his ankles together. He hissed from one yanking his head up by the hair. The new angle finally gave him a full view of his surroundings.

Necrem knelt before several men sitting in chairs, the man in front of him with the biggest. He sat at an angle, with one leg propped on top the knee of the other. While the other men around him wore fine suits, he wore a bright orange, silk robe hanging slightly open enough for the tuffs of his linen shirt underneath to poke out.

The sprinkle of gray in his dark hair and thin beard that ran down the edges of his jaw and chin, along with the wrinkles around his eyes, marked him as nearing early middle-aged. His wavy hair stuck out in several direction as if he had just gotten out of bed. His thick eyebrows hung over his eyes as he gazed down his sharp nose at Necrem with curiosity.

"He doesn't look much like a beast, does he?" the man said disappointedly, followed by a ripple of chuckles around them. "What's your name, beast?"

Necrem hesitated, swallowing from his throat being dry. His instincts warred within him; one voice saying he needed to answer, while the other said he should keep his mouth shut.

The provost guard beside him cuffed him across his good cheek. "Answer Si Don, beast!"

Necrem stared back at the man sitting in front of him. He had never seen Marqués Emaximo Borbin up close. His request from a baron had been a stroke of luck, but meeting the marqués in person felt impossible. A common steelworker was beneath the notice of the ruler of the marc.

"Necrem," he replied. "Necrem Oso."

The marqués frowned. "Necrem Oso," he repeated, sounding disappointed. He pursed his lips and worked his jaw from side to side. "Doesn't sound very impressive. I expected something *grander*!" He slapped his right arm down on the arm of his chair.

Grander? Necrem frowned. He laced his fingers together, his skin sticking and peeling off each other as his hands started to shake. Something about his tone didn't sit right.

Marqués Borbin straightened his back against his chair, his eyes narrowing sternly. "You killed four noble calleroses." His gaze shifted to his right. "I that correct?"

A provost guard stepped up with a snap of his heels then made a sharp nod. The pointed tuffs of his thin mustache twitched. "Yes, Si Don," he said. "My patrol came upon the scene. It was . . . a *grizzly* sight. We found *this* man"—he jutted a finger down at Necrem—"sprawled over the corpses of two dead men in a wagon, covered in their blood. Neither man was clothed or armed. One had been punched repeatedly until he no longer had a face!"

The crowd growled as the provost continued.

"Two other bodies were outside the wagon. One man had the back of his head smashed in. The other . . . The other was Cal Suiro Pela."

Marqués Borbin sat forward in his chair, pulling off the leg he had propped on the other. "Go on."

"Cal Pela's neck had been crushed, Si Don," the provost guard said. "Wrung like a chicken by powerful hands."

Everyone was glaring at Necrem. All around, as if their swords were already plunging into him.

He shook his head then turned back to the marqués, staring back at him. "They raped my wife."

Marqués Borbin raised an eyebrow. "Excuse you? Are you calling Cal Pela a rapist?" He snorted disdainfully then sat back in his chair. "Don't be absurd."

Necrem began to shake. His chains clanked and jingled softly together. "He did. They *all* did!" His voice sounded desperate to his own ears. The words themselves left a foul taste in his mouth, saying it out loud for everyone to hear and knowing what they had done to his darling Eulalia.

Yet, the marqués frowned back, unimpressed.

"Nonsense." Marqués Borbin waved dismissively. "Absolute nonsense. Why, how many challenges did Cal Pela take up in the Bravados, Marshal Ribera?" He looked to the man sitting beside him.

Marshal Fuert Ribera was a tall, thin man. His knees were pointed up in the air, the back of his legs not fully touching the seat. The chair was too low for him. The White Sword, as he was called, was dressed like his namesake—all in white, matching his white hair, obscuring his age. He sat with his left hand balanced atop the hilt of a sword hilt; the simple, steel handguard the perfect resting post for his arm. The functional metal design and lack of any jewels or crest on the plain, wooden scabbard stood in sharp contrast to the fancy swords worn around him.

His gray eyes looked Necrem up and down, giving away nothing behind emotionless face.

"Five, Si Don," Marshal Ribera replied, his voice higher pitched than Necrem had expected, just below a squeak.

"Five," Marqués Borbin repeated, grinning and nodding his head. "And did he take any injuries?"

Marshal Ribera frowned deeply before shaking his head. "None, Si Don."

"None!" The marqués threw up his hands. "Yet this beast of a man strangled him with his bare hands." He leaned forward in his seat and growled, "You should tread very carefully, sir. Speaking so ill of a calleros so gallant. So honorable."

Necrem gaped up at the marqués. He looked around at the men sitting around him, all of them staring back with contempt for him.

"But . . ." he stammered. The last bit of sense he had left screamed at him to be quiet. That lost out to the roaring demanding to speak his peace. The demand of a wronged husband, speaking for his violated wife. "He had no honor! I found him standing watch while his three . . . friends *raped* my wife!" His cheek stung, and he felt fresh blood slowly oozing from it. "They were holding her down. Sh-shar . . . *sharing* her like animals with a piece of meat." He spat out the words, disgusted for saying them, yet that was the only way he could describe it. Drool leaked out and ran down his chin.

Men shifted around him. The provost guard nearest him ground the dirt under their boots as they moved their weight, and chairs squeaked. Marqués Borbin sat unmoved, his shoulders slouched, and his eyes glazed over, as if bored.

"Did you find this man's wife?" Marshal Ribera asked the guard's commander.

Marqués Borbin shot his marshal a glance then shrugged to the provost.

"We did find a woman in the wagon," the provost replied. "But—forgive me, Si Don"—he made a respectful nod to the marqués—"but the whore was too hysterical to get anything out of, possibly from seeing the carnage this man did."

"She's not a whore!" Necrem snapped. "Don't you dare call her *that*!" He instinctively tried to lunge to his feet, but the chains held and nearly made him tumble onto his face. The guards around him grabbed his shoulders and hoisted him back up.

"If he yells like that again," Marqués Borbin said, "bludgeon him."

"Yes, Si Don," one of the guards holding him replied.

Marshal Ribera gave Necrem a frown then turned back to the commander. "How do you know she was a whore?"

"She was completely naked when we found her," the commander said. "Clearly in the middle of performing her services with only a bedsheet around her. Also, we have the word of several of Cal Pela and the other calleroses' footmen who've stated that their masters were seeking out the company of a camp follower who had offered her services to them in the past."

"That's a *lie*!" Necrem roared and glared at the provost commander, standing there with a smug, assured look on his face.

"Silence!" a guard ordered then cuffed Necrem across the cheek again.

Necrem shook his head and squeezed his eyes shut. *There're not listening! Why won't they listen to me?*

"Is one of Cal Pela's footmen here?" Marqués Borbin asked, looking over the crowd around them and clearly ignoring Necrem.

Necrem jerked his head up to look over his shoulder. The onlookers still looked at him with contempt, arms folded, noses in the air. He had cried out that his wife had been raped, yet he couldn't spot a single look from any man that hinted they gave a damn.

What kind of men are these?

"Aye, Si Don!"

Necrem rolled his head to spy over his other shoulder, seeing a young man, possibly early twenties, step out of the crowd. He wore a light green suit, like his master had worn, with bushy black hair that needed a comb. He was blurry-eyed, with dark bags under them. He held his fist in the air, as if trying to be seen.

"And who are you?" Marqués Borbin asked.

"Capitán Joso Audre," the man replied.

Marqués Borbin motioned him forward. "Do you have anything to add to this . . .?" He waved his hand over everyone in front of him. "Please be brief. I haven't had my breakfast yet."

"Yes, Si Don," Joso replied. "My master, Cal Pela, joined his companions last night to seek out the company of a . . . camp woman of ill repute. He remembered her from several interactions in the camps' very market. I, myself, saw one of these very meetings before the battle. She promised him a very . . . *thrilling* night should he return victorious in his challenges."

Marqués Borbin hummed. "As many do to keep the soldiers' spirits up. I doubt many had to collect on such promises after yesterday's glorious work, eh?"

Laughter broke out in the crowd; deep, gruntled approval with several slapping others on the shoulders. The soft chuckles of the provosts holding his shoulders echoed in Necrem's ears.

"Are you certain the woman your master talked to in the camp and this man's wife are the same?" Marshal Ribera asked.

The chuckles and laughs died. Necrem caught the marqués roll his eyes before the footman answered.

"Yes, Marshal. I said so to the provost guards when they showed me her. She's the woman."

"Begging your pardon, Si Don," the provost commander said, stepping forward, "but it seems clear to me what occurred. The woman offered herself to Cal Pela, who felt obliged to take his companions out for a night of celebration after your victory yesterday. This man"—he pointed at Necrem—"whether her husband or simply another patron of hers, came around to visit at the same time and discovered, to his shock, the simpleton that he is, that the woman he thought he had feelings for was nothing more than a common whore.

"So, in a fit of jealousy, he killed the unarmed and unclothed calleroses before they could properly defend themselves. Sadly, we provost guards have seen and broken up many fights like these in the camps, but there is no excuse for how extreme this man took out his rage on your Si Don's noble warriors."

Grunts and nods of approval rippled about the crowd, joined by a few sitting around the marqués.

"Well, beast," Marqués Borbin said, tilting his head to the side then folding his arms, "anything you have to say to that?"

Necrem's head had slowly fallen lower and lower with each passing word and accusation. Through strands of oily hair, he spied the calleros's footman, standing with his hands behind his back, chest out, and head raised, as if receiving a medal. To the provost commander, his thin mustache twitching again above his smirk, holding back a mocking laugh. Lastly, up at the marqués, still bored and uninterested.

They're all together on this.

"*Lies*," he gasped. "Liars and thieves, all of you." His neck muscles tensed and throbbed from his hard grimace. The coppery taste of blood from the cut on his cheek seeped through his tightly pressed lips, and then he snarled, "You're all *liars*! None of you know my Eulalia! She would never—"

"You dare call *me* a liar!" Marqués Borbin roared, storming to his feet. His face was a thunderclap, baring gritted teeth down at Necrem. "Who do you think you are, you . . . what are you?"

Necrem knew he should bow his head. A still voice told him to beg for pardon, that he had lost his head. Instead, his chest swelled against his chains and his grimace remained.

"I'm a smith," he replied.

"A smith." The marqués's snarl drooped, his contempt returning. "I expected you to be some bull-headed farmer who didn't know how the world works, not a smith who's supposed to know his place." He folded his arms again while working his jaw, studying Necrem. "What should I do with this fool? Hang him?"

"Aye!" someone shouted.

Hang me? Necrem's chest tightened, his quickened breaths whistling quietly through his teeth. *He's going to—*

Marqués Borbin snickered. "No. A beast his size would break the rope. That would be a waste."

Laughter followed.

The marqués grinned, shaking his head. His eyes suddenly went wide, and he held up a finger. "Do you think he would make good sport for Rojo?"

More clapped and whooped in agreement.

Marqués Borbin laughed and gestured to his far right.

Necrem looked to see a large, iron cage with its own wheels welded into the base. The thick iron bars told him it probably weighed half a ton, at least, impossible to load into a wagon. A chill ran down his spine when the long tail, covered with feathery, yellowish-brown quills, moved and he spied a great *mellcresa* laying curled up inside.

Its serpentine neck allowed the beast to rest its head on its hip. Its large, red twin crests rose like two large ovals from its snout to behind its closed eyes. Its nostrils flared as it took deep, slow breaths, its sides rising and falling, showing off its yellow spotted and deep orange leathery hide. It sporadically snarled as it slept, showing of the cork at the tip of his upper jaw and the recurved teeth behind its lips. It kicked its three-claw-toed feet. Its hook-clawed forelimbs scraped against the metal bottom its cage.

Marqués Borbin sighed disappointedly. His arm dropped against his side with a plop. "It seems Rojo is too full after last night to be excited about breakfast."

Some in the crowd groaned, while others laughed.

Necrem breathed only a small sigh of relief at not being fed to a great *mellcresa*, but it turned soar in his gut.

What kind of men are these? he asked himself again.

"Well then," Marqués Borbin said, stepping down to lord over Necrem, "how about we send him to the Bowl? Him and his beloved whore. See if they claim to be husband and wife then?"

Necrem glowered up the man. The Bowl was a massive desert, hundreds of miles to the east. Ringed by mountains, the marcs sent prisoners that either committed heinous crimes, those they hadn't any need for, didn't want to give the mercy of a quick execution to, or wanted to make an example of to die in.

Blood pounded in Necrem's ears from hearing him call Eulalia a whore. The sight of her thrown into the hot dunes to crawl and suffer flashed before his eyes. The taste of blood and spit collected in his mouth.

He pulled his head back then spat. The gob of drool and blood struck the left side of the marqués's face with a *splat*, making the man flinch and blink.

"*Damn* you, you bastard," Necrem growled. He flashed a grimace at all the shocked faces around him. "Savior damn all of you!"

Marqués Borbin stepped back. He raised a trembling hand to his cheek to wipe it. He pulled his hand back, staring at the blob smudged across his knuckles. A flame burned in his bright, amber eyes when he turned back to Necrem.

"That's a nasty cut you have there," he said coldly. Then, fast as snake, he seized Necrem's face, his fingers stabbed into his cheek. "How'd you come by it?"

Necrem felt the ends of the gash splitting, pulling wider as he snarled into the marqués's palm.

"He had the cut when we found him, Your Excellency," the provost commander said. "We discovered a dagger next to Cal Pela's body and suspect he tried to gallantly defend himself against this scoundrel."

"Did you? Then it's a shame that he didn't get to finish what he started." The fire in Marqués Borbin's eyes danced like flames in a furnace being worked by a bellow. He wrenched his fingers off Necrem's face, the fingernails coming away red with drops of blood.

He held his hand out to the commander. "Your knife."

The provost commander fumbled at the command, quickly and eagerly drawing his belt knife and placing its hilt in the marqués's hand.

Necrem gasped when Marqués Borbin yanked him back by the hair, pulling it by the roots and making him gape up at the man.

The knife was plunged into his left cheek before he could prepare for it. The blade pierced into his soft flesh then grated against his teeth. His face felt like it was on fire. His mouth quickly filled with blood, making him gargle and spit to breathe.

"Si Don!" Marshal Ribera yelled, leaping from his seat. The tall, thin man towered over everyone around him. His face pale, astonished, he yelled, "Don't do this! I implore you, don't sully our victory yesterday by torturing a man today."

"This beast has already sullied *my* victory!" Marqués Borbin yelled. He yanked the blade out, spraying blood as he spun about to point it up at his marshal.

That only made more blood pool in Necrem's mouth, forcing him to spit more to breathe with his head still being held back.

"He killed *four* of my calleroses!" Marqués Borbin waved the knife about. "*Four*! One a champion of the Bravados! We have pushed the Quezlians out, yes! But the Campaigns will go on. And for that, for the sake of the marc, each must remember his place!

"A smith is meant to fashion our weapons so that our soldiers, so that all of you, my noble calleroses, can keep fighting. Not murder you over some whore." He turned back to Necrem, snarling, "Not questioning, slandering, or *spitting* on his marqués."

He gave Ribera a glare from over his shoulder. "If you don't have the stomach for this, Fuert, well"—he snickered—"then your services are no longer required."

Ribera glowered back. His face grew paler by the second. Then he gave a sharp nod, snapped up his sword, and stormed away.

Marqués Borbin watched him leave then turned back to Necrem, holding the knife toward his face. "Where was I?"

He started cutting, and Necrem started screaming.

Chapter 18

15th of Andril, 1019 N.F (e.y.)

Recha's hand was numb, her arm quivered, yet she refused to let go of the giant man's hand, despite his grip having loosened some time ago.

"Eulalia," he whimpered through the shredded remains of his lips while also not moving them. "Eulalia."

"The reaction's run its course," Doctor Maranon said.

"Most confusing case of delirium I've ever seen," Doctor Wertae, the Lazornian doctor, commented. "More like a long-held confession finally pouring out of the man."

The two had bonded while Necrem had spun his story. The more he had spoken, the less he had moved, giving the doctors and their assistance a chance to tend to his cuts and gashes around his thighs and arms. They'd taken care to stitch up what they could of his face. It was easy in the beginning, but when the horrors started, he began to thrash again, and only Recha squeezing his hand had calmed him down.

He'd refused to let go of her hand in the beginning, leaving her no choice but to remain seated and listen to the entire tale. While the doctors had their task to distract them, she could do nothing but sit and listen. She could feel the busted knuckles under his skin with her thumb every time he squeezed, the bones shifting and grinding out of their joints.

With the tale finally over, Recha felt as drained as the poor man looked. Her cheeks drooped, chapped from the tears that had dried on her face. Her shoulders slumped. The small of her back ached from longing to sit back. Her eyes burned, wanting to blink. Worst of all, her dry throat scratched whenever she breathed.

"Is—" She suddenly hunched over in a coughing fit.

"La Dama!" Doctor Wertae cried. "Are you all right?"

Recha waved him away. "Is he all right now? Can you do anything for him?"

Doctor Wertae frowned and looked back at the injured man. "He's lost a lot of blood."

"He'll make it," Doctor Maranon said, rubbing some oily paste over Necrem's cheeks, dabbing them between the scars and lightly across the stitching. "He's a hard man. Some food, water, and attention, and—"

"He's still an enemy soldier," Doctor Wertae said. He glanced about the tent, at the attendants now huddled together in the corner; to Harquis standing a few paces away with his arms folded and white eyes watching; to Sevesco smoking a pipe and blowing long, white streams of smoke out of the front of the tent; then lastly to Recha. "Forgive me, La Dama. I don't know what your interest is in this man, but he is an enemy soldier, and I understand the armies will be on the move again soon. We can't spare the needs to make sure he heals properly."

Recha peeled her hand away from Necrem's. Her fingers popped and trembled from the blood finally returning, rushing through each one.

"I was told of someone being hailed a hero among the Orsembians," she replied, glancing over at Sevesco, who was peeking outside the tent. No sunlight slipped in when he did, only darkness. "And instead, I found a delirious, wounded soldier with a . . . horrible story for his life."

She sat back and wiped her hands on her knees, returning feeling to her arms. She pressed against the chair to soothe her lower back. She gasped a sigh of relief when it popped, and then pushed off her knees to stand.

"Sevesco, I need to—"

"He's not a hero," Doctor Maranon said, finishing dabbing the last bit of fatty paste on Necrem's cheeks. "No matter what those fools say, charging a group of soldiers with nothing but his fists was a terrible idea."

Recha arched an eyebrow. "He fought my soldiers barehanded?"

Doctor Maranon grimaced while wiping off his fingers then shooed away a fly buzzing around Necrem's face. He gently spread the cloth over the man's injuries, Necrem's soft breaths pushing the cloth up and down, yet it stuck to the paste on his cheeks and stayed in place.

"Late into the attack"—the doctor's shoulders sagged as he stared down at his battered patient—"your soldiers were rounding the last of us up when, out of the darkness, he just came . . . *charging* out. Raging. Almost like he was now. He tossed men aside, hammered on their shields, driving them back. Even when surrounded, he kept fighting, yelling they wouldn't touch a camp woman. I think he . . . thought it was his wife?"

Maranon paused to swallow. "But it was a sight to see. More men, ragged soldiers, came after him, fighting back. Him roaring in the night, 'Stand with me!' It was something everyone suddenly got caught up in. Charging out with nothing in their hands. Utter stupidity." He shook his head. "And the soldiers fled."

Recha watched him closely, the look he gave Necrem especially. His eyes gleamed. Through the welling of tears and the doctor's disdain for fighting, there was something else.

A flicker.

A piercing light.

A spark of pride.

Almost . . . admiration.

"He rallied," she said. "*He* rallied the camp followers. Not Don Givanzo."

Maranon took a deep breath, as if waking up. He rubbed his eyes. "Probably best if he hadn't. Would have saved you and your officers a lot of time this morning."

Recha looked Necrem up and down, noting again the cuts and slashes from swords on his thighs, arms, and legs. "And him a lot of blood," she replied, turning back to Maranon.

The Orsembian doctor upheld his stoic demeanor, though his chin faintly wobbled when he nodded.

Recha turned on her heels, her mouth open to say something to Doctor Wertae, when she spied Harquis facing her out of the corner of her eye. She glanced to make sure, and those white eyes were focused on her.

She flashed a soft smile at Wertae and whispered, "One second."

She walked over to the cultist and stood shoulder to shoulder with him, keeping her back to the doctors. "What is your interest here?" she whispered.

"I saw him through the crowds," Harquis replied, voice hauntingly low. "A soul Scorched to its core. His pain, held in for years. Such a soul needed to be saved. Their betrayal avenged." His head turned stiffly, slowly, until those white orbs bore into her. "You did a great thing today. Such souls are what you need to tear down this world of lies. Keep him close, Mandas. He will help bring Truth."

He stepped around her, and Recha sharply turned her head to keep him in view, yet the cultist appeared content with his cryptic babbling.

Sevesco scooted his chair out of the way then pulled back the tent flap for the cultist to exit. Harquis, however, walked into the other flap without pausing, the cloth pulled against his shoulder as if he didn't feel it.

Recha's shoulders shook once he was gone from a chill that she'd been holding in.

Sevesco shrugged, let the tent flap fall back, then stood up. "Always such a *charmer*," he said walking toward her, pipe in hand.

When did he start smoking? Recha shook her head, chocking up the stray thought to exhaustion.

"I trust you had a purpose in bringing me here." She folded her hands in front of her.

Sevesco came up beside her, shoving his pipe in his trousers pocket before she could get a whiff of what he was smoking. "Well, I first thought us capturing an Orsembian hero was a boon that required your personal attention. And after hearing all of that, I'm glad I was correct."

"Oh?"

Sevesco hummed. "A story like that, it's perfect to rile up others with resentment toward Borbin."

Recha frowned, knowing what he was hinting at. "This is not the time to indulge that *particular* pet project of yours. Trying to foment a popular uprising now while we're marching through Orsembar can lead to more trouble than we can handle." She gave him small, warning smile. "Papa would be furious if the generals started reporting they'd been slowed because the peasants had started rioting over rumors you spread."

A network of espis wasn't the only thing Sevesco wanted to set up in Orsembar while Recha had her hands full keeping Lazorna together. He made countless requests with plan outlines to spark popular uprisings in the meantime. Recha wasn't sure of the methods or if the outcomes would help their end goal. She couldn't afford him sparking a fire that either got out of control or somehow slipped to Borbin that they were responsible. It risked drawing Lazorna into conflict too quickly before she was ready.

Recha couldn't risk it.

"Don't worry," she said, elbowing him, "if this campaign goes well, you'll have other chances for such projects."

Sevesco shrugged, looking back at her with an obviously forced smile. "Very well," he said. "We'll save those for projects for later. But what I was also thinking is that man could be an excellent propaganda tool."

Recha raised an eyebrow at him. "Propaganda?"

"A story like that . . ." Sevesco shook his head. "And those scars . . . Even better, look at how that doctor is treating him."

She gave one more look at Necrem. The giant Orsembian was breathing in slow, deep breaths now, likely asleep. Maranon was checking over the other stitches down his body with a critical eye. Recha's eyebrows shot up, the doctor's attentiveness to his patient giving her another idea.

"It could be an excellent recruitment tool, too," she whispered.

Sevesco stared at her, his mouth slightly ajar. "You'd recruit . . . Orsembians?"

"I know," she replied, shaking her head, "I'm skeptical, too. And, considering our plans, it may not be the most successful endeavor. However, Hiraldo and some of the other generals did request if they could pick through the captured troops—the conscripts especially—to see if there were any soldiers more willing to fight for pay than marc. But perhaps there are those"—she turned back toward Necrem—"who've got just as many reasons to fight against Borbin as we do."

A wide grin slowly spread across Sevesco's face. "*Exactly*. We can use his story for recruitment along our entire line of march. I can send my riders out and spread the story through the towns ahead of our columns, telling the people there we've come to make Borbin answer for such atrocities like what he did to that poor man." He chuckled from deep in the back of his throat. "We can even slip the story into Puerlato and see if it festers their defenses while under siege."

Recha's eyes slowly widened at thinking of it, slowly grinning herself. *We can call ourselves an army of liberation. Not only for Puerlato, but for everyone under Borbin's boot. Who knows how potent it will be against any resistance? It may sap any of it before Borbin sends any force to stop us. What if we can slip it into his very camp? It could—*

Necrem groaned a hollow bellow from Maranon moving back a bandage on his left thigh, examining the stitching and poultice.

Recha's grin slipped. "It would mean taking advantage of his tragedy," she said.

"It's for a greater purpose," Sevesco replied nonchalantly. "Besides, you've used your tragedy to your advantage and look at everything you've accomplished." He gave a low chuckle then froze.

Recha glared daggers at him.

"Sorry." Sevesco swallowed then hung his head. "That was too far."

Recha said nothing, merely holding her relentless stare.

Sevesco rolled his lips around, as if working out his next words carefully while avoiding eye contact. "I work in the dark, Recha," he said softly. "Sometimes, it's hard for me to come out. I use every method, every tool, to get the job done. Using another man's tragedy to topple an enemy is . . . just another method."

He finally met her eyes. The fun, prank-loving boy she remembered growing up was gone from those haunting eyes.

"It's another way to bring Borbin down," he continued. "I'll do anything to make that happen. For Sebastian, for Hiraldo, for Cornelos . . . for you. I'll do the dirty stuff to keep the rest of you clean."

By the Savior, Recha blinked, *what have you done that you haven't told me about, Sevesco?*

She turned away so her curiosity wouldn't make her ask him, keeping her focus on the choice at hand. Her lips tightened, and her hands became clammy pressed together. In the end, for the larger sake of war effort, throwing one more method in with the others was something she couldn't pass up.

"Very well," she finally said.

"Doctor Maranon."

The doctor perked up.

"Can you keep him alive?" she asked.

Maranon looked Necrem up and down. "With the right attention, rest, and food, I believe I can."

"Then, until he's recovered, that man is your only patient." She pointed at Necrem. "Consider it an observation period. If our army doctors find you have the proper skills and can be trustworthy, then you can tend to our wounded."

Maranon stood up, sticking his chest out. "Thank you, La Dama!" He made a sharp nod. "I promise, he will make a full recovery!"

Recha turned to Wertae. "Make sure Doctor Maranon knows where he can request what he needs from our camp stores," she ordered. "And make sure he *gets* them." She added that in case someone took offense to an Orsembian getting treatment and tried to prevent it.

"Yes, La Dama," Wertae replied with a respectful bow.

Recha nodded contently. "I shall leave you gentlemen to it then."

She turned sharply on her heels, suddenly eager to get out. She left Sevesco to trail behind her as she burst through the tent flaps before he could reach them to open for her.

The cool night air struck her face instantly. A gentle breeze swept across her face and through her hair, forcing her to stop in her tracks to feel it. She took a deep breath, taking in the crisp freshness with the underlining scent of woodsmoke. She'd been in the tent for too long and hadn't noticed how stale the air had gotten.

The hard thump of footsteps coming up beside her snapped her back. Her guard formed around her during her moment of indulgence.

Yes, she reminded herself, *back to it.*

She was about to head off when, from the corner of her eye, she noticed the corralled Orsembian soldiers from earlier. They stood out with lights of the small campfires ringing them. Her soldiers still patrolled around them, watching.

They hadn't disbursed to sit around in small groups. A great number of them was massed up, looking into the camp.

At Necrem's tent.

Recha looked back at the tent then at the Orsembians. *They're waiting for word.*

She slipped around her guard and to the edge of the tent, cupped her hands over her mouth, and shouted, "He's going to live!"

A ripple of relieved sighs and slumping shoulders spread through them. Soon, there were nervous chuckles, slaps on the backs, and sparks of conversations.

Recha watched them. They suddenly didn't look like enemy soldiers. Just ordinary men thrown together by coincidence and now bonded over a shared experience.

"Come," she ordered her guard as she headed back toward the command tents. She put determination in her stride, walking with a quick pace, and failed to see if Sevesco was going to return with her or not. "I must talk with some generals."

Chapter 19

His head was laying on a hard, flat surface. That was the first thing Necrem felt—the back of his head balancing the floor. At least . . . he thought it was a floor. It was too level to be ground.

The first thing he felt after the hard floor under his head was the rocking grinding his shoulder blades into the floor. Slight jolts shifted under him, swaying his body from side to side.

More sensations flooded him then. Everything was stiff, from twitching a finger to readjusting his shoulders, nothing wanted to move.

A piercing itch on his thigh changed that.

Necrem gasped from the irritating, crawling sensation. With his left hand, he reached for the spot without hesitation and rubbed it. There was some patch or cloth under his clothes. He also felt his skin pulling and rubbing over a line sewn into the flesh.

Stitches? He knew the feeling. However, he remembered them being higher up.

He cracked his eyes open slowly. His blurry vision prevented him from taking in everything at first glance. Everything was shaded in a dull yellow that slowly focused into the canvas covering of a wagon, offering shade and light at the same time.

A hard knock of wood striking stone came from under him, and the wagon jolted upward, its right wheel rolling up over something then coming down hard. Necrem groaned from his head being tossed back and forth from the hit.

Who's driving . . .? Why am I in the back of a wagon?

Someone else groaned beside him.

Necrem turned his head slowly to the right, discovering a booted leg. He followed the limb upward, arching his back the best he could and craning his neck back to see Stefan dosing above his head. He wore the clothes of a laborer. He sat leaning against a box at the head of the wagon, his arms folded over the box's top, and his head pressed down on his arms.

Necrem could make out the side of his face enough to recognize him.

"Stef—"

He rasped and coughed hoarsely. His throat scratched, begging for water. The coughs reverberated down to his gut and made his body tense and pull in on itself. His legs and arms sprang up to wrap around him but stopped from the muscle aches of moving so fast after being still for too long. Necrem groaned and rolled his head, dropping his limbs back against the wagon's floorboards with thuds.

A sharp sniff and snort came above him, followed by a gasp. "Oso!" Stefan squeaked, his voice cracking.

Necrem rolled his head back up to see the lad hunched over him, looking him up and down with wide, shocked eyes.

"You're awake!" Stefan said excitedly. "Are you hurting anywhere? Are you bleeding? Do you need anything? I should get the doctor, right? You need the doctor. Is everything all right with your face?"

The tirade of questions sped by too quickly for Necrem to catch them all. Barely able to swallow, his body screamed for one thing above everything else.

"Water?" he asked hoarsely and heard a soft whistling sound in his voice.

"Yes, sir!" Stefan nodded vigorously.

He scrambled to turn around, his boots scraping the floorboards in the confined space. One of his feet slid past Necrem's head, the rush of air brushing his face.

Stefan ripped the hanging cloth back, spilling yellow light into the wagon, and yelled, "He wants water! Doctor Maranon, he wants water!"

"He's awake?" Maranon exclaimed, startled. "Pull over there!"

"But that's—"

"I don't care!" Maranon shouted over the driver. "I need to check on my patient. Pull this wagon over there!"

The wagon jolted hard to the side. The force lifted Necrem's head up, and it bounced against the floorboards. He groaned, rolling onto his side to get his head off the floor. His stomach and inside his head swam. He smacked the remains of his lips together from the sudden nausea.

He froze. He snapped his eyes open. A stiff tug pulled on his left cheek from a dry stitch.

My mask?

He reached to touch his face. His hands were as heavy as irons. His fingers stubbornly refused to bend, and his knuckles felt like they were grinding against each other. Several of them popped when he finally got his fingers to ball then touched his face.

The sticky residue of the salve clung to his fingertips. He ran them across a couple of new stitches in places he hadn't sewn up before. Some of the scars felt longer than he remembered.

Did they . . .? Did I rip my scars again?

His hands began to tremble. From there, the shaking spread throughout his body. His breathing quickened. The air whistled through the holes in his cheeks. His fingertips lightly touched his scars. He tried to measure them, but they just felt gaping, wide open. He wasn't even sure how much was there.

The image of the last of his cheek, attaching his skull to his jaw, being severed and gone flashed through his mind. The sight of him having to wrap a wire under his jaw and around his head to keep it from falling off burst from the dark recesses of his mind where he thought he had forced that nightmare years ago. The years of oppression struck him all at once, his throat clenched tight, and he started to cough.

"Necrem!" Stefan cried. The boy tumbled beside him, slamming his knee against the floorboard then stifling a hiss. He grabbed Necrem's shoulder and started shaking him. "Necrem! What's wrong?"

Necrem rolled over, peering over his hands that were wide across his face. "Mask!" he hissed.

Stefan jerked his head back. He held a leather-cased, wooden canteen in one hand. "What? Water?" He held out the canteen.

"Where's . . . my mask?" Necrem repeated, ignoring the canteen. "Where's my mask?"

Stefan stared back at him, mouth slightly agape and hand trembling. "I . . ."

"How is he?" Doctor Maranon shouted, pulling back the wagon's rear covering. He jerked his red face back once Necrem turned his wide-eyed look at him.

"He . . . .. He wants his mask back," Stefan stuttered.

Necrem shot his gaze between the boy and the doctor, hands pressed over his face.

Maranon grunted, unhitching the wagon's tailgate. "Demanding a drink and demanding his cloths." The tailgate dropped open with a loud rattle of chains and shook the rest of the wagon when it hit. "Sounds like a recovered patient to me."

Maranon struggled to haul himself up onto the tailgate, pulling on one of the anchor chains while crawling up on his belly. He took a deep breath when he finally got up then walked on his knees into the wagon, dabbing his sweaty forehead with a rag he had pulled out of his pocket.

"But we best check to see if you're ready to get up," he said, crawling up beside him. He frowned and motioned down with his hands. "Well? Take your hands down. I need to check those stitches before I can say you've recovered."

Necrem held his hands closer to his face and backed away from him. "Where are my masks?" he demanded.

Maranon snorted. "Gone. Remember? You lost all of them when the Lazornians attacked."

Necrem leaned back against the wagon. The memories of the mad rout at night, the struggle to get through the camp, avoiding and fighting Lazornian patrols through the dark rows of tents, and the morning after all rushed back in. The fight for the wagons was still vague, like a dream. Yet, he roughly remembered what had happened then, as well. All of it felt like they had happened for months on end. A long trail of misery that refused to end. Not something that all had happened in one night.

After all that, something else stood out to him.

"What happened?" he asked, glancing around the wagon. "How'd I get here?"

Maranon worked his jaw then turned to Stefan and said, "See if you can fetch a clean towel. Something big enough he can put his hands down. I'll keep the water."

"Yes, Doctor!" Stefan eagerly replied, passing the canteen. He crawled out of the wagon through the front, kicking and scratching his way over a couple of trunks and the driver's seat to get out.

"Typical," Maranon said, shaking his head. "Good lad, but typical. Could have just asked for a pardon and stepped around me, but no, had to do things the hard way and get out that way. Here." He held out the canteen with a concerned look on his face. "I've seen your scars, Necrem. Worked on them. You don't have to hide them from me. Drink."

Necrem looked at the canteen then back at Maranon. He turned his face away when he lowered his hands. His fingers, laced together, refused to pull apart, yet Maranon simply set the canteen in them.

"Thank you," he said softly. He peeled his fingers away, pulled out the canteen's plug, then tipped it back to drink. Water leaked between the holes in his cheeks then trickled around and under his jaw as he gulped down as much as he could. The canteen was over half-empty when he pulled it away, gasping. "Sorry for wasting some of it."

Maranon waved him away, though frowning deeply. "What's a little spilt water? With injuries like that, you must have the Savior's own patience. I did the best I could, but after so many years, there's no way to close them up. I may have stop them from splitting more, though."

Necrem held his head away. He worked his jaw a little and flexed the remaining muscle he could. He mentally pictured all the cuts and gashes on his face, feeling the tugs and working his hacked lips.

Some of them did split wider. He slumped his shoulders.

In the quiet moment, he gazed out the back of the wagon. He caught the rolling shadows of wagon wheels crossing the ground, visible from the gap between the dangling covering canvas and tailgate. The clomping of horse hooves, creaking axles, and muffled stream of passing voices drifted through air.

All too familiar sounds.

"A convoy," he said, breathing heavily. His heartrate finally decreased, and his nerves relaxed. His body still felt stiff, especially around his waist, hips, and left forearm, but his breathing became easier. "Where are we?"

"With the Lazornians," Maranon replied. "After the battle, the survivors were divided. The camp followers were free to join their armies as workers or be sent east to work on their siege. Your fellow soldiers were split up between going to work on the siege, too, or being recruited into the Lazornian armies. Many of your fellow conscripts are still here. Although, from what I hear, they are still being kept apart from everyone else. Those who were too wounded, though, were left at the nearest village."

Necrem looked over his body, checking the injuries he could see and trying to remember the others. His hands were sore and knuckles were wrapped. However, he could bend his fingers and make fists. The telltale tugging of healed-over stitches pulled at his side and his forearm. His legs ached like they had been laying still for a long time.

"I guess I wasn't injured enough to be too wounded," he said.

Maranon snorted. "Those Lazornian doctors didn't give you a few days. But you were deemed . . . important to keep alive."

It was Necrem's turn to snort. He shook his head, too. "Who would think I'm important?"

The doctor opened his mouth but didn't speak. His jaw hung open, and his gaze slid off to the side.

Running feet skidded on the gravel outside, up to the wagon's tailgate. Stefan, huffing and puffing with sweat glistening on his face, shoved his arm up in the wagon, holding a bundled cloth.

"There you are," Maranon barked yet sounded relieved. "Where'd you run off to? The rear of the convoy?"

"Sorry it took me so long," the lad said. "Had to make sure I found a clean one."

Maranon snatched the towel, inspected it, as if expecting it to be covered in dirt, then held it out to Necrem. "It'll have to do until you can have a new mask sewn for you. At least it's clean."

Necrem set the canteen away then took the towel. The dark, tanned cloth had various splotches and old stains dotting it, darkening and lightening the rough fabric in several places. Several of them overlapped.

No point in being choosy, he told himself. *Not the worse I've had to make do with, anyway.*

He stretched the towel apart by its far corners then wrapped it around his face. The heavy smell of soup and brine water flood his nostrils. He pulled the cloth tight to get as much slack as he could to tie the ends together. There was barely any room, and the rough edges of the cloth rubbed against his upper cheeks, snagging the ends of his scars and the few remaining stitches there. He breathed a sigh of relief either way once he had them covered.

Stefan stepped up on the tailgate then pulled the covering back, a big smile on his face. "I also found Sir Hezet!"

"You did *what*?" Maranon snapped.

Necrem looked past Stefan, and his eyes widened. He had expected to see guards escorting Hezet. Instead, the veteran and former squad mate wore a violet uniform, the shoulders, black buttons, and black trousers powdered with dust from the road. He lacked any sign of a weapon, but he walked a little taller. He was certainly far better than the ragged appearance Necrem remembered him from the morning after the surprise attack.

"Oso!" Hezet barked, stepping up to the tailgate. "Finally awake, Blacksmith?"

"Hezet." Necrem nodded. He ran his hand across his left forearm and felt the thin, scabbed-over cut. "You look well. Joined . . . another army?"

Hezet's shoulders slowly dropped, his chest fell. "It was an offer," he replied. "They only gave it to us conscripted men. Didn't even bother with captured provost guards or calleroses men-at-arms." He snickered. "First time I ever heard any of them complain about not getting what *we* got."

"Still"—Necrem shook his head—"how could it be any better?"

Hezet shrugged. "Some things are the same. The Lazornians do like to march faster. And they're still nervous about us carrying weapons. But"—his eyes softened, reflective—"the officers . . . act proper."

Necrem snorted, not understanding what that meant. "Figured they'd be nervous with any of us near weapons. Funny they'd try to recruit anyone after slaughtering most of us a night or two ago."

Hezet gave him a blank stare. He glanced to Maranon, who folded his arms, then back at Necrem. "Oso, you've been out for over a week. Near two."

Necrem's hand froze on his arm. Flakes from the scab clung or peeled off against the hard calluses on his palm. He glanced at everyone around him. Hezet frowned deeply, Stefan looked on with concern, and Maranon simply nodded.

"At first, I thought it was because of your age," the doctor explained. "I told Stefan men of our years take longer to get over things." He chuckled, but then his cheeks drooped. "But after a few more days, you still hadn't woken up, and you muttered in your sleep. I figured you were healing what you've been holding inside you more than everything else. If . . . that's even possible."

Goosebumps ran down Necrem's arms. Every strand of hair on his head stood up at the way the doctor had said that.

What I've been holding inside? Muttering in my sleep?

"Doctor," he said hesitantly, his voice soft and low, "what did I—"

"Riders coming!" the wagon driver snapped from his seat. "Important ones. Calleros and officers by the look . . . By the Savior!"

Necrem heard the galloping hooves before the demands started to fly.

"You there! Identify yourself! Why is that wagon blocking the lane?"

Multiple hoofbeats slowed to a trot up to the wagon.

"Injured tent, sirs," the driver replied timidly. "Carrying wounded and had to stop to check on him. Doctor's orders."

"For the love of the Savior's own backbone," Maranon growled. The old doctor crawled and wobbled on hands and knees to the tailgate. He stubbornly slapped Stefan's hand aside when the lad tried to help him to his feet while he struggled to pull himself up then peered over and around the wagon's covering.

"Pardon us, sirs," he said a little gruffly. "My patient has just recovered, and I required a place off the road and steady to check on him instead of a bumpy highway. I promise we didn't mean to inconvenience anyone or tread where we weren't supposed to."

"One wagon for one patient?" someone asked.

Necrem's ears twitched at the tone in the man's voice. It was inquisitive rather than skeptical, with a hint of more questions to follow.

The wagon shifted, coming from movement on the tailgate.

Necrem looked up and found Maranon gawking, his face growing pale. He shot a glance to Hezet. The veteran had gone rigid at attention, arms pressed to his side, his chest barely moving to breathe.

"*And* a personal doctor riding with the patient," the person said. Slow pings of horseshoes walked beside the wagon, slow enough Necrem could follow them with his ears as the horses passed by. "They must be important."

The riders rounded the rear of the wagon. Hezet took a respectful step back, his head lowered. Maranon and Stefan both climbed down from the tailgate to join him.

Without Maranon in the way, Necrem spied the horses' heads and bridles through the back of the wagon. Their riders remained out of sight, but the three horses he could see wore head armor with the black horse in the center having a bridle and reins of violet and gold colored leather.

Must be important themselves.

"Are you well enough to come out?" the person asked.

Doctor Maranon looked in at him, his mustache pushed up against his nose, and nodded.

Necrem dropped his head, groaning deep from his chest. Instead of rolling around to crawl out on his hands and knees, he placed his hands under him then scooted out with the combined effort of his legs. He came out on the tailgate and sat, legs hanging off the end. He winced and held his hand up against the glaring Easterly Sun.

"So, you're the giant Orsembian I've heard about."

Necrem squinted through his fingers at the man on the center horse. He sat taller than the armored calleroses sitting beside him. He wore a deep violet uniform jacket, a polished steel helmet with cheek guards and no visor, and armor on his thighs and legs rather than full plate.

He was broad in the chest and shoulders and sat straight back in the saddle, a natural officer's pose. His square jaw stuck outside the helmet's cheek guards. He studied Necrem up and down, his hazel eyes returning to the towel wrapped around his face.

He's young, he realized.

The shallow bags under his eyes almost threw him, but beside the obvious want for sleep, the commanding officer was younger than he would have thought for someone getting such reverent reactions out of Hezet and the others.

"I'm . . . not sure what you've heard, sir," Necrem replied cautiously. "But—"

"You're the man who forced one of my companies of sword to retreat." The officer shifted in his saddle, the leather rubbing and stretching as he pushed up in the saddle then sat back down. "Charged them alone, they say. Got men to rally. And all with your bare hands. I must admit, even to a former enemy soldier, such things are admirable."

Necrem's eyes adjusted to the light, and he dropped his hand into his lap. He hung his head. "Begging your pardon, sir, but I wasn't—" He clenched his teeth, catching himself. "I'm not much of a soldier. I don't recall much of what happened that night. Mostly running and hiding for our lives. I know I . . . hurt . . . someone. More than one. But I wouldn't say what I did was . . . admirable."

Everything hung in the air after that. The passing wagons, yards away, barely put a dent in the quiet.

I shouldn't have said that. Hezet's opinions aside, calleroses were calleroses, officers were officers, and he was an Orsembian prisoner surrounded by Lazornian soldiers. *Awake for barely twenty minutes, and I've said the dumbest things just I've said in years.*

He set his shoulders, waiting for whatever punishment or orders were bound to be coming.

A horse snorted then shook its mane, chomping on the bit in his mouth.

"Humble, too," the officer said. "You are an interesting man, Sir Oso. It's not every campaign a man is hailed a hero. Lesser still not take some pride in it."

Necrem's head jerked up. "I'm *not* a hero."

The calleroses around the officer sat up sharply in their saddles, tugging on their reins, as if preparing to dash between him and their commander. The snorting of more horses alerted Necrem to other calleroses on the other side of the wagon, watching him and keeping an eye on the others. There was no telling how many other calleroses were out of sight, blocked by the wagon canvas.

The commanding officer, however, softly smiled. "I'm afraid you don't get to decide that. I heard someone say once, 'It's not up to you if people call you a hero or not. It's up to them. It's their recognition of your deeds. The moment others call you a hero, you're a hero in their eyes from then on.'" His eyes lost their focus. "I knew another man who I called a hero."

The stillness returned. This time, it was turned in on the commander. His eyes misted as he sat there, lost in whatever memory he had invoked.

These Lazornians are strange. Necrem cautiously looked at Hezet, standing more relaxed than before yet still at attention. *Was this what he meant by the officers acting proper?*

"General," one of the calleroses beside the commander whispered, "we shouldn't delay if we're to take command of the city."

Necrem sat up straighter. *General?*

The young general drew himself up in his saddle, taking a deep breath. His eyes blinked rapidly. "Yes. Quite right."

He fumbled his horse's reins in his hands before giving Necrem one last look. "You say you're not a soldier, Sir Oso, and I know your . . . wounds probably make being one miserable, but we could use any man we can get to bring Borbin down. If you think we can find common cause in that, come by the First Army's tents when you're able. Tell the provosts there that General Galvez promised a place for you." He gave a sharp nod. "Make sure you turn your wagon off this path and return to the main camp. Good day, gentlemen!"

The general wheeled his horse back, slipping from between his two retainers then taking off at a determined trot. The calleroses jumped to catch back up. The rumble of hooves soon surrounded Necrem and the others as over twenty of them galloped around the wagon in a column of two, flowing to the road then turning left down it, heading in the same direction as the convoy.

Necrem was left sitting there. Eyes wide, staring at the general's back as he rode away. The general had reluctantly looked down at Necrem's covered face when he'd mentioned wounds. It was faint. Almost a flicker. But Necrem had seen it.

When he had mentioned Borbin by name.

He knows!

Necrem's heart began to race. The towel around his mouth fluffed about wildly from his short, heavy breaths. His arms began to shake.

They know!

His body folded in on itself. He dropped his head down until it was almost between his legs. His chest felt like it was collapsing in on him. His throat tightened as if he were being strangled. He gasped for breath. Pricking stings sprung up across his face. Then they all began to burn. Searing until he could picture the outline of every scar.

Screams raced in his mind. They had once come from the depths of his memory. Now they sounded fresh. He felt each, singular, *agonizing* cut.

A strangled gargle hissed out of his throat until it blossomed into a deep bellow. He clutched his face, his thick fingers blocking out the light.

"Oso!" a muffled voice yelled. "Oso!"

"Breathe!" another encouraged. "Calm down! You're all right! You are all right!"

Hands shook him by the shoulders.

Necrem jerked up, throwing his arms in the air.

"Easy, Oso, easy!" Hezet yelled, dashing in front of him with his arms raised. Near panic streaked across the veteran's face, along with his sweat. He flickered glances at Necrem then above his head.

Necrem sat there, unmoving. His breathing slowly came back under control. Then he looked up. His hands were balled into fists. He was holding them high, like dual hammers, ready to come crashing down.

The joints in his fingers and knuckles popped as he forced his fists open. Then he brought them down, dropping his arms on his legs. His forearm muscles bulged and throbbed.

He looked from Hezet, keeping his hands up and watchful, to Doctor Maranon now sitting beside him, drawn back with his arms up defensively. Their eyes met. The doctor's were trembling, with his brow furled, conveying one look that Necrem recognized.

Pity.

"You know, too," Necrem said softly.

Maranon lowered his arms, scowling deeply. He nodded then hung his head. "When we were finally able to treat you, we gave you something for the pain before we could . . . help. You had a *terrible* reaction. You rambled. You yelled. You kept calling out for one person. Eulalia, I recall. Over and over.

"Then the story just came pouring out. Like . . . festering puss that had been hiding under a tumor. It was as if the reaction forced it to the surface, and you couldn't calm down until you forced it out of yourself."

Necrem went numb. Besides the people who'd been there that day, who had seen or witnessed the aftermath, he had never told anyone what had happened. Not about what had happened to him. And certainly had never uttered a word about what they had done to Eulalia. The violation was too much. The mere trying to pick up the little pieces left over and building anything afterward had been hard enough, especially with her condition taking hold of her. Dredging up the past wouldn't have done them any good.

He turned back to Hezet, standing with his shoulders slumped and face angled away from him. Stefan was hiding and watching from around the side of the wagon.

"You two . . . heard, as well?" Necrem asked.

"Probably not the whole story," Hezet replied. "But enough. The story began spreading through the camp about why the La Dama herself had come down and met an enemy soldier and ordered the doctors to keep him alive. Told about what happened to your . . . wife, and how Borbin himself did"—he pointed at Necrem's face—"*that* to you when you killed the men responsible and demanded justice. They tried to use it as recruitment speech, like just now."

Necrem gave Hezet a skeptical look. "The marquesa herself?"

"She visited you when you were . . . being treated."

Necrem turned to Maranon.

"I told you, didn't I?" The doctor shrugged. "Important people wanted you alive."

"They said you and the marquesa had something in common." Hezet snickered. "A personal grievance with Borbin. And they offered anyone else who had one to join up."

Necrem snickered back. "Always figured they would have personal grievances with each other by staring in each other's direction. What could I have in common with one of them?"

They just want to use me. A good, shocking story.

They sat there a moment longer in uncomfortable silence. Hezet worked his jaw, as if he wanted to say more but didn't.

"Well," Maranon grunted, hopping off the tailgate, "we best do as the general says. I'll check your other injuries once we've gotten to the campsite. Best if you go back in and—"

"I'd rather stay right here," Necrem said. "The sun feels too good."

It was a lie. His body was still stiff, and he didn't feel like forcing it to crawl back in the wagon.

Maranon gave him a concerned look. "Road's awfully bumpy. You sure you can hold on there?"

"I'll ride with him," Hezet volunteered. "Make sure he doesn't fall off."

"All right." Maranon grunted, passing a look between them. He threw an arm around Stefan then began leading him away. "Come along, boy."

Stefan dragged his feet. "But I—"

"There's plenty of room next to the driver and me." Maranon's voice carried a no-attitude tone, and he successfully kept his grip on the lad's shoulder.

Necrem remained hunched over, arms pressed on his legs. Hezet walked up and sat down on the tailgate beside him without saying another word.

Reins cracked a few moments later, and then the wagon started moving, slowly turning around on a gravel path that led deeper into a wooded lane off the main road. They rejoined the main convoy without any fuss from the other drivers, and then it was back to rocking and swaying.

"You going to say anything?" Necrem asked Hezet after a while of riding in silence.

"Nuh-uh," Hezet grunted, shaking his head. The veteran wasn't watching him with curiosity or sitting on edge, as if expecting Necrem to push himself off the wagon. He was simply there.

Necrem took a deep breath then hung his head. "Thank you."

Chapter 20

"You may keep your servants, baroness," Recha said to the cowering, homely woman before her. "Your cooks, your nurses, your maids, everyone necessary to look after your family and home. I'm afraid your guards are already being disarmed."

Baroness Sa Manta shot nervous glances at Recha's soldiers posted around her foyer. All the household servants were cramped together on the bronze tiles, the maids and nurses to one side and the gardeners, butlers, cooks, and handymen on the other. In all, forty-six people were employed to keep the three-story house and fifteen-acre grounds in order.

That didn't count the guards or the *sioneroses*.

"Thank you," the baroness said with a hush, "La Dama."

The woman was a few inches shorter than Recha. Her woolen dress was fine, light blue with a high collar, long sleeves, and smooth skirts. Not something one of her station would wear meeting a marquesa. However, Recha and her armies hadn't announced they were coming beforehand. She held her head down, her light brown hair spun and held up in a tight bun, though stray strands stuck out of it, as if made in haste. Her round, plain face showed signs of going fat, along with her hips and waist.

Although, that could have been from having six children, all of which stood behind their mother along the wall, arranged by age. The eldest son, probably a boy around fifteen, stood as tall as he could with his chest out, scowling at everything that moved. His siblings, though, were less defiant. The youngest, two girls no older than five, huddled together, clutching each other's hands, and their chins wobbled as both were on the verge of tears.

Recha tore her attention away from them to finish her little speech. "I'm afraid we are going to have to commandeer your home for a night or two while we move through the area. We shouldn't be long. Just enough to take in the lay of the land before we continue our march. Only my senior staff and I, along with our guards, will be taking up any form of residence."

The baroness jerked her head up, eyes wide, and gasped, on the verge of speaking.

"We won't take anything," Recha assured her, throwing her hands up to try to calm the woman. "We'll be bringing our own servants to not take away from yours. You have your hands full as it is, don't you?" She motioned to the children behind her while forcing a small smile and gently put a hand on the baroness's shoulder.

The baroness's shoulders seized up. Her breath hissed sharply between her teeth at Recha's touch alone.

Recha snatched her hand away. She caught the eldest son fixing his scowl on her out of the corner of her eye.

"Apologies," she said.

"No, no," Baroness Sa Manta stammered, shaking and lowering her head. "Nothing to . . . apologies for . . . La Dama. Nothing at all! Thank you for your . . . for your understanding and generosity."

Recha put her practiced mask on, though the corners of her lips strained from the pressure. "There's no cause to be upset." She made her voice as calming as possible. "We only request—"

"We will not give aid to an enemy of our marc!" the eldest son yelled. "When our father hears you've invaded our home, he'll return and drive your curs out! Sa Manta has the finest calleroses of Orsembar, and you will rue the day you trespassed!"

Baroness Sa Manta wailed and rushed to the boy in a panic, throwing her arms around him and lowering his head.

"Forgive him, La Dama!" she cried, pleading eyes on the verge of tears. "He's only a boy who's trying to be strong while his father away. Please! He didn't mean any offense!" The baroness pulled the boy's head closer to her chest, shaking as those tears finally gave way.

Despite her mother's pleas, the boy peered daggers at Recha through his mother's embrace.

Being strong indeed. Recha held back a pleased smile. *And with any luck, that's exactly the same reaction your husband will have when you send him a message that we've marched through here. Pity those calleroses won't find an easy fight when they come.*

"This is a very stressful situation," she replied understandingly. "His outburst is natural for the eldest to defend his family when the father is away. I would only warn him to be more tactful in the future. It's especially unwise to make threats like that in a room full of enemy calleroses." She glanced at her guard, all of which watched the mother and son pair intently.

The distant boom of volley fire drifted through the air.

Recha spun to stare down the long, north-facing corridor to her right. The last remaining echoes bounced off the varnished wood paneling to the open balcony, the gleaming speck of light beckoning to her.

I'm missing everything again!

"That will be all, Baroness," she said hurriedly, backpedaling toward the corridor. "Tend to your children and household. If you have any concerns you need to speak with me about, send word to my secretary. Take care of the rest, Cornelos!"

Cornelos had been standing at the entrance with a rank of her guards behind him. Recha was sure he was trying to make her look imposing, yet now he gawked at her as she sped down the corridor.

"La Dama!" he protested after her.

It was too late. Recha took to her heels after her fourth step, the hard leather of her riding boots thumped against the floor tiles. She hadn't bothered dressing formally by any stretch of the imagination today. She'd had her fill of riding dresses and instead had a pair of sensible trousers made for her. They, along with the boots and light blue blouse, gave her the appearance of a camp worker instead of the marquesa of a marc. She didn't care. Not since she had three armies at her command. Running was also easier without having to worry about tripping over skirts.

The balcony's patio table came into view first, covered in maps and papers, followed by Baltazar's cutting figure, standing next to the balcony's railing and looking through a thin, brass spyglass and down into the valley.

"What's happening?" she demanded, bursting out onto the balcony.

The guards flanking both sides of the exit jumped, startled from their posts. Sevesco sat in unform with his boots propped on the table. He nursed a glass of wine in one hand while fingering though several leaves of parchment in the other.

"Are we retreating?" he asked, peering worriedly over his messages.

"What?" Recha gave him a confused look as she rounded the table. She rolled her eyes when Sevesco slipped behind his messages, chuckling with his shoulders shaking up and down. "I'm sure if we have to retreat, you'll be the first to hear about it, Sevesco."

She slipped up beside Baltazar, who was still gazing through the spyglass intently.

"We're not retreating, right?" She kept her voice low to avoid Sevesco eavesdropping. "I heard musket fire."

A gust of dry wind swept up from the cliff drop below. The air flung her hair, tightly woven in a thick braid, upward with its draft. Feeling the air brush her misshapen earlobe, she hastily tugged her braid back over her shoulder.

"We're not retreating," Baltazar grumbled, unmoved from the wind, save for the tufts of his mustache flaring up. "We didn't push into the Crudeas fast enough, and now there's a barricade in the city center. Someone ordered their muskets forward. Either Hiraldo got down there and ordered it or another First Army officer's trying to put pressure on them before this becomes a real fight."

Crudeas sprawled out below, taking up the valley center. From her elevated view, Recha could see the intersecting highways running southwest by northeast and south by northwest through the brick- and clay-slated rooves of the city. Columns of the First Army were marching up from the south. The drummers beat in quick time to make them hurry. Calleroses circled the outskirts toward the southwest highway through cotton fields that stretched on for miles westward.

The city's old walls facing the southern highways had buildings and outlaying districts grown up around them, with seemingly no regard for the city's defense. While, in contrast, no houses or buildings had been built out along the northeast highway.

Musket fire erupted below again.

Recha pressed herself against the balcony, clutching and pushing up on the railing. She lifted herself up on her tiptoes.

A gray cloud of smoke drifted up from several city blocks below the center of the city. Despite the roads widening in the center of the crossroads around a bronze statue in the middle of the city square, the taller buildings obscured Recha from getting a clear view of what was happening.

She shaded her eyes against the Easterly Sun, yet all she could make out were the tiny figures scrambling through the streets and diving behind large obstructions thrown across them. There were banners flapping in the wind around the statue but, again, the distance made it impossible to see what was depicted on them.

"What are those banners?" she asked. "Did we catch a relief force in the city? What's *happening*?"

She glanced at Baltazar who, instead of watching the fighting, was slowly sweeping his looking glass around it, focusing on the cotton fields to the west, the vineyards stretched over the hills northwest of the city, then back around to the dense trees east of the city.

Recha tracked his eyeglass's every movement, squinting to see what he was looking at, but the distance was just too great.

"Do you see something?" she asked.

Baltazar let a reserved, deep growl rumble from the back of his throat. He lowered his eyeglass to grimace over his shoulder.

Recha let out a sharp sniff, realizing she had slipped up behind him to follow his gaze. She jumped away with a bashful and apologetic smile.

Baltazar's grimace melted away with a sigh. "Time for a lesson."

Recha's shoulders sagged at his tone. It was his teaching voice. She had heard it many times growing up. Mostly from overhearing him using it with Sebastian and the others, but she had received it a fair number of times personally.

Please don't be long, she prayed.

"Patience and calm," Baltazar said, looking back into the valley. "These are the two hardest and most important things to have while in command. If a commander has no patience, you will run into situations without thinking. And if you behave excitedly, you will be constantly reacting to situations rather than anticipating and planning for them. Take the information you get as you receive it and make the most rational decision you can. Be patient and have faith in your field officers. Let them react and respond quickly to the enemy they are facing.

"In the meantime," he brought his spyglass up again, "you look for the enemy they're not . . . if they're out there."

Recha rubbed the back of her hand with the other's thumb while holding them in front of her. She cautiously checked over her shoulder. Sevesco had slid deeper into his chair, hiding under his messages, the papers too close to his face for him to be reading them. The guards by the doors stood stone-faced, and the few dispatchers crowding together off to the side didn't dare meet her eyes.

Terrific. They just watched their field marshal lecture their marquesa. No telling what's going on through their heads.

She drew herself up then cleared her throat. "Field Marshal, I wish to be informed on what's going on. How goes the battle?"

"More of a skirmish than a battle, La Dama." Baltazar remained focused through his eyeglass. "However, contingents of the First Army have it controlled to the center of the city. The rest of the army is sweeping through the rest while the Second Army is moving to the west to secure the cotton fields and the hills north of the city. No sign of any other enemy force. Hiraldo needs to send a company of calleroses to check those woods to the east.

"Dispatch!"

343

"Sir!" one of the dispatchers yelled, running up to him.

"Send word to General Galvez to order calleroses to clear those woods east of the city." Baltazar never broke contact with the eyeglass.

"Yes, sir!" The dispatcher raced off the next second.

That left the balcony uncomfortably quiet afterward. Baltazar kept watching everything unfold, the guards stood silently, and Sevesco occasionally sipped his wine.

Recha thought she caught movement in the city and clenched her hands tighter to hold back her irritation of not being able to see it all clearly.

"Do you have another one of those?" she whispered.

"Sorry," Baltazar whispered back. "No."

Recha pressed her lips tightly together, and her right leg began to shake, tapping her foot.

Someone cleared their throat.

She looked sharply over her shoulder to see Sevesco holding a brass cylinder in the air, his uniform jacket flapping open.

You've had that this whole time?

She gave him a dry look, which didn't deter him from setting the spyglass on the table then rolling it across with a flick of a finger. She caught it before it neared the edge and mouthed '*Thank you*' as she twisted and extended it. Sevesco gave her a big smile and nod before tossing his messages away to mull solely on his wine.

Recha spun back around and raised the spyglass. She twisted the lenses back and forth until the city came into view. The southern outskirts were densely packed with her soldiers, companies, mostly swordsmen broken up into squads and filtered off the main road and into the side streets, sweeping toward the east.

She followed the highway up, finding the derelict old city wall. Her banners were already mounted and waving on the battlements. She grinned at that.

Another volley made her jump. Her vision through the glass waved and bounced, blurring from the speed until she came to rest at the city center. She sniffed sharply, twisting the lens out for a wider view.

This new volley had come from the northeast highway. Two lines of her musketeers were pulling back behind a column of pikemen, struggling to form a hedge with their polearms to claim the road. Fortunately, enemy soldiers didn't come pouring through the musket smoke. Instead, townspeople and soldiers alike were scrambling back to the nearest barricade in the city center. Not until the dense smoke dissipated did the bodies littering the street between the two groups become visible.

"Push them!" Recha said excitedly under her breath. "Take the barricade before they—"

A strong hand gently pulled her back by the shoulder.

"Careful," Baltazar warned. "Don't lean too far."

Recha stepped back, swallowing after realizing she had pressed herself against the balcony railing and had been leaning further and further over.

"Thanks," she said then brought her spyglass back up.

Her soldiers hadn't taken the initiative. The hedge of pikes held the road, yet all the city's soldiers had gotten to safety behind the barricade of hastily overturned wagons, tables, chairs, and whatever else could be dragged out from the nearby buildings.

"Narvae's taken the vineyard," Baltazar said.

"Huh?"

Recha pulled back then focused her spyglass on the hills north of the city. She picked up calleroses galloping through the long lanes of grapevines. She followed the lanes up to the top of the hill where her banner flew from the top of the large winery there.

"You sent Narvae to personally take a winery?"

"No," Baltazar replied. "I gave Ramon personal command to secure the highest point north of the city and cut off the northwest highway."

"But . . ." Recha lowered her spyglass and gave him an uneasy look, "you sent him to capture a winery."

Baltazar exhaled deeply from his nose. "He hasn't had a drop of hard liquor in the past ten days. And he needed time in the field. He was antsy just riding with the command officers and nothing to do but sort dispatches. Taking a forward hill and cutting off one of the important highways was just what he needed. He should be about to . . ... Calleroses are already moving down the hill, taking the highway."

Recha quickly looked to see squadrons of calleroses riding down the hill, three columns of horsemen flowing downward to the winding highway below. Her hair stood on end at seeing the road crowded with people on horseback, in wagons, and on foot, fleeing the city. Many fled before her calleroses in every direction, but most were corralled by the horsemen back toward the city. Following the road back, she saw a fight breaking out over the northwestern gate as her soldiers inside the city moved in to secure it.

"Crudeas should be secured"—Baltazar closed up his spyglass with several twisting clicks—"within the next couple of hours."

Recha tore her attention away from everything going on below to watch Baltazar step away from the balcony. He stood his spyglass straight up on its lens on the table then frowned at Sevesco. Or rather, his boots on the table.

Sevesco caught his expression, winced apologetically, then took his feet off.

Baltazar grunted in approval before sliding his chair back and sitting down, instantly going back to his waiting reports.

"That's *it*?" Recha asked, feeling her heart sink from her excitement draining out. She looked back and forth between the ongoing struggle below and Baltazar's back. "There's still a battle going on down there."

"The battle's already over," Baltazar said with an assuring tone, flipping through a couple of hastily drawn maps. "We'd have found any hiding force already if there was any hiding in wait. Ramon wouldn't have divided his force to secure both the northern high ground and the road if there was something waiting beyond. The Second Army will face anything from the west. And, last I looked, my dispatcher finally reached Hiraldo."

Recha angled her spyglass south of the city. She caught the tail end of a column of calleroses, trailed by three columns of pikes from the rear of the First Army, heading for the thick grove of trees east of the city.

She lowered her spyglass and took in the valley below, now knowing her soldiers' movements and knowing where everyone was. The outline of the cotton fields, the lanes of the vineyards, the layout of Crudeas's buildings, and the two highways dividing it, all laid out in front of her. It all felt . . . clear.

"It's like a jedraz board."

Baltazar chuckled. "Better. No jedraz board could ever be as detailed or a replacement for the real thing."

Drawn in by everything going on below, Recha took a final look through the spyglass, focusing on the city. The fight for the northwestern gate was over, her banners flapping proudly over them. That highway was completely secured with a long trail of city-dwellers being marched back inside. The road inside the city was theirs, as well. Though clogged with people, her soldiers were trickling around toward the eastern side, closing in the northeast main street from both sides.

"The barricades around the city center don't matter," she said. "As soon as we take the last main street, they'll be utterly surrounded."

"And if they break," Baltazar added approvingly, "they'll have no defenses whatsoever when our troops give chase. If they wanted to try an escape, they should have tried at least thirty minutes ago. They'll either make some small fight of it or perhaps whoever is in command down there will surrender. Either way"—there was a brief pause. and Recha's ear twitched at a gulping sound—"the city *will* be ours within the next couple of hours."

Recha lowered the spyglass, twisting and clicking it closed while giving the city one more look. More musket volleys rang out, from both the north and southward roads. Even from her distance, she saw the columns of pikes begin to gradually inch forward.

Hiraldo's tightening the noose now.

Hurrying footsteps came from behind her. She turned around to see Cornelos marching out onto the balcony. In a brief flash, she caught him replacing a scowl with a cold, expressionless look. He tossed a dispatch pouch around the arm of a chair then sat down without a word or courtesy to anyone.

"Cornelos," Recha said warily, arching an eyebrow as she came up behind the chair next to him. "Has something happened?"

"No, La Dama," Cornelos sourly replied as he pulled more dispatches and letters from his pouch. "Everything is well."

Recha noticed how set his jaw was and his lips pressed into a thin line. He shuffled the papers in his hand without giving her a glance. She looked at Sevesco, who was watching him over his cup.

"Guards," she said, "leave us. Messengers, too. Wait inside, please."

"Yes, La Dama!" the guards said in unison. The messengers snapped to attention then hurriedly followed the guards off the balcony and into the corridor beyond, out of sight.

Recha waited a few moments longer to be sure they were out of earshot to speak. "Cornelos, what is it?"

Cornelos paused sorting through his papers, hands holding them in the air between two piles. He briefly held them there, unmoved. Then, he dropped them, letting them flutter down without a care where they landed as he rounded to look up at her.

"You shouldn't have handled Baroness Sa Manta like that," he snapped.

Recha blinked at him. "Excuse you?"

"She had more questions," Cornelos added. "And you *ran* out of there the first chance you got. It was . . . unbecoming."

Recha propped her right hand on her hip while leaning against her chair with the other. She matched Cornelos's brave stare, yet he held without blinking.

Everything grew quiet. Strangely quiet. Then she realized she couldn't hear Baltazar's pen scratches anymore.

She broke from the staring contest to look over her shoulder. Her field marshal had tossed his pen aside and was leaning back in his chair while folding his arms. An inquisitive look gleamed in his eyes.

"Don't stop now," Baltazar encouraged. "As her commandant de marquesa, it's your duty to advise and inform her on matters you believe are being overlooked or not being given their full due."

Recha pursed her lips at the return of his "teaching voice."

This feels coordinated.

She straightened back up then turned back to Cornelos. "Well?"

Cornelos hadn't moved a muscle. Lines of sweat had run down the sides of his face. "Recha," he said, letting out a deep sigh, "with all due respect, you're giving all your attention to the campaign and avoiding your other duties. Ever since the battle at the Compuert Road Junction, you've seized every chance to get out of answering these dispatches."

"My armies were going into battle," Recha retorted, gesturing out toward the valley behind her. "They're still engaged. I *had* to know what was happening."

Cornelos slammed his hand down on a stack of papers, shaking the table. "You have requests and letters *weeks* old! If you answer them today, it will take weeks to get back to Lazorna. Situations could be worsening, and Esquire Valto is not able to answer them all. You're the only one with the authority to answer these.

"Lazorna *needs* its marquesa. You *don't* need to watch the war. You have the rest of us for that." He nodded at Baltazar and Sevesco in turn.

Recha dug her fingernails into the headrest of the chair in front of her. She couldn't deny she found the daily actions of the armies more interesting and exciting than answering requests and writs. The movements of the troops, waking up every morning to hear where they were heading, if anyone had found the enemy, if Puerlato had surrendered, it all thrilled her unlike anything had for the past three years.

She gazed at the two piles of papers with trepidation, knowing exactly what they held. Long lists of requests. Long descriptions, stories, and pleas for aid for one thing or, in most cases, multiple things. Long platitudes in hopes of flattering her ego that she would agree to them. One after the other. And, most likely, she would have to deny most of them or allow a compromise, yet not give the petitioner exactly what they wanted.

Cornelos kept his firm look, the fading remnants of his boyish features pushed away by a stoic seriousness and determined expectations.

He's not going to let this slide. Recha dropped her shoulders, studying the stacks again. *And they're not going to get any smaller.*

She looked over her shoulder again. Baltazar still sat with his arms folded, but with an approving smile and soft look in his eyes, for both her and Cornelos. A fatherly look.

"I thought you trained them to be calleroses," she quipped. "Ride horses. Wield swords. Take orders. Not demanding, overzealous secretaries."

Baltazar lifted one hand back in gesture that was half-wave and half-shrug. "He's good at both."

Recha couldn't help but grin. She looked back the stacks and sighed. "Come on then." She pushed away from the chair then started around the table. "Let's see if there's a room I can take over and get those done."

"Yes, La Dama!" Cornelos said excitedly, hurriedly gathering up the stacks with a mass ruffle of papers.

"Not going to stay out here?" Sevesco quipped.

Recha paused at the mansion's threshold then longingly looked back. She felt the draw of the maps on the table, the curiosity of how the battle was going below. She turned back, shaking her head. "I'll just be distracted."

She beckoned back to Cornelos to follow. "Come along, Cornelos."

Cornelos followed behind her as she walked into the corridor, her bootheels instantly echoing off the close, wooden panel walls. The guards snapped to attention as soon as she passed.

"Dispatch!" Baltazar yelled, sending a shiver across her shoulders.

A messenger respectfully waited for her pass before running to take the field marshal's message.

Recha pushed down the last bit curiosity and put more determination into her stride, away from the balcony.

I better find a room on the other side of the mansion; otherwise, I won't get anything done. She rolled her shoulders, getting them ready for what she knew was coming. *This is going to be a long day.*

~~~

Strands of hair hung loosely between Recha's fingers. The braid she had spent nearly an hour on that morning had long unspooled, and now her hair fanned across her left shoulder and clung to the back of her neck. There was undoubtedly a bright palmprint on her forehead from her propping her head against her left hand as she struggled to scribble her signature, answering another petition.

She sat hunched over a small table that barely reached above her knees while she sat in one of the room's armchairs. Propping herself up on one arm and writing with the other were the only things keeping her balanced. She had gotten used to the dull pain in the curve of her back, combining it with the throbbing between her temples and the numbness of her left arm, which was asleep.

Her entire body was clammy. She had loosened her blouse's sleeves and slipped her boots off under the table, yet those offered little comforts in the humid room.

Recha wasn't sure if it was intended to be a sitting room or waiting room for the Sa Mantas' guests. It was too small to be a reception room, and a few armchairs and one long, short oak table running down the center of the room were originally the only pieces of furniture. Nothing to say this was a room the family regularly used.

She slid the latest petition aside, the sheet of paper fluttering across the tabletop to the waiting staffer at the foot of the table. Then her eyes fluttered at the sight of another waiting for her.

"You're punishing me, aren't you?" she said with a groan. "You're making me sign the same petitions twice." She angled her head to the side to keep her head propped against her hand and to look up across the table at Cornelos.

Another button of his uniform had been undone since she had last looked. It hung open, revealing his tan undershirt with light damp spots around its collar, as he leaned against one of the arms of his chair. He squinted through his spectacles at the petitions he held up in the air, angling them in the light from the room's oil lamps. That was making the bags forming under his eyes grow.

"I'm not that petty," he replied. "Or cruel." He shook his head and set both aside.

Another staff member was there to scoop them up and rush them back to the others. Seven women sat in a circle, scribing out draft responses on writing planks, filling the room with sounds of their pen scratches. Most of the draft responses were denials. After three years working together, Cornelos was able to pick out the ones that shouldn't come to her because of some reason or ones he knew she would deny off-hand. Simply setting those aside helped speed things along.

And *still*, there were so many for her to address personally.

"I'm not so sure about that." She snickered.

She rolled her head back down, and her eyes instantly lost focus in the swirling script. Her shoulders slumped, suddenly too heavy to keep straight. She lost strength in her fingers. The spine-like quill of a *mellcresa* rolled back into her hand as her fingers loosened their grip. Her eyelids began to drift.

"Does *anybody* around here stop working?"

Recha lulled her head up. The skin of her forehead peeled away from her palm, and strands of hair fell over her face, making it even more difficult to see through her half-lidded eyes.

Her vision cleared to find Sevesco waltzing into the room, uniform jacket thrown over his shoulder, undershirt collar soaked with sweat, and rubbing a towel around his neck. He saw her then jerked back, grimacing.

"You *definitely* should stop working," he said.

"Huh?" Recha grunted, realizing her mouth was lazily hanging open. Holding her head up was suddenly too much, and she let out a low, pleading groan as she rolled her neck in a circular motion.

She took one more look at the papers in front of her and couldn't make sense of the words. Her eyes and brain were either conspiring or warring with each other, but the results were the same as she couldn't read the letter before her.

"Oh!" she weakly protested, slamming her hands down on the table. Her arms spasmed as she flung herself back into the chair. The curve of her back popped instantly. She gasped from an icy spark shooting through her body, forcing her to arch forward until it ran its course and allowed her to collapse back into the chair.

"No more," she begged. She waved her left hand in the air, trying to be dismissive, but her limb dangled limply. "Send them all away. I'm finished for the day."

"Day?" Sevesco said, pausing from pulling up another chair for himself to look toward the windows. "The Easterly Sun set two hours ago."

Recha rolled her head to her left, craning her neck to see the room's two windowpanes blackened by darkness. She rolled back around, sighing deeply before settling back into the corner of the armchair. "*Oh*, absolutely! No more for today."

"You're being dramatic," Cornelos said, giving her a dry look over the rim of his spectacles.

"No, I'm not." She shook her head, rubbing her hair against the cushion in chair's back. "That will be all, ladies. We can finish this tomorrow."

"Yes, La Dama," a few of them said.

"Thank you, La Dama," a couple of the others said, sighing.

Recha indulged in the several minutes the staffers took stretching, sorting, then shuffling to leave on stiff legs that many obviously were struggling to awaken and walk on after sitting for so long.

Recha let her eyelids drift closed and enjoyed a moment to simply not think about anything.

Her bliss was shattered when Sevesco let out an obnoxiously loud groan, followed by two thumps against hard wood. She cracked an eyelid to see him stretched out in his commandeered chair, slumping down in it and propping his feet on the table. There was no sign of his boots. Instead, he wiggled his toes underneath his clinging black socks.

"*Must* you do that?" Cornelos demanded, pointedly glaring at him.

Sevesco snorted. "I've had to sit for hours in the hot sun going over every report, every rumor, every whisper of news I've received since we invaded Orsembar. I don't care whose table this is, whose house this is, or if Baltazar comes through that door scowling at me some more, I am *going* to relax!"

Both Recha and Cornelos stared unflinching at him.

Sevesco squirmed deeper into the chair, briefly folded then unfolded his arms before finally letting them hang over the chair arms.

"That bad?" Recha asked.

Sevesco rolled his eyes. "He's getting anxious. He thinks we should have met some resistance by now. He wants every espi I have looking for an Orsembian army and refuses to accept that I haven't heard anything from my agents in Borbin's camp. If Borbin has sent an army our way, *one* of them would have gotten a message to me by now."

"Are you certain?" Cornelos asked while sorting more papers again, despite Recha declaring the day's work to be over and dismissing the staff.

Sevesco's eyes narrowed, and his lips twisted. "I know my people. One of them would have gotten word to us. If my agents in Puerlato can keep getting messages out to me, then those outside Compuert should—"

Heavy thuds from bootheels out in the hallway announced Hiraldo's approach before he loudly requested the guards outside, "Is La Dama available for an audience? If she's not—"

"Come in and join us, Hiraldo!" Recha called then giggled. "We're not doing anything important."

The door creaked open as Hiraldo stepped into the room. He looked around in a wide sweep, checking the corners and behind the door when he pushed it back. It swung around but didn't latch, standing slightly ajar. He strode up to the end of the table with a perplexed look on his face.

"I thought you were still working?" he asked.

Another tired giggle crawled up Recha's throat, and she smiled. "I'm refusing to do any more tonight, Cornelos is refusing to stop working, and Sevesco is refusing to stop complaining."

Sevesco grunted. "I'm not complaining."

"No," Cornelos cooed mockingly without looking up from his sorting. "You're just . . . *lamenting* over your toils in life. Isn't that how you put it?"

"I didn't sound like *that*," Sevesco objected. "I was discovering my eloquence and wanted to practice."

"Then Baltazar added fifteen minutes to all your exercises," Hiraldo said, hooking his thumbs under his sword belt and shifting his weight to one leg, "*then* made you clean out the stables."

A soft hiss escaped through Sevesco's gritted teeth. "Who knew horses could shit so much?"

Cornelos snapped his head around and loudly cleared his throat.

"What?" Sevesco raised his hands, as if to shrug, but he was too deep in the chair to lift them high.

Recha caught their eye movements as something unspoken passed between them. Finally, Sevesco looked at her.

"Oh," he grunted. "Excuse me, Recha."

Recha rolled her eyes. "I've heard you all say worse."

She spotted Hiraldo still standing and sighed. "Find a chair, Hiraldo! You're making me more exhausted just looking at you."

"I'm . . ." Hiraldo hesitated, "not sure—"

"*Sit.* Your marquesa demands it." She chuckled.

Hiraldo didn't say another word. He took a chair from the corner, a servant's chair with a high, wooden framed back, no arms, and a round cushioned seat.

"You've been waiting a long time to use that one, haven't you?" Sevesco asked, a crooked smile on his lips.

Recha snickered. "Waiting? I started ordering I wanted things done because I'm the marquesa the day after I took over the marc."

"Even at times when it wasn't appropriate," Cornelos commented dryly.

"Hush," she shushed him then rolled her shoulders against the back of the chair. "Spoiling my fun."

Cornelos gave her at telling look, peering up between his eyebrows and spectacles without lifting his head. She smiled teasingly back at him.

In hindsight, some of those things he warned her weren't appropriate or argued against were correct. The sting of not always getting what she wanted was there, though they did fade over time. And, while she would never openly admit it, some of his advice on those matters were the better course of action. She couldn't risk him getting *too* big of an ego. He would drive her crazy with more of his recommendations and the prospect of possibly having to find someone else to take over for him so she could get some peace was a nightmare she didn't want to have. She couldn't do that to one of her Companions.

Hiraldo sat in his chair at the end of the table. He unbuckled then wrapped his sword belt on the back of the chair. A low groan escaped him as he stiffly sat down, rubbing his legs before doing his best to sit up straight.

With him no longer towering over them, Recha could see that his uniform was wrinkled, pressed into his body with sweat patches and marks outlining where his armor had been strapped over his legs, shoulders, and arms. His hair was matted, dried, and flattened against his head from his helmet. Sprinkles of dust still coated his cheeks, reddened by the Easterly Sun. His eyebrows drooped wearily.

"You're as exhausted as us," Recha commented.

"It was a long day," Hiraldo replied then nodded. "But good."

The corners of her lips slipped at his response. "Did we lose many?"

"Casualties were light." Hiraldo rubbed his legs once more before folding his arms and sitting up straight. "On both sides, casualties were light. They probably would have been lighter if that group of calleroses weren't there to rally the city garrison. Reports from our vanguard state they rode into the outlying city and through the southern gate before garrison had even realized what was happening. If they'd only just moved quicker."

"At the rate of our march, that's impossible," Cornelos commented.

Sevesco snorted. "We'd outrun our rumors. My agents are starting to complain to our outriders that they're moving too fast. Some are saying they're getting into towns and hearing rumors about our march they *haven't* even made up yet!"

"It adds to the fire," Recha said then snickered. "Keeps everybody on their toes."

Sevesco rolled his head toward Hiraldo and asked, "How many interrogations do I need to plan for?"

"Hmm?" Hiraldo grunted.

"The calleroses you captured," Sevesco clarified. "I assume you took some prisoner. How many interrogations am I looking at for tomorrow?" An intense, dark expression crossed his face.

"None," Hiraldo replied offhandedly.

"Oh?" Sevesco's eyebrows raised, his expression softening.

"They surrendered unconditionally. Their commander—Oh yes!"

Hiraldo snapped around and pointed at Recha, startling her. "I was going to tell you," he said excitedly. "Fuert Ribera's grandson was the calleroses' commanding officer."

The White Sword.

Recha raised her head at the name, suddenly finding a well of energy deep inside her. "Is the White Sword here?"

Hiraldo shook his head. "I"—"he bashfully lowered his head—"asked him the same question. But he said he hasn't seen or talked to his grandfather in months. Hard to believe he was leading a squadron of calleroses; he looks barely old enough to shave. Luziro's got the White Sword's height, though." He suddenly winced. He seized his upper right leg, wrapping his hands around and under the lower muscle, squeezing it while sticking his leg out as straight as he could. His face darkened red from the grimace. His body shook. Finally, after a torturous minute, Hiraldo gasped and let go. His leg throbbed, but the rest of his body had stopped shaking. He leaned back with lines of sweat running down his forehead.

"That was a bad one," Sevesco commented first, naturally. "Hadn't had one those in a while."

"Cobblestones don't have any give to them," Hiraldo said haggardly, sucking air through his teeth. "It makes those bounces in the saddle hurt that much more."

"Well, at least you didn't have to worry about your saddle sliding out from under you," Cornelos said, shooting an accusing glance at Sevesco.

Sevesco flung up his hands. "Of course he doesn't have to worry about his saddle sliding out from under him." He slid his own accusing look at Hiraldo. "He's *always* been an expert at saddling horses."

"Yes!" Hiraldo boomed proudly. "And I've always saddled them properly. Now, if someone didn't come along behind me, critical of everything, and mess with straps he *wasn't* supposed to"—he glared burning spearheads at Cornelos—"then nothing would have happened!"

"I didn't do any such thing!" Cornelos tossed the papers in his hands aside, spilling them across the tabletop. "We all know playing with someone's saddle straps is just the sort of practical joke Sevesco would do."

Sevesco grabbed the arms of his chair then pulled himself up with a frustrated growl. "Not when Baltazar was drilling us on how to ride. I was never *that* stupid! If something happened with the straps, then the logical fault lies with the person who saddled them." He swung his head around toward Hiraldo.

"And I did them right." Hiraldo folded his arms again and held his chin in the air. "Although, not everybody believed I was doing most things right then."

The scene dissolved before her after that. Recha bounced her eyes back and forth between her three Companions, trying to follow the strange triangle of accusations and twisted logic the best she could. Her jaw dropped as her head started to swirl and their voices grew louder.

"Stop," she said but was swallowed up under the men's overlapping voices. "What—"

Her question was cut off by Sevesco calling Cornelos something that should never be repeated. Recha's head fell back against her chair. She bit her lips, jutting her jaw out as her Companions' voices became noise.

"*Shut up!*" she screamed, throwing her head forward and her hands in the air. Her hair flailed around her face, and she had pull it back to see all three men had gotten out of their chairs, pointing at each other in a comical display, and now staring down at her.

Recha growled, dropping her hands in her lap and letting her shoulders drop as she tiredly looked up at them. "What, in the Savior's name, are you three talking about?"

The men drew themselves up. Each went to fussing and straightening their own clothes. None of them looked each other in the eye, or her.

Recha shot looks at all of them. "I'm *waiting*."

Sevesco broke first, signing loudly then plopping back into his chair. He leaned forward with his right elbow propped on his leg and hand out. A storytelling pose if ever there was one. "It was about seven . . . or eight years ago now—"

"We shouldn't let Sevesco tell the story," Cornelos grumbled.

"Sevesco, tell me the story!" Recha snapped.

Cornelos and Hiraldo groaned simultaneously as they eased themselves slowly back into their chairs.

Sevesco gave each a look then an appreciative one to Recha. "Thank you. Now, where was I?" He snapped his fingers a couple of times. "Oh yes. You remember that brook that ran through the Fareras' field, right? They were farms on—"

"They're Papa's oldest tenants." Recha nodded her head and waved her hand. "I know the place you're talking about. Go on."

The brook came easily to mind. A deep, winding trickle of water with steep banks and lined by thickets and trees. It denied the Fareras from ever plowing straight rows but, to her knowledge, they never complained about it.

"Well," Sevesco continued, "one day, I think False Fall had just begun because I remember something happened at that year's Simem Harvest Festival, but . . . I can't remember what at the moment—"

"*Sevesco,*" Recha said lowly, warningly as she folded her arms.

"Hmm?" He blinked rapidly then shook his head. "Right. Anyway, it was late. The Easterly Sun was setting, it was getting colder, and we had this field we had to go around to get home. Well, someone—can't remember who—suggested we cross the brook—"

"Sebastian," Hiraldo said.

"Right," Sevesco agreed. "Sebastian's idea. And immediately, this guy says it wasn't safe"—he thumbed at Cornelos—"and this guy worries about the horses"—he thumbed at Hiraldo—"and I—"

"Wagered twenty deberes that none of us had the *stones*, as you put it, to leap across it," Cornelos interjected.

Sevesco frowned at him. "I didn't do that."

Recha joined the other two, giving him a disbelieving look, not being there yet completely believing he would have.

"Yes, you did!" Cornelos shot a finger in the air. "You wagered it, you encouraged it, and when he slipped, you laughed the hardest and was the last to rush to help. More proof you orchestrated the *entire* thing!"

"I did not!" Seveso's face started to redden.

"Don't start that again!" Recha pled, holding out her hands as if to separate the two. "Especially since I don't know the entire thing. Sevesco, continue."

"Savior help us," Hiraldo grumbled.

Sevesco straightened his shirt before continuing, "We finally found a break in the thickets, but the bank on the other side was a bit higher than ours. So, Sebastian decided to go first because . . . he was Sebastian and . . . you know . . ."

Recha nodded. "I know."

Of course, you would have gone first, she thought of Sebastian, *you idiot. You had to go first for these three to follow you.*

"Well, he wheeled his horse around us a few times, building up speed, and then *charged*!" Sevesco shot his arm out. "He leaned down in the saddle, flicking his horse's reins all the way. He got to the bank, kicked the horse, it jumped"— he held both hands in the air, holding the moment—"and, in the air, Sebastian's saddle lifted off the horse." He threw his hands back as he fell back into the chair.

Recha's eyes shot wide, realizing the full severity of the story's moment.

"The horse made it to the other side just fine. As for Sebastian"—Sevesco bashfully shrugged—"he landed on the hill of the bank, the saddle hitting first with him still in it and holding on to it. Then he rolled back and toppled into the brook, saddle and all." He snorted and chuckled, his lips pressed together in a wiggly smile, holding back his laughter.

The room fell quiet. The scene played out in Recha's mind—Sebastian sailing through the air, hitting the dirt bank still in his saddle, the pain from the impact, then tumbling head over heels backward into the water.

She hadn't realized she'd been holding her breath until she coughed and cracked into laughing, doubling over from where she sat. Her hair fell around her, and she felt her laughs deep in her gut. She was quickly joined by the others, and she sat up, whipping her hair back to see them all laughing.

"Was . . . was . . . Ah!" She had to stop and take deep breaths, whipping her teary eyes to calm herself. "Was he mad?"

"*Furious*!" Sevesco cheered.

"Wouldn't even let us help him out of the brook," Hiraldo said.

"Or check to see if he was hurt," Cornelos added.

Sevesco let out a loud, exhausted sigh. "And then the accusations started to fly."

"He blamed all of us, in one way or another." Hiraldo made a dismissive wave. "His horse had run off to the stables, so he just threw his saddle over his shoulder and said he'd walk the rest of the way home."

Recha's heart fluttered as the thought of Sebastian walking home, muddy and wet, carrying his saddle over one shoulder wasn't something she had to imagine. Instead, a memory blossomed in her mind. Her back went rigid at the flood of memories that poured to the forefront, and things she never knew were missing pieces clicked into place.

"And you three . . . have been arguing with each other about this . . . for eight years?" she said.

"Mmhmm," Sevesco hummed.

"Yes," Hiraldo replied.

"Correct," Cornelos pointedly said.

Recha felt the curls of her lips tug, heralding the start of a grin. She clapped her hands in front of her face, burying her nose in them. Yet her grin grew. Laughter bubbled deep in her belly again, and she felt it starting to rise. Her Companions watched with growing curiosity and confusion as she started to snicker and snort into her hands.

Finally, she shook her head excitedly. "None of you messed with his saddle," she squeaked out. "That was *me*!" She threw her head back and laughed. She clapped her hands and stomped her feet.

When she looked back, her Companions' gaping faces made her laugh harder. She drew herself up as she calmed and went into her own story.

"Eight years ago," she said, "you four snuck out to Lupa."

All three men's faces went pale. Their bodies went stiff.

Lupa was a small town, south of the Vigodt estate, known to the farmers around there for having certain places of . . . ill-repute.

"You . . . knew about that?" Sevesco nervously asked. His voice cracked, and he had to clear it.

Recha molded her grin into a knowing smile and folded her arms. "Of course. A woman in love will *always* learn if her beloved's snuck off to places he shouldn't." She let them chew on that for a second before she continued, "And I let him know that I knew."

All three of them slowly turned their faces away from her while pushing themselves deeper into their chairs.

"We had a bit of fight," Recha admitted, describing their shouting match as lightly as possible. "And I didn't think he got the message. So, I loosened his horse's saddle straps that day. I mean"—she shook her head—"horse riding training in the evening sounded ridiculous. I figured all of you were sneaking off again, and I knew Papa had instructions that all his horses knew to return to their stables if anything happened to them.

"The idea of the saddle falling off and leaving Sebastian in the road as the horse left him there was the best thing I could think of at the time. It was right there for me to loosen. And when he came back, soaking wet, covered in mud with just his saddle"—her giggle was a little darker sounding than she meant, but it felt good—"I knew I had made my point."

"Except, he blamed us for it," Hiraldo said.

She raised an eyebrow at him. "He never went back to Lupa after that, did he?"

Her Companions turned to one another, eyes locking, realization sprouting.

"He knew," Hiraldo finally said.

"And kept making us argue with each other," Cornelos added.

"That clever bastard," Sevesco cursed yet sounded in awe.

Cornelos pointed at her. "He turned your prank against him—"

"—into his own joke against us," Hiraldo finished.

"I wish he were alive." Sevesco scratched his chin, his eyes out of focus, clearly in thought. "So I could kill him."

Her joy in the moment was snapped up, and Recha gave him a narrow-eyed glare.

Sevesco glanced at her. "Too far?"

"*Yes*," she growled, joined in concurrence by Cornelos and Hiraldo.

"That's it." Sevesco stood up in a long stretch, sticking his arms up above his head and groaning then slapping them against his sides. "I know when it's time to leave." He gathered his uniform jacket that had been laying on the floor beside his chair and flung it over his shoulder. "Have a good evening, all," he said then headed for the door.

They all gave him their goodbyes, but when he reached the door, he stopped and said, "Don't play any more pranks, Recha. You can start lifelong feuds."

"Get out of here," Recha said back, shaking her head.

Hiraldo slapped his knees then grunted as he pushed off them. "I best be going, too. The First Army may still need its general for . . . something."

"All right," Recha sighed understandingly, not envying his prospect of having to ride back to his army's headquarters at all.

Hiraldo gathered his sword belt then put his chair back where he had found it. "One more thing I almost forgot," he said. "I met that Orsembian hero that those rumors have been talking about."

Orsembian—?

Recha spun in her chair. "Sir Necrem Oso? He's recovered?"

Hiraldo nodded.

"What did you think of him?"

"Older than I thought," Hiraldo replied then thought some more. "Also, he's . . ."

"Yes?" Recha tilted her head.

"Beaten." Hiraldo's tone became somber. "Never thought a man that big would sit like he was about to crumble."

"He's been through a lot," Recha agreed, remembering that terrible story through those dreadful scars. "Thanks for letting me know."

Hiraldo nodded again then turned for the door. "Pleasant evening, Recha. Cornelos."

When the door closed, Recha sat back to find Cornelos scooping up the stacks and putting them into different satchels.

"Finally decided to stop working?" she asked.

"Who could work after all that?" Cornelos replied, putting his spectacles in his breast pocket.

Recha snickered, smiling, then leaned her head back against the chair. "First time all three of us were in the same room in what . . . over a year?"

"And look at the mayhem you caused."

"*I* caused?"

Cornelos gave her a telling look through his eyebrows again and smirked.

Recha rolled her eyes. "Fine, blame me for everything. Give Sevesco a reprieve."

Cornelos's head shot up. "Oh, if it's like that, then *yes*, it was all Sevesco's fault." He nodded excitedly.

Recha chuckled, grinning broadly. She rubbed her hands together and was reminded of how clammy her body felt by the way her palms stuck together.

"You did work out the details with Baroness Sa Manta of me taking up residence here while we're in the area, right?"

Cornelos lazily nodded as he picked up the last of the papers. "I did clarify you would be taking rooms here. Assured her you had your own staff and servants, and her household need only keep out of our way. Why? You ready for your rooms?"

"Yes." Recha exhaled deeply, thinking of finally having a real bed to sleep in and a roof over her head. "I've also been thinking about what you said earlier. Maybe there is a way to make up for being . . . what did you say? *Unbecoming* as a marquesa?"

Cornelos swallowed. "I didn't mean to be that harsh—"

Recha raised a hand, stopping him from going into a long, apologetic tirade. "I think I know just how to make up for it. Possibly even help the war effort, too. We might also want the invite of Crudeas's city officials, as well . . ." She groaned and shook her head. "But that can wait for tomorrow. I just need one thing tonight."

Cornelos straightened, exhausted yet still attentive. "What do you need?"

"*Please* tell me my rooms have a bath."

Chapter 21

Why am I here?

Necrem sat on a fancy wooden bench with a cushioned seat, hunched over with his elbows on his knees. He rolled his shoulders, failing to soothe the itch between his shoulder blades.

It was his new clothes. The soft cotton of his shirt rubbed against his skin and was making him itch all over. He had never worn a finer suit. The white shirt without a stain on it didn't stretch or strain from his broad shoulders, and the sleeve length was just right. The trousers were professionally hemmed. The black jacket could remain buttoned while he sat and wasn't too tight. *Brass* buttons at that! The boots shined with a fresh polish, and he guessed he could walk from where he was to Manosete and not wear out the heels.

It didn't feel right wearing any of it.

Except for the boots. Never turn down a good pair of shoes, of any kind.

He wished he could have turned down being where he was.

He sat up, pressing his back against the flowing woodwork of the bench, hoping to soothe his itch and hide in the background against the wall. A nervous tick traveled down his right leg, making it tremble, and his heel tapped sporadically against the floor tiles. The sound was blessedly covered up by the multiple conversations, the gentle melody of flutes, and soft plucks of bandias— a fourteen-stringed wooden instrument.

He could have fit his entire forge in the room he was in.

People milled about in small conversations on the bronze tiles. Lights from candles and oil lamps danced off crystal chandeliers in the ceiling and along the walls between the wooden columns holding up the room.

Necrem figured a whole forest had been cut down to build the exorbitant mansion he sat in. He had been stunned when he'd seen the size of the mansion as the wagon that had picked him, along with a great many camp workers, up along the road and onto the grounds.

Although, he'd been in a constant state of stunned confusion ever since he had awoken in the back of that wagon three days ago. After waking up, he'd been driven to a new camp with a view of another battle displayed before them.

Everybody had been in such a rush. Hezet had been called back to his new company, leaving Necrem alone with the doctor and Stefan. After the battle, nothing had happened, though. It was the first time Necrem had seen a city taken. He'd expected more damage, yet no buildings or homes had been plundered or burned. Its people weren't being divided, sorted out as *sioneroses*. Instead, those who tried to flee were forced back *into* the city.

In the meantime, everyone seemed to have forgotten about him, which Necrem didn't mind. He enjoyed finally being left alone. He'd made a new mask for himself, endured Maranon's checkups, and was pleasantly surprised that the Lazornians had better food.

Then, yesterday morning, a Lazornian officer had informed him that he'd been summoned to a reception tonight.

By the personal request of the marquesa herself.

His entire day after that had been snatched from him. He'd been rushed to a tailor in Crudeas where the officer and soldiers had watched over him as he was measured and accidentally poked with sewing needles that he had to wonder if they had done it on purpose. They had sewn him a new mask that fit better than his makeshift one. It breathed better than his old ones, too, but he wasn't sure if the thin cloth would last long. It felt too delicate against his scars and skin.

Now, he was in some baron's conquered mansion. He felt more out of place sitting by the wall than he did in that fancy tailor's shop.

Men in fine suits, jackets of silk with sleeves of lace, knee-high pants and hose, and polished buckled shoes sniffed and sipped wine while talking business ventures and road conditions since campaign season had started.

Women in dresses of shimmering silk, with bare shoulders and their hair done up to show off their jewelry, necklaces of gold and silver, and sapphire and emerald earrings, talked behind their hands. There were gleams in a few of their eyes for the Lazornian officers walking around in groups of twos and threes.

The Lazornians were easy to pick out in their violet and black uniforms. Each group kept to themselves. The Lazornians only mingling when either a group of city officials or ladies stopped them to briefly talk.

Water and oil, Necrem thought. *Water and oil.*

They were trying to mix, but the hesitancy was there. Necrem found it funny and odd at the same time. From what he had always seen, calleroses and the gentry always got along together, no matter if they were from a different marc or not. Them being standoffish from one another made him want to shake his head.

But someone might notice him if he did that.

He hadn't moved from his seat since arriving. It didn't matter which side was water and which was oil, he was hot steel, and both sides would give him the cold shoulder and distant, disdained glances.

The bench was just inside the room, no more than ten feet from the door. He stiffly turned his head, gazing longingly at the freedom beyond.

Maybe I should leave? He gripped his knees, squeezing them to stop his heel from trembling. *They wouldn't notice, would they? Or maybe I should wait until someone—*

"Sir Oso?"

Necrem snapped his head around. A Lazornian officer was beside the bench who hadn't been there a moment before. He stood straight with his hands folded behind his back. He was slender, but his uniform fit him perfectly. A glint sparkled off the metal rim of his spectacles in his unform jacket's breast pocket. Necrem noticed marks on the bridge of his pointed nose that the spectacles had made.

He was young, too. His dark hair was combed, and his face freshly shaven. There were bags though under his eyes, though, which Necrem suspected were possibly from this being his first campaign.

Ah, finally, Necrem breathed a soft sigh of relief, *he's going to tell me this was a mistake and to leave.*

"Yes?" he replied hopefully.

The Lazornian sharply nodded. "Permit me to introduce myself. I am Commandant Cornelos Narvae, La Dama Mandas's commandant de marquesa. On the behalf of my marquesa, I can tell you she is delighted that you could join us. Are you having a pleasant evening?"

Necrem sat there, staring at the man. His mask hid his jaw tightening. "Huh?" he grunted.

"The reception." The young commandant blinked rapidly. "Are you enjoying it? Have you eaten?" He gestured to a side room where the scent of roasted meat and baked bread wafted out of. Groups of people drifted in and out, eating and drinking while standing. "There is plenty of food—"

"I ate earlier." Necrem's throat tightened, realizing who he had interrupted. He lowered his head respectfully. "Sir."

He hadn't known there would be food, but he still would have eaten before being forced to come. He avoided eating with the men he was conscripted with; there was no chance, under the threat of Oblivion, that he would eat among the people filling this room.

"Ah." Commandant Narvae nodded. "Well then, if you'd be so kind to come with me." He held his arm out, motioning toward the back of the room. "The La Dama is about to give an address to all the guests and *personally* requested I bring you up front to hear."

Necrem knew a command when heard one. Through all the polite, confusingly formal, and long, unnecessary words, the message was clear. He'd been summoned, and there was nothing he could do about it. He had gone from playing the whims of a marqués to playing for whims of a marquesa.

Only this one remembered his name.

The commandant stood there with his arm out, waiting.

Necrem patted his knees a couple of times then eased up on them with a grunt, slowly rising to his feet, his legs shaking, as if he were hoisting barrels of coal on his shoulders.

The young commandant followed him as he rose, his head tilting back further and further. His calm demeanor remained the same, yet his eyes widened ever so slightly until Necrem towered beside him, his shoulders looming over his head.

Conversations around them, though, suddenly cut off. A few of the women stopped whispering about the Lazornians and gawked at him. Men who had walked by him, deep in conversations, whether it be the war, money, or the weather, without a second glance, pointed at him like he was a statue come to life.

Necrem let his shoulders hunch down, trying to make himself look smaller from all the attention.

"How are your wounds?" the commandant asked suddenly. He was looking him up and down with a concerned frown. "Have you fully recovered?"

Necrem's legs wobbled from sitting so long, and he forced down his body's pleas to stretch. He was drawing enough attention. He didn't want to draw more from stretching and showing everyone how big he really was.

"I'm just getting old," he replied. "Doctor Maranon said my wounds have healed up, but it might take me a while to get over them."

"That's good to hear." Commandant Narvae smiled politely. "The La Dama will be pleased. Shall we?" He turned sharply on his heels then strode forward through the crowd, the clusters of people parting for him as he came upon them.

Necrem's brow furled, and his eyebrows creeped down into his eyeline from the path the young man was taking. Yet, he had no choice. He followed, with shoulders slouched and head down.

"Who's that?" a woman with a nasal voice whispered.

"He's not a soldier," one man mumbled.

"Or a calleros," another man agreed. "Walks too humbly."

"I wonder what's under that mask?" A young lady giggled with a group of friends.

You don't want to know, girl. Necrem shoved his hands in his trouser pockets to stop them from shaking.

However, it did bring him a little relief. Hearing them gossip and speculate assured him they didn't know who he was. Therefore, the truth about him was safe. There were a hundred rumors in the camp about his scars, about how he had gotten them and why. Some were outlandish, while others terrifyingly close to the truth.

Only one thing was the same in all of them—Marqués Borbin was the one who had carved his face.

Why? The frustrating question echoed in his mind. *Why did they tell everybody? Just to make everyone pity me more?* That steelworker pride roiled inside him. No bigger than a lump of coal now, but it was enough.

Maybe . . . if I get the chance, I can ask—

Necrem failed to see the commandant had stopped and stepped on his heel. The young man jumped forward, startled.

"Sorry," Necrem apologized, stepping back.

The commandant cleared his throat and straightened his clothes. He frowned at a large group of people, mostly women, huddled around someone buried in the center.

"No need to apologize, Sir Oso," he said, bobbing his head back and forth at the crowd. "I stopped without saying so. Would you be so kind as to wait here for a moment? I will tell La Dama you're here." He gave a sharp nod then strode away before Necrem could say anything.

Leaving him alone.

Out on the open floor.

He glanced this way and that. The groups of people gossiping about him seemed to have lost interest, yet he spotted an older woman in a cluster of ladies near him turn her head his direction a few times.

Over to his right, he saw two tall young men in deep conversation with each other. One man was a Lazornian officer, while the other wore a fine suit with pressed trousers and stood with a confident bearing. A semi-circle of men surrounded them, half Lazornians by their uniforms, behind the man doing most of the talking, and the other half wore suits matching the other. By the way they all stood—confident, arms stiffly to their sides, and heads held high—told Necrem what they were. Calleroses. Lazornians and Orsembians alike.

Calleroses are calleroses, no matter what marc they come from or if they are campaigning against each other. It made Necrem's scars twitch hearing them laugh together. *Nothing really changes.*

He pondered slipping away when another laugh made him look again. He got a good look at the Lazornian in the center—square-jawed, broad-shouldered, tall yet shorter than him by a head. His carrying voice stirred a memory.

That general on the road . . . what was his name?

The commandant rounded the gathering in front of him, walking back with an apologetic frown. "Sorry to make you wait," he said, "but La Dama is wanting to make a small speech first. She got detained by more guests than she expected and figured now would be the best time to address everybody."

"Speech?" Necrem grumbled, raising an eyebrow.

The sharp tings of metal against glass rang throughout the room.

As the multiple conversations slowly quieted, the crowd in front of him flowed back, their heads tracking someone moving toward their right.

A Lazornian servant appeared and put down a wooden crate a few feet away from where the calleroses had mingled.

As the crowd pulled back, Necrem finally caught sight of the person who held everyone's attention.

She was a young woman, much in her prime. She walked with her head and her supple nose up with dignity. The light from the ceiling reflected off her smooth, tanned cheeks, catching her dimples formed by her small smile. Her dark hair was combed smoothly back, displaying her heart-shaped face yet covering her ears, and rolled into a bun that sat at the back of her neck.

Her clothes weren't outlandish or exposing. While most of the other ladies wore dresses with bare shoulders, white lace formed a collar around her neck. Her deep violet dress swallowed the light rather than shimmered when she moved, and there was no swish or loud ruffle of multiple layers of skirts and fabric underneath.

The servant stepped away from the crate with his hand out. The woman took it and pulled up on the hem of her dress with the other. When she stood up on the crate, she passed a roaming glance around the room, her dark eyes catching everyone.

Necrem thought he saw her thin eyebrows twitch when she passed over him.

"Good evening," the marquesa said, "and thank you all for coming. I . . ." She paused to shake her head, lowering it slightly. "I know it's odd for me to say that to all of you, especially after the events of the last few days."

She turned and stuck her hand out to her right. "I especially wish to thank Baroness Sa Manta for allowing me to call this gathering at her home. This has been a very trying time her and her family. I wish to commend her and her household for bearing and caring for our needs with grace and courtesy. She and her family are true paragons of hospitality." The marquesa started to clap, and the rest of the room followed.

The homely woman who she had gestured to stepped forward, bowing with her hand over heart and pulling her left skirt to the side. When she stepped back, though, Necrem caught the trembling traces of strain as she smiled softly.

It's not as if she had a choice. He probably wasn't the only one having that same thought.

"And this has been a difficult time for her," the marquesa continued. She folded her arms in front of her. Her smile slid away as she faced the guests. "It has been a difficult time for all of you in Crudeas, having your home invaded and then invited here while my armies surround you. I know what you fear. Your homes destroyed. Your loved ones taken." She shook her head. "That won't happen."

Soft whispers ran through the guest with cautious glances shot toward the Lazornian officers spread throughout the room. Some were having to mind their tongues.

The marquesa cleared her throat. "Some of you many know I have freed the *sioneroses* in your city. I tell you now that I did not do that to swell my army and put your people in their collars. I did so because they deserve to be free. As do all of you.

"Free of the Rules of Campaign. Free of this endless cycle of year after year of sacrificing your wealth, your food, your children to this senseless season and seeing *nothing* in return. No end in sight, no goal to strive for. We of Lazorna wish to change that."

The marquesa drew herself up, her shoulders rising and falling as she breathed heavily through her nose. "We are *not* your enemies!" she exclaimed boldly. "Nor are you ours. The people of Orsembar have nothing to fear from us. Our grievance"—her eyes flashed in Necrem's direction—"is with Marqués Borbin."

A spike of ice coursed through Necrem's body at hearing the name. He balled his fists in his pockets, stretching and straining the fabric as the rest of the room grumbled. Many around him frowned, shaking their heads, having trouble finding a difference between her being an enemy of their marques and them.

"He has campaigned only through guile and betrayal," the marquesa accused. "Being needlessly ruthless when he didn't need to, betraying ally after ally, and hiding behind the Rules of Campaign when faced with opposition. You stand alone, Orsembians, with vengeful enemies all around, all for Borbin's profit. But I ask you: where's yours?"

She placed her hand on her chest then leaned toward the guests. "I have seen the burdens he's placed upon you. Every town we have marched through, granaries are under lock and key. Commerce is ground to a halt because no one has the deberes to pay, and the prices for goods are exorbitant.

"And where are your men? Gone. Squatting in trenches or laying in ditches in front of another wall so Borbin can add another acre of land to his name. While what do you get? Fathers who don't return. Sons who come back mutilated. Fodder for officers who see them as a quota they must bring to eat the scraps from Borbin's table. Scarred forever by whoever Borbin points them at, or Borbin himself."

Her gaze fell upon him, and Necrem's breath clawed in his throat. Those dark eyes consumed him, swallowing him as deeply as the sleep he had awoken from days ago. They screamed to him from their very core.

She knew.

A quiver ran up from the soles of his feet to top of his head. Everything shook. His heart raced. His teeth clattered together.

"Please," he hissed under his breath, unable to keep the thought silent. "Don't."

The commandant and others around him shifted. Most gave him cautious looks, as if he had shouted. The commandant, however, frowned worriedly.

The marquesa's eyes glistened, her eyebrows drooped, and her lips pressed tightly together. She braced, on the brink of tears for an instant. Then she shook her head, blinking and taking a deep breath before raising her head, and the small smile had returned.

"I won't ask any of you to change your allegiances," she said. "I won't demand you rebel against your marqués to set you against your neighbors. Especially, again, with your homes and families surrounded by my armies.

"I only ask this. When we leave here tomorrow, and you spread word of our time here, tell them what I said, and then tell them what we did. Tell them we came in like a whirlwind but left your homes standing. Tell them thousands of men struck as a steel but honored surrender. Tell them we tore the collars from the *sioneroses* but did not put them on your children's necks. Tell them our fight is not with them but with *Borbin*. All I ask is that you wait to see the outcome. After that, you can make your choices."

She nodded sharply then hopped off the crate. She strode to join the calleroses to her left, her shoes tapping on the floor as the crowd watched her silently. No claps or cheers, nor whispers or grumbles. Everyone watched, faces struggling to remain placid while chewing on her words and obviously not ready to swallow.

Necrem found them hard to swallow himself. *An enemy of Borbin himself? Wait and find out? What difference is that from year to year? Marquéses and marquesas are always enemies. They just choose which year to strut before each other, and the loser sells out to the victor.*

A still voice in the back of his head whispered to him, however, *That didn't happen at the junction.*

Conversations began to resume, small whispers grew louder and built on top of each other, after the general introduced the marquesa to the Orsembian calleroses. The calleroses clicked their heels together, nodding sharply and respectfully.

Necrem felt his sleeve being tugged, and the commandant beside him cleared his throat.

"This way, Sir Oso," the commandant said, ushering him toward the marquesa. Again, the young officer didn't wait and proceeded to walk ahead of him.

Necrem kept his head up so not to step on him again.

"I'm glad you're enjoying yourself," the marquesa said to the tall Orsembian calleros.

The commandant stopped behind the marquesa and clicked his heels together. "Pardon me, La Dama, but I've brought Sir Oso, as requested."

The marquesa turned on her toes, keeping herself able to address both groups with a turn of her head. She gave him an assuring smile, looking up at him in the eye without a glance at his mask.

"Good evening, Sir Oso," she said, her voice as smooth as a touch. "I'm glad to see you're better."

Necrem swallowed, unsure of what to say. Everything inside him screamed to say nothing, yet she could see that as insult, as well.

"Thank you," he said lowly, "La Dama."

He remembered his hands were still in his pockets and took them out with a jerk to perform a hasty bow.

"You needn't be so formal," the marquesa said with a wave. "I'm not as . . . snobbish as some of my contemporaries." Her smile grew to a grin, bright with an air of charm.

Necrem kept silent, rising only slightly yet keeping his head tilted. She was being nice, which only made him more nervous.

Does she . . . want something? What? What could I have?

The general on the other side of her cleared his throat. "Excuse me, La Dama, but may I . . . ?" He nodded at Necrem then at the calleros beside him.

"Oh, but of course, General Galvez," the marquesa replied happily, taking a step back.

General Galvez held out his hand, as if presenting Necrem to the other calleroses.

"Luziro," the general said, "may I introduce you to Sir Necrem Oso. He is the Orsembian soldier who rallied against us at our battle at the junction.

"And Sir Oso, may I present Cal Luziro Ribera."

Necrem's eyes widened upon hearing that name. The calleros's own piercing hazel eyes widened, as well. He certainly wasn't the White Sword. However, he was as tall and slender as the famous marshal Necrem remembered. The calleros was the opposite of the general, however. His shoulders weren't as wide, and his face was all sharp angles, with his high cheekbones, pointed nose, and cleft chin. There were also specks of white in his dark hair, blending with his gray clothes.

Cal Ribera looked Necrem up and down then turned to the general. "Is this the man?"

"He is," the general assured.

Cal Ribera snapped his heels together, going instantly to attention. "Bravo, sir!" He gave Necrem a sharp nod then stuck his hand out to him. "To hear a man stood alone against a whole company and got others to rally, with your bare hands, no less. It's truly an honor. You did your marc proud."

Necrem stared at his hand. *It's an honor?*

The words sounded strange to his ears, as did his gesture. Yet more things to add to the pile of things that stopped making sense since that terrible night at the junction.

Everyone waited. While Cal Ribera kept his hand out, Necrem saw his fellow calleroses watching him as cautiously as they did the Lazornians. It would be rude not to take the man's hand.

Still.

He was a calleros.

Whether it was that kernel of steelworker pride or his old scars, Necrem couldn't.

"I don't rightly remember what I did," he said, turning his head away, "but it was nothing to be proud of."

He kept his head down. He saw Cal Ribera's hand wavering in the air and heard boots shifting on the floor tiles. He was sure they were glaring at him. However, in his current situation, maybe being accused of being rude would make them force him to leave sooner.

"I'm sorry to hear you feel that way," Cal Ribera said softly, his hand falling away. "And I beg your pardon, La Dama, if I offended you."

The marquesa shook her head. "Think nothing of it, Cal Ribera," she replied. "While it was a slight against my soldiers, I must admit it was a small one. And, unlike the other rulers of the marcs, I am no stranger to calleros bravado. I grew up hearing it." She shared a small look with both the general and the commandant. They were faint and quick, yet Necrem had caught them thanks to his head's angle.

"By the way," she continued, "I do apologize for our field marshal being absent tonight. While I assure you that he wanted to be here, the pace of our march has left him in need of some rest. I'm sure he would have been honored to meet the grandson of such a famous marshal."

"Thank you, La Dama," Cal Ribera said cheerfully. "I, too, would have been honored to meet the field marshal. My grandfather spoke highly of only a few commanders outside Orsembar, and Baltazar Vigodt was always one of them."

The marquesa laughed softly; a small, happy, practiced laugh. "You are too kind. I hope your grandfather is doing well?"

"Last I heard. I haven't seen or had word from him since a couple months before the exchange. In fact, it was . . . ."

The conversation was leaving Necrem further and further behind. Worse, he found himself caring for it less and less. The courtesies. The formal addresses. The polite apologies followed by polite disagreements. They all left him standing there, wondering the same thing over and over.

Why am I here?

"If I may ask, Cal Ribera, what did you think of my speech tonight?" the marquesa asked.

There was a pause.

Necrem lifted his head to see Cal Ribera with his arms folded, his head tilted forward, and brow furled.

"To be honest," he began, "I'm not quite certain. You've campaigned against my marc. It is my duty as a calleros of Orsembar to defend it. And, while it is commendable for you to say you are not an enemy of my people, I'm still left with my duty." He chuckled, a smirk breaking his frown. "I'm afraid that doesn't matter now, though. No matter how much leniency you give us, we're still your prisoners."

Everyone's attention slowly slid back to the marquesa.

She pursed her lips thoughtfully. "Something to be said for the honest response of a dutiful soldier. I'm afraid I probably won't get any such honesty from the rest of the people in this room. The baroness is merely praying for us to leave to write to her husband about how dreadful we've been, and he and his ilk will likely not take kindly to me upending their world.

371

"All the merchants and this city's important families are probably too uncertain to say they would be for or against. They'd probably just tell me what they think I want to hear."

Her gaze shifted, locking eyes with him. Necrem knew what was coming before the words left her mouth.

"What of you, Sir Oso?" she asked. "You are neither baron, calleros, nor rich. What do you think?"

A knot formed in the small of his back. After being left out, the conversation suddenly engulfed him again, and when he lifted his head a little more, hard stares greeted him. Both Orsembians and Lazornians gave him warning looks and, caught between them, they made his response that much more obvious to him.

"It doesn't matter," he said.

"Oh"—the marquesa raised an eyebrow—"I think it does."

"That's not what I meant." He shook his head. "You win. Borbin wins. It doesn't matter. There will always be next season. Another marc. Another tax. Another order for a pound of flesh. On and on it goes. It's just not worth it."

The warning looks softened into blank stares. The marquesa's face became expressionless, no hints of her inner thoughts escaped her. Finally, her soft smile returned.

"Walk with me, Sir Oso," she requested.

She passed between the two groups, giving the calleroses a respectful nod as she went by. Her commandant beside him gestured to follow.

I should have stayed quiet, Necrem berated himself. His entire face twinged under his mask, fearing what was coming next.

Again, he was led through the room, and again, people parted. The marquesa, though, turned right down a corridor, out of the room and away from the exit. Voices grew louder behind them as they left, the guests more at ease to talk now that their benevolent captor had left.

The wood-paneled corridor echoed with the sound of bootsteps, more than just his and the marquesa's commandant. Necrem looked over his shoulder. Two soldiers were following, wearing black breastplates over their uniforms. Their sleeves had black stripes, and their helmet's black visors covered their faces, save for the eyeholes. The farther they got from the guests, the louder their bootsteps, accompanied by their swords slapping against their legs.

Necrem paid for not paying attention again and missed the marquesa stepping into a room off to the left. He walked past it a few steps before the commandant cleared his throat to alert him that he had gone too far. He bashfully turned back and cautiously walked into the room.

It was small room, about the size of Eulalia's bedroom. Except, it was filled with chairs instead of a bed, all spread out through the room as if invisible people were having conversations with each other. There was a long, low table in the center of the room where two armchairs sat facing each other on either side.

The sound of pouring water grabbed Necrem's attention to the right, and he looked to find the marquesa filling two wooden cups.

"That will be all for now, Cornelos," she said.

The commandant snapped his heels together, nodded sharply, then drew the door with him as he stepped back out into the corridor. He didn't close it. Instead, he left it slightly ajar, wide enough for Necrem to catch sight of one of the soldiers standing beside the door.

Still, he was left alone with the marquesa.

"I know you probably don't want to drink in front of me," she said, carrying the cups of water around the table and toward the armchair on the left side of the table. "But I would have felt it rude if I poured a cup for just myself." She placed one of the cups in front of the chair on the other side of the table then sat down in her chair, already tilting her head back to drink. She took a couple of large, loud swallows then pulled her cup away with a relieved sigh.

"The worst thing about these events is that it nearly aways leaves me with nothing to drink," she said. "A downside from my oath." She gestured at the armchair opposite her. "Please, Sir Oso, sit."

Necrem did as bade. He dragged the chair back a little more from the table to give his legs space then sat down. He folded his hands in his lap, his elbows resting on the armrests, leaving the water she offered on the table. He raised his head and found her studying him. She crossed her legs under her skirts, held her cup in her lap, and watched him.

Finally, she blinked then glanced down at her cup. "When General Galvez informed me that you had recovered, I asked him what he thought of you. He described you as being . . . beaten." She leisurely swirled the water in her cup. "But I didn't know how beaten you were until just now."

Necrem rubbed the back of his knuckles. "I . . . didn't mean—"

"You said nothing wrong," the marquesa interjected. "Hiraldo—General Galvez—and the rest of the calleroses have all lived in a world where they are taught how to fight and know how to fight on even after a loss. But you"—she winced—"you've never been given a chance to fight for yourself, have you?"

Necrem was as lost as if he had awoken in the middle of the Desryol Sea. He listened the best he could, but he had no idea what she was talking about. There was only one resounding question that kept nagging at him, and he found that was the only response he could make.

"What do you want from me?" he asked. "Doctor Maranon said I might not be alive if you hadn't ordered it. Why?"

The marquesa frowned into her cup. She took a small sip then placed it down on the table. "Because we share a similar pain," she replied.

Necrem sat straighter and watched her rise back up. Her gaze was stone, yet a fire burned within those eyes.

"Three years ago," she began, "Borbin violated an alliance he made with my uncle. He invaded us, marching in virtually unopposed and stormed the city of Puerlato. The commander of Puerlato's garrison, the one my own uncle abandoned without help, was my beloved." Her mouth twisted, and her chin wobbled. "He was killed trying to guide soldiers he thought were his retreating. Instead, they were Orsembians. They dragged him from his horse and butchered him in the mud."

They sat there for a moment. Her pain was plain, yet talks of alliances, campaigning, and loss of cities meant nothing to him. As for the death of a calleros, Necrem felt nothing.

"Another campaign where the marcs betray each other," he said.

The marquesa gave him a searching, dismayed look. "Is that . . . all you have to say?"

Necrem knew he shouldn't have said that. He also knew he shouldn't answer. He knew he should apologize. He did, anyway. "We common folk face such things every season. There's not a family that doesn't have someone fail to come back from the campaigns. It's just how it is."

The marquesa leaned forward, her face bright. "What if we could change that?"

"Change it?" Necrem snickered. "By you beating Borbin? How does that change anything?"

"No." The marquesa shook her head. "Ending the Rules of Campaign. Everything."

Necrem blinked at her. "What are those?"

The marquesa's expression went blank. Then she snickered, halfheartedly chuckled, and lastly laughed; a desperate, sad laugh.

"It's the boot on all our necks," she said. She rubbed her forehead, causing a few strands of hair to come loose and fall across her face. "What all the marcs agreed to when the Desryol dynasty collapsed to see which ruling family could take its place. The reason for the yearly negotiations, the yearly declarations, and the meaningless campaigns. They set out the Bravados for the calleroses, the dealings between the marquéses, even who is chosen as a *sioneros* and who is not. All of it."

What is she talking about? He understood some, other parts sounded ridiculous.

She looked at him as if he did, possibly expecting some passionate response. Instead, Necrem turned away.

The marquéses, the barons, and their calleroses all seeing everyone as having their job to do, some more important than others, was just how it was. It didn't matter if was by whim or law.

He shook his head, feeling suddenly tired, and that they were getting nowhere. "I don't understand what any of that has to do with me?"

"Do you not hate Borbin?" she asked coldly.

Necrem snapped his head up. The fire in the marquesa's eyes was now an inferno.

"I saw how you looked at the Cal Ribera. And Hiraldo. The other calleroses. Even my guard outside." She pointed at him. "You *hate* calleroses."

"I—"

"That wasn't a question." She waved him off. "I remember every word you said that night in the clutches of the laudanum. You may not remember, but I do. You tore your scars, grimacing and snarling at every mention of them. For . . . what they did to your wife. You snarled and growled talking about Borbin, too.

"That same hate, the same loathing, I've felt that for *three* years, waiting for this campaign." Her voice dripped with venom. Her face became a serene mask, yet her lips jerked and spasmed, fighting not to pull back into a snarl.

"So, because of that . . . you want me to join your army?" Necrem ran his fingers through his hair, pulling them back, damp with sweat. "I'm not a soldier! How many times must I tell people *that*?"

"No," the marquesa replied in a hushed tone. "You're much more than some conscripted soldier to be traded back and forth." She ran her tongue across her lips then suddenly reached down to seize her cup, draining the last of her water in one gulp. When she finished, she held the cup to her chest, folding her other arm around herself. "That night, after the laudanum had run its course, Doctor Maranon told me what you did during the battle. I saw the look in his eye as he told it. He was . . . *proud* of you."

"Proud?" Necrem grunted. "He called me an idiot."

"All doctors call their patients idiots." The marquesa snickered. "But he was proud of you that night. The other Orsembian soldiers, they stood up the whole night to hear if you had recovered."

The tops of Necrem's cheeks around his scars warmed. He looked down and rubbed his palms against his knees. "Can't imagine why they'd do that."

"You *inspired* them." A hint of awe laced the marquesa's voice as she leaned forward, returning her cup to the table. She kept the pose, leaning with her arms against her legs. "You charged a whole company, alone, with your bare hands. And instead of running or slipping away in the dark, you inspired men who had no reason or desire to be there, no hope of winning, to *fight*." She gleamed brightly. "That's special, Sir Oso. That's why the soldiers keep talking about it. Why even Cal Ribera wanted to shake your hand."

"And why you want me to join you," he said.

"Yes, but *not* to fight." She held up a finger pointedly. "I want you to tell your story. Everywhere we march, as we draw out Borbin's army bit by bit, I want you to tell everyone in Orsembar what he did to you. How he let his calleroses *rape* your wife. How he *mutilated* you for defending her. I want you to show them your scars and tell all Orsembar who did it to you!" She spoke louder and louder until she was yelling. She paused to take a breath, panting as her shoulders fell up and down, the fire returning to her eyes. "And I want you to be there. I want you to be there that day when we face Borbin himself and tell him, '*Vengeance* comes for him!'"

Necrem's hair stood on end. Every scar on his face throbbed, tugging the stitches. Fire raced down his spine, forcing him to sit up. The lump of coal, which was left of his steelworker pride, ignited from it. His heart pounded in his chest like a hammer. It resonated with the marquesa's words and the fire in her gaze.

A singular hatred in common. It roared deep within him, long buried yet refusing to be contained. The roaring demand of a wronged man wanting retribution.

The memory of Eulalia flashed before him, as she was before and as she was when he had left her. The memory of her bedridden deafened the roar. Eulalia and Bayona were home, alone and waiting.

"My wife . . ." he said softly, "needs me."

The marquesa had sat up, as well, head high and assuredly feeling the same connection he did. Her fire blew out, and her shoulders fell.

"Your wife? She's still . . .?"

Necrem gripped his knees, stopping his legs from shaking again. "She has her good days . . . but most are bad. It's been . . . challenging. Especially for Bayona."

"Bayona?" The marquesa raised an eyebrow.

"My daughter."

The marquesa paled. "Is . . .? Is she—"

"She's *mine*!" Necrem's words came out harsher than they should, but he'd been plagued with others who knew what had happened back then, asking the same question. His fingers dug into his knees. "I see it in her face, in her eyes, how she's grown. She's mine. My . . . little miracle."

"They conscripted you"—the marquesa sat back with a disgruntled expression, folding her arms—"even though you had a family and your age."

Necrem's mangled mouth twisted. "Couldn't pay the tax. Borbin made it so high. They left me no choice." He folded his hands together tightly. His knuckles went white. "I couldn't leave my family without a roof over their heads." He licked his misshapen lips, his breath going hoarse from his dry throat. He reached for the cup but stopped short of grabbing it.

"Would you excuse me for a moment?" he asked her.

The marquesa nodded.

Necrem took his cup and got out of his chair, walking over to a corner of the room. He kept his back to the marquesa as he lifted his mask only above his chin. He held his head back then poured only small trickles into his mouth, enough to quickly swallow yet not worry about overflowing and spilling from the holes in his cheeks.

The lukewarm water rushed down his throat, soothing it in streaks as he took one sip. Then another. Then another.

"Do your scars hurt?" the marquesa asked.

Necrem lowered the cup then lowered his mask back over his mouth and chin. "If I don't keep them clean. Or if I don't keep them salved. Or if I make any sudden movements and raise my voice. They hurt at least once a day."

"I'm sorry."

Necrem glanced over his shoulder, finding her with her hands folded in her lap, her head down, contemplating.

"I didn't know they'd taken you from your family," she said. "I assumed you'd lost them. And despite what I believe you can bring to my cause"—she shook her head—"I can't ask you to abandon them."

Necrem turned, his heart pounding again.

"We're moving out tomorrow," the marquesa continued. "When we leave, I'll make sure you're able to get back to them. You can stay with us until we reach a part of the road that's safe to leave."

Necrem's jaw dropped, pulling on his mask. *Is it . . .? Is it really that simple? Just like that?*

He tried to speak, but his words came out as grunts. "Thank you, Marquesa," he finally got out.

She gave him a knowing smile. "You needn't thank me. You can stay here for the night to rest. That way, you don't have to—"

"Is she in there?" a man demanded outside.

Both Necrem and the marquesa's heads spun toward the door.

"The La Dama's busy," the commandant replied. "Come back—"

"*Damn* that!"

Boots scraped against the floor tiles in the corridor. The loud thump of someone hitting the wall made it shake. The marquesa was already on her feet when the door swung open.

From his angle, Necrem couldn't see whoever was holding it open. He saw the marquesa's eyes narrow, glaring at them, her fists balling around handfuls of her skirts.

"What is *it*?" she demanded pointedly.

Something unspoken passed between her and the person holding the door. Whatever it was made her take a deep breath before putting on a serene expression and turning back to Necrem.

"Please excuse me, Sir Oso," she said. "Something important has come up. I do thank you for letting me speak with you."

Necrem was about to thank her, but she turned on her heels and strode out of the room. They didn't close the door all the way, though, and he was able to hear them outside.

"This better be important, Sevesco," the marquesa warned.

"One of my informants outside Compuert finally got word back to me," a man said. "Borbin is marching straight for Puerlato."

Chapter 22

"*What*?" Recha hissed through her tightening throat. "What did you say?"

"Borbin's marching on Puerlato," Sevesco repeated. His expression was cold. His eyelids sporadically twitched, as did his jaw, slightly ajar to keep from gritting his teeth. Every hair on his hair stood on end. His fists were tight, white balls at his hips.

He wasn't in uniform. It hadn't been wise for him to mingle with the crowd considering his position. Anyone could remember his face. His trousers and boots were covered in dust. His shirt was unlaced, and sleeves rolled up.

Recha's brows rose sharply at the red stain miring his left side. "Is . . .? Is that—"

"It's not mine," Sevesco said. "Toreta, one of my espis in Borbin's camp, rode in with a crossbow bolt in her side and her horse two steps away from dying under her. But she brought messages back."

"Is she . . .?" Recha doubted the need to ask the question, given the size of the stain on his shirt.

"The last I saw, the doctors were trying to sew up her remaining insides." Sevesco's voice was haunting. His eye twitches became stronger. "Luckily, she wasn't awake to speak. She won't see the morning."

Recha ran her tongue along the roof of her mouth, the moisture from her cup of water suddenly evaporating. She tried to think of words of comfort.

However, seeing Sevesco's state, she knew they would do little. Offering any praise that she made it to them at all would garner even less. It was best to move on.

"Have you reported this to anyone else?" she asked.

Sevesco snickered. "Narvae stopped me outside, nursing a pipe. He had the front guards detain me until I handed over all the coded dispatches Toreta brought." His lips twisted. "The message about Borbin on the move wasn't in code, though."

The hairs on the back of Recha's neck stood up. "Narvae *detained* you?"

"He said I wasn't allowed in out of uniform. But after he took off with my messages, I slipped around the side and got in." He shifted on his feet, his hands opening. "Took me about twenty minutes."

"Twenty minutes!" Recha's shout echoed off the wooden paneling. It was her turn to ball her hands into fists. "And no one's come to tell me, except—"

She spun on her heels then marched down the hallway. After taking quick steps to catch up, Sevesco, Cornelos, and her two guards fell in behind her. Their combined footfalls made it sound as if an entire column was storming down the corridor. She kicked her skirts out in front of her while gripping them to stop herself from swinging her arms.

How? Her mind reeled. *How could Borbin . . .? How could his barons . . .? This* shouldn't *be happening!*

The campaign was over. Baltazar's warning of Borbin making this move echoed in her head. She was certain of what she would find once they made it to his chambers. That meant she had to get to the other side of the villa, beyond the reception hall and all her invited "guests." If she was in a clearer state of mind, she probably would have avoided them.

She wasn't.

She marched out into the hall, cutting a line across the back toward the other side of the room and the hallway, which was fastest route to Baltazar. A man, possibly a local merchant or wealthy member the city, turned in her direction, wine glass in the air, smiling mouth open to speak. Whatever expression Recha wore killed his words in his throat, and her hard glare fixed him in place until she passed by.

A few others noticed her. Whispers broke out once her back was to them, but she didn't care. The war called to her now, and Sevesco's fateful message had turned everything upside down.

They were losing.

The question now was: could they recover?

Baltazar's room was all the way down the hallway, flanked by guards. The field marshal had picked it because it had a better view of the city and valley below, and it was on the bottom floor for easy access. Excited voices drifted from it down the corridor.

A courier suddenly dashed from the room, a young man, possibly his first time on campaign, clinging a satchel close to his side. He skirted around Recha and her party without a word of acknowledgement, fixated on his mission.

Papa's not wasting any time.

That was the only comfort she had. Her armies and officers had all proven their competency. However, competence mattered little when you were cut off by a larger enemy who was positioning themselves to destroy both you and your home.

"I want every map we have on this table *now!*" Narvae yelled. The abrasive shout slapped her in the face the moment she turned the corner to look at the whirlwind inside the room. "Get every courier that we can scrounge up! Tell General Galvez what's happening! And somebody find that damn Capitán Viezo! I can't make out a sentence of these 'important' messages."

"That's because they're in code," Sevesco quipped. He slipped by Recha and into the path of scrambling staff members unrolling and unfolding parchment after parchment of maps on the large, round table in the middle of the room, possibly a dining table for guests. "My people write their messages like that to keep their information safe."

Narvae sat at the table, a short-stemmed pipe stuck firmly out of the corner of his mouth with smoke rising from it. Beside him, Marshal Manel Feli was circling and marking items laid out in long supply lists in front of him. They were both in uniform, though Recha didn't remember either being at the reception.

Narvae held a thin slip of paper up to an oil lamp, as if he'd been trying to see through it, but now he glared at Sevesco with his one good eye.

"Watch your tone, Capitán," he growled. "I ordered you to remain outside. Where'd you—"

"He came to tell me that our campaign's in peril," Recha announced, stepping into the room. All the staffers stopped what they were doing, several hastily moving out of her way to the table. "Why is it that I had to hear Borbin was on the move *twenty* minutes after it was reported?"

Narvae rose to his feet, ripping the pipe from his mouth then stamping his feet together.

"Don't shout." Baltazar's calming, commanding voice reverberated from the far side of the room to her left. That side of the room was dark, save for a small candle next to a water basin in the corner. Her field marshal slowly walked out from the dark, wiping his face with a towel wrapped over his shoulders.

His uniform jacket hung over a chair. Only one strap of his suspenders was wrapped over his shoulder. His shirt showed signs he had slept in his uniform again, by its pressed wrinkles. He ran his fingers through his hair, several strands on the right side of his head refusing to lay down and stayed sticking out in all directions.

"If the Orsembians hear us yelling at each other, some may try to make trouble for our withdrawal," he added, pulling the remaining suspender over his shoulder then straightening his shirt in his trousers.

Recha frowned at the bags still hanging under his eyes.

He's getting too old to push himself this hard. She winced at the thought, not wanting to think that of Baltazar Vigodt. Yet there was no denying he was tired.

All the armies had been ordered to hold their positions for the past few days, gathering supplies and intelligence. Resting. But not Baltazar.

She glanced at the cot in the dark side of the room, the bedroll flung off onto the floor. It was his tradition on campaign to always sleep in one, even if they captured a villa like this where his station gave him the authority to claim a real bed for himself. He claimed it kept his mind focused on the campaign, but it did little for his rest.

"Now, everyone *calm* down," he ordered firmly. "Sevesco, sit down and start decoding those messages. I want every word cyphered before morning. Has anyone gone to get Hiraldo?"

Narvae grimaced at the staffers now standing around the room. "I ordered someone to do that an *hour* ago!"

The staffer closest to the door sprinted off. Recha felt the air rush behind her as he ran.

She smirked. *It was more like a few minutes ago, and then I walked in.*

"Thank you," Baltazar said.

Recha snapped back to watch Baltazar take a mug from a staffer. The dark brown coffee steamed, filling the room with its pungent, vanilla aroma. Baltazar brought it to his lips and, without blowing on it, took a sip. Only a flex of the nose hinted he felt its heat.

Recha's mouth suddenly felt dry again. She licked her lips at the coffee but knew Papa's had always been a little on the strong side for her, never sweet enough, and always too hot. She didn't have to look at the table to know there was a bottle of wine out with Narvae around.

Dammit! She rolled her eyes. *I'm going to need something—*

The pitcher of water back in her commandeered office sprang to mind.

Not wanting to be loud about it, she turned over her shoulder and whispered, "Cornelos."

"Yes?" Cornelos said, stepping closer and keeping his voice down.

"I'm sorry to ask this," she began, "but can you go back to my office and fetch the water I left in there? I'm going to need it."

Cornelos gave her a studying look, as if determining if she was being serious or not.

She gave him an apologetic smile and said, "Please."

"I'll get it," he replied without a hint of reluctance.

Recha mouthed "*Thank you*" to him as he slipped out the room then turned back. Sevesco was already seated beside Narvae, his head bouncing back and forth between a message to his left and writing on another sheet of paper on his right. Narvae had his pipe back in his mouth as he squinted at Feli's stock and supply lists.

Baltazar was the one she came to rest upon. He stood staring down at several maps spread out for him on the table, one fist holding his coffee and the other on his hip. His grimace made his mustache bristle.

"What do you suggest, Field Marshal?" she asked, walking over to join him.

Baltazar raised his eyebrows and gave her a warning look. "You know what I have to do," he pointedly replied. "All armies are to march hastily back to Lazorna. I need to plot out the logistics first to make sure we don't clog the roads and bog ourselves down. We can't spare a single minute on roadblocks we cause ourselves.

"Ramon!" He snapped his fingers and pointed at his second. "Did you send a courier to the Third to order them to halt and wait for further orders?"

"Sent him out of here ten minutes ago when you were . . ." he trailed off and shot Recha a glance, "relieving yourself."

Baltazar grunted then took a sip of coffee, possibly to hide his expression.

Recha strained to hold back a grin. It was obvious what he had meant, and being that she was raised in the Vigodt household, things like using a chamber pot shouldn't have been that embarrassing.

"I think he ran by us on the way here," she said to restore the conversation's course.

"Good." Baltazar leaned down to move some of the maps around. "General Ros's last report had him too far west. I'm not sure if the lack of resistance made him too eager or if Tonio's doing the encouraging, but they're the ones in greatest danger now."

Recha tapped her palms on the head of a chair's back. She looked down at the map Baltazar was studying. She made out the highway they had marched from the Desryol Sea up to Crudeas, the small villages they had passed, the villas, the sparse farmlands, and few connecting roads. Holding and resting the army at the city had been a wise as well as a strategic decision. While the armies rested, the enemy would have either been forced to march directly from the northeast road to be hampered by the forest to the south, hills to the north, and Crudeas's single well-maintained section of city wall, or swing around far to the north, around the hills, where they could be ambushed in several points.

Their second engagement would have been as beautiful as their first. Recha bit her lip, seeing it play out in her head.

And now it was all gone.

"There must be some way to salvage this," she said, tapping her fingernails on the top of the chair. "If we take the northeast road toward Compuert, threatening their rear might just make them turn around and chase us?"

Baltazar shook his head. "Too risky. And too many things could happen. There is no guarantee that Borbin would turn to chase us or send a contingent to hold us or chase us while he marches in force to cut us off from Lazorna, or simply use his numbers to pincer us.

"No"—he set his cup on the table then leaned over it—"we must retreat. Get back to Puerlato before he does and use the narrow gap of the coastal road and mountain range. If we get there in time, we can force Puerlato to surrender and free up all our forces." He let out a deep sigh. "We're going to need them."

Recha's grip grew tighter and tighter on the chair. Her fingernails dug into the wood as she listened to him, to the tone of his voice. Baltazar was resigned to his course, and his regretful sigh reverberated inside her.

No! No! No! This can't be it! She bit her lip harder, the dull, growing pain from her teeth adding to her frustration. The bridge of her nose started to twitch.

She ran over their original plan in her head, thinking of everything they could have missed. She kept coming back to one conclusion.

It doesn't make sense! She shook her head, her hair bun feeling too tight. A sharp sting sprang up from her middle finger on her right hand. Her fingernail had caught on the chair's wood.

She hissed, snarling down at the chair for its offense. She picked the chair up then flung it into the dark corner of the room.

Crack!

A wooden leg, splintered on one end, rolled out into the light.

"*Dammit!*" Recha yelled.

She raked her fingers into her hair, undoing the bun and spilling her hair across her shoulders. The pressure around her head was relieved but little else. The bridge of her nose kept twitching, and she had to rub it to make it stop.

She sighed from the relief then stopped.

Her sigh was too loud.

Rather, the room was too quiet.

Cautiously, she peered from the corner of her eye. Everyone in the room was staring at her. The staff stood frozen again in whatever duty they were carrying out. The guards peeked into the room, curious. However, the moment they caught her looking, they ducked back out of the room. Everyone at the table sat straight, watching her cautiously.

Baltazar glared at her, his eyes as hard as iron and his mustache bristling.

Dammit, Recha cursed again.

She looked away, ran her fingers through her hair, spreading it out again, and then gripping her hips. She heard Baltazar's approaching footsteps but didn't turn to look.

"Recha," he said lowly, stepping up beside her, "if you need to step out, you can, but you know better than to make such an outburst like this in front of your officers."

"It doesn't make sense," she repeated, ignoring his chastisement.

"I warned you before we invaded," Baltazar said. "It was the best countermove against us he could make, a sure military decision."

"But Borbin doesn't make *military* decisions!" Recha kicked the broken chair leg back into the shadows. She spun around, matching his gaze. "Borbin is a political monster. He invaded us in the first place because my uncle made political deals to look after Lazorna first over their sham of an alliance. He forced a marriage between Marqués Narios daughter and his idiot son so Saran would attack Quezlo for him. And he's had a personal grudge against Marqués Dion for years. He wouldn't have gone through all this effort, amassed the largest army he ever has and marched them in front of his prize, just to leave now!"

"Unless that same political monster heard of our attack and decided to plunder our homes in return," Ramon said, folding his arms. "Teach us a lesson for butting in."

Recha stalked back to the table. "Maybe next year, if we hadn't finished him off, but Borbin couldn't give a . . . second thought about Lazorna. He scoffed at every ambassador I sent to Manosete. Those yearly campaign negotiations were all jokes." She sniffed sharply. "He stopped taking us seriously when we didn't counterattack Puerlato the year after he took it."

"Well, he's taking us seriously now," Narvae said.

"By abandoning his siege *and* the heartland of his marc!" Recha exclaimed, throwing up her hands. "Don't any of you see it?"

The blank expressions from the staff—except for Sevesco who had gone back to deciphering his messages—made her grit her teeth under her grimace.

She started stalking around the table. "Borbin's been planning to take Compuert for over three years now," she explained. "Perhaps even since his campaign ten years ago when he first pushed Quezlo to the city. Now, engrained with the largest army he's ever assembled, he hears we've marched in, and instead of seeing us as a nuisance, he abandons the prize he's been wanting for all these years in an instant?

"And what of his *barons*? This is the fourth estate we've marched through, taking their crops, releasing their *sioneroses*, disarming their home guards. Baroness Sa Manta should have already sent a frantic message to her husband, and she shouldn't have been the first. There is no conceivable way that Borbin's barons aren't up in arms, demanding they be sent to defend their estates! They should be taking their retinues and companies and rushing to face us. All of it doesn't make sense!" She made a full circuit around the table, staffers edging out of her way as she paced, coming to rest where she had started.

"No offense, La Dama," Narvae said, his arms still folded and seemingly unfazed by her quandary, "but it is possible they learned how far we are from Lazorna and, believing the marc exposed, Borbin and his barons now see a greater prize than Compuert."

Recha could see that. An entire marc was worth more than a single city. She could also see Ramon was missing something.

"Borbin might," she agreed, "but not his barons. Orsembian barons are just as, or perhaps more, greedy and petty as Lazornian barons. Believe me; I've been dealing with both for three years. Borbin can make all the promises he wants of how they would divide the spoils, but there aren't enough promises he can make to convince *all* of them to ignore us marching through their estates while they attack ours. Some of them would have to break rank."

Baltazar stepped up beside her, stroking his mustache in thought. "Promises of spoils alone might not have convinced them," he said, "but offered with a strategy that would force us to withdraw or lose everything, checking us and protecting the barons' property in the same move, that could have convinced them."

Recha snorted. "Doesn't sound like Borbin. He might think of a strategy, but he's not the sort of man who makes strategies to protect anything other than what he wants. It just doesn't feel like him."

"No," Baltazar grunted and nodded in agreement. "It doesn't feel like him. It feels more like . . ."

"*The White Sword*!" Sevesco gasped in a crisp hush.

Recha joined the rest of the room and swung her attention to her espi master. Sevesco's neck rigidly craned over his decoded messages. His eyes bounced frantically between the papers in front of him, as if convincing himself he was reading his reports correctly.

"Sevesco," Recha said warningly, hoping this wasn't a joke of his to break the tension, yet also praying he wasn't seriously implying what she thought he was implying, "this is no time for jokes."

"Who's joking?" Sevesco said under his breath then began to read his decoded message.

"'*Seventh of Andril, joined advance force to Compuert.*

"'*Eleventh of Andril, Compuert reached, observation of siege preparation commenced.*

"'*Twelfth of Andril, preparation of siege has commenced strangely. Marqués and prominent barons have yet to arrive, yet command of advance soldiery took the fields outside Compuert from a larger Quezlo force. Counterattack quashed without reinforcements. No banners fly over command position. Investigation of command needed.*

"'*Sixteenth of Andril, Marqués arrives with main force. No update on command structure.*

"'*Twentieth of Andril, Orsembian army is dug in for siege. Cannot possibly move out with haste. No update on command structure.*

"'*Twenty-first of Andril, contact made with fellow merchants. Claims to have witness Marqués observing the status of siege. Claims to have seen the White Sword in his retinue. Verification needed!*'"

Sevesco stopped reading and rummaged around in his notes.

"Don't tell us you've gotten them out of order," Narvae snapped at him.

"That was the last entry made in that handwriting!" Sevesco growled back. "Either they didn't make confirmation, or something happened to them, or . . . Either way, another espi should have carried on."

He flipped over more papers. A grimace spread across his face, forcing the veins on the side of his head to become visible.

"Sevesco," Baltazar said.

"*What?*" Sevesco snapped.

"Calm. Down." Baltazar's spoke softly yet firmly. "Read what you got. You can't afford to miss anything."

Sevesco stopped and took a deep breath. Once. Then twice. His grimace faded to serious focus, and then he started methodically flipping through his reports again.

"'*Twenty-first of Andril*'," Sevesco read, "'*missed contact with two fellow merchants. Another has disappeared, along with all their belongings. Question of dispersing being considered. Rumor of Fuert Ribera's presence leaving several to remain. Verification needed.*'"

He flipped over to another report. "'*Twenty-first of Andril, Compuert's wall was attacked today. Marqués and entire retinue observed. Fuert Ribera among them. Only member without personal retainers or banner. Why?*'" He thumbed through the last few reports then dropped his hands on top of them. "That's the last mention of him."

A somber spell fell over the room again.

Another piece of terrible news after the other. Recha braced herself against the table, her hair spilling over her shoulders then falling around her face.

"How did I miss this?" she asked aloud. "We made our entire battle plans around Borbin, not Ribera. How did we miss Ribera was still—?"

"There was nothing to *miss*!" Sevesco slammed his fists down on the table. "Ribera *is* retired. He hasn't shown his face in Manosete once in three years! Everyone rumored he was in disgrace."

"He's not in disgrace now," Narvae said.

"Perhaps," Baltazar said. "'*Only member without personal retainers or banner. Why?*'"

Recha peered through her hair at him. He stood with his hands on his hips, frowning deeply into space with a distant look. His eyelids narrowed and expanded.

Recha picked herself up, tilting her head as she watched him. "What is it?"

"More questions," Baltazar replied softly.

Let's not ask them, she inwardly sniped. *We've received too many terrible answers for one night.* Yet, a part of her was already wondering what he meant and rolling it over in the back of her mind to figure it out.

Baltazar returned out of his thoughts and turned to Sevesco. "Your informants did well, Sevesco. They stuck to their mission, found quandaries to answer and stuck out to answer them on their own, and got the information back to us. We couldn't ask more than that."

"I want to know how they were found out," Sevesco said darkly, deciphering the last remaining messages.

Bootheels stomped together behind her.

"General Galvez has arrived!" a guard announced.

"Send him in," Baltazar replied.

Hiraldo stepped slowly into the room. Gone was his cheerful, almost comradery expression he wore back in the reception hall. He held his chin up, his jaw hardened to granite. He went to attention without a word.

"You heard?" Baltazar asked.

"The guards advised me to wait while"—he glanced at Recha then into the dark corner where she had thrown the chair—"heads cooled off. A wise general doesn't stroll into someplace where his men are cautious to go."

Recha smiled despite how horrible the evening was going.

Baltazar grunted in approval. "Well then, you know what we're up against. How fast can you pull the First Army out of Crudeas?"

"Tomorrow night," Hiraldo replied after thinking for a moment. "That, of course, depends on how fast we can load up the stores we need, the weather, and road conditions."

"Weather's not a problem," Narvae scoffed. "No rain for nearly two months and hot as sin. Should be able to march out by nightfall."

"Still," Hiraldo added, "I think it best if the Second Army departs first. The sooner, the better. They're camped outside the city and should be in a better position to move. If they get out ahead of us, we don't risk the roads getting clogged."

"That'll make the First Army our rear guard," Narvae warned. "If we need to get our best troops back to Lazorna as fast we can, we may have to wait until the First Army is ready to pull out."

"With respect, Marshal, we can't wait." Hiraldo shook his head. "The armies need to move fast. If the First Army must be the rear guard to push the others along, we'll take that role."

Recha raised her head, feeling a sense of pride in her Companion's selfless duty.

Baltazar chuckled deeply from his chest. "See to it, General. Marshal Feli should have a list of supplies to commandeer sometime . . ."

"Before dawn," Feli confirmed, handing a checked list to a staff member.

"Yes, sir!" Hiraldo nodded sharply then moved to leave. Yet, he paused. "One more thing, the prisoners we took while taking the city, what should we do with them?"

"The city guard can be released once we withdraw," Baltazar replied, picking up his mug then taking a sip.

"The calleroses, as well? None of them surrendered under the Rules."

"Their enemy calleroses, Hiraldo," Baltazar said. "If we released them, too, they would either pursue us with the intent to slow us or rendezvous with their main force and tell them where we are. We'll have to take them with us."

"Yes, sir—"

"Wait!" Recha exclaimed, throwing her hand out toward Hiraldo. A spark flashed in the back of her mind. "Something else doesn't make sense."

Hiraldo stood there, eyes darting between her and Baltazar in silent confusion.

"Something *else* doesn't make sense?" Baltazar inquired, eyebrows raised over sipping his coffee.

Recha nodded then pointed at Hiraldo. "Luziro said he'd last spoken to his grandfather before the Exchange. He said his grandfather was no longer campaigning."

"Prisoner or not," Hiraldo said with a shrug, "he's still an enemy calleros. He wouldn't divulge such information."

"But he said it with such certainty."

Recha thought back on her little chat with the young calleros, maybe a few years behind her Companions. He had behaved as a model of nobility and soldiery. She wouldn't have thought him as clever. That spark in the back of her mind hummed, as well, coming to the forefront.

"And then there's him being *here*," she added, "with a company of calleroses while his own grandfather is taking part in a grand siege without *any* personal retainers. Why?" She bit her lower lip again as the question repeated itself in her head.

"We could interrogate him," Sevesco suggested.

"Put him to a more serious questioning," Narvae concurred, puffing on his pipe.

"No," Recha, Baltazar, and Hiraldo replied in unison.

"He surrendered under the codes of war, not the rules of campaign," Baltazar said. "I won't have the codes of honor broken for something we already know."

"Also, he's a calleros, just like us," Hiraldo added, staring down Sevesco. "I doubt he would break easily."

Sevesco mouth opened, but he kept silent, biting his tongue on whatever cutting remark he almost made.

Recha kept her reasoning silent. Unlike the person or honor of either man, she mostly disagreed because, after their little introduction, she found him likeable. She didn't want to admit that, but a calleros who acknowledged the bravery of a conscripted man and spoke highly of Baltazar couldn't be all bad. Even he was an Orsembian calleros.

"Still, why is he *here*?" she asked. "He said he was here for training. But wouldn't the best training be with his grandfather at an actual battle? That's what doesn't make sense to me."

"I could speak with him about it," Hiraldo suggested.

"You have an army to move out." Recha pursed her lips, thinking. Then she slid her gaze toward Baltazar. "But maybe if he spoke with a field marshal that his grandfather always spoke highly of, he'd let more slip than he would talking to another calleros."

Baltazar gave her a dry look. His shoulders slumped momentarily then rose back up as he turned to Hiraldo. "Bring the lad here," he ordered.

"Yes, sir," Hiraldo replied then left.

Recha looked Baltazar over while he took a long slurp of coffee. "You may need to put on your uniform jacket," she suggested. "Seeing a field marshal in his suspenders might not be the best . . ."

Her words dried up at Baltazar's warning stare. She grinned apologetically and blessedly Narvae snickered, drawing the look away from her. She took the reprieve to beat a hasty retreat and slipped across the room near Sevesco.

"*Very* brave," Sevesco whispered over his shoulder at her.

"Shut up," Recha retorted out of the side of her mouth.

"Recha."

She snapped up straight, almost stomping on the floor. She spun around, expecting Baltazar to have something more to say. Instead, she found Cornelos setting a water pitcher on the table and holding out a cup to her.

She breathed a sigh of relief. "It's just you, Cornelos."

She ignored his concerned look at her statement and seized the cup, downing the lukewarm contents in several long, spaced-out gulps. Her eyelids instinctively closed as she felt the rush of water flow down her throat and throughout her body. She hadn't thought she was that thirsty, yet she drained every drop.

"That bad?" Cornelos asked once she lowered the cup from her lips.

Recha nodded. "Worse."

She held her cup out, which Cornelos graciously refilled.

"I would have returned sooner," Cornelos said, "but I'm afraid he wanted to speak with you some more."

"Hmm?" Recha gave him a confused look, raising her cup to her lips again.

Cornelos gestured to the door.

Recha coughed into her cup when she saw Necrem Oso standing in the hallway, shoulders hunched and head low, at a careful distance from the guards at the door.

Did I just leave him . . .? She cursed herself for her own forgetfulness and hurriedly slipped out into the hallway.

"Sir Oso," she greeted, putting on the best smile she could manage. "I'm so sorry. I didn't mean to run off and leave you in that small room alone."

"Begging your pardon, La Dama," Sir Oso replied, his voice a rumble behind his mask. He folded his hands in front of him, but that did little to diminish how giant he was. "You don't have to apologize. I . . . overheard what happened."

Recha's smile slipped. "It's . . . the ever-changing tides of war, I'm afraid. But in the very least, I still thank you for hearing my offer. I promise you'll be given transportation back to your family when we march out. There's bound to be a wagon we can commandeer around here somewhere. *And* provisions for your journey and deberes for your family, too." She forced herself to smile, showing him some comfort. The poor man deserved that much.

"Thank you . . . La Dama," he replied bashfully.

That was how Recha interpreted it at least. It was hard to tell with his mask, but his speech was soft, and he couldn't look her in the eye, glancing off to side at the floor.

"For understanding," he added, rubbing his broad knuckles with his palm.

He reminded her of a shy child unused to receiving compliments, blushing when he finally received one. Except, Sir Oso was a walking mountain and likely over a decade older than her. In his lack of response, though, an awkward quiet settled over the hallway.

Recha tapped the outside of her cup while thinking of anything else that needed to be said. "You're welcome," she finally replied. "I mentioned before, we can provide you a room here tonight so you won't have to bother traveling back to camp in the dark."

"Oh no!" Sir Oso said sharply, throwing up his big hands and shaking his head. "I . . . couldn't ask that. I wanted to ask if it would be all right if I *could* leave, actually. I . . ." He folded his hands back. "I really don't want to be a bother." His eyes shifted wearily to the guards behind her then looked away in a flash. He shifted his weight, making him sway.

He is extremely uncomfortable here.

"Very well, Sir Oso." Recha nodded, understanding. "I'll send word for a carriage or wagon be brought around to take you back. Thanks again for accepting my invitation and hearing me out."

Sir Oso hung his head, and a short snort escaped from under his mask. "You're welcome, La Dama. I . . . hope I didn't offend you for not joining you. I do feel bad for not repaying you for saving my life." A hiss of air and a wet smack came from under his mask, the fabric sinking into his cheeks briefly before he breathed out. "I just . . . I just need to—"

Recha grabbed his hands. His skin was rough, brittle, and hard as stone. The joints of his fingers and knuckles were coarse nubs. She squeezed, anyway.

"It's fine," she assured him. "You have a family to take care of."

Sir Oso's eyes widened. His body was stiff, yet his hands trembled. His mask shifted as if his jaw was opening and closing, but he didn't say anything. He simply nodded.

Recha nodded back then let his hands go with a small shrug. "I'm afraid, even if you'd agreed to help us, these new events have killed that plan entirely."

"Sorry I couldn't be—"

"*Stop* apologizing!" Recha snapped.

Sir Oso jumped back. Sweet broke out on his brow.

I shouldn't have done that. Recha took a sip of water then sighed softly to calm herself.

"You don't have to apologize for things you have no control over," she said.

That seemed to work. Sir Oso shifted his weight again, and his shoulder fell, although he kept silent and watched her closely.

I guess he's been beaten so much he won't lower his guard even if a marquesa tells him to, she thought. *Best to send him on his way then.*

"Anyway," she said with forced cheer, "there's nothing anyone can do to help us now, unless they have a faster way back to Lazorna. I'll send for a servant to—"

"Ribera's Way might be open," Sir Oso said with a shrug.

Recha blinked from hearing that name again. She had heard it repeated far too many times tonight. *"What?"*

"Open may not be right." Sir Oso shook his head. "I'm not sure if it's called that—"

"Sir Oso," Recha said firmly. "What is Ribera's Way?"

"It was what we called the route the army took ten years ago when Marqués Borbin first fought Quezlo. The ground was pretty rough, and many of the heavier wagons broke down. Eulalia was scared ours would . . ." He cleared his throat, as if to shove the memory aside. "It was a dried river that opened up to passages around the hills to other side above Compuert Junction."

That could save us some time!

"Do you remember the name of the river?" she inquired.

Sir Oso's brow furled. Then he blinked a few times. "Se . . .? No. Medseca. The Medseca River, I think."

Recha spun on her heels and rushed back into the room, straight for the maps on the table. She caught a few surprised looks as she slapped her hands on the table to flip through them.

"Do we have any map of the Medseca River and the hills between the two highways?" she asked.

"I don't recall," Baltazar replied, stepping out of the dark corner of the room and buttoning up the collar of his uniform. That made Recha smile. "Why?"

"Well, Sir Oso mentioned—"

She glanced over her shoulder to see Sir Oso was still standing out in hallway. She beckoned to him. "Come in, Sir Oso. You don't have to stand out there."

Sir Oso hesitated but reluctantly stepped into the room. Although he held his head low, he had to stoop a little lower to enter. The staff gave him a wide, wary distance, either from his size or the sight of the mask over his face making them uneasy.

Recha went back to shifting through maps.

"Sir Oso says there is a passage Borbin used ten years ago to get around the Quezlians," she explained. "Probably how he managed to push them back so far. He out-flanked them. Or rather, Ribera did."

She stopped flipping through the maps, frowned, then turned over her shoulder at Sir Oso. "Why did you call it Ribera's Way?"

"It was a joke," Sir Oso replied. "When another wagon broke a wheel, a horse threw a shoe, or a soldier fell out of line, everyone asked why the route was so tough. They would say it's Ribera's way. It just stuck after that."

Baltazar snorted. "Not the first time an army complained about a march to name it after their general."

"Or a marshal." Recha snickered.

She ignored his pointed look and resumed digging through the maps. Most detailed small areas, square acres around towns or estates along the roads. Some would mark streams if they got close, but few had names. Fewer still showed grand stretches across Orsembar.

She found some that laid out the highway they were on, marking towns by the milage, and didn't depict everything. One or two had the hills to the east between the highway they were on and the one to Compuert. The hills stretched wider the farther north one went and narrowed and fell away the closer one traveled toward the Desryol Sea. None showed a passage through them.

Dammit, do we have nothing?

She flipped through them so fast she barely had time to fully look at them. She just knew they didn't mark what she was looking for and that was it. Her hands trembled with the urge to throw the whole stack across—

She breathed sharply. She pulled one map out, holding it in the air. It certainly stood out. Whomever the cartographer or scout was had sketched out rather than doodled or marked down places and landmarks. Little houses marked the towns, along with their names along the road. Crudeas was depicted with its round walls toward the northernly roads and with houses spilling out along the southernly roads. The hills between the highways were more detailed, as well.

There, halfway between Crudeas and Luente, was a river marked the Medseca. It ran down from the hills, alongside the road, and into the tributary around Luente.

"Here it is!" Recha said but then thought aloud, "I don't remember a river on the side of the highway as we were marching up, though."

"Last year was terribly dry," Cornelos suggested. "And we haven't had to march through any rain, either."

"There was a drought the same year we marched through that way, too," Sir Oso added.

Recha turned excitedly to Baltazar. "The passage could be open! We could cut across to the junction faster than Borbin or Ribera could expect."

Baltazar gently took the map out of Recha's hands, frowning. "A cartographer or scout is trying to be an artist instead of doing their job."

Recha gave him a dry look. *Seriously?*

"There's something on the back," Narvae said, pointing at the map with his pipe.

Baltazar flipped the parchment over then snorted. "Definitely trying to be an artist. Who is Joaq Estavan? He needs to be instructed on scouting protocols."

Recha's ear twitched, hearing a grunt from Sir Oso.

"What name did you say?" Sevesco asked, snapping his head up with a stunned expression.

"Joaq Estavan," Baltazar repeated.

"One of yours?" Recha asked, raising an eyebrow.

"No . . ." Sevesco replied, his expression shifting from intrigued to confusion. "No, it's just that name. I could swear . . . There was this painter during the Liamena affair." He pursed his lips, pondering for a moment, then shook his head. "Couldn't be the same person. Or could it?" His head started twitching from side to side, and his gaze grew distant.

"Well, while you're dealing with that," Recha said, determined to avoid whatever was going on in Sevesco's head and returned her attention to Baltazar, "this still could be Savior sent."

"It's a reach," Baltazar said. "We don't know the land, if there is a definite route, or whether it leads above Compuert Junction."

"That's what we have scouts for," Recha said.

"There's no way they can have all those hills scouted by the time columns of the Secord or Third armies get to the entrance." Baltazar shook his head. "There are too many unknown risks."

Recha ground her teeth together. Baltazar was being cautious, not setting his marching orders on a whim, which she would generally applaud as a sign of competence. Yet, in her heart, she knew this wasn't the time for that. They could be as cautious as they want, have all the information they could gather, make all the right moves, and still lose.

I won't allow that, she told herself firmly to give herself confidence before stomping in front of him.

"We *must* risk it," she urged. "We knew before we started this that we were going to have to take risks. This is just like that."

"Going that route could leave the entire army stranded in the hills between here and Compuert Junction with Ribera between us, Recha," Baltazar retorted.

"We can also have that happen going back the way we came! That path leads us in the same position as we found Givanzo. Only, this time, we could be the ones caught out in the open and destroyed if Ribera reaches Compuert Junction first!"

"*Could*!" Baltazar jutted a finger in the air. "But not certain. You shouldn't let any new piece of information and speculation blindly lead you. Snatching victory from defeat is not so simple."

Recha drew herself up and raised her head higher. "Neither should we resign ourselves that we have lost without fighting back."

Baltazar held her stare, standing motionless. He didn't frown. He didn't grimace. His stare was icy steel. "You're flirting on the line of our agreement," he warned, his voice low yet hard. "If this passage is something we can use, our scouts will alert us. But I will *not* order the armies to march toward unknown course until then. And you need to be prepared for their reports to come back that it's not, Recha. You can't suddenly hear you are losing a war and expect to think of a way to win in the next moment."

Recha's body was shaking. That was not what she had wanted to hear, and that wasn't what she was doing. At least, it wasn't what she thought she was doing. She wanted him to see this information as it was—a chance.

"I simply request it's something we *should* consider, Field Marshal," she said measuredly.

"And it will be, La Dama," Baltazar replied. "I promise, it will be."

Taking what she could get, Recha stepped away and noticed everyone staring at them.

"Back to work," she ordered without thinking of waiting for Baltazar to give the command.

None questioned it as the staff returned to their duties.

As they did, Sir Oso stood out more than . . . being himself, simply standing awkwardly in the way. Recha put the best face she could then waved Cornelos over as she walked over to the man.

"Thank you, anyway, for your assistance, Sir Oso," she said. "Commandant Narvae here can show you the way out and find you passage back to camp. We'll see about getting you to your family some time tomorrow."

"Thank you, La Dama," Sir Oso replied eagerly then looked to Cornelos expectantly.

Cornelos gave Recha a look, which she retorted with a curt gesture.

"Very well," he said then gestured to the door. "This way, Sir Oso."

There was no hesitation this time. Sir Oso stepped lively after Cornelos, his boots stomping nearly on his heels. He ducked back through the door without any word or recognition to Hiraldo returning with Luziro Ribera in tow.

Recha stifled a tired sigh at seeing them. *One thing after the other.*

She hastily drank some more water to refresh herself before smiling broadly as Hiraldo showed Luziro in.

"Ah! Cal Luziro!" she called, bringing her hand up for him to take. She felt a soft crick in her neck for again having to look to another tall man.

"La Dama." Luziro snapped his heels together then sharply nodded before respectfully taking her hand. "It is a pleasure to see you again. And when General Galvez informed me that you wished to introduce me to Field Marshal Vigodt, I knew I dare not refuse either such a gracious lady as yourself or such an illustrious calleros of honor. I thank you." He clicked his heels together again and kissed the back of her hand.

Recha laughed. It just came out of her. She wasn't sure if it was because of everything else that had happened, how suddenly exhausted she felt, or just Luziro's mannerisms. She laughed and grinned.

"You're too kind, Cal Luziro," she said. "And speaking of the field marshal." She pulled her hand away to gesture toward Baltazar.

Baltazar gave the map in his hands one last look before flipping it over then setting it back on the pile with the other maps. Normally, they would worry about an enemy calleros, even a prisoner of war, seeing their maps; however, with them scattered around the table after Recha's mad hunt, Luziro probably wouldn't be able to make out any meaning to them.

Baltazar walked over with his hands folded behind him, his head raised, the cutting image of a superior officer. "Cal Luziro Ribera," he said, snapping his heels together and sticking his hand out. "I have heard a great many things about you, young man. You live up to family name."

Luziro's jaw dropped into a wide smile, and his eyes gleamed, elated. He grasped Baltazar's hand and shook it vigorously. "Thank you, sir! It's an honor, sir!"

Baltazar nodded in agreement and, with Luziro still shaking his hand, he pulled the tall young man along with him as he slowly walked back into the room toward his side of the table. Sensing Baltazar was taking control of the situation, Recha and Hiraldo stepped away. Recha returned to her cup and water pitcher by Sevesco, and Hiraldo went to stand next to the door.

"It was actually quite the surprise finding you here, Cal Luziro," Baltazar said.

"Not half as much as us seeing you coming, sir," Luziro joked.

Recha smirked at that as she refilled her cup. She also took a glance around the room. Sevesco held his head down and sat with his body angled away from the talking pair. Narvae snoozed with his head hung, his chin propped on his chest and arms folded, soft, deep breaths came from his nose.

Recha shook her head but took a sip of water instead of saying anything, more intent on listening to the conversation than anything else.

Baltazar chuckled. "Well, surprise campaigns do happen. Can I offer you some coffee?"

"Why, thank you, sir," Luziro replied, respectfully nodding.

Baltazar waved for one of the staff to bring another mug as he fetched his own. "Wine is for young calleroses, but we older ones need a lot of coffee to stay fresh." He chuckled again at his own joke then sipped his coffee.

Luziro laughed, too, and cautiously sipped his own when the staff member brought it. He winced when he did, which made Baltazar laugh.

"We have to take it strong, too," Baltazar added. "Keeps us awake. Right, Marshal Narvae!"

Narvae snorted awake, throwing his head back. "Right!" he yelled back. His arms unfolded then spilled out on table. "Right! Must stay awake." He looked over everything in front of him, his one eye blinking. "What was I . . .?"

Recha bit her lip, hiding her bemused smile behind her water cup, and wrapped an arm around herself to stop herself from giggling. Some of the staff members were distracting themselves in different manners, as well, to prevent from chuckling.

"By the way," Baltazar said, nudging Luziro with his elbow, "another thing we were surprised by was your lack of strength. Not of marshal strength, of course, but lack of numbers. We wouldn't have been surprised in finding a company or two of calleroses stationed in vital cities, but from my reports, your numbers barely made up a squadron."

"Well . . ." Luziro dropped his head and shuffled his feet, "don't take me rude, sir, but if you're asking me to divulge what our mission here was, I can't—"

"I wouldn't dream of asking you that." Baltazar raised a hand assuredly. "It would be an insult to your family heritage and your personal professionalism. Besides, General Galvez"—he gestured at Hiraldo—"has already reported that you and your men were undergoing some training in the city, and that's enough for me.

"My only curiosity is why you would be training *here*, so far away from the frontlines of campaign, and you undoubtedly being trained by the finest calleros of all Orsembar—your own grandfather—"

"You do my family too much honor, sir," Luziro said, suddenly sticking his chest out proudly with his chin held high then respectfully bowed.

"Not at all." Baltazar waved. "Not at all. But considering your grandfather, what more training could you benefit from being here and not the front?"

Recha grinned at the show. She causally rubbed her bottom lip with the rim of her cup.

Three years of choosing every word out of my mouth carefully, working to pacify my own barons, and playing the surrounding marcs, yet Papa can talk to an enemy calleros for a few minutes and their guard is gone. She shook her head then sipped her water.

"Actually, sir, this was something I brought up with the rest of the men in my unit," Luziro replied. "The siege of Compuert must be a massive undertaking, and the marc could surely use every man we can muster. Alas, the last word from our honorable Si Don—" He stomped the floor then thrust out his mug. "Savior guide Marqués Borbin!" He shifted a look at Recha and lifted his mug at her. "And you, too, La Dama."

Recha raised her cup to him, struggling to keep the smile on her face. They all drank—her, Luziro, and Baltazar.

Baltazar shot her a look over his mug, and Recha shrugged back at him.

"As I was saying," Luziro continued, "our honorable Si Don regrettably instructed us to remain at our posts."

"The marqués *himself*!" Baltazar raised both his voice and his eyebrows. "You must be very honored to be under such a command, and not a local baron or marshal."

"Yes, sir, we are! Our whole unit was handpicked by Si Don himself."

"You were, were you?" Baltazar sipped his coffee.

Recha tilted her head, listening while things spun in the back of her mind. Something, some instinct, whispered that pieces to a larger picture were there, needing to be put into place.

"Yes, sir! Si Don summoned me to Manosete a few years ago to induct me into this company." Luziro beamed like a young boy eager to share war stories and compare medals to an older veteran. "I was extremely honored. I raced to tell my grandfather about it, but he wasn't home that day."

Recha's ears twitched at that. She caught herself from interrupting and asking questions, too. Luckily, Baltazar was just as inquisitive.

"A shame he wasn't there," he said. "Were you ever able to give him the good news?"

Luziro nodded, almost spilling his coffee that he was sipping. "Oh, yes! Last year, we were stationed on our side of the Saran border. We trained all campaign yet, unfortunately, were never called up. Me and a few of the other calleroses went to see him after the end of the season. He seemed . . . proud."

"Well, of course he would be," Baltazar said. "You're his grandson. Any words of wisdom? I wouldn't mind meeting Fuert Ribera myself one day." He smiled up at the young man. His eyes, though, were sharp, and he stared intensely.

"My grandfather wouldn't mind meeting you, too, sir," Luziro replied, setting his mug down. "I can assure you of that. He simply told me, 'Do your duty. Be strict with your training. Keep your eyes and ears open. And I will take care of the rest.'"

"Really?" Baltazar stroked his mustache then passed Recha a knowing look. "'Keep your eyes and ears open. And I will take care of the rest.' Sounds like he still has some fight left in him, for a retired marshal."

Luziro snickered. "I don't think my grandfather will ever be retired, sir. He just says he is."

Baltazar grunted then gave him a lopsided smile. "Fascinating."

"Not as fascinating as your march through Pamolid! If I may ask, how did . . .?"

The conversation was turning elsewhere, but Recha's mind was stuck in a whirlwind.

Keep your eyes and ears open. And I will take care of the rest.

It struck her as obvious what he meant.

His grandfather was trying to warn him. Other things spun in her head. Fuert Ribera was out of favor with Borbin, yet he was at Compuert, giving advice without his own retainers or standard.

Maybe he's not out of favor. Maybe he went into retirement to recuse himself from service. She shot a glance at Luziro, carrying on a conversation in happy oblivion. *And Borbin found a way to—*

Muffled, convulsing snickering drew her out of her thoughts. She glanced to find Sevesco shaking his head, his shoulders twitching, as if fighting a fit of laughter.

Recha causally turned then gracefully bent down with her knees beside him. He was rubbing the bridge of his nose, with a large grin on his face.

"You're thinking the same thing, aren't you?" she whispered dryly.

Sevesco snorted, holding back that much. "He's precious, isn't he? So naïve and full of daydreams of honor. Are we sure he's even Ribera's grandson?"

Recha smirked then took him by the shoulder and leaned in close to whisper directly into his ear, "I want you to take a group of guards and, one by one, gather up all the calleroses we captured with Luziro. They're all in this villa and being escorted by one of ours, so they shouldn't be hard to find. Take them all. Put them to the question."

"They're war prisoners." Sevesco dropped his humorous tone, becoming stone. "Baltazar and Hiraldo may not like it."

"I don't care." Recha squeezed his shoulder. "They may have surrendered under false pretenses. Besides, Papa will probably agree with us on this . . . just so long as we bring back certainty that they were holding Luziro for Borbin as leverage against the White Sword."

"That may take some doing. And we're short on time."

"Use the Viden." Recha's voice sounded cold, even to her ears. However, he was right. They didn't have the time and needed all the information and tools they could get.

Sevesco icy chuckle matched her tone. "Done."

He slipped around in his chair, gathering up all his papers and reports in one sweep before rising. He walked calmly around his chair and her, keeping his face angled away from the conversation still going on between Luziro and Baltazar.

Recha watched him each step of the way. He gave Hiraldo a small nod that one could mistake for respect to a higher officer then slipped out on his new mission.

Seeing him go, Recha caught the sounds of laughter from the reception going on down the hallway, the one she'd called for.

That's still going on, she inwardly groaned and let out a deep sigh, knowing with all the catastrophes that had just hit, she still had a duty to be out there. One Cornelos would undoubtedly remind her of the moment he returned and learned all the storms had abated.

Might as well beat him to it.

She spun back around, finding Baltazar deep in his reminiscing of his Pamolid Campaign, and she held up her cup.

"Excuse me, gentlemen," she said, cutting Baltazar off, "but I'm afraid I still have a reception full of guests that I must attend to. If you will all excuse me, I'm sure you officers and calleroses have everything well in hand."

All the calleroses in the room stood to attention, snapping their heels and sharply nodding.

"We thank you, La Dama, for your time," Baltazar said respectfully.

Recha returned his smile then headed for the door, cup of water in hand. She raised it to Hiraldo on her way out.

When she stepped out into the corridor, she paused and took in deep breath. She spied both her guards stepping up behind her.

"Come," she instructed, breathing out deeply. "Let us pray nothing more earth-shattering happens tonight, and that the guests leave soon."

Her guards chuckled under their visors and followed behind her, back to the reception.

401

Chapter 23

Necrem shifted the drenched handkerchief hanging around his neck for the hundredth time. The Easterly Sun bore down on him mercilessly in his coachman's set of the bouncing, rattling buckboard. He missed the shade of a covered wagon, although he wouldn't dream of complaining. He greatly preferred the option of riding home rather than having to wander back on foot, especially since the wagon had been granted to him by the marquesa herself.

A hot gust blew in from the west. It stripped the remaining brittle, brown leaves from the withered husks of corn stocks littering the expansive fields bordering the rocky road and flung them along with the grainy dust and into the faces of men and beasts alike.

Necrem angled his head away, desperate to keep the tiny grit from finding a way through his mask. A column of pikemen marching beside him cursed and coughed. Those who could shuffled up against the side of his buckboard to avoid the brunt of the gust.

Necrem's mule, Malcada, snorted and whipped her head back and forth. Her blinders protected her eyes, yet the sudden swirling mass of dust and debris from the field made her pull up and cry loudly in protest.

Her previous owner had warned she could be an ill-tempered nag when she wanted to be. Necrem had said she had her good days and her bad days. He'd given Necrem a queer look when he laughed and told him they'd get along fine, patting the mule's neck.

"Hey!" someone yelled behind him.

He peered over his shoulder, squinting against the last remaining swirls of dust. The wagon driver behind him was on his feet, raising his fist at him. The man's four-horse team were neighing, biting their bits, and stomping their hooves against the rocky, packed road. The covered wagon, heavily laden with crates that pushed out against the covering, rocked from suddenly coming to a halt.

Necrem waved apologetically then gave Malcada's reins a flick. The mule snorted and flipped her head back at him, needing another slap of the reins to start moving. He gave the reins some slack as the wagon rolled on, bouncing and shaking on the rocks.

Must've been holding too much again, he chided himself.

After a decade, he was surprised he could remember how to drive a wagon and take care of the animal. He had taken the benefit of how not having to provide for an animal as large as a mule or horse for granted during his poverty. Malcada needed food, water, and rest every day, same as him, and he had to provide for it before tending to himself every night. That meant sticking with the Lazornian army for as long as he could, because they were the closest ones around with grain to feed the ornery thing.

His gaze wandered to his left at remembering the Lazornians. The files of pikemen were moving again, pikes on their shoulders and dust covering them from their faces to their boots. Their armor, violet uniforms, and dark trousers were all turning brown.

None of them spoke. No jokes or songs. No officers cursing them or demanding them to move faster, either, blessedly. Grim determination hung on their faces, like men set off to work on a hard job, and it was too hot to do anything else but be about it. Necrem caught a few of them longingly eyeing his empty buckboard as they trudged along. Their column moved faster than him behind the line of other wagons.

He dropped his feet down from the footrest to nudge the iron chest under his seat with his heels. The chest's heavy lock tapped against the leather of his boots. He knew the soldiers were only interested in riding instead of marching, yet Necrem couldn't help his protective urge toward the chest's contents. He had never dreamed Marquesa Mandas meant to keep her word to provide him a way home or give him coin for his travel.

Five-hundred gold deberes sat in neat rows, flawless and freshly minted. *Five hundred*! He absentmindedly rubbed his heel against the chest to remind him yet again it was still real.

That should take care of us for four or . . . five years? The calculations returned. They always did when he thought about the amount of money with the dull passage of time moving with the Lazornian army. *Maybe more?*

He shoved down the dreary thought that it could last for less. Yet he had known what to do with it the moment he had lain eyes on the treasure in that chest.

When he finally left that villa, his worry and thought of Eulalia and Bayona, that he had desperately tried to ignore during his conscription, had come flooding back. Sleep had rejected him that night, his mind plagued with fears of how they must have been managing, whether Sanjaro was looking in on them, if Eulalia had gotten worse, if something had happened to Bayona, and on and on. Worst of all, again, that he wasn't there.

Necrem's chest suddenly felt tight. He sucked in air in short, hissing breaths. A familiar sense of hopelessness pressed down on him, like an anvil, with the thought. It cracked open the worst nightmare of all—the thought of getting back to find his home and shop deserted, with no one knowing where his family had gone.

He clutched his chest. His heart slammed against that anvil with all its might, threatening to burst from his chest. He squeezed his eyes shut to force the fear away and took long, drawn-out breaths. He rubbed his heels against the iron chest again, reminding him of the feeling he got when he'd first lain eyes on the treasure inside.

It was an old, familiar feeling, same as this fear. Every man had that fear. The fear of not having what it took to provide for your family. Of becoming destitute. Of losing them. Touching his boots against the iron chest again, a comforting feeling pushed back against his fear like warm arms embracing his shoulders, whispering that he had a way to provide for them now and all he had to do was get back home.

"Driver, look out!"

Necrem snapped his eyes open. Malcada was veering left, toward the column of infantry. He yanked the reins, pulling the mule back on course, then looked to his left.

"Are you well?" a Lazornian officer walking beside his wagon asked. He rested a hand on the coachman's seat, as if to pick himself up into it, looking Necrem up and down with occasional, concerned glances ahead of them. Necrem could tell he was an officer because he walked out of formation and didn't carry a pike.

"I'm fine," he replied, sitting up straighter. "Heat got to me for a moment."

The officer gave him a doubtful look. "Best not to push yourself. If it happens again, drive your wagon off the roadside. We don't want to risk any accidents, do we?" He slapped his hand against the side of the wagon then rushed ahead to rejoin his men.

Necrem nodded and watched him go, breathing a sigh of relief. His shoulders relaxed at that. He hadn't remembered them becoming tense, likely a reflex from expecting a scolding. Yet it had never come. It reminded him of something Hezet had said, that the officers acted like officers.

Maybe we shouldn't stay in Manosete? The strange consideration came over him as he watched the soldiers marching beside him. *Maybe we should move. Better than saving this money to pay more campaign taxes to Borbin. Away from Borbin and all of this. The Lazornians aren't too bad. Marquesa Mandas . . . was fair.*

Sparing his life was proof enough without the wagon he drove and the gold under his seat.

Perhaps . . . somewhere else is what we need.

The daunting task flooded his mind all at once. That would mean trying to leave Manosete, if they could. They lived in the slums, but the need for people and taxes was always on the nobles' minds. Same with leaving one marc to another. Then there was convincing Eulalia. He had no idea how she would be when he got home, if she had gotten worse or frail, or if she could travel at all. Then there were their belongings, how much they could carry with them, how much they would have to leave behind. Bayona would probably be upset by it, too, with it being such a big change.

Still, a chance at a better life. Perhaps, oh perhaps, they could make it.

Necrem let out another deep sigh. *I'm not going to sleep tonight.*

"You there!"

Necrem groaned at the sight of two calleroses on horseback. They trotted along the roadside in the opposite direction as the rest of the army, and one was pointing at him.

Not again. He pulled Malcada to a halt, the mule snorting in protest of being handled repeatedly. He ignored her and reached into his back pocket to pull out a now well-worn piece of paper.

"What is the purpose of this wagon?" the calleros who had pointed at him asked after trotting up to him. They investigated the empty buckboard, where only his bundle of remaining belongings sat nestled in the corner just behind him. "Which army are you assigned to?"

"The wagon's mine, sir," Necrem replied, "I'm—"

"All wagons are needed for official use," the other calleros recited.

"If you aren't offering or meeting a need for the army," the first calleros said, "then I'm afraid we're going to have to commandeer this wagon. I'm sorry, but there's been a breakdown up the road and—"

"Sir!" Necrem held the paper up so they could see it. It drooped from being folded and refolded several times and was starting to yellow. "I beg your pardon, but this should explain everything." He held it out to them.

He knew reading it or trying to explain what it said was pointless. They wouldn't believe him. It was best they read it for themselves.

The first calleros twitched his hooked nose. His horse kicked and stomped against the rocks as he snatched it. His eyes went wide the moment he unfolded the paper and saw the seal at the bottom of the page.

"Pardon us for bothering you," the calleros said, handing the paper back.

Necrem took it back then watched them closely as they rode away. He could get along with most of the Lazornians, the common folk in the convoy, the workers, the soldiers, but the sight of a calleros still made his scars pull taut.

He glanced down at the paper in his hand. Marquesa Mandas's flowing signature was the largest thing on it, underneath the declaration stating that the wagon and mule belonged to him and were not to be seized for any reason.

That makes the tenth time, he mused, folding and tucking his saving grace back in his rear pocket. Despite being a well-provisioned army, everyone noticed his empty wagon and several, especially calleroses, seemed keen on finding a use for it.

The road became rockier and narrower the further they continued. The soldiers on foot moved closer or were forced to walk in the ditches and around steep inclines from the first foothills marking the larger hill and rock formation to the east.

The heat was starting to get to him when voices of men arguing came from up the road. The wagon ahead of him swerved to the left, avoiding a crowd of workers trying to get another wagon's back wheel free from being lodged in the gap of a large boulder embedded in the ground and part of the road.

That's a forge wagon! He recognized the slanted, wooden roof on the wagon to keep the tools and movable forge dry.

The workers grunted in unison as they pulled on ropes and pushed down on timbers they used as levers to try to dislodge the wheel. The wagon creaked and shook. Wood strained against iron in protest.

Necrem guided his wagon around the group while watching them work. The heavy-laden wagon refused to budge with its wheel remaining stuck at an angle in the red clay rock.

How'd they manage that?

A loud snap made him jerk around in his seat. One of the timbers they were using as a lever had snapped. The wagon fell back, the stuck wheel grinding deeper into the crevasse.

"What did you *do?*" an older, grizzled man wailed.

"Dammit!" one of the workers yelled. "The axle's broke."

"We're going to have to saw this wheel off!" another yelled.

As Malcada pulled his wagon by, Necrem caught sight of the man with his fists on his hips, glowering at the workers. The scowl slipped into agony as he looked at the stuck wheel.

Do I . . . know him?

Necrem frowned at the man, obviously the owner of the wagon and fellow smith. He racked his memory, trying to place the face with a name, yet nothing came to mind.

Malcada pulled the wagon along, carefree of everything. A few feet away from the wreckage, he spotted a shaggy-haired boy squatting on a stump on the side of the road in a smith's apron, hugging his knees to his chest.

I do know him!

The sight of the boy with the old smith was enough to jog his memory of the smith who had let him repair his armor, saving him from Raul's whip. The broken axle meant the wagon would likely be pulled off the side of the road and abandoned to allow the rest of the army to move on. The calleroses were probably looking for another wagon to put the smith's forge and tools in.

They'll probably find one, Necrem thought. *The Lazornians don't seem to have a shortage of much right now.*

He drove down the road a little farther. and the lingering thought festered in the back of his mind with each step Malcada took. He knew if they couldn't find another wagon, everything would have to be abandoned—the tools, the forge, everything. The poor smith would be out of everything.

He helped me . . . once. He shook his head and touched the chest with his heels. *Eulalia and Bayona need me. I've been away for so long, and . . . .*

Something the old smith had said to him echoed back to him. *Smiths take care of our own.*

He pulled Malcada to a stop, much to the mule's annoyance, stomping and throwing her head back. Neither she nor the people behind him were happy with him turning back around in the road to head back toward the wreckage. The other wagon drivers gave him sour looks, while he simply gave them an apologetic wave.

The boy remained motionless on the tree trunk. His neck was noticeably paler and pinker than the rest of him, free from the *sioneros* collar. A lethargic look clouded the boy's eyes, as if he were staring off into a great distance, unable to see the world passing him by or Necrem's wagon rolling mere inches from him.

Necrem shook his head and drove on toward the wreckage.

The workers were removing the timbers, giving up on the idea of lifting the wedged wheel out. Several were taking a break in the shade of a withered willow tree.

"You don't have to cut off the wheel!" the old smith argued with the officer in desperate anger. "I told you, just let me unload the wagon and *then* we can move it."

"This is holding up the convoy," the officer replied with his arms folded. "And blocking part of the road. The armies need every smith we can, but we need speed, too. I'm sorry, but—"

The officer turned his head at Necrem's approach. "You're going the wrong way. Move that buckboard out of here!"

"Need help unloading?" Necrem asked, pulling Malcada to a halt. The horses hitched to the forge wagon snorted at her.

The officer frowned at him. "Are you sure that buckboard is sturdy enough? If not, then it'll cave—"

"Steel Fist!" the old smith blurted out. He gaped at him, pointing with a trembling, age-gnarled finger.

The officer grunted and raised a questioning eyebrow at the man.

The smith passed a look between him and Necrem, working his jaw until he finally stuttered, "He's—"

"Another steelworker." Necrem calmly slapped Malcada's reins and guided her around the lodged wagon so the empty buckboard was accessible to the back forge wagon.

The workers watched from underneath their shade, sweaty rags in hand from where they wiped their necks and faces.

Necrem pulled the break on the buckboard, in case Malcada got any ideas of wandering off, then began to rummage all his belongings that he could reach and pulled them up into the driver's seat.

"You really going to let us use your wagon?" the old smith asked, rushing after him, almost bouncing with each step.

Necrem looked down from his driver's seat. The old smith was more grizzled than he'd been back when they were in the Orsembian camp. He looked tired, too, with bags under his eyes and a stoop in his posture. He was either working too hard or pushing himself too much. Maybe a combination of both.

"Smiths look after our own," Necrem repeated to him, bringing his last bundle of clothes, the fancy ones the marquesa's officers had provided for him, into the driver's seat.

The old smith stood a little straighter, bracing his hands on the small of his back to do so. The patchy whiskers on his chin trembled as he smiled and gave only a knowing nod.

The officer cleared his throat. "Come on, you men," he ordered, sounding annoyed and waving at the workers, "let's unload this wagon into the other and get this damned thing out of the road."

More annoyed groans followed from the men under the willow tree. They took their time, leisurely standing back up, stretching, and wiping the last bet of old sweat before returning to work. Necrem caught a few annoyed looks shot his way as he climbed down from his seat with a feedbag for Malcada.

"Thank you," the old smith said.

"You joined the Lazornians after the junction," Necrem said, putting the feedbag over the mule's head.

The smile slipped from the smith's face. "I needed more work after . . . after my son ran off with that *camp* woman." He spat off to the side. "Campaigns still go on, and the Lazornians pay just as well."

"That they do," Necrem agreed, remembering his chest under his driver's seat. He unbuttoned his sleeves and rolled them up as he went to lend a hand with the other workers.

"Savior, this heavy!" one worker complained, straining to drag the cast iron forge closer to the edge.

"How do you lift this, old man?" another complained.

Both men grappled with the forge's handles, welded to the side of the large cast iron box with several gaping holes for the flue for the bellows, the opening to work the metal, and the funnel shaped top for the flue. The forge's black iron was warped and scarred by age, use, and heat.

"We generally get help loading and unloading," Necrem replied, stepping up beside the first man.

The worker jerked, staring up at him in surprise. He let go of the handle at a gesture from Necrem then joined his fellow on the forge's other end. Necrem grabbed the handle and braced his other hand on the forge's back to gage its weight.

About as heavy as my old one, he reckoned. He shifted his feet to ensure his balance, bending his knees a couple of times to prepare.

"Lift with your arms and legs," he warned them.

After a few nods and grunts, they picked up the forge. The iron groaned from being moved. Necrem's arms trembled under the strain of the weight and sweat burst across his face and down his neck. His knuckles popped. He fixed his jaw, nose flaring from the excursion. His mask sucked into his cheeks, nicking and pricking against his scars.

The other workers huffed and groaned, too, through gritted teeth. Others joined in once they moved it off the edge of the forge wagon. They groaned and heaved, shuffling and skidding their feet against the rocky road to quickly slide the forge out then hurriedly put it in the back of Necrem's buckboard with a metallic *pang*! They stopped pushing and heaving the moment the forge was entirely sitting on the board, a few inches from the edge.

Many of the workers fell back, gasping for air and letting their arms dangle free.

"Thank the Savior that wasn't loaded farther up," one said, much to the agreeing chuckles of the others.

"Forges are always loaded near the rear of the wagon," Necrem said, working his arms in circular motions to ease their throbbing. "The heaviest thing to load is the first thing off and the last thing on."

The other men let out snorts of relief at hearing that and went about unloading. A pair of anvils came next, followed by the flue and bellows, sawhorses, stools, and boxes of tools, hammers, tools, coal, and used coke. Necrem's smaller wagon creaked and shuddered under the weight as it was slowly filled up.

The Easterly Sun was starting to descend by the time the last man crawled out from under the forge wagon's covering with the old smith's and boy's personal belongings. The officer paced the entire time, his arms folded and jaw set. His harassing barks to hurry didn't do a thing to help.

"That the last of everything?" he asked impatiently. "Then you men get back on the timbers, you men guide the horses, and the rest lift on the end. We needed this road cleared hours ago."

Necrem joined the men at the back of the wagon. His damp shirt clung to his back, and he blinked sweat away from his eyes as it dripped off his brow. He planted himself in the center, squaring his feet and arms, as he had the forge, and rolled his shoulders to prepare them.

"Ready!" the officer yelled. "*Lift!*"

With one, unified groan, the men on the timbers pushed down and the men gripping the rear of the wagon pulled up. The forge wagon groaned from the two forces, its wooden frame straining. The lodged wheel ground against the rock until it finally popped out.

"It's free!" one of the workers on the timbers yelled.

"Forward, driver!" the officer ordered. "Walk with it, men! Move it over here, off the road!" The officer waved his arms behind the ditch near the willow tree.

The horses jerked their heads and stomped their hooves when their bridles were pulled but followed. Necrem walked with them. The wagon wasn't too heavy, not with other hands helping.

A loud, grinding squeak came from underneath the wagon as they pushed it off the road. The broken wagon rolled at an odd angle and pulled off toward the side. It fell off when they finally made it to where the officer was standing.

Necrem was as eager as the others to set the wagon down. It leaned sideways because of the fallen wheel. He rubbed his neck with his handkerchief. The soaked cloth did little to wipe away the sweat. He turned away and found the old smith frowning at his broken forge wagon, the boy standing a few feet behind him.

"Axle's broke," a worker confirmed, stooping over to look under the wagon.

"What should we do with the horses?" another asked.

"They'll be turned over to the calleroses," the officer said. "If they can't find a use for them as mounts, then they'll be added to the herd for the other supply drivers."

"Those are my horses!" the old smith yelled as he stormed up to the officer, gesturing with his fist protectively.

"We need every horse," the officer replied pointedly. "Now that your forge has been reloaded and the wagon out of the way, we need to make use of the horses."

"But their *mine!*" the old smith snarled up at the officer. However, Necrem felt it was all bluster. The older man surely had worked with armies long enough to know, once its officers wanted to take something, they would take it. Unless the owner carried an impossible document that said they couldn't, anyway.

He looked at his small wagon, completely loaded, if not precariously, with the old smith's forge and tools. His cheeks trembled worriedly, especially when he studied Malcada. The old girl was having trouble keeping up with the convoy's pace without the heavy load.

One good hill, and then . . ..

"We need the horses," he said.

The officer and the smith turned to him.

"My mule can't pull that heavy load," Necrem explained. "We'll need the horses to pull it."

The officer frowned at his wagon, and then at Malcada. "And what about the mule?"

Necrem reached for his back pocket before the question had left the officer's mouth. He showed the man the order, and the officer had to read it twice. His face darkened, and he shoved the order into Necrem's chest.

"Switch out the horses," he growled, brushing past Necrem to vent his frustrations on the tired workers. "Make sure everything is unloaded, and then see if there's anything of value left. I want to be back with the main body before nightfall."

The old smith snorted, smiling crookedly. "That's another thanks I owe you."

"That was more for Malcada," Necrem admitted. "She's past her prime of hauling loads like this."

As the workers were finishing up with the derelict forge wagon and unhitching the horses, Necrem walked over to unhitch Malcada. The mule had finished her meal and now stood with her head hung close to ground. Necrem peeked and discovered the old girl was snoozing, her eyes closed, and deep snorts ruffled her feedbag.

"What was on that paper?" the old smith asked, rushing up with an iron chest of his own under one arm and a bundle of ropes under the other. "Did the Lazornians just let you go? Too old to recruit or something?"

"Or something," Necrem replied, unhitching Malcada.

"Well, at least you're not in an army anymore. No offense, but I still remember your work on that breastplate you brought in. Worked it all into shape in one evening. That was something." The old smith whistled sharply through his teeth. "Mind if I put my earnings up on the driver's seat? You know, for safety."

Necrem glanced at his driver's seat, knowing his chest was lodged there, as well. The smith's chest was iron, but he could distinguish it for not having a lock on it.

"I won't mind," he replied.

He rubbed Malcada's neck, waking the mule with a few snorts and hoof stomps. He removed her feedbag, which Malcada shook her mane at him for, then took her by the bridle to lead around to the back of the wagon.

"There, there," he comfortingly told her as he tied her bridle to the rear of the wagon, "this isn't a load you want to pull."

"Here, lad!" the old smith called, throwing one of the ropes over the back of the wagon, tying down the parts of the flue and toolboxes. "Make sure the knots are tight."

The boy, still in *sioneros* fashion, raced off to do as he was told.

"I can't thank you enough for this," the smith said near gleefully, tying down his side of the wagon with a large, relieved smile. "If you hadn't . . . If you hadn't . . ." The old man's hands began to tremble as he retied the same knot he had finished.

"I'll get you to camp tonight," Necrem said, bracing his hands on his hips. "We can see if we can find you a replacement wagon for your forge then."

"Replacement?" The old man straightened, blinking at him confusedly. "We can make it together if . . . if it's not too much of an inconvenience."

"I'm not staying with the Lazornians," Necrem said. "Once we reach Luente, I'm heading west to Manosete."

The other man gawked at him. His hands trembled around the remaining ropes he held. "You're . . . you're *leaving*? Why?" The man caught his voice as the workers brought his horses around to hitch them to Necrem's wagon. He stepped closer and whispered, "I know the Lazornians are odd, and warring through our marc, but . . . for Savior's sake man, they have *deberes*!"

Necrem brows came together. "So?"

"This army's a gold mine!" The old smith threw up his hands, forgetting to keep his voice down. "And every smith in this army can tell you the same. I have made more in the two and a half weeks I've been with them than I did the whole time I served in the Don's army." He shook his head, cackling under his breath. "I've never *seen* such a well-paid army. Their soldiers are walking around with gold in their pockets."

Necrem rubbed the back of his neck. "But I'm not looking for work."

"You're not? Why, man? There's good money to be made here. *Damn* good money! Much better than as a conscript, and these Lazornians will take every smith they can find." The old smith put his hands on his hips, a boss clearly expecting an answer.

"My family needs me. My wife . . . she's ill. And my daughter's young." Necrem's hands fell to his sides, balling into fists. "I need to get back. Make sure they're well. And maybe"—he glanced toward his chest under his driver's seat—"maybe take them someplace safer."

"That may take more deberes than you think," the old smith suggested.

"We'll manage." They had before. They could do it again.

The old smith snorted in resignation. "All right then. If that's what you want. But we're going to need to find another wagon before we make camp. I heard the Lazornians have changed their marching route, going off road and cutting through the hills."

"*What?*" Necrem stood straighter, his eyes widened. "They *are* taking Ribera's Way?"

He figured the Lazornian marshal would have kept his decision not to go that route. He had seemed hard set about it when Necrem had left the marquesa that night.

Maybe the marquesa convinced him after I left? Or he just changed his mind? Or—

He growled in frustration. That threw off his plans. He was waiting for them to reach Luente before he stocked up on supplies and left the army to head west. They were days away from Luente. He didn't have enough provisions to reach the town before departing for Manosete alone. There was no guarantee that there would be food at Luente for a stranger passing through to buy, being campaign season already had multiple armies of two marcs marching through it.

"Thinking about the miles now, aren't you?" the old smith asked.

Necrem jerked his head up, having been pulled out of his thoughts.

The other man's grizzled features softened, and he patted Necrem on the arm. "I know it's hard, being away from them like this," he said. "And I understand the urge to get back to them as fast as you can. Really, I do! My wife had my first kid when I was away, working on campaign, and I couldn't keep my mind on my work for an instant for the worrying. Now, though, this is the time to earn what we can to provide for them.

"This could be your chance! Think about it. You were taken away as a lowly conscript, barely getting any pay, but now you can be a smith in an army that pays good. Think about what you can bring home after this campaign's over." There was a gleam in the smith's eye, a shining, desperate gleam, and his salesman's voice hid a hint of desperation.

Necrem glanced at his hand on his arm, feeling it shake.

"You're not making good money, are you?" Necrem asked.

The old man went stiff. He worked his jaw to finally squeak, "What?"

"You sounded like you wanted me to stay and work with you, more than simply finding work for myself."

The old man stepped back, wringing his hands together, head cast down. "I was . . . I was going to ask," he said. "I am making more money, but . . . most see an old smith like me, my small forge with just the boy to help, and we get the small jobs. If you were staying . . . looking for work, I thought of asking . . .."

The man's ramble became mutters. His eyes went misty, staring at his tools and forge. "This was supposed to be my last year. Until my son ran off. If I don't make enough this campaign . . ." He withdrew into himself, yet his last sentence didn't need to be finished.

Necrem recognized that feeling. The distant look of a someone thinking far off and seeing hardship ahead. He thought he was giving the man a good turn in stopping to help, but it seemed they needed more help than he had to offer.

I need to get home, he told himself. *Eulalia and Bayona need me. Even if the Lazornians are using Ribera's Way, some part of their army will have to camp outside before going through. There's no way they can move this entire mass of people through in one day. We can find them a replacement wagon at camp, and then . . .*

He would have to depart with whatever supplies he could purchase, as well. He would have to travel without the safety of an army to Luente and hope to resupply before going on to Manosete. Alone.

The distance began to add up in his head again. Those were a lot of miles, open road with no telling what was on it. Campaign season wasn't the safest to travel great distances. And then there was his money.

Do I have enough once I reach Manosete to move? The price of everything has likely gone up. And traveling alone with so many deberes . . . He shuddered at the thought of anything happening to that money. If it did, then his family was back to being destitute.

The same thing the older smith was facing.

"If I stayed to help," Necrem said, "I would need an equal share of what we make."

The old smith jerked up. "You mean you'll . . .."

"It's a long way between here and Luente," Necrem replied.

"And the road can be a dangerous place," the other smith agreed.

Necrem rested a hand on the forge, the rough iron digging into his calluses. "You know, I can't guarantee you'll get more customers just by me helping you."

"Heh!" The old man stuck his chest out. "Don't be sure of that. Why, when customers see a tower of steelworker like you in action, fix one breastplate like you did yours, and the provosts will have to be called to stop them from fighting each other. By the way, whatever happened to that breastplate?"

"Lost it," Necrem grunted, rubbing his thumb against the corner of the forge. "Never got the chance to put it on. As for the shares—"

"Equal! Yes, yes, I heard. But with your work, there should be plenty to go around." The old man barked a laugh and stuck out his hand. "Radon Noe."

"Necrem Oso." He took Radon's hand firmly and shook.

Radon nodded then gestured behind them. "The boy's name is Oberto."

Necrem looked over his shoulder to see the boy petting Malcada's neck. The usually fussy mule looked be enjoying it, too.

"You can ride her, if she'll let you," Necrem told the boy.

Oberto's head popped up, eyes wide with excitement, and he smiled. He said nothing back, just resumed petting Malcada.

"He's an odd one," Radon said, shaking his head. "Think he dreams of being a calleros someday."

"Let's not wish something so horrible on the lad." Necrem shook his head and headed for the driver's seat.

Radon barked another laugh and followed. "You do have a sense of humor. Say! You know, if we tell everyone that Steel Fist is forging, that might bring in more customers."

Necrem stopped, one foot off the ground. "The Lazornians might not take too kindly to that."

"Just a thought," Radon agreed with a shrug. "Can't help an old salesman when he's desperate, eh?"

It took a few minutes to get everything sorted in the driver's seat for them both, moving personal belongings behind the seat, making sure each deber chest was secured. When everything was stowed away, Necrem checked to see Oberto on Malcada's back. How he had gotten there, without a sound or asking for help, was anyone's guess, along with Malcada allowing it.

Finally, he snapped the reins and guided the horses back into the convoy.

Wait for me, Eulalia, Bayona, he silently begged, staring longing at the road south. *I'll make it back. And then I'll take both of you someplace where we'll never have to worry about it again.*

Chapter 24

12th of Iam, 1019 N.F (e.y.)

Recha shifted in her saddle and repositioned her parasol, angling it to keep the Easterly Sun out of her face as they rounded a bend. She hated having to use it. The red silk, stretched out across the wooden poles, was too bright, the white lace hanging from around the circular rim too flimsy, and her wrist ached from having to hold the parasol's wooden handle steady.

It also felt out of place.

She, her personal guard, and a company of calleroses walked their horses in a stretched-out column along the winding path through the Orsembian hills.

Sir Oso had been right about Ribera's Way being difficult. They walked their horses carefully through the dried-up riverbed, cautious not to get a loose rock caught in their horses' hooves. Centuries of waterflow had carved a smooth, wide, yet twisting path, revealing a running mosaic of multi-colored strata streaking through the polished rock. Fortunately, the passage was big enough for columns and wagons to travel, if not with a bit of effort and muscle power in a few places.

The Easterly Sun was their main enemy. The ridgeline and rocky hillslopes offered little shade. Few clouds graced the skies to offer them relief, but it would spell disaster if rain came now with their need for this passage.

Still, it was *damned* hot!

Recha peered out from under her parasol. Clouds of dust from the marching columns ahead of her swirled in the air. An oppressive, shimmering haze hung over them, obscuring her vision to a mere mile, although there wasn't much to make out except another bend where water had once flowed around rock and slope.

All she could make out was her infantry, rows of men with pikes on their shoulders and heads down, marching at a steady pace. No company sang a marching song for their fellows to echo down the line. No jokes were made. No urging from their officers to quicken the pace. Not even a complaint. Each man silently trudged along, each knowing they were heading back toward home and why.

Baltazar had made it clear that each armies' commanders and officers explain why they were heading back to Lazorna and the urgency. Recha had agreed. Something of this nature couldn't be held from the men. They needed to know the worst had happened and their homes were in danger. She just wished they didn't look so defeated.

"Damn this heat!" she hissed under her breath, her head sagging.

Sweat ran down the back of her neck. She kept her hair tied in a bun on her head to keep it off her neck; otherwise, it would be truly unbearable. Wearing a hat was unbearable, hence the parasol for relief from the oppressive rays. She'd forgone lace under her dress and hose for her legs, left her sleeves unbuttoned and hanging open, and had left her blouse's collar button and the one under it undone. Any more than that, and she would have her soldiers commenting how scandalously dressed their marquesa was.

Maybe that would lift the men's spirits. She snickered. *It'd give me relief from this corset.* She shook off the unseemly thought as delirium from the heat.

"Water?" Cornelos offered, holding out his canteen.

Recha licked her lips at the sight of the wooden bottle, the plug hanging by a leather cord. However, instead of accepting it, she pushed his arm aside.

"That's the third time you've asked me," she complained. "You know we need to save water, including myself."

Poor Cornelos appeared more in need of water than she did. In both armor and uniform, Recha could only imagine how sweltering it must be under all that. What parts of his face the round brim of his helmet and cheek guards left exposed was red and sunburnt, glistening with sweat dripping from his nose.

"You're more important, La Dama," he said firmly, offering his canteen again.

Recha frowned, not wanting to get in a battle of wills over being offered water. It was much too hot for that.

418

The pathway widened with a round-pebble-strewn bar, possibly an overflow patch between the hills when the river flowed through here, over to their right. An escape.

"Let's rest the horses."

She guided her horse across Cornelos's path, cutting him off and making him follow behind. Just her guard of twenty riders followed. The rest of the calleroses carried on. Her horse snorted gratefully when Recha pulled her to a halt and began situating her skirts to dismount.

"Recha," Cornelos said dryly, canteen still in hand as he rode up to her. "You need to drink. Last thing the army needs to see is their marquesa collapsing from her horse."

"I was complaining about the heat, Cornelos," Recha growled in frustration. "That's *all*. I don't need to be babied." It took her a few infuriating attempts to get her left foot out of the side stirrup so she could go through the annoyingly long process of dismounting.

She dropped down onto the soft, dry ground with a thud. Her bootheels sunk into the pebbles and made her shift her weight and wave her arms about to keep her balance. Once she regained it, she looked about from under her parasol to see if anyone was laughing. Instead, she found her men sitting on horseback, shoulders slumped and heads down. Their faces just as red as Cornelos's.

"Stretch your legs and rest your horses," she ordered. "Take those helmets off to cool your heads."

"We thank the La Dama," one guard said.

Others echoed him as they slowly slid out of their saddles, as if their limbs had sludge flowing in their veins. A collection of groans, grunts, and clanks of metal followed as they stretched their legs and backs, followed by eagerly unclasping and stripping their helmets.

Recha snorted, holding back a chuckle at the sight of them shaking their sweat-soaked hair, reminding her of wet dogs trying to dry themselves.

Cornelos cleared his throat, suddenly beside her with canteen still in hand. She sighed, propping her parasol on her shoulder in resignation.

She took the canteen and brought it to her lips. The lukewarm water slipped between her lips and ran down her jawline while what she caught flowed down her throat. She meant to take just a sip but took gulp after gulp instead.

Until Cornelos snatched it away from her.

"Hey!" she gasped. She glared at him as she wiped her chin.

"We do need to save *some* water," Cornelos replied, plugging the stopper back into the canteen.

Recha held her glare as he walked away to his horse to stow the canteen. *Now you're responsible with our supplies after nagging me?*

She rolled her parasol's handle between her fingers, sending the canopy spinning above her head. The sunlight bleeding through the silk cast her in a deep, shaded red.

Hoofbeats changed to marching feet, and she lethargically turned to watch the men march by to pass the time. They were riding with the Third Army, the first to enter Ribera's Way. Baltazar's dispatches had reached them in time for them to turnabout. Whether General Ros or Marshal Olguer had set the fast pace, it was starting to slow now.

The next column of pikemen, as heat-stricken as the others, walked by. They quietly moved along without any drums to keep pace to. Their pikes were propped against their shoulders. Their heads bobbed, with some finding refuge under the small brim of their helmets or their hats, and . . ..

Hats?

Recha blinked, refocusing her eyes in the heat. Most of the men in the passing company were wearing hats. Not just that, only a few had violet uniforms under their breastplates, and not all their armor matched. An officer, who was properly uniformed and armored, snapped an acknowledging salute as he walked by.

Recha lifted her hand to wave back but forgot when she saw the column's banner was black instead of Lazornian purple. It did bear her red sigil, though.

"Cornelos!" she called.

A thousand pebbles ground together under the feet of her guards, who snapped around at her voice. That was followed by the rustling of armor from Cornelos jogging around the horses.

"La Dama?" he said, looking around for trouble.

"Who are they?" Recha pointed at the out of place column of men. "They aren't properly outfitted, and their company standard doesn't match the rest of the army's."

Cornelos looked, and then noticeably swallowed. "Probably a recruited company General Ros formed on the march. Possibly in haste before we changed direction and had to make do with equipping them the best they could."

It was logical enough. Materials to forge and equip new companies was in short supply now that they were in the mountains and most materials were going toward maintenance. However, Recha stared at Cornelos, who stood too stiffly, avoiding her eyes.

There's something else.

She slid her gaze back to the column, studying it more closely. They resembled a company a baron would throw together, a stingy, uncaring baron. Besides their pikes, the company lacked a unifying quality without uniforms. Their clothes were drab browns, whites, and blacks.

Black.

There were black wraps around their arms, above their elbows. They weren't sleeves or armbands and wobbled on their arms as if they were ill-fitting. Some were worn and cracked. Like leather. Thick, black leather.

Collars.

"*Sioneroses*!" She snapped around to Cornelos.

Cornelos squeezed his eyes closed for a moment. "Former *sioneroses*," he said. "Former. The Third Army freed several estates in their drive westward, but when they got the order to withdraw, many of the freed people were worried about where to go and if they'd be safe. General Ros requested permission to recruit those able enough to fight."

"And I wasn't told of *this*?"

Cornelos flinched. "The field marshal approved it. And with everything going on . . . our current situation . . ."

He withheld it to protect her. It was clear in his tone.

He didn't want to risk another argument between me and Papa.

Baltazar had kept his distance from her ever since their disagreement at the Sa Manta villa. Even though he had decided to take Ribera's Way to cut across the hills to Compuert Junction, they hadn't had another war council nor had a meal together once on the road. True, there was little to council over—their course, destination, and goals were clear—and Recha usually collapsed at the end of a day's march.

Still, it hurt.

The column of former *sioneroses* disappeared around the bend. A column of musketeers trailed behind it.

"I should've been told," she said, swinging around without waiting for Cornelos's apology and arduously began climbing back into her saddle.

Cornelos offered a hand, but she swatted it away. She refused to let him take her parasol from her, no matter how much more difficult it made mounting for her. Finally, she folded it down and stuffed it under her arm, enduring the Easterly Sun to get her feet in the sidesaddle's stirrups.

"Mount," Cornelos ordered her guard.

Recha, however, didn't wait for them. She snapped her horse into a quick trot.

"La Dama!" Cornelos protested after her.

She knew it was reckless. The ground was smooth, and her horse could throw a shoe or slip, but she wasn't going to wait until they reached whatever spot the scouts had picked to camp for the night to find Baltazar.

He was at the head of the column. They might not be calling war councils or having supper together with their staff every night, but she still got reports on where he was. The forward scouts had reported the path was widening, and there were rumors of a water source up ahead. Baltazar wanted to see that for himself.

Water and answers, Recha thought, *that's worth risking a horseshoe.*

She kept her horse to the side, riding between the columns and hillside. The officer of the company of former *sioneroses* saw her coming and urged the closest line of men back to give her space. Recha caught a few looks of the men as she passed.

They were drifting. Despite their different ages and appearances, they all had the same unfocused, emotionless look in their eyes. They weren't men who were proud to be soldiers, or marched with a purpose to reclaim what they had lost, or even with hatred for what had been taken from them. The collars were off their necks, but not their hearts. They walked as men set out to do another mindless job.

Recha's heart sank at seeing them like that. She winced in pity for them instead of waving in salute.

They're not soldiers.

"La Dama!" Cornelos yelled.

She had slowed her horse to study the men's faces and her guard was catching up.

"Keep up, Cornelos!" she yelled back then set her horse back to a quick trot.

The winding trail continued in a gradual slope. She maintained the quick pace despite it. They were in the middle of the Third Army's column, placing the head at least two miles ahead of them. Their horses snorted, gasped, and flailed their manes at the pace and the dust. Recha kept her parasol under her arm, refusing whatever comfort it offered to press on.

Until she couldn't.

Her horse faltered. The gelding slowed, snorting and foaming around his bit. She grimaced in frustration. Patting his neck and his rump did nothing to hurry him along.

"Recha," Cornelos complained lowly, riding up beside her, "it's too hot to force the horses up such an incline like that."

Recha grimaced. "Then how can they be expected to ride into battle?"

"Hopefully, they won't be riding into one *immediately* after the day's march." Cornelos rubbed the sweat from his brow.

Recha groaned loudly. Maybe a little exaggerated, but she would never admit that. Nothing else could make her horse move faster, and she absolutely didn't want to talk. Thus, she had to settle riding at the sluggish pace in silence.

~~~

Time crawled. Another curse of the oppressive heat. Recha's sudden burst to move up the column had gained her nothing, and she had fallen back to her original spot in line. She didn't remember when, but she had reopened her parasol to shade herself from the Easterly Sun again.

They topped another rise and, miraculously, there wasn't another bend around a rocky ridgeline waiting for them. The path leveled out and opened wider. Recha sat up straighter at the better view from her saddle through the field of pikes lumbering in front of her.

The hills were giving way on their right while, to their left, the ridgeline shot upward, rising above their heads into a sheer cliff. Before them stretched a large lake or, rather, the remnants of one. Half of it was shrunken under the overhanging cliff, as if hiding from the sun. Impressions of rings were notched in the gentle, sandy slope of its bank to mark each step of its evaporating retreat without any water to fill it. Calleroses watered their horses while the infantry officers led their companies around the lake, heading instead to the steep rise on the other side.

Recha guided her horse over to the side, out of the column, to get a better look. Her horse chomped at his bit, and his nostrils flared at the smell of water. The lake was a dark blue and grew darker the farther back it went under the overhanging ridge. She glanced down at the sound of soft sand under her horse's stomping hooves. The same lines from the lake's former edge were there, almost eroded.

This is the source of the river! She lifted her head, taking in the lake in a different light.

"Recha," Cornelos whispered, "Baltazar's up there."

She lifted her parasol to trace where he was pointing.

On the other side of the lake, atop the highest point of the steep rise that forced the large lake's runoff west, between and under the shade of two twisting cypress trees, stood a group of men. They were silhouettes in the sun, yet it was a commanding position of both the columns marching up and the ground beyond. A place where she would expect Baltazar to be.

Recha kicked her horse into motion. The curved incline and sandy ground of the receded lakebed denied her from making her horse gallop. It infuriated her further by stubbornly veering off toward the water. She repeatedly, and forcibly, pulled his reins to steer him back on track.

"I'll let you drink in a minute," she told him between gritted teeth. "Just get me up that hill, and you can drink the entire lake."

That hill was steep. Her horse snorted and stomped from the first step. She pressed him through, patting his romp and his neck to put one foot in front of the other. As the hill rose, she leaned forward, not caring about her skirts or blouse wrinkling or smelling of horse. Recha fixated only on the men at the top, whose silhouettes became clearer with every inch of hill she climbed.

Baltazar stood in the center, with everyone surrounding him. The other marshals stood to his left. Marshal Bisal's tall figure stood out as he pointed to the land beyond, and the others were looking over Baltazar's shoulders, presumably at more hastily drawn maps of their forward scouts. General Ros and his staff stood to Baltazar's right.

Excellent, she thought, *just the audience I wanted.*

Marshal Narvae peeked over his shoulder at her approach. "Oh shit," he said, not soft enough, turning quickly away.

"Good afternoon to you, too, Marshal Narvae," Recha said loudly. She pulled her horse to a stop and let the poor beast have a well-earned rest. "Gentlemen."

The marshals, General Ros, and their staffs turned and gave her quick and respectfully snaps to attention. All save Baltazar. He snapped around, eyebrows up to his hairline with a perplexed look on his face that quickly morphed into a thunderclap.

"*Recha!*" He slapped the scouts' small sketches together, his hands balling into fists. "You did *not* force your horse up that hill! It could have slipped and fell on top of you. And look at it! Your mount's about to collapse. I taught you better than—"

"You went behind my back!" Recha snapped, keeping her head raised in the face of the scolding. "There are *sioneroses* in my army."

She met Baltazar's fiery glare with her own. She refused to blink. Baltazar's eyebrows started to twitch, then his mustache, and finally his chin. Recha's eyelids wavered, but she caught them from narrowing each time and forced them open.

"Marshal Bisal!" Baltazar said, thrusting out the scouts' sketches. "I need more. Send the scouts farther out and make sure they verify every stretch of ground."

Eager to depart, Bisal took the sketches and hastily retreated, taking a party of scouts who'd been standing in the background, unnoticed.

"Marshal Olguer! See to it that every company of horse cools their horses and waters them before bringing them onto the plain."

Olguer silently and sharply bowed before departing.

"General Ros! Continue to bring your infantry into the plain. The further we push, the more space we'll have for camp. We'll see to their watered as soon as a parameter is established with enough room to get all armies out of that spillway."

"Yes, Field Marshal!" General Ros saluted, and then he and his entire staff marched off.

Baltazar looked Recha and her horse up and down then turned to his left. Cornelos and the rest of her guard were making their way up the ridgeline toward them, taking it slow.

Recha frowned. *Guess I lost them.*

"Marshal Narvae," Baltazar said, "take La Dama's horse to her commandant, then make sure he and the rest of her guard cool and water their horses with the rest. They've been pushed hard enough for one day."

Recha flinched, feeling the sting in that one.

"The rest of you are dismissed," Baltazar ordered, to the deep breaths of relief of the remaining staff.

Narvae walked reluctantly up to her horse and held a hand up to her. "Need a hand, La Dama?"

Recha pointed her parasol at him, forcing him back. She tossed her reins to him then began the arduous process of dismounting again. In true, irritating fashion, her right foot got caught in the stirrup, and she had to kick then manually force it free, keeping Narvae at a distance.

When she finally hopped down, she waved him off then folded her arms as she waited for him to leave. She ignored him snorting and shaking his head as he led her horse away and matched Baltazar's stare until they were at last alone on the hill.

Droplets of sweat glistened on Baltazar's forehead, and yet he stood in full uniform and breastplate, as if he didn't feel the sunlight on his back. He stepped closer. His eyes bored into her.

Recha held firm. She was used to this old command tactic. She had grown up with it. But she wasn't a child being stubborn anymore. She was the marquesa, and he was her field marshal. He was going to answer for going behind—

"Get a hold of yourself," Baltazar said, his voice low and cold, heedless of the heat. "Forget yourself once more, and I will order your guard to detain you in your tent for the rest of the march."

Recha suddenly didn't feel the heat. Her arms fell to her sides. Her mouth dropped open and, for a moment, she couldn't find her words. But then the heat returned. Not from the Easterly Sun but from inside her. Her jaw snapped closed, grinding her teeth in a grimace.

"You *threaten* me!" she yelled. "I'm your marquesa!"

"My marquesa who has forgotten her own promise to me!" Baltazar roared back. "These armies are not yours to swoon over as they parade for you. These armies are going into battle against an army possibly over thrice its size with a renowned field commander. As commander of these armies, I will take every man I can get on the field, regardless of where or how they were recruited."

Recha shook her head. "Battle? What are you talking about? We haven't reached Lazorna yet! We'll have plenty of—"

"No, we won't." Baltazar ran a hand through his hair, sending sweat flying everywhere. "We're not going to make it, Recha. If Borbin is moving his army, like I suspect, he should reach the junction in two days."

The admission made Recha's skin crawl, not only by it being said but the way Baltazar had said it with such surety, as if it was absolute.

"Did the scouts report that? Have they found the rest of the path through these hills?"

"No," Baltazar replied.

"Then how do you know?"

"I've known a day into our retreat."

Recha's eyebrows shot up, but Baltazar kept going.

"There was no other conclusion," he said. "With that straight road to the junction and not a force strong enough to block it, Borbin was going to reach it before us. Ordering the Fourth Army to abandon the siege to blockade the road would only put them in danger from the remaining garrison at Puerlato, and no force to mount any defense at Lazorna's border. We are on our own."

"Then what are we doing here?" Recha demand, gesturing back at the men still trudging up through the dusty, dried riverway.

"To improve our position for battle. You were right about taking the road back to Lazorna. Approaching the junction from the west would have put us at a disadvantage. Once the scouts confirmed this route was passable, I determined approaching the junction by the high ground these hills provide would give us a better chance of striking where Borbin would least expect it."

"And you didn't think to consult me on that, *either*!" Recha squeezed the handle of her parasol. The wood groaned from the friction of her grip. "What else are you keeping from me?"

"What I've had to!" Baltazar yelled. "I've had to make these decisions for this campaign to be successful. Your concerns about what the common Orsembians think, or preserve, or aid us are meaningless now. We must *win*, on the field, when faced with Borbin's entire army! Nothing else matters. Not what I've kept from you, and not what you've kept from me."

A fire raced up Recha's back from the shimmering look in Baltazar's eyes. He had never raised his voice like that to her. It was as if he had doubled in size, as well, standing like a giant over her. Her mind spun from the way he had spoken about her keeping things from him, as if he knew everything, every secret she kept.

Elegida!

"Such as?" she asked softly.

426

"Don't play coy, Recha." Baltazar frowned. "I've let you step over the line into my authority many times since we invaded Orsembar. You allowed the Viden to execute prisoners at the hill fort outside Puerlato. You dictated whom the armies could and could not be recruited after Compuert Junction. You rushed heedlessly to observe and issue orders at every small engagement you could reach all the way up to Crudeas. You neglected your correspondences back to Lazorna!

"But worst of all"—he gasped for air, his shoulders rising up and down— "you ordered prisoners of war seized and interrogated without consulting me first, and then directed me on which way the armies should march. Without any intelligence or forward scouting, you set your mind to it and openly debated with me in front of my staff. It was bad enough when the generals were requesting approvals from both me *and* you, but then Feli said the same about our final requisition orders before leaving Crudeas.

"That's why I've been keeping you at a distance, Recha. The chain of command needed to be reinforced before we found the Orsembians." He looked about at all the officers he'd dismissed. "I would say I've been successful in that."

Recha's grip on her parasol had grown tighter and tighter. Her palm stung, and when she loosened her grip, she realized she'd been holding it like a sword. Her jaw muscles started to twinge. She opened her mouth to loosen them, and her cheeks ached.

"And—" She coughed and cleared her throat. "And you've waited until now to tell me all that? We could have talked about this at any time before now!"

Baltazar's expression softened, and he folded his hands behind his back. "Because it was you."

Recha's grip slackened, lowering her parasol until the tip of its head brushed the dirt.

"You grew up in my house," Baltazar continued. "I knew you weren't acting out of egotism, not out of some need to remind everyone that you're the marquesa. This has been something you've wanted for three years, and I know that call to the battlefield. I've seen it in you at every engagement. Something you got from your father, probably, enflamed by your mother's fire, and I *let* you step over the line. These past days of march have been my way of making up for allowing it to get this far."

Recha's chin trembled. "That's not fair."

Baltazar arched an eyebrow.

"It's not fair to scold me then make me feel sympathy for you," she explained, her lips pursing in an attempt not to pout.

The ends of his lips curled under the tips of his whiskers, the first fatherly expression she had seen in weeks. "I didn't mean to put you on the back foot and then flank you. I couldn't very well berate you and not recognize my own faults in it. The only thing that matters now is we keep moving forward. Since I can't send you out of harm's way, I can only ask that you leave everything to me, Recha. That's why you came to me to be your field marshal in the first place, remember?"

"Yes." Recha turned her head away, her cheeks puffing as her pursed lips became the pout she sorely tried to prevent. And failed. Luckily, or rather unfortunately, a thought made her cheeks deflate, and the pout slipped away. "But those men, Papa, those former *sioneroses*, they're not soldiers."

"They're fresh recruits, Recha," Baltazar replied bluntly. "They need time and drilling."

"I've seen their faces. The look in their eyes." She shook her head. Her sweaty hair slipped their knots and spilled around her. "They're going through life still merely following the orders of anyone who gives them. Can we rely on them? If Borbin sends calleroses riding on top of them, will they hold?"

Baltazar drew himself up. His chin rose in the air, and he kept his hands behind his back. "We could say the same thing about most of the companies in our armies, considering how fresh most of them still are, having not yet faced a pitched battle. Everything up until now has been small engagements where we held nearly every advantage. We probably won't have that when we march down these hills to face Borbin."

"The men of Lazorna are free men, Papa. Recruited of their own choice before I declared war. Those former *sioneroses*, they—"

"Will stand." Baltazar's tone was iron, as sure as a mountain. "A commander must believe in his men. The moment he doubts them, he doubts his ability to lead them. Defeat then is certain."

A hot gust of wind blew up from behind her, swirling dust and making her eyes water. Baltazar stood there without flinching.

Recha wiped her eyes then snickered. "Another personal quote? Which of your early campaigns did you come up with that one?"

"I didn't," Baltazar replied.

Recha cleared up her watery eyes to see him smile again.

"Your father said that to me . . . oh . . . on our second campaign together." Baltazar chuckled. "Our company was ragtag and disorganized. We looked like we pulled the dregs of a prison out and put spears in their hands to call it a company. Part of me is still amazed we weren't dismissed and stripped of our duty for that." He shook his head. A misty look came over him as he revisited that time in his mind.

Recha watched him. Then came a snicker. Then another. And finally, a soft chuckle. "You win," she sighed out, resigning to leave the responsibilities up to him.

Baltazar snorted. "This wasn't a fight."

"Wasn't it?" Recha raised an eyebrow. "I bet if we looked down the hill, Cornelos and Ramon both have squads ready to rush up here to pull us apart."

Baltazar's frowned then cleared his throat, putting back on his dignified, commanding persona. "As if it would ever come to that."

"Right!" Recha laughed, rolling her eyes.

Baltazar smirked but refused to laugh with her. He sighed and opened his mouth to speak—

Hoofbeats rushed up the hill.

Baltazar spun to reveal a courier riding hard toward them.

"Field Marshal!" the man yelled. The man's face was covered in sweat, as naturally expected, however it was hard set. The courier was bouncing out of his saddle despite the hill's incline. "Field Marshal!"

"Calm down," Baltazar ordered. "What is it, soldier?"

"Word from Marshal Bisal!" the courier replied, pulling his horse to a halt. "The Orsembian army's been sighted!"

"*Where?*" Baltazar rushed away. "Compuert Junction?"

"No, Field Marshal! Our forward riders scouting the western pass came upon the outriders of their vanguard. The Orsembian army is moving through the passes, marching straight at us, sir!"

Chapter 25

"How great is their vanguard?" Baltazar demanded. "What's its composition?"

Recha remained motionless. Her body refused to move while her mind screamed for action. As the two impulses fought, she became numb to the incessant heat.

"Calleroses, Field Marshal," the scout replied. "Our outriders merely got a rough estimate, but they were certain at least three thousand calleroses are riding through the easterly gap. Infantry is following them, sir. However, we couldn't get a good count before having to report."

In their argument, Recha had failed to notice the sweeping landscape beyond the rise. The scout's gesture at what he called the easterly gap forced her to take it in.

Finally free from the winding remains of the riverbed, the hill's sloop widened into a rolling plain, stretched between a vertical cliff to the north and more steep hills to the south. Farther east, the plain expanded and split from the rise of steep, jutting ridges, creating two passes—one continuing east while the other trail curved southeasterly.

Another hot breeze rushed over the rise Recha was standing on and into the plain. The blades of tall, yellowish-brown reeds and grasses swayed in the wind, holding fast in the dry ground in the vain hope for rain.

The Third Army's vanguard was filtering down into the plain. Companies of calleroses dotted farther out, dismounted and letting their horses rest as they stood guard at predetermined positions ahead of the army's advance.

"How soon does Marshal Bisal expect the vanguard to reach us?" Baltazar continued.

"He can't be certain, Field Marshal," the scout apologized. "However, he fears the calleros companies will reach us within the hour."

Baltazar pivoted on his heels and stormed away. Recha followed him to see Narvae and Cornelos rushing up the hill with every staff member they could find behind them, undoubtedly alarmed at the sight of a scout rushing through all junior officers and protocol to report to the armies' commander.

"Marshal Narvae!" Baltazar bellowed down at them. "Order battle formations! And get General Ros and Marshal Olguer back up here!"

Narvae skidded to a halt. He grabbed several of the staff officers around him and dragged them back down the hill, sending them scurrying in different directions.

"Send word to Marshal Bisal," Baltazar ordered the scout. "All outriders are to converge on the last sightings of the enemy's vanguard. I want constant reports on their movements! Go!"

The scout saluted then turned his horse around in one motion. He galloped down the hill, sending dirt flying in the air. A bugle sang out in the distance. One of the calleros companies in the plain was saddling up.

Drums began to tap. The company of sword marching over the hump of the rise was the first and, like a ripple, it spread forward and behind them. A hurried, quick-paced beat of sharp raps. Officers sprang alive, waving and urging their men forward. Lone officers on horseback raced up the column, outpaced by the drums as they galloped toward the calleros companies in the field.

The taps filled the plain below by the time answering bugle calls from the other calleros companies in the plain mounted up. The company at the head of her army's column turned and peeled off to the left in square formation. The company behind did the same, except marching off to the right.

On it continued, the drums urging the marching column into line, stretching farther and farther across the plain. Baltazar's intent was obvious.

He's going to march them across in battle lines. The thought was enough to spring her into motion.

"I need to *do* something!" she blurted out. "I'll set up our camp preparations. Are you suspecting casualties? No! We need to get the water wagons up here to fill and resupply the companies coming up." She raked her fingers through her sticky hair as she racked her brain to hastily think of everything that needed doing. "Maybe even get army cooks, as well. The men in the back must be hungry by now! We need to make sure—"

"Recha!"

"*What?*"

Baltazar took her by the shoulder with a firm squeeze. "I need you to stay right here."

"*What?*" Her voice cracked. The tremor ran from her throat down to her hands, making them tremble until she balled them into fists. She gripped her parasol like a sword again. "I can't just stand here and do *nothing!*"

"You won't be doing nothing." Baltazar's voice was both gentle yet firm, a combination in tone with a commanding presence and fatherly touch. "You'll show the men what they need to see—their marquesa standing firm on this hill, waiting for the men coming up to join her and watching those in the field fight for her. They need to see you standing confidently right here, as if there is not a force alive that can move you off it. Stand fast, Recha, and let your armies do the work."

Recha didn't know why, but her heart was racing. She felt she could run a mile. No, she could leap from hilltop to hilltop and soar.

How does he do that? One minute we're venting our frustrations, and the next, he's making an inspirational speech.

"Very well," she replied staunchly, putting on a commanding tone of her own. "I'll heed your advice, Field Marshal. See to our advance. I'll have Cornelos and my guard tend to whatever needs I might have." The Easterly Sun glaring down on her head was one need. She popped open her parasol to shade herself.

Baltazar took his hand away and snapped his heels at attention. "Yes, La Dama! I promise you I will take as much control of the field as I can before the enemy's vanguard arrives."

They shared a nod, and then he was off, marching quickly down the slope toward General Ros and his staff waiting on horseback.

"Make sure the battle lines aren't spread too thin!" Baltazar roared. "We need to stretch over as much of the plain as possible, but leave the wide flanks to the calleroses. Once Olguer is satisfied with resting the horses coming up, he'll send them to reinforce them." He groaned loudly as he heaved his old body up into the saddle.

"Yes, Field Marshal!" General Ros replied. "Should we leave any men in reserve to make camp preparations?"

"Keep your men coming!" Baltazar swung his horse around, and the rest joined him. "Leave making camp until we claim as much ground as possible. We need all the men we have . . . ." His voice drowned out with distance.

Recha watched them go. Baltazar pointed out across the plain in multiple directions. Here and there, a staff officer or dispatcher would peel off, riding back to some unknown destination behind her or up to the still forming battle line now stretched out across the plain. And more companies were moving up.

"Did everything get resolved?"

Recha jumped, snapping her head around to find Cornelos had snuck up on her while she was contemplating. "Hmm?" she hummed.

"Between you and Baltazar," Cornelos clarified, "did you get everything worked out? Uncle and I nearly got into an argument of coming up here to pull you two apart."

Recha allowed herself a small smile at the thought of both Narvaes throwing themselves into danger to protect their commanders. "It could have been worse," she admitted. "But what was said was said. Some of it doesn't matter anymore."

Bugle calls and a change in drumbeats drew her attention back out to the plain. A forward battle line had completely formed and was advancing at a march, a company of calleros led the center ahead of the pikemen with two more companies at each flank. As they began their march, another battle line began to form out of the steady flow of more infantry.

A cry of horses came from her left, and Recha looked to see calleroses ride up from the other side of her rise and gallop onto the plain. She then noticed her banner, posted into the ground a few feet away and leaning slightly at an angle. She frowned at it.

"Cornelos," she called.

"Yes, La Dama?"

"Send someone to find a bigger banner," she ordered. "The biggest they can get their hands on. And plant it"—she checked for a spot on the hill that would be seen by the men marching up and the men in the plain then stomped her hill to mark it—"here! For everyone to see. Is my guard seeing to the horses?"

"Yes."

"Once they've been taken care of, I want them to bring their horses and form two lines on the forward slope of the hill." She pointed down the hill facing the plain. "I want everyone to know that I'm here, both our men and the Orsembians."

"As you wish." Cornelos gave her a sharp nod then turned on his heels to perform her orders.

"Oh!" She remembered one more thing and yelled after him. "And Commandant! Fetch my looking glasses! I'm going to want to observe what's happening!"

"Yes, La Dama!" He yelled over his shoulder without looking back to rush on down the slope.

Recha remained behind, planting her heel in the impression to remember where she wanted the new flag placed. She angled her parasol to keep her shaded and squinted against the haze farther into the plain.

She couldn't be sure, but she thought she spotted dust clouds drifting up over the eastern horizon.

~~~

Recha's knees ached. A hot throb pulsed in her heels. Her feet desperately wanted her to sit, but she couldn't take her sights off the plain in front of her. She only moved to periodically switch her hands between holding her eyeglass and the other holding her parasol.

She scanned the line of Orsembian calleroses stretched out across the eastward passage and advancing at a trot. They held their lances high, broad heads gleaming in the Easterly Sun, adding to the haze and swirls of dust. A dozen banners of barony families she didn't know flapped in the air among them. While she would admit three thousand calleroses advancing in stretched-out lines were impressive, they lacked a sense of intimidation as her battle lines continued their advance, as well.

"Any word from General Priet?" she asked.

"None," Cornelos replied, standing beside her, as always. "The last of the Third Army is still moving up. The path should be clear for Priet to send an estimate of the Second Army's arrival then."

"Marshal Feli," she called, "how goes setting up the camp? Are the wagon trains still moving?"

"Well, of course," Marshal Feli replied, hesitantly puzzled, "as you can see . . ."

Feli sat at a field table under one of the trees with some of his staff, the last Recha had checked. He likely looked back to find her fixed on her eyeglass and chose to change his initial response.

"The Third Army's wagon train continues to be brought up, La Dama. The rise is more manageable now that we got block and tackles to help pull up the heavier wagons. We should be able to take full advantage of the ground the field marshal is gaining and bring up the Second Army when it arrives."

"Have the last of the Third Army's calleroses been deployed?" she inquired.

"Marshal Olguer's checking on them now," Cornelos answered.

Recha clicked her tongue out of annoyance. "Send another request for them to hurry. Most of the Third Army's infantry is deployed, but Baltazar *needs* more cavalry."

"Yes, La Dama." The crunching of boots against the hard-packed ground signaled Cornelos's departure.

Recha knew most of her demands for updates were probably becoming incessant. Everything was well in hand. Everyone was still moving forward and following their orders. Necessary tasks were being taken care of and seen to with the best speed they could under these conditions.

And yet, she couldn't contain herself. Her being an encouraging figure for advancing troops had lost some of its glamour the instant she'd peered through the eyeglass and spotted the Orsembians riding up from the eastern passage.

She swung her eyeglass down, passing over the tall grass and rolling patches between the approaching armies, over the front columns of her battle lines to the men on horseback behind them. A body of officers rode in a wedge formation, with lower ranked officers surrounding the higher ranked in the center, where Baltazar was.

He was ordering a steady march across the plain. Behind the wedge marched a second line, though more spread out with gaps between the company squares. The two lines weren't comprised of the entire Third Army. A third line stood between the forming camp of army wagons moving onto the plain and the rest of the army, held back to guard the wagons, Recha deduced.

Her ear twitched at the clumps of approaching footsteps, heralding Cornelos's return.

"Marshal Olguer reported back," he said. "The calleroses' horses have been watered and fed. The remaining companies should be mounting up soon."

"Very well."

Recha's focus returned to the distance between the Third Army and the Orsembian vanguard. She bit the inside of her cheek as she struggled to pull the eyeglass's field of vision out, but that did little to help. She struggled to judge their exact distance from one another from the angle of hill and the plain's rolling slope.

At a casual glance, the plain deceptively appeared to stretch on for miles to the east. Upon a closer look through her eyeglass, however, Recha saw it had a gradual slope to it. In a situation where they needed every early advantage they could seize, having the high ground was a fortunate boon. However, they lacked any maneuverability to retreat, and the angle made it difficult to judge distances the farther the battle line advanced.

If only I could move closer—

Cornelos cleared his throat then whispered, "Olguer also respectfully asked if we didn't send him requests to hurry every five minutes."

"Then he needs to get all our available cavalry out there," she quietly sniped back. "That vanguard can't be stupid enough to face our battle line head-on. Sooner or later, they'll remember they're calleroses, see they have more horses on the field, and try to drive ours away to go for our flanks. It's *obvious*. We need more calleroses!"

A bugle rang out from the left, answered swiftly by another on the right. The steady rhythm of drums changed to swift claps and fell silent. As one, the forward line stomped to a halt. Pikes swayed in the air, and the companies' standards flapped in the breeze.

"We've stopped," she mumbled. "Why?"

"The Orsembians have halted, too," Cornelos said.

Recha pulled her eyeglass up. The enemy calleroses pulled their mounts to a stop. Their distance from her soldiers was still obscured, yet she assumed there was enough for them to build momentum should they charge. It would be reckless, but she wouldn't put it past some calleroses to be arrogant in the face of infantry.

"There's movement on the horizon, too!" Feli said.

Recha glanced away from her eyeglass. Feli stood from his seat, peering through his own eyeglass. Several other staff officers on the hill did the same, the rest resorting to shading their eyes in a momentary pause in duty to take in the change to the battlefield.

Free of the eyeglass's narrow view, the broader picture opened to her. The forward battle line stretched from ridge to the left to last of the hills to the right before they fell away and led to the southeast passage. She estimated they had to be a few miles away. Maybe more. Plenty of space to move out the Third Army's wagon train and have enough space for the Second Army when it arrived.

A holding action then?

It made sense. This was Borbin's host. While her armies individually worked splendidly in smaller engagements, they would need them all combined to face what was coming over that horizon. Holding the best ground to build up their strength was a good move.

But that feels too timid.

She choked down a frustrated growl for not being out there to suggest they give the Orsembian vanguard a bloody nose before their infantry support joined them and brought her eyeglass back up.

Feli was right. Blocks of infantry marched steadily over the eastern horizon and in a battle line of their own. They were too far away for her to make out what kind of troops they were, though their formation told her someone down there had some sense.

"Do you think the White Sword's commanding them?" Cornelos asked.

Recha sharply shushed him. "Don't say that too loudly," she whispered. "But yes, I think we better assume so. Baltazar probably is."

After all, it stood to reason that Borbin would have Ribera lead his vanguard again. Borbin wasn't a complete incompetent. Sevesco's reports depicted the effectiveness of that move in seizing the fields outside Compuert. He was out there, either with the infantry coming up or the calleroses.

He must be. Stay sharp, Papa.

Thumping hooves sent tremors up the hill and rumbled under her heels. She peeked to make sure the last of the Third Army's calleroses were riding up, beside the wagons, and into the center of the plain to join the other companies.

"Finally."

"The enemy's moving on our right!" a staff officer yelled.

Recha joined everyone on the hill, swinging their eyeglasses in that direction. Close to five hundred Orsembian calleroses on the far right peeled off from their line. They walked their horses at a slow angle, keeping their lances coached and pointed at Recha's battle line. Their measured movement made their intentions clear.

They meant to circle around the eastern ridge and into the southeastern passage.

"They can't flank us," Feli assured his officers. "They're not sending enough calleroses to dislodge ours on the right."

"But if they take command of the southeastern passage, too . . ." Cornelos said under his breath.

"Yes," Recha whispered back, "they'll have more room to move, and we'll be trapped in here." If Borbin was bringing the numbers Sevesco's espis had reported, it was likely they were going to be trapped in eventually.

A rider broke away from the wedge around Baltazar. It rode off to join Recha's calleroses on the right, and they began to move. One company moved out in a slow walk, matching the Orsembians. They didn't charge out to drive them back, just kept pace, stretching out the battle line into the southeastern passage.

Recha expected the Orsembians to stop and form up when they saw her calleroses move. They were evenly matched and farther away from the threats her infantry posed. Instead, they kept stretching out into the southeastern passage.

Where are they going?

"Recha, there's a hole." Cornelos said, alarmed. "Our calleroses are moving too far out!"

She widened her eyeglass's focus. A widening hole in her battle line expanded the further her calleroses followed the Orsembians. If the Orsembians pivoted and charged, they could smash into her battle line's far right or attempt to sweep behind it.

They could make an attack straight at Baltazar.

"I need a dispatcher!" Recha yelled. "Someone—"

"Wait, La Dama!" Feli said, pointing to the middle of the field. "Look to our center. The second battle line."

Recha took his advice. The center right of the second line was moving forward. They creeped without the rap of drums and curved inward toward the hole. The tempting gap to strike at Baltazar and his command was still open, however, the right side of the second battle line curved in to face it.

Waiting at an open door. Recha smirked. *He's trying to lure them in.*

If the Orsembians charged through that hole, Baltazar and his staff could quickly swing their horses around the opening in the second battle line. As the enemy came face to face with the second line, her calleroses could sweep in behind them, effectively closing the door on them.

But will they take the bait? She bit the left corner of her lower lip. *They can't keep moving into the other passage like that forever.*

A sharp bugle call sounded on the left.

Recha snapped around too quickly. Her left foot nearly slipped out from under her, kicking a few pebbles in the air. Her knee buckled, but she fortunately caught herself. Everyone's focus absorbed with the battle beyond to see her almost falling over was another blessing.

Her calleroses on the left were moving straight forward, not swinging around to charge the Orsembians. They resumed their steady advance as before and, within several minutes, they were completely exposed out of the battle line.

Recha shifted from foot to foot, trying to work out the strategy in her head. *Is he trying another bait?*

Before the calleroses got too far forward, the infantry column on the far left started to advance. It took minutes for the faint echoes of their tapping drums to reach back to them.

They marched at a steady pace. Pikes still raised. Once their rear column stepped beyond the battle line, the company beside them began their advance.

The cascading maneuver became apparent. When the advancing company marched completely ahead of the battle line, the one beside it followed. They formed a creeping wedge, encroaching on the Orsembian right.

"He's moving around their right flank," she said, grinning. "Either they'll move to stop us, or they'll have to pull back."

"They could always charge," Cornelos suggested.

"Right into our pikes and shot." She giggled and shook her head. "If only Ribera could be so accommodating."

Recha figured that would be convenient. If Ribera was among the calleroses, he surely had a grasp of what he faced. Hiraldo's formation design was meant to put an end to the calleroses' bluster. No longer would the threat of a heavy calleros charge carry the same weight as before. No more will calleroses gallivant in a Bravados to intimidate the ranks. Not without getting stuck on the end of a pike!

"If we get in close, our calleroses can charge and swing around their flank." She bounced on her heels. "If the pikemen charge with them, we could crush their—"

The Orsembians sprang in multiple directions. A quarter of their number wheeled their mounts and charged her calleroses leading the encroachment on the left. The rest aimed for the gap on the right, including the company encroaching into the southeast passage.

The plain erupted into a flurry of activity. Recha's calleroses on both sides of the field countercharged. The advancing infantry companies halted. Officers scrambled across the line, and the front rows lowered their pikes, planting them in the ground and forming a bristling wall of outstretched spearpoints.

Baltazar and General Ross wheeled around with their trailing command staff behind the second battle line. Those companies nearest the gap lowered their pikes, as well, unable to make quick march to plug the hole and not wanting to be caught when the enemy calleroses dashed through without their pikes down.

The thundering of over forty-five hundred horse hooves drowned everything in the field. The tremors vibrated under Recha's feet. She winced at the impact as horses collided and reared. Lances shattered or found their marks. Men were pulled out of their saddles, flung into the air, and came crashing down in heaps or disappeared under the maelstrom of hooves.

On the left, the charge was evenly matched. Lazornians and Orsembians collided like combining torrents of water. Some calleroses were able to charge all the way through to the opposite side of the enemy, but most of each side hit and wheeled away. From Recha's distance, it appeared they bounced off each other and rode back the way they had come in wide circles.

Her calleroses on the right fared worse. They charged into the enemy they had followed into the southeastern passage, making an even fight of it, like their comrades on the other end of the field.

They didn't have the numbers to match the rest of the Orsembian vanguard charging down on them. Her calleroses, their momentum lost after their first impact, were crushed by the Orsembians' second charge. Those who weren't unhorsed fell back the only direction they could—into the southeastern passage, away from the safety of their infantry's battle lines.

And the Orsembians pursued.

"We need more *calleroses!*" Recha screamed, grimacing.

"Reinforcements are galloping to the flank," Feli pointed out.

The calleroses who Olguer had held back raced for the flank, but they weren't in an attack column, and thanks to the deceptive distance of the plain, they were minutes away.

Not enough time!

Her hands trembled, shaking the eyeglass and the world as she could do nothing but watch her calleroses be overwhelmed.

Musket fire erupted over the roar of galloping hooves. A plume of mingled, gray smoke rose in the wind from a line of her musketeers on their far right. They stood outside the protection of the pikes, and another line stepped forward, leveling their muskets at the mingled Orsembians struggling with their startled mounts.

"Fire," Recha hushed under her breath.

Another eruption and plume of smoke came. Orsembians twisted and tumbled out of their saddles. Horses reared, throwing their riders. A few collapsed, as if their legs had fallen out from under them, rolling over their riders.

The combined Orsembian pursuit of their fleeing calleroses fell apart. Only a quarter continued the chase, oblivious of their rear being filled with shot. Half of it turned to face the new threat, out of the protection of the pikes.

The musketeers sensed the danger and raced back behind the hedge of pikes before the Orsembians could charge. They charged, anyway, around their right flank.

Recha traced their trajectory.

Four companies of her second battle line were moving to plug the hole in the line. They weren't marching in step—one was too far forward, another too far back. The reinforcing calleroses were still minutes away.

More calleroses from their left were galloping around the battle line to join them, but they were too far away, as well.

"Ribera's *insane!*" she hissed back to Cornelos. "Even if they break our second line, how does he expect to get away from our calleroses?"

"Maybe breaking our battle lines is all he wants?" Cornelos suggested. "If he breaks our line, he may suspect we'll pull back and leave more of the field to them."

"With our numbers?" Recha shook her head. "We can recover—"

"A company's breaking!" Feli shouted.

The day's heat disappeared. Goosebumps raced up Recha's arms.

Men were fleeing from the company too far forward. One man. Then a couple more. All from the back of the square, like grains spilling from a ripped bag. That rip was growing, too.

"*No!*" she gasped. "They'll get run down! They'll . . ."

Their company banner caught her eye.

It was black.

The freed sioneroses!

"I warned you, Papa." She gritted her teeth. Her throat clenched to swallow her yells. "I *warned* you!"

The remaining men lowered their pikes in an uneven hedge. The calleroses guided their horses toward the fleeing men. Hunters barreling down for a slaughter.

"If any man from that company survives," a staff officer commented, "they should be flogged."

Another grunted in agreement.

"*No!*" Recha pulled her eyeglass away to snarl at them.

All of them, including Marshal Feli, jumped.

"None who survive this will be punished!"

"But with respect, La Dama," an officer said, head bowed, "the discipline of the men—"

"*None!*"

The officers returned to their duties and vigil. Recha, begrudgingly, returned to hers.

The Orsembians dashed around the isolated companies, avoiding the square of pikes to chase the lone, fleeing men. Several of those fleeing had abandoned their pikes and were brutally rode down. Those who kept their pikes were ganged up on, their lone pike outmatched by the calleroses combined efforts. Only those men who stopped running and, out of desperation, held their pikes firm stood a chance.

A trumpet call, repeating four short blasts from the eastern passage, cut the Orsembians' sport short. They turned their horses and galloped around the way they had come, but not before the Lazornian reinforcements finally arrived.

Lazornian calleroses charged in from two directions—the right and front. Again, lances unhorsed men and toppled horses. This time, however, the Orsembians got the worst of it. Their signal to withdraw had come moments too late, and now they were the ones being pursued.

"*Get* them!" Recha snarled. "*Chase* them! Let them *feel* what it's like to be run down!"

"Recha," Cornelos whispered warningly, "you're scaring the—"

"I don't give a damn!" She sucked air through teeth, her heart thundered faster and faster in her chest. "I want them to *bleed* for what they did! Drive them into the dirt!"

She knew this was a cost of war. Infantry that broke became the target of cavalry. A fact as old as warfare, even under the twisted Rules of Campaign. But the fire in her breast would not abate with the mere knowledge. Those were *her* men. They flew *her* banner, despite the color. And the Orsembians had run them down like animals.

The fire inside her wanted one thing—for them to receive the same.

The musketeers in the first battle line took the Orsembians' withdrawal as another opening. They sprayed them with shot from the safety of their pikes. Only two of the far companies had the range and, while only a few Orsembians fell from their horses, every one of them was one more to feed the hunger inside her.

The Orsembians abandoned the southeastern passage entirely, hounded by her calleroses.

"Drive them," she gasped. "Drive them all the way back to their infantry and make them run."

A bugle call dashed her dreams. Her calleroses drew up at the entrance to the eastern passage. Behind them, the infantry reformed their lines. Officers on horseback were riding up down the second line, moving the injured companies back and those intact to the right flank to plug the hole in the calleroses' absence.

Another bugle sounded on their left flank, followed by drums. The infantry companies that were stretched out in an angle were pulling back in an ordered withdrawal, back to their original positions, reforming the forward battle line.

Recha followed the withdrawing Orsembian calleroses with her eyeglass. They galloped to join their advancing infantry, now closer with spears leveled. While Borbin's *mellcresa* skull banner waved in their center, the shimmering orange silk flapping like a dancing flame in the air, it was the smaller black banner with a white, unsheathed sword that caught everyone's attention.

The White Sword had finally made his presence known.

~~~

Recha eyed the dispatcher galloping up toward them. She sat at the table with Marshal Feli and some of his officers. A lull had fallen over the field.

The Orsembians held their battle line across the entrance to the eastern passage. Baltazar held his original battle line. Both armies had stared at each other for nearly an hour now, unmoving.

Recha's feet couldn't take it anymore, and she had to sit down. Her heels still throbbed when Baltazar and his commanders trotted out to meet with the Orsembians in the space between the two armies. By the time she managed to stand and get her eyeglass up, a dispatcher was racing back to her.

Terms, undoubtedly. She tapped her eyeglass to her lip. *Maybe to retrieve the dead? If they're terms of surrender . . . .*

She shook her head, finding that unlikely. Orsembian arrogance aside, she was sure they would all leave Borbin that pleasure. Someone depriving a marqués's fun never boded well them.

"Any word on the Second Army?" she asked again.

"Their vanguard should reach us within the hour," Cornelos replied, still standing off to her side.

Still not fast enough.

The enemy's vanguard, infantry and cavalry combined, outnumbered the Third Army one-and-half men to one, with more coming up.

The dispatcher rode through Recha's mounted guard and dismounted. He raced up, dripping sweat from his face, and hastily saluted. "La Dama," he said, breathing deep and out of breath, "Field Marshal Vigodt reports he has parleyed with the commander of the Orsembian vanguard. If you agree, La Dama, the commander wishes the battle lines be acknowledged and gives his word to not molest ours if we likewise do not molest theirs. If you agree, the Orsembians will retire, and they offer to allow us to collect our dead and ask to collect their own."

Recha pressed her eyeglass into her lip. Retiring from the field with respected battle lines would give them time to rest the Third Army and fortify the camp while waiting for the Second Army. It meant food, rest, and treatment for her wounded. Reason begged her to accept instantly, but caution sparked in the back of her mind.

"Whom is the enemy commander that offers these terms?" she asked, knowing the answer but wanting to be certain.

"Fuert Ribera, La Dama," the dispatcher replied. "The White Sword himself."

Several of her staff officers grumbled under their breaths. A quick look from Marshal Feli made them hush.

"Also, La Dama . . ." the dispatcher added hesitantly.

"Yes?"

The dispatcher wetted his lips. "The field marshal ordered me to relay that he advises us to accept these terms. He holds them agreeable."

It was Recha's turn to wet her lips, from all the stares she was getting. "What does Ribera want to show I agree to terms?"

"Your seal, La Dama," the dispatcher instantly replied. "Your seal was all he said was sufficient."

A press of her seal into hot, red wax later, and the dispatcher was galloping through the plain again. The day's battle was over, and blood for blood, Recha felt they had bled more. She *hated* it.

"Marshal Feli," she said softly, "start—"

"Tell the army doctors to expect more wounded," Marshal Feli told one of the staff officers. "We got those who crawled back here, but there are probably some still out there. Tell the cooks they're about to get a lot of hungry mouths and they better have started cooking an hour ago, like I told them. And get the reserves ready. When the field marshal gets back, he's bound to have the third line stand guard of our lines."

He turned back to her. "Pardon me, La Dama, were you saying something?"

Recha gave him a soft smile and shook her head. She stood to get up, and her trembling legs gave out. She braced herself against the table with a hard slap, making everyone jump.

"La Dama!" a unified chorus of concern went up as every man in ten feet rushed toward the table.

"I'm fine," she said, waving them off, though secretly finding it flattering that so many men would leap to her aid. "I'm fine. Just the heat. Cornelos, with me."

She walked slowly away from the table, desperately hiding her limp from her stricken heels.

Next battle, I'm watching from a chair. No! Horseback. Definitely horseback.

"Do you need a hand?" Cornelos asked. "An arm to lean on?"

"No," Recha replied. "I need someone to send a message to Sevesco and Harquis. I want every prisoner we've taken brought here before tomorrow morning."

"That may be difficult."

"I don't care." She'd had enough time during the battle's lull to go over preparing for the next, and those prisoners were vital for what came next. "Either tomorrow or the next day, Borbin's going to be here, and he's going to want to follow those forsaken Rules to the letter. We need those prisoners up here. Especially Givanzo."

"It'll be done," Cornelos agreed. "In the meantime, will you please go to your tent and lie down for a while. You need rest, Recha."

Recha pulled up short. She was tired, and her aching legs and throbbing heels begged her to get off them. A lingering fire from the battle earlier still gnawed at her, though.

"Men died for me today," she said somberly. "Poorly equipped and unprepared. Another conversation with Baltazar might see to the prepared portion for next time, but that still leaves the matter of their equipment."

Cornelos frowned. "That sounds like a duty for their officers."

She drew herself up under her parasol, as straight back as she could manage. "I am going to my tent to lie down for an hour. When you wake me, I expect to see every smith in the army you can find assembled for me. I have work for them to do."

Chapter 26

Necrem guided the team of horses by flickering lantern lights through blurry eyes. A twinge throbbed in the small of his hunched back. His legs were asleep from leaning his elbows down on them.

Can't we stop? His exhausted mind and body begged for it. *The sun went down over an hour ago and the horses are spent.*

The officers were insistent that the convoy keep moving. A provost stood every hundred yards or so, paced out with lantern in hand to light the winding path and usher them on. They hadn't done this before, which lent credit to those rumors that had been trickling through the wagons earlier that day.

Calleroses on horseback had raced down the convey, ordering everyone up from their noon rest and break from the Easterly Sun to eat and tend to the horses. The army's pace became relentless after that. They refused to let the wagons stop for more than a few minutes to rest and water the horses. The soldiers got no rest at all.

Whispers came later that there was a battle. No one was sure of from who or how many. Some said it was Borbin's main army, a hundred thousand strong. Other claimed it was a scouting force and either the field marshal or La Dama herself wanted all the armies to race after them.

Whatever the reason, Necrem only wanted one thing—a place to sleep.

His ear twitched, and he angled his head away at the gravelly snoring beside him.

Radon sat folded up in the seat, his arms hugging his chest, his legs propped on the footrest. The old smith showed his long familiarity with traveling by wagon, his drooped head barely wobbling with the bumpy trek.

Necrem had let their scheduled exchange of driving duties slip by so the older man could sleep. He would need it if they were rushing toward a battlefield.

A shiver ran across his shoulders. His nerves warned him to be ready to flee or make it obvious he was a smith. It was an old instinct he'd never forgotten, like so many others, but wished he had.

With Radon sleeping beside him, Necrem glanced over his shoulder to check on Oberto and Malcada. The boy *loved* that mule. Necrem couldn't explain how or why it came to be, but Oberto spent every moment he could around her. He lay on her back, facedown in her mane, and limbs dangling over her sides. The seasoned mule took it all in stride. She seemed to love the attention, much to the jealousy of the horses.

"Watch the road there!" an officer yelled.

Necrem snapped around in his seat in time to catch the road bending and the horses walking forward heedlessly. He quickly pulled the reins, guiding them over and back on track. He bashfully nodded to the officer in thanks as he passed.

Radon groaned. "Are we stopping yet?" he asked groggily.

"I'm not sure they're ever going to let us stop," Necrem replied. He exhaled deeply to stifle a yawn, not wanting to pull his scars. His mask was still damp from the day's sweat and clung to his face.

Radon hawked up a glob of spit and spat off into the darkness. "They're going to make the horses lame."

"The path's winding, but not rocky and as steep anymore," Necrem tried to explain. "We've passed the worst—"

"Hey!" Radon yelled heedlessly to the next soldier lighting the way. "When do we make camp? My horses need to rest, and I need to piss!"

Tired laughs and agreeing grumbles came from the wagons ahead and behind them.

Necrem snorted. The older smith was far too used to his protected place with an army. Smiths might always be needed; however, soldiers were soldiers. Talk out of turn too often and, sooner or later, you are bound to catch one of them on a bad day. Or night, after a long, hot march.

"Shut up and keep the convoy moving!" the soldier yelled back. "Piss off the back of your wagon, for all I care. The generals want this path cleared."

More grumbles followed, but no one was brave enough or at the breaking point to demand they stop.

Radon plopped back down against the back of the seat and wrapped his arms around himself. "Damn officers," he sneered. "Keeping us moving all night.

Don't know what they expect us to do for them when we get to wherever they're herding us. By the time we get there, we'll be too worn out to work or do anything except feed the horses and collapse."

"Probably just want the road cleared," Necrem suggested. "If there's really been a fight, then they probably want the soldiers behind us to move up faster."

"Then they should have put all the soldiers up front." Radon snickered. "Lazornians are odd. They run their armies all over the place, and then try to squash them together up these hills. What were they thinking?"

"Just trying to find a better route home."

The wagon rolled over a large rock in the trail, lifting it up then bringing it down with hard a thud and rattle. Both Necrem and Radon bounced in their seats.

"They sure picked the bumpiest," Radon growled.

"Ribera's Way." Necrem shrugged. "At least the worst is behind us."

Once off the main road, they had come to five major humps in the path, boulders in the way that required wagons to need the aid of block and tackles to winch them over and keep the wagon train moving. Several wagons didn't make it.

"Unless the entire Orsembian army is waiting on us," Radon said.

Necrem glanced at him out of the corner of his eye. The old smith had kept his voice low and soft. He hung his head, his chin going into his chest as he vacantly stared off into the darkness. He likely didn't mean for Necrem to hear that.

We're Orsembian smiths with another marc's army. The scars on his right cheek twinged as he blew air through that hole to loosen his mask's fabric gripping his skin. *No telling what they would to us if they found out.*

Although, he had more ideas than Radon probably did.

We might need to unload the wagon tonight, he considered, his cautionary instincts returning. *Keep the horses close and easy to hitch. If something goes wrong, we can try to . . .*

The nostalgia ran up his shoulders like crawling hands, adding weight to his back. It quickly soured, his stomach roiling at recalling the last time he had such a fear and what had come afterward. Then it rumbled from hunger.

Around another bend, the ground began to slope upward. Drifting clouds blocked most of the stars, making the night's darkness more oppressive, and yet the path seemed to be widening. The clomps of hooves against the rocks, the squeaking of wagon wheels, and the clatter of their contents softened to a hush.

Necrem sat up straight upon rolling over the crest of the slope. The ridge and rocky cliffs fell away, opening to a large, round enclosure. Small fires and braziers outlined the sandy, sloped shoreline of a great pool, the slumbering heart of the river awaiting the rains to flow again. The convoy pivoted away from it, hugging the curved side of the cliff where the ground was level.

The horses neighed and flung their head up in the air. Necrem tugged on their reins to keep them on the proper route.

"They smell the water," Radon commented.

"Once we're in the camp, Oberto can water them," Necrem said.

Radon snickered. "Sure. If they don't run him over first. He still sleeping back there?"

"Last I—"

Necrem remembered Malcada was probably as thirsty as the horses, and the only thing keeping the mule bound to the wagon was the lead of her reins, tied in a knot that Oberto made. It could be loose. An image flashed in his mind of the mule stubbornly pulling free and galloping down the slope to drink and throwing the boy off, breaking his back or tossing him in the water to drown.

He jerked around . . . only to breathe a relieved sigh at Malcada still tied to the wagon, trotting along with Oberto snoozing none the wiser.

"He's still asleep," he confirmed. He cleared his throat and turned back in his seat.

Radon softly chuckled.

Necrem glanced, bouncing his attention from driving the horses and the old smith who was grinning broadly beside him, his shoulders jiggling up and down.

"What?" he asked.

"Your reaction just now," Radon replied, tilting his head up, a knowing light reflected from his eyes in the passing campfires. "An act of man gripped in that sudden spike of panic of not knowing where their kid was and had to look for them. Felt it myself a few times. So"—he elbowed Necrem—"how many do you have, anyway?"

Necrem hunkered in his seat. He had kept quiet about his family. While his business-partner-of-convenance was talkative about his family woes and how much he missed, was disappointed, and nearly despised his son, thinking about Eulalia and Bayona still waiting for him was too painful to think about for long. Rather, knowing he had a chance to risk the dangers and go back to them, but instead didn't, hurt the most.

Radon waited expectingly, letting the question hang in the air as that grinning look made it clear he wouldn't let it go.

"One," Necrem reluctantly replied.

"Just *one*?" Radon cackled. "Figured a big man like you would have a dozen, even with your . . ." He waved at Necrem's face.

Necrem ignored the gesture. "Just one. A girl."

Radon's cackle grated Necrem's ears this time. "Thought you had several boys after jumping to look back for Oberto like you did."

"Not particular to one or the other, I suppose." Necrem shrugged off the lie. Nothing was more precious than his little miracle, and he wouldn't trade Bayona for anything.

"Comes with being steel working men, eh?" Radon elbowed him again. "We care about people." He let out a rasping laugh.

Necrem shook his head and rode on.

The trail of wagons rounded the cliffside to a sharp, rolling incline. Horses struggled to pull their loads over the hump. Necrem precariously guided his team in, their hooves digging into the hard, packed dirt, smoothed over by countless horses that had come earlier. They snorted and struggled, shaking their heads in the air as the wagon ground to a halt.

"Take the reins," Necrem said, tossing the reins to Radon. He jumped out of the seat and off the wagon to lighten the load.

"Get up there!" Radon yelled, cracking the reins.

The horses snorted and flared their manes. They kicked and pawed at the dirt but made little gain.

"What's going on up there?" the wagon driver behind them yelled.

Wagons were backing up behind them. Soldiers, who'd been standing around, watching the convoy roll in, pointed at them and started walking their way.

Necrem jogged up to the front of the team, took hold their leads, and pulled. His tired back went stiff. Firelight danced in the whites of the horses' wide eyes from the sudden force. Radon cracked the reins again.

The horses gained an inch. Then another. Necrem gritted his teeth and pulled, digging his heels in to drag the horses up inch by inch over the rise. His arms burned, and the backs of his legs tensed with every step. It took several minutes of constant heaving and multiple cracks of the reins to get the horses over the hump.

Necrem jumped out of the way once they had, and the horses kept barreling forward. The one on the left brushed his shoulder as they passed.

"That must be a heavy load you got there."

Soldiers jogged up. The one in the center was shorter and struggled to keep up yet was the only one wearing a helmet and stood out from the rest. He walked through the others who got there before him to stand in front with his hands on his hips.

"Smithing forge and tools, sir," Necrem told the officer. He rubbed his shoulder and lowered his head respectfully. "We didn't mean to hold up the convoy. The horses are tired, and I didn't see how steep the hill was in the dark."

"No need to apologize," the officer said, shaking his head. "We've been"—he paused to hastily gulp down some air—"helping pull wagons up this hill all evening. You said you're a smith?"

"Yes," Necrem replied hesitantly.

"Right, well, once you get situated, they want all smiths to report in the center of the camp." The officer pointed out into a large, open plain that stretched for miles, outlined by campfires dotting through it.

Necrem squeezed his shoulder. "Can't it wait until morning?"

"Order said it came from the La Dama herself." The officer shook his head. "Can't say what she could want with all of you after a day like today, but"—he shrugged—"what are the reasons of marquesas and generals to us, ay?"

An awkward pause hung in the air. He suspected from the officer's tired, lopsided grin that he expected him to agree. Necrem was too tired for small talk and left the conversation there to trail after his wagon.

~~~

The gathering was bigger than Necrem had expected. After the frustrating process of following one provost after another, directing where to stop their wagon, where to make camp, when they could see to their horses, the order finally came for both Necrem and Radon to assemble with the other smiths in front of the command tent.

He counted at least fifty-five men of all ages standing around the open space cleared out in front of the large tent, three times the size off the smaller ones surrounding it in straight, laid-out lanes. Many of the men milled around, shaking hands and talking to one another like old friends, which most probably were.

"You don't say," Radon said to another elderly smith a few feet away. The old man had complained each step of the way from their wagon that they were having to do this. He quickly changed his mind the moment he saw all the smiths from two armies gathered in one spot and went to mingling. "I always thought you should smelt with . . ."

Necrem snorted, amused. They weren't sharing trade secrets or techniques. Smiths as old as Radon and the other man, in his late-fifties, bald and red-faced from the merciless Easterly Sun, save for the gray stubble of a beard, never did that. They were boasting about their work, while the other tried to knock them down a peg.

"Steel Fist."

Necrem's ear twitched at the whisper, and his amusement vanished.

A body of younger men, possibly fresh from their apprenticeship, were gathered over to his right. One in the back pointed straight at him.

"What kind of tradename is that?" One of them snickered.

"That's not a tradename, *idiot*!" one of his fellows hissed.

"The Orsembians at the junction gave him that name," another explained. "He took on one of our companies with nothing more than his bare hands. He punched through their shields and breastplates as if they were made of *tin*!"

"But we still won that battle," the disbelieving youth added.

"That company had to retreat, though. All because of . . ." The man retelling the story shrugged at Necrem. His face went white when he caught Necrem staring back him. They all did.

I'm not far enough back.

He lowered his gaze and backed away.

"He's an Orsembian?" the questioning youth bravely whispered the moment Necrem's back was turned. "What's he doing with us?"

A fair question, son, a fair question.

He moved farther to the back of the crowd, next to a tent. No snoring or faint signs of anyone asleep came from it, nor any other signs of life.

Soldiers are probably off eating or taking care of things. No one could sleep with the rumbling crowd of steelworkers right outside, and because they were ordered here by the marquesa, there would be no point in cussing at them until they left.

The rows were neater than those at the training camp, hastily pitched as they were. He guessed the soldiers belonging to these tents were recovering from the day's march, tending to their tender feet and sunburned faces. He shifted his weight from one foot to the other, recalling the blisters.

A shudder crawled across his shoulders, forcing him to shake it off, along with the memory. He squeezed his hands in fists. His prickly calluses ground together. It'd been less than a month since the relentless days of constant drilling but seemed like years.

"Attention!"

Necrem glanced over his shoulder.

An officer stood in front of the tent. His uniform was pressed against his body with deep wrinkles outlining the straps and pieces of his armor he had worn that day. His hair stuck up in the back, molded in place by sweat. Necrem recognized him, despite how red his face was.

The marquesa's commandant.

"Gather around," the young officer ordered, motioning them closer. "La Dama has a request to make of you."

One of the marquesa's guards stepped out of the tent, in full armor, and held the tent flap open. Lantern and candlelight cast the shadows of multiple people moving about a large table inside. Necrem couldn't make out how many, but he pictured a similar scene as the room back at the villa, with all the staff running around and officers too important for him to be near congregating around maps and such.

The marquesa slipped out of the tent, followed by another guard.

Every conversation died as she walked up to the edge of the platform, the heels of her shoes tapping against the wood. The men broke up from their groups to come in closer, their heads bobbing respectfully as she surveyed them.

She held her back straight and shoulders high. However, her hair hung over her left side in a wavy curtain, with wayward strands sticking out in various directions. Her hands folded in front of her couldn't hide her riding dress's wrinkles, the front having the deepest pressed in as if she'd been wearing armor, too. Her sleeves were unbuttoned and left open. Swollen bags hung under her eyes.

She's tired, too.

Necrem fold his arms to keep his own shoulders from sagging.

"Thank you all for coming," the marquesa said. "I know, after such a forced pace like today, you're all probably as tired as the soldiers. However, time is of the essence. As some of you know, the Third Army met the Orsembian vanguard today."

Necrem jerked his head straight. Whispers passed through the smiths in the back who had arrived late, like him. The soldiers hadn't told them why they'd been forced to hurry, but now it was clear.

"We held our ground and secured our battle line," the marquesa continued. "However, five miles east of here, the Orsembian army is growing. This mountain pass is about to become a battlefield, and we're going to need every soldier we have properly equipped."

She motioned to her commandant. "Commandant, if you please."

The commandant turned to his right and shouted, "Capitán, bring in the men."

The smiths parted to let an officer lead ten soldiers through the crowd. The capitán lined the men in front of platform, facing the smiths.

The soldiers looked tired. A couple struggled to stand up straight. They stood out from the capitán and marquesa's guards. They lacked the violet uniforms under their breastplates. None had pauldrons for their shoulders, and some were missing faulds to protect their waists and hips.

The capitán snapped his heels together. "Detail formed as ordered, La Dama," he said.

"Thank you, Capitán," the marquesa replied.

She ran her eyes across the line of men before her. A deep frown formed, and her brow lowered as a flash of pity crossed her face.

"These men fought well today," she said. "However, as some of you smiths can see, their equipment is in dire need of repair and refitting." She lifted her head up at them, the pity replaced with determination. "These men make up three freshly recruited companies, close to a thousand men. I want their armor repaired and properly equipped for the next battle."

Raised eyebrows went up all around, like a furnace fire catching a strong bellow gust. Murmurs broke out as men turned to each other from their individual companies.

"Do we have enough supply?" one smith asked his partner.

"Do we have enough fuel?" a smith asked his apprentice.

"Pardon, La Dama," one man called out, raising his hand from close to the center of the group.

Men drew back to give him space, but Necrem could only make out the back of the man's head.

"Speak," the marquesa granted.

"Thank you, La Dama," the man said respectfully. "This is an enormous task you bring us. And meaning no disrespect, but I'm not sure if we're up for it. How much time do we have? How are we expected to outfit so many?"

"Let me worry about time," the marquesa replied. "As for how this commission is to be done, before you leave, Commandant Narvae will require the name of each of your companies. In the morning, you will each receive a list of soldiers you are to equip and their needs. All three companies will be divided among every smith company equally."

"But what if the Orsembians attack tomorrow?" another smith asked. "We can't refit a thousand men in one morning."

The agreements were soft, few, and begrudging. No smith wanted to say loudly what they couldn't do. Bad for both pride and business.

"The Orsembians won't attack tomorrow," the marquesa replied, a slight smile on her lips. She raised a hand to cut anyone off from questioning her. "Leave the Orsembians to Field Marshal Vigodt. These men need your skills. I call upon your duties as smiths to complete this commission."

More soft grumblings came.

The marquesa's smile slipped. She danced her eyes across the gathering at the guarded whispers spreading through the smiths. Most were spoken behind another's back and abruptly cut off the instant the marquesa looked over them.

"You have more concerns?" she asked, frowning.

Many shuffled their feet and turned their heads away, staring off into the night to avoid looking up. Some sulked. Others shoved their hands in their pockets or folded their arms.

What's wrong with them? Necrem watched in disbelief. He leaned in to catch a stray whisper, but it was too soft and quick. *A marquesa gives you an order, you do it. Is this how they take work in Lazorna?*

"Begging your pardon, La Dama," a hesitant man on the far right of the crowd said with his hand raised. "But how are we to be paid?"

The marquesa's cold stare could have warped steel. "What . . . did you *say*?"

"Please, La Dama!" the man begged repentantly with his head lowered. "I meant no disrespect. I only ask on behalf of my colleagues who won't. We're being asked to put in many hours and use the remains of our supplies. And these men are—"

"*Free!*" the marquesa shouted. "As free as you and me! As free as every man, woman, and child in these armies and Lazorna! As free as they *always* should have been!"

Necrem looked at the soldiers again, beyond the state of their armor and lack of common uniform. They were tired, yet each one stood a little taller with the marquesa's outburst. Some of their eyelids drooped with bags under them, and yet there was something more. All held a distant look in their eyes, as if they had stared longing into a void, knowing whatever they sought, they would never reach.

Necrem knew this look.

Oberto occasionally looked that way.

Sioneroses! He stood up straighter. *They're freed sioneroses!*

"Let me make this clear to you all," the marquesa continued, causing many to jerk their heads up. "In next few days, the deciding battle of this campaign is going to be fought here. I know it. The field marshal and his staff now it. And tomorrow, when the soldiers fully realize our position, they will know it, too. When Borbin and the Orsembians figure it out is none of my concern.

"What is, is to make sure we fight at our fullest. The purse of Lazorna will pay your commissions. This is *my* commission to all of you. Arm these men for war!"

"Yes, La Dama!" rippled through the smiths as individuals felt compelled to comply.

The marquesa took a deep breath. Her shoulders slumped, as if they were heavy. "Thank you, gentlemen. That's all I wish to ask of you. Get plenty of rest tonight."

"Before you all leave," the commandant announced, stepping up to the edge of the platform, "please give the name of your company to one of the officers. That way, we will know how many of you there are and how many men to assign to you." He gestured, and the ten officers in the back descended the platform with paper and graphite in hand.

Smiths started flocking to the nearest one to put their names in first, elbowing each other until a few officers motioned them to get in line.

Necrem shook his head at them. *Now they're eager. After being assured payment.*

Not all the smiths acted like that. Most waited to put their names down then left with their company members in tow.

As the smiths finally got themselves organized to give their company names, the former *sioneroses* were led away. Normal soldiers would probably have broken rank and walked casually away after being dismissed and gained some distance. These men, though, stayed in a single file line as they walked out of sight.

Someone nudged his shoulder.

"What are you waiting for?" Radon cackled, suddenly beside him. "Let's get our names listed, too."

Necrem stubbornly, and rather easily, held his ground, despite the older man's tugging. "They don't need both our names," he pointed out. "You can put down your name for both of—"

"Sir Oso?"

Every scar on his face went taut. He had come straight here after being ordered to and had forgotten to salve his face. His scars prickled against his mask's fabric as he hesitantly turned to see the marquesa staring wide-eyed over the others at him.

The name collection came to a halt as everyone turned to look at him.

Radon held on to his sleeve, his fingers turning white and arm trembling. "You . . . *know* the marquesa?" he whispered.

She was already moving. She hiked her divided skirt up and hurried off the platform, her guards on her heels.

"Continue with the name collection, please," her commandant ordered, remaining on the platform with a tired look on his face. The officers went back to asking the smiths' names, yet most watched the marquesa walk around the crowd.

She grinned crookedly while looking him up and down with both curiosity and disbelief. She walked right up to him without a glance at anyone she passed or Radon.

"Sir Oso, whatever are *you* doing here?" she asked. "I imagined you to be halfway home by now."

Necrem swallowed and lowered his head. His throat caught, trying to think of the proper way to explain himself. He didn't want her to think he received her leave and money, and then decide to go back on his word.

"Yes," he replied, wincing immediately after. "I mean . . . begging your pardon, La Dama. I meant to go home. It's just . . . things happened on the road, and I don't want you to think I lied or . . . went back on my word."

"Oh, not at all, Sir Oso," the marquesa said, waving his dismay away. "Not at all. I would like to hear about these things that happened on the road, though. Would you mind joining me? Somewhere away from all the prying . . ."

She blinked at Radon standing stiffly beside him, eyes wide at the whole conversation.

"Hello," she greeted the old smith. "And, who are you?"

"*Noe!*" Radon squawked, as if being chocked. He bowed his head and cleared his throat. "Radon Noe, La Dama," he replied. "At your service, La Dama."

The marquesa's grin broadened, and she shot a look up at Necrem. "You made a friend, Sir Oso."

"Yes," Necrem said, "well—"

"More like business partners of circumstances!" Radon added, lifting bent figure and chuckling. "Business partners of convenient circumstances, to be accurate."

The marquesa raised an eyebrow. "Is that so?"

"Yes!" Radon nodded. He pat Necrem on the shoulder. "I'm going to go put our company's name on the lists. *If* you don't mind, La Dama?"

"Not at all." The marquesa gently waved him away, and Radon hastily, and happily, slipped away.

Necrem watched him go. There was an extra spring in the man's step.

He's running off to brag to the other smiths that we're partners, and his partner knows the marquesa personally.

"What a curious partner you have," the marquesa said, shaking her head. "Come tell me how this all happened." She gestured as she turned.

Necrem read her intent and followed. There was no use arguing, and he hoped she would take him out of sight of the other smiths.

"Did something happen to you on the road?" she asked him seriously once they were walking around the command tent. "You weren't accosted, were you? Did one of my officers refuse to believe the order I gave you?"

"Hmm?" Necrem grunted then shook his head. "No . . . No. Nothing like that, La Dama. No one—"

"Relax, Sir Oso," the marquesa calmly said. "This day's been too tiring on all of us to be so formal. Just call me Recha."

Necrem stopped. His stitches tugged until one threatened to snap as the top of his cheeks, around his nose, warmed. "I . . . No. No . . . I can't."

Marquesa Mandas rolled her head, letting out a low sigh. "Very well. La Dama it is. Please, tell me how you're still with us."

Necrem let out a deep breath of relief, and the faint stinging on his face soothed. "I had planned on staying with the army all the way to Luente, but I was caught off guard when the army took Ribera's Way. I thought your general said he wouldn't go this way that night at the villa, but . . . I guess he changed his mind."

"Scouts came back saying it was passable," Marquesa Mandas said matter-of-factly.

"Yes. I supposed they had. I hadn't prepared any provisions for leaving your army so soon and . . ." He lowered his head, considering what he should tell her.

Marquesa Mandas arched an eyebrow. "*And*?"

"Roads during campaigns aren't the safest things to travel," he replied. "I saw a hanging on the road, the day before the armies turned off it."

Marquesa Mandas's eyes widened.

"They were claimed to be thieves who had come too close to your camps and were caught," Necrem explained. "I thought of traveling alone with . . . what you gave me. Thank you for that, again."

"You stayed to keep yourself and your belongings safe." Marquesa Manda's face softened. "Oh, Sir Oso, I'm sorry I didn't offer you protection."

"Oh no, La Dama!" Necrem shook his head. "I couldn't have asked you for that."

She softly smiled at him, a tired, grateful smile. "If only so many were as understanding."

Necrem kept quiet, unsure of what she meant and knew it wasn't his place to ask.

"And now you're left with my army, serving it as a smith." She snickered. "I asked you to help, you decline, and yet you help in another way. Papa's right; war has a curious way of throwing people together."

"I . . . wouldn't know."

"Don't you?" She sighed tiredly, her shoulders slumping. Before he could react, she took him by the arm and urged him on. "You were conscripted in Borbin's army, survived a terrible battle, was saved by the grace of an enemy marquesa, and now smith in her very army. *After* declining my offer to be a part of it, may I add."

"I meant no offense, La Dama." Necrem dropped his head.

Marquesa Mandas slapped him on the arm. "Didn't I tell you to stop being so formal? How did you come to smithing for me?"

"I met Sir Noe on the road again. He was a smith with Borbin's army when I was . . . a soldier. He looked after me when I was in trouble. His wagon had broken down, and the soldiers were going to take his horses. I wanted to return his kindness."

"You're a good man." She squeezed his arm. "Had any good business?"

"I suppose for an army on the move." After ten years of being banned from working on campaign, he didn't know what a good earning was for an army smith.

"Had much to fix?" she asked.

"Mostly horseshoes," Necrem replied dryly.

Damned. Horseshoes!

He blinked, remembering something. "And this."

He fished a gold, oval nugget, fixed to a steel chain from his pocket. They stopped in front of a brazier on the other side of her command tent for her to see it dangle from his broad hand.

"I still need to work on the clasp," he explained. "My wife"—he swallowed—"once had a locket that . . . I don't know how to smith two tiny pieces of gold to open and close together, but . . . I think this will do."

Marquesa Mandas stared at it, mouth slightly open and a blush forming on her cheeks. Her eyes glistened with droplets of tears hanging on the corners. She warmly smiled.

"You're a good husband, too, Sir Oso," she said.

Warmth returned to Necrem's face again, and he had to look away. "You're . . . Thank you, La Dama."

"Fixing thrown horseshoes must be good business then," she said. "To get the gold to make that."

"Actually," he said, "I used a few of your deberes that you gave me."

Marquesa Mandas snickered and whispered, "They weren't actually mine. They were Borbin's son's. We captured them at the junction."

"I guess we know how to spend it better," Necrem said.

Marquesa Mandas pulled away. "That was a *joke*!" She pointed up at him, eyes glistening with glee, mouth open in merry excitement. She started giggling. "You joke! Oh, I will have to tell Hiraldo. Steel Fist is still with us, forging and telling jokes."

"Please, La Dama," he softly begged, curling his fist around the necklace, "please don't."

Marquesa Mandas patted his arm again. "I'm not teasing you, Sir Oso. After all, we're not the monsters." She stepped forward, gazing off into the distance. Farther east, over the gently sloping tents and beyond, twinkling lights danced and moved back and forth along an invisible horizon in the darkness.

"Borbin will be here tomorrow or the next day," Marquesa Mandas said, the gentle warmth gone from her voice, leaving only cold determination. "Probably with most of his army, or at least more than what I will have tomorrow."

A pit formed in Necrem's stomach from the old rule of campaign. *The biggest army wins.*

"What . . . will you do?" he asked hesitantly.

"Buy time," she replied pointedly. "Borbin will want to talk, banter, and *show off.* His calleroses will insist on their Bravados while we do. I just got to drag it out to get all my armies up here."

"Will you have enough to match him? Borbin's army?"

"No." Marquesa Mandas shook her head, shaking her hair about. "He'll still outnumber us. Two, maybe three, to one."

The biggest army wins. Yet Necrem recalled that night at the villa, the way she had looked when crying for vengeance. It wasn't just his she was offering. It was hers. Only personal pain burned that hot.

"And you will still fight," he said.

She turned to him, face placid like washed steel, yet that same fire as that night reflected from the brazier's light. "I will have my vengeance." Her voice was a soft hiss. "Either I get it, or I die here, Sir Oso. Victory or death. That's all that matters now."

It sounded crazy. In the face of such odds, her knowing the odds, a marquesa would spit on the rules to not save herself.

It also sounded like the most honest and sincerest words Necrem had ever heard. No steel he had ever forged had been so pure, so permanent.

He squeezed his closed fist around the necklace, the nugget burying itself deeper into his palm as the chain cut against his calluses.

"I promise to forge you the best armor I can for your men," he swore.

"Thank you," she said but frowned. "I only wish there was more I can do for them. The more time I buy, the more they will have time to drill and equip, but . . ."

"They're still getting used to being free again," he said.

"Yes." She nodded with a grateful, small smile. "Broken men can't put themselves back together again in a day. Some can return to life faster than others, but some need more than being told they're free and asked if they want to get back at those who held them. They need more than a common purpose or direction. They need a leader. A . . ." An envisioned spark flamed in her eyes, making every hair on Necrem's hair stand up and his scars to prickle. "A Hero."

Necrem wilted back from her, shaking his head. "I'm no hero, La Dama. No soldier, no leader of others. I'm just a *smith*!" He wanted to yell and shout it out to the stars above until it echoed around the suns.

How many times do I have to tell people this?

"You don't get to decide to be a hero, Sir Oso," Marquesa Mandas said. "Others have seen your actions and declared you one. There is no going back. A heroic action comes from a heroic heart. If someone has one, then it's not something they can stop being. Trust me"—she wrapped her arms about herself—"I know."

"So, you want me to be a hero for you?" His brow furled, finding the whole thing ridiculous, and snickered. "A hero for those former *sioneroses*? They don't even *know* me."

Marquesa Mandas tilted her head to the side, lips pursed in thought. "Do people still call you Steel Fist?"

Necrem grunted. "Some," he mumbled, still disliking the name.

"You bent steel with your bare hands," she went on, "and punched dents into breastplates with your fists."

"I'm a *smith*! Of course I can work metal with my hands, hammer, tongs, or not."

"But, what if you'd been in armor that night?" Marquesa Mandas stepped closer. "Fully armored, you certainly wouldn't have received the wounds you did."

Necrem sensed where this was going and couldn't help but laugh. "Forgive me, La Dama, but you can't be asking me to do that for you. That was one night of . . . terror and . . . blood." He shook his head as flashes of that night at the junction repeated in his head—the death, the fear. "I can't do that again."

"Do you still hate calleroses?" she asked gently.

He jerked his head up. Marquesa Mandas stared back at him, calculating. The truth was obvious, and she knew it. He *loathed* them and would for the rest of his life.

He breathed heavily, shoulders slumping, tiring of this argument. "What do you want of me, La Dama? To be some new hero general?"

"No." A grin lit her face, one that made the fires around them seem to burn brighter, glinting off her teeth. "I want to offer you a chance. Just like those freed *sioneroses*. A chance to demand retribution against the men who wronged you all those years ago. And I want you to forge something to scare all of Borbin's calleroses into the arrogant cowards they are. After all, what good is living when you've been wronged and won't make it right?"

Necrem trembled. His earlier exhaustion faded away, and at the thought of retribution against Borbin's calleroses, and those same calleroses before them, he listened to her request.

Chapter 27

14th of Iam, 1019 N.F (e.y.)

"Why couldn't we have done this, this *morning*?" Recha hissed under her breath, dabbing her forehead with a small handkerchief.

It was *too* small. The white linen was already turning yellow from her repeated attempts to keep some of her makeup from smudging away and revealing the bags under her eyes. She couldn't afford to show an ounce of weakness to Borbin, including fatigue from sporadic naps while waiting for the parley to *finally* happen.

"If we'd have done it this morning," Baltazar whispered beside her, "half of the Second Army would still be shaky on their feet."

"So, instead, we're all *roasting* and waiting," Recha retorted, to which Baltazar chuckled.

Once again, the Easterly Sun brutally glared down on Recha and her army. Not a cloud hung in the sky to challenge its oppression. She sat on her horse behind the second battle line stretched across the plain.

The majority of the Second Army stood in two lines along the battle lines the Third Army had staked out yesterday. She and most of her command staff waited with the Second Army's calleroses massed to their right and the Third Army's calleroses to their left. Behind them, the infantry of the Third Army formed two more battle lines. Even without Hiraldo and the First Army absent, Recha and Baltazar agreed that they needed to make the biggest show of force possible.

A stray ray of sunlight reflected off a nearby soldier's helmet and shined directly into her eyes. Squinting in frustration, she nudged her horse forward and angled the floppy brim of her velvet bonnet to block it out. She had left her parasol in her tent, wanting to keep her hands free.

"Don't be hasty," Baltazar warned.

Recha tilted her head to speak back at him. "I'm just keeping the sun out of my face. I'm not going to dash off and demand Borbin come out."

"That's comforting to hear." Baltazar's lips faintly curled under the tips of his mustache. Metal clicked against metal as he switched his horse's reins from one gauntlet to another. He sat straight back, armored and uniformed pristinely, as if again he didn't feel the heat or the sweat sprinkled across his exposed face between his helmet's cheek guards. Ever the picture of military stoicism.

"They still don't look like they've gotten their act together over there," Narvae complained, followed by the sound of wet spit, behind them.

Recha frowned. As poorly mannered as his observation was, he was also right. Across the plain, the Orsembian battle line appeared to be a churning mess. What had started out as random infantry companies and pickets guarding their line that morning was now flowing with calleroses moving up and down the line.

There were over fifty individual banners the last she counted, from minor calleros companies to barony houses, each one more irrelevant than the other. There were only two banners Recha cared about—the White Sword's and Borbin's.

The White Sword's banner, she easily spotted off to the left of center of the Orsembian line. While other calleroses and barons moved their horses about, the standard with a white sword against a black field sat motionless, like a waiting predator.

Borbin's *mellcresa* skull, however, had *yet* to make an appearance. Regardless, there were over fifteen thousand calleroses milling about their line, and more gathering. A lot of horses. Annoyingly, their gathering, combined with the gradual slope, obscured the enormous amount of infantry undoubtedly forming up behind them.

"Wouldn't it be wonderful"—General Priet snickered—"if they all just charged onto our pikes and got it over with? All those bloviating barons right on our pikes. We could hold our shots until their line was impaled and turn their charge into a charnel house."

"Just save some for my boys," General Ros requested. "Some have scores to settle after what happened the other day."

"You can leave whatever you two leave alive for me and the calleroses to mop up," Marshal Olguer jumped in.

Agreeing hums, grunts, and chuckles broke out behind her among her commanders.

"Now's not the time for wishful thinking," Baltazar gently warned. He turned in his saddle, and Recha caught the hard stare he threw back over his shoulder. "Or overconfidence."

Hesitant coughs and clearing throats followed. Leather squeaked from shifting rearends as the members of her command staff glanced off in odd directions like scolded boys.

Recha pursed her lips and leaned in closer to Baltazar. "It would be wonderful, though," she whispered.

"Hmm," Baltazar grunted, but his face gave away nothing.

Recha bit back a smile for him, having wished the same thing to happen the day before, and glanced over her shoulder. The quietness of the jovial moment made her realize something.

"Where's Marshal Bisal?" she asked, not finding the tall, blusterous man.

"He and his best scouts are exploring that ravine," Baltazar replied, gesturing to his left with a tilt of the head.

The northern ridge of sandstone cracked open with grassy mounds, leading into a narrow passage that wound up then turned sharply back behind the ridge.

"That wasn't there before," Recha commented, turning her memory over and over, but couldn't remember it.

"You couldn't see it from the height," Baltazar corrected. The height being what he called the hill she had watched the battle the day before from. "I saw it when we marched through here but couldn't do anything about. We needed to establish a perimeter first."

"Are you seeing if it leads behind their lines?" Recha sat up straighter. "Planning to raid their rear once Hiraldo gets here?"

"Best we know the ground before we make any strategies. That's one lesson I learned the other day." His frown darkened to a scowl, directed across the field at the White Sword's banner.

At least he's speaking now.

Recha picked at her lavender skirts, fussing with them to ensure they obscured her riding boots while ignoring the urge to back away from him. The only thing Baltazar had said after returning from the field yesterday were orders. If anyone asked him *anything* other than a military question, they received a fiery glare.

"The skirmish wasn't a defeat, Papa," she whispered gently.

"Yes, it was," Baltazar bluntly replied. "I underestimated Ribera. I took his reputation of that being a master tactician. A thoughtful marshal." He snorted disdainfully. "I rode out as if I was going to play a game of jedraz with the man, but the White Sword doesn't play games.

"No." He shook his head. "Ribera is decisive action. He thinks about his decision, yes, but once he makes it, he follows through with it with all his might. That's how he drove off my right flank and turned my trap against me. He holds nothing back, moves fast to gain ground, and leaves little room for counterattacks. That's how he generals. Some might think it reckless, but when most commanders are barons or marquéses timidly wanting to avoid a battle, such tenacity can end a battle before it even begins."

"I trust you have a strategy to counter him today," Recha said. "In case this goes poorly, and we have to fight."

She hadn't been at the war council that morning. Cornelos had let her sleep after staying up later than she should have, mind swirling with competing ideas of what she was going to say to Borbin when they met.

She was surprised with herself. She had envisioned a version of this coming moment for three years. However, now with it staring her in the face, her mind warred with itself about her and her army's current situation, what she needed to say, and what her heart desperately wanted to say.

"Hit them," Baltazar replied. "Hard and straight. No tricks, traps, or gambits. We don't have the numbers, and I'm not giving Ribera any openings. But, if you have your strategy worked out like I think you do"—his eyes slid across to her—"then we won't have to worry about that."

"You think I have all this planned out?" She nervously chuckled, but Baltazar didn't join her. A few awkward moments passed for her to clear her throat and take a deep breath. "We need time."

"As much as you can get for Hiraldo to arrive to the field," Baltazar agreed.

"I'm going to stall any way I can," she explained. "While I do, listen for anything he lets slip—how many forces he has, how desperate he sounds. Gage his state of mind."

She twisted in her saddle to address the officers behind her. "No one else speaks but me," she ordered. "I don't care what insults they make, do *not* speak. We must show a united front, unlike Borbin who's bringing"—she glanced back at all the different banners crammed together and fighting for space across the field—"an *exorbitant* number of barons."

They all laughed in agreement at that. Cornelos, sitting behind her, grinned broadly.

Recha grinned back then turned forward. "And, as for Ribera," she added for Baltazar, "maybe I can find an opening to let him know about his grandson."

Baltazar hummed thoughtfully. "Just be careful on your wording. If I understand what you plan to do with Borbin's son is any indication, Ribera may misunderstand your meaning if you aren't precise."

"I've had three years of practicing my wording with Orsembians," Recha assured him. "If Borbin brings him, I'll make sure he gets the message."

A bugle blared from across the field. The mingling of horses and banners split apart in the center of their mass, allowing a procession of more riders through. The *mellcresa* skull banner of Borbin led it, three times the size of any other banner on the field, the orange cloth rippling back from the simple effort of carrying it forward.

In the center of the procession rode a man alone with a soldier carrying a large parasol spread out wide enough to shade the man and most of his horse from the Easterly Sun.

Borbin.

Recha squeezed her reins in her fists, and her body shook.

Borbin's procession fanned out across the front of his line, the barons and calleroses filling in the gap behind him, jostling again for several minutes for positions before they finally got themselves in order.

Another bugle blast came.

The field went silent.

Recha stared. The field, the heat, the multitude of people and horses on it, they all seemed to fade away. The faint echo of heavy breathing grew in her ears. There was only that man across the field, sitting in his saddle as if he were lounging under the shade of the parasol.

"Recha!" Baltazar gripped her shoulder.

She gasped, her shoulders rising and falling as she breathed heavily. Baltazar kept hold of her, watching her worriedly.

"I'm fine," she said, shrugging him off.

She straightened her lavender blouse and skirts to calm herself. She needed to make it obvious on sight that she was a regal marquesa, even in this blazing mountain plain. She had picked her clothes specifically to match her violet banners while also being light enough to wear.

She checked that the lace of her long sleeves were thin enough to let air seep through but not a wandering eye. She left her top collar button undone, refusing to be strangled in this heat. To pay for letting her neck breathe, she had pinned an oval, violet gem brooch on her blouse under her chin, centered on her collarbone.

Her finger lingered on the golden *M* engraved on the gem. The sight of Borbin waiting, finally in sight, reminded her of her small hand pistol, primed and loaded, nestled in her pocket.

"Papa," she said darkly, "if this does go poorly . . . if I'm unable to . . . If you see me reach for my pocket, stop me. I don't think I'll be able to stop myself."

Baltazar pulled back, studying the Orsembians. "Sometimes in war, there are times where it is best not to outright kill your enemy," he recited, causing Recha to relax. "Sometimes you must face him in the field and defeat him utterly. Decisive victories are necessary to make it absolutely clear to everyone that you defeated him."

"Are you quoting yourself again?" she asked, crookedly smiling, her head tilted to listen to him recite.

"An ancient Desryol king," Baltazar replied. "Morcourn Desryol, I think his name was."

Recha frowned. "I don't remember that one."

"He's from long ago, maybe over five hundred years or so. Not much is left from him, but I've always remembered that quote. It always let me focus on what's required for a real victory, instead of"—he shook his head—"whatever small things everyone else was after."

"Borbin doesn't deserve to simply die," Recha said, piecing together his meaning and coming to an agreement. "He deserves to be *utterly* defeated."

The image of his entire army crushed and littering the field around him played in her mind. She envisioned Borbin kneeling in the middle of their bodies, looking up at her while she pressed her pistol to his forehead. It made her grin,.

Taking another deep, calming breath, she ordered, "Drums."

"Drums!"

The drummers of the companies in front of them filled the air with a long, unyielding flurry.

Tap!

Tap!

Rap! Rap! Rap!

Officers of the four infantry companies in front of them on both battle lines shouted orders. As one, blocks of men stepped forward in time with drums. The companies marched forward until their formations had cleared the battle lines.

"Right face!" officers on the right yelled. "Quick! Turn!"

"Left face!" officers on the left yelled. "Quick! Turn!"

The companies in front of her turned as commanded and, like four great sliding doors, marched in opposite directions, opening a wide path for Recha and her command staff. The plain echoed with the sound of their matching footfalls and drum taps until they completely cleared the path.

"Companies! Halt!" the officers yelled, followed a second later with a combined last stomp of two hundred men.

"About face!"

The companies turned, facing out at the Orsembians. In unison, their heels stomped, the ends of their pikes slammed into the dirt, and their drummers made one last rap, reverberating a crescendo throughout the plain and off the ridges of sandstone surrounding them. An eerie silence followed.

"My compliments, General Priet," General Ross whispered, ruining the stillness.

"My thanks," General Priet replied, "General Ross."

Recha pressed her lips together tightly until they started to burn, all to stop herself from turning around to glare at them.

Couldn't either of you take in the moment and wait until we were moving to share compliments?

Not to disparage the men, all four companies marched superbly, and she hoped it had an intimidating effect on the Orsembians. She wanted to soak in the quiet for a little longer.

Baltazar raised his hand. On the signal, Recha's standard-bearer rode before her, lining up beside a bugler and accompanied by her own guards, fully armored with black face visors closed.

"Bugler," Baltazar ordered, "conversar!"

The bugler lifted his bugle. He played long, overly drawn-out notes, blaring them across the field. It was the most unfitting bugle call Recha had ever heard. The wailing call made it sound like someone's joking attempt to make a ballad into a military call.

Although, it wasn't a military call at all. The conversar was an invitation to talk, part of the Rules of Campaign. After ignoring them for so long, it was jarring having to go back to them. She bit her tongue to prevent herself from spitting at the sound of it and being neither ladylike nor distinguished as a marquesa should be.

A minute into his call, the bulger was answered by the receiving song across the field. The standard-bearer and his entire line nudged their horses into motion, and Recha followed with Baltazar, her command staff on their heels.

They casually walked their horses through the gap her infantry had lain open for them, and the Orsembians mirrored them. Borbin's own standard-bearer walked out ahead of him as he leisurely guided his horse out in the middle of the plain, surrounded by his flocking entourage.

The infernal conversar played on well after Recha rode out into the field. She gritted her teeth at each wayward note and flat-blaring burst the buglers made from bouncing in their saddles. They were walking slow, but the ground was uneven, leading to plenty of bumpy, missed notes.

As if the call couldn't get any worse! Her ears started to ring as the buglers blew harder, competing in who could play the loudest. *I'm going to have that infernal call banned. Then completely forgotten!*

The buglers played their clashing song until they were within ten feet of each other, and both lines reined their horses to halt. Guards, buglers, and standard-bearers stared at each other. The banners themselves hung limply without any wind. Although, because of its exaggerated size, Borbin's fell over his standard-bear's shoulders.

When both retinues finally gathered, both sides' guards peeled off to the side, letting their rulers through.

Borbin sleeked forward. The metallic sheen of his horse's white-gold coat made every horse around him look like a mule. His servant carrying the enormous parasol stepped lively to ensure his marqués never rode out into the sun.

Recha rode out to meet him with Baltazar trailing her. She had met Emaximo Borbin at a reception in Manosete a few years before becoming marquesa. It had been the first and only time they had been face to face and the beginning of her uncle's imbecilic attempt to form an alliance with the man. She was loathed to admit that he didn't live up to her odious expectations.

He rode comfortably in the saddle, leaning back but still sitting straight. His armor was more ornate than she would have preferred, with a golden *mellcresa* skull that had emerald eyes encrusted on his sleek breastplate. Armor covered him from neck to toe, a full suit, which was rare these days, but wearing it confirmed he was still fit for a man of his age. His long saber hung from his hip, its gold, ornate handguard matching the gold on his breastplate. A vibrant orange cape hung from clasps on his shoulder pauldrons, flowing neatly over the rump of his horse.

Despite the heat, Borbin wore a felt, red hat with golden tassels along its stiff, wide brim and one on the top. Black and gray curls of hair poked out from edges of the hat. His angular cheeks were free of fat, age spots, or deep wrinkles. His pointed nose made his smirk and pointed beard stand out more.

Recha bit her tongue to keep her features smooth and unrevealing as she caught him gazing at her up and down with amber eyes.

"La Dama Recha Mandas," Borbin greeted, "how fortuitous to find you here, of all places. I expected you to remain in Zoragrin when this season started, like every year."

"Like son, like father," Recha said under her breath.

Borbin raised a thin eyebrow and tilted his head at her. "What was that?"

"Pardon me, Si Don Borbin"—Recha grinned, holding back a laugh—"but I've heard that same remark countless times for the past month. From Puerlato to Luente all the way up to Crudeas." She threw her head back with a laugh, unable to hold it in any longer and letting everyone in Borbin's entourage know where her army's marched. "Everywhere we've gone, people were absolutely *astounded* to see us."

The mob of barons and calleroses broke out in a plague of frowns and disgusted sneers. Yes, it was unwise to antagonize the other side in a negotiation, yet it was all too wonderful for Recha to stop herself.

All of you kept me waiting until the heat of the day to do this. Only serves you right that I get to gloat in your faces.

Borbin's upturned face, however, never twitched a muscle. "Indeed," he said. "I'm sure you've had yourself a grand adventure, like any young woman craves. However, I'm afraid the real challenges of campaign have caught up with you."

"Oh really?" Recha feigned concern and fanned herself with her hand. "If you're referring to the heat, none of us would have suffered so if you'd have risen earlier."

The squeaks of over fifty rears rubbing against saddles ground over the field as calleroses shifted in their seats. Men cleared their throats but held their tongues. Everywhere Recha glanced, there were defiant Orsembian eyes staring back for her audacity.

"I would have thought a lady, especially a marquesa as *young* as yourself, would appreciate the comfort leisurely resting before facing a day as hot as this," Borbin calmly replied.

Recha shook her head. "You needn't have worried so, Si Don. After a month of blazing campaign, I can assure you that I've grown accustomed to placing army needs first. As *any* commander should."

"But as a ruler of a marc, you must realize there are rules for these things." Borbin's nostrils twitched, and a faint snort escaped them. He worked his jaw, as if holding back a snide remark. He gave her an expecting look, leaning forward in his saddle. "Proprieties must be upheld."

"But we have been upholding proprieties." Recha raised her eyebrows coyly. "We played the conversar and now we're conversing, aren't we?"

Borbin stared blankly at her. "La Dama, by the Rules, as the aggressor, it is your obligation to introduce your delegation to the conversar first, and then the defender. While I don't see any member of your delegation worthy of note." He made a quick, dismissive scan of her general staff.

"That's because I was rather hoping we could dispense with that formality, Si Don," Recha replied through a strained smile. "It is so terribly hot, after all. But, if you're calling my field marshal, Baltazar Vigodt"—she held her hand out, as if presenting him—"as someone unworthy of note, then I must admit you are a poorer judge of character than I thought." *And I never thought you were a good judge of anything, anyway.* She held her tongue not to add that.

Borbin's entourage grumbled to each other.

"Must we endure this upstart's remarks, Uncle?" a young man behind him called, one of the few barons not in armor, wearing a bright, azure blue jacket, buttoned down his right breast with gold buttons and a similar hat as Borbin, save for it being blue, matching his jacket. "Tell this wench what she can do with her sharp tongue, or let her taste Orsembian steel."

The man propped his fist on his hip as the men around him grunted and nodded in agreement. He smiled crookedly, making the thin lines of his mustache stand out even more under his large, pointed Borbin nose.

"Ah, ah, gentlemen!" Borbin shouted back, raising a hand to silence them. "The Rules must be given their due."

He tilted his head at Recha. "You must pardon my nephew, La Dama," he said cheerfully. "Timotio suffers from the overeagerness so prevalent with youth. I'm sure you understand. He meant no disrespect."

"Oh, I'm sure he did," Recha said, narrowing a glare back at Borbin's nephew. The smirk he returned her made her want to order Cornelos to strike it from his face, but she held her tongue.

Timotio was nothing more than Borbin's hound. At least, that's what Sevesco gathered. While Borbin doted on his son, grooming him to take his place, Timotio was always the one sent out to do the demanding, and sometimes dirty, work.

He could be a problem. If Borbin likes him just a little more than Givanzo, then . . .

"As for my retinue," Borbin said, holding out his right arm, "may present—"

"No," Recha whined, shaking her head. "By the Savior, please no."

Borbin stared back her, wide-eyed and aghast. "La Dama, you forget yourself. The Rules—"

"It's *too* hot! How many times do I have to say that? Besides, you don't recognize any of my army commanders of note. *I* don't recognize . . ." She sat up in her saddle, craning her neck to look over Borbin and at the barons lined up behind him, shaking her head at them one after the other. "No. No. Don't know that one. Him, neither. Oh! Baron Irujo! Fancy meeting you here, scowling as always."

Baron Valen Irujo was indeed scowling at her from under his helmet, his hooked nose sticking out between his cheek guards. The former ambassador probably felt personally perturbed from her lying to his face and now this engagement the only thing to save it.

Recha went on by him. "No. No. No, no, no. Nope. Wait!" She pointed sharply into the mangle of horses and armored riders. "There he is!"

She held her finger on an elderly man sitting two horses deep behind the front line of the Orsembian delegation. His tall, thin frame, even in armor, helped her spot him. His armor was simple, no ornamentation or designs upon it. However, the visible clothing underneath was shock-white, matching his mustache, wisps of hair sticking out from under his helmet, and sword on his hip. The sword's hilt and scabbard were fashioned with white wood, as pale as bleached bone.

"Marshal Fuert Ribera," she called, grinning at finally laying eyes on the White Sword, "well fought the other day, sir! You have our compliments. Until then, we hadn't met an Orsembian force that could give us a proper battle."

Her compliment didn't help the sneers she was getting from the barons and other calleroses, which she was glad to see. She was also glad to see the sideways looks they were giving the White Sword and the frown on Borbin's face.

That's right, growl and frown. None of you like him. And if you remove him from command, then Baltazar can mop up the rest of you incompetent buffoons. Wishfully thinking, she knew. However, seeds had to be planted everywhere she could.

"Cal Ribera is merely the commander of my vanguard," Borbin pointed out. "Think of what you received as merely a taste of what my entire army is capable of."

Sneers turned to snarky grins and dark chuckles behind him. The Orsembians' horses kicked at the dirt, feeling the aggression of their riders.

Recha raised an eyebrow. "*Cal Ribera*? You would demote one of your marc's most renowned Heroes, Si Don?"

"Careful, La Dama. Your youthful ignorance is showing again." Borbin snickered. "A true marqués must utilize all his resources for the good of the marc. A calleros who shows exceptionalism on the field mustn't simply be elevated in rank but placed where their exceptionalism can continue to benefit the marc. Elevate them too highly or too often, and you risk losing their benefit."

You mean risk them becoming more popular than you.

The hairs on the back of her neck bristled. Her uncle embraced the same logic in casting off Baltazar and putting her beloved in harm's way. She wanted to call him out for his shallow selfishness and spit at his empty platitudes to make him seem grander in the eyes of his bootlicking entourage.

"I never took you for a philosopher, Si Don," Recha said instead.

"The wisdom of experience, La Dama," Borbin replied confidently. "That same wisdom, I'm sorry to inform you, says you are in a regrettable position."

"I think my position isn't as regrettable as you may think." Recha held back from smirking, not wanting to boast or give too much away but also refusing to surrender the dominate position to their conversation entirely to him.

"La Dama, you are miles from home. Trespassing deep into my domain, and you've been caught!" Borbin pointed at her, his tone that of a lecturing parent. "Generations of chroniclers will mark this as the biggest campaign blunder in half a century. This and not being bold enough to face me at Compuert, at your supposed ally's defense."

"Caught? I wouldn't say caught. I would say . . . bumped into you by surprise."

"Don't be coy with me, La Dama." Borbin gave her a dry look. "I'm not another imbecilic ambassador you can wag your eyelashes at."

The whispering and smirks on his men's faces behind him told her plenty of them were thinking the opposite, if not with other obscene comments. Baron Irujo, however, remained scowling.

"I assure you, Si Don, you are the *last* man I'd ever wag my eyelashes at." She dropped her smile and let her disdain shine. "Or be coy with."

They stared each other down. Borbin squinted at her over his nose. Recha was amazed he could keep his head raised back like that. The back of her neck ached from looking at him.

"It seems we can dispense with pleasantries as well as the proprieties then," he said, leaning back in his saddle. "If your army stands down, here and now, I will allow you to return to Lazorna with a third of your men. Your guard, staff, and servants included."

"That almost sounds like you were demanding me to surrender," Recha said.

"You *are* going to surrender, La Dama," Borbin said, bored. "My offer is the only one where you surrender and save as much face as you can. If you force my hand, then I promise you, my terms will become less and less generous."

"Si Don, you've been called many things, but never generous." She worked her mouth, wanting to sneer. "You shouldn't be so certain in war. Even as we speak, I have more troops arriving."

She nudged over her shoulder. She could hear the drums beating to a steady rhythm men could march in formation to. Either they were the last of General Priet's rear guard, moving up from spending their night in fissures, or some of General Ross's men.

"La Dama," Borbin sighed out, shaking his head tiredly, "because you are clearly new at this, allow me to explain a simple Rule of Campaign." He sat up in his lecturing pose again. "You taunt that you have more troops arriving on the field, but it's clear to me that *I* have more men and will continue to have more. By the Rules, *I* am the authority here. *I* have the larger army. *I* set the terms!"

Recha sniffed disdainfully. "Sounds like an obscene joke than an actual rule of war."

Uncomfortable and shocked coughs burst around her, including behind her, likely from some of her guards and lower staff officers, stunned to hear their marquesa talk like that.

That may have been too much for them, she mused at the wary looks she was getting. It also might have been too much for this negotiation. She needed to stall for time, not completely throw Borbin over the edge.

"And besides, Si Don," she said, "you forget what happened at the Márga's ford. You outnumbered us four to one then, but after an entire week, not one Orsembian had crossed. Unless they were a corpse that had floated downstream and got caught on some driftwood."

That was one of many memories of her first battle she could never forget. The Orsembians had been desperate to get across that ford after she had destroyed the other bridges across. After Baron Irujo had relieved Ribera, Recha had believed it became a point of pride of breaking them instead of building makeshift bridges around. There were still corpses littering the bottom of the Márga, both Orsembian and Lazornian.

Borbin took deep, long breaths. His shoulders rose and fell. He worked his jaw, moving his dimpled chin side to side, as if he were grinding his teeth. With one last, deep breath, he pulled his hat from his head, sending tuffs of sweaty, curly hair in all directions.

"Mandas," he growled, straightening his hair, "you are an *utter* disappointment."

"Excuse you," Recha said, giving him a narrowed glare, "*Borbin?*"

"I thought you'd learned your place," he replied, dropping his hand back into his lap, unfazed by her stare. "I admit, when I heard three years ago that you had killed your uncle, proclaimed yourself marquesa, and ordered your army south, I thought you were another brash, young child. Head too full of dreams of the world that she couldn't wait to conquer. I planned to take all Lazorna then, before the others carved it up.

"But then"—he raised a finger—"then you surprised me. You held our advance. Then you held what you had left of your . . . speck of a marc together. And to top it off, when the conversar was called, you agreed to hold the lines as they were.

"I had to reconsider, 'Maybe she understands. She's nothing more than some hideaway between two mountain ranges and a few rivers, hardly to be considered an actual marc. She'll understand her role from now on, unlike her idiot uncle who thought himself my equal.' Your uncle, indeed, was an idiot, by the way."

Recha's mouth twisted. Not so much for her uncle—she'd killed him—just the way Borbin talked about her.

"I always thought you took advantage of my uncle," she said. "Lured him into a false sense of security before humbling him. I never imaged you'd take Puerlato, too."

"Puerlato was always going to be taken." Borbin waved dismissively. "If not by me, then someday by Pamolid. I took it to teach your dimwitted uncle his place. In the months before our shared venture, he'd been sending ultimatums to Marqués Dion on how the campaign shares were to be split evenly between himself and me. Declaring we were equal *partners* and made demands in *both* of our names!" Spit flung from Borbin's lips, and his eyes flashed. "No one is my partner! No one makes demands on what *my* claims will be!"

Recha's glare turned to disgust. "That's your reason? Not because my uncle . . .? You killed so many . . . for *that*? And you call *me* brash!"

"Because you are!" Borbin laughed. "Do you think I don't know about your own petty oath, Recha Mandas? Do you think I don't know why you're *really* here? What was his name?"

The heat around her vanished, as if the Easterly Sun was no longer in the sky. Every muscle contracted, stiffening her in her saddle.

"Your son, was he not?" Borbin asked Baltazar.

"You don't address my officers, Borbin!" Recha snapped, lifting herself up in the saddle to make herself as tall as possible. "You talk to me, and *only* me! I am here for Lazorna—"

"Don't insult me," Borbin scoffed. "If you had wanted to reclaim Puerlato, you could have by now. And I know that because I know the strength I left there. Or, I should say, the lack thereof, another testament to how I misjudged my recalculation of you knowing your place."

"I will choose my own place, Borbin," Recha hissed through clenched teeth.

"That's where you're wrong, child. For the last three years, we've all been humoring you. Me, Marqués Dion, Marqués Hyles, we've let you sit in your little corner without having to be any real fuss for any of us.

"Hyles saw you as a relief from having to deal with your uncle's ridiculous ideas so he could tend to his own personal grudges eastward. Dion saw you as a suitable bargaining chip, patting you on the head with words of friendship in case I ever decided to finish what I started." Borbin chuckled. "As if I'd ruin such a garden."

Recha arched her brow. "Garden?"

"Yes." Borbin fluffed out his hat and straightened it back on his head. "A quaint little garden, fit for young girl playing at being a marquesa. Where she can sit out her days and get over her youthful delusions before properly marrying.

Because *that* is where you belong—safely nestled away and not being a nuisance."

Recha snarled at the jeers and mocking chuckles from Borbin's men. They added to her anger at the man himself.

"You dare think of Lazorna as your buffer state?"

"That's what you *are*!" Borbin's shout echoed across the field. "That's what I made you three years ago! That's what I made Saran last year and what I will make of Quezlo, either this year or the next! As marqués of Orsembar, this will be done!

"You"—he pointed at her again—"*will* stand down! You *will* lift your siege of Puerlato and sign a binding document relinquishing all claim to the city and lands I held! You *will* sign a binding document never to ally with Quezlo against me again! And you *will* return to Lazorna and stay there!"

Recha visualized his hand being cut off, his horse throwing him to the ground, and the last shocked look on his odious face as she—

Her hand clutched her pistol through the cloth of her skirts, her fingers wrapping around the natural feel of the grip and trigger.

"And if I refuse?" she hissed.

Borbin gave her a flat glare. "If you waste my time here any longer and force this issue, I will lay waste to your army, parade you through your former marc, before shipping you back to Manosete to live out the rest of your days as an example of what happens to those unfit to rule. Don't be stupid, Mandas. Accept my terms and be grateful."

Shoot him! the longing, bloodthirsty screech echoed in her mind, blocking everything else out. *This bastard deserves it! Shoot him! For Sebastian! Shoot—*

"La Dama." Baltazar's gentle voice cut through the screaming. He sat as firm as the rocks surrounding them, unmoved by Borbin's threats and boasts. He merely glanced down at her hand and made a minuscule, barely a twitch, shake of his head.

He needs to be more than just killed, she recalled. *He needs to be utterly destroyed.*

She let go of her pistol to take hold of her saddle horn instead.

"I must say, Si Don," she said coldly, "you are more competent than I originally thought."

Borbin smiled and nodded his head.

"Of course"—she shrugged—"besides yourself and Fuert Ribera, there aren't any other competent leaders in Orsembar."

Borbin's smile slipped. "Mandas, you're making this worse for yourself. Accept—"

475

"This isn't about me anymore! This is about incompetent leaders." She peeked behind him at the barons and calleroses frowning and shaking their heads at each other, not sure if she meant them or not. "Do you have an eyeglass, Si Don? I can lend you mine if you—"

"I don't need an eyeglass to see you don't have the troops to face me." Borbin waved dismissively.

Recha grinned. "It's not my troops you should be looking for, Si Don, but rather someone you've misplaced."

Borbin frowned and glanced over his shoulder.

"He's not back there," she teased. "But if you do have an eyeglass, look behind me, as far back as you can. I promise you, there's someone waiting under a pair of trees who's been missing his . . . papa."

Multiple stunned uproars rippled through the entourage. Men shook their heads as they reached and pilfered through saddlebags for eyeglasses or demanded them from subordinates. Borbin held her with a fiery amber stare, unflinching.

"You lie," he said.

Recha giggled, her cheeks hurting from how wide she grinned. "No, I don't."

"Uncle!" Timotio cried, peering through an eyeglass. He launched his horse forward the few feet separating them then jerked the poor animal to a halt beside Borbin, nearly trampling the servant holding the oversized parasol. "It's true! Givanzo is up there!"

Borbin snatched the eyeglass away and cast his sight to the back of the plain. His jaw slowly opened as he took it in.

"And he's not alone," Recha continued. "We caught several barons trying to play calleros and failing miserably with him. And, as for calleroses, we captured plenty of them, too! Some fought, while others tried to flee or hold captives rather than fight like real soldiers! Those you'll find joining Givanzo, where they belong. Those few who fought valiantly and yielded their swords with dignity have been given the honor they deserve and are now safely away from those cowards on the hill."

She shot a look into the gathering of Orsembian calleroses, locking eyes with Fuert Ribera for only a second.

Please see it! We captured Crudeas and your grandson is safe! Please understand!

The look was all she was able to give before a hiss drew her back.

"You bitch!" Timotio spat. "You dare treat my cousin this way!" He reached for his sword, followed by everyone else.

Metal hissed against metal as blades inched out. Horses snorted at their riders' hostility. Cornelos was at Recha's side in an instant.

"*Stop!*" Borbin roared. He backhanded Timotio, cutting his nephew's cheek with his gauntlet. "*Stop!* Sheathe your swords!"

Timotio clutched his face, his sword slapping back down into its sheathe. "Why, Si Don?" he cried.

"No one draws weapons at the conversar!" Borbin snapped.

"Especially when a marqués's son is being guarded by the Viden de Verda," Recha gloated.

Timotio's face paled, save for the red streak of blood running down his cheek. Borbin's face became stone, the eyeglass shaking in his hands.

"They make excellent sentries," Recha explained. "Impervious to all promises of wealth or threats against family. They also make excellent questioners. So many truths to find. So many ways to find them." She forced away her grin, making herself as cold as possible. "They are also very good at killing my enemies who I have no further use for."

Borbin's fingers squeaked against the eyeglass's metal casing. The instrument groaned and trembled, as if about to spring apart. "Half of your army for—"

"I think we've talked enough for today." Recha gathered up her reins, ignoring Borbin's glare and Timotio gaping at her. "Any more would be pointless, and we both need time to think. You can send me a more sincere offer tomorrow. Preferably in the morning. I hate being kept waiting."

Reins firmly in hand, she kicked her horse. He sprang into a gallop, and she turned him in time that his back hooves threw dirt and dust up at Timotio.

Cornelos and her guard were quick to follow and join in behind her. She left Baltazar and the other officers to return with her standard-bearer, but she wanted to be the first to return to her soldiers.

She raced back through her battle lines' gap and ripped her hat off, sending her hair spilling out behind her.

"Stand firm, Lazornians!" she yelled. "Yell out! Let them hear you don't give a damn about their numbers!"

A ripple of pikes slamming down into the ground flooded over the plain.

"Huzza! Mandas!" her soldiers roared. "*Huzza!*"

Recha galloped her horse in a circle, waving her hat and laughing as the men's chant grew louder. Her heart boomed in her chest when she finally pulled her horse to a halt, in time to see Borbin withdrawing.

Baltazar and the rest of her retinue were returning, as well, much more orderly and professional in comparison to hers. The forward companies of infantry filled in the gap on the line behind them.

"That could have gone better," Baltazar said lowly, frowning as he pulled up beside her.

Recha panted and wiped the sweat from her forehead. Her wet hair clung to the back of her hand. "Could it?" she gasped then laughed. "If I had to suffer through another minute of that, I was going to shot him. Or at least try."

Baltazar looked over his shoulder at the withdrawing Orsembians. "Borbin's not going to be in an open mood to negotiate long," he said, blinking sweat out of his eyes. "We may only have two . . . three days at most before his patience runs out."

Recha breathed deeper and slower. Her heart slowed. Her momentary rush of excitement faded, leaving her with a chill. "Then you best send word to Hiraldo to hurry."

Chapter 28

17th of Iam, 1019 N.F (e.y.)

The rough surface of the slender steel file bit against Necrem's thumb as he smoothed out the holes in the cheeks of a metal facemask. Steel flakes flicked into the air with every scrape. He studied the hole, making sure to carve out just enough to let air pass through but keep the metal sturdy.

Three more, and then hammer in the cord clasps.

Fortunately, the clasps wouldn't be too hard.

The faint touch of red lingered on a few of the drifting clouds above. However, the first morning rays of the Easterly Sun were still an hour away from peeking over the horizon. The last of his fellow smiths had put out their forges and gone to bed hours ago.

Necrem should have, too.

He sat, leaning over in a chair and against the anvil off to the right of the forge. Besides the scraping of his file and the occasional *pop* from inside the forge, the night outside was deathly quiet. The early morning quiet that beckoned people to sleep.

His eyelids drooped, and his hands trembled. His filing slowed. The red glow reflecting off the metal from the burning coals in the forge began to blur.

His shoulders grew heavy. His head threatened to fall, but he caught it in time, forcing it back up over the objections of his stiff neck.

I need to finish, he stubbornly told his weary body. *So close. So . . . close.*

His entire vision blurred and winked out.

He hovered there. The smell of earthy, heated metal and burning wood in his nostrils. A dull pressure built on his elbows and slowly crept in to run across the length of his chest in straight line. Something cool and . . . metallic pressed against the side of his face and ear.

It was as if he hung off the edge of a steep cliff, a sheer drop, and instead of feeling terror, everything was simply . . . heavy.

"Boss?" a soft voice called, muffled through a fog.

Something touched his shoulder, pushing against him.

A small hand.

"Boss Oso!" The young voice grew louder.

A child's voice.

"*Bayona*!" he exclaimed, springing awake.

He tried to stand but was no longer sitting in his chair. Instead, he was on his knees, his arms hanging over the anvil. A dull pain lingered on his chest from where he'd been laying against the edge. His hands were empty. The steel mask and file laid on the ground on the other side of the anvil.

Instead of his forge, he was back in the war camp. Instead of finding his little miracle trying to wake him, Oberto stared back at him, his arms wrapped around his chest and shivering.

"Sorry, Oberto," Necrem groaned. He ran his hand across his face, rubbing the tiny grains of sleep from the corners of his eyes. He straightened his mask, hissing from the hem being pressed into his cheeks and pulling his scars. "I didn't mean to scare you."

"You . . . you were laying over the anvil," Oberto stammered.

"I just fell asleep," Necrem assured him.

The boy trembled, as if he had awoken the dead.

"I've done it—Ah!"

A loud pop came from the small of his back. The soothing ease rippled through his stiff upper body and threw him into a convulsive stretch. His back arched, his shoulders pulled back, his arms flung open wide, and his biceps tightened to knots, pulling forearms in and balling his fists. As every muscle in his upper body rebelled, his lungs joined, burning inside his chest until he let out a yowling yawn.

He clenched his jaw muscles as hard as he could; however, the yawn had won out and forced his mouth open, stretching his face. Every stitch strained to hold fast. The ends of every scar pulled against their corners, sending fiery stings across and into his cheeks.

His yawn became a yell, breaking his convulsion. He doubled forward and slapped his hands over his face. He pressed down as hard as he could, daring not to rub in fear of pulling or making a rip worse, but simply held and cupped his face in his hands.

Blessedly, after a few moments, he didn't taste iron nor feel his mask become warm and damp. His gasping, heavy breaths hissed against and under his leather mask.

"I'm getting too old to work all night," he groaned. His hands and fingers slid off his face, collapsing into his lap.

He looked out of the corner of his eye and found Oberto now on the far side of the forge, still shivering, his wide eyes watching him intensely.

"Sorry again, Oberto." Necrem weakly chuckled, shaking his head. "Falling asleep hunched over an anvil isn't the brightest thing you can ever do."

Oberto shook his head like a twitchy pavaloro, his shaking and excitement making his head wobble on his shoulders.

Necrem took hold of the anvil with both hands and, taking a few preparing breaths, pulled with as much strength as he could muster while simultaneously lifting with his legs. Tears formed at the corners of his eyes from his aching knees. The joints bit and popped. His legs spasmed as he lifted one foot then the other under him. His knees throbbed from blood pumping into his lower legs and continued as he pushed himself up.

Finally on his feet, he kept hold of the anvil, not trusting his legs to keep him standing yet.

Poor Oberto remained at a distance.

"What are you doing up so early?" Necrem asked, attempting to ease the skittish boy.

Oberto stared blankly up at him. "It's . . . The sun's been up for a few hours now."

Necrem grunted and looked over his shoulder. Outside the forge stall, the Easterly Sun loomed over the morning horizon, warming everything it touched to a sticky humidity in the promise of another hot day. The mumble of men's voices, the deep whooshes of bellows working to start fires, and horses neighing mingled together, the sound of a camp coming alive all around him. He looked back at his forge to the coals, now dark and lifeless.

"Well," he coughed, "that explains that."

He hung his head. His body was taking longer to regain its strength. His file and the metal mask he'd been working on stared up at him, on the ground, from the other side of the anvil, taunting him.

"Boss Oso?" Oberto said meekly.

"Hmm?" Necrem hummed.

"Are you well?" The lad pointed at the anvil. "You were laying over . . ."

Necrem softly laughed, smiling behind his mask. "I'm fine, Oberto. Not the first time I've refused to stop working and fell asleep by a forge. I've scared my daughter a few times, too, for waking me up."

"Oh." The boy frowned, rubbing his hands together. A meek, distant look fell over him. "I didn't . . . I thought you were . . ."

"It's all right." Necrem kept his voice low, his best attempt to be calming. "Say what's on your mind, boy."

Oberto rubbed his hands faster, nervously glancing at him. "I thought . . . I didn't think you had a . . . a family."

"What gave you that idea?" Necrem raised an eyebrow. He pushed off the anvil, his legs' strength able to hold on their own. "Because I look so frightening?"

"*No!*" Oberto's voice cracked in a squeak. His cheeks flushed red. "I thought . . . because you were a conscript, you were . . . you were . . ." He rubbed his neck shyly.

No, not shyly. The boy rubbed his neck where the leather brace used to dig into his skin. His neck's skin color was finally matching the rest of him after days of riding Malcada in the sun, yet the thin line that had once separated the two was still faintly visible.

He thought I was sioneros.

"Do you have a family, Oberto? A home?"

Oberto opened his mouth but said nothing. He became distant again, his eyes wandering across the forge yet looked at nothing, as if searching for something but couldn't remember what.

Necrem walked around the anvil and startled the lad when he knelt in front of him, patting his shoulder and grunting from bending his stiff knees.

"Oberto," he said, "if something happens, if they start fighting today and it goes bad, I want you to go to the horses, pick the fastest looking one, and ride back down Ribera's Way as fast as you can. Don't look back. Don't stay around here to see what happens. You *run*. Run home."

Oberto's eyes glistened, welling with tears. "What . . .?" His chin wobbled. "What if I don't know where it is?"

Necrem wished he could smile for the boy. His mask hid the horror underneath yet gave him little to show comfort, save a furled brow and sad eyes. He settled for squeezing Oberto's shoulder as tightly as he dared.

"Home is where you want to go the most," he replied. "The place you see every time you close your eyes."

Eulalia and Bayona flashed before him, and in that moment, Oberto's breath caught, his eyes widening. The distant cloud that had hung over him was gone. For a brief time, both stared at each other, yet they saw only their distant homes.

Oberto looked away first, glancing back into the corner of the forge. "What about you?"

Necrem turned. A suit of armor hung in the back of the forge, its many parts hanging from a long rack. There were more pieces than most, and all of them— the breastplate, shoulder pauldrons, leg and shin plates, helmet, and especially the gauntlets—were made for a large man. A big man.

"I gave my word," Necrem said. "You look out for yourself. If anything goes bad, you're only going to have yourself to depend on. Understand?" He gave an extra squeeze to drive home the message.

Oberto nodded.

"Go see to them horses." Necrem patted his shoulder then waved him away.

Oberto's gloomy face lit up. The small tears running down his round cheeks forgotten. He took off in a quick burst then skid to a stop.

"I pray you make it home, too . . . Boss Oso," the lad nervously said from over his shoulder, and then off he went again. This time, he didn't look back.

Necrem watched him go, one arm hanging propped over his leg. He turned back and frowned at the armor. "I pray so, too."

***

"I beseech you, La Dama," the deacon courteously pled. "Please accept Si Don Borbin's offer. If you don't, I fear there is nothing that will save thousands of your men's lives."

Recha tapped her fingernail against her large command table. Baltazar sat to her right with the rest of the general staff sitting around them. General Ross, General Priet, and their staff were absent, tending to their individual armies' needs.

She was failing not to look bored. She leaned back against her chair, shoulders slumped, and sat with her legs crossed. Her left foot joined her finger by tapping against one of the table's legs from below. She desperately resisted the urge to plant her free elbow on her chair's arm and rest her face in her hand.

He's too clean.

She frowned through her eyelashes, studying the deacon. She ignored the man's begging grey eyes and bent posture while holding his black staff and lantern. Instead, she took in his cream-colored hat that he held by the wide brim to his chest, his nearly pristine-white dust cloak and cream-colored suit underneath. He sweated like the rest of them. The faint breeze they tried to foster through her command tent by opening two walls failed to materialize. However, the deacon lacked a telling amount of dust and dirt.

"Pardon me, Deacon . . . Gelome, was it?" she asked.

"Yes, La Dama," Deacon Gelome replied happily. "That's correct." He nodded, wobbling his double chin. The average-height man wasn't going to fat. He simply missed the road-weary look she would expect from a deacon. No bags under his eyes, days-old stubble on his face, or gaunt appearance from making do with light meals. He looked too well rested and fed for Recha's tastes.

"Deacon Gelome, how long have you been accompanying Si Don's armies?" she asked.

"Only recently, La Dama," Deacon Gelome said. "My normal outreach surrounds Manosete and the road west of our ancient, shared capital. This is the first time I've been granted the privilege of comforting souls on the campaign trails."

The Santa Madre sent him to counsel Borbin.

His outreach could only reach down the coast of the Desryol Sea, Orsembar's safest corridor, lined with luxurious villas for Borbin to escape from Manosete with his favored barons, if he was favored by both the Santa Madre and Borbin, too.

"Pardon me again, Deacon Gelome," Recha mused, "I have little doubt you've been sent here as Si Don's representative for today"—she glanced at Borbin's latest offer, the parchment folded and sealed with red wax, a *mellcresa* head molded into it—"but how am I to interpret a deacon bringing me this, especially if this is your first time campaigning?"

"Interpret, La Dama?" Deacon Gelome blinked, keeping his unintrusive smile as plain as he could. "Whatever do you mean?"

"A couple of days ago, a ragtag group of calleroses galloped in here, making demands and saying everything short of threats of what they would do to my person should I not accept Si Don's offer." Recha's lips twisted as she recalled that morning. It had taken Baltazar an hour of arguing with her not to order an attack in response. "That evening, a couple of barons came apologizing for their calleroses' actions and repealing the offer their men had delivered. These same barons returned the next morning, with another offer.

"Barons and calleroses sending me messages, I well expected, but a deacon of the church acting as representative of one marc to speak with another, I find *that* . . . peculiar." She wanted to say *alarming*, but that might have conveyed too much. Deacon or not, she had received him as Si Don's representative and, as with her years staring down Valen, she couldn't show any weakness to him. She couldn't let him think she could be cowed by the mere presence of a member of the church.

"It's not peculiar at all, La Dama," Deacon Gelome said assuredly. "Not in the least. Deacons have long offered themselves to be independent arbiters between the marcs in these strife-filled times."

Recha tilted her head. "I thought you said this was your first time on campaign?"

Deacon Gelome's mouth hung open. Tiny droplets of sweat bloomed on his brow. "Yes, La Dama, it is." He swallowed. "But I know from other deacons this is so. Si Don himself confided to me that he only chose to send me here today because of how dire the situation is. He grieves from your mistrust in him. So much so that he wholeheartedly believes you will only listen to an independent voice, such as mine."

Recha stared at him, sorting his platitudes from his nonsense. *Borbin sent you to tell me to surrender to his terms and how many soldiers I get to keep in exchange for his son. You couldn't be less independent, save your clothes not being gaudy orange!*

"What does Si Don offer me today?" she asked, moving on with the useless discussion and picking up the sealed parchment. She sliced apart the wax seal with a table knife then tossed the blade on the table with a clatter. The leaves of paper shifted in her fingers, now free of the wax.

"Hmm," she hummed. "*Four* pages today."

Borbin had sent two pages the day before and one page before that, not including the several slips of notes and tears of parchment from several of his belligerent calleroses. She flipped through the first two pages, consisting mostly of greetings, honorifics, and platitudes. She slid those pages on the table and stopped to read the third page more thoroughly.

Borbin had a practiced hand. His writing was neither blockish nor artistic. He thought out his words without scratching out one or showing any signs he had to write a sentence.

Where is it?

Recha picked at her fingernails. Her left pinky and thumb clicked together as she looked for the faint hint of him warning her to surrender. She could call it a threat, hang her denial on it, and send Deacon Gelome on his way. Instead, Borbin's language read like a concerned parent, worrying about the safety of his son, concerned about the safety of his soldiers, urging her to think of the same.

That could be a threat? She struggled with the idea, though. *A bit of a stretch since any side would urge another to think of their soldiers in a situation like—*

She turned the page and finally came across Borbin's offer for today.

She read it once.

Then twice.

485

Her left hand, holding the third page in the air off to the side, began to shake as she read it thrice to make *sure* she was reading it correctly.

She shot a glance over the page at Deacon Gelome, patiently waiting with a soft smile. He lifted his head upon seeing her look at him, eyebrows raised expectantly. Recha bounced her eyes between him and the offer for a moment, collecting the running implications in her head.

"Deacon Gelome," she said, clearing her throat, "have you read the contents of this offer?" She held up the fourth page.

"I am but a humble messenger, La Dama," Deacon Gelome replied, pressing his hat to his chest. "Si Don Borbin took me into his confidence only to let me relay how sincere his intentions are that this ordeal be brought to a swift and peaceful end. Nothing more, I assure you. I have no idea the nature of his offer, only that it's meant to bring peace. Si Don asked me to deliver it, along with any words of wisdom I may impart, and then return with your reply. Do you have a reply?" Deacon Gelome leaned forward, as if suddenly standing on his tiptoes. "Is Si Don's offer satisfactory? I pray it is so. Hmm?"

Recha forced a smile.

He could be lying.

She fought the temptation to glance into the distant corner of the tent. Harquis sat huddled there, observing everything through his mystic blindness and a stone expression. The Viden priest could sense out the lie, but she chose against asking him.

She slipped the third page behind the fourth to free her hand so she could straighten and run her fingers through her hair over and around her misshapen ear. While looking a little embarrassed, she hoped she looked more flustered than the truth.

"Si Don's offer today is . . . very generous," she replied, ignoring the soft, subtle movements and shuffles in the seats around her from her general staff. "One that I'm afraid I . . . must think on before giving any sort of reply. Forgive me, Deacon, but I really *must* think on this one. When you return to Si Don, please tell him that for me *and* assure him that I will give him my response by this evening."

Deacon Gelome's smile slipped to a concerned, almost wounded frown. His mouth worked, opening and closing, yet nothing came out. "Are you sure, La Dama? Are you certain a more . . . immediate response cannot be given? A hint, perhaps?"

He's either fishing or desperate to bring back a definite reply.

Recha shook her head. "I'm afraid not. Trust me, Deacon; if you knew what this offer was . . . any marquesa would request time to consider it." She gave him a measured smile as she smoothly passed the offer to Baltazar.

Deacon Gelome longingly watched the offer being passed off. He turned his sad expression back on Recha, but she held firm. "Very well, La Dama," he replied with a sigh, "if that's your wish. May I request I remain in your camp until you do come to a decision? I would so happily like to converse with my brethren deacons accompanying your—"

"No." Her curt response was probably sharper than it needed to be; however, there was likely no alternative to lighten it.

"But La Dama!" Deacon Gelome stammered. "I'm a deacon of the Savior!"

"You're also a representative of Si Don Borbin." Recha sat up in her chair, straight back, head high, and hands folded on the table. "I accepted you into my camp to hear your sovereign's terms. Now that I've heard them, you may leave."

"But . . .!" Deacon Gelome's face paled, along with his knuckles from gripping his staff tighter. "I'm a *deacon*!"

"And your ability to serve two masters is impressive." Recha bit her tongue at her own quip, keeping her composure. "Sadly, while one is welcomed here, the other is not. And I can't have someone who openly serves a rival marc wander freely in my camp."

She rose to her feet. The legs of her chair scraped the wooden floor as she pushed it back, cutting of anything Deacon Gelome had to say.

"Escort!" she called.

Two calleroses, armored from boot to helmet, stomped in to flank the deacon.

"Thank you for coming, Deacon Gelome," she said, folding her hands in front of her. "Please tell Si Don Borbin that I am *seriously* considering his offer. And I promise him, I *will* send him my answer before the sun sets."

Deacon Gelome pressed his lips into a thin line, yet in the end, he merely nodded his head. "May the Savior guide you, La Dama Mandas."

"Same to you, Deacon."

The deacon's staff tapped on the floor, and the lantern softly creaked as he was led out. He doffed his hat upon leaving the tent and needed a hand climbing back into his awaiting saddle. Borbin had sent ten calleroses as escort, all of them watched under guard and hadn't been allowed to dismount.

Recha waited until her calleroses were leading them away to push her chair farther back and walked around the table.

"That was nice and short," Narvae said, in typical fashion to be the first to comment.

Bisal snickered. "First Orsembian I've had to watch my manners with."

"About time you realized keeping silent was the best way to be polite," Feli said dryly.

Bisal laughed briefly before the chuckles caught in his throat with a loud grunt.

Recha shook her head. *Papa really did raise my Companions to take after his friends.*

She walked over to a small table and picked up a wooden cup. A servant dashed in before her hand was reaching for the silver pitcher of water, head drooped apologetically as he silently offered to fill her cup. She softly smiled and allowed him to fulfill his duty.

"What's today's offer?" Narvae asked.

Recha peeked over her shoulder, readying a response, but Narvae was looking at Baltazar.

Baltazar stared down at the paper through a pair of spectacles balanced on the bridge of his nose. He looked to his second then raised his head to look back at her.

"You can tell them, Papa," Recha said, taking a sip. "I'm sure you've grasped its meaning." She wrapped her free arm around her and slowly began to pace around the tent.

"Borbin's new terms," Baltazar started to summarize, "are that for the return of his son, he will not require us to surrender and lay down our arms. Instead, he will permit us to retire to Lazorna with seventy-five percent of our forces and arms. He still demands a quarter of our forces be turned over to him as *sioneroses* for transgressing into his marc; however, he offers to allow the La Dama to choose the quarter to be turned over."

"Generous," Feli commented, tapping his fingertips together. "Especially considering the previous demands."

Bisal snorted. "Yes, *very* generous. We hand over Borbin's son and a quarter of our own good men, and then we just expect them to let us march out of here, waving fare-thee-well." He threw up his hand in an overdramatic gesture that only for Bisal could have been considered a wave.

"Bisal's right," Narvae agreed. "Not that I'm saying we should accept Borbin's offer"—he shifted in his chair and carefully avoided looking in Recha's direction—"but if we're *seriously* considering terms, we need some security."

"*Which*," Recha piped up, stopping on the other side of the table where Deacon Gelome had stood, "Borbin actually offered this time." She took another drink, expecting Baltazar to continue. However, everyone in the tent watched her in intense silence. "Well, go ahead, Papa, tell them."

Baltazar frowned but acquiesced. "Borbin is offering a political alliance between Orsembar and Lazorna in the form of marriage between Recha and . . . his nephew, Timotio Borbin."

Nervous coughs spread throughout the tent, and everyone suddenly found anything but Recha to look at. Except Cornelos, standing in the back. A compressed grimace spread across his face, the bridge of his nose trembling, and his grip around the stack of papers he carried squeezed, crinkling the paper.

Bisal, on the other hand, snorted then burst out in roaring laughter, his tall shoulders bouncing. "Ain't that just like a woman?" he barked, slapping the table. "Leave a man waiting even when everyone knows the answer's going to be no!" He slapped the table again.

Recha gave her jovial marshal of scouts a flat stare, with the rest of the tent joining her. It didn't help. The oblivious man enjoyed his joke in ignorance.

"That's not why the La Dama said she'll give her response later!" Baltazar snapped, cutting off Bisal's laugh.

"Eh?" Bisal raised an eyebrow at her. "Are you really considering the offer, La Dama? No offense if you are, but I thought—"

"Never fear, Marshal Bisal," Recha cut in dryly, finding any more of that unbearable. "That part of Borbin's offer doesn't interest me in the least. The meaning behind it, though, *that* is troubling."

"Meaning?" Bisal grunted.

Recha sipped her water. It was going lukewarm, now free of the silver pitcher. "The offer of a political alliance changes everything. For us, in the short term, it looks like we've traded one valuable hostage for another, despite the sacrifice, to withdraw the bulk of our forces back to Lazorna. The long-term effects would be very different.

"If I agreed to the marriage, our neighboring marcs would see it as a change in Lazorna alliances, even if I locked Timotio in a tower and cut off his hands so he could never touch me." There were a few smirks at that comment, which she appreciated. "The other marcs, Quezlo especially, would see us as nothing more than Borbin's ally. A part of Orsembar in everything but name, waiting for something to happen to me so Timotio can bring it into the fold.

"In short, agreeing to the marriage cements Lazorna the eastern buffer Borbin sees it as." She gulped down the rest of the water, the large gulp forcing her to cough into her elbow to clear her throat and make sure it all went down correctly.

"The inverse of what he did with Saran," Feli iterated.

"Precisely," Recha agreed. "We save ourselves now and become subservient to Borbin for the foreseeable future."

"We're still saying no, right?" Bisal asked, turning this way and that to everyone around him.

"Yes, Bisal," Olguer piped up softly beside him, patting him on the shoulder. "She's still going to reject the offer."

"It's only our current position that makes that difficult," Recha clarified. "Under normal circumstances, I could easily refuse the proposal." She had refused several in the past year. "However, considering where we are and what else we'd be refusing to accept, or rather whom we're holding, if I reject this offer, there won't be another.

"It's ridiculous to expect Borbin to alternatively offer Puerlato for his son. He's not going to offer anything I *actually* want in a trade. And he's expressed his intent for this proposal in nature of an alliance. I reject it, we show our intent."

"Borbin will know battle is a certainty," Baltazar said plainly. "Our delay will be over."

And Hiraldo's still not *here!*

"That's why I'm . . . being a woman, as you eloquently put, Marshal Bisal."

For his part, Bisal dipped his head and apologetically shrugged, but Recha moved on.

"The stall may not work long and, at most, we'll be fighting tomorrow. Unless"—she turned to Harquis—"Deacon Gelome was lying about knowing Borbin's offer."

The cultist lifted his head. His milky eyes stared at nothing yet incapsulated her entirely. "I did not see the blue flames," he coldly said. "Whether he had prior knowledge or not, the deacon's intentions were genuine, if not misguided."

You're supposed to tell if he was lying, not state your belief that his intentions were made in good faith. You claim to serve a spirit of truth, but you can't tell if someone's simply lying or not by just hearing them?

She shook her head to put that frustrating conundrum away for another time.

"Cornelos!" She spun around, setting her empty cup on the table. "Any update on the First Army's arrival?" They had awoken to the ecstatic surprise of a group of Hiraldo's forward scouts riding into camp before dawn. That was three *hours* ago!

Cornelos's expression had soften over the past few minutes. His papers, though, were badly wrinkled. Upon her asking, he instantly went to shuffling them, searching for their report.

"Last reported," he read, "they estimated the First Army's vanguard to be at least an hour's march away." He lifted his head, frowning. "That was three hours ago."

Dammit! Nothing new!

She folded her arms around her, restraining herself from touching her ear.

"If we attack like we planned, how far can the Second and Third Army go alone?" she asked Baltazar.

Baltazar tossed the offer on the table, frowning deeply. "The battle lines will be strained. Each company will have less time to recover once pulled off the line.

Regardless, we must strike first for any chance of victory. The less men we have, the sooner our initial strike may stall. The longer we can postpone the battle becoming one of attrition, the better, and we'd have better chances of postponing it with all three armies on the field."

"And we'll be able to watch that north trek better," Bisal added.

"How far back does it run?" Narvae asked.

"Miles." Bisal folded his arms and leaned back in his chair. "I had the boys run down as far as they could, but they still weren't able to find where it ends. A couple of them came in last night saying they thought they saw movement in it but had to fall back and report before they could confirm exactly what they saw and how many."

"Could that passage reach behind Borbin's line?" Baltazar asked.

"I'd wager it does," Bisal replied.

"We need to plug that passage," Narvae urged. "Tear some wagons apart to make stakes, plant them in the passage, and set a company of pikemen behind them to bottle up anything that may try to get through it."

"Might have to." Baltazar drummed on the table with a thoughtful expression. "The trouble is, without the First Army, that'll mean we'll have one less company to rotate on the line."

"*Actually*"—Bisal sat up excitedly—"your Capitán Viezo gave me another suggestion about that trek. He and one my scouts, my new map maker, came up to me yesterday morning." He started fishing through his pockets, dragging them out until pulling out a wad of yellow paper. "They have a farfetched idea, but"—he unrolled the papers the best he could to slide over to Baltazar—"it would free up the pikemen."

Sevesco's thinking up battle plans now?

Recha hurried around the table. She caught a glimpse of etchings before Baltazar turned over the thin sheets of paper, over to pin scratches.

"Instead," Baltazar read, squinting at the tiny writing, "he's asking for spare musketeers and anyone who can use the Third Army's old crossbows they turned in."

Bisal shrugged. "It frees up pikemen. And gives the calleroses in reserve something to look forward to."

Baltazar hummed in thought.

Recha creeped up behind him to peek over his shoulders, but the writing was too small and, without the illustration, she couldn't make out what they meant.

"What . . .?" she cautiously asked. "What's Sevesco's—"

A piercing bugle call cut through the air.

Recha sprang her head up and peered out through the open tent wall to the perimeter line. The Bravados was still going on. She could faintly make out some lone Orsembian calleros trotting his horse back and forth in the center of the open space between the two armies. He had a small entourage with him, men under his direct command or a second, calling challenges and curses at her men, standing stone-faced on the line.

That didn't come from—

She spun around.

A body of riders were riding around the tall hill in the back of the plain to turn down the center of her camp. Her banner went before them, along with the army's symbol "*1*." The tall figure riding at the head of the column stuck out, as well.

"Hiraldo!" she exclaimed, rushing out the back of the command tent. She left her parasol behind, but she beamed like the Eastern Sun when she watched a column of infantry following behind Hiraldo's calleros vanguard, drums beating to their locked steps.

He didn't leave his army to ride ahead. Her shoulders fell up and down as her relief matched her excitement. *The First Army's here. We're all here!*

The rest of her command staff formed around her to watch as men of the other armies came out to raise their helmets and hats in cheer as Hiraldo led his vanguard down the center of the camp. He even started waving at them.

"There's a battle to start," Narvae grumbled behind her, likely to Baltazar. "We need to do more than parade."

"Don't spoil this, Marshal Narvae," Recha warned from over her shoulder.

A stifled grunt followed.

Hiraldo did take his time riding up to them. He reined in his horse before her, fist raised so his vanguard could muster to a halt behind him. Moments later, shouts from company officers ordering the column to halt roared up and down the line and the drums beat to a resounding stop.

"Welcome to the battlefield, General Galvez," Recha greeted. "You've kept me waiting long enough."

"Apologies I couldn't get here sooner, La Dama," Hiraldo replied, smiling just as wide as she was. "I would have been here sooner, but with all due respect, Ribera's Way is a tasking trek for an army to move fast on."

"Well, you're here now. I pray the entire First Army is at your back."

"All the way." He stretched his arm back behind him. "They're squeezing their way through the best they can. It's fair to say, they're all ready to be out of that dried of riverbed."

"Even with a battle at the end of it?" Recha arched her eyebrow, teasing him more than anything.

Hiraldo sat up taller in his saddle and placed his fist on his hip. "Your First Army is always ready for the battle. Just point us where we need to be, and we shall go."

Recha grinned. "Glad to have you back with us, General."

"Glad to have made it, La Dama. I was afraid we'd miss the initial assault, so I told the men they'd be paid double if we got here in time."

A cold sweat broke out on Recha's brow. "Hiraldo, I swear, you're going to bankrupt me—"

She drew herself up, folding her hands behind her back as she took deep breaths and turned to Baltazar. "Field Marshal, I leave their deployment to you. I must prepare my response to Borbin."

Baltazar nodded, and Recha left them, waving Cornelos to follow her as drums started up behind her.

"Go to Sir Oso," she instructed him as they reentered the command tent. "Tell him that it's time, and make sure his escort is prepared for him."

"Anything else?" Cornelos asked.

Recha rubbed her chin and spotted Harquis, still loitering in the corner of the tent. "Just make sure Sir Oso is still willing to do that task I asked him about."

"Yes, La Dama." His boots thumped against the floorboards as he rushed out.

That left her alone with the Viden. The servants were watching the First Army march in, along with the rest of the command staff. Harquis, though, gazed in her direction, silent and knowing as death.

Recha slowly made her way around the table, seeing if her soft footsteps would let her get close without him noticing. Instead, Harquis's milky stare followed her every move. She stopped before him, folding her arms to keep her stomach calm. The Viden tilted his head up at her with a look akin to longing, for a blind man.

"Are you ready to deliver my response to Borbin?" she asked.

"Time always comes for all betrayals to be answered for," Harquis replied, unfolding his arms and stiffly rising to his feet. His white, void pupils took everything in. "Your word is all that's required."

A rumbling rolled in Recha's stomach. She pressed her arms against her belly to keep it settled. One last queasy question in her plans. Yet, it was far too late for questions. She had a battle to win.

"Vengeance comes today," she replied.

Chapter 29

Every muscle in Necrem's upper body tensed as the breastplate slid over his shoulders. His violet shirt, damp with sweat, clung to his body. Fastening the belt around his waist glued the formed metal plates against his chest and back from the wet cloth.

I didn't fight in my last breastplate. He flexed his arms, making sure he had full range of movement and that the two plates didn't pinch or dig into his sides. There was no time to fix them if they had.

A low grumbling piqued his interest. Radon was perusing the rack of armor and picked out one of the pauldrons.

Necrem could tell immediately it was the left set. After all, he had forged them.

He raised his left arm, sticking it out from where he sat on his stool so Radon could fit it over his shoulder and bicep.

He's still upset.

Radon's reddened scowl gave him the appearance of a dried grape. His scraggily, days-old beard added to the grimace. Tiny hairs stook out in all directions over his face from neither of them having time to shave with the demanding work. His face had taken on that expression the moment after the commandant had told him the marquesa said it was time.

Necrem winced as Radon buckled the pauldron's leather strap under his arm. He bucked the other strap holding the three plates across his bicep himself. That plate on, Radon returned to the rack, the muttering starting up soon after.

"You shouldn't be mumbling to yourself," Necrem said. "Everyone will think you're going senile."

Radon hawked spit off to the side and hefted the other pauldron off the rack. "You joking at a time like this isn't good either."

Necrem held out his right arm for the old smith as he stormed back and slammed it down on his shoulder.

"You told me," Radon grumbled, this time loud enough for Necrem to catch, "and everyone else with ears, that you *weren't* a soldier."

"I'm not," Necrem grunted from how tight Radon was securing the buckles.

"Then *why* are you doing this?" Radon dashed in front of him and clapped his hands down on the pauldrons. The metal sang out, but the minor impact was blunted. "If you're not a soldier, then you have no business going out there in front of *calleroses*! You may be big, and you may scare everyone that looks at you, but that won't do you any good in a Bravados. You know *that*! Those bastards out there will be riding around on their horses, looking down at you as some idiot bumpkin they get to boast about killing. And they'll do it, too, Oso—you know they will! The Bravados is their sport."

Necrem's ears twitched from quiet metal ticks. Radon clutched the top plates of his pauldrons, his shaking grip failing to reach through the padding while the metal clicked together.

The soft scrubbing of a brush against leather stopped. Necrem glanced down at Oberto knelt beside him, stiffly shaking as he tried to remain as still as possible. He held the shoe brush over the toe of Necrem's right boot with his ear slightly raised.

A loud knock came from the front post holding up the stall.

"We're closed!" Radon growled.

Hezet pulled the canvas flap back and stepped inside. The veteran paused at the entrance, swallowing at the grizzled smith snarling at him. He wore Lazornian armor and uniform now, carrying his helmet under his arm with a round shield strapped to his back and sword on his hip. His spirit brightened when he spotted Necrem.

"Well, smith"—he laughed—"finally decided to enlist right at the end, huh?" He put his hands on hips, smiling as if an old friend had come for a visit.

"It's nothing like that," Necrem replied.

Hezet raised an eyebrow. "Then why the armor? Good armor, too."

"What business is it of yours?" Radon demanded, pointing back the way Hezet had come. "This forge is closed and likely won't reopen. Go somewhere—"

"Radon!" Necrem snapped. "This is Hezet. We were conscripted together before Compuert Junction."

"Guess you were one of the lucky ones." Radon snorted, dropping his arm and looking Hezet up and down. "Got taken in by the Lazornian marquesa, too, did ya?"

Hezet shrugged. "Her officers did make recruiting sound better than being taken as a laboring prisoner of war. The pay's better, too."

"That makes sense." Radon softened at the talk of money and wandered back to the armor rack, mumbling to himself again.

Hezet looked between him and Necrem, perplexed at what to do next.

"Did they make you an officer?" Necrem asked, attempting to change the subject.

"Hmm?" Hezet raised his head up, blinking. "They did, amazingly. Talk started about making me a sergeant after I showed a few I had some knowledge with a blade as well as a pike. Even sparred with some to prove I can hold my own. These Lazornians do have some peculiarly high standards for common footman."

"And yet, you seem to have met them."

Necrem meant it as a compliment. The Lazornians had a higher standard for the armor the marquesa wanted fitted on those former *sioneroses*. Despite the limited time and resources, the officers weren't shy of looking over the finished work and throwing plate back, demanding it be redone.

"I did," Hezet said proudly. He dug into his pocket and pulled out a folded piece of paper. "However, upon receive my rank, my new capitán pulled me out line with transfer orders to report to a newly formed company to escort someone called"—he unfolded the paper and squinted down at the writing—"Steel Fist for further orders." The veteran raised his eyebrows over the scrap of paper, back at Necrem. "I thought you hated being called that."

Necrem squeezed and released his knees, his shoulders hunched, rubbing the pauldrons against the breastplate.

Oberto began brushing his boots again. It was something the commandant had suggested, and the boy had become strangely set on trying to make the worn leather shine.

"I think that's as good as they're going to get, Oberto," he said. "Fetch the shin plates."

Oberto hastily nodded. He tossed the brush aside in his scramble for the armor rack, getting a chuckle out of Hezet.

"I've been asked to challenge the Bravados," Necrem said blankly.

Hezet smirked. "Right."

Necrem sat straight and kept his gaze from wavering.

Hezet blinked. His smirk turned from confused frown to stunned, mouth-gaping shock. "What? That's *impossible*!"

"That's the most popular opinion of the day," Radon chided, bring over Necrem's elbow plates while Oberto brought the shin plates. Necrem pushed off his knees to stand up and make it easier for them fit the arm on him.

"It was a request," he explained. "From the marquesa."

"The Lazornian marquesa *herself* asked you to go into the Bravados?" Hezet said, still gawking at him.

"Yes." Necrem bent his elbows, one after the other, once Radon had strapped on the plates. He needed to move his arms if he was to do what the marquesa had asked of him.

Oberto strapped on the shin plates over his bootlegs, tugging them as tight as he could make them.

"Is she wanting you to challenge Borbin's calleroses?" Hezet shook his head. "Recruiting you is one thing, but to throw you against calleroses . . . that's *insane!*"

"That's what I've been telling him!" Radon piped up, finished with the other elbow plate. He pointed at Hezet. "I knew I liked you from the moment you walked in here. Good luck talking sense into this one." He thumbed up at Necrem. "Head's made of adamant, it is."

I'm not that stubborn. Necrem grunted, watching Radon go to the rack and pick up the knee plates.

"The way I understand it," he explained, "the marquesa doesn't want me to fight."

"Then, with all due respect, she doesn't know what a Bravados is," Hezet said dryly with a skeptical look. "Campaigns have been decided on Bravados' victories alone."

"She knows that."

Necrem knew it, too, having witness several years ago. The Bravados always felt archaic. Calleroses challenging each other in front of their respective armies, dueling each other as their men shouted insults, as if they were fighting in a tavern. All the while, their marquéses were talking behind their backs to determine whose men would be sold off.

"But not all Bravados end up in a fight," he added.

Both Radon and Oberto paused in buckling his knee plates.

Hezet studied him. He looked at his armor, more akin to the heavier plate of calleroses. He turned to the remaining plates still hanging on the rack and stared.

Necrem followed it to the pair of darkened steel gauntlets hanging from leather cords off the rack. When his knee plates were fastened, he walked past the rack to a side table. He didn't wear all the armor pieces yet, and they were heavier than his former plate and better made. On the table sat a metal canister of his face salve and the steel mask he had finished that morning, now with a cloth lining the inside and leather cords dangling from the corners.

"You're not going to answer a calleros's challenge," Hezet said. "*You're going to make your own challenge!*"

"Welcome to the madness," Radon said.

"Oso, you can't *do* that!" Hezet exclaimed.

"Do you remember that night at the junction, Hezet?" Necrem asked, reaching behind his head to undo the knot holding his leather mask. "All that talk, you and the other old soldiers telling the young boys what was going to happen, how the Bravados worked?"

Hezet snorted behind him. "That feels . . . long ago now."

"It does," Necrem agreed, laying down his leather on the table and letting his face breathe. Each of his hissing breaths drew air in from all three sides of his face. His scars were dry and crusty, in need of a heavy layer of salve before he put the steel mask on. Flabs of skin hung down, and drool pooled around the gaps in his cheeks.

"Remember how you told it?" He picked up the metal canister, popping open the canister's lid with his palm. "In a Bravados, the calleros making the challenge makes the rules, while his men cuss." He frowned into the can, finding only enough salve for this coat. He could make out the bottom of the can beneath the thin layer of fatty, yellow paste.

Too late to ask Doctor Marron for more.

He dipped his fingers into the salve, the greasy gob squeezing between his fingers as he scooped out a hefty portion.

"How do you plan on making your challenge?" Hezet asked. "Or is the marquesa doing that for you?"

"I wanted to ask you"—Necrem smoothed out the salve across the right side of his face, working the sticky mess into every crevice of scarred flesh and holding in the urge to spit from the invading, salty taste—"if you could do the challenging for me."

"*Me?*" Hezet's voice cracked, followed by a thud from dropping his helmet.

Necrem smiled, despite his taut skin.

A dry, retching gargle came from his left. He caught himself from turning his head, yet watched Oberto slink away, hand over his mouth, face paling.

Necrem turned his face away, gathering more salve to lather that side. "Not a pretty sight, is it, lad?"

"That's what you get for not minding your own business," Radon whispered a hiss, presumably at Oberto.

"I just . . ." Oberto softly whined. "I didn't know . . ."

"I'll need to know why, Oso," Hezet said. "I can see why the marquesa would want you, a man who did what you did at the Compuert Junction. Stories like that would be a boon to any company's morale. But . . . you're a smith." He cleared his throat and snickered. "I'm an old soldier that had nowhere to go, no family to get back to, and needed the deberes. But you . . . you got a family, Oso. If you're ever going to see them again, you should just stay with the other smiths until this is over. One way or the other."

Necrem's fingers fell still against his face. The salve seeped into his scars, bringing moisture back around the stitches. In a shock to all of them, he turned around and displayed his face, every scar, pulled stitch, and gaping hole, to them.

Hezet winced and, with each passing second, withered under the flickering impulse to look away. Radon's sour scowl evaporated, replaced with wide-eyed paleness as he instantly turned away.

"Borbin did *this* to me," Necrem hissed. His chest swelled against his breastplate, heart hammering against bone and steel alike to say that aloud after all these years. "I've lived with . . . *this*, and I . . . *refused* to say anything about it. All I ever wanted was to . . . just live with my family." His chin wobbled. The stiches on his face, though lubricated, stretched taut, stinging him as his jaw clenched. "But *Borbin* and his calleroses ruined our lives." He sharply swiveled his head to Radon, making the old man jump. "I forge scrap, horseshoes, nails, and knives for people who have nothing. My little miracle, Bayona, though she smiles all the time, she has gone to bed hungry once too often.

"My wife . . ." He turned, shaking from head to foot and hands balled into fists, to Hezet, "Eulalia . . . She can't stand the *sight* of me!" His armor rattled from his body's tremors. Angry tears escaped and rolled down his face, joining the salty salve in his scars. "I haven't held my wife in ten years! How's a man supposed to *live* like that?"

Hezet swallowed, bowing his head. Radon couldn't face him, and Oberto hid behind the old man's legs.

"I want to go home, but there's no safe way home." Necrem shook his head. "And that Lazornian marquesa, she plans to fight to the end. No matter what, there's going to be a fight. And she was also right. I hate calleroses!

"It wasn't Lazornians I fought that night at the junction, Hezet. No. I never saw one of their faces. I saw the calleroses who laid their hands on my Eulalia. I saw them that laughed and called her a whore! I saw Borbin *laughing*!"

He stood straight and reached around, picking up the metal mask. He pressed it against his face, the inside cloth clinging to the salve while the steel fell below his chin so he could move his jaw and speak if he needed. He tied the cord back behind his head with a tight yank.

"It's not enough just to go home," he said. "Go back and keep my head down and accept this is all there is."

He moved over to the rack and picked out the right gauntlet. He turned the heavy-plated glove down and slid his forearm into it. His fingers clicked the small, overlapping plates together as they filled them. One sharp tug after the other fastened the greave's buckles to his forearm. The gauntlet's weight was that of a hammer, coating his entire hand and forearm.

He raised his hand, forming it into a fist. Metal plates scraped against each other, grinding and groaning under the tightening pressure until he could close it no further.

"The Bravados is supposed to test the mettle of each side, right?" he said lowly, his vision briefly narrowed and reddened around his raised fist. "I'm going to make them look at what they did. And if any of those calleroses answer me . . ."

He raised his head. Radon was as white as a canvas, having backed away several steps and shielding Oberto behind him. Hezet, however, stood taller, hand on his hilt and eyes beaming as if enthralled.

"Today, I will be Steel Fist."

His last words hung in the air. Outside, marching footsteps, hurried voices, distant drums, and neighing horses clamored together, only to hush after leaking into the covered stall.

Radon hung back, trembling. Hezet's breathing grew louder. His breastplate stuck out from his rising and falling shoulders. His beaming eyes burned with fire, and his lips twitched as if holding back a scream.

In an instant, his head snapped around to Radon, causing the old smith, and Oberto, to jump.

"You heard him!" the veteran barked. "Get the rest of his armor on! We have a Bravados to interrupt, and probably a battle to start. Move!"

His demanding, officer's voice sent Radon and Oberto scrambling. As they hastily fitted Necrem with his remaining plate, Hezet picked up his helmet from the dirt.

"Master Sergeant Hezet, reporting!" he exclaimed, tying the helmet's cheek guard strings underneath his chin. He snapped to attention, and a bright grin spread across his face. "Shall we interrupt the Bravados, Steel Fist?"

Necrem held his left forearm out for Radon to finish buckling the other gauntlet. He flexed and curled the fingers, testing them out, as well as the right again. Satisfied, he gave Hezet a hard look from over the rim of his metal mask, air hissing through the holes.

"Yes."

~~~

Necrem struggled to keep up with the drumbeats through the long, dried stems of grass covering the field. He was getting used to the extra weight of the shin plates and had to make a conscience effort to lift his foot higher to step over or through the grass threatening to trip him with every step.

The last thing I need is to trip and fall.

"Light your matches and fall in!" an officer shouted.

The camp was in upheaval. Tents were coming down and being moved to make way for another army to march in. While they did, fresh companies formed up along the old outskirts, preparing to relieve those guarding the battle lines.

Musketeers formed single file lines, lighting their matches one after the other from a sergeant holding a lantern.

"Come on!" another officer yelled, waving his arm to guide them into line behind two rows of pikemen. "Move!"

"Load!"

To Necrem's left, another company's musketeers hastily rammed long rods down the barrels of their guns.

"Keep your powder pins closed unless ordered to open them," their officer instructed. "And keep your matches burning."

"Our company doesn't have those new muskets," Hezet commented beside him. "Well armed, but after drilling with them for a day, I can tell they're a newly formed company."

Necrem turned his head, but his pauldron and the rim of his helmet, joined with the uneven ground, made it impossible to look over his shoulder. "They're former *sioneroses*. The marquesa commissioned every smith in the camp to improve their armor. I think they've been drilling them ever since we got here, too."

In-between forging his own armor, Necrem and Radon had forged what they could for the *sioneroses*. Within the second day of the stalemate, the men they got had been happy to be measured, some mentioning it was better than being marched and carrying pikes all day.

Behind them marched three such companies. Most of their armor gleamed from polish, the army's smiths having used up most of their stores to make it happen. Most lacked the uniforms of the other soldiers, though some had tried to dye their jackets or shirts purple with various results. All of them wore leather neck braces around their biceps like badges. To make them stand out even more, their company banners were black.

"Here's hoping their drilling was enough," Hezet whispered.

Other companies accompanied them marching out on the field. Here and there, square blocks of men made their way down, moving casually at their own pace, each on their way to relieve their designated counterpart on the line. A couple had already been relieved. The relieving company would wait patiently as the company on the line beat a disciplined withdrawal out of line until there was enough space for their counterpart to march in and replace them.

After the exchange, the newly arrived company would stand at rest, pike butts resting on the ground and men glaring at their counterpart yards away from them. The old company beat a steady march back to camp, keeping out of the way of other fresh companies.

"Rotating out in battle won't be as easy as that," Hezet mused. "Companies will have to merge with one another. The new boys rushing between the holding company's lines and ranks to take their place while the tired men hold out the best they can."

"Sounds complicated," Necrem said.

"It requires a great deal of drilling. That's why most try to avoid the hard battles."

Beating hooves over the drum taps announced the calleroses before they rode up behind them.

"Column, halt!" one of them yelled.

Necrem stomped his feet into the ground with the rest. Being in armor brought out some of the training that had been drilled into him. Unfortunately.

Calleroses galloped around both sides of the column. As they formed their own column in front of him, a small group rounded in front of him, one bearing a large banner of Lazorna.

"Sir Oso!"

Necrem raised his head.

General Galvez rode up to him with his guard close behind. He held his hand in the air, which Necrem assumed was a greeting, and a wide smile shined from between his helmet's cheek guards.

Necrem thought of moving aside for a second before the general turned and reined his silver stud to a halt a foot or two before running into him.

"Attention!" Hezet roared. His order was echoed by officers down the line, followed by bootheels stomping together and pike shafts slapping against shoulders and breastplates.

Necrem followed suit by standing straight and keeping his head up.

General Galvez looked him up and down then let out a whistle. "Sir Oso," he said, "if ever a man was a sight on the battlefield, it is *you*! If I wasn't horsed and saw you coming at me, I'd"—he shook his head and glanced at his guard behind him—"curse my sword as useless and pray to the Savior I'm faster than the next man."

The calleroses behind General Galvez laughed.

Necrem spied Hezet faintly smirking out of the corner of his eye. As for himself, he remained silent.

General Galvez let the laughter die and sighed down at him. "Still stoic, I see." His smile faded, and he straightened in his saddle. "Do you understand the battle plan for today?"

Necrem matched the general's stare. "With respect, General, I'm not going into battle. Marquesa Mandas offered this to me, and I gave her my word I'd do it."

The other calleroses frowned and mumbled to each other. General Galvez gave away nothing.

"That's a strange way of looking at it," the general said, "while you're also walking out onto a battlefield. And believe me, Sir Oso, a Bravados is the *center* of a battlefield."

Necrem looked out past the general and over the field. Two Orsembian calleroses were galloping up and down an empty corridor between the two armies' battle lines, jeering and insulting the Lazornians as they rotated companies off. A smaller square of men stood out in front of the Orsembian line, the calleroses' footman carrying their patron's personal flag.

Necrem turned back to the general, gauntlets balling and tightening at his side. "As I said, I'm only keeping my word."

General Galvez nodded. "I've been ordered to escort you onto the field before taking command of the left. Neither I, nor any other calleros, have been given permission to interfere with the Bravados. You'll be on your own if you go through with this and if your challenge is met. However, once it is over, you are to pull back behind the battle line and stay there until ordered. Is that clear?"

"Yes, General."

"Very good." General Galvez spun his horse around then abruptly pulled it to a halt. "And if any of them are crazy enough to fight you," he shouted over his shoulder, "*crush* them, Steel Fist!"

The calleroses fell in behind their general, passing hard glances as they rode by. He might march with them now, but the stares proved they remembered he got the name from crushing Lazornians.

Once the horses were moving, Necrem followed.

"Column, forward!" officers ordered behind him.

Drums started up again and marching feet resumed. The beating grew louder the farther Necrem went into the plain. Squares of companies marching toward the battle line. Squares of companies marching away. Each in step with their own drummers tapping out the same beat.

It was almost . . . *maddening.*

Not one man's step was his own. Rather, they all walked as if reduced to blocks and shapes, crawling along the ground. Even the horses, plodding along in files of three, were included.

Necrem's own heels found the drums' call irresistible, falling in with the others, as if he were being drawn to the Bravados instead of choosing to go.

He rolled his shoulders, shifting his pauldrons, and looked about, desperate to satisfy his mind's demand to take hold of his situation, to not get swallowed in.

"Have you ever been a part of a Bravados before, Hezet?" Necrem asked. A little late, but any respite from the drums around him would do. "Any calleros ever pick you for an entourage?"

Hezet snickered. "I've cussed up a storm a time or two from the lines."

"Will you be all right speaking for me?" Again, it was too late to ask, but Necrem felt he should.

"I'm getting a chance to cuss right at a calleros's face or two." Hezet barked a laugh. "Who wouldn't jump at a doing something so crazy? What about you? What are you going to do with *that*?" He thumbed behind them.

Trailing between them and former *sioneroses* were two three soldiers carrying an armor rack, a breastplate and helmet, and a shield.

"The marquesa asked if I could repeat what I did at the junction," Necrem explained. "So, I will."

Hezet hummed.

"What does that mean?" Necrem gave him a sideways glance.

"Just coming up with ideas before we stroll out there."

Closer to the battle lines, the drumming became less intense with more and more companies rotating out, the relieved ones getting farther away and the replacements simply taking up their place.

General Galvez and his calleroses peeled off, revealing the line and waiting company capitán at the rear of his company. The officer stood at attention for the passing general, yet frowned concerningly as Necrem approached.

"Column, halt!" officers yelled behind him, and Necrem stopped with him.

The waiting capitán bounced his eyes between Necrem and Hezet expectingly.

Before he could say anything, a young officer, the company's true capitán, rushed around them from the column and snapped a hasty salute.

"Company three-three-seven of the Third Army, reporting to take its place on the battle line!" the young capitán shouted. "You are relieved, sir!"

The waiting capitán gave Necrem and Hezet another wary look then gave his fellow officer a sharp nod. "We stand relieved," he said. "Drummer! Beat rotation!"

Necrem wanted desperately to cover his ears from the infuriating taps. The image of putting his fist through the top of the drum also flashed through his mind. He would have walked into from behind if Hezet hadn't jerked his elbow to alert him.

The exchange happened just as smoothly as rest, the old company pulling back and letting the first *sioneros* company to step into its place. Yet, the other two *sioneros* companies didn't replace the companies to either side of the old one. Instead, they remained in squares behind the first on the line.

What are they here for?

Galloping hoofbeats killed Necrem's curiosity. He spun to see an Orsembian *calleros* barreling toward the new company, crouching in the saddle, head down, and lance leveled in a charge.

"Pikes down!" the company capitán yelled, dashing into the middle of the ranks.

The first three rows of long poles fell in waves. The front rank planted the ends of their pikes in the dirt and held them at an angle. The second rank held their pikes out straight, and the third held theirs high over the heads of those in front of them. The rest behind them braced the backs of their comrades, their pikes' wooden shafts knocking together.

"Pikes down!" The order echoed down the line as the Orsembian charged on.

The *calleros* was within ten feet before he reined in his horse. The animal screamed, its eyes wide and white from its head being jerked back. Its hooves dug into the dry ground, flinging clouds of dirt and dust into the pikemen's faces. The *calleros* threw his head back and laughed, ignoring his horse prancing and kicking under him.

"You sniveling black-flaggers finally grew a backbone?" he yelled. "Or did they send the rest of them to stand behind you so you couldn't run away this time?" He stuck his lance out and trotted his horse down their line. His lance's head pinged and tinged off their pikes as he galloped by. One pikeman lunged. However, the *calleros* knocked him away with his lance as he passed, guiding his horse away before others could try the same.

And still, he laughed. Always laughing.

"Look at that!" he yelled, prancing his horse back out into the field with his lance raised in the air. "They *did* grow backbones and guile!"

Calleroses from across the space between the armies laughed. There were five other calleroses on horseback, nudging each other and pointing at the former *sioneroses*. Each's armor was a little different in color and shape, signs they'd had their suits forged specifically for themselves. Behind them were personal retainers standing in small, separate squares. The calleroses joined their fellow in laughing and pointing at the pikemen, with their retainers adding in.

"They finally think themselves solders, do they?" one yelled with his gauntlet cupping his mouth.

"They certainly *weren't* soldiers a few days ago!" another yelled. "Running like squealing pigs."

"And ending up as stuck pigs!"

They shared a boisterous laugh, and Necrem glowered over his mask. *Laughing.*

His fists balled until the plates in his gauntlets squealed in protest and their edges dug into his fingers through the gloves' thick fabric. The laughter buzzed in his ears, drowning everything out as those from ten years ago answered them in his mind. *Always laughing.*

Someone grabbed him by the elbow. He jerked it away, forcing Hezet to jump back, warily looking up at him.

"This is your last chance," the veteran warned. "If you walk out there, you'll have to go through with it. Otherwise . . ." He cautiously looked over his left shoulder to watch General Galvez and his calleroses trotting toward that side of the field.

"I'm fine," Necrem replied lowly. His breath hissed through the mask's steel holes.

Hezet swallowed then took a few deep breaths. "Well then"—he straightened his armor, running his hands along his belt to loop his thumbs under—"I best go smart off before they all run away. I am rusty at this. I might make a fool of myself."

"Be honest to them," Necrem advised. "A common man giving them an honest opinion is something they can never stomach."

"You sure *you* don't want to tell them off?" Hezet smirked. However, it drained away when Necrem looked at him and shook his head.

He cleared his throat, set his shoulders, then made for the gap between the companies on the line. Necrem followed a few paces behind with the men carrying the extra suit of armor at his back.

"Stand easy, men," the different officers of each company urged.

The men, glaring across the field, took easy breaths as they stepped apart and raised their pikes to rest them on the ground.

Necrem caught confused and wondering looks as he walked between them.

"Pardon, calleros!" Hezet shouted firmly and directly, the tone of a soldier to a superior with his shoulders back and head high. He snapped to attention in front of the former *sioneros* company. "Pardon, but we men of foot would have words with you!"

"What's he doing?" someone whispered to Necrem's left.

"We were ordered not to talk back," another whispered. "Weren't we, Sergeant?"

More whispers spread, and officers in the ranks hushed the men. It was too late, anyway, as the Orsembian calleros turned his horse around.

"What's this?" the calleros spat back. "No Lazornian calleros has the courage to face us, but they send a footman to talk for them?"

"Apologies if you are disappointed, Cal," Hezet shouted back. "The calleroses and officers of Lazorna have more important duties. But speaking for the footmen, if you're going to make charges like that, you would kindly give us some relief!"

"Relief?" The calleros couched his lance in the crook of his elbow with a bored sneer visible under his helmet.

"Yes, Cal! If you would kindly plant yourself on the end of our pikes, it would save us from having to listen to you, Cal! Such a thing would be a relief more Savior blessed than rain to all of us right now!"

Sporadic, surpassed snickers sprinkled through the ranks.

Then a chuckle.

Then a bursting hiss.

In a company over, someone slammed his pike butt into the dirt. More joined in the beating, and those carrying shield slapped their fists against them. Men shouted throughout the ranks in agreement, waving their pikes or muskets.

"You forget your place, footman!" the calleros spat, thrusting his lance at Hezet. "This is the Bravados. Unless your calleros have finally come to answer our challenges with one of their own, run back to your sniveling marquesa before I waste my time running you down for speaking so impertinently to your betters!"

"Pardon, Cal, but I was unaware there were any who could call themselves my betters on the field. Permit me to confer with my comrades."

Hezet sharply spun on his heels, never breaking his straight posture. "Gentlemen!" he shouted. "Company three-three-seven of pike! Do any of you see anyone one the field that are our betters?"

"*No!*" men yelled, in the company and up and down the line, in response, brandishing their weapons at the Orsembians across the gap. A floodgate of pent-up frustration had been opened, snarls, spitting, and rude gestures abound from the men.

Necrem snorted at watching Hezet rile everyone up. *And he said he was rusty.*

Hezet spun back around, snapping his heels together and faced up at the calleros now glaring at him. "To the calleroses of Orsembar!" he shouted. "We, footmen of the Lazornian Third Army, bring you a challenge. Sir Necrem Oso!"

He beat his fist up into the air, shouting and chanting in fury, "Steel Fist! Steel Fist! Steel Fist!"

The men in the ranks shared looks at one another.

"What's he doing?" one whispered to Necrem's left

"Who is he shouting for?" another asked.

"Wait! The junction! Men in the First Army talked about a man . . ."

Necrem slipped out from between the companies.

Hezet saw him, his face red from hollering. The veteran kept yelling, pumping his fist in the air at the men behind them and the calleroses across the gap.

The men in the front ranks watched Necrem in silence, their heads craned upward and turned with his every step.

"Steel Fist!" a soldier yelled to the company in the left. "Steel Fist!"

More shouts rose after the first, though most watched quietly, more intrigued than excited.

Men set up the armor rack, and Necrem pointed at two of them to stay; one held the shield and the other stood behind.

"What was *that*?" the calleros mocked.

"They don't have any calleroses to challenge us, Enostio!" One of his fellows behind him laughed. "Looks like they brought out an armorer instead!"

"And he's brought his wares to sell!"

The calleroses' following laughter sounded pretentious, yet still grating.

Hezet grimaced, first back at the ranks and then to Necrem.

"Let's get on with it," Necrem reminded him.

Hezet snorted, casting one last disappointed glare at the ranks before facing the calleroses again. "Calleroses of Orsembar," he yelled, "a challenge is made! A Bravados of fists!"

The laughter stopped, followed by the calleroses sharing confused looks.

"There's no such thing, you ignorant footman!" the one called Enostio, the calleros who had charged, yelled. "The Bravados is of the sword! Of the spear! Of the horse! None of this fist nonsense." He waved dismissively. "If you're going to be a bore, do it to your calleroses too stupid not to tell you the difference."

"Since they obviously fraternize with their lesser ranks and allow you to wander where you don't belong!" another calleros added.

Necrem ground his teeth together. Drool pooled out between the gaps in his cheeks, dampening the cloth mask pressed against his face and making his every breath a wet hiss.

Always. Laughing.

"*Cowards*!"

His bellow shocked him along with everyone else. Hezet flinched and stepped away. Men shifted their weight, their armor rustling. Some cautiously coughed. The calleroses across the way and their men stood in stunned silence.

Necrem had thought to let Hezet do all the talking, but he couldn't stop the words flowing out of his mouth.

"*Cowards*!" He pointed his gauntleted finger at them. "*Thieves*! *Liars*!" His cheeks warmed, and his hot breath blew back in his face, unable to fully slip through the mask holes. "All of you calleroses! All of you, always sitting and ordering working men about and providing *nothing* in return. N*othing*!"

He shook from the bottom of his souls to his shoulders. Heart pounding in his ears, he could barely hear himself, making him shout louder. Ten years of holding his tongue. Ten years of accepting things as they were. Ten years of trying to put shattered pieces back together while ignoring something he was too proud to admit he held. Resentment poured out him like molten iron, bubbling hot and hissing.

"Year after year, we try to build!" His hands stretched out before him, the interlocking metal plates clinking and tinging from the excessive shaking. "And year after year, *you* take it away! You take our food! You take our *deberes*! You take us from our homes! You've even *taken* our families! And for *what*?" Necrem raised his fists in the air. His teeth clicked together. His entire face burned and stung, but he ignored it as the world took on a red hue.

"Prove that you are men! On your own feet with your own two hands, like working men. Get off your comfy saddles, where you look down on us. *Laugh* at us! *Always* laughing! *Prove your steel*!" His demand turned into a roar. His knuckles popped inside his gauntlets from his tight squeeze. His teeth cracked. There was a stinging snap against his right cheek. One of the scars had cracked.

It all added fuel to his roar, more coal to the furnace inside that had been shut up for so long. The pressure building.

He needed to hit something!

He spun on his heels, rearing his fist back. The two men carrying the shield raised it in defense of themselves, faces pale and eyes wide with terror. Necrem crashed his fist against the shield's rounded surface. Metal on metal grated the air with the powerful boom of a parish bell. The men holding the shield crumbled under the blow, collapsing onto each other. The shield itself now had a large dent in the center.

Yet, it wasn't enough.

Necrem jerked the shield away from the men who were cowering and scrambling away. He turned around and held it up in the air, his grip tightening more and more around the rim.

Tighter.

Tighter.

Metal groaned. The leather and wood of the forearm straps inside moaned. Necrem's biceps bulged, and the straps of his own armor soon joined the shield's, crying from the strain. Sweat soaked his face, dripping off his mask. The taste of iron invaded his mouth. The cracked scar had started to bleed, yet still, Necrem *pulled*.

The shield let a yawn as metal bent.

Necrem let out a bellow and—

Snap!

The wood for the forearm brace exploded, raining splinters above his head. The shield's round frame gave way and folded outward in screeching cry. Necrem held the bent metal over his head, arms throbbing against his armor's straps with every heartbeat, and each breath a heavy, fuming hiss.

The calleroses stared at him. Their men shared nervous glances at each other while the Orsembian soldiers along the line looked between their calleroses and Necrem.

"Get off your frickin' horse," he spat.

The calleroses remained in their saddles, one of them looking back and forth at his fellows as if searching for someone else to dismount first.

Enostio fumbled with his reins. His horse snorted and pawed at the ground with a hoof, the animal recognizing a challenge his master ignored.

"Get off your *frickin'* horse!" Necrem yelled, thrusting the misshapen scrap of the former shield at Enostio. "Prove you're a man with your own two hands!" He threw the shield down with a reverberating clamor, leaving the metal sheets wobbling in the dirt, the rim bent and molded with the shape of his fingers.

Enostio's horse snorted and danced under the calleros. Likely bred to fight, the animal wasn't afraid. Enostio struggled with the reins, growling and muttering curses too low to reach across the field for Necrem to hear properly.

"Such a display of strength," he said, finally getting his mount under control, "for a common rank. So common you *obviously* don't understand. The Bravados is meant for civilized and honorable combat, that between warriors! Between calleroses! Not brawling in a saloon. But, if you're so intent on bending your own arms, don't let us stop you!" He let out another pretentious cackle, glancing over his shoulder too obviously. His fellows were a bit slow to join and not as loudly as before.

"Scared of getting your own armor bent?" Necrem called, cutting them off. "Or scared of taking it off?"

Enostio spat off to the side. "Watch your tongue, scum. You may have a strong arm, but your armor's shit compared to ours!" He thumbed his fist against his breastplate. "Orsembian steel is the finest of all the marcs, and our smiths are the best. I can slice through your armor before mine even dents!"

Necrem locked eyes with the man.

He snorted.

A grating snicker later, and he threw back his head and laughed, rich and deep. It was a sick joke hearing a calleros compliment Orsembian steel after so long.

Hezet backed farther away from him, and grumblings went through the ranks behind him.

Enostio and the other calleroses pointed at him, shaking their heads as if he were mad.

"Awfully proud of your fancy suits, aren't you?" Necrem gasped. "I should know. I've forged many of them!" He reached around and grabbed the top of the breastplate hanging on the rack, driving the rack's prong feet into the ground. "But if you're so proud of it, let *me* test it for you! Come on! Get off your frickin' horse and let a steel-working man test *your* metal!"

He reared back and slammed his fist into the center of the plate. Crashing metal rang out again over the field. The gauntlet cushioned the blow for his knuckles, but the plate held. The rack held also, barely wobbling where it stood.

Necrem let go of its neck, pulling back and striking the other side of the breast with his left. The plate held. The rack remained standing. Metal sang in his ears. The world narrowed around the plate and that fading tune. All so familiar, but with a sharper feel.

He lashed out at the plate, raining blow after blow into the chest. The metal song drowned out the laughter, although he could see their faces. They flashed in the armor, changing with every punch.

The calleros guarding the steps of his and Eulalia's wagon. His right fist dented the plate over the heart.

The calleros inside watching. An uppercut with his left bent in the plate against the ribs.

The calleros holding her down. A crack formed at the center of the plate running to the top of the neck.

The calleros violating her.

Necrem let out a roar. Moisture—spit mixed with blood—stained across the inside of the cloth mask, sticking it to his face. He punched faster. *Harder*! Not pulling all the way back before beating the plate now riddled with dents and the growing crack.

The rack snapped. Before it tumbled to the ground, Necrem seized it by the neck again and, with a yell, sent a right uppercut into the gut of the plate. His gauntlet struck. The plate caved in with a scraping screech.

When Necrem tried to pull back, the gauntlet's metal plates hung in the armor. He pulled and jerked, snarling at the breastplate refusing to let go. He flexed his fingers, and the steel gave, revealing a caved-in hole punched through the plate.

Turning to face the calleroses across the field, he wrapped his fingers in the hole and heaved. At first, the steel held, an estimate of how well he had forged it. Necrem's arms bulged once again and, keeping a firm grip on the neck, he pulled all the harder.

The steel croaked and creaked.

There was a pop.

Then—

Shriek!

The steel ripped louder than any piece of parchment as Necrem gutted the plate, pulling a long, curling sheet up the center to the crack. The ripped portion of metal rolled and curled around itself, the tear losing momentum at the neck rim, and Necrem left it there to hold up in the air.

"Let a steel-working man test the metal you're so proud to wear!" he bellowed. "Get off your horse! I challenge *you*!"

He had never challenged another man to fight. His own past meant he couldn't deny he had fought before. Those few times had always been after someone had done something to him or after they had hurt someone whom he cared about.

His throat tried to hold the words back, yet the desire forced them out. He couldn't deny it. He *wanted* that calleros to get off his horse. He *wanted* to fight.

The field was quiet. The distant sounds of the camps behind the lines never reached them. Up and down both lines, all eyes turned toward the calleroses. Not a man coughed or spoke. Even their breaths were hushed and low.

Enostio turned his horse and spat.

Necrem tossed the ruined breastplate aside, seeing that as his answer. He took a step forward—

Enostio wheeled his horse without a word. He waved to his entourage and fellows, riding past them and between a gap in the Orsembian line. One by one, the other calleroses followed, spitting at Necrem as they wheeled their horses to ride back behind their lines, their soldiers watching and following them with their heads.

Necrem stared, shaking. His fists pulsed inside his gauntlets from using them as hammers against the breastplate. No matter how deep he breathed, no amount of air could calm him.

"Cowards," he growled, glaring at their backs. "*Cowards*!"

"Cowards," Hezet agreed.

"Cowards," someone behind them echoed.

Another man repeated it. Then another. Men companies down the line spat in agreement.

"Cowards!" a soldier yelled.

"Cowards!" a group shouted in unison.

"Cowards!" an entire company roared.

"*Cowards*! *Cowards*! *Cowards*!" The chant grew up and down the Lazornian line. Pikes beat in the dirt. Drums sounded, tapping out. Fists slammed into shields. Swords waved in the air.

Ever muscle in Necrem's body swelled. Every hair stood on end. Every breath of air he sucked in tasted sweater than the last. At last, the world saw the calleroses as he did. At last, other men had joined him.

At last, vindication!

In the thrall of the chant, he pumped his fist into the air and walked down the rank of former *sioneroses*, each man yelling with crazed eyes and spitting snarls.

"*Cowards*! *Cowards*! *Cowards*!"

His voice cracked, but he ignored it. His face burned, but he ignored it. His throat begged for water, but he ignored it. He could have kept yelling until his lungs burst and every calleros rode away in shame.

Men in red and black walked through the Lazorna line, two companies down from him. Those companies they walked between fell quiet.

Officers?

His fist hung in the air, missing a yell when he spotted the pink eye on the men's chests.

Not officers.

Viden de Verda.

Behind them, they led disheveled men in once lavish and silk clothes by a long chain interconnected to collars on their necks. The Viden led the men out and forced each of them to their knees, kicking their legs out or driving fists into kidneys, whether they protested or not.

The last Viden to emerge wore steel vestments over his red robes with the pink eye emblazoned upon his chest. The Easterly Sun reflected off his bald head, but what was most striking, even at a distance, was his wide, milky eyes. He walked up to the prisoner kneeling in the center, out of nearly twenty, and raised his hands out to his sides.

"Hear me!" he yelled, his voice carrying as well as any deacon's. "Hear me, Orsembians! Before me kneels Givanzo Borbin! Before me kneel betrayers! Men who claimed to take on the duties and lives of other men but did *not*! When the time came, these men offered to barter and sell their own!"

513

He reached to his side and slid a hammer out of his belt with a head too small for metal work, but a wicked spike on the end of it. He thrust it at the Orsembian line.

The calleroses who had ridden away had returned, gawking over the heads of the ranks in front of them.

"Hear these words, Orsembians!" the Viden yelled. "I bring you the words of La Dama Recha Mandas, Marquesa of Lazorna! She will *never* surrender a single soul under her charge! She will *never* betray her people! This is her answer to your Si Don." He raised his hammer over his head. "Begone with the Rules of Campaign. Vengeance comes . . . *now!*"

His hammer swing was smooth, a technique fit to be seen in a forge. The song of steel didn't ring when he struck, the hammer's spike driving into the top of Givanzo's skull before the man knew it. In stunned silence, his skull cracked open and sprayed blood on the faces of the men beside him.

The prisoners gawked in shock. The men with blood on their faces stared in stunned disbelief until the Viden wrenched his hammer free and smashed Givanzo's skull in with a second blow.

"Wait!" one begged as another Viden pulled his head back by the hair then drove a dagger into the man's eye, forcing the entire blade in man's head.

The other cultist fell on the prisoners with all the ferocity of *mellcresas*. Knives slit throats. Daggers gauged out eyes before being driven into brains. Hammers crushed skull. The hapless, chained men wailed, thrashed, and begged, but the Viden butchered in absolute silence. No cruel, mocking retorts. No curses. No righteous sentiments. No pity. No hesitation.

Just cold slaughter.

A cry came from across the field, followed by pounding hooves. Scattered Orsembian calleroses rushed between their soldiers ranks, lances leveled or swords waving, toward the killing ground.

"Musketeers, front!"

The order was repeated down the entire Lazorna battle line. Two ranks of musketeers filtered through each company and took up positions a few feet into the field.

"First rank!" an officer yelled. "Blow match!"

Red embers blazed as each man blew on their matches. Small wisps of smoke drifted around their faces. All down the line.

"Present!" the officers yelled and, as one, the front ranks leveled their muskets.

"Open pans!"

The musketeers made a flicking motion on the side of their stocks.

The calleroses were closing in. Drums beat down the Orsembian line. Officers stepped out in front of their companies, waving their swords across the field. Spears dropped and men started to—

"*Fire!*"

The world erupted!

In a bellowing pitch of smoke and flashes of fire, a thousand muskets went off. Calleroses tumbled from their saddles. Horses, tripped by an invisible hand, rolled head over hoof, crushing their riders. Their charge fell apart, and men who hadn't begun to move dropped where they stood.

"Second rank!" Lazornian officers yelled. "Step forward!"

The process repeated. Matches were blown, muskets were leveled, pans were opened, and then—

"*Fire!*"

Necrem envisioned the ground splitting open to engulf the space between the two armies from the fire and sulfur. Added to that was the cry of wounded and shocked men. He stood and watched men across the field drop—some holding their limbs, their heads, their sides; some dropping to the ground and never getting up.

"*Pikes, forward!*"

Lazornian drums tapped the march. Every company, except the one behind him, moved forward, absorbing their musketeers and stepping over the butchered Orsembians whom the Viden had left to rot on the field. Pikes dropped, and men yelled as the Lazornians pressed to attack.

Necrem turned back, finding General Galvez pointing and giving orders to the subordinates around him. More Lazornian companies were marching down from the camp, now in their own lines.

The general's words came back to him. The Bravados is the center of a battlefield.

Chapter 30

Recha's hands *refused* to stop shaking. They were as incessant as needy children, demanding to hold something. To *do* something!

When Sir Oso stepped out between the battle lines, she had ordered water served to her, fearing she would spill it if she poured herself. Her trembling hands shook half the cup out, anyway.

She tried pacing with her hands folded under her armpits. However, the pacing made everybody nervous, Baltazar included, watching her out of the corners of their eyes as more companies formed up in the camp.

When Sir Oso's angry roars reached back to them, she had fetched her riding crop. She twisted and bent the hard leather with every punch Sir Oso threw. A tremor ran down the back of her spine, down her legs, and into her heels. She couldn't sit down. She bounced on the balls of her feet, watching Sir Oso rip a breastplate apart with his hands and demand the Orsembian calleroses face him.

What are you going to do, Orsembians? she teased, biting her lower lip. *You have a challenge. Calleros or not, do any of you have the honor to face a man unhorsed and without weapons?*

She conceded fighting a man as big as Sir Oso without a weapon would be insane. However, no more insane than the Bravados itself. It made no sense to her why the marcs allowed such a waste. Something to shake the morale of the side that loses a calleros to go into the background negotiations. Pathetic.

She growled when the calleroses left the field, denying her the opportunity for a spectacle. It didn't affect any of her plans, though. That had always been the most likely possibility, save for the calleroses disregarding the challenge and answering with weapons. It turned her stomach to watch them leave the field in utter disregard of the challenge after all their bluster in demanding one.

Sir Oso's furious bellow followed. Her whole battle line joined.

Cowards! Cowards! Cowards!

It buzzed in her ears and, unbeknownst to her, she began slamming her riding crop against the command table in time with the chant, and the drums, and pikes pounding.

Cornelos took her by the wrist, startling her. He respectfully took it away, shooting warning looks across the tent.

Recha didn't have to ask. Baltazar wanted her to stop. The command tent's walls had all come down. More companies were steadily moving out onto the field. The fury of the forward battle line was what those men needed, but the companies in reserve needed order to not tip their hand too soon.

Then came Harquis delivering her message.

She was too far away to make out the details, and it happened too fast for her to reach for her eyeglass. She knew what had happened, though. They had told her everything she was going to get out of them and, as promised, she had let Harquis have them when she was done.

She screamed *fire* in time with the officers. The thunderous eruptions of over a thousand muskets at once sent her jumping up and down, yelling, "*Into them!*"

Baltazar seized her arm. "*Recha!*" he growled lowly for only her to hear, eyes flashing like thunderclaps. "Don't. Do that. *Again.* If one officer mistook that as an order for all-out assault, we could lose the entire army in an undisciplined charge."

That was how she ended up being forced to sit at the table, hands still shaking, and with no need for her eyeglass. She could make out the battle just fine.

Their initial charge was a success. Sir Oso had offered the perfect distraction, along with striking the first blow against the Orsembians' morale. Then came Harquis's executions afterward. A blow to their confidence in their leadership, followed up by a blow to their courage with a shocking demonstration. And there was little more shocking than Harquis's methods. The volley fire had riddled the Orsembian front lines with gaps from wounded or dead men, leaving them vulnerable when the pikes marched into them.

The Orsembian battle line bulged backward against the longer reach of the pikes. First on the right. A couple in the center. More musket balls tore up their cohesion, and by the time the swords had moved in, the enemy was breaking. Disorder spread from the disorganized front ranks, and companies broke apart.

Ripples spread to the neighboring Orsembian companies as one retreated or broke apart. Within ten minutes, there were five gaps in their line. In twenty, half were in retreat; some in fighting order and others running fit to be routed. In twenty-five, the entire Orsembian line took to their heels.

Recha would have been on her feet again had she not seen a second Orsembian line moving to take the place of the first. Neither she, Baltazar, or any other officer needed to rush messages down to the front. The generals and the other officers on the line must have spotted them, too, because, within five minutes, her companies went to chasing the retreating soldiers to reforming ranks to resume their steady, measured advance at the enemy's reinforcements.

The initial attack and rush were over. The slogging struggle commenced.

Recha's hands still demanded something to do. She propped her elbows on the table and interlaced her fingers in front of her face yet, still, they quivered.

Battle has commenced. Officers are rushing around everywhere. Camp workers are being called to every task imaginable. While I, the marquesa herself, am relegated to just sit here like a spoiled child! She reached into her pocket and pulled out her pistol.

"Cornelos," she called over her shoulder, "can you bring me my cleaning kit?"

Cornelos jerked, eyeing her pistol. "I'm not sure this . . . is the best time—"

"*Cornelos.*" She squinted back at him. "I need *something* to do. Please bring me my cleaning kit."

He swallowed and took a step back. Then he nodded without a word and marched off into the organized madness revolving around the command tent.

Recha bit the inside of her cheek, watching him go. She might have been too forceful but wasn't in the mood to be told what to do by her direct subordinate.

She pulled out her handkerchief and pistol's loading pouch, laying them out on the table. There was no breeze threatening to whisk her handkerchief away, so she left it spread out without having to weigh it down. She turned up her pistol's steel cap and tapped out the fine black powder into a neat pile in the middle of handkerchief, likely ruining the thin cloth.

"Recha," Baltazar said lowly.

She turned her head up. Baltazar stood beside her, dispatches in hand, eyeing the upturned pistol in her hands.

"What are you doing?" he asked.

Recha shot a sideways glance at her pistol then back up at her field marshal, replying, "Cleaning."

Baltazar raised an eyebrow.

"*And* keeping myself busy," she quickly added.

Baltazar frowned, puffing up his mustache and giving her pistol a squinting glare.

"Field Marshal!" a staff officer yelled.

Baltazar snorted and gave her a sharp nod before seeing to whatever new situation had arisen. Everyone else around them were going about their duties, fixated on the battle below them. The command table might as well have been the only quiet place left in camp. The tranquil eye of the tornado.

Once he was away, Recha was alone again, but she could still overhear the reports.

"We're losing visibility of the front, sir!" the officer reported.

"What?" Baltazar snapped.

"It's the musket fire, sir. The smoke is lingering over the line, and the forward observers are having difficulty making out the enemy's movements behind their secondary line. They say each volley is adding to the fog."

Baltazar tossed the dispatches on the table, stomping his way around it to the front of the tent. He pulled out his eyeglass from a loop in his trousers and put it up to his eye.

Recha could make out the front from where she sat, a mass line of men, pushing and shoving each other. Their banners and different colors differentiated them from being a crashing mob of bodies. Above them hung a dense gray cloud, stretching from end to end of the mountain walls of the eastern passage.

Taking this moment of being unsupervised, Recha set her pistol on table as gently as she could to avoid noise and cautiously stood up. She picked up her eyeglass on the table, got a bearing on where Baltazar was scanning, and brought the glass up.

The fighting mass came alive the second she did. Her pikemen dueled an array of Orsembian company formations. Some matched pikes with pikes in a frantic duel for each to get inside the other's reach before the other side could strike back. Others made do with spears in desperate attempts to fight the Lazornians' longer reach, and many failing, never getting close enough with their spears before a pike struck them down. Those who managed the best deployed shields.

In that pushing, crashing struggle, sporadic volleys went off, aiming to break up the cohesion of an enemy company's ranks for the pikemen to smash. Each volley added to the hovering smoke cloud, which indeed blocked out what was going on behind the Orsembians' second line. Recha thought she could make out shapes. However, in the constant, sometimes orderly, sometimes chaotic, movement of battle, they could have been anything.

"Send orders to all company commanders of the second line," Baltazar instructed, which the staff officer hurried to write down, "upon rotation, all musketeers are to hold their fire unless absolutely necessary to eliminate the haze."

The staff officer scribbled down the order until his hand paused mid-writing. "The second line, sir? What of those in the front?"

"The front lines will be rotating soon," Recha explained without thinking. The companies on the front line had been engaged for close to the thirty minutes. She knew a company in combat shouldn't be on the front for longer than forty; otherwise, they would start to tire, and the men in front ranks would become exhausted and unable to withdraw to rest. And in the pitch of battle, an exhausted man was a dead man. "By the time the order reaches the front, the second line will already be rotating in. If the orders aren't given to them, then it will have to be repeated and a waste time."

She swallowed, realizing what she had done. Cautiously, she moved her eyeglass slightly to the side to peek around the brass rim, while keeping her other eye firmly closed. The staff officer stared at her, holding his pyrite aloft the small parchment strip in his hands.

Baltazar still studied the battlefield. When he finally broke his attention from his eyeglass, it was the staff officer he turned to.

"You heard the La Dama!" he snapped. "Issue the order!"

The staff officer jumped, hastily saluting with a sharp nod. "Yes, Field Marshal!"

Recha watched him run out of the tent.

Baltazar kept his back to her, scanning the battle line again as that order and a host of others trickled down to the front by dispatch riders or bugle calls.

"I"— she struggled with the words but knew it was better to say them now than later—"didn't mean any—"

"You didn't," Baltazar grunted. "There was nothing to offend. And, more importantly, you were right."

Recha tapped the eyeglass against her forehead. "Then why did you yell?"

"Officer had his orders and wasn't moving. We don't have time to waste like that." He scanned the battle line again, a deep growl resonating in his throat. "Damn smoke. At the worst time, too."

Recha crookedly smiled at the sense of being vindicated, yet that slipped away when she looked through her eyeglass again. The smoke wasn't clearing, and worse, more sporadic volleys added to the lingering haze. She knew why Baltazar was on edge, another insight from growing up in his household.

A battle line is at its most vulnerable when rotating, she recalled.

Exhausted, bloodied men pulled back while the relieving company filtered through their lines to take their place. For a moment, the fighting company lost the support of their rear ranks, and more pressure was placed on those in the front to hold until the front ranks of the new company joined them. If the enemy pressed their attack at the right moment, or the front ranks were struck by their exhaustion while the two companies were bleeding through each other, it could spell disaster for both.

Whistles screamed and bugles sounded. Here and there, companies from her second line marched up and began to filter through the front line. The process would likely take twenty minutes to finish for the entire line, as only every second company switched out at a time. No two companies fighting side by side could be relieved at the same time to reduce any weakness to the front.

"Your cleaning kit, La Dama."

Recha jumped, snapping her head back to wheel around at Cornelos.

Cornelos dropped the silver case on the table with a clamor, raising a startled hand.

Recha blinked at her pistol's cleaning kit, the silver case holding various small, thin steel brushes, cloths, and oils to keep Sebastian's gift in proper order.

"Oh," she grunted, "thank you, Cornelos. I'll use it in a moment."

"Hmm?" Cornelos hummed, arching an eyebrow.

Recha arched her own back at him. "I'm behaving."

She didn't wait for a retort and resumed checking the battle line again. One last look to make sure the rotation was going . . .

Their far right was losing ground.

When they'd first attacked and crushed the Orsembians' original line, her line had marched into the eastern passage, using the cliff faces to cover the flanks. On the far right, the farthest three companies were inching back, their musketeers putting up volley after volley, obscuring whatever they were facing on the other side.

Yet, no matter how much shot they poured out, the companies still inched back.

"Papa!" Recha yelled. "Something's happening on our—"

"Far left flank is faltering!"

What!

Recha wheeled her glass, going too far and moving it in a long arch to find the battle again. Just like the far right, the companies on the left were frantically trying to hold their ground, firing volleys as fast as they could and striking out with their pikes. Their intensity made rotation impossible, and they were being threatened with being pushed back into the secondary line or dislodged from against the steep ridge slope on their flank.

The smoky haze thinned over them, and Recha's eye widened to see rank after rank of Orsembian infantry piling behind their line. Where Recha's companies were around twenty ranks deep, she counted the enemy ranks to be nearly twice as that before the haze obscured their true numbers.

"They're deploying oblique formations against *both* our flanks!" Baltazar roared, snapping his eyeglass shut. "Stop all rotations across the line! Send orders to General Galvez to move all the companies he has on the left to bolster the companies engaged! He's ordered to hold, understand? He *cannot* let the Orsembians dislodge him from the cliffside for *any* reason!"

A pair of riders hopped onto their mounts. Their horses' hooves kicked up clouds of dust as they bolted onto the field.

"But Papa!" Recha yelled. "The far right!"

"Can wait!" Baltazar snapped.

Recha jerked back, her mouth falling open, but he was moving before she could disagree.

"Ramon!" Baltazar marched off to the other end of the tent. "Get me another rider! General Priet needs to move!"

Recha turned her head, following him. The corner of her right eye twitched in a frustrated spasm as he stormed into a crowded group of staff officers surrounding Narvae, pointing at the battlefield.

In a huff, she gathered up her things on the table, hurriedly poured as much of the priming powder she could back into her pistol's pan, then slammed it shut. She stuffed the weapon in her pocket, turning on her heels—

Cornelos grabbed her shoulder, pulling her short. "Please, Recha," he softly implored. "Baltazar has everything in hand. You don't have to . . ."

Recha seethed, breathing heavily through her nose. Every hair on her head stood on end, and her glare narrowed more and more the longer he held her arm.

Hesitantly, Cornelos released his grip, visibly swallowing.

"Stay," she ordered, snatching her eyeglass as she turned again to follow her field marshal.

Baltazar was ordering another rider, pointing out into the field in a sweeping motion to the right. "He needs to prepare to form a screening line," he instructed, in mid-explanation. "Once he's in position, we can give the signal for the far right to give ground and siphon off the pressure, understand?"

"Give ground?" Recha cried. She couldn't believe what she'd heard— Baltazar Vigodt returning ground to an enemy.

Staff officers spun around and hastily gave her space. The rider stiffened in surprise upon seeing her.

Baltazar, however, slapped the rider's chest. "Do you *understand*?"

"Yes, Field Marshal!" the rider yelped.

"Off with you!" Baltazar waved, and Narvae delivered the rider a shove on the back for good measure to send the rider sprinting to his mount.

Recha's head spun, and the rider was away before she could say anything.

"Find Feli," Baltazar said to Narvae, both standing with their heads together. "If Borbin, or Ribera, is throwing this much pressure on us already, the men down there can't pull back to rest where we plan. Tell him—"

"Baltazar," Recha demanded.

"One moment," he replied, lifting a finger to her and returning to his instructions.

"Tell Feli to move the cook fires, water barrels, and powder supply closer, about"—he pointed to the middle of the field, at least twenty yards forward from where a line of wagons carrying barrels of water, black powder being put into resuppled bandoliers, and cooks wearily tending pots over small fires stood— "there."

Recha tapped her foot.

"That's mighty close to the rear line," Narvae said, squinting. "If something happens . . ."

Recha's grip tightened around her eyeglass, the brass work biting into her palm.

"The faster the men are cared for and resupplied, the faster they can get back into the fight. If Feli has the same concerns, then you tell him—"

"*Field Marshal Vigodt*!" Recha snapped. "I *demand* to know why you're ordering to give ground on one of our flanks?"

Every staff officer around the tent stopped what they were doing to stare at her. Those around Baltazar and Narvae took a few steps back. Baltazar kept his focus on the battlefield, unmovable as stone, yet his mustache puffed up.

Recha's stomach grew queasy with each passing second, having only the distant sounds of battle to keep the silence from becoming awkward. She held her ground, though, waiting, *demanding* with her very presence an explanation.

"Get it done, Marshal Narvae," Baltazar calmly ordered. "The rest of you, to your duties."

Quick, snapping salutes followed without a single reply uttered. They were all eager to step away. A few jogged into the camp, while Narvae made a quick march with a pair of officers trailing to keep on his heels.

Recha remained determined and stood her ground. *I'm not going to be shut out. Promise or no, this battle is more important.* She bit her tongue, wanting to scream but determined to keep her dignity. *I won't be sent to watch from a corner.*

"With me," Baltazar finally said, cold as steel. He brushed past her, eyes never leaving the battle.

Recha frowned and watched him walk to the center of the tent.

"What do you see, Recha?" he demanded, holding his hands out toward both far flanks.

Recha's brow furled. She took in the battle again. Hiraldo was moving. Companies were being driven in behind the three on the line, adding their numbers to a swelling column of men. The more men who joined the press, the less ground was lost. And where the two sides clashed, men were pressed and packed in so tightly that she couldn't discern where the battle line was.

The far right was a different story. They were losing ground, and no great rush was being made to add more companies to slow it. Instead, while a few companies were placed behind the third company on the front line, others were being pulled back, angling themselves around the edge of the ridge and into the southeast passage.

"I see us doing all we can to save one flank," she replied, stomping up beside him, "but preparing to surrender the other. We should be saving both."

Baltazar turned his head, finally breaking away from the battle below. His face was tight, every muscle strained, showing the outline of his cheekbones and veins on the side of his head. Every whisker in his mustache stood on end.

"That is a *tactical* response," he replied, sharp and low, snapping his head back around to the battle. "Not a *strategic* one. The enemy's aim is not to dislodge our flanks"—he waved his eyeglass at the two flanks—"but to *smash* our center!" He wielded his eyeglass like a baton, jutting it out toward the center of their battle line. "Their oblique formations are threating our flanks and threaten to encircle our front line if they dislodge them, *but* the enemy outnumbers us three to one! We can hold the flanks but look at the effort Hiraldo's having to put into holding the left."

The press was tighter than ever. Men desperately fought and shoved, and still more companies were being waved in to add their bodies to the world's biggest shoving competition. The holes those companies left behind in the second and third battle lines stood out like a beacon.

"We're weakening the rest of our lines," Recha said.

Baltazar hummed with approval. "Just the left flank. But if we do that for both flanks, we'll weaken the entire line. Our rotation schedule is already behind because of this attack. Once the center is weak enough, I suspect the enemy has a third formation to thrust into it.

"A break there with the pressure boiling at our flanks will ensure the entire front line is lost. What would remain of the second will be caught in a rout if discipline cannot be maintained. Likely, half the defending companies on the flanks would have the strength to withdraw. We could lose an entire army's worth of companies by the time we recovered. We would have to draw up defensive positions in our passage with the men we had left, and that would be it."

He grimly turned to her. "We would *never* have the initiative again, Recha."

Goosebumps ran down her arms. Her eyeglass slipped in her sweaty grip, and she had to press it against her hip to keep hold of it.

Checking on the battle, her companies on the far right were pulling back. Rather, they were backing away like creeping open a door. "So, we're giving up one flank to protect our center and prevent a disaster?"

The corners of Baltazar's lips curled. "I don't recall ordering the flank surrendered." He extended his eyeglass and peered at the far right. "Fighting men on a line are like water. They flow in waves and crash upon one another. If they fight another line that resists or repels them, they will be cautious and slowly increase the pressure. But, if they find an opening, a break in the enemy's line, they will rush forward without hesitation. That mentality has won many battles. However, it can also lead men to slaughter. Look."

Recha hung on to every word, captivated. She had heard Baltazar talk of battles and tactics many times, yet *this* time, there was a taste of blood to his words.

She jerked her eyeglass up, taking moments to find what he was hinting at.

The Orsembians were rushing against the ridge, squeezing through with the Lazornian far right no longer holding against it. The Lazornian front companies were angled, protecting their flank and forcing the Orsembians to attempt to rush around them to have any chance of attacking the rear of the front line.

That chance was nonexistent. General Priet had elements of the second line connected with companies of the far right, creating another line, a funneling corridor for the Orsembians to rush through, like cattle into a stockyard. That new battle line ran all the way to the end of the ridge and into the mouth of the southeast passage, waiting for the Orsembians who made it through the gauntlet.

Once an element of an Orsembian company made it around an engaged Lazornian company, musketeers of the waiting Lazornian company delivered volleys into the rushed enemy. Orsembians fell in rows, and the remaining men in the company had to stop rushing through the gap and engage the Lazornians or never make it through.

On and on it repeated. The crushing oblique formation, those columns upon columns of Orsembians were filtered through the gap between General Priet's new flanking line and the ridge face.

"They think they're winning," Recha said breathlessly, her lips twitching as she watched the repeated slaughter and filter of the enemy's numbers.

"They will for a time," Baltazar agreed. "The more men they send in that pocket means less down the rest of the line. And any enemy that makes it into the southeast passage will have no place to go, no relief or supply. We just need to—"

He grunted sharply. "Savior dammit! Who gave *that* order?"

Recha jumped, nearly fumbling her eyeglass. She pulled away and saw Baltazar grimacing with exposed clenched teeth, the veins in his neck bulging out.

"Bugler!" he bellowed. "Sound off to hold the line! Stop the rotations, dammit!"

"Rotations?" Recha swallowed, shaking her head back and forth but not seeing any as the bugler let out several sharp, blasting notes.

"The center!" Baltazar waved, fuming. "The damned center! Messenger!"

Recha raised her eyeglass. Three of the center companies on the front line were in the process of rotating, files of men blending, some back and others forward, moving through the gaps in the lines to exchange places. The fighting was tepid there, compared to the flanks. Each side kept their distance, thrusting and dueling each other with their pikes and spears.

In watching their process, Recha angled her eyeglass down to see how many companies they held in reserve. The third battle line was still intact, waiting to fully take the second's place once fully rotated. Her eyeglass stopped upon a column of men, three companies deep, all under black flags.

The former sioneroses *are in the center. They haven't been ordered to move since the Bravados.*

A line of sweat ran down the back of her neck.

Sir Oso was also—

"Rush as many riders down to the center as we have!" Baltazar ordered. "*Stop* that rotation! Go!"

Five dispatchers raced away to their mounts. A couple of the horses felt their riders' urgency and took off in a gallop before they were fully in the saddle, waving their arms in the air for balance as they thundered through the camp.

"Will they make it in time?" Recha asked.

Baltazar frowned grimly. "No."

"New enemy oblique column advancing toward our center!" a prophetic lookout yelled.

True to Baltazar's deduction, another long column of Orsembian infantry marched toward the center. Their forward companies engaged suddenly broke off, scrambling back in disarray to withdraw.

Fortunately, the Lazornian company commanders saw what was approaching and didn't rush to pursue. The miserable rotation suddenly halted as men scrambled to jut out as many pikes as they could before the new enemy advance made contact. The enemy in the front, however, weren't wielding spears or pikes.

They wielded halberds.

Recha twisted both her hands around her eyeglass as she watched the Orsembian hack at her men's pikes, closing the distance to hack then push against their bodies. Her soldiers resisted, throwing away chopped pikes to draw swords and daggers to get in close with their attackers. Men with shields moved up, and musketeers fired volleys at point-blank range, adding more smoke to obscure the field.

Nothing could obscure her center line was starting to bow backward.

"Papa," she gasped, struggling for breath yet unable to look away. "Papa, we must do something!"

The company in center was on the brink. Men backed up in good order, only to trip over others who suddenly lost their feet. Exhaustion was striking with the Orsembians bearing down on them, and any man who fell was crushed underfoot.

"We're committed on both flanks," Baltazar said softly, as if going through his options in his head as fast as we could. "Too late for withdrawal, and we'd be crushed if we don't. A calleros charge will hardly hamper their advance."

The center companies were starting to pivot out of the way of the oncoming tide, desperate to keep their formation yet unable to hold the line for long. The one at the precise center was down to a quarter strength.

"General Ross will have to engage."

The center company was collapsing. Wounded men struggled to retreat, limping away, using their pikes as overly long canes.

Recha followed them back to the *sioneroses*. "Order the center reserve to engage!" she implored, tearing her eyes away from the battle.

Baltazar wasn't watching the center anymore. Instead, he was scanning the entire width of the field and their camp, as if doing calculations in his head. His furled, sweaty brow and darkening face told he wasn't liking the results.

"After what happened in the last engagement . . ." He shook his head. "They should withdrawal and give General Ross room to maneuver. Dispatch!"

"*No!*" Recha grabbed his arm. "They're right there!" She pointed out into the field. "They're the closest units to counter while we reorganize. They must engage!"

Baltazar frowned, a glint of pain in his eyes. "A few days drilling and new armor doesn't mean they can stand against Borbin's best. They didn't the last time."

Recha's body trembled. "*But—*"

"Field Marshal!" a lookout cried. "Our center reserve is moving without orders!"

Baltazar grimly brought his eyeglass up. "The company officers probably ordered the withdrawal after—"

His mouth dropped open. His face began to lighten. Another day of firsts for Recha—seeing Baltazar Vigodt speechless.

She brought her own eyeglass up and sniffed sharply.

The former *sioneroses*, three companies in a long column, were moving. Forward!

And a few paces in front of them, even at a distance, strode a big, *big* man.

Chapter 31

Necrem's ears buzzed from the den of hundreds of roaring men all around him. The battle at Compuert Junction was a street brawl compared to what he stood in the middle of now.

He had never watched a battle before. In his union days, he would tend to his forge, keeping it lit during the Bravados and packing it up if fighting broke out. The risks had been too great, too foolish, to watch one side try to kill another, especially if he ended up on the losing side and suddenly needed to flee. A camp worker could be killed in a rout the same as a fleeing soldier. Or worse.

Now, Necrem watched a battle from the center of the battlefield. Finally witnessing a pitched battle, they were a terrible thing to see.

The Lazornians first volley cut deadly swaths through the Orsembians. The war yells began moments afterward as the pikemen charged across the field, followed swiftly by Orsembians desperately crying in agony, fear, or anxious fury.

Those men were mostly dead now, their bodies mingled together on the ground where they'd fallen, marking their old battle line. Others laid beyond, either having fallen while trying to hold their line or where they had collapsed from their wounds and unable to make it back to their camp.

The Lazornians, fighting in their dense squares, were now twenty yards ahead of him within the eastern passage. Pikes rattled and jabbed. Swords sliced. Drums and shields competed over which were beaten the hardest. The musket fire, fortunately, had slackened off. The air was thick with the acidic smoke of burnt powder that wormed through Necrem's mask to scorch his nose and throat and made his eyes water.

Most of the firing came from the right flank, which Hezet keenly watched, standing on his tiptoes and craning his head over the helmets of the men beside him.

"Something's happening over there," the veteran anxiously whispered over his shoulder. He bobbed and weaved his head over the man's head next him then fell back on his heels with a grunt. "I think they've turned the flank but don't see where they've broken through."

Necrem cautiously glanced at the men standing in ranks beside them. A few worriedly watched Hezet and shot looks across the field. He bent down and said softly, "I think you need to calm down."

Hezet tilted his head back with a crooked, puzzled look.

Necrem nodded at the men beside them, which Hezet glowered upon seeing.

The veteran faced forward, clearing his throat in a low growl and rolling his shoulders, his pauldrons rising and falling. "It's the waiting, especially when the fight is on and we're just waiting our turn. Except"—he grunted—"do we even know when our turn *is*?"

Necrem exhaled deeply through his nose. After the attack had begun, both he, Hezet, and the men behind them had found themselves at a loss for what they should do. He remembered General Galvez's order to go behind the battle line should fighting break out, but that battle line had moved twenty yards in front of them.

Unsure of what to do and certain it would look bad if he simply walked back to camp with more and more soldiers marching onto the field, Necrem took up a spot beside Hezet in the front company of former *sioneroses*, who likewise had been seemingly and strangely forgotten.

The last orders they had gotten was from an officer riding by on horseback, simply yelling, "Remain in your positions until ordered!"

They were an island in the middle of two colliding rivers.

Behind them, companies of men hurried under the urgent orders of calleroses, riding along to break them off to either of the field's far sides. Other groups of calleroses trotted between the tight squares, some to waiting officers on horseback to deliver messages while the larger groups of horsemen galloped off into the southeast passage.

To their right, companies formed a long line that now stretched into that passage. Muskets went off at strange intervals, followed by battle cries as if they were suddenly fighting the sloping ridge face into the southeast passage itself.

The fighting over there couldn't have been worse than that on his left, though. Necrem was hesitant to glance that way. The massive press made him wince. Rank upon rank of men pushed against the rank in front of it, all the way to the struggling front line. The scene was gruesome, both sides heaving their shoulders into the other to the point where several men on the front lines were no longer pushing back.

Here and there, the mass of shoving men had squeezed the bodies of men at the front of their feet and only the tightness of the press held them in the air. The squeezed men hung like dolls with dangling limbs and slumped backs over the man in front of him, whether he be friend or foe. The Savior alone knew if they were alive or too exhausted to push back and miraculously ended up there instead of trampled underfoot.

Yet still, calleroses galloped up and down the column, waving swords and shouting, "*Heave!*"

A sharp whistle snatched Necrem's attention forward where a second line of infantry waited. The company directly ahead of them began to move up, pikes held high as they slipped into the ranks of the company on the front line.

"About time," Hezet said. "Those boys up front must be ready to collapse."

Necrem watched with curious fascination as men in one company slipped between the men in the other, staying in ranks the best they could. The men in the other company slowly moved back through the other company's ranks, again doing their best to stay in line with their fellows. It didn't feel like it should be possible, and yet, one company was taking the place of another by them simply walking through each other.

It's a wonder they don't trip each other up.

Sharp bugle calls trumpeted distantly from the back of the field, adding more noise to an already confusing mess.

Or shove each other out of the way.

It was another thing they'd never been taught when conscripted. Another example that Gonzel and Raul had merely cared about them looking like soldiers, to just run around in ranks and thrust spears instead of treating them as soldiers. Or worse, they'd just been there in case they needed men to sell off.

"*Stop!*" A calleros thundered down the line, waving his arm in the air and bouncing in his saddle. "*Stop!*"

Men in the rotating company stopped and threw their hands in the air as the calleros came barreling toward them.

Necrem held his breath, expecting the officer to ride into the dense pack of shifting men, only for him to wheel his horse around at the last moment. The man trotted around the companies, standing in his saddles.

"Stop the rotation!" the calleros roared. "Company capitáns, dislodge your companies and keep the frontline firm until ordered!"

Whatever retort or complaint the tired men gave was lost in the sea of war cries.

The calleros thrust a pointing finger toward the Orsembians over and over, yelling at someone below him.

The men around him looked up with weary, sweat-soaked, and some blood sprinkled faces.

A blaring trumpet from the Orsembian side of the field cut the argument short.

"Savior, help us," Hezet hissed under his breath.

Necrem jerked his head up and squeezed his hands together until his gauntlet plates bit through the gloves.

Rank upon ranks of Orsembians marched in a long column, out of the lingering haze of musket smoke, straight at the two companies trying to trade places.

"Reform the ranks!" the calleros cried. "All companies, *hold the line*!"

A mad scramble ensued. The companies' capitáns took up the order, shouting and waving their men together. Men in the mangled companies had to reform ranks together, standing shoulder to shoulder until the companies were indistinguishable from each other, save for their banners.

The Orsembians on the frontline suddenly broke away, giving a few parting thrusts before they scattered back, some with their backs turned. Necrem was sure, after being around soldiers long enough, the Lazornians would have been eager to chase after them. However, that long Orsembian column was coming on, and through the haze, Necrem finally got a good look at them.

The front three ranks were heavily armored with pauldrons, forearm greaves, and shin plates over their boots, along with their breastplates and helmets. They carried halberds instead of spears, and the *mellcresa* of Marqués Borbin waved above them in a fiery orange and gold banner.

A hedge of pikes lowered to meet them, many with bloodstained heads. The Lazornians jabbed and waved their long poles, claiming the twenty feet in front of them.

The Orsembians came on. Once in range, they lowered their halberds and went to swinging. Not at the Lazornians, but at their pike shafts. They swung their halberds like oversized axes, and cracks of wood followed wherever their axeblades fell.

The Lazornians speared and jabbed back, striking under armpits and grazing necks, dropping a man into the arms of their comrade behind. Still, once a pole was snapped or knocked out of the way, an Orsembian would rush in. They roared as they came on, hefting their halberds again to hack into the Lazornians' frontline. The Orsembians behind pushed their mates in front forward, some into pikes, in the mad dash to get inside the pikes' reach.

Another hard press formed in seconds, like on the left. Only here, there weren't enough men to hold the Orsembians back. They pushed and they pushed as if they were a nail driven by whatever hammering force kept their drums beating.

"Hold the line!" the calleros ordered. He leaped from his horse, drawing his sword, and shoved into the fray. "*Hold the line!*"

"Brave officer," Hezet mumbled.

Desperate.

That was what Necrem saw. Desperate men thrusting, punching, stabbing, and *clawing* to keep a few inches of ground. Men staggered out of the fray, using bent or splintered pikes as canes. Some limped, and some held their hands fast to wounds on their sides, their faces, their legs, a couple to their groins. Many couldn't get out of the way fast enough from the frontline bowing back.

It was bending like a persistent hammer blow dented a plate of steel. The companies to either side of the onslaught were giving way, too, curving backward as the companies in front of Necrem gave way step by step. Something became apparent with each of those steps.

Necrem and the men beside him were the only ones standing in front of Borbin's soldiers if they broke through.

"Capitán!" a man yelled from the company beside him. "What do we do if they get through?"

"That's the marqués's flag!" another cried. "We can't hold against his personal soldiers!"

"Capitán!" more cried. "*Capitán!*"

"Quiet in the ranks!" the young capitán yelled. "We hold until ordered! We will not run! We will not break! We will not disgrace ourselves again!" As commanding as he tried to be, the young capitán's voice cracked.

Many a pale face lingered, and knuckles remained white-gripping their pikes. Some trembled in their armor while other silently prayed.

"This is bad," Hezet whispered up at him. "That line's going to break, and the first thing that column is going to do is come at us." He cast a wary eye at the men beside them. "These men won't hold."

"Then"—Necrem paused, yet the answer was still the same—"someone should order them back."

Hezet looked up at him in horror. "If they pulled back . . . three whole companies in a column . . . that could start a rout!"

Necrem hung his head. "Guess that would happen if we went back, too, huh?"

"Well . . . I don't know." Hezet shook his head. "Never had the choice to just leave a battlefield." He swallowed and brought his shield around. "Doesn't really sit right to just . . . leave."

The Lazornians were losing ground. The remaining companies tried to stretch themselves out, desperately thrusting pikes and swords into the mass of Orsembians. They fired muskets into their bellies, yet still the Orsembians came on, fighting all the harder. The stretched lined reminded Necrem of that white ring steel got after being dented in a certain spot over and over, just before it gave way.

"If we leave," he said, "everything falls apart. Borbin wins."

Hezet nodded, drawing his sword. "Pretty much."

Borbin wins. He would likely be killed, or worse. And Eulalia and Bayona . . . their lives would remain in the same, disheveled state. Alone and hopeless.

Victory.

Or death.

Necrem's legs moved on their own, carrying him forward, toward that driving nail of men.

"Oso!" Hezet shouted after him. "Where are you going?"

Necrem looked over his shoulder, stopping in the middle of the field. Hezet stood a few feet in front of the square of curious men, as if he had begun to chase after him but stopped short. They were all watching him.

"We can't go back," Necrem replied. "And you said it wouldn't be good if we just stayed here and let them fight through." He pointed at the Orsembians, sucking in as much air as he could to bellow through his mask, "So, I guess I'll lend them hand. And *hammer* back a nail!" He didn't know what compelled him to do it. His arm rose on its own and held his gauntleted fist up in the air.

Hezet stared blankly at him. The men behind him, their capitán especially, stood speechless.

Hezet broke the awkwardness by bursting out with a laugh, throwing his head back with all the carnage and pain around them. "I guess I'll come along with you then," he said, shaking his head and trotting toward him.

Necrem wasn't sure why, but he felt a bit of comfort in the veteran's response, uplifted.

"Stop!" the young capitán yelled at them. "Your orders are to stay behind the lines!"

"Pardon, sir," Hezet yelled back from over his shoulder, "but at times like these, a soldier has to fight the battle in front of him, and damn the orders!"

"You men were sold out once, right?" Necrem yelled back at the former *sioneroses*. "This could be your best chance to get back at the men responsible for that."

534

Hezet waved his shield back at the men and bellowed, "*Come on*! Come and get the fight you were all denied!"

When Hezet joined him, Necrem took off toward the fight. The front was bulging to the brink. More and more men were scrambling away with bleeding wounds and exhausted faces. Those who were left jabbed their pikes over their compatriots' heads to strike at the Orsembians, unable to lend any support to their backs to keep from losing ground.

"You know this is stupid, right?" Hezet asked, fixing his shield strap tight to his forearm. "Even for a smith."

"I figured," Necrem grunted, swinging his arms to keep his stride long and heavy. "Just couldn't keep standing there. Waiting."

Hezet snickered. "Congratulations! You're now a soldier."

Necrem snorted but couldn't slap the comment down this time. In his armor, in the middle of a battlefield, and after the things he'd just said, no one would believe him. "What a terrible thing to be."

"Still, you better pick up a pike." Hezet gestured at a man lying slumped on the ground, his pike the only thing keeping his body propped up. "Better than going into *that* with just your fists."

Necrem grimaced, earning him a sting from cracking the dried blood on his scars, as he plucked the pike up. The slumped man fell forward and remained motionless as they passed by.

"Any more suggestions?" he asked, hefting the long pole. He recalled a little of his training and grasped it with both hands. However, the pike wobbled in the air with each step.

"Well—"

Men rushed up beside them. In moments, they were enveloped in the front ranks of the former *sioneroses'* company. Necrem peeked behind him and let out a relieved breath at the other ranks following, more than one company worth. He didn't know why, but striding in with a group of other men was comforting.

"Glad you boys could join us!" Hezet laughed to the nervous chuckles around him.

The laughter died instantly from the cries of the frightened men ahead of them.

The Orsembians broke through the line.

Those wielding halberds swung the long axe heads from side to side to open more gaps or to rain down blows on those who refused to budge. Swords flashed and hissed against blades from small duels breaking out. Spearmen and pikemen batted each other, the Lazornians desperate to hold any Orsembian back while the Orsembians clambered to make the breach wider.

"As I was saying," Hezet called out, "we better—"

"Company!" the capitán yelled, cracking his young voice, holding his sword in the air. *"Charge!"*

Necrem sprinted, swept up by the ocean around him. His long pike wobbled violently in his hands, threatening to slip from his grip with every step. He held it out level with the ground, along with the men around him. They shouted liked crazed men, eyes wild, faces flushed, barely breaking to breathe and just yelling.

It was infectious.

As they closed the space, an Orsembian knocked down a Lazornian with the butt of his halberd. He spun around in time for Necrem to see his blood-splattered snarl shrink in shock, his halberd held aloft as if momentarily forgotten.

The furious shouts around him raced up Necrem's spine and seized his throat. Without any concerns for his scarred face, he roared with every ounce of strength his lungs could give him and *rammed* into the Orsembian. The impact on the pike was jarring, but the force of his sprint and everyone coming in behind propelled him forward.

The man's eyes bulged, and his head dropped. The wobbling pike had made aiming the massive weapon impossible. The pike head grated against the abdomen of his breastplate, slid down under the metal, and through the man's thigh. A second later, Necrem slammed his shoulder into him, knocking him back into his comrades and driving his pike into the mass of bodies.

The man whose thigh was impaled hobbled backward, dropping his halberd and crying in pain, snarling and drooling. More Orsembians joined him in agonizing screams as the former *sioneroses* smashed into them like men possessed, shoving pikes into the mass, driving the pointed heads into any flesh or soft armor they could reach.

Necrem was driven farther into the fray. His pike shoved deeper and hit against more resistance, making the shaft jerk and stop before eventually shoving through. So close were they packed together that he couldn't tell whether he was stabbing someone else or sliding against armor. He grunted and snorted in his mask, struggling to pull the pike back. Every sound reverberated and echoed under his helmet. Everything was so close.

Including the enemy!

The impaled soldier finally got to his senses and snarled at him, mere inches from his face. He reached for his belt, grappling for his dagger.

I can't pull the pike free!

So, he let go.

The impaled soldier wobbled on his feet without any support. His hands fumbled to get his dagger out.

Necrem acted without thinking. He drew back, and the last thing he saw on the impaled man's face was wide-eyed shock before Necrem's gauntlet crushed the man's nose in. The soldier's head snapped to the side, but the pike held his body in place. His head wobbled back and forth, blood pouring from his crushed nose, the splintered bone visible, and then he collapsed, falling underneath everyone's feet.

Necrem didn't have time to see what happened to him. The shoving propelled him over the man's body and farther into the fray. Now without any weapon.

Save his fists.

The next soldier in line ran into him, slamming his pauldron into his chest. Necrem's breastplate absorbed the blow. He dug in his heels and, with the added support of the men behind him, barely gave an inch. The soldier held his spear high, unable to thrust. He batted the shaft into Necrem's belly, but the blows were cushioned by the breastplate.

Necrem raised his fist and dropped it like a hammer blow, crashing his gauntlet onto the man's shoulder. Pauldron and gauntlet clapped together. The soldier let out a strangled yowl and crumbled to the side.

The struggling press was too tight for the next soldier in line to step over his fellow, nursing his shoulder, on his knees. The next soldier wasn't in any hurry. He stared up at Necrem, pushing back against the ranks behind him, as if holding a tide threatening to topple him over.

Necrem kept his hands up. That tide would win sooner or later, and that soldier would have to fight.

His every breath was a struggle to suck more and more air through the holes in his mask. His legs burned from running, and his chest swelled and pounded against the bounds of his breastplate. He took a glimpse around him during the breather, taking advantage of standing head and shoulders over everyone.

The Orsembian nail had been blunted, but not fully stopped. There were still more pressing in behind and attacking the other Lazornian companies to either side. The fight around Necrem was quickly becoming like the grueling fight over on the left end of the field—men tightly packed, pushing and shoving, both sides desperate to be the one that pushed the other back.

That's the job, I guess, Necrem reasoned with himself. *They're yelling to push them back. They must mean it literally.*

That tide broke at the next soldier's reluctance. He stumbled over the crumbled man in front of him, spear in the air and unprepared.

Necrem swung an uppercut into the man's gut. His breastplate took the blow. However, he still folded over, and Necrem's follow-through lifted him off his feet. As the soldier reeled, doubled over, he grabbed the nape of the man's neck and flung him.

He didn't see where he ended up as another soldier came charging in, screaming.

Necrem threw his hands up to punch, but the soldier rushed in and rammed his shoulder into his gut. Again, he dug in his heels and held, grabbing the man's pauldrons as the man kicked and squirmed furiously to push Necrem back.

You're too small—

Clink!

Necrem grunted. Something was pressing against his side, squirming and wiggling between his chest and back plates. He raised his arm, and his eyes widened at the soldier's dagger. The soldier's wrist worked back and forth. The dagger's blade wiggled like a silver snake trying to burrow and squeeze through, between the plates.

There was a sharp sting. The point had found flesh.

Necrem raised his left hand high and backhanded the soldier across the side of his head. The soldier whipped and rolled from the blow. Teeth flung up in the air and were lost in the crush. The soldier went down in a heap under the feet of his fellow soldiers, leaving his dagger lodged between Necrem's plates.

Something warm, something wet, trickled down his skin. A trickle he knew well.

He was bleeding.

Dammit!

He wrenched the dagger free. Only the tip, barely a few centimeters, had made it through, and fresh blood stained it.

"*Oso!*"

He spun. A couple men behind and to his right, Hezet cracked the pommel of his sword into an Orsembian's face.

"The *banner*, Oso!" Hezet yelled then delivered a few more smacks. "Borbin's banner! It's right there!"

Necrem looked. A soldier was waving Borbin's banner furiously as the man beside him, the company's capitán, yelled and waved his sword, ordering his men forward.

"Get it, Oso!" Hezet roared. "Take Borbin's banner! They *will* break!"

Break?

Another hollering Orsembian rushed to fill in the gap. Necrem barely had time to raise his hands to catch the man's spear thrusting toward his face. The sharp head slid into his gauntlet fingers, the thick gloves protecting them as he struggled with the waving shaft in his grip.

The Orsembian yelled in frustration, yanking his weapon back—

The man grunted. His mouth dropped open, and his head drooped.

Necrem followed his gaze to the pike shaft lodged in his gut, punching through the plate. He hadn't seen him do it, yet the soldier behind him must have slid his pike around him and now skewered Necrem's latest attacker.

"Drive through, Steel Fist!" Hezet urged on. "*Break* them!"

Necrem flung the spear out of the way. Borbin's banner was a few ranks away, but of those in front of him, there were only two.

Break them, and we hold them, he worked out. *Break them . . . and we win.*

He cast a look over his shoulder. The soldier behind him determinedly held the Orsembian on his pike while the others behind him bobbed their heads to get a look at what was going on.

"Follow me!" Necrem yelled, waving behind him.

He shoved the skewered Orsembian off the pike and roared as he bulled forward. He kept one hand on the pike, guiding it along, and stuck his right shoulder out as he drove through the press.

He plowed into the first soldier he met, breaking his spear shaft on impact with his shoulder. The man tumbled head over heels, and Necrem ran over him.

The next soldier he hit stayed on his feet, and the pike skewered him. He clung to Necrem's pauldrons to keep his feet, but Necrem kept moving. The soldier gasped and sucked air as the sickening squish and scraping of metal on wood came from his gut. Necrem was forced to fling the man off, losing the pike in the process.

Two soldiers away from banner, and the Orsembian company capitán finally noticed him.

"*Kill* that huge bastard!" the capitán ordered, pointing his sword at him.

Necrem didn't wait. He plowed forward. Fists raised.

One soldier leapt out from the side, and he backhanded him. The next received an uppercut to the jaw that snapped his head back under his helmet, teeth and blood flying in every direction.

A rhythm settled over him. Everywhere he turned, he threw a punch. He struck flesh or plate, it didn't matter. His fists were hammers, and their bodies were mailable metal. They couldn't use their spears in such a close space, and the few with daggers found his plate stronger than they could stab through. At least in one try, because that was all Necrem gave them before his fists came down on their heads.

He roared, and his face burned. His mind, though, was clear. The fury was there, but it didn't consume him. The nightmarish visions were quiet. He fought with the same clarity as if he were in his forge. He wasn't destroying anything. He was creating.

He drove his gauntlet into a soldier's gut, plate squealing under the blow. He grabbed the man's shoulder and hit him again, and again, and *again*! Plate groaned and cracked. The soldier gargled a gasp, and his eyes rolled back.

Necrem let him fall, and another solder tackled him, wrapping his arms around his waist.

"*Capitán!*" the soldier cried.

Necrem raised his fists together to come down on the man's back, certain that would make him let go.

The glint of steel flashed before his eyes!

Cling!

Necrem's eyes went wide at the point of the sword embedded in one of the breathing holes of his mask. The Orsembian capitán glared up at him, arm stretched as far his could over his man holding Necrem's waist, sweat streaking down his brow.

He tipped forward. The sword pushed Necrem's head back, but by the Savior's miracle, the mask held.

Necrem seized the sword in one hand, pushing back to get the point dislodged from his mask but also keeping a hold of it so the capitán wouldn't be able to stab him with it.

More men yelled from behind him. The former *sioneroses* came in through the opening he had made and started fighting all around him, likely saving him from being jumped or daggered by the rest of the waiting Orsembians.

"*Capitán!*"

The standard-bearer rushed in, dagger raised in the air, underhanded.

Necrem hissed, finally pulling the sword free, and raised his forearm. The dagger sliced across his brace. The plate turned the blade's edge away. The standard-bearer lacked the strength to knock his arm down, and Necrem backhanded his hand away. The dagger clanged against gauntlet, tumbling through the air. Seeing a chance, Necrem seized the banner's pole wavering in the standard-bearer's hand.

"The colors!" the capitán cried. "He's trying to steal Si Don's *colors!*" He lunged forward, scrambling to climb over the man holding on to Necrem's waist to shove his sword into his face.

Necrem squeeze harder on the blade and flagstaff. He could make out the impression of sword's edge pressing through the gauntlet's palm.

A mad tug-of-war broke out. The capitán struggled to pull his sword back. The standard-bearer jerked and whined, trying to seize the flag away. Necrem squeezed his grip as tight as he could and held on to both.

They heaved and shoved while the battle around them raged. Necrem caught glimpses of Lazornians pushing forward around him one moment, and in the next, the Orsembians pushed back. He twisted and turned. His biceps and forearms began to burn.

"He's stealing Si Don's *colors*!" the capitán yelled again. "Stop him! Stop *him*!"

Necrem flung the standard-bearer back, but the man kept his grip.

Suddenly, Orsembians from both sides jumped on him, wrapping their arms around his and punching at his gauntlets and braces. The added weight made Necrem snarl, and it didn't help with the man holding his waist punching his ribs. Necrem's armor held off the worst blows, but no armor held out forever, and his strength was seeping from his arms *fast*.

His muscles burned and trembled. His fingers grew numb in his gauntlets. He snarled and hissed through his mask. Drool pooled in his cheeks. The edges of his scars pulled taut, stinging his face.

Don't let go, he told himself. *Don't let go!*

"Put steel in that big bastard's face!" the capitán ordered. "Kill *him*!"

Necrem snapped around, locking eyes with the officer. He wasn't sure how he appeared, but the capitán's face went white, and he froze. His trembling arm ran shivers up his sword blade.

"You want *steel*?" Necrem growled. His breathing rose to panted hisses. His pauldrons rose and fell with every gasp through his gnashed teeth. He worked his lungs like bellows to draw every ounce of strength he had left.

He had to get that flag!

He had to break them!

He had to stop them!

He had to *win*!

A roar broke loose from deep in his gut, and he thrashed. He pulled and jerked with all his might, swinging his fists to either throw the men holding his arms off or punch them with his full fists.

"Hold him!" one of the soldiers cried then desperately again. "Hold *him*!"

His left wrist twisted. His right hand squeezed. Metal squeaked. Wood groaned. He squeezed as tight as he could, losing all feeling in his fingers.

Squeak.

Groan.

Cling!

Snap!

Shards of metal and splinters of wood rained in the air. The tussle around him paused. Men held their breaths. Eyes widened in shock.

Necrem stood in the middle of the chaos with the broken blade of the *capitán's* sword in one hand and the broken-off shaft of the flag pole in the other . . . with Borbin's flag.

I . . . got it!

"Get the *colors*!" the capitán screamed.

No longer in a tug-of-war, Necrem's fists were free to use. He hoisted them in the air, flinging off the men latched to his arm from their grips loosening upon seeing him with their marqués's flag. He brought them high then *slammed* them into the back of the soldier holding his waist. He put his full force of his back into the swing, bending his legs to make the drive as hard as possible.

The soldier crumbled to the ground, finally releasing him.

A crazed yell made Necrem shoot his head up to see the capitán charging in with his broken sword, raised to thrust. Necrem swung a left uppercut . . . and buried the broken tip of the capitán's sword under the man's jaw and into his head. The officer gaped. His jaw worked, yet no sound came out. Only blood oozed from below his jaw.

Necrem pushed the man, stumbling back into the men behind him, and began to swing again. He backhanded the soldier to his left then swung around to slam his fist into the blocking forearms to his right.

When he got some space, he raised the stolen banner in the air and yelled behind him, "I *got* it!"

Amazed shouts went up, demanding those around them to look.

"He's got it!"

"He took their colors!"

"We've taken their colors!"

"*Charge into them!*"

Necrem got caught up in that ocean again. A surge of war cries, maddening roars, and triumphant laughter the likes of which he had never heard. The Lazornians pushed, and this time the Orsembians gave. Necrem prepared for another fight, but the Orsembians around him were pulling back wounded comrades, and the standard-bearer tossed away his useless pole to drag his capitán's body away.

They're . . . breaking?

Musket fire belched from around the edges of the retreating Orsembians. Sulfuric clouds filled the air and men collapsed to the ground. The former *sioneroses* flooded around him, lowering their pikes now that they had room and began their deadly screwing.

They're breaking.

Necrem's arms burned. His fingers pulsed. He tasted copper on his tongue. The telltale warm lines streaked down his face, sticking the cloth mask to his cheeks. His face was bleeding. *Again.*

Yet all he could do was . . . laugh.

"*Oso!*" Hezet came running up behind him, slapping him on the arm. His sword was gone, and in its place was a halberd he must have picked up along the way. The veteran beamed like a man seeing the birth of his first child. "Oso, you magnificent bastard! You did it!"

Necrem looked down at the banner in his hand. It felt so light, almost as if it weren't there. He lifted it up just be sure, and the long, orange fabric ruffled as he did.

He chuckled. "I guess I did."

Hezet chuckled with him.

More laughs broke out around them. The former *sioneroses* formed around them. Their faces were bloodied and bruised. They held their pikes sticking out in every direction. While officers down the line shouted orders to reform ranks, they all laughed.

An exhausted laugh. A shared laughed that no order could stop.

It felt good to laugh. To be alive. To have won—

The ground shook.

A thunderous pounding came from beyond the haze of musket smoke.

Horses screamed.

"*Pikes down!*" a distant officer cried.

Men around Necrem scrambled. Those in front knelt, buried the butts of the pikes into the dirt, and held their long poles at an angle. Those behind stuck theirs out as far as they could, and those farther back held theirs above the other's heads. They fell like waves, wavering in pockets. Hezet joined those kneeling with his halberd.

Necrem had nothing but the flag.

"I need a pike!" he yelled behind him. "A spear or—"

"*Oso!*" Hezet cried.

Necrem turned around—

And a horse ran into him.

Chapter 32

Everything was numb. Everything was black. Everything was distant.

Where . . .?

Necrem's lungs screamed at him from trying to breathe.

What . . .?

A muffled groan rumbled up from his belly. He tried to move, but he didn't know what exactly. An arm? A leg? His head? Or he simply tried to breathe? He couldn't be certain. The only thing he was certain of was that he was sore, and that soreness was spreading throughout his body.

Where—!

A ragged, violent cough ripped through him. His spine convulsed, forcing him up over his weak limbs' objections. He shot up on knees and elbows, coughing and spitting from his lungs' desperate cry for air. When he finally cleared his throat, the cool taste of air was laced with a coppery aftertaste.

Blood filled his mouth.

His torment continued as the numb cloud lifted from his head and a stinging fire replaced it across his face. He yowled at the sudden slap of feeling it all at once. Not one scar could have been left unripped.

He clapped his hands on his face, his gauntlets pressing against the masks.

That did nothing to soothe his face. It did, however, give Necrem the strength to open his eyes.

A shin kicked into his side.

Necrem hardly felt it, his plate taking the blow that equaled to a pat on the back compared to the aches he already had.

Another kick made Necrem angle his head, squinting up. An Orsembian soldier jabbed a spear over him. His kicks were nothing more than his footwork as he lunged to bat away a pike lunging at him.

Necrem rolled his head the other way and found a Lazornian at the other end of the pike. The rest of the world around him was a mash of legs, men and horses alike, all jumbled together without any sense of order. They all danced back and forth with one another until, here and there, one of those pairs of legs slipped and another body came flopping down to join the many the dancing legs either stepped around or on.

Wounded men crawled in every which direction. They hunkered as low as they could, their armor weighing them down as they used their good limbs to claw away. Every now and then, the butt of a pike, or the head of a spear, or the tip of a sword rained down on one of them from above.

Not five feet from where he lay, a sword struck down into the back a wounded soldier's neck. Sudden and quick, cutting the man's struggle short.

I need to get up!

The Orsembian soldier above him kicked him in the side again. This time when Necrem looked up, the soldier looked back at him. The man's eyebrows leaped, realizing he was still alive. His reaction of pulling his spear back was enough to spur whatever strength Necrem had left to raise up, hands outstretched to grab ahold of the spear shaft.

The wood slid through his gauntlets' thick gloves. His fingers struggled, and his biceps burned after using them so soon. His right hand meeting the soldier's saved him, allowing him to get a grip on the spear before the metal tip drove into his face.

Necrem focused on that sharp point, wavering inches from his face. They struggled, and that point grew closer. He pulled his head back. His legs wobbled. His hamstrings especially screamed in protest from being tightly stretched with him leaning back on his knees. But it was either that or allow a spear through his face.

Necrem leaned back, pulling the spear with him. He tried to push it up, but that resulted in bending the shaft, but the Orsembian soldier stepped forward, drawing the spear back for another thrust. Necrem's grip slipped. He shook back and forth, sticking an arm out for balance.

The Orsembian soldier came again—

A pike caught him under his neck. The soldier's head jerked. His jaw fell open as if he was holding the pike against his chin. Blood squirted and ran down from his neck along his breastplate.

Necrem watched his eyes roll back as he tipped to his side. His spear slipped from his grip, tumbling into Necrem's. When the pike pulled free, the soldier's body followed the direction he was leaning and joined the others at everyone's feet.

Necrem gasped in a mixture of revulsion, exhaustion, and relief. He took up the man's spear and used it as cane, planting it in the dirt and climbing hand over hand to get to his shaky feet. His chest ached, his lungs burned, and his head grew foggier the higher he climbed. None of it mattered. He knew he *had* to get up.

His head wobbled as soon as he stood. He kept both hands clutching the planted spear for support, not trusting his quivering legs an instant.

The scene that greeted him above was just as confusing as the one below.

Only a few feet in front of him was visible through clouds of dust and musket smoke. Men fought everywhere and everyone. There were no lines, no ranks, no squares of men. Men fought back-to-back, facing every direction, batting each other with spears and pikes, thrusting with swords, smashing with shields, stabbing with daggers, and some simply punched at one another.

Calleroses were among them, too. Some in groups, hacking anyone around their mounts with swords. Here and there, a horse came galloping through the dust. There was a whoop, a slash, a cry, and off they sped, leaving some poor soul cut down without knowing what struck him.

It was Compuert Junction all over again.

I got to get out of—

He caught a glint of metal out of the corner of his eye in time to move his head. The pike head grated across the rim of his helmet and sent his head reeling.

"Hey!" he yelled back at the Lazornian who had just saved his life. "I'm on your *shide*!" The blood pooled in his mouth and slurred his speech as he yelled.

The wide-eyed Lazornian looked up at him, face pale-stricken with terror. He didn't have a leather collar around his arm, so he wasn't a former *sioneros*. He had to be a soldier from the next company over on the line.

"What?" the Lazornian yelled.

"I'm with"—Necrem beat on his chest, wincing at a dull pain, then pointed at the soldier— "*you*!"

"How do I know that?" The Lazornian waved his pike at him.

Necrem went slack-jawed under his mask, unable to remind the soldier of the Bravados or what had happened earlier. His mind went blank. "I . . . don't—"

A calleros came pushing through the men behind the Lazornian, swinging and slashing his sword in curving arches down on every man he passed.

"*Look out!*" Necrem yelled, pointing behind the soldier.

The soldier saved himself by spinning with his pike. The spiked head thrust level with the horse's, spooking the animal and making it jerk back. The calleros wavered in his saddle, clutching his reins to get control of his horse.

The soldiers surged in around the calleros, no longer able to hack at them.

Necrem stepped to join them, but before he took two steps or picked the spear up, the calleros was knocked from his horse by several pikes, including the Lazornian who he'd been yelling to.

The calleros flailed and swung his sword as he fell to the ground with thud of metal from his plate. A stabbing barrage of pikes followed where he landed, his wails covered up under all the furious shouting and cussing around him.

"*Oso!*"

Once again, Hezet had found him.

The veteran elbowed his way through the press, having lost his shield. The spike and axe head of his stolen halberd was covered in gore, bobbing above his head.

"Damn it, smith!" Hezet growled, stumbling up to him. He planted the butt of his halberd into the ground and leaned on it just as much as Necrem leaned on his stolen spear. He gasped, struggling for breath with sweat coating his face. "How are you *not* dead? You got ran over by a *horse!*"

Necrem's gaze trailed down to his chest. There was a great dent in his breastplate, and the curve around his belly was pressed flat against him. He couldn't be certain with the angle, but he wouldn't have been surprised to find the impression of a horseshoe now in the center of his plate.

"That explains why my chest hurts." He coughed, spitting more blood into his masks.

Hezet shook his head. "Where's the banner?"

Necrem grunted. All around them was mobbish fighting, and when he looked, the banner he had worked so hard to get was nowhere to be seen. "Lost it."

"You should have held on to that," Hezet groaned.

"I think we should get out of—"

Eruptions roared all around them. Streaking, whizzing sounds filled the air. Calleroses cried, tumbling from their horses while soldiers on the ground dropped without a sound, Lazornians and Orsembians alike.

"*Get down!*" Hezet screamed. He took hold of Necrem's pauldron, dragging him down with his weight as another round of eruptions roared.

Men around them collapsed; some clutching their sides or limbs, while others never moved again.

"What's going on?" Necrem cried.

547

"The melee's too thick," Hezet replied, making Necrem shake his head, not understanding. "Keep low and crawl!" He slapped Necrem's pauldron as he began to crawl on his hands and knees, dragging his halberd with him.

"Where?" Necrem yelled over another round of musket fire, following the veteran's example.

"Anywhere but here!"

That was the simplest thing Necrem had ever heard, and he agreed wholeheartedly.

***

Recha held her eyeglass limply at her side.

I'm killing them. Her hand shook, tapping the eyeglass against her thigh. Her gaze fixed on the last black banner still waving, the other two having disappeared when the calleroses came crashing in. Yet, it, too, now wavered to remain upright in the center's madness. *They fought so gallantly, and I'm . . .*

Another concentrated volley roared in the center. Swaths of men dropped in clumps, the frantic melee making it impossible to tell which were Orsembian and which were Lazornian.

The former *sioneroses'* sudden charge had given them the time they needed. They had stopped the center from collapsing. They had given General Ross time to move up, forming another battle line for the center to fall back to and reserve companies waiting to be deployed where needed. They had broken all the way into the enemy's ranks.

Borbin's banner fell!

Now she was forced to fire upon them.

General Ross had formed musketeers up in blocks, three ranks deep with one firing at a time, on all three sides of the bulge in the center. They couldn't feed more men into the melee. It would become a meatgrinder and a battle of attrition they didn't have the numbers to win. She didn't need Baltazar to tell her *that*. The melee also prevented them from withdrawing her men in any semblance of order.

However, with so many Orsembians trapped in one spot, infantry as well as calleroses, they were in a similar position. They were bogged down just as much as Recha's soldiers were. Trapped at a distance and ripe for the pickings.

It left Recha wanting to scream and curse, yet she saw two consolations in the deployment. After each volley, the Lazornians around the edges of the melee were able to break free, many dragging wounded comrades with them behind the ranks of musketeers.

Another volley, and she watched with a sneer as calleroses tumbled and jerked out of their saddles.

"Tell them to aim high, Ross," she mumbled, callous to the calleroses' plight of being unable to cut or ride through the melee. They made excellent targets perched high in their saddles. "Don't let any of them ride out of there."

"Hmm?" Baltazar hummed, raising an eyebrow from over his shoulder as he scribbled his signature on a random order. "You say something?"

"No," Recha replied, folding her arms. She held her eyeglass up to rest her chin on it while she watched the battle continue across the field.

Baltazar shooed the dispatch away and took up his bowl of soup that a staff officer was holding for him while he signed the order. He stepped closer, following her gaze while slurping a spoonful of his meal—a mix of meat, potatoes, rice, and whatever else the cooks had decided to toss in the pot to fill the rotating soldiers' stomachs.

"Has something changed?" he asked.

Recha sighed. "No."

"Good." Baltazar munched down another spoonful, this time finding something crunchy. "Two crises averted in just an hour, and we are still holding. After the next rotation, we can start our counterattacks."

Recha frowned, tapping her chin against her eyeglass's lens. "While we wait, send an order to General Ross. Tell him to shoot every enemy calleros in the center he can. Even if they surrender, I don't care. Shoot them."

"I'll do no such thing," Baltazar replied as he chewed.

Recha slid her gaze across to him, squinting at him from the corner of her eye. "What?"

Baltazar casually stirred his soup, unfazed by her glare. "You're upset—"

"*Obviously,*" she hissed.

"But now's not the time to make such rash orders." Baltazar tapped the rim of his bowl with his spoon. "General Ross needs to keep focused on untangling that knot and holding formation across the center. If he focuses on cutting down as many calleroses as he can, he will leave his wings unattended. Hiraldo and Priet need him to keep focus across his line while they tend to the flanks. Another near break in center could be enough for them to collapse, as well."

The fight on their flanks had lost their urgency with all the commotion in the center. Hiraldo's counter oblique formation had blunted the Orsembians with both pulling back from the line, leaving bodies trailing behind them, and a mound where the press had been the thickest. Hiraldo had reformed a line, anchoring their left flank against the cliff face, rotating his tired troops out with reserves as men in squads took turns rushing out to gather up wounded from the mound and pulling them to safety.

There was still a fight on the right flank. The Orsembians weren't in a hurry to send more men down the corridor General Priet had lain open for them.

Nonetheless, they had their backs to that ridgeline now, and a little trickle of Orsembian troops were slipping into the southeastern passage. While calleroses of the Second Army waited there to harass them, those who made it formed squares to hold their positions. It would take a concentrated push to stop more Orsembians from making their way into the passage, an effort Priet lacked the position and resources to make presently.

"Those calleroses in the center can't get away," Recha said, stubbornly pressing her eyeglass's lens into her chin. "They turned the center into a charnel house, and for *what*? This is the perfect chance to cut down as many as we can."

Baltazar struck the rim of his bowl with his spoon loudly, the sharp, wooden clap loud enough to cut off officers talking over their own soup a few feet away. "Look to your armies, Recha," he warned. "The men are starting to tire. The enemy, as well. It's best we make use of this lull to recover as many as we can before the next engagement."

Her armies did look tired.

That passionate zeal they'd had when they first charged appeared to have burned out. Now they moved as men going through practiced motions, following orders without much thought. Relieved companies made their way to the cook fires. They racked their weapons and descended on the pots, eating and drinking as quickly as they could before laying on the ground for short naps.

Meanwhile, musketeers switched out their bandolier, and men carrying wounded made their way to the army doctors. Fortunately, those grizzly sights were quartered on the far-right side of the camp, away from where she could casually glance in that direction.

"The melee is breaking up!" an observer shouted. "The enemy's withdrawing!"

Baltazar turned to exchange his soup for his eyeglass that his waiting staff officer held. "Put that on the table and get yourself some food," he told the officer.

"Yes, sir!" the officer replied. "Thank you, Field Marshal!"

Recha pursed her lips, watching the exchange. With a *harrumph*, she opened her own eyeglass and joined Baltazar in surveying the center.

General Ross's musketeers were falling back behind their second line. The companies of pikemen stood ready, the front rows of pikes lowered in case another charge or breakthrough came from the untangling knot in the center.

Streams of men trickled out of the melee on both sides. In twos, in groups, in limping lines, they pulled themselves out of the fighting, making their way to the gaps between the companies on the second line and to safety.

The Orsembians, likewise, broke away from the melee, hurrying out of the press and into the haze below. Not just in the melee, but the Orsembians attacking down the rest of the center were withdrawing, too, in much better order than those running out of the knot.

The smoke would clear soon now that the musketeers had stopped. If there was a second line behind it, Recha was sure it would be visible soon.

"Calleroses are getting away," she grumbled, biting the inside of her cheek at seeing the number of them riding free of the fighting.

"Let them," Baltazar remarked. "They're riding away bloodied. They'll go back to camp, rest their horses, lick their wounds, and talk to the other calleroses about how their charge couldn't break our lines. We need to take advantage of this lull.

"Dispatch!"

A rider dropped his food and came running.

"Send word to General Ross," Baltazar ordered. "He is to use this moment to rotate the entire front line! Not company by company or one at a time. *Every* man who was in that fight is to be pulled back to rest!"

"The men on the front may not wait for those orders," Recha commented.

Watching through her eyeglass, the melee had completely broken up. A few companies on the front line orderly fell back, making their way, step-by-labored-step, to the second line to rotate. Those lumbering out of the melee didn't look to see if they were being replaced as they headed for the rear.

However, while most men lumbered back behind the second line, the last remaining black flag remained standing in the center. Those who didn't rush to get behind the second line instead formed up around it. As they did, a second black banner reappeared, reclaimed from the battle, though with far less men around them than when they'd had charged in.

Recha peeked away from her eyeglass to spot the dispatcher still there, scribbling Baltazar's order down as fast as he could. "Relay a message from me, as well," she said. "After General Ross rotates the men out, he's to deliver my personal compliments to those men in the center. They're the saviors of the line, and they have my gratitude."

The dispatcher wrote frantically to get it all down.

Baltazar shot glances to him, to her, then back to him. "That's enough. Just relay the messages. General Ross is to rotate the entire center, and La Dama wishes him to convey her compliments to the survivors. Go on!" He waved the dispatcher off, sending him jogging to his horse. Then he turned and gave her an odd, crooked smirked. His mustache whiskers twitched.

"What?" she asked, shrugging.

"Deliver your *personal* compliments?" He arched an eyebrow.

Recha's shoulders slumped. "I know," she replied with a sigh. "After what they've been through, they may not care about any compliments or praise from me." She straightened her shoulders. "But my recognition is all I can give them right now. I dare anyone on this field to say they haven't earned it."

Baltazar studied her for a moment. "You should get something to eat."

"I'm not hungry."

"Doesn't matter." Baltazar shook his head. "You will be and need to eat like everyone else. I'll send—"

A sharp trumpet call pierced the air from across the field.

Recha's eyeglass was up in an instant, along with Baltazar's and every other observer's.

Ten riders trotted out of the drifting musket haze, led by Borbin's banner and a white flag of parley. The stopped yards away from the dead left from the melee, and their bugler let out another call. Their formality made their intentions obvious.

"Borbin wants to talk some more," Recha said, frowning.

After everything that's happened? The hairs at the back of her neck stood up, and she bit the inside of her cheek. *You're up to something again, aren't you, Borbin?*

***

"Come on!" the pikeman yelled, waving his arm.

Necrem and Hezet scrambled, dodging and weaving to avoid the calleroses riding out of the carnage. The shooting had blessedly stopped, and the soldiers were all eager to get out of the maddening brawl, as if every man on foot had silently agreed they had had enough.

The calleroses, however, didn't share the same view. Those still in their saddles broke free from the melee with fanfare, yelling and slicing at anyone in their path. A soldier waved his spear to fend them off or spook their horses and was ran down for his trouble. His armor and clothing marked him as an Orsembian.

"*Hurry!*" pikemen yelled.

Hezet had spotted the Lazornians rallying around a flag as the shooting stopped and the mad dash to get out of the mayhem began. They thought they could simply make their way to join the rally. It would be much safer than trying to walk out of the press and into whatever awaited them on the other side. That was if the Orsembians didn't get their fight back.

Necrem huffed and sucked in air in fast, sharp hisses. His lungs screamed for more, but he could only pull so much through his mask. His legs burned from running, and the rest of his body was numb. He'd worked through nights of endless hammering and had never felt as tired as he did now.

The hoofbeats grew louder. The yowling yells grew closer.

"*Run*, Oso!" Hezet screamed. "Run for your *life!*"

They both sprinted. Necrem's legs were longer, but his armor was heavier. He'd never been much of a runner. Hezet hefted his halberd on his shoulder and raced beside him.

Sweat pooled in Necrem's eyes. His vision blurred. His lungs demanded more air. The hooves grew louder! The hairs on the back of his neck stood up! The horses were breathing down on him. He could barely see the pikemen or their outstretched pikes.

"*Come on!*" men yelled.

Necrem roared. He ignored his screaming body, his burning face, blurring eyes. He lost feeling in everything but his legs. He squeezed his eyes shut and ran!

Faster. Faster! *Faster!*

He slammed into two men, and they all went tumbling over each other.

Others flooded around them, one stepping on Necrem's back. He felt a telltale tremor rumble through the ground before hearing a horse bay and the sound of hooves grind against the dirt. Seconds later, the hoofbeats resumed, trotting away.

"Get 'em up," someone ordered.

The boot left Necrem's back, and someone slapped his pauldrons.

"You all right?" someone asked.

Necrem pushed himself up onto his knees, groaning along with the men he had run over. Hands reached down all around him. A couple snatched up the other two on the ground, but Necrem fetched his stolen spear, used it as a crutch, and attempted to crawl back up it again. His wobbling knees threatened to topple him back over, and his gauntlets slipped on the spear shaft. He sucked in air and his pride, and then took a hand to get back to his feet.

Men backed around him, giving him space while also staring up at him.

"His face," someone whispered.

Necrem shifted on his feet, looking about him but couldn't find the man who had spoken. Most of their faces were drenched in sweat and dust. Specks of blood only reached a few without any around him having head wounds.

He reached up and touched his mask. His fingers found the metal holes. The gauntlet's flexible plates tapped against the mask's steel.

He snorted in relief that it was still there. His cloth mask underneath was sealed to his face, thanks to the blood drying to his cracked skin.

"What about it?" he asked lowly.

Men passed wary looks at one another. Most returned to watching out for any more calleroses riding by, ignoring him.

"You're . . . bleeding," one man said, pointing at him.

Necrem looked at his hand. Droplets of blood painted across his gauntlet's fingertips. It must have seeped through his cloth mask and dripped onto the metal. Now some was leaking through the holes. Here on a battlefield, though, there was little he could do about it.

He shrugged and said, "Who ain't?"

A round of snorts and grumbles broke out around him.

"Order!" someone demanded, cutting over the men. "The calleroses have passed! Withdraw in steady order!"

Drum taps started up from somewhere in the center of the pack. Men moved together. Their feet drawn in step with the beat. Its infectious tone reached Necrem, and he didn't need to be told to follow. He glanced over his shoulder, making sure Hezet had made it. The veteran was following a few men behind.

The men on the edges held their pikes out as they walked in more of a large circle than a square. They waved in and picked up any stragglers they met, absorbing smaller groups of Lazornian soldiers as they went.

Any group of calleroses that came galloping by was greeted with rows of pikes and roars of curses, whether they chanced a charge or kept their distance. Orsembian soldiers hurriedly ran away, some frantic to keep their distance.

Again, Necrem had an advantage being head and shoulders taller than everyone. He spotted where they were going before those around him could. The Lazornians had made another line, squares of infantry waiting and letting their embattled comrades through gaps between them. Safety was yards away.

A sharp trumpet call split the air. The drums stopped, and Necrem joined every man around him in spinning to see where that call had come from.

"*Calleroses*!" a man yelled. "They're charging again!"

Not again. Necrem groaned and felt the soreness of his chest, not wanting to test the strength of his plate like that ever again.

"Square!" an officer ordered. "Form ranks and lower pikes on all sides!"

Drums rapped urgently, and exhausted men struggled to move at the pace. Necrem was swept along, finding himself, thankfully, three men deep and nowhere near the front row.

They waited. Men breathed hard, and poles rattled against each other as arms shook, expecting to hear that rumble again.

Instead, another trumpet blast sounded, accompanied by a group of calleroses walking their horses through the haze of dust and musket smoke to stop in the middle of the field. Two flags waved above them—Borbin's and a white one.

"They're not charging!" someone yelled.

"They want to talk!" Another laughed. "Maybe they've had enough!"

"Steady men!" an officer ordered. "It could be a trick! Orderly withdrawal! Keep your ranks!"

"Keep your ranks, boys!" someone repeated as the drums began tapping. "Keep your ranks!"

Necrem felt awkward backing away one slow, measured step at a time. The bottom rim of his shin plate dug into the top of his boots, and he repeatedly backed into the man behind him.

The slow pace was maddening. He kept glancing over his shoulder at the safety behind the second line of Lazornian squares, and it felt farther and farther away with each glance.

Another trumpet sounded, this time behind them, followed by drums.

A line of Lazornian calleroses trotted by, their marquesa's flag and a white flag waving in front of them as they headed toward their Orsembian counterparts. Three of those calleroses broke away, riding toward them.

"Companies, halt!" an officer shouted.

What now? Necrem took a deep breath, wanting desperately to plant his spear into the ground and lean on it.

He spotted Hezet watching him, frowning.

"Well fought, men!" the calleros in the center yelled, reining in his horse a few feet from them along with his compatriots. "Well fought! Where are your officers?"

"Here, sir!" someone shouted deeper into ranks, which was echoed by several more men calling out all around.

"Continue your withdrawal to the rear," the calleros ordered. "Pick up any stragglers and walking wounded you can, then reform, rest, and wait for further orders!"

I don't think we needed to be told that. Necrem held his tongue. Although, from the rolling eyes and frowning faces around him, he wasn't the only one thinking it.

"Yes, sir!" an officer shouted. "Thank you, sir!"

The calleros nodded and waved at all of them. "La Dama Mandas's compliments you all! She has declared each of you as saviors of the line! Rest well." He wheeled his horse around. "We may still have need of you this day!" With that, the calleroses galloped off to join their fellows in the talks happening in the center of the field.

"Can't we just get paid and sleep the rest of the day?" a soldier joked, drawing some chuckles.

"With a woman!" another added, followed by more laughs.

"Two women!"

The burst of laughs, smirks, and a dozen conversations of each man trying to top the other of what they wanted spun quickly out of control.

"All right, knock it off!" a stern voice shouted. It sounded like Hezet to Necrem, but he couldn't be sure.

"Companies, to the rear!" an officer shouted. "*March!*"

The drums picked up again, this time a more measured pace. As they made their way off the battlefield, they passed between the second line of Lazornians, marching up to take over. There were waves and nods as the groups passed, but it was mostly done in silence.

Necrem shouldered the spear he was carrying, unsure of what to do with it, or even what to do with himself, for that matter.

Should I . . . just go back to camp? Despite fighting with the men around him, he wasn't a part of any of their companies. He wasn't entirely sure if the men around him were the same ones who had fought around him when he'd first charged into that mess.

He looked over his shoulder. Hezet nodded back at him.

He sighed. *Maybe I should just follow them to the rear and see what I can do then.*

As he contemplated further, with every step, the calleroses who went out to talk galloped back behind the lines. Those carrying banners joined a column of over two hundred, mounted and watching behind the squares of men, while three broke away and kept riding into camp.

***

Recha scooped spoonful after spoonful of soup, barely chewing the stray carrot or bite of pork before swallowing. The soup was a touch too salty and needed to boil more of the water out. However, her demanding stomach didn't care. The moment she had stubbornly relented and taken her first gulp, she'd suddenly become ravenous and attacked her bowl without a care of how unladylike she appeared. She didn't even rise from her seat when the calleroses came riding in with Borbin's latest overture.

"Who did you receive this from?" she asked, wiping her lips with the back of her hand. "Did Marshal Fuert deliver this personally, or was it another officer?" She pushed her bowl away to take up the folded missive on the table in front of her. Then she sat back and unfolded the unsealed parchment.

"Neither, La Dama," the foremost calleros replied, clicking his heels together. "The message was delivered by a baron, Baron Valen Irujo. The baron wished to relay that we have fifteen minutes to offer a response."

Recha snickered and smirked. *Still delivering Borbin's letters, are you, Valen? I wonder if it's because you fought to keep your position, or if you're being punished . . .*

Her smirk slipped as she read. The message lacked a seal, yet after days of reading other correspondences, she instantly recognized Borbin's own handwriting. She pursed her lips and read the message again. Her hunger suddenly disappeared.

"Thank you, gentlemen," she said, rising to her feet. The back of her legs pushed her chair back before Cornelos caught it and drew it back the rest of the way. "You may all return to your duties."

Dozens of heels snapped together around her, and officers sharply nodded in salute. "Yes, La Dama," they parroted before breaking away. The calleroses put their helmets back on and headed toward their horses, and staff officers returned to their duties.

Baltazar remained standing to her left, watching her.

Recha handed him the missive as she snatched up her eyeglass and walked around the table to overlook the battlefield again. She twisted the glass, extending it, and brought it to her eye as her ears twitched from Baltazar's heavy bootsteps walking up beside her.

"He wants his son's body retrieved," Baltazar said lowly, a hint of understanding in his voice. "For that, he's requesting an hour reprieve for us both to tend to our wounded. It sounds . . . reasonable."

"You hesitated," Recha noted.

She slowly passed her eyeglass over the field. The left flank and center stood unengaged. The First Army was clearing the last of the dead and wounded from the where they had stopped the Orsembian oblique from dislodging them, and squares of companies were forming up on the battle line they had preserved. General Ross was forming up his second line where the center had held, making sure there was barely any gap between his arm and the First and Second on his flanks.

"Borbin doesn't say whether he's going to withdraw from the right or not," Baltazar said, followed by the clicks of his eyeglass extending.

The fighting on the right flank had devolved into light skirmishes. General Priet was more focused on rotating out his companies at the front of the line, especially those on the corner, keeping the corridor the Orsembians held around the ridge on the right as small as possible.

Instead of fighting across the line, the Orsembians had banded together in tight pack squares, three companies strong. They formed tight pockets with spaces between them, and anchored their backs to the ridgeline all the way down and around into the southeast passage.

"We can't accept the reprieve and let those squares remain in those positions," Baltazar commented. "If we do, it will give them time to regroup, reinforce, and possibly widen their position. It could risk the entire right flank. Priet should never have let up the pressure."

"And if we ordered an attack on the right now, we can tear up that offer of reprieve for the rest of the line while we're at it," Recha said.

"Not just that." Baltazar coughed and cleared his throat. "Ordering an assault on the right with the enemy in tight squares like that would require fighting against each individual square. It'll be a fierce bloodbath for each one. If Priet is pushed by Orsembian reinforcements, we could just be throwing men away without dislodging them completely. We need to plan across the entire field . . .

"Recha! Across the field. The *center*!"

Recha took her eyeglass down to reposition and brought it back up again, focusing across the field at the Orsembian center. The haze of musket smoke and dust kicked up by withdrawing calleroses had wafted away, revealing what amassed beyond.

A new Orsembian formation came into view. In the center massed three calleros columns, five horses across and stretching down the slope. Their lances were held high, along with a multitude of banners from barons and high-ranking calleroses. In the center column, ten horses back, waved Borbin's largest banner on the field, three times the size of the others, and sat in a commanding, protected space among the calleroses.

Lines of infantry flanked the calleroses, at least six lines deep, amounting to at least forty thousand strong. A couple of lines were positioned on each wing of the massed formation, but the bulk of that army was pointed like a broad sword at the center of her line.

"He still intends to destroy our center," Recha said, interpreting the obviousness of the formation.

"Yes," Baltazar agreed. "Either now or an hour from now." He hummed to himself.

Recha lowered her eyeglass, finding him standing with his arms folded and eyeglass under his arm. Unlike before when the center had appeared to be breaking, Baltazar's dark eyes scanned the field back and forth repeatedly. His face was carved from unmoving rock, unshaken at the prospect of the Orsembians doing the same thing again, only in most likely overwhelming numbers this time.

"I don't think we're going to get that reprieve, are we?" she said.

"I don't think so, either," Baltazar agreed. "I think General Ross needs to prepare to hold, and then orderly withdrawal. Hiraldo and Priet, on the other hand . . ." He raised his eyeglass again. He twisted and turned the lens, grimacing. He growled after a moment and pulled it away. "Your eyes are better than mine. Can you look for something for me?"

Recha suppressed a small smile. "Sure, great Field Marshal." She brought her eyeglass up. "What are we looking for?"

"White Sword," he growled. "I don't see his banner anywhere!"

Recha sniffed sharply, her bemusement instantly snuffed out as she tightened her eyeglass's focus on all the banners waving in the Orsembian center. It was nearly impossible to distinguish individual banners from how they hung around each other, the lack of a breeze prevented them from unfurling so she could see them all clearly. However, there was only one Orsembian banner that was black and white.

It was *nowhere* to be seen.

"It's not there!" she exclaimed, dropping her eyeglass. "The White Sword's *not* on the field!"

Baltazar crumpled Borbin's message in his hands, tossing it back on the table as he spun. "Dispatchers!" he roared. "I need dispatchers! General Galvez needs to—"

A piercing, echoing trumpet call came from Recha's left. She looked back to the field, yet Hiraldo and the First Army stood unopposed and unmoved from the last time she had looked. There was no attack. There was . . .

She spun on her heels.

Squads of soldiers that they had left stationed near the narrow passage on the left were darting away from it. A few riders galloped out it, their arms flailing in the air and bouncing in the saddle without any sign of fear of slipping off or breaking their horses' legs. Or perhaps they feared something else.

"Beat to arms!" Baltazar shouted. "Get the men eating and resting up! They're coming—"

Another sharp trumpet blast, followed by the shouting, yelling, and thundering hooves echoed out of the tight passage and into the plain. They grew louder and louder over the hurried drumbeats breaking out across the camp.

Recha kept her eyes on the passage, waiting for what she knew was coming.

Men scrambled, kicking cookpots over to fetch their racked pikes and muskets.

Another trumpet blast echoed!

The hooves grew louder!

Suddenly, calleroses by the dozen spilled from the narrow passage in a fast, endless stream. They came on, waving their swords and lowering their lances, eager for the slaughter. They broke into multiple lines, some flowing toward the rear of the First Army, others around the cliff face at the rear of the camp, and the main force, waving the White Sword's banner . . . came *straight* at her tent.

Orders were shouted on top of orders. Men raced back and forth, grabbing every weapon they could find. In an instant, Cornelos and her guard surrounded her and Baltazar, swords drawn.

"We should withdrawal, Recha," Cornelos urged.

"No," she replied.

"What—" Cornelos grunted and pulled back at seeing her.

She grinned broadly from ear to ear. Her heart raced with the pounding of the hooves coming to take her life. She couldn't hold it any longer.

"*Now, Sevesco!*" she screamed. "*Now!*"

Boom!

Both sides of the narrow passage *exploded*!

Chapter 33

Explosions tore across the cliff faces above the narrow passage, showering the oncoming Orsembians with rocks, from pebbles to boulders. The calleroses' horses screamed and reared out of their charge in a panic. Their riders desperately whipped and kicked their mounts, driving them forward until the moment the rocks fell upon them.

Raging avalanches of rock, dust, and smoke bellowed down the slopes of both cliff faces. The rumble of cascading rock drowned out everything—the trumpets blaring, the drums beating, the hooves pounding, and—Savior be praised—the calleroses screaming. The last sight Recha caught before the tide of dust and smoke engulfed the entire trek was the unfortunate calleroses who had turned the bend in time to be caught, their hands outstretched above their heads before being swallowed up.

No manner of plate could survive such an onslaught. Horses shrieked and men wailed, many of which were cut off short and suddenly.

Recha didn't count the minutes. What felt like hours had happened in the span of seconds.

"It worked," she said under her breath, still grinning from ear to ear. She laughed. "Sevesco, you . . . magnificent madman!"

More rumbling explosions echoed from back inside the pathway.

Sevesco had been setting it up for a couple of days. They had known Ribera knew these paths. They had suspected that path led to their rear and likely connected farther east. Their scouts had reported movement. However, they couldn't be certain of what. They couldn't ignore the obvious threat the path posed, nor guard it completely.

Recha shook her head at Sevesco being the one to have suggested turning the trail into a trap.

Now for the second part.

The avalanches' giant, combined cloud of dust and smoke merged and wafted in the air, taking minutes to drift high enough to reveal the carnage below. The ground was littered with crushed bodies under rock, yet not all were dead. Many of the survivors struggled and coughed through their helmets' visors. Some led horses while others staggered on their feet.

A couple drew their swords and trudged forward—

A high-pitched whistle pierced the air!

A steel-barbed crossbow bolt struck into a calleros's pauldrons with a *thunk*! The man staggered, dropping to his knees.

As his compatriots raised the alarm, more crossbow bolts whistled down from the west- and north-facing cliffs. The calleroses' charge was demolished, their path blocked, and now, as for the second part of Sevesco's plan, the surviving calleroses were being treated with a hail of steel from above.

"Excellent call giving Sevesco all our spare crossbows, Papa!" Recha praised over her shoulder. "We're finally putting them to use."

The Third Army had been carrying around their crossbows and bolts since refitting with the muskets before Compuert Junction. It had felt like such a waste to have them hauled around and unused. Sevesco's plan had offered the perfect opportunity to deploy them again, along with any camp worker able to volunteer that could use the weapon, either firing or loading them.

Of course, Sevesco found no shortage of volunteers, Recha mused. *They got to climb up to the highest, safest place during a battle.* With *weapons!*

"This battle *isn't* over!" Baltazar bellowed, storming through Recha's guards surrounding them. "Dispatchers! Ride to Marshal Narvae! He must charge *now!*"

A man sprinted to a horse, galloping off as Baltazar seized two more dispatchers by their collars.

"Find Marshal Olguer and General Priet! Marshal Olguer's to take command of all of Second Army's calleroses and take control of the southeastern passage. He's to harass all Orsembians who've made it in there until they are driven off, crushed, or taken prisoner! General Priet is to prepare all his musketeers and swordsmen to keep those squares of Orsembians divided and unable to link up. He's to prepare the rest of his army, all his pike to attack forward. Off with you!"

He didn't give them time to reply. He shoved them toward their waiting mounts that were nervously kicking the dirt from all the excitement around them, and marched back to the command tent. He moved hurriedly, like a man half his age, grim determination scowling his face.

I should be doing something, Recha thought, sweat streaking down her forehead. *I know I should be doing something!*

"Don't just stand there!" Baltazar shouted, rushing by. "Commandant Narvae! Get La Dama to her horse! All staff officers, to your horses and prepare to defend yourselves and this position!"

The whirlwind that had engulfed the camp now swept through her tent. Every officer and soldier around the tent dropped whatever they were doing and rushed about. Papers went flying. Plates and bowls clattered on ground. Men sprinted to their horses, fixing helmets over their heads before soldiers helped them into their saddles.

Someone seized her shoulder.

"This way, Recha!" Cornelos implored. "Hurry!"

Hurry?

"*Wait!*" she yelled, realizing what Baltazar had meant. She stumbled a few steps then dug in her heels, turning a snarling glare at Baltazar a few feet away, shooing some officers. "Baltazar! I'm not running!"

"Neither am I!" he yelled back, glaring through his grimace. He thrust a finger at her. "But you're getting on your horse!" He shifted his finger, pointing behind her. "The White Sword's *still* heading this way!"

Recha spun around. Despite the explosion crushing most of the enemy calleroses in the passage, despite being behind enemy lines with his means of escape cut off, despite Recha's soldiers rushing off to face the calleroses who had gotten through, Ribera was still charging toward her tent.

After the explosion, the calleroses who'd been aiming to swing around the rear of her camp had pivoted and joined up with him. It was too late for the calleroses charging toward Hiraldo's rear to change their course. Hiraldo's rear guard was already countercharging.

Yet, even without those men, Ribera and close to five hundred calleroses were charging straight for her. Her soldiers in camp were still forming up, and those resting in reserve were still rushing to cut them off.

They're not going to make it! Recha realized, judging the soldiers' distance and the calleroses' speed.

A dozen trumpets called at once. Piercing, sharp-noted cadences.

Recha stiffly turned her head.

Borbin's host was moving, straight for the center of her armies.

***

Necrem hissed. The damp cloth stung his face with every light dab.

"Hold still!" Doctor Maranon scolded. "You're bleeding from a dozen rips." He spat to the side, wiping his sweat drenched brow with a stained sleeve before dabbing the other side of Necrem's face with the cloth. "Whatever possessed you to do something as insane as this?"

"The La Dama asked him, Doctor," Hezet replied, standing off to the side with two bowls of stew.

Doctor Maranon shook his head. "Stupidity. I took you to have more sense, Necrem."

Necrem winced and said nothing as Maranon dug the cloth between the flabs of scarred skin, cleaning out the dried blood and dust. He sat on his knees on the slope between the battle lines and the camp. Cookfires dotted the land, along with wagons filled with water barrels and barrels of black powder.

Men sat around in the hundreds, eating, drinking, sleeping. Some ventured off to take care of releasing themselves. Men and women with bandages and buckets of water for washing moved about, tending to the lesser wounded, if they could, and helping the more seriously wounded limp back to camp, if they couldn't.

The healers had descended on them upon reaching the rear, checking everyone. The sight of him bleeding through his mask's holes was enough for one woman to become insistent, believing he had either been struck on the head or in the face.

No amount of warning from him or Hezet could persuade her it was something she couldn't handle. Not until Necrem knelt on the ground, removed his helmet to allow her to untie his mask's knots did she get to see the grizzly truth for herself. Necrem's cloth mask made wet, sticky, suction sounds as it peeled off his face.

Surprisingly, instead of repulsion, the woman's face, tanned like bronze from being out under the Easterly Sun all day, had hardened. She furiously demanded him down to his knees and began washing his face with the cloth carried in her water bucket.

Necrem could do little but wince at every dab and wipe, unable to keep his face out of sight from the men passing by. Although, on a field where so many gruesome sights lay strewed about, his face probably amounted to one of the hundreds, probably thousands.

Hezet left to fetch some food, and on his return, he brought Doctor Maranon. A few stubborn words passed between the doctor and the healer woman before he informed her there was little more that she could do and sent her to tend to the wounded she could help. The woman did so in a huff then raced toward another group of limping soldiers. Maranon, meanwhile, instantly went to scolding Necrem.

"I don't have any salve," Maranon grumbled, pulling a glass bottle of yellow liquid out of his satchel. "I ran out of stiches an hour ago"—he uncorked the bottle and dabbed his washcloth into the liquid—"and I can't send you to the surgeons. For once, I agree with the soldiers—you've been cut up enough."

Necrem grunted at the joke, opening his mouth to retort. His nose wrinkled at the strong, heavy scent of—

Liquor!

Maranon dabbed and wiped his face. A searing, stabbing pain shot through his face with every wipe of the cloth, forcing a gasp through his clenched teeth and tears to swell around the corners of his eyes.

"Don't move!" Maranon demanded. "This will clean you up and stop most of the bleeding—"

Bugles blared. Echoing shrieks sounded like they came from everywhere at once. Men stumbled and groaned to their feet, twisting and turning about in search of the direction of the bugles.

Maranon continued to clean Necrem's face with a stubborn scowl on his own face as he remained focused on his work . . . until he flickered a glance over Necrem's shoulder. His hand froze in the air. His scowl dropped as his eyebrows leapt up.

"Savior, shield us," he whispered.

Necrem angled his head to check on Hezet. The veteran, likewise, gawked at something behind him.

Necrem shuffled around. His armor felt heavier with him on his knees, the plates clinking and knocking together, weights dragging him down by their straps. He was also exhausted. His muscles strained and burned with every twitch and jerk he made to hobble himself around and . . .

The largest army Necrem had ever seen stretched across the other side of the field. Rank after rank of infantry. Columns of calleroses. The number of banners swaying on poles equaled the number of spears. Necrem lost count of how many must have been out there instantly.

His shoulders slumped at the sight of them. *Was . . . was everything we did down there . . . was it all for nothing?*

He curled his hands into fists, popping his knuckles. The gauntlets' leather groaned and plates rattled. He breathed deeply from his nose once, twice, *three* times before realizing he was mad. From that simple question, one which he must have shared with most of the men around him as they, too, looked, pointed, and shook their heads at what they saw across the field.

Still, he was mad, like working on a commission for days, only to be told it was not what the customer wanted. The waste of steel, sweat, and time. This anger felt worse. It stung deeper and tasted bitter.

Explosions ripped him back to the present, and he snapped his head around, as did everyone else.

Those are behind us!

The north cliff line was exploding! The bugle blaring cut off.

As Necrem followed the rock fall, he jerked to his feet.

Calleroses were behind them!

He couldn't count how many, though a stream of them were charging toward the Lazornians over on the left, while more joined together and charged into the camp. Necrem stiffened at the banner waving over those charging into camp.

"White Sword!" someone yelled.

"Calleroses are behind us!" another yelled.

Drums furiously rapped across the field. Officers shouted. Men cursed as bowls were sent flying, and it became a mad dash as every man raced to take their pike or musket from their racks, their swords out, and their helmets on.

"Here!" Hezet shouted, nudging something insistently against Necrem's arm.

The veteran held out one of the bowls of stew while tipping his head back, gulping down the other. Necrem watched, blinking in wonder as Hezet sucked gulp after gulp, barely needing or trying to chew. He pulled away coughing after a minute.

"Hurry!" Hezet coughed. "Eat as much of it as you can!"

Necrem took the bowl and was still holding it after Hezet finished devouring the rest of his.

"Eat, Oso!" Hezet demanded. "If you don't, you won't have any strength for the next fight." He turned his head back and forth at the calleroses behind them and Borbin's massive army across the field, frowning grimly.

"Wait!" Maranon protested, grunting to his feet. "He can't fight with his face like this! He could bleed out from these. They could become infected! Besides"—he looked up at Necrem with a pleading look—"you're a blacksmith, *not* a soldier."

Bugles blared across the field.

"Form up!" an officer galloping across the slope bellowed. "Form up, Third Army! All reserve companies form up!"

As company capitáns repeated the order and drums tapped, Necrem passed looks between Hezet and Maranon, holding the bowl of stew in his gauntlets.

Despite having scooped water through them, he picked out the stained varnish of dried blood speckled between the small plates on his gauntlet fingers.

He looked behind him at the sound of thundering hooves. The Orsembians' calleroses across the field were charging. All three columns roared over the field of dead that Necrem and so many others had left barely twenty minutes ago.

The Lazornians lowered their pikes. Their tight squares grew tighter. Drums ceased.

The calleroses roared in, waving swords and lowering lances. Their banners waved in the air against their colorful sets of plated armor. A volley of musket fire erupted from one Lazornian company. Then another volley from beside it. Calleroses pulled up on their reins. Some jerked and fell out of their saddles. Horses stumbled head over heels, rolling their riders under them. But more came on after them.

Necrem gritted his teeth, watching every second. Until . . .

Impact.

The Lazornians, to their credit, didn't budge. Most of the calleroses horses wheeled away, refusing to run into the bristle of barbed steel. A few unfortunate beasts had no way of turning. They slammed into the pikes, screaming out across the field as the force of their charge took over after their legs failed them. Two or three pikes snapped off and lodged in their bodies.

Calleroses swarmed around the squares, hacking with their swords and thrusting with their lances. In response, the Lazornians kept their squares and stabbed at horse and rider with eager vigor. Any calleros who fell from his saddle, whether it be from caught by a pike or musket ball, was brutely set upon by more stabbing pikes.

However, the calleroses keep storming in, riding between the company squares and getting between the lines. Drums began tapping, and the second line of Lazornians in the center lowered their pikes and began marching forward to meet those who got through.

"Third Army, form up!" a Lazornian calleros yelled, waving and pointing at the battlefield from his horse. "Those men are going to need all of us! They're holding back all of Orsembar out there! For the love of the Savior, *form* up!"

Necrem turned back. More men had formed their companies. Their drummers rapped taps, and they began to march down the slope again, in step. The healers and cooks were all jogging away to their wagons, rushing off to whatever their duties were and avoiding watching the soldiers leave and the battle beyond.

Hezet and Maranon both stood there, watching him. Hezet stood with his body turned, one foot pivoted toward the marching companies. He frowned determinedly, his fists shaking while his eyes twitched at every drum tap, as if they called him. Maranon, though, held his pleading look, holding his washcloth up.

Necrem dropped his head. His grip tightened around the bowl of stew as the sounds of battle raged behind him.

It couldn't have all been for nothing.

"Yesterday, I was a blacksmith," he said. He brought the bowl up to his mouth. His ripped and sliced lips made slurping impossible, and he didn't have time to use the spoon. He tipped his head back and lifted the bowl. The stew was mild, and he poured it into his mouth. He strained it through his teeth, chewing what he caught, and swallowed what he could. Half of the salty, milky contents spilled out of the holes in his cheeks, running down his jawlines and dripping onto his armor. He pulled the bowl away with a sigh. "Today, I'm just another man with a job to do."

Maranon hung his head, dropping his arm to his side.

Hezet stood a little straighter and held out Necrem's steel mask and helmet. "You're going to need these. And we need to find ourselves some pikes."

***

Recha finally discovered something positive about sitting sidesaddle—holding her pistol's ammunition in her lap. She held her pistol under her other hand that was holding her horse's reins. She rubbed her thumb along the pistol's hammer as she watched Ribera's force storming toward her.

"Form up across here!" a calleros ordered. The officer guided soldiers with his sword between a lane of tents that led straight into the open surrounding Recha's command tent. "Across here, men! Hurry! Fix your pikes once you take up your positions!" The calleros trotted his horse back behind the infantry as they rushed to fill in the gap with their pikes.

They made three rows. The first row bent over and planted the butts of their pikes into the ground, the second held theirs straight out, and the third over the others' heads.

"Order all reserved units in camp to converge around the command tent," Baltazar ordered to one of his few remaining dispatchers. "Understand? Every group you can find in camp is to rally here." He passed messages to his last two dispatchers. "Make sure these orders reach General Galvez, Ross, and Priet! *Go!*"

The dispatchers galloped away before a wagon was overturned in the center lane. Rallying around the command tent was the best strategy, rather than having every soldier in reach try to put themselves in front of the charging calleroses. They would meet the same fate as the current squad of soldiers.

A mixed group of pikemen and swordsmen struggled in a tight knot as the calleroses flowed around them. They had run out to block the lane from the

Orsembians, but they didn't have the numbers, and half of them were trampled upon contact. The survivors kept close together, holding a portion of the lane.

The Orsembians followed their horses around the path of least resistance, striking out with their swords to knock the jabbing pikes out of the way or thrusting their lances at the soldiers as they rode by.

A lance found its mark. The unfortunate soldier was jerked out of the defensive knot and into the path of oncoming hooves. In an instant, the soldier was snatched from his feet and sent rolling on the ground underneath the calleroses' hooves and out of sight.

Recha bit the inside of her cheek. *Damn them!* She cocked her pistol's hammer. *Savior damn them—!*

"No, Recha!" Cornelos warned, grabbing her saddle horn. As always, he was by her side, mounted with his helmet's vizor down. She could only make out his wary eyes through the holes in his helmet's black mask. "You can't move! No matter what happens, we can't have you move from this spot."

She had inadvertently nudged her horse forward. She was surrounded by her guard and nearly every mounted calleros left available in camp, amounting only fifty riders. They had more infantry that could be mustered, yet . . .

Not enough! Recha bounced her eyes this way and that, counting. *Not enough! How is it we read the enemy's movements, performed an ambush, and they still have enough men to outnumber us?* She gently squeezed her pistol's trigger and guided the hammer back down to avoid setting it off accidentally in the heat of the moment.

Baltazar trotted his horse in front of her, beckoning more soldiers into their packed formation with his sword. He had donned a breastplate and helmet in all the confusion and, although he was less armored than the other calleroses, he still managed to appear born to command by his poise alone.

"Form up across the lanes!" he ordered, directing with his sword. "Use the tents and wagons as barricades! Once they hit the first line of pikes, they will try to race around us."

Recha swiveled her head to see. Somehow, in the short amount of time, they had formed a square around the command tent in-between the lanes of tents. However, even with more soldiers rushing in to join it, the question remained.

Do we have enough?

She stood in her stirrups, searching for any relief coming from beyond the camp. The calleroses Hiraldo had sent from his rearguard were still engaged with those Ribera had sent. Despite Hiraldo's rearguard outnumbering the Orsembians, there was little chance of them defeating them and coming to her aid before Ribera reached her.

Rather than seeing relief, she gritted her teeth at the sight of groups of enemy calleroses in twos and threes, barely managing to doggedly walk their horses through the hail of crossbow bolts and rubble out of the trek. They remounted the moment they cleared the trek and raced on Ribera's trail.

"Baltazar!" she shouted. "More of them made it through the trek. We need more men!"

"We need to hold!" Baltazar said back from over his shoulder

"*What?*"

"We must hold here!" He raised his sword in the air, shaking it. "Stand your ground, men! Stand shoulder to shoulder and don't show your backs! Stand for Lazorna! Stand for La Dama! Stand for your *lives*! *Lower*! *Pikes*!"

Men roared as a forest of pikes fell into position.

The thunder of hooves grew louder. Recha could pick out individual riders now. They filled the entire lane, and those in front charged abreast, each with lances couched low under their arms. They whipped and kicked their mounts into a frenzy.

They smell glory. Recha bristled in her saddle. It took more than courage or madness for a calleros to incense his mount to the point it would charge a formation of pikes. *They think they've won.*

Her bristles turned to shivers. She clenched her jaw and teeth together. Her snarl split wide to a compulsive grin. Every panting breath came as a hiss. Her chest tightened, threating to burst.

The howls of the Orsembians drifted over their crashing hooves. Every Lazornian officer yelled to hold.

"No *quarter*!" Recha screamed. Her arm thrusted into the air, as if it had a mind of its own, waving her pistol. "No *withdrawal*! No *fear*! Let them hear you, *Lazornians*!"

Her guards roared around her, lifting their swords in the air. Their bellows spread like fire through the ranks. First, through the calleroses mounted around them. Then the officers shouted at their men. And like a dam, the soldiers holding the lines and makeshift barricades let loose roars and curses until they were red in the face. The infectious fever broke through her stoicism, and she screamed until her throat squeezed shut and her voice cracked in the dust-filled air.

They yelled over the charging hooves, over the calleroses' howls, until—

Crash!

The front row of Orsembian calleroses ran into the wall of pikes. The soldiers' yells were overcome by wailing horses impaled on the end of a pike, a few from breast to jutting out of their sides or backs. Most of their riders had no time to dismount before dueling off the second line of pikes thrusting to knock them into the dirt.

However, some of those impaled horses rolled over a few of her men in the front row. The loss of a horse also equaled the loss of a pike or two, opening a gap for another calleros to dash their mount through to fight the pikemen up close.

The Orsembians weren't satisfied with waiting to break through one lane, either. Those riding in from behind quickly turned their horses between tents and rode around to the other lanes, charging in and probing the defensive perimeter.

In a matter of seconds, a swirling cloud of dust surrounded them. The center of Recha's camp became a twister of sand, screaming horses, and desperate men. The Orsembians threw all their numbers at every line and against every barricade. Lances rattled against pikes. Swords sang against swords.

Calleroses around her dashed off, one by one, wherever they could lend a hand. One filled a gap in the line across the lane behind her. One rushed up to an overturned wagon and traded sword thrusts with the Orsembian on the other side of the barricade, both men still on horseback.

Fight, Lazornians! she wanted to scream. She wanted to ride her horse up and down the line of men yelling until she lost her voice. But in all the shouting, crying, and swearing, it would only get lost.

Is this it! she raged in the only place she could—inside herself. *Is this all I can do? Even in the middle of a battle, fighting all around me, I can only just . . . sit* here!

She spun toward Baltazar, expecting him to be shouting order after order, directing with his sword as if he were everywhere at once. Instead, her field marshal sat straight-backed and calm, staring forward as if it were a tranquil False Fall day, immune to the carnage and struggle around him.

Recha followed his gaze to a calleros, sitting tall and lean in his saddle. His horse, his armor, and his sword were all bone white. The thin face stood out from under his helmet. Ribera, like Baltazar, sat on his horse, as unmoved as death. The great men held each other's gazes, as if silently speaking to one another. Then his eyes slid across and met hers.

Recha's shoulders compulsively rolled at the sudden rush of spikes racing down her back. Her horse snorted, sensing her move, and stomped his feet. She was forced to look away to rein the animal in, and when she looked up, Ribera held his white sword out toward her.

His words cut through all the noise around her, "Mandas is there! Forward, men! Seize Mandas, and this day is *ours*!"

***

Fighting raged everywhere. To Necrem's right, volleys of repeating musket fire erupted. To his left, the Lazornians marched over the remaining lump of bodies from the press, advancing along the cliff wall with pikes down, ready to meet anything. However, the fight in front of him was a frantic mess.

The charging mass of calleroses had squeezed through the gaps between the companies on the front line. They raced their mounts around them, picking at the squares of fighting men with their lances. The pikes kept them at bay, and the second line of Lazornians edged forward, their own pikes down to catch any wayward rider between them before they could dash away.

Necrem watched, nestled shoulder to shoulder in a company square that made up a third line. They were more spread out than those fighting. It was as if they were a drifting island, watching everything around them but too far away to do anything. Except knowing exactly what it was like to be in such tightly packed fight.

"Do you think we'll be able to take their place?" he asked Hezet, who was standing beside him, motioning toward the companies fight. "When the time comes?"

Hezet hummed and moved his head back and forth, taking everything in. They had joined the rear of the company when it had been called up, figuring they would be in the back row. Instead, they had found themselves in the front when the company had been ordered to turn and put into line with the other companies. It gave them a view of what was happening, but no comfort.

"I think," Hezet replied, "when the time comes, they'll just order us in to join the fight."

"That bad, huh?" Necrem shifted his stance to ease his throbbing heels, aching for him to be off them. He balanced against the pike he had planted into the ground to lighten his weight.

"That bad," Hezet agreed. "If they break through this time"—he shook his head—"I don't think another crazy charge from you is going to stop them." He snickered and elbowed Necrem.

Necrem grunted. "No. No more charges for me." *I'm too worn out.*

He leaned a little more on his pike. His heels weren't the only things aching. The backs of his legs were sore from running and constantly standing. His heavy arms demanded to hang to his sides. He kept his grip tight on the pike's shaft to make sure they didn't, or risked falling over with them.

His shoulders slumped under the weight of his pauldrons. Every strap holding his armor on chaffed, and his sweat made every plate feel stuck to his body. Sweat also dripped off his eyebrows, into his eyes and onto his metal mask. The mask holes pricked at his scars now that he no longer had the cloth mask under it. Every breath he took brought in hot, dry air, which did nothing to cool him down.

I should have drunk more water.

From the tired panting around him, he wasn't the only one needing water.

Musket fire cracked from in front of him. He lifted his head to the sight Orsembian calleroses tumbling out of their saddles and those left spinning their horses around. The Lazornian companies of the second line forced their way between the companies on the front line, driving the calleroses back with their pikes and skewering man and beast alike.

Necrem squeezed his hands around his pike until his arms trembled. As much as he sympathized with the foot soldiers fighting for Borbin, he felt nothing for the calleroses being knocked out of their saddles.

"Get 'em," he growled.

The man beside him grunted in approval.

A horn sounded.

"Shoulder!" an officer yelled. "Pikes!"

Necrem glanced around to make sure before joining everyone else in lifting and propping their pikes on their shoulders. It was just the same as carrying spears, except the pike's extra length made it wobble more.

"Here we go," Hezet said.

Necrem looked down at him. Hezet nodded at him, and he felt obliged to nod back.

"See you when this is over, blacksmith," Hezet said.

Necrem snorted. "I'm not a blacksmith today, remember?"

Hezet smirked.

Another horn blew.

"Company!" the officer yelled. "Forward! March!"

Drums furiously rapped down the line.

Tap!

Tap!

Rap! Rap! Rap!

The drums' call was the same as when they had left the field. Now they drew him back.

Necrem's steps fell in line easily with the rhythmic cadence as easily as his arm fell into rhythm hammering steel. Their footfalls thumped on the ground as one on the stomped-over ground.

While they marched closer, the fighting on the front changed. The calleroses were dashing back. Their horses eagerly galloped away from the jabbing pikes. The Lazornians didn't cheer or rush after them, though. They didn't get the chance.

Those ranks of infantry behind the calleroses stormed in across the entire center line like two colliding waves. The Orsembians charged in from the sides of the front line and, gradually, as the calleroses moved out of the way, more and more companies squared off against their Lazornian counterparts.

Pikes clashed against pikes this time. Some Orsembians did wield spears, and there were several halberds in the mix, chopping at whatever came into reach, but most brought pikes. Both sides dueled and prodded each other. The Lazornians' musket fire was sporadic, and as Necrem marched closer, he caught the sounds of crossbows being released, metal clicking and bows strumming, along with the whistle of a bolt cutting through the air and random pops of powder firing.

This was different than the press. Men weren't packed against one another. Instead, they either jabbed forward with their pikes or staggered away from any enemies'. The cries of pain were the same, though, growing louder the closer Necrem got.

A man shrieked as if he'd suddenly been caught by surprise.

"No!" another begged. "No! Get bac—!"

"Hold them, boys!" an officer encouraged. "We can hold these bastards!"

The line weaved and bobbed. As Necrem's company approached, a few of the companies on the front took a step back. Then a few around those inched back. Any company from the second line that hadn't squeezed between those on the front line to push the calleroses out, stepped up and braced the front line. Like folding metal, the ranks of soldiers merged with little say they were combined companies, save their banners.

Horns blared. The drums rapped furiously and suddenly fell silent.

"Company!" the company capitán yelled. "Halt!"

Necrem stopped, and his heels immediately resumed throbbing, fatigue raced up his legs. It took all his strength to keep from planting his pike into the ground and leaning on it again. The heavy panting resumed around him. However, it couldn't compare to the battle cries in front of them.

Galloping horses snatched his attention. A column of Lazornian calleroses were riding between them and the second line. At every square, three calleroses would break off from the rest of the column and two dismounted. One pushed his way into the dense fighting while the other jogged to join the company in Necrem's line. The third calleros took their horses and led them away by their reins.

"They must be carrying orders," Hezet surmised aloud as they watched a calleros rush through their company's ranks.

"To everybody?" Necrem grunted.

"Must be something big to include the entire army." Hezet looked up and down the line. "Or a big maneuver. Savior, I hope it's not a big maneuver."

"*Company!*" someone yelled, different from the capitán, probably the calleros. "At the volley, you will join with front line! From here on, all companies are on rank rotation! Move with the rank in front of you! We fight as one army now! We will *hold* this center! We may give an inch! We may give a yard! But we, the Third Army, will *hold* this center!" A similar speech was parroted down their line to the other companies.

"Oh Savior," Hezet mumbled under his breath, "we're in for it now."

"In for what?" Necrem whispered.

"Rank rotation," Hezet replied, "it means, instead of fighting as companies, we're all going to rotate rank after rank every so often. I haven't seen or heard of it being used in"—he shook his head and snickered—"years. But we're not going to be pulled off the line to rest. We're not going to have any reserve to back us up. We're all going to fight sooner or later, and none of us are leaving this field unless we win . . . or we break."

Necrem's gaze traveled past the fight and over the heads of the Orsembian soldiers waiting for their turn. He looked over the wounded and struggling men, hobbling out of the fight, and the line of calleroses behind them, waiting like razorbills to swoop in on dying flesh.

There, in the center, the calleroses ringed around an open space where the largest of Borbin's banners was on a towering pole planted in the ground. The vibrant orange fabric draped down under its weight, nearly quadruple the size of every other banner on the field. While men rushed in and out of the square, only one man sat on a horse, watching.

Borbin.

"Then we better win," he growled, his face growing taut. The few stinging pricks flared across his cheeks, forcing him not to grimace.

"That's the spirit, Steel Fist." Hezet chuckled, joined by the other man standing next to Necrem.

Two volleys exploded on the far ends of the line. Others followed in a cascade. Musketeers in the company next those on the end fired, followed by the companies next to them, and then those next to them. The volleys flowed inward toward the center of the front until at last the musketeers in the company in front of Necrem fired. The concentrated fire dropped ranks of Orsembians.

Once again, Necrem's nostrils wrinkled at the sulfuric gray cloud of burnt powder rising over battlefield.

"Third Army!" the calleroses yelled. "*Forward!*"

The Lazornians at the front rushed in with their pikes to reclaim the ground they had given up moments before. Drums rapped along Necrem's line.

Tap!

Tap!

Rap! Rap! Rap!

Necrem stepped forward without a thought. *We have to win!*

***

"They're cutting through the tents!" Recha yelled, pointing at a couple of Orsembian calleroses hacking through a tent in the corner of the lane.

Three calleroses surrounding her broke away. They maneuvered their mounts around men, rushing between the barricaded lanes and those staggering away from the fighting to charge the enemy before they carved through the tents. Sword blades hissed and clashed off one another as the horsemen dueled each other from their saddles. Their horses finished the enemy's job, trampling the shredded tent under their hooves and leaving a gap in their defenses.

Such fights were breaking out all around them.

After Ribera's declaration, his calleroses had charged and probed their entire perimeter, pushing for a breakthrough. The pikemen blocking the lane behind her had withstood five separate charges already. Those in the lane in front of her were still fighting off Ribera's main body. The calleroses willingly risked their mounts to get in close and thrust or slash down at her soldiers.

An enemy calleros gasped. A Lazornian calleros had found his mark, getting under the enemy's arm and thrusting his sword into the man's armpit above his arm. The Orsembian folded over and slipped from his stirrups in a crash of steel.

A wrenching *crack* jerked Recha's head around. One of her pikemen fighting to hold the lane facing the battlefield, took two shuffling steps back then fell backward. His pike fumbled from his grasp, and his head tipped back, revealing the carved gash through his helmet and into his skull.

The victorious Orsembian attempted to force his mount through the now open gap in the line, only to furiously defend himself as her soldier's compatriots closed in on him from both sides. Their curses were lost in the other noises of battle, yet their determined pike thrusts spoke for them.

The wounded and the dead were mounting. Those who could were dragged or hobbled back out of the lines or barricades. Many collapsed around Recha's banner, laying sprawled out in the Easterly Sun. Without any doctors, they made do with ripping cloth from either their clothes or the uniforms of others to wrap around their wounds. Those who could bandaged themselves up and went to kneel or sit behind a barricade. They couldn't remain standing, and several at least held their pikes firmly in the dirt.

As for the dead, they were left where they fell.

We need more men.

Recha stiffly clenched her jaw until her back teeth ached from gnashing together. She had to keep her face placid, though. She couldn't grimace or show any fear or frustration. Her men were fighting so desperately; they couldn't look behind them and see their La Dama had given up.

Still, their situation remained the same.

Three years of planning. Three years of preparing. Knowing the odds, finding the ground to match them, using tactics to even them . . . and it's still not enough!

She pushed herself up in the saddle, longing to catch a glimpse of Hiraldo's calleroses rushing. All she caught, though, was dust clouds kicked up from whirling Orsembians riding around them.

A snarl cracked her calm mask, and she nudged her horse up beside Baltazar's. "We can't keep taking these loses!" she declared.

"They're holding," Baltazar replied, hard as stone and never taking his eyes from the fighting.

"We must fight back!" Recha urged. "If this keeps up . . ." Her chin wobbled, not wanting to say it aloud. *We'll be overwhelmed.*

She took a deep breath and raised herself up in her saddle. "We got to break this encirclement and take the fight to them. We gather the remaining calleroses we have, even my guard. When the Orsembians pull back from a line, we charge them."

"We hold."

"We *can't*!" She grimaced at her outburst, but as another shriek of pain carried through the air, she couldn't let it go. "They're going to break through if we do nothing but defend our lines. We *must* attack!"

"We must *hold* our lines!" Baltazar snapped back, his harshness making her jerk back in her saddle. "Any attack we make now will only cost us lives. If we send our calleroses outside the perimeter, they'll be cut off, outnumbered, and destroyed. The longer we hold them here, the longer we hold Ribera's attention here."

He leaned back in his saddle, looking around Recha, and pointed. "They're trying to tip that wagon over!"

Recha spun where she sat. At least seven Orsembian calleroses, from what she could see, were dismounted and pushing against one of the toppled wagons blocking the lane behind them. The few soldiers left on the barricade were dueling other dismounted calleroses to stop them.

Two of her guards led ten calleroses charging the barricade. Swords from horseback fell on the enemy that had made it inside the perimeter, and several of the calleroses leapt from their saddles to fight the enemy away from the wagon.

That was close. Yet they were straining to hold every lane.

Recha's mind raced with all the excitement, taking everything in. She perked her head up and spun back around to Baltazar.

"What do you mean, *the longer we hold Ribera's attention here*?" she asked.

"For Ramon to get into position," Baltazar replied offhandedly. He twisted this way and that in his saddle, as if searching for something.

"Ramon?" Recha shook her head. "Papa, Ramon's not—"

"*Mandas!*"

Three Orsembian calleroses charged through a gap in the line facing the battlefield. The calleros leading the charge roared, waving his sword over his head.

Baltazar moved his horse in front of her, drawing his sword. "Every man that can stand, prepare to defend yourselves!"

Wounded men all around struggled to their feet.

Undeterred, sensing glory, the enemy pressed on.

From the corner of her vision, a pikeman with a ripped uniform sleaves wrapped around his head charged into the path of the oncoming horsemen. He weakly raised his pike.

Not high enough.

The calleros on the far end rammed him with his horse. The beast stumbled as the man's body was thrown feet in the air.

A few members of her guard countercharged, kicking up swirls of dust and came in with swords swinging. They cut off two of them.

Horses circled and snorted at each other as their riders traded blow for blow. Blades sang against each other as all riders searched for openings to thrust between armor plates or knock the other out of the saddle.

One enemy escaped.

"For *Orsembar!*" He leaned in his saddle, arm outstretched, his sword leveled directly at her.

Shoot him! Recha screamed at herself. Her hand gripped her pistol. Her thumb, slick with sweat, slipped on the hammer, failing to cock it. Her arm froze, spasming. It turned to rock and refused to move. *Shoot!*

Baltazar kicked his horse. It screamed, spinning about. Its rear bumped into her mount and forced her to move, turning with him.

The calleros charged in. Sword level.

Something flashed.

A clash of metal, steel kissing steel.

Baltazar leaned back in his saddle, farther back than Recha believed possible for a man of his age. His sword arm flung back.

"*Papa!*" she screamed.

They got him! a part of her wailed while her mouth hung open, eyes wide, shaking in the saddle. *They got—*

Baltazar sprang forward, the movement almost too fast to follow. His sword followed up the enemy's as he charged by. A spring forward, a turn of the wrist, and Baltazar swung under the calleros's arm.

Clang!

His sword struck and sliced against the edge of the enemy's breastplate. His sword's tip ripped through the man's shirt underneath and staggered him, but the calleros kept in his saddle.

"Missed," Baltazar grunted.

Recha gawked at him. Her vision blurred until she couldn't see.

"*Baltazar Vigodt!*" she screamed, shaking her head to clear her eyes. When they were, she snarled at him, face burning, but she'd been in the sun all day, so she brushed it off. "What were you thinking? You're too old for those kinds of stunts! Don't *ever* do that to me again!"

Baltazar raised an eyebrow at her.

A horse screamed behind them.

Her fears of the calleros charging again eased at the sight of his horse thrown to the ground. Cornelos and another of her guard had rammed into him. The enemy's mount had lost against the combined force of two horses slamming into its side. The enemy calleros scrambled in the dirt to stay mounted and get his horse up, fortunate his leg hadn't been crushed.

His fortune ran out when Cornelos guided his horse around, and its raging hooves kicked the man in the head. The horseshoe cracked against the man's helmet and sent his head rolling around on his shoulders. When his horse regained its feet, the calleros slipped out of the saddle, and her guardsman dismounted to finish him on the ground.

"La Dama!" Cornelos cried, trotting up to them. A bright sheen of sweat gleamed across his worried face, looking her up and down. "Are you unharmed?"

Recha blinked. "Yes," she replied.

"Rally!" Baltazar shouted, holding his sword in the air. "Every man still standing in the perimeter, rally here! We'll stop every enemy who slips through, one at a time!"

He snapped around, glaring at her. He seized her reins and ripped them out of her hand. "Commandant! Get the La Dama to the center and make sure she *stays* there!" He threw her horse's reins at Cornelos.

"Baltazar!" Recha protested.

"Yes, sir!" Cornelos eagerly replied, raising his sword hilt to his forehead.

Recha glared at him. "Cornelos, don't you *dare*—"

Cornelos kicked his horse and dragged hers along with a jolt. Recha's head snapped back, drawing an embarrassing yelp. Her cheeks flushed warmly, and she clawed to take hold of her saddle horn to keep her seat and her pistol's kit in her lap.

"Cornelos!" she growled. "When we get out of this—"

"You can reprimand me all you want!" he finished.

He waved at her few remaining guards as he led her horse to stand right beside her banner in the center of their square. Cornelos put his horse in front of hers, still commandeering her reins. The other three guards surrounded her. Two put their mounts beside her; one facing forward and the other facing behind her. The last guard put his mount behind hers.

Terrific, Recha fumed. *Now I have my own personal square and look completely desperate.*

"Cornelos! We can't—"

"They're breaking through!"

The crash of wood and axle springs announced one of the wagons being turned upright and rolled away. The calleroses whom had rushed to defend the barricade had all dismounted and now were backing away in a line. They fought in line with each other, several picking up shields left over from the wounded and dead.

"Form a square!" Baltazar bellowed. "All defenders, fall back in order and form a square! Rally around the banner!"

The order filtered through the defenders. Those around the overwhelmed barricade fell back quickly, while the pikemen struggling to block the lanes took measured steps backward at a time to keep their lines.

The Orsembians became maddening, desperate to keep up the pressure, some recklessly charging in the moment the defenders eased back. A few were knocked out of their saddle or had their horses cut from under them by thrusting pikes for their brashness.

Her calleroses holding the corners took the worst of it. They couldn't wheel their horses out of the tight pockets they dueled in, and showing their backs was suicide. They were trapped defending corners they couldn't hold.

When the infantry had backed away enough for a tiny gap to slip through, a few charged straight at her calleroses, attacking them from behind.

Recha panted and sweated from her saddle. A fixed snarl stretched across her face, unable to utter single useful word as her men yelled in desperation and wailed in pain. Swords slid under armpits. Blades sliced between helmets and plate. One by one, her men in the corners fell as the rest pulled back around her banner.

Her calleroses, who withdrew to safety, dismounted and turned their horses loose to keep the formation tight. They, and every wounded man who could stand, gathered as many pikes as they could find to ensure pikes bristled every side of the square.

The tighter the square became, the less the Orsembians attacked. They pushed the barricades away, clearing the lanes. However, when they saw the forming square, they sprinted back to their horses instead of pressing the attack. The pulled back from all four sides.

The dust cloud swirling around them began to subside. A few of her calleroses lucky enough to survive were able to break away as the enemy did, leaping from their saddles to dash into the safety of the square.

They're withdrawing?

Recha turned her head back and forth, watching the Orsembian's pull back. In their withdrawal, they left the bodies of the fallen, both theirs and hers, marking the boundaries of the old perimeter. She faced forward.

Ribera remained there, under his banner, as his remaining calleroses formed up across all the lanes.

They're preparing.

***

Necrem grunted and heaved, swinging his pike over the heads of the two men in front of him.

Being the third man in line from the front, it was his job to hold his pike over the men ahead of him and knock away the enemies' pikes by swinging down on them. His height gave him an advantage in being able to see over their heads and handle the pike better than those in line beside him. The long poles wobbled clumsily as mostly everyone either waved them about or aimless jabbed over their comrades' heads.

An enemy's pike made a thrust, aiming for the man at the front. Necrem heaved his pike to the side, striking the oncoming shaft and knocking it aside.

"Keep at 'em, men!" a calleros yelled, wandering back and forth through the ranks. His repeated words of encouragement were nearly lost under the crashing of thousands of pikes clashing down the line. "They may make us take a step back, but they'll *never* break us! Put your backs into your thrusts and drive them back!"

"Skewer those cowards!" an enemy calleros shouted from atop his horse behind Orsembian ranks. "Are all of you going to let these dirt Lazornians stand up to you? In front of *Si Don*? Get in close and *break* them!"

The Orsembians heaved forward, some weakly shouting while the rest grimly charged in silence. Necrem braced the back of the man in front of him, and that man likewise braced the man in front of him. Pikes, breastplates, and shoulder pauldrons crashed together.

"Keep your feet, men!" the company officer encouraged. "Hold them! *Hold them!*"

Necrem dug his heels in. He held on to the top of soldier's breastplate in front of him, steadying him as he steadied the man in front.

Unlike the previous press, instead of the entire company pushing in from behind and all the enemy bearing down on him, only the first three rows pushed and shoved against each other. Men at the front of the line grunted and cursed over thuds and smacks against armor and flesh, both sides struggling to heave the other back for the slightest inch.

"Hold the line!" officers yelled. "Hold the line!"

A musket fired somewhere in the distance.

"Push 'em in tighter!" Orsembians yelled desperately.

Musketeers tried to slide in their muskets where they could between the struggling forces to shoot into the densely packed ranks. Necrem didn't smell the acidic smoke of burning powder, so the shot didn't come around him. He kept his ears sharp for other things.

A hard *thunk* of a blunt impact against metal made him jerk to his left.

"Crossbows!" came shouts farther down the line.

"Don't give them any openings!" someone else yelled.

Necrem had watched this same cycle from halfway through the rotation. The Orsembians would rush the line, pushing and shoving. The Lazornian musketeers would take advantage and shoot, and Orsembian crossbowmen would take advantage and release some bolts. Both adding to the struggle, until—

"Front line, *heave!*" the company officer ordered.

Necrem rushed forward, pushing the man in front of him as hard as he could while not running over him. The man groaned and pushed into the man in front. For a moment, they all pressed together, shoving forward as if against a cliffside.

Then that cliffside gave.

The Orsembians slipped backward, and the rush was on. Necrem hauled his pike over the men's heads again and stabbed blindly. Every man in front and around him did likewise. It was a test of strength and a race to see which side could push the other off then stab with their pikes.

Necrem jabbed, unable to aim where he was thrusting while using one hand and everyone being so close. His pike was struck. The reverberating wobble raced up the shaft, being turned aside, and shook in his grip. He pulled back again and stabbed.

Resistance. His pike hit and stayed put.

He drew back. Stab. More resistance, followed by something giving way and a pained yelp. He knew that feeling. It was the same as the spear drills and running his pike into the press. It was the feeling of a steel-tipped pole driving into a body, almost the same as hammering a post into the ground. However, Necrem repulsively discovered that, after the initial strike, there was less resistance sinking steel through flesh than a post through dirt.

The resistance came when pulling the pike out.

Something pulled on his pike. A foot of pike slipped through his grip before he grabbed it with both hands to keep hold of it. He twisted and jerked back, just as he was drilled, and the resistance released.

"*Forward!*" the company officer ordered. "Entire line, *forward!*"

Pike shafts rattled as they fell and batted into the enemy.

The men in front of Necrem stepped froward, giving him room to finally see over them. There was a gap in the enemy's line. A man was missing.

The first man in front had enough room to lower his pike and thrust into the enemy company. The second man joined, stabbing the Orsembian soldier to their right as he held his arm up, blocking another battering pike.

"We have a hole!" someone shouted beside him.

"March into it!" a calleros roared.

Necrem joined the surge around him. Men yelled and jabbed. Necrem did his job, thrusting his pike over the heads of the men in front of him. He knocked flailing pikes away as their line surged into the gap. The men in the first two rows did the stabbing and . . . killing.

We can't let them win, he told himself as men yelled and cried from the broad pike heads stabbing between their armor, under their bellies, or into their faces. *We can't let them—*

A dozen metallic springs and releases filled the air. Multiple *swishes* followed.

Thunk!

Clang!

Both men in front of Necrem fell; the one in front was thrown back while the second twisted, clutching his shoulder. The metal spike of a crossbow bolt jutted out, lodged through his pauldron. The man in front took one squarely in the chest, the bolt jutting through the breastplate.

"Crossbows!" a man cried.

A running roar was all the warning Necrem got.

Three Orsembians rushed in at him, stepping over the bodies of their comrades laying and crawling away on the ground in front of them.

Necrem shoved the injured soldier aside, grabbed his pike, and swung it downward with all his force. The long shaft swooped through the air and came down on the first man's head. It smacked against his helmet like a gong, sending waves wobbling down his shaft. The man collapsed, sprawling facedown on the ground. With him in the way, the man behind him tripped and ran into Necrem's pike.

Necrem winched as he watched his pike spear into the man's side, piercing the plate to shred the man's flesh. The opposing soldier stumbled a couple of steps then stopped, dropping his own pike to weakly grab Necrem's. With him blocking the way, the soldiers behind the man were stopped in their place.

Necrem paused. He took deep breaths through his mask, taking advantage of the lull his pike blocking the space in front of him bought.

"Oso!" Hezet yelled.

A pike slid across his vision and slid past him, over his own, and into the enemy soldier he hadn't seen on his left. The soldier stumbled back, dropping his own pike to hold his belly.

"You're the front of the line now!" Hezet chastised. He held his pike over Necrem's shoulder as the man directly behind him did the same to his other shoulder. "You can't stop or hesitate!"

"Sorry," he gasped. "I got tired." He twisted and pulled his pike out of the enemy soldier.

A soldier elbowed his way between them, yelling as he leveled his musket at the ranks of enemy soldiers. Necrem didn't have a chance to pull away before the trigger was pulled.

The blast made his ears ring, but worst was the burning smoke. The gray cloud made his eyes water, blurring his vision. His face stung from the sulfuric haze seeping through the holes in his mask. He coughed and gagged. Unable to use his hands to wipe his eyes because of his gauntlets, he was forced to blink them clear.

"Are you *insane*?" Hezet yelled angrily at someone. "You blinded *us* firing that thing off like that. Get back in line and wait for orders! Oso, get back in this fight!"

Necrem turned to catch the musketeer being dragged back in the ranks. In front of him, though, Hezet and every other soldier around him swiped their pikes into the gap between the lines. A couple of Orsembians waved their own pikes around, trying to bat their way in.

Necrem shook his head, took up his pike, and stepped into the gap. No thrusts were required. Leveling his pike in the gap, the Orsembians couldn't bat the other pikes and stave off his. They scrambled backward, avoiding his pike, and into those behind them, nearly tripping over each other.

"Huzza!" someone cheered. "They're pulling *back*!"

Necrem stopped. He had lost all sense of the fighting all around him while focusing on what was just in front of him. He cautiously looked away from the Orsembians hastily backing away from him to glance side to side.

The other Orsembians were backing off, too. Not down the entire line; only those facing Necrem's company and the two beside it. More cheers went up at the retreating soldiers, yet Necrem's hands started to shake.

Not again, he tiredly groaned at a familiar, warning feeling.

He leaned his head back, peering over the withdrawing enemy to beyond them. The fluttering banners in a valley with no wind blowing confirmed what he was sensing.

"Calleroses," he said loudly. "Calleroses are coming!"

The exhausted cheering around him died to exhausted and frightened groaning. More exhausted than frightened, but the fear was there. Seconds passed, and the horses trotting and forming into columns came into the sight for everyone else. There were at least eight of them, all aiming to ride into the different companies at different points and cut them apart.

"Don't buckle now, men!" a Lazornian calleros yelled, stepping out of the ranks and walking down the line. "You've faced down calleroses before! You withstood their charge *and* turned it away! You can turn them again!"

No one cheered.

We're too tired. Necrem swallowed, his dry throat desperate for water. *And it's too hot for speeches.*

"Muskets to the front!" the calleros ordered. "Two ranks; one kneeling, one standing. Both ranks load your shot and keep your matches burning!"

Musketeers filtered through the lines to form up, their faces blackened from powder, and they smelled no better.

As they formed ranks, they pulled out their ramrods and began loading their powder and lead balls. Necrem and the rest kept their pikes high.

"Sir," one musketeer called the calleros, "we're running low on powder and shot. Some of us are down to are last shots."

The calleros frowned. "Then, after this, use your muskets as clubs. Just prepare to shoot what you have."

A bugle blew, and pounding hooves drummed through the valley. Eight clouds of trailing dust cut through the field as if it were being ripped apart, cracking open and heading straight toward them.

"Take your positions!" the calleros roared, racing down the line. "Each pikeman, lower your pikes between the musketeers! Musketeers, hold fire until ordered!"

Being on the front line, Necrem did as he was told and followed the others' example, lowering his pike between the ranks of musketeers.

That dreadful waiting set in again. This time, though, he was at the front of the line, waiting for the calleroses to ride down on him. No surprise charge through the smoke. No sudden, horrifying attack. Necrem stared straight ahead and saw them coming. The hot haze of the Easterly Sun shimmered on their helmets and plate, obscuring their distance and number. He couldn't tell if one of those columns was heading straight for him or around him, but they were coming.

Closer.

"Steady!" the calleros ordered. "Hold your fire!"

The nearest charging column spread out a little. Now closer, Necrem could tell the right side of the column was coming right at him.

Closer.

The shimmer caught the calleroses' lances now, lowering into a charge. The hooves grew louder.

"Hold!" the calleros ordered.

Closer!

The calleroses shouts and hollers echoed over their charging mounts.

"*Hold!*"

The earth vibrated under Necrem's boots. He set his shoulders and stance, gritted his teeth, and held his pike as firmly as he could.

The calleroses waved their swords above their heads and held their lances low, hollering like the madmen they were.

Necrem could make out faces and visors of individual riders!

"*Fire!*"

Chapter 34

Smoke and dust swirled in the air. Calleroses yelled, twisting out of their saddles. Horses screamed, their legs collapsing out from under them. Several tumbled and rolled over their riders. Their combined wails were swallowed under the horses charging behind them.

"Second rank!" a Lazornian calleros shouted, his voice cracking. "*Fire!*"

The second rank of musketeers fired. Again, the air was filled with smoke, lead balls streaked through the air, and men and horses fell. The difference this time was that Necrem didn't flinch. His ears didn't ring. Despite his eyes watering from the burnt powder, he kept them open, watching and waiting.

The added bodies littering the ground tripped some of the horses that had escaped the deadly hail. They crashed headfirst into the dirt and rolled over onto their sides, throwing the lucky calleroses off yet crushing the rest. Regardless, the head of the calleroses' charging column was blunted, and those coming in behind had to slow and guide their horses around the mass of corpses.

"Pikes!" the Lazornian calleros rushed out of the ranks, sword waving behind him. "*Charge!*"

Hundreds of roaring voices lifted around him as everyone sprinted forward. Necrem had no choice. It was either be swept up or be trampled. Yet again, he was running with a long, unwieldy pike stretched out in front of him and into a gray cloud of smoke with little to nothing telling him what awaited on the other side or what was coming through it.

He squinted his watering eyes against the haze, angled his shoulder to ram anyone he ran into, and tightened his grip on the pike's shaft. He burst through the smoke and—

His pike slammed into a man's gut with the wrenching screech of metal prying metal. The calleros stared wide-eyed through his visor's eye slits at him. He was hobbled over, propping himself up on his sword from dragging his left foot behind. The armor on his boot was twisted and mangled. Despite having rolled in the dirt, the calleros's armor still had a shining polish to it.

Calleroses always did want their armor to shine.

Necrem's blow tore the calleros off his feet, driving his pike farther into the man. His sword flew out of his weak grip as he gargled under his vizor and doubled over around Necrem's pike. Necrem charged a few more feet, carrying the calleros, and then slammed him into the ground. He twisted the pike as he was taught to pull out a spear.

"Rules!" the calleros wailed, one hand grabbing the pike's shaft while the other reached up at him. "*Mercy!*"

Necrem froze. Hearing a man wail like that made his hands shake, sending the tremors down the shaft of his pike.

"Unhorsed calleroses!"

Men let out crazed yells as they charged from the smoke. Pikemen stormed into the carnage, finding calleroses on the ground and wildly stabbing them with abandoned. A maddening glee was on many of their faces.

Necrem turned back to the calleros pinned under him. The man clawed at the pike's shaft, unable to push back against his strength. A swift twist and pull wrenched the pike out. The calleros gasped and gripped his side.

Necrem held the pike up, watching him writhe on the ground. The man curled in on himself, bringing his knees as high as his armor would allow. His shaking body made his plates clink together. Tears streamed out of the man's pleading eyes staring up at him.

Any other man, Necrem would have felt something for. Pity. Regret. Perhaps even disgust for himself. But this was a calleros. The memory of Eulalia that night clawed its way back from the man's curled posture and weeping expression, the same as hers.

You gave none to her.

Necrem lifted his head. The charge had passed him by. While some soldiers fell on injured calleroses with vengeful abandon, the others climbed over and charged around the bodies of the dead horses to attack the calleroses still riding in. Lances and pikes clashed. Swords hacked and slashed. The pikemen were eager to knock every calleros out of their saddles while the calleroses pressured their reluctant horses to the pikes to run down or hack any man they could.

Why should any of them have mercy.

"No," Necrem replied coldly. He drove his pike between the rim of the calleros's breastplate and helmet. The steel head crushed the man's windpipe and speared through his neck before he could scream. He held his pike in place until the calleros twitched his last.

***

"La Dama!" Fuert Ribera's voice was a graveling drawl. The elderly calleros held his head back, his Adam's apple sticking out of his scrawny neck and wobbling with his every word. "La Dama Mandas, I, Cal Fuert Ribera, beseech you, please order your men to lay down their arms and surrender. They have fought valiantly in your defense, and you have shown them more dignity than . . . I have seen from many by staying with them.

"But this fight is over." Ribera lowered his head. The bone-white wisps of mustache framed his long face as his grim gaze cut over the distance at her. "Please, surrender. Under the Rules of Campaign, you and your general staff will be taken into my custody and your soldiers will be disarmed and detained until such time as terms are agreed upon."

Recha and her remaining guard were surrounded. Ribera and his calleroses had moved in closer.

Despite all the killing, the glory-seeking calleroses throwing away their horses by trying to run over her pikemen to get to her and her men holding their lines, Ribera still held his numeric advantage.

Over half of the remaining enemy calleroses stood in ranks, forsaking their horses to face her pikemen and guard on foot. They held their lances like spears, and behind their ranks sat the rest of their compatriots remaining mounted. Ribera sat in the center of such a line, with an additional rank of mounted calleroses behind him.

They're not going to risk any more of their horses, Recha easily surmised. *First comes those on foot, and once they force open a gap, those behind will charge in to break our square. However, . . .*

"Marshal Ribera!" she yelled. "If you permit me, I will address you in the rank I believe that is rightfully yours."

Ribera held her gaze, unmoved. A few tiny, shimmering dots on his leathery-tanned face hinted that he was sweating under the Easterly Sun's oppressive heat.

Recha blinked streams out her eyes and dripped droplets from her lashes but refused to wipe her face or look away.

Finally, Ribera nodded.

"Marshal Ribera," she said, "I thank you for your compliments. More so about my men than myself. They deserve it." She glanced around at them. She could only make out the back of most of their heads, all facing away from her and toward their side of the square. Those too weak or injured to stand sat or lay hunched near the flag. On her horse, she couldn't tell if they were watching, but she was certain they were all listening. "But as for your demand, I cannot accept it."

Ribera's mustache twitched. A brief flicker that instantly disappeared. "Field Marshal Vigodt, well fought, sir. Both this day and the other."

"My compliments, Marshal Ribera," Baltazar replied with a respectfully nod. "And well fought to you, as well, sir."

"If I may ask," Ribera said, "one marshal to another, is there any chance you can advise your marquesa on changing her mind? To some, they would find that . . . not our place. However, men such as we, who have commanded real battle and seen the aftermath, have a duty to advise our lieges of when the battle is over. Do we not?"

Baltazar's horse snorted and shook its mane, as if agitated from Ribera's question. Baltazar, however, sat a few paces to her left with his back to her. His helmet obscured his face. A few of the soldiers around him threw nervous glances over their shoulders up at him.

"We have many duties," he replied. "And while I would voice my advice regardless, I must respectfully disagree with yours, Marshal Ribera. This battle is not over."

"That would only lead to more blood." Ribera scowled. His bushy eyebrows drooped over them, making him look . . . tired, despite keeping straight in the saddle. "Why prolong this?"

"Sometimes," Baltazar replied, "that blood is needed to determine who the real victor is."

Ribera's scowl melted. A placid reflection crossed his face. He pushed himself up in his stirrups and stiffly turned, gazing out at the ongoing battle below.

Recha's ear twitched at a timely spaced, repeated roar of musket fire. The volleys were in coordination and good order, not the kind made in panic or desperation. She couldn't see them behind the enemy calleroses' heads, but she knew her armies were still holding, still fighting.

If they're still fighting, she reasoned, *there's still a chance we'll be reinforced. And if Ribera sees them coming—*

"Marshal Ribera!" she shouted.

Ribera remained standing in his saddle, surveying the area without a hint of acknowledgment.

Recha drew herself up. She scowled angrily and took a deep breath. "*Marshal Ribera*! You attend a marquesa when she addresses you!"

Ribera snapped around. His steely glare could melt stone, yet Recha held it.

"Very good. I want you to understand," she explained, "that I'm not rejecting your offer out of stubborn pride or personal vanity. I hold you as an honorable man who would keep his word. Nevertheless, I have thrown away all conventions of the Rules of Campaign. From the very first battle, I neither honored them or anyone who tried to claim them. I will not now submit to them now that I'm cornered." She snickered. "Nor will I submit to Borbin under any circumstances!"

She lifted her pistol for Ribera and everyone to see. "I had it decreed at the start of this battle that I will only uphold the Rules of War. I will not barter my men's lives away for my own. I will not barter the submission of my marc for my own freedom. Try and seize me, and I will fight until you have no choice but to kill me. Should all my men throw down their weapons and beg me to throw down mine, I will kill myself! I will *not* yield!"

Her thumb, pressing hard on her pistol's hammer, jerked on reflex. The loud clicks made everyone around her—her guards, the soldiers, and Cornelos— flinch. A grin split her face. She couldn't smooth it back or regain a calm composure.

She might have lied a little. There was some stubborn pride and some personal vanity in refusing to surrender. Yet, mixed in with the two was her own heart's determination. She poured it out in gasping blasts of honesty. At least, it kept Marshal Ribera's attention on her.

"Did you not hear what I had decreed before?" Her breaths came out short and hard. Her heart drummed in her chest. "Victory or death! Those were my terms at the start of this battle. And I will uphold that decree until the end. No matter what amount of blood it takes, those are my *only* terms!

"If you can't match them, if *you*, Marshal Ribera, the White Sword of Orsembar, cannot stand the blood, then it should be *you* who throws down *your* weapons! You'll be treated as prisoners of war, to be held and confined with the honors your station deserves, just as your grandson now enjoys, until this war is over. But if none of you Orsembians can do that, then I only have one thing to say to you."

A tremor ran up her spine to the tips of her fingers. Her pistol shook in her grip, and she kept her finger away from the trigger so as not to squeeze it. Every hair on her head stood up. The corners of her grinning lips quirked and jerked. She felt a vibration in her throat, threatening to make her burst in a giggling mess.

"What are you waiting for?" she yelled before being overwhelmed. "Come and get me!"

Her lungs burned. Her heavy breathing was all she could hear. Sweat burned her eyes, forcing her to blink rapidly. The salty droplets flung off her lashes. That vibrant clawing in the back of her throat still warned she was the verge of bursting into uncontrollable giggling or tears. Or both.

I must look crazy, she guessed. Her sweaty visage coupled with her unbridled grin and shaking in her saddle. All of that *and* her screaming, she had to look a sight.

Ribera was frozen in his saddle. The heat around him was unbearable, yet the seasoned marshal appeared colder than any True Winter. His tiredness evaporated, and his facial features were sharpened edges, staring right back at her.

He silently raised his sword. Glints of sunlight reflected off his blade's polished, white scabbard in defiance of the dust. He raised it high in the air and held it there. The calleroses around him tilted their heads toward him, watching.

Here it comes. Recha lowered her pistol, hands still sweating, but her grip on its handle was solid.

Ribera brought his sword down in swift *swoop*.

The swish of slicing air in the hushed silence made her scalp crawl. She gripped her saddle horn, bracing herself. She expected the calleroses to rush in from all sides, bellowing like madmen.

Instead, the enemy inched forward. Their heavy footfalls stomped and scraped across the hardpacked dirt. They mimicked footmen without the need for officers shouting for them to keep their lines straight or step together. Their lances wobbled, closing the space between them and her soldiers' pikes.

The closer they got, the smaller their steps became. The heads of their lances and the heads of her soldiers' pikes wavered back and forth, aligning with each other but also avoiding touching the other.

"*Ha!*" a calleros to her left yelled. He lunged. Pike and lance crashed together then slid apart.

Another battle cry came behind her. Metal clanged against metal from a lance head striking a shield. More shouts and grunts erupted around her, some from her own men making preemptive strikes. They grew to a boil. Yelling, cursing, and taunting, each man working himself up—

"Have at them!" an Orsembian shouted.

"Come on!" a Lazornian spat.

Every man charged, Lazornian and Orsembian alike. Pikes batted against lances. Swords clashed against both blades and shields. Men threw themselves at each other with little restraint.

In moments, angry, curse-ridden battle cries became cries of pain as men were impaled on pikes and lances. Duels between swordsmen devolved into slamming into each other's faces with either the pommel of their swords or rims of their shields.

An Orsembian calleros pushed through the square's first rank and blindly charged into a pike held up at an angle by an injured Lazornian sitting on the ground, no longer able to stand. The Orsembian took the pike in the gut, dropping his sword in a struggle to pull himself free. The injured pikeman lunged forward from where he sat, plunging the pike deeper into the calleros. When the calleros toppled, he took the pikemen's pike with him, pulling it out of the wounded soldier's grip. Too weak to retrieve it, the pikemen simply crawled back farther into the square.

Although, its protection was shrinking by the minute. As furious as the first attack had been, the Orsembians' answer was just as ferocious. The initial attack hadn't bought them any ground and now the front ranks of the square were all being pushed back. At least, those left standing were.

"Guardsmen of La Dama!" Cornelos suddenly yelled. He held his head at a high angle and sat leaning back, as if to stick out his chest despite his breastplate hampering the pose. "Even if we are overwhelmed, so long as the Savior guides you to draw breath, strike down anyone who means harm to our marquesa! Don't let a single enemy lay a finger on our La Dama!"

The guardsmen surrounding her shouted in unified reply, lifting their swords in the air. Several soldiers surrounding them joined in, as well. Rank and actual troop assignment didn't matter here. They were all pretty much her guardsmen. After all, they were fighting and dying because she refused to surrender, and they still stood beside her.

Regardless, she frowned at Cornelos.

He looked this way and that, turning in his saddle at every yell. Finally, he noticed her. "What?" he asked.

"You need to work on your speeches," she said. "That was too personal."

"Too personal?" Cornelos flinched at the clang of swords near him. The square was still holding, though, and he turned back.

Recha arched an eyebrow. "*Our* marquesa? *Our* La Dama?"

Cornelos's face flushed. It was already reddened from the Easterly Sun, and the added blush almost turned his face purple. "I was . . . rallying your guard! As Commandant de La Dama, it was part of my duty. I wasn't thinking about what I was saying!"

Recha held her frown for as long as she could. She held her breath until her nose wrinkled and air escaped her twisting lips as she burst into gasping laughter.

Cornelos stared at her dryly, his face darkening more. "You were teasing me? At a time like this?"

Recha threw her head back and wiped tears out of her eyes, cursing her emotions for running amok at a time like this. "It seemed like . . ." she stuttered, catching her breath, "like a good idea. With everything—"

Movement caught her eye. "*Cornelos*!"

Cornelos spun in time to meet the Orsembian rushing him through a gap in the ranks. He swung his sword in a wide arch to knock away the calleros's lunging thrust. The enemy managed another swing that Cornelos also parried before a Lazornian soldier intervened. The Orsembian clashed blades with the man, yet his sword was held there, leaving him open. Cornelos drove his sword into the man's shoulder and into his body from above.

"Secure the line!" he demanded the soldier, gesturing to the opening in the ranks with his blood-streaked sword.

"Tighten your ranks!" Baltazar ordered over the symphony of battle cries and clashing weapons. "Don't let yourselves be drawn out! Stand together and face them as one!" The field marshal was an unmovable rock in the sea of upheaval around them.

The ranks obeyed, inching back while staving off the enemy's attack. The enemy themselves continued their onslaught, driving forward to claim every step her soldiers gave up. Several charged in.

An Orsembian slammed into the shield of one of her soldiers. The enemy's fury was too great and he was too close. Her soldier had no choice but to drop his sword, pull out his dagger, and stab at his attacker's eye slits in his helmet and neck.

A pikeman waved his pike wildly between two calleroses, swatting away their lances. The calleroses stepped closer every time the pikeman's attention was diverted to the other until—

One of the calleroses lunged. The pikeman reacted too slowly. The lance speared his hip. Twisting in the pain, he could do nothing to parry the other lance. It took him in the neck, and together, the calleroses pulled him out of the square.

That left an opening near Baltazar.

"*Baltazar*!" Recha yelled, pointing at the hole. "Get over—"

The yell of men and horses snapped her around. That wasn't the only hole in the square. Another of her fallen soldiers had created one to her right, and two of the waiting Orsembian calleroses remaining on horseback leapt into it. A couple of her soldiers jumped out of the way. A poor injured soul screamed as the raging hooves crushed him.

Her guardsman beside her met the first calleros, sword stroke to sword stroke, the uproar giving him plenty of warning. The second calleros kicked his horse to get around his compatriot to join the fight when a pikeman aimed too low and speared the horse instead of the enemy. Undeterred by the beast's screams, the pikeman drove his pike deeper into its chest until the horse reared, ripping the pike from his hands.

The calleros was thrown into the air. His impact on the hard earth rang out over the battle. The horse continued to scream, becoming a greater danger to everyone as it collapsed, writhing and kicking. Men scrambled to get away from those lashing hooves.

The fall of his compatriot's horse threw the other Orsembian calleros off balance. Her guardsman was likewise forced to keep control of his horse instead of attacking the enemy, but the Orsembian was too distracted to react when a soldier leapt up, wrapped his arms around the man's waist, and pulled him from his saddle. The calleros flailed out with his sword wildly, to no avail, and a dagger stabbed under his helmet ended him.

Recha hissed sharply, watching. *That's about to be this entire battle!*

"Baltazar!" she screamed, twisting back around. "Get over here!"

Baltazar was dueling another Orsembian on horseback. The enemy pressed him, swinging blow after blow. Baltazar focused on parrying, unable to wheel his horse with the square's tight courters and risk the soldiers or their formation.

"*Baltazar!*"

Recha kicked her horse without thinking. The steed jolted forward, bumping into Cornelos's. The dense square denied them any space to move and, in frustration, drive, or panic, Recha's horse reared.

She yelped, throwing herself forward. She squeezed her right leg wrapped around the saddle's pommel as tightly as she could. She seized it for good measure with one hand. Her other hand flew into the air, keeping her balance.

She kept in her saddle, yet when her horse came down, her pistol's ammunition spilled from her lap.

"Savior *dammit!*" she hissed, hastily grabbing everything she could catch. She grabbed her pouch of lead shot and thumb of power, but her cleaning kit slammed into the dirt below. Worse still, when she pulled her meager catch up, the shot pouch opened and spilled half of the small, lead balls.

"Recha!" Cornelos cried, getting his own horse under control. "What are you *doing?*"

She fumbled to preserve her remaining ammunition, pressing it in her lap, and then growling back, "Baltazar needs—!"

An Orsembian calleros came screaming through the square. His horse snorting. His sword waving above his head. Cornelos clenched his teeth and jerked his horse's head sharply to the side, barely wheeling it to meet the charge. The horses slammed against each other. They bayed, snorted, and nipped at each other. Their swords clashed, scraping their blades together.

More wild yells announced other calleroses charging into the square. Some forced their way in, whereas others were repulsed by the ends of pikes or being impaled on them. The fighting grew more desperate with each successful incursion.

The defensive square was losing its shape.

Recha swung back toward Baltazar to catch him make another successful parry and, in a flash, his blade sliced his opponent's reins. The Orsembian flailed backward, losing his balance. He reached for his saddle horn and took a sword thrust in his side from an intervening soldier.

"Fight!" Baltazar encouraged, letting his opponent slide from his saddle with a second look. "Fight for your lives, men! Just a little longer!" He swung his sword down into the slowly devolving melee.

A little longer?

A pain-laced shriek that suddenly cut short snatched her attention. Another Orsembian calleros was charging in, leaning forward in the saddle, lance couched under his arm at full tilt, his head down. His face was concealed behind his visor, set on his target. In the short span, the distance was easy to judge and his target easy to see.

The lance was aimed straight at Cornelos's back.

Cornelos was still dueling with the other Orsembian. If she called out to him, the distraction would give his current opponent an opening. She turned to her other guardsman beside her, but he wasn't in his saddle. Instead, he was locked in a fight of his own, punching and stabbing at an Orsembian who had fought his way into the square on foot.

Two of her soldiers threw themselves in front of the charging calleros and were thrown aside themselves. The charging horse slammed into both. Its rider's kicking spurred it on, and the impact didn't slow it.

Cornelos!

Recha's mouth went dry. Her tongue stuck to the roof of her mouth.

Soldiers scrambled out of the horse's way. The pikemen were too desperate to keep the square from collapsing. None could make it in time.

The lance aiming for her Companion's back brought an image to the front of Recha's mind. Sebastian's pale, clammy face. The gaping hole in his back where he'd been impaled.

Not again!

Recha turned her horse, throwing her arm up, and everything slowed. The world around her shrank as she stared down her arm and the barrel of her pistol. The drumming of the incoming hooves matched her breathing. The calleros's head lifted slightly.

She squeezed the trigger.

The hammer sprung, and sparks flew.

Pow!

The powder's ignition was louder than the demolition of the mountainside to her ears. The flash of burnt powder turned the world white. Her pistol's kick gently ran up her arm.

The puff of powder drifted up like a curtain, unveiling the Orsembian calleros tipping farther and farther back in his saddle, his head snapped back. The farther he fell, the more his horse slowed, its head being pulled back by the reins. The animal snorted and shook its head, and its rider's grip slipped. The calleros spilled off his saddle, rolling to the side with his lance dragged along with him.

Recha watched him fall. Her arm stiff as a pike, her tensed muscles spasming but unable to move. Every quick, sharp breath sucked in burning gulps of powder. The calleros hit the ground with a thud, his lance falling on top of him. As he rolled onto his back, Recha saw the small hole punched through his visor above his left eye slit.

"Huh," she grunted.

She looked around, her wider surroundings coming back to her quickly. Several soldiers stared up at her. The calleroses in front of the square, mounted around Ribera, shifted in their saddles, regarding her. The fight continued against the other sides of the struggling square. Cornelos was still locked in his duel. However, for that moment, she held the attention of everyone at the front of the square.

"*Victory* or *death*!" she shouted.

"Victory or death!" some of her men repeated then charged the nearest enemy with renewed vigor.

The enemy answered. Several more calleroses charged their mounts into the square. Her soldiers on the edge moved to let them in then closed the holes to keep others from following. It preserved the square for a little longer, trusting their comrades inside the square to deal with the enemy they had allowed in.

"Recha!" Baltazar wheeled his horse toward her. His dark grimace was heart rendering.

As was the sight of an Orsembian calleros decapitating one of her soldiers in a downward, arching sweep of his sword as he kicked his horse.

Recha sniffed sharply and finally dropped her arm. Her sweaty hands grappled with her pistol, turning it up to reload. Her thumb repeatedly slipped on her powder charge's plug. Growling in frustration, she took the cork-like plug in her teeth and wrenched it out.

Come on.

She glanced up as she tapped powder down her pistol's barrel. The calleros was still approaching, kicking a wounded soldier's feeble attempts to stop him, undeterred to finish the man to get to her.

Come on! Come on!

She filled her charge pan then closed it. She fumbled for a lead ball next. Desperate, she spilled the few she had left in her lap to get one and shove it down the barrel.

Got to pack it. Come on! My musketeers can load and fire two shots a minute, why can't—

The calleros lunged his mount forward. Instead of his sword, he came at her with his hand stretched out.

Recha recoiled, snarling and jamming her pistol's ram rod home. *Don't you—*

Baltazar charged in from the left. His sword would have taken the man's head had the Orsembian not leaned too far forward in his attempt to grab her. The whoosh of air from his slicing blade struck her face.

The Orsembian pulled his hand away, easily switching the reins with his hands as he rolled up to parry Baltazar's back stroke. Both men wheeled their horses with each other, kicking up dust in the center of the fighting. Recha pulled hers away to avoid one of them running into her or the wayward reach of their flashing swords.

Baltazar furiously lashed out at the younger calleros. He put weight behind every stroke. His sword clanged and pinged loudly off the Orsembian's. While Baltazar darkly grimaced, the younger man's sweaty visage was one of earnest concentration. Every parry left him reeling in his saddle, yet he kept his sword up to turn Baltazar's next attack, lest he lose a limb or his head.

Reload! Recha reminded herself.

Her ramrod was left sticking out the pistol's barrel, and she rammed it in a few more times to make sure everything was packed in tight.

Charge. Powder. Shot. Where's the wad? She frantically looked through her remaining kit in her lap. *Savior! Where is my wad?*

The wad was a small bit of cloth packed in after the shot to make sure neither it nor the powder poured out of the barrel. The only cloth in her lap was her dress.

Savior forsake it! I'm just going to have to—

"*Ah!*"

Recha shot her head up at the pained grunt, and she went numb.

The Orsembian's sword was lodged under Baltazar's left arm.

Baltazar's arm pressed down on the blade from above, holding it from going any deeper. His eyelids trembled in a pain-stricken wince, exposing his clenched teeth. His body started shifting sideways, threatening to slide out of the saddle.

The Orsembian held his sword in place, neither pressing the attack nor withdrawing. His face was a mask of concentration, but his gray eyes were wide, as if surprised his thrust had struck.

A painfully hiss escaped between Baltazar's teeth, snapping Recha back to reality.

"*Papa!*" she screamed. Her pistol was up the next instant.

Her scream jarred the Orsembian back, as well. He gaped in surprise at her gun aimed at him and jerked back. He pulled his sword out from under Baltazar's arm, its tip and several inches red with blood, to raise his arms in front of his face.

"At *this* range"—Recha cocked the hammer and aimed—"that won't save you!"

She squeezed the trigger. The hammer fell, sparks flew, and powder flashed. But there was no ignition. No kick. No *shot*!

The mere whiff of powder blew away instantly, leaving both her and the Orsembian staring at one another.

A misfire!

Goosebumps ran up her arm, adding to her reeling inside. *A flash in the pan at a time like* this*!*

"The field marshal!" someone yelled as a horse cried.

Baltazar was leaning sideways, pressing his left arm tightly to his side and pulling his horse back with his sword arm. The mount had no choice but to follow his rider and, in a sideways stagger, bend his knees and drift to the ground. As the horse eased down, Baltazar slid out of his saddle, releasing the reins and collapsing on the ground. His horse sprang up once freed.

Recha's face burned. Her breaths became louder and louder. Her lips peeled back in a snarl. She looked between the Orsembian and her pistol. He seemed distracted, looking over her shoulder.

He's . . . ignoring me!

It would take too long to prime it again. She recalled what Sebastian had told her when he'd first given it to her. She had made the comment about it for one shot and useless after that.

"*Well,*" he had replied, "*then use the pommel. Swing it hard enough, and you might put a dent in someone's skull.*"

She turned the gun in her fingers, gripping it by the barrel. She reeled back and swung with a scream.

The Orsembian blinked, remembering she was there.

The silver butt of her pistol struck him across his cheek, the end of the pommel hit bone. To her frustration, the blow left him shaking his head instead

599

of sending him out of his saddle. It *infuriated* her! She pulled back and swung over and over.

Metal pings rang out from her pommel striking the rim and then the top of his helmet. The calleros yelped and brought his forearm up to fend her off as he struggled to sheath his sword, the movement making his intention clear.

"You'll never take *me*!" she spat, changing the angle of her next swing.

The Orsembian peeked out from his guarding forearm and took her pistol's pommel on the bridge of his nose. Recha grinned at the sound of crunching bone and his head snapping back. As he recoiled, she kicked his horse, sending it bolting forward with its rider off balance. She laughed at the sight of the horse bucking the Orsembian out of his saddle and sending him flying backward.

She was denied the joy of seeing him slam into the ground as everyone surged around her. Men ran into her horse, forcing her to focus on keeping it under control unless she would be thrown, too. Everything grew louder—the shouting, weapons clashing, the charging horses—

Charging horses?

Recha's ears twitched. There was no mistaking it. The rumble of charging hooves filled the air. And it was growing louder!

She turned over her shoulder in time to see Lazornian calleroses crashing into the backs of the Orsembians blocking the path to the main battle beyond. Lances and swords cut a bloody path into the enemy, and in their center, waving his sword above his head and cussing with every breath, was Ramon Narvae.

"Cut every one of these frickin' sons of bitches down!" he bellowed.

The thumping of crossbows releasing echoed behind her. Men were rushing up the lane to the southside of camp, toward the infirmary. It was a mass assortment of walking wounded with swords and pikes; camp workers with pikes, shovels, hammers; a random calleros charging with them on horseback; and Viden in their red robes, sending crossbow bolts into the backs of the Orsembians blocking that path.

The Orsembians' attack broke.

Recha swiveled around to catch a glimpse of Ribera. The marshal again proved his rational nature by doing the only thing one could do in this situation. He calmly wheeled his horse around and, along with everyone he could gather, fled.

"After them!" Recha yelled, pointing her pistol after the withdrawing banner.

Some of the Narvae's calleroses did break through to pursue while most joined the fight against those Orsembians who couldn't get away. There was no need to send them all, though. With Servco covering the mountain trek, Hiraldo's calleroses in-between, and Narvae's in pursuit, Ribera had no escape.

"Recha!"

She tiredly turned. Her shoulders slumped, unable to keep straight with the pressure of death no longer closing to keep her edge up.

That is . . . until she saw Cornelos wrapping strips of cloth around Baltazar's armpit and shoulder. Baltazar winced with every pull of cloth, and even from her distance, Recha could see him struggling to breathe.

"*Papa!*" she cried, leaping from the saddle. The little of her pistol's ammunition and kit left went flying, but she didn't stop to care, shoving her pistol into her dress's belt.

She sprinted over and collapsed beside him. Baltazar's face was drenched. His short, heavy panting rang in her ears. A pool of blood soaked the ground under his arm, and it was growing.

"He needs a surgeon," Cornelos said, wrapping as fast as he could and packing more cloth under Baltazar's armpit. "He may have nicked an artery. Press down, Field Marshal. Hard!" He shoved Baltazar's arm in and pressed the wadded cloth into his side.

Baltazar grunted and hissed. His head rolled around on the dirt as he curled his arm and held it against his side.

"*Stretcher!*" Recha yelled. "The field marshal needs a stretcher!"

The fighting around them drowned out the demand. She pushed herself up, but Baltazar grabbed her wrist and pulled her back down. He reached and took her by the back of the neck, pulling her down.

"Ramon . . . made it?" he grunted.

"Yes," she replied frantically, patting his breastplate. "Yes, he made it, Papa. You rest here, and I'll get you to the surgeons—"

"*No!*" He squeezed and shook her neck. "The battle comes first! I gave orders to the armies. Look for Hiraldo and Priet pressing against Borbin's flanks. If Ross is still holding, then there is only one order to give." He opened his eyes, glaring up at her with raging fire. "Attack, Recha! *Attack!*"

Recha shook her head. "Yes. Yes, I'll give the order, but first—"

"No! Now!" Baltazar threw her off. "Go, Recha! *Attack!*"

Recha scrambled away, Baltazar's urgent order ringing her ears. Clawing her way on hands and knees, she came up, sprinting to her horse.

"Marshal Narvae!" she screamed, digging out her eyeglass and pulling herself up into her saddle with a tired groan. "*Marshal Narvae!*"

She extended her eyeglass and stood in her saddle. She brought the glass up as Narvae rode up.

"La Dama!" he replied, out of breath. "Good to see you're still alive. Where's the field marshal—?"

"Baltazar's wounded, but he'll be fine."

601

Or he better be, she prayed, scanning the field the best she could.

"But right now, I need dispatchers!" she demanded. "Baltazar left orders and, wounded or not, the armies need them."

"Calleroses! To me!" Narvae shouted.

The clomping and skidding of hooves announced them gathering around her.

"What are their orders, La Dama?" Narvae asked.

"To Generals Galvez, Ross, and Priet"—she grinned, unable to tear her eyes away from the sight through the glass—"*attack!*"

Chapter 35

Necrem jabbed his pike into a snorting horse's face. The panting animal's wild eyes roamed this way and that from its rider forcing it forward. The calleros's wayward, downward thrusts with his lance were easily met by another pikeman's parrying blow. The calleros swayed in his saddle, pulling on the horse's reins.

Necrem jabbed again over another pikeman's head, the pike head stabbing the horse's face. The horse screeched from the sharp point slashing across its cheek and reared. Pikemen hurried back, bumping and pushing Necrem back in their scramble away from the incensed animal's kicking hooves.

The calleros flung himself forward. All the calleros's calming pats and attempts to soothe his mount proved futile as it began to buck and kick out behind him.

"Lower your pikes!" a soldier yelled. "Drive the crazy animal into the others!"

Necrem rushed to join them, forming a bristling wall that made the horse scream and snort at seeing. It shook its mane wildly, refusing every command his calleros gave.

Other calleroses struggled to pull their horses away. Several fighting to stave off the pikemen thrusting at them couldn't. The injured horse leapt into the air, twisting and bucking. A few kicks found their marks and struck several horses around it.

The horses that were kicked screamed and reared. The rage and fear spread through them like fire, and the calleroses were forced to abandon any hope of fighting to tending to their mounts. The horses bucked and turned. Pikemen edged forward to prod those they could reach to enrage them more.

Finally, they broke.

Here and there, a calleros was thrown from the saddle. The horses stampeded the way they had come, running through other calleroses still stubbornly trying to press their failed charge and into a waiting company of Orsembian soldiers behind them. The wild horses tore gaps into the soldiers' formation, forcing many to spear them to death to save themselves from being trampled.

"Get 'em!" a soldier yelled.

Several men around Necrem picked up the call and charged forward. Their blood was still up from charging the dismounted calleroses from earlier, and seeing more crawling on the ground renewed their vigor. They fell on the thrown calleroses, struggling on hands and knees after their fall and their helmets' poor visibility, with the same vengeful, and some gleeful, abandon.

No mercy. Necrem took a step to join them.

"Reform your lines!" an officer urgently ordered. "You men get back here! The other calleroses are—"

A calleros charged in and struck a pikemen's head off with sword. The pikemen's decapitated body flopped to the ground. His pike stayed erect in the air in the calleros's body he had just impaled.

More calleroses charged back in, hunting down the pikemen like *pavaloros*. They ran down the pikemen with equal vengeance, running them threw with their lances or cutting them down with their swords. The pikemen who could dashed back to the safety of the line, but the calleroses pursued.

They hacked and pushed their horses forward in the face of more and more pikemen rushing up to join the line. The line bulged here and there under the renewed pressure. The pikemen's orderly ranks were long broken, and they fought more as a disorganized mob stretched across the front.

Necrem held his pike out, ready to face another charging horse. *We can't let them break through!*

A calleros crashed into the line a few feet away from him. His lance speared one man, and his horse trampled another. He batted away the pikes nearest him with his forearm braces. His armor proved its worth, shrugging off the assaulting shafts with ease as the calleros drew his sword.

The soldier next to Necrem lashed out with his pike. He swung again and again to knock the calleros out of the saddle. The calleros grabbed the pike's shaft, pulled it in, then stabbed downward with his sword. The blade drove into the soldier's chest.

A wet gasp escaped from the soldier. His hands slid down his pike, and his shoulders slumped. The calleros's sword hissed against the rim of the soldier's breastplate as he pulled it out, leaving the soldier to fumble backward into Necrem.

Necrem reached his arm out to catch him, but all strength seemed to have evaporated from the man's limbs, and he folded into a collapsed heap. The soldier's scruffy face pointed upward at the sky. He never got a last glimpse of it. His eyes, half-closed, revealed only the whites from them rolling back in his head.

The calleros paid him no thought, hacking and slashing at the other soldiers around him. Another soldier, too close to spear him with his pike, received a cut across his face. The soldier wailed, dropping his pike to clutch his face, blood running out between his fingers.

Necrem picked out another sound under the screams and yells—muffled laughter.

Laughing, he growled. *Always . . . laughing!*

He raised his pike from where he stood and swung. The length of the pike made it wobble and unwieldly, but its weight couldn't compare to a hammer's. Necrem bellowed and put all strength into the swing. His biceps bulged and tightened against his armor's straps, digging into his arm.

His pike knocked several others away, clapping and whooshing through the air, and slammed into the calleros's back at an angle. The impact sent tremors down the shaft, but Necrem's gauntlets protected his hands. He brought his swing all the way around.

The calleros doubled over in his saddle. His backplate cushioned the blow and his helmet saved his head from being cracked open as the pike slid up his back and over him.

Necrem brought the long, wobbling pole around, gritting his teeth at it trying to slip from his grip and the calleros still in his saddle.

His head's probably ringing like a gong, Necrem surmised, knowing the claustrophobic sense of wearing his own helmet. *I can't let him get his bearings!*

He stepped over the corpse of the slain soldier and swung again, using the momentum of his last swing into a back stroke.

The calleros was pushing himself up, shaking his head—

Crack!

Necrem's pike slammed into the calleros's head. The visor bent inward around the splintering shaft. Wood and metal wrenched against each other as the calleros was ripped around, his head bobbing and twisting backward from the blow, and fell out of his saddle. He flopped to the ground in a heap of metal and groans, his sword flung from his grip.

The soldiers around Necrem roared, thrusting their pikes in the air. They pushed the riderless horse out of the way and rejoined the fight against the other calleroses, leaving the one Necrem knocked off at his feet.

The man rolled over. Trails of blood dripped and ran out from under his helmet around the chin. Necrem picked up faint coughing and wheezing under the caved-in visor.

Necrem glanced at his pike. It was badly bent, looped over toward the right. Visible cracks webbed along the outside curve of the bend. The shaft would snap if struck against a strong plate.

"Help."

The weak voice made Necrem look down. The calleros fumbled to push his visor up, his gauntlet scraping against it.

A pike impaled the man in the neck before he could raise his visor.

Necrem jerked his head up to find Hezet next to him. The veteran put his boot on the calleros's chest and pulled his pike out, leaving the man to suffocate on his own blood.

"You broke your pike," Hezet said.

Necrem planted the butt of the bent pole in the ground and leaned against it. His shoulders suddenly felt heavy and slumped forward. His legs trembled. His breaths became long and haggard, and he blinked lines of sweat out of his eyes.

"I held the line," he replied.

Hezet smirked, shouldering his pike with a sigh. "One battle, and you're already talking like a—"

His smirk vanishing, Hezet leapt forward, ramming his shoulder into Necrem's gut. Necrem jerked back, partially from being shoved and partially from Hezet's wild expression. He turned in time to see another calleros barreling into the ranks just in front of him.

This one was clad head to toe in plate, along with his horse. The horse wore a metal mask over its head with a barbed spike in the center of its forehead. When it charged in, it bucked with its head, slamming the soldier in front with the spike.

Men screamed under the beast's iron-clad hooves. Worse, the calleros charged in, swinging a halberd. The axe-headed weapon cleaved men down left and right as the rider tore into the forest of pikes without any hint of slowing.

He's coming right at me! Necrem saw the halberd raise in the air. His body, too tired to move fast, tensed in place. *Eulalia!*

"*Oso!*"

Hezet dashed in front of him. He brought his pike up. The steel barb pointed straight for the calleros's gut. The calleros would be impaled on it by his horse's own momentum, raging forward like it was. It was impossible to avoid the impact—

The calleros's tug on the reins was subtle. As hard as the horse charge in, it slammed its hooves in the dirt, sending dust and rocks everywhere, including into Hezet's face. The veteran burst into a fit of coughing. Necrem's own eyes watered, forcing his hands up to protect them.

He watched the halberd come down through his fingers. The axe head tore through Hezet's left shoulder, pauldron, armor, bones, and all. The pike was cleaved in two, and once it dropped uselessly into the dirt, the calleros kicked his horse into gallop again, running past Necrem without looking. He made a half-circle, carving into, around, then out of the ranks.

Once behind the pikemen, all they could do was dive out of the way or get cut down, their long pikes too cumbersome to defend themselves against the overwhelming onslaught. As the calleros galloped out, he waved his gore-trailing weapon over his head, and the other calleroses flocked to him, riding away and finally breaking off from their attack.

Hezet crumbled to the ground at Necrem's feet. His entire left side was a bloody mess. His shoulder was gone, cleaved off with his arm lying feet away among the other bodies, the cracked pauldron still attached to the limb. Blood squirted out in three trails from his body, pooling on the ground, and bone stook out from the gaping wound.

Hezet stared up at him. His sweaty, glistening face drained of color. His eyes were wild, bouncing this way and that. He shivered in the dirt. Hot and fast breaths hissed out of his mouth. He was joining all the other soldiers who had fallen to the ground, never to get up. He was dying right in front of him, and there was nothing Necrem could do.

He let go of his splintered pike, and his strength vanished from his knees. He fell beside Hezet with a thud.

"Why?" he asked. He had only known the man for a couple months. He hadn't seen him in weeks. He had left him with the army. He'd been *going* home and hadn't spared a thought for those he had been first conscripted with who had chosen to still fight. He wasn't even sure if they were friends.

Yet Hezet had thrown himself in front of that calleros.

"*Why?*"

Hezet's wild eyes snapped straight at him. His head weakly shifted, failing to raise. His facial muscles jerked and twitched, his chin spasmed, and his lips smacked together. Air hissed from his throat, breaking his quick, staggering breaths. He was trying to speak.

Necrem leaned closer.

"Break . . . break . . ." Hezet's voice was soft, barely a whisper. Only leaning over him could Necrem hear the words over the noise of battle. "Break . . . 'em . . . Break 'em . . . Steel . . . Fist." His sharp breaths quickened into a long, final exhale. His body fell still. No color remained in his face, and his eyes, turned glossy, rolled upward.

Bugles blared across the field. They started from the left, then from the right, and finally behind him. Their loud ringing drowned out the cries of battle all around.

Tap!

Tap!

Rap! Rap! Rap!

The drums followed, rapping in unison. Necrem felt them through the ground and his knee plates.

"*Fall in!*" an officer ordered. "Fall in behind the ranks moving up!"

Marching feet approached in unison. Although all the companies had merged into one line, only Necrem's had charged. The others now marched, pikes shouldered to allow the wounded and survivors to pass between the ranks. Men eagerly left the line to the relief of the rear.

A hand clapped him on the shoulder.

"Come on, soldier," the officer urged. "If you're able to stand, pick up a pike and fall in. The enemy's reforming." The officer slapped his shoulder again then walked away.

Necrem looked across the field. The remaining calleroses were dispersing. Some rode off either toward the other sides of the valley or off their rear. Those who stayed were dismounting and reforming the companies of soldiers, taking positions in front of them.

The oncoming soldiers marched in. They stayed in their ranks and walked around him, their column swallowing him as he remained kneeling on the ground. He watched them step lively over the bodies, cautiously glancing to make sure they didn't trip or step on any of them.

He took one last at Hezet's face and said, "Goodbye, Hezet." Then he pushed himself to his feet, knees wobbling, body shaking. A groan ripped through him as his tired limbs threatened to fail him. He'd been ignoring it for so long, but the stinging and burning across his face returned with the lull. He took deep, haggard breaths to keep himself standing.

He took no notice of the soldiers marching past him. They were all nameless faces now. Grim men carrying on with a grim job. He gave the direction they were heading in one last glance then turned for the rear.

Maybe I should leave. His steps were slow, cumbersome. His shoulders slumped. His hands hung from his sides from the gauntlets' weight. *Go back to the doctors and wait my turn. What else can I do here? I'm not a soldier—*

"*Break 'em, Steel Fist.*"

Hezet's last request stopped him.

"*What good is living when you've been wronged and won't make it right?*"

"*Break 'em, Steel Fist.*"

Necrem's hands curled to fists. *Why? Why after everything today? We've been fighting for hours. Why?*

A bugle trumpeted. The drums sped up. Sporadic volleys of muskets erupted. Men roared together.

Necrem looked over his shoulder. The first ranks for the column surged forward, meeting the Orsembians charging. Pikes smashed together. However, this time, the sides pushed into each other's with raging abandon. The Orsembian calleroses threw themselves into the fray, trusting their better armor to hack at the soldiers' pikes.

One of those calleroses in the center swung a halberd. And behind them, rippling in a meager breeze, was Borbin's banner.

"*Break 'em, Steel Fist.*"

The first step made him grunt. The second, he gritted his teeth at. He ignored the back of his legs burning. He forced his arms up. He shoved the stings clawing at his face aside. And he ran straight forward!

"Show these peasants how true warriors fight!"

"Push into them!"

"Orsembians—!"

"Lazornians—!"

"*Attack!*"

The encouraging drive of the respective officers, the battle cries of the soldiers, the beating of the drums, the wails of the wounded and dying, all boiled down to a dull buzzing in Necrem's ears. Each step forward, his focus narrowed. Each step forward, he heard less and less. Each step forward, he saw the calleroses in front of him, off their horses, nothing standing between them, and nothing to hold him back.

He shoved soldiers out of his way, his legs pumping, his arms waving back and forth as he ran. *Sprinted!*

A cascade of images ran through his mind. Eulalia smiling. Eulalia teasing him. Eulalia waiting for him. Eulalia as he found her that night. Eulalia as he left her.

"*What good is living when you've been wronged and won't make it right?*"

His tear-filled vision blurred red. Something between a wail and a bellow tore out of his throat.

The halberd-wielding calleros hooked a soldier by his shoulder, flipped him on the ground, and raised his halberd over him to hack the soldier's chest open.

"Break 'em, Steel Fist!"

Necrem burst through the soldiers' line, roaring, and wrapped his arms around the calleros, tearing him from his feet. He barreled on, into the other calleroses in front of him, not stopping for an instant.

They were finally close.

Finally in reach!

Finally . . . he had his *hands* on them!

With the halberd-wielding calleros off his feet, Necrem pulled back and slammed his fist into the man's gut. Breastplate and gauntlet slammed together. Steel screamed. One punch wasn't enough. It could *never* be enough! He swung again. And again. *And again*!

This was no fatigue and nightmarish dream. This was no repression held delusion. This was no conscripted Orsembian forced to fight or else. This was an actual calleros whose breastplate was caving in with every punch, who grunted and gargled with every punch! *Borbin's calleros*!

"*Eulalia!*" Necrem roared, grabbing the calleros by the top of his breastplate, letting him bend over as he reared his arm back.

Clang!

A sword came down on his left arm. The blade bit into his elbow plate but failed to slice between the joint. The intervening calleros stared at his caught blade with pale shock, clearly having expected to cut Necrem's arm off.

Necrem shrugged off the blade, letting go of the halberd-wielder's breastplate to seize the top of the intervening calleros's helmet. "You think you can cut my steel?" he yelled, spitting through his mask's holes and twisting. "Do *you*?"

He drove his fist into the calleros's face. Bones crunched. Blood squirted. The man's body jerked, and his limbs flailed. His sword slipped from his fingers and clattered on the ground. Necrem held him by the helmet, reared back again, unfazed by the man's bloody face— he had seen worse for ten years—and hit him again.

Twice.

Thrice!

Teeth flew in all directions. Pieces of flesh clung to his gauntlets' knuckle plates. The calleros's helmet strap was the only thing keeping the man on his feet.

Something thumped against Necrem's gut. He jerked down to find the halberd-wielding calleros kneeling on the ground and pressing the spike of his halberd against Necrem's breastplate, the spike digging into the steel yet not penetrating.

"You're still mocking my steel!" Necrem backhanded the halberd-wielding calleros. The plate covering the back of his fist smacked side of the calleros's head, bending the cheek guard inward.

The calleros's head snapped to the side. He twisted on the ground and fell backward, pulling his halberd back with him. The spike grated upward against Necrem's breastplate, spinning and falling on top of its wielder.

More calleroses rushed him, swords raised in the air. Their muffled curses lost in all the noise. One leveled a lance like a spear, yelling out of his visor.

Necrem bellowed back at them. Still holding the one calleros up by his helmet, he threw him into his comrades. The charging lance-wielder had to lower his weapon to prevent spearing his fellow calleros. The opening was enough, and Necrem dove into it, swinging out with both fists.

It was just like the press from earlier. Heads and chest were in easy reach, and with how close they pushed in, there was little chance he could miss or that they could dodge. A jabbing left hook to a calleros's unprotected face sent the man spinning. A right uppercut under the jaw of another lifted the man off his feet and into his fellow calleroses behind.

He grabbed the calleros's lance before he could bring it back up, pulled him in close, and drove his fist into the man's gut. The man doubled over, and Necrem took hold of the back of his plate and tossed him, tripping others for his fists.

He couldn't stop, not even to catch his breath. A calleros stabbed him in the side with a dagger, the point blunted against his plates. Necrem caught the calleros's arms, wrapped own his arm around them at the elbow, and held them.

He squeezed his arm up. As he did, the calleros's arms bent back at the elbow. Armor and limb bent backward, and the man threw his head back and wailed. His cries grew louder and louder. Screeching metal joined. Necrem gritted his teeth, added his other hand to the press, and *squeezed*!

A glint of light caught his eye. He lifted his head—

Clang!

A sword struck him across the face. The force of the blow jerked Necrem's head around. The blade scraped across his mask and caught one of the holes. The mask's rim ripped across his cheek, followed by the cord. The taste of copper leaked into his mouth, followed by the dry, dusty air swept through the holes in his cheeks, instantly drying them out as he snarled.

He glared down at the calleros he was holding. Heavy droplets of blood dripped down on the man's visor. Terrified eyes stared up at him through visor eyeholes, blinking rapidly and dancing wildly.

"What?" Necrem growled. "Isn't my face funny?"

The calleros squirmed, kicking and digging into the dirt, pulling on his arms, unable to get them free.

Necrem held him tight and lifted his head. The other calleroses groaned and gagged. Several recoiled, shifting their feet and turning their heads away. The calleros directly in front of him, the one who had struck him, took a few steps back, holding his sword out.

"All of you thought it was funny ten years ago," Necrem spat, blood and drool clinging to his chin. "You laughed at *every* cut! Why aren't any of you laughing now? Go on. *Laugh!* Let me hear you *laugh!*" Necrem squeezed, pulling his arm up. His hold grew tighter and tighter the louder he yelled, only outmatched by the calleros screaming in his grip.

The armor caved.

Snap!

The crack of bones echoed from under the arm, bringing the calleros's wail to a fever pitch until his voice cracked, too.

Necrem dropped the man to the ground, leaving him there with his arms bent backward at the elbow, and regard the other calleroses.

They edged away from him, weapons raised and pointed at him, but none eagerly or vengefully charged him. He caught faint flashes of sunlight dancing off their steel.

They were trembling.

More blood pooled in the side of his mouth from the fresh cut, forcing him to spit. Instinctively, he pulled his hand up to wipe his mouth with the back of his hand and stopped at the sight of gore on his gauntlets. He caught his reflection in the metal, face torn to shreds, scars held together by years of stitching. Those were his scars, but his weren't the only ones they had scarred.

"Eulalia . . ." he growled, hands shaking into fists.

Some calleroses drew up short from inching forward, cautious with their weapons raised. Others, like the calleros in front of him holding out his shaking sword, stood motionless. All Necrem saw, though, were calleroses. Calleroses who defiled his wife.

"*Eulalia!*" He charged in, abandoning any sense or planning. He just swung. His fists were hammers, and their bodies the steel. The jabs, swings, and thrusts of their weapons didn't matter. Not once he was close. Not once he got his hands on them.

He punched one calleros in the chest, denting the breastplate and sending the man staggering backward. He wrapped his arm around a lance, pulling its wielder close, then backhanding the man, caving in his visor. He took a sword blow to the shoulder to grab a calleros by the helmet, kneed him in the groin, and then furiously punched in his helmet.

Blows came from every direction. A lance thrust to his side. A sword slash against his helmet. A mace blow to the back. He took them all. He would withstand everything to keep hold of them and swing.

He swung punch after punch. Blow after blow. He lost count of the number of breastplates he dented, of the helmets he bent, and visors he cracked. If he caught one without a visor, he instantly went for the face. It just took one blow, one punch, and his gauntlets crushed them to the point the man was unrecognizable.

He blocked a sword swing against his left forearm brace, and a right hook tore another calleros's helmet from his shoulders. The man's head snapped back from the force, his neck jutting forward in a strange position. He took two steps back then toppled over. His head still snapped backward where he lay. Necrem walked over him, searching for the next calleros.

However, there wasn't one.

He spotted a few of them running back toward their waiting horses, yet there were none left around him. At least, none left standing. He glanced over his shoulder. A trail of mangled, beaten-in bodies laid behind him. Pikemen picked among the bodies, stabbing any who moved. More lingered behind him, cautiously watching him, and not a soul appeared willing to get close to him.

The sounds of musket fire, drums, bugles, and galloping hooves all flooded back to him. Loudest of all was his heavy breathing. His lungs worked like heavy bellows to keep him standing.

And yet, as he looked back at what he had done, as he held his hands up, no longer able to feel his fists clenched in his gauntlets, an overwhelming desire burned inside of him.

It's not enough. Necrem spat and swallowed, his throat too dry to be picky about swallowing his own blood. *It's not enough!*

He froze.

Borbin's erected flagpole was twenty feet away, with the marqués's banner looming over them. Under that banner, surrounded by a few riders and guards, sat Marqués Borbin himself on his horse. He sat in plate armor from neck to toe, without a helmet. A cape of shimmering silk draped from his shoulder pauldrons like a curtain that reached and covered his horse's rump. They were all gazing and pointing at something happening to Necrem's left, where loud musket fire was coming from.

None of them took notice of Necrem. More importantly . . .

Nothing stood between them.

No company of soldiers.

No mounted calleroses.

Just open field.

His legs moved on their own. His arms swung at his side as if he were on a stroll. His tired knees buckled with every other step through the clumps of marched-over field bushes, but he pushed through them. He caught himself repeatedly, clapping hold of his knees and pushing himself straight.

Borbin sat right in front of him. Every scar stung as if every cut was still fresh. His teeth clenched from the man's voice whispering in the back of his mind. He had called him a beast. He had called Eulalia a whore. He had *refused* to say her name.

"Plug up that hole!" an Orsembian officer cried.

"Hold them!" another officer furiously ordered. "*Hold them!*"

Necrem glanced at the fighting. He was walking behind the Orsembian's line, as bold as he pleased. He snickered despite himself. The soldiers were all focused on the Lazornians in front of them.

Though they rushed to fill the hole Necrem had made, the Lazornians met them with pikes and swords. More and more of them pushed through, attacking and pushing the Orsembians back.

Here and there, an Orsembian soldier in the back row tumbled out of line and ran. A couple rushed past Necrem without giving him a second look.

Necrem ignored them and focused on Borbin on his big horse.

"We must stop their advance," one of the men next to Borbin said, pointing at something on the left side of the valley. "They've advanced along the cliff face, and now they're pushing in on our flank."

"This wouldn't have happened if Baron Delazar had dislodged them!" another man flanking Borbin spat.

"It's too late for that." Borbin waved away their concerns. "We need more men on that flank. Any word on Barons Ortiga and Suerez? We need their companies."

"None, Si Don," the first man replied, shaking his head. "Ever since Ortiga withdrew from the right flank, he hasn't responded to any of our requests."

"Baron Suerez reported his companies stood ready a few hours ago," the second man added. "Last word I received said they hadn't left the camp yet."

"I'll strip both of them of their lands after this," Borbin growled.

Necrem breathed deeper, working his lungs hard, needlessly stoking the fire raging within at recognizing the tone. Just a few more feet.

"*How* are they pushing forward?" Borbin hit his saddle horn in frustration. "We outnumber them three to one. We should have crushed them *hours* ago! Bring up—"

"Halt, soldier!"

Necrem froze.

One of Borbin's guards hurried in front of him, putting himself between Necrem and Borbin, planting his halberd in the dirt.

"State your business!" the guard demanded. "Are you a messenger or—?" The guard winced and hissed, recoiling at taking in Necrem's face. "Injured go to the rear." He pointed back toward Borbin's camp.

"I don't need a doctor," Necrem said lowly. He kept his head low and took careful, leisure steps forward. He needed to get closer. "It's ten years too late for that."

The guard tilted his head, avoiding eye contact and looking at Necrem's face. "What—"

The guard gasped, his eyes widening at something behind Necrem. "Si Don!" he yelled over his shoulder. "The center is—"

Necrem seized his halberd by the shaft and drove his fist into the guard's turned jaw. The odd angle made the jaw pop and crunch. A tooth flew into the air as the guard's head jerked aside, followed by the rest of his body collapsing in the dirt, leaving Necrem with his halberd.

"What are you doing?" the first man with Borbin, a baron by his shining, decorated armor and sword, demanded.

Necrem brought the halberd up, remembering how he swung his pike, and charged. The other guards were spread out too far, and the baron's hands were tangled up his reins. Necrem swung the halberd's axe head into the baron's back. The edge bit into the baron's backplate, snagging on it.

Necrem pulled hard, dragging the man out of his saddle with a startled yelp. He fell in a calamity of metal and plate, rolling over on his head, his armor weighing him down. Necrem wrenched the halberd free and left him there, seeking his true target.

"He's an enemy!" the baron still on his horse cried.

"*Guards!*" Borbin yelled, turning his horse around.

Necrem's heart raced. *He's trying to run!*

"*Borbin!*" he yelled, shoving past the fallen baron's horse and swung his stolen halberd as wide and hard as he could. His eyes danced between the axe head and the marqués, judging the distance in the meager seconds.

He's out of reach!

The halberd lacked the reach of a pike. Borbin was leaning back in his saddle, wheeling his horse. The axe head was going to swipe harmless through the air, and Necrem was committed to the swing. There wasn't enough time to get closer for another one!

He's going to get away!

Thunk!

The halberd struck the head of Borbin's horse. In wheeling his horse, Borbin had pulled out of the halberd's reach and had put his horse in its path. The axe head crushed the plate on the horse's forehead and sliced through the bone. Necrem followed through with the swing, bringing the axe head through the beast's skull and slapping it aside.

Borbin's horse jerked and swung its head from side to side. Its eyes rolled wildly. A strangled screech came from his gaping mouth, tongue sticking out from the bridle.

Borbin struggled with the reins as it danced under him. As suddenly and violently as it started to thrash, the horse's legs caved under the weight and flopped sideways on the ground. Borbin groaned and gasped from his leg being pinned under the horse's corpse.

"*Si Don!*" the mounted baron cried.

Necrem looked down at Borbin, trapped and clawing in vain to get out from under his horse. His face stung in a hundred places, but for the first time in ten years, Necrem grinned broadly.

A couple of Borbin's guards roared as they charged around the horses at Necrem, halberds lowered like pikes.

"*Get out of my way!*" Necrem yelled back at them.

He swung his halberd. The guard charging his left pulled back, but the one charging his right wasn't as quick. Necrem's extra height brought the polearm around higher than his and struck the man in the chest, sending him flying and twisting in the air.

Necrem used the momentum to step forward and swing again. The remaining guard brought his halberd up to parry, but the strength of Necrem's swing slammed into his halberd, moving it aside, and the axe head cut into the guard's arm. The man wailed as the heavy edge broke through his arm and sliced into his flesh. The man dropped his halberd and scrambled away, clutching his bleeding arm as if it was about to fall off.

"Come back here!" Borbin yelled at the guard. The marqués stared up at Necrem in terror then twisted away, reaching out to the mounted Baron. "Valen! Help me!"

Baron Valen turned back around in his saddle after watching the fleeing guard. His helmet-covered head moved this way and that, looking at the dead bodies, looking at his trapped marqués. He said nothing. He didn't reach for his sword. He kept swiveling his head in the wide circuit of a man unsure of what to do.

Musket fire grew louder around them. Battle cries filled the air.

"Si Don has fallen!" someone screamed.

"We can't hold!"

"Calleroses!"

The familiar pounding of galloping hooves rumbled through the valley, yet they were coming from behind Necrem this time.

"Fall back!" The shouting grew desperate. "*Fall back*!"

Orsembian soldiers started running past them without a second glance. Baron Valen still sat there, swiveling his head.

"Valen?" Borbin called.

The baron suddenly sat straight, gathered his reins, then wheeled his horse around in a gallop, kicking dirt in both Necrem's and his marqués's face.

"*Valen*!" Borbin screamed. "Savior damn you!" He beat the ground with his fist and frantically tried to pull his leg free.

Necrem watched him. He planted the halberd in the ground to lean against. His breathing slowed, and the aches and weariness returned. But he couldn't rest yet. Not yet.

He let the halberd go, letting it clatter on the ground.

Borbin spun around, raising his hands defensively. "I yield under the Rules," he said, reluctantly yet also assertively. "And under the Rules, it is my rights to be taken and properly treated in accordance with my station. I demand you—"

"I don't care about your rules," Necrem said, leaving Borbin to gawk up at him as he stepped over him. "And I don't care about your demands." He put his foot down on Borbin's horse and pressed down.

"*Stop*!" Borbin let out a yelp and rolled his head back. He reached and pushed against his saddle, as if to lift the weight. It only made Necrem press harder. "Please! What do you care about? Name it, and it'll be yours! I *swear* it!" he hissed, clawing at his trapped leg.

"What do I want?" Necrem suddenly planted a knee into Borbin's chest. The two plates came together with a loud clash, driving the air out of the marqués and leaving him coughing and gasping. He leaned in, looming over the man, and dripped drool down on him from his snarling, scarred lips. "I want to hear you say something. Is my wife a whore?"

Borbin gulped air and blinked up at him. "What? I don't know—"

Necrem slammed his hand down around Borbin's neck, and he yelled in the man's face, "Is my *wife* a whore?"

Borbin's eyes bulged. His mouth gaped. The man trembled in his grip. "I don't—"

Necrem's grip tightened, pulled him back, then slammed the back of his head into the dirt. "Is"—slam—"she"—slam—"a"—slam—"*whore?*"

"*No!*" Borbin cried, voice cracking to a squeak. His head bobbed and rolled with every impact. Tears welled up and streamed from his eyes. "No! No, she's not!"

"Then say her name!" Necrem's spit rain down the marqués. His face burned as if on fire, but he didn't care. Nothing mattered but having his hands around the man's throat.

Borbin gawked up at him in a mixture of panic and terror. His head shook back and forth. "I don't know—"

"*Eulalia!*" Necrem tightened his grip and slammed Borbin's head in the ground again. "Say"—slam—"her"—slam—"*name!*"

Borbin's eyes rolled back after the second impact. When they rolled back down, he started to whimper and cry, "Eulalia! Eulalia! *Eulalia!*"

Necrem squeezed tighter and tighter each time his wife's name left Borbin's lips. "And is she a whore?"

"*No!*" Borbin shook his head, flinging tears in every direction. "No, she's not!" He deflated in his grip, sobbing.

It wasn't enough. The world around Necrem was becoming smaller and smaller, and hearing the man who had ruined his and family's lives admit those words aloud wasn't enough.

"Then why"—his grip gradually grew tighter, popping a knuckle, and squeezing Borbin's neck—"*why* did you call her one!"

Borbin squirmed under him. His armor plate scraped on the rocks and crushed stocks of grass. His arms flailed, and his free leg uselessly kicked in the air. Wet, gasping sounds escaped his gaping mouth. His eyes bulged wider and wider with each passing second as his face grew redder and redder.

"*Why?*" Necrem's own voice sounded strangled in his ears. He wasn't certain if it was from his demand to the marqués or questioning why he couldn't squeeze any harder. More of his knuckles popped, the joints going numb, and refused to let his grip tighten any further. The longer he held Borbin's neck, the more his arm started to shake.

Borbin worked his jaw, desperately gulping like a fish out of water. His wet gasps became long hisses. His face was turning purple, and his bulging eyes started rolling back in his head.

Necrem stared down at him, his body frozen and trembling. Everything was muffled under the pounding in his ears, but just underneath it was the rumbling of a voice drifting around him. There were footsteps, cautious and uncertain. Clomping of horse hooves.

"Sir Oso?"

Necrem's ear twitched. He didn't move or release his grip, but *someone* had spoken his name.

"*Sir Oso!*"

There it was again.

Necrem looked up, stiffly turning his neck. He was surrounded by Lazornians watching him at a distance, leaning against their pikes, resting their muskets lazily on their shoulders, or hanging their swords and shields at their sides. Men winced and turned away the moment he raised his head. A group of officers sat on their horses, their swords still resting in their scabbards and armor covered in dust.

General Galvez sat in the center of them, leaning forward in his saddle and frowning down at him with concern. "Sir Oso," the general said calmly, "that's enough. You've done enough."

"It . . . It . . ." He had to swallow. Necrem wasn't sure if he shook his head or if his shaking had reached it. He couldn't keep still, though. "It'll never be enough."

"I've heard reports," General Galvez said, sluggishly dismounting and walking around the bodies over to him, "about a mountain of man in armor who fought with his hands alone to hold the center. They say this man led a charge that kept it from collapsing."

"He charged the calleroses," a soldier added. "Caved in their armor and helmets with just his fists, he did."

"He broke through their ranks by himself!" another yelled.

General Galvez laid his hand on Necrem's pauldron, pressing some weight down on his shoulder. "And now you captured the enemy marqués singlehandedly," he said comfortingly. "That's more than enough for any soldier. For any Hero."

Necrem jerked his head back. "I'm not a Hero! I'm not even a . . . a soldier."

"Today, you were both." General Galvez smiled. "And it would be a shame that your last act of the day was strangling someone pathetically in the dirt."

Necrem looked down at Borbin, hanging on to life by a thread. Just a few more moments . . . and that thread would snap.

"It's not enough," he said. His body's spasming intensified, and he clenched his teeth. "It's not *enough*! Why does *he* get mercy? Why does *he* deserve it?"

General Galvez's shadow fell upon him. The man leaned down, putting more pressure on his shoulder. "Who said he'd get mercy?" the general whispered.

Necrem's shaking instantly stopped.

"All I said," the general continued, "was that you've done enough this day. And he has more to answer for. Let him go. The credit will always be yours." He patted Necrem's shoulder, gauntlet and pauldron clapping together. "This glory will *always* be yours."

The talk of credit and glory was all calleros and soldier nonsense that didn't mean anything to Necrem. The general's tone when he mentioned mercy, that made the hair stand on end.

He remembered how the battle had started, the priests and their prisoners, including Borbin's own son.

He let out a long, deflating sigh. The air hissed through the holes in his face. His hand relaxed, and he pulled away. After a few, dragged-out seconds, Borbin suddenly convulsed into a raging, coughing fit.

General Galvez slapped Necrem's pauldron again. "Huzza, Steel Fist!" he shouted to the men with his fist raised in the air. "Hero of the center and capturer of Si Don Borbin!"

"Huzza!" the soldiers shouted, raising their weapons in the air. "Huzza, Steel Fist! Huzza!"

Necrem shuffled off to the side and collapsed to his knees. His arms fell out on his lap, every ounce of strength in his body completely spent.

As the soldiers gave their last cheer and the general returned to giving orders—one being to give up his horse to take Necrem to camp doctors—Necrem knelt there on the ground, content to let the world move around him.

I did it, he lamented, hanging his head. *I did it, Eulalia. Your husband did it. I made those cowards pay. I made Borbin eat his words.*

His shoulders, though burdened under his pauldrons, felt a weight—a resigned, unconscionable weight—lift from them.

The sounds of fighting were growing more distant. When he raised his head to check, he closed what remained of his mouth, feeling his cheek muscles lift, trying to form a smile. The Lazornians were pushing all the way into Borbin's camp. Yet, all Necrem saw was his way home opening.

I'll be home soon.

Chapter 36

Recha snapped her eyeglass shut and dropped it into her lap with a deep, exhausted sigh. She leaned forward in her saddle, letting strands of hair fall over her face, and softly laughed.

Beautiful. Her shoulders bounced as her chuckles grew. *Absolutely beautiful, Papa!*

She blinked tears from her eyes, brought about from peering through her eyeglass for over an hour. She could feel the circular indention from the eyeglass's lens on her face and would likely remain for a while. Her left eye was tearing up from being squeezed closed, and it struggled to regain focus. Neither bothered her. They helped keep everything she had witnessed fresh.

A double envelopment! A Savior-inspired double envelopment!

General Priet had marshaled nearly every pikeman he had and split the enemy's line on the right flank. Those Orsembian companies left along the ridgeline were cut off and in divided pockets for the Second Army's musketeers and swordsmen to maim.

Musketeers fired volleys behind the swordsmen's shields, witling down the enemy until they made desperate attempts to break out and were crushed or surrendered.

Those companies that reached the southeast passage fared little better. The Second's calleroses harassed them, forcing them to keep tight formations, unable to move swiftly to reinforce the companies left along the ridge. When the musketeers were able to turn their attention to them, a couple were left surrendered, while one disintegrated and men fled deeper into the passage. The calleroses gave chase, scattering them further before being recalled. There were likely many Orsembian soldiers still running into those hills.

Meanwhile, General Priet drove his pikemen along the ridgeline, turning Borbin's left flank. The pikes' long reach with the Second Army's momentum made the Orsembian companies wheel and bunch together, their numbers working against them, making them easy pickings for her pikemen.

On the right, Hiraldo pushed forward. His hold and command along the cliff face on the right allowed him to turn the enemy on that flank, as well. Although, he deployed the First Army more aggressively. His army's units weren't divided like Priet's, and the First Army's rhythm was unparalleled.

Pikemen smashed into the enemy's front line. Musketeers tore holes into those behind. Swordsman finished the rest. Each company and unit moved like seasoned bailer dancers, to the beat of their drums. Enemy companies either turned aside or got mowed down under their dance.

Yet neither armies' success would have been possible had Borbin not been determinate, or maddingly *fixated*, on her center. While the Orsembian flanks buckled, more companies were sent against her center.

Calleros columns charged pikes head-on! It was insanity!

And the Third Army held.

That was how she found the field after Marshal Narvae's rescue, and Baltazar had been right. There was only one order to give. *Attack*!

There was little for her to do afterward but watch.

Priet and Hiraldo simultaneously brought their men inward from both flanks. Ross, after all the Third Army's punishment, ordered the center forward. The three armies squeezed in together like two hands squeezing a neck; the First and Second Armies being the hands and the Third Army the thumbs.

The Orsembian's numerical advantage had become a liability, as the companies on the flanks were pushed against each other until they fell over each other, compacted in a tightening space and unable to fight back. Those in reserve in the center saw what was coming, and instead of countering to threaten Hiraldo's and Priet's flanks, a trickle of men started pulling away, running for their camp.

First, it was a handful of men. Then a few companies' entire rear lines took to their heels. When the Orsembian center line was breached, Borbin's entire formation crumbled like a hole in the bottom of a water sack.

Recha still shivered from the cheers that had erupted around her. She hadn't been the only one watching. Officers and soldiers who, not half an hour before, fought for their lives around her were all standing around her, yelling . . . until Marshal Narvae stormed in and ordered them all back to their duties of seeing to the prisoners and putting the camp back in order. Even after giving the fateful command, Recha found there was little need for her intervention.

Afterward, she watched the battle's fall-out. Orsembian companies crumbled and surrendered en masse. Some held up in the center. Companies of her soldiers had paused from pursuing the enemy and stood around Borbin's banner. She couldn't get a good look through the crowd at what exactly had happened. However, Hiraldo came in from the left to sort everything out.

Then it was a race to the enemy's camp. No counteroffensive was launched. The Orsembians' camp was taken. The day was theirs.

She had won.

Victory or death. She threw her head back up, tossing her hair out of her face. Her arms twitched and spasmed out of soreness from keeping her eyeglass raised until the Easterly Sun was disappearing behind the cliffs behind her, depriving her of light. Her shoulders, though, remained slumped forward.

She giggled. "We did it."

"Should we retire?" Cornelos asked. "The cooks may be overworked, but I can still order something served to you."

"After a day like this, I'm too exhausted to eat," she lied. Her stomach growled the moment he mentioned food.

She shook her head and looked up, expecting to see red streaks of setting sunlight against the sparce clouds. Instead, she grunted at peering at the inside of her parasol. "Where did . . .?"

She followed the parasol's holder down to Cornelos's hand, discovering he was holding it over her head.

"How long have you been holding *that*?" she asked.

Cornelos shrugged.

She gave him a sly stare, which made him turn his head farther away, acting as if he was watching the surroundings.

"I wondered why the Easterly Sun wasn't as hot as before," she lied again, taking the parasol from him. She'd been too enthralled with watching the battle to have noticed.

She set the parasol handle on her shoulder and straightened herself. She put her eyeglass back in her saddle while keeping her pistol in her lap, just in case. With the battle over, the worry she had kept at bay flooded in.

"I must check on Baltazar. After that—"

Cornelos cleared his throat.

"What?"

Cornelos pointed, and Recha looked to see Hiraldo riding up through the center lane of the camp. Among his command staff and entourage, his calleroses carried a trove of captured banners. Bolts of cloth flapped in the air, representing baronies, individual calleroses, and Orsembian companies, all presumably captured in the battle, surrendered in the development, or captured when their camp had been stormed. Chief among them, flying just behind hers and the First Army's standard, were Ribera's White Sword and Borbin's *mellcresa* skull.

"Huzza!" Men in camp rushed in from all sides, lining along the sides of the lane to cheer and raise everything from their weapons, fists, and tools in the air. "Huzza! Huzza!"

In salute, Hiraldo raised a scabbarded sword in the air. Its bone-white polish gleamed in the last of the Easterly Sun's rays and made the men shout louder.

"Huzza, La Dama!" Hiraldo yelled, spurring his horse quicker upon seeing her.

Recha's horse snorted and shook his head at the oncoming hooves, probably still anxious and tired after all the excitement. Recha comfortingly patted his neck and smiled at Hiraldo from under her parasol.

"Come to show off your trophies, General?" she teased.

"Show off?" Hiraldo barked a laughed and pulled his horse up to hers. "Never, La Dama! Merely coming to offer the prizes of battle to their rightful victor!" His tone was a mix of showman and formality. His command staff formed a column behind him, allowing for the onlookers to gather in and watch. "La Dama Mandas"—he stuck out the white sword, long ways by the scabbard, rattling the blade within—"it is my honor to present the white sword of Marshal Fuert Ribera!"

Recha took in the sword. The scabbard was bleached white from age yet held a polished shine. Same with the hilt, polished from constant handling. It lacked any orientation and was larger than most swords. Older. It only had simple handguards that extended out at the top of the hilt instead of one that encased around the wielder's hand.

Recha placed the handle of her parasol in the crook of her elbow to reach out toward the sword with both hands. Hiraldo waited until she had a firm grip then let go. Recha's eyebrows jumped, surprised by the weight. The hilt tilted down, threatening to slide out, and she was forced to reorient herself to prevent it.

Loud and startled grunts went up around her. Men jumped in their saddles, Hiraldo included, hesitatingly reaching forward to catch the falling blade, and others took sharp steps forward. Recha caught it in time, though, and pulled it close. She felt her cheeks flush.

"Got you!" She giggled, grinning broadly to play off the slip as a joke.

Hiraldo blinked at her with his protective hand still outstretched.

Fortunately, Cornelos broke the silence by laughing. "La Dama got you, General."

Other men started to laugh, and finally, realization struck Hiraldo.

His eyebrows shot up. "Oh!" he said, smiling and leaning back, joining in with the laughter. "Pardon me, La Dama. You know I can be too serious at times."

"I do indeed," Recha said, letting the men laugh while she rearranged herself. She swapped the parasol handle for her left hand and firmly gripped the sword by the scabbard just below the handguard with her right. It also gave her flushed face some cover, as well. "What of this sword's former owner, General?"

The laughter died down, and Hiraldo straightened in his saddle to report, "Marshal Ribera surrendered it and himself upon engaging combined companies of calleroses from the First and Third Amies. Both companies closed in on him, and his retreating force, before they made it back to the pass. Instead of fighting, he surrendered."

Recha breathed a soft sigh of relief. Although he'd led a force that had almost captured her, it would have been a waste to be forced to kill such a renowned man. Also, he shared a resemblance to Baltazar.

"When the field is fully secured and the prisoners sorted, reunite Marshal Ribera with his grandson," she ordered. "I understand they've been separated for far too long."

"Yes, La Dama!" Hiraldo exclaimed, a little too loudly. "But it won't be necessary to wait. All enemy forces have been routed from both valleys. Any remaining companies have surrendered and are being disarmed, and their camp has been seized and secured." He beamed broadly, prouder than Recha had ever seen. "Recha, the field is *ours*!"

Recha grinned back just as broadly, unable to contain herself, and lifted Ribera's sword in the air. "The field is ours!"

"*Huzza!*" the men around her cheered.

"With your permission, La Dama," Hiraldo interjected, "may I order my command staff to store the banners taken this day, and then dismiss them to enjoy the festivities?"

"If you're that certain the field is secured, and they can be excused from their duties." Recha shrugged then paused to point behind him. "Although, I must insist on claiming Borbin's banner for myself."

"Of course!" Hiraldo nodded. "Stow the banners!"

The parade behind him broke apart. Men whooped and hollered, waving their captured banners. A thousand stories started up in every direction as men relayed how each had been taken in, each more exorbitant than the other.

Recha waited for the crowd to disburse before turning to Cornelos to say, "I'm going to check on Baltazar."

"You may want to summon him."

Recha snapped around to Hiraldo suddenly pulling his horse alongside hers, towering over her in the saddle. His jovial expression was gone, replaced with a sharp, cautious frown.

Recha raised an eyebrow. "I thought you said the field was secured?"

"It is," Hiraldo replied. "But I held back something from my report. Something . . . I'm sure you'll want to see to personally. Without much fanfare."

"You're terrible at being vague and secretive, Hiraldo." Recha's eye twitched. She cradled the sword in her arm to rub the frustrating spasm. "Just tell me. We've been through enough excitement for today."

"Marqués Borbin is being held, secured and alone, in your command tent."

Recha's eye twitch instantly stopped at Hiraldo's cold as steel tone. She glanced up from underneath the rim of her parasol, seeing Hiraldo staring down at her, as serious as an executioner. She then looked over her shoulder at Cornelos, who was sitting as stiff as a statue in his saddle.

"Did you have the ammunition I spilled picked up?" she asked him.

Cornelos swallowed. "As much as we could recover."

Recha turned away, hiding herself for a moment under her parasol.

Borbin can wait, she debated. *Papa's been with the surgeons for what . . .? A couple of hours, at least? He needs to be there, too. I should wait until . . . until . . .*

She tightened her grip around Ribera's sword until her arm shook, rattling the sword within its scabbard. Borbin's armies were routed. Borbin was captured.

Borbin killed Sebastian.

Sorry, Papa. Her arm instantly stopped shaking. *I can't wait.*

~~~

Her command tent had been put back up and in order after the attack. A couple of the anchor ropes had been cut, and one side had collapsed, but the tent, fortunately, hadn't been ransacked.

Recha spotted a few tears leaking lantern light out of the side as she and the rest rode up to it. Seven calleroses stood guard around the tent. The flaps were closed to prevent anyone wandering by from peeking in.

"It's a good thing Narvae is busy coordinating all the after-action," she said to Hiraldo, who rode on her left while Cornelos took her right. "What of these men? Do you trust them?"

"As much as you trust your own guard," Hiraldo replied sternly.

"Very well. Cornelos, my guard can join Hiraldo's at their stations." Eight of her guard remained fit for duty; the rest were among the wounded under the care of the camp doctors or dead. After today, she trusted them explicitly.

"Are you sure you want to do this now, Recha?" Cornelos asked. He winced and frowned with concern when she snapped around toward him. "It's been a long day. Your life was in jeopardy multiple times. You haven't had time to eat or check on Baltazar. Surely, this can . . . can wait? Maybe tomorrow morning?"

Recha fixed him with a flat stare. "Yes, I am hungry. I'm tired. I'm worried." She swallowed. "But I've waited for three years, Cornelos. I'm not waiting another morning. If you don't have the same resolve as you had when you led soldiers through Zoragrin, then you can stay out here. Take command of my guard and—"

"That won't be necessary," Cornelos said coldly.

His resolve returned as he turned over his shoulder to order, "Take stations around the tent. *No one* is to be allowed entry!"

Her guard kicked their horses, surrounding the tent and dismounting beside Hiraldo's calleroses. Both gave each other wary looks, keeping their distance between one another with hands on their swords.

"You have my ammunition, correct?" she asked Cornelos.

"Yes," he replied, nodding. "The ammunition, powder, and cleaning kit." He reached back and tapped his saddlebags with a muffled tap.

"Good." Recha picked up her pistol from her lap and handed it to him. "Put this in my kit and bring it all in with you. Just put it on the table."

"Yes, La Dama." Cornelos took her pistol and began digging out her kit.

In the meantime, Recha closed her parasol, took both it and Ribera's sword under her arm, and arduously dismounted. Her right leg was asleep from being wrapped around the side saddle, and her knee nearly gave when she pushed out of the saddle and caught herself against Hiraldo's horse.

Hiraldo reached his hand down to her, but she waved it away. Instead, she planted Ribera's sword in the ground and used it for balance.

Huh, she grunted, closing her parasol, *swords make good crutches.*

At least while standing still. When she started toward the tent, she had to switch to her parasol because the sword wanted to slide out of its sheath.

Hiraldo and Cornelos fell in beside her, leaving their horses to the calleroses rushing up to meet them.

"La Dama!" one of the calleroses snapped to attention in front of them, the officer Hiraldo had left in charge, Recha assumed. "General! As ordered, the tent has been kept secured. No one but those under yours and the La Dama's orders have been granted entry."

"Very good, Lieutenant," Hiraldo replied. "La Dama's guard will be joining your perimeter. Divert everyone away from here. *No one*, not even the general staff, is to be allowed entry. Do you understand?"

The lieutenant clicked his heels together and sharply nodded. "Yes, General!"

Recha walked around them, leaving Hiraldo to have everything well in hand. There was no need to order the same from her guard.

Commotions were growing in the camp—laughter and cheers from the soldiers coming back from the field, distant screams and yells from the wounded in the camp hospitals, faint instruments starting to play.

After a battle like today's, everyone should be too occupied to notice—

"Here's to you, Si Don, and the women we've loved."

Recha stopped. *Sevesco!*

She dashed for the tent, thrusting her parasol between the flaps and tearing them aside.

Sevesco was pouring wine into a silver cup, sitting before a man in chair with his back facing her and left leg splinted and raised in another chair.

Sevesco was dressed like a vagabond. His black trousers were uniform-issue, but his white shirt hung unlaced around his neck and rolled up at his sleeves, the front of which was stained from dirt and sweat. He wore a maroon bandana over his head, turned darkly brown from his sweat.

"And speaking of women, there she is!" he cheered, raising his bottle of wine to her in salute. "The woman of the hour! Please, come in. Your table is almost set, La Dama."

Recha glared back at him. "Capitán," she said in a calm, warning tone, "what *are* you doing?"

"Keeping your distinguished guest company, as ordered, La Dama," Sevesco replied. "We were just discussing our mutual acquaintance with Baroness Liamena over some refreshments."

He turned to Borbin. "You must pardon La Dama if she abstains from sharing a glass, Si Don. It's been three years since she's partook in wine with anyone. Although"—he shrugged and strolled around the table with a smile—"after a day like today, she may break that fast tonight."

Recha's cheeks warmed. She bit her lip to keep from yelling. She wasn't in the mood for his machinations. Not in front of . . .

Borbin hadn't moved since Recha had entered. Not even a glance back at her. He sat as straight as he could manage with his leg propped up. His clothes were wrinkled and pressed to his body, likely from being compressed by his armor. He rested one arm on the table. The tips of his fingers rubbed the bottom of a silver cup, like Sevesco's. His hair was a disheveled mess, especially in the back of his head where a large knot had formed.

Did he fall from his horse?

"Capitán Viezo!" Cornelos exclaimed upon stepping into the tent behind her. "Explain yourself!"

Sevesco smirked at him and stepped away from the table. "At the cost of repeating myself," he whispered to them when he walked over, "just keeping Borbin company until you arrived."

"And how did you learn Borbin was here?" Hiraldo asked warningly, having slipped in without Recha hearing.

"You don't really expect me to answer that, do you?" Sevesco winked at him then shot glances at all three of them.

For her part, Recha stared flatly at him, weighing the options of having Cornelos and Hiraldo throw him out. The flush on his cheeks was more than being in the Easterly Sun all day. She didn't want his behavior to spoil this, yet he'd been one of Sebastian's Companions, one of hers, too, and had been there for her three years ago. He had just as much right to be here as Cornelos and Hiraldo.

She slammed her parasol into his chest, holding it there. "Put this away for me," she ordered. "And *behave*."

"Yes, La Dama," he replied, taking her parasol. "Your audience awaits."

With him taken care of, Recha turned attention to Borbin. The captive marqués still hadn't moved, facing forward as if patiently expecting to be waited on. His head bobbed, as if it was difficult to keep raised. Besides that, his poise remained regal.

Recha watched him for a moment. Her grip gradually tightened around Ribera's sword. Her heartbeat rose louder in her chest. She licked the roof of her suddenly dry mouth.

I have him! Sebastian, I finally have him! And yet, she didn't know what to say first.

Cornelos softly cleared his throat and whispered, "This can still wait, Recha. If you want?"

She broke away from him, stalking around Borbin. She watched him like the *mellcresa* he was, looking for the slightest movement. Borbin kept his gaze forward, not sparing her an acknowledging glance until she stood directly in front of him.

His thin mustache bristled in every direction. Puffy bags hung under his eyes. The sides of face were smeared with dirt, dried and caked to his skin from his sweat. His head strained to look up at her, as if his neck would break, revealing a great purple bruise wrapped around it.

629

He looked . . . tired, lacking the arrogance, resentment, terror, or hate she would have if she were in his place.

Say something! she yelled to herself to speak. *Three years of planning, finally winning, and* now *I can't say what I've been wanting to all this time? Say* something*!*

"Thank . . . you," Borbin said hoarsely, his voice barely a whisper, lifting his cup at her, "La . . . Dama Mandas. For your generosity." He brought the cup to his lips and sipped with shaking hands.

Formality then.

"You're welcome, Si Don Borbin," she replied.

In an instant, Cornelos walked around her to pull out a chair for her. Recha gave him a thankful nod, placing Ribera's sword on the table in front of her before sitting.

"The famous Ribera family heirloom," Borbin commented, his voice clearer after the sip of wine. "When I received reports that his standard was spotted charging out of the pass after the explosion, I still expected his strike to succeed."

"He nearly did," Recha admitted. She crossed her legs and smoothed out her dress. "But he ran out of time."

Borbin frowned and set his cup down. "So, he fell, too."

Recha studied him for a moment. Borbin's gaze grew distant, staring down into the contents of his cup.

Is he regretful or disappointed? She folded her arms and leaned back against her chair.

"He wasn't killed," she clarified. "He pressed his attack for as long as he could but withdrew when my reinforcements arrived. He surrendered to my calleroses after they cut off his retreat."

Borbin drummed his fingers on the table. His eyes wavered back and forth, sorting out his rapid thoughts. "Very well, to the matter at hand," he said, lifting his head, his frown vanished. "The battle is yours, La Dama. As such, Puerlato will be conceded. I will sign any declaration to that effect. The question I have, and one I wish you to consider yourself is: how much more are you demanding? This campaign of yours has been . . . unusual. How far did you *actually* march, and did you leave garrisons anywhere or just marched through? If neither of us knows preciously who holds what, I'm afraid some things can't be fully agreed on until—"

"Are you . . . *negotiating* with me?" Recha asked, surprised.

"My dear La Dama, I have been trying to negotiate with you since the start of this tragic affair." He folded his hands in his lap. "As you recall, it was you who rejected every proposal I sent without you returning one. However, now that the events of today are settled, it is only right that I offer the obvious concessions before we get to the final details."

Recha stared at the man. He sat there calmly, as if they were discussing some menial trade agreement.

She searched his eyes, expecting rage or contempt to be staring back at her. Yet, there was none. Not even a hint of hate. She'd had his son killed, *executed*, and he patiently waited for her. She bit the inside of her lip, not understanding why, but it was . . . frustrating.

"I would think, after everything that's happened, you'd finally realize I'm not interested in negotiating," she replied. "And now, my armies have shattered yours in the field. Those who remain free are in flight. And I have you. You're in no position to negotiate anything."

Borbin snorted. "*That* is a most disagreeable assertion. La Dama, we are rulers of marcs, *we* are always in a position to negotiate."

Recha arched an eyebrow. *There's that arrogance.*

"Oh really? I doubt you would say the same thing if our places were reversed."

Borbin shot her a sharp look. "You can accuse me of being many things, La Dama—a traditionalist, a pragmatist, a manipulator. *But*, what no one can ever accuse me of being is a *hypocrite*. You are the marquesa of Lazorna. Were you in my position, I would lay out the terms of your surrender the same, and likewise expect negotiations on them."

Recha tilted her head. "That seems pointless. You would take all of Lazorna. There would be no need for negotiations."

"You're overestimating my resources." Borbin waved his hand dismissively. "I would have only insisted that a third of Lazorna's lands be ceded directly to Orsembar. You would have remained marquesa of what had been left. Only the manner of your position would have depended on your acceptance or refusal of my second offer."

Recha grimaced, easily guessing the second offer. "Whether I agreed to marry Timotio."

"Precisely." He softly smiled. "I know the two of you weren't introduced in the best of circumstances, but time and your similar stations could have worked that out."

The edges of Recha's lips curled. She snickered. Her laughter poured out of her that only putting a hand over her mouth and tightening her other arm around herself could stop it.

"*Never!*" she gasped, her shoulders fell up and down as the laughter refused to stop. She took long, deep breaths, slowing her breathing down to calm herself. "Pardon my outburst"—she slid her fingers off her face and straightened—"but after everything that's happened today, that's the most absurd thing I've ever heard!"

"How fortunate for you then that you don't have to make such a decision." Borbin warily watched her, his posture slightly recoiled in his seat. He cleared his throat to regain his composure. "Well then, La Dama Mandas, with our current positions, what are your terms of capitulation? I've already conceded that Puerlato will be yours, but how much more do you think you can—"

"All of it."

Borbin blinked at her. His mouth hung open in mid-speech. His eyes searched her face for a moment. Recha remained perfectly still, waiting for him to realize.

"Clearly, you jest, La Dama," Borbin said, shaking his head. "I may be your captive for the time being, but if you believe this grants rights to my entire dominion, I must warn you that is a youthful simplification of war. Victory in one battle does not mean victory over an entire marc."

"I strongly disagree, Si Don," Recha retorted, dropping her smile to be as stern and serious as her tired body could muster. "My victory here today, along with your capture, *does* grant me rights to your entire domain. At least, it will if I *take* it."

Borbin stared at her. All expression, emotion, and nearly his color, save for the bruising around his neck, drained out of him. Yet, he didn't give any spark of fear. Almost . . . disappointment.

"That would be unwise, La Dama Mandas," he warned.

"It's nothing less than what you intended to do Lazorna if you had won."

"On the contrary, I stated you would have ceded a third of your territory directly to me. The rest would have remained to you—"

"Either through a forced marriage or as your hostage," Recha snapped. "If I was to be dictated on how to rule my own homeland, then all of it would have been yours."

"Delegated." Borbin raised a finger. "You are correct that certain policies would be out of your hands; however, rule of your lands would have been left up to you under your current laws. But I would have delegated certain duties to you, as well."

"My opinion on that remains the same," she replied dryly.

"And yet, in our reversed positions, you find yourself in the same place I would have been. You are in a place to dictate the most favorable terms for yourself. However, instead, you declare you want all of Orsembar. I say that is unwise because, frankly, that's impossible."

Recha snickered. "After what was accomplished today, are you sure you should use that word so freely?"

"It's true that you won an impressive battle today." Borbin took up his cup. "You defeated an army three times your size. A terrific upset!" He saluted her with his cup then sipped. "However, you still have a limited size army to try to seize control of a marc over thrice the size of your own. I say this is impossible, La Dama, because you have neither the manpower nor the resources to take and hold all of my marc."

"Do you think it wise to lecture me, Si Don?" she asked warningly, eyeing his wine cup.

"Lecture you?" Borbin raised an eyebrow over the rim of his cup then set it down. "No. This is part of the negotiations. It is best for both of our interests to point out terms that wouldn't do either of us good."

He really thinks he's going to talk his way out of this!

It struck her like a lightning bolt. His poise and demeanor were the same as when they had met on the battlefield. His tone, mannerism, everything screamed he still held control despite his defeat.

Recha worked her jaw, finding it all unsatisfying.

"Except you keep forgetting, Si Don," she growled, "this *isn't* a negotiation. And our interests are *not* the same."

"Our mutual interest now is peace, isn't it?" Borbin said bluntly. "For you, the peace of Lazorna, and to me, the peace of Orsembar. However, if I ceded all of Orsembar to you, that would grant us neither."

Why couldn't you have cursed me when I first came in? Spit at me! Declare some form of vengeance! Beg! Any of those, and I could have ended this already. She could still end this. A simple order to Cornelos, a few final words, and then

. . .

It didn't sit right. It was too quick. Too easy. She had loathed this man for three years, and now, when he was at her mercy, he showed not an ounce of fear or remorse.

I want to see that smug arrogance ripped from his face.

"Please, enlighten me."

"If Orsembar were ceded to you," Borbin began, "that would require you to garrison the entire marc. My army may be shattered, but I'd wager a remnant managed to withdraw. You would have to fight them, along with the rest of the Orsembian barony who didn't march with me. This campaign would continue, and Orsembar would be engulfed in war.

"As for Lazorna, once our neighboring marcs learn of your victory today and become aware of your intentions to conquer my marc, they will turn against you." A wide grin spread across his face that made goosebumps run down Recha's arms. "Your days of sitting out the Campaigns are over, La Dama. You're in them now, whether you plan to sustain from them or not.

"Your treaty with Quezlo will likely be voided. Saran will try to reclaim the lands I took last year before seeing what else they can quickly claim. Pamolid will also have to reconsider its western border with you. If you are overextended trying to cement your hold over my marc, you'll be less prepared to defend yourself when the others attack. And they will *attack*, Mandas. Maybe not all together, maybe not all with the same strength, maybe not all at the same time, but they will."

I should just shoot him now! Recha leaned forward with her arms still folded. Her hair fell over her face so she wouldn't have to look at him. She squeezed her elbows, biting her tongue to stop from screaming. *I should—*

"However," Borbin's tone reverted to formal, "take my offer, and you avoid all of that. You reclaim Puerlato, I cede a portion of my western territory, preferably along the coast of the Desryol Sea up to the Compuert Junction, and your position with the other marcs becomes more . . . manageable. That's why it's impossible for you to claim all of Orsembar, Mandas—you need me in Manosete. You need me to be the balancing force to keep all the other marcs from coming against you. You need me for the same reasons I needed you for my eastern buffer state. If you put your emotions aside and look at the larger picture, you'd agree this negotiation would be best for your marc."

It was all so reasonable. So pragmatic. In a grand scheme, the offer would be agreeable. Any other marc would jump at the chance to regain whatever they had lost with a little extra territory. Any other marqués or marquesa would have happily agreed to take the tremendous victory, the settlement, and keep the status quo so that the other marcs would be kept in check.

However . . .

"Cornelos," Recha called and tapped on the table, "my kit."

She waited until she heard the thud of the silver box on the tabletop. She turned and lifted her head around to the kit, avoiding looking at Borbin altogether. She raised the kit's lid, flicking it back with her fingernail. Despite being in complete disarray, she easily dug in and pulled out her pistol.

"I shot my uncle with this pistol," she said, holding it up. She ran her index finger across the pistol's lock, watching the candlelight flicker on the silverwork. "It was at his campaign feast, surrounded by his picked barons and chosen marshal. They were laughing and drinking as if we hadn't just been invaded. As if Puerlato was still ours. As if . . . they hadn't just attended my beloved's corpse."

She set the pistol on the table and peered sideways through her draping strands of hair to check on Borbin. He shot wary glances between her and the pistol. A trail of sweat ran down the side of his face.

"Neither my uncle, my cousin, nor any of their barons or calleroses showed an ounce of concern about your invasion," she retold. "My uncle announced that evening that he was in communication with Si Don Dion to jointly invade you from Compuert. He said"—she snickered—"we could negotiate a trade with the land you took with the land he would take."

"A common response." Borbin nodded approvingly.

"A *fool's* response!" Recha snapped. "Ribera would have had Zoragrin surrounded in weeks. But worse, none of them cared that Puerlato was lost. No *remorse* that they had left a man they'd hailed a Hero a season before without any help. To fight alone. To . . . die." She straightened back in her seat. "I shot my uncle in his forehead, watched my cousin's skull be smashed in, and the favored barons and calleroses were slaughtered at their tables."

Borbin was pale, stiffly leaning back in his seat and eyeing her as if she were the *mellcresa* now. "Why—" He swallowed. "Why are you telling me this?"

"Because"—she ran her fingers through her hair, pulling it back out of her face and behind her shoulders, exposing her misshapen ear—"I want you to finally understand what kind of woman I am. What kind of marquesa you're talking to." She leaned her head back against her seat with a deep exhale. "I *despise* the Rules of Campaign, but that doesn't mean I don't understand them. And after three years, balancing between you, Dion, and Hyles, I've become a pretty good watcher of how each of you follow them, too. Tell me, if I accepted your offer, how many years would you give me, Borbin?"

"I . . ." Borbin's frowned. His brow furled. Either what Recha meant was completely lost on him, or his practiced composure was finally starting to crack. "I'm not sure what you're implying?"

"I've waited . . . planned . . . *dreamed* of this campaign for three years. Three years for *this* moment, to have the last man responsible for killing my beloved in my hands." She lifted her head. "How many years will you wait before you retaliate and campaign against me? The woman who killed your son?" She held up her fingers, counting down. "Three? Two? *One?*"

Borbin's frown darkened. The last of his calm demeanor slipped, and glaring vitriol filled his eyes.

"I suspect one." Recha wagged her finger. "I accept your offer, and we will be at war again this time next year, over the same ground you claim to be ceding tonight." She curled her fingers into a fist. "But I'm not here for ground. I'm here for *you*."

Borbin let out a deep sigh, his shoulders slumped, and his face drooped into a long, disappointed look. "Mandas, one victory doesn't make you a conqueror."

"I'm not a conqueror," Recha agreed. She dropped her hand into the pistol kit, digging her fingers in until she brought out a second pistol. Sebastian's pistol. "I am the woman whose beloved you took from her. And like my uncle, you *will* pay." She flicked the firing pan open with her thumb and reached for her priming powder.

"La Dama." Borbin's voice was hoarse, and Recha ignored him to fill the pan. "Mandas! You cannot be serious! You're being naïve. *Unreasonable!* The other marquéses and marquesas will—"

"Do what?" Recha slammed the pan closed. "Declare war on me for killing one of their rivals? *Please!*" She pushed up on the table, rising to her feet. Her chair grated against the tent's floorboards. "I'll face them all, be it in schemes, trade, or war—I don't care which. Those who join me, I'll welcome on conditions. But those who fight me, if *anyone* tries to hurt or take away the people I love, I'll remind them"—she leveled the pistol at his head—"of how I dealt with you."

Borbin trembled in his seat, his lips and jaw quivering, and his hands folded and unfolded in his lap. Then, just as briefly as it'd started, he fell still. He glared up at her, straight down her pistol's barrel, with the vitriol returning and turning his eyes into burning amber coals.

"You petty, conniving *girl*," he cursed. "May you be cold and lonely for the rest of your days. May you know nothing but betrayal and paranoia. May the others drag you down and suitably rip you apart like the bloody marquesa you are. And on that day, on that *gloriously justified day*, may the Savior himself forsake you, *Recha Mandas!*" His voice had risen until it reverberated in the tent. It drowned out the drifting camp noises from outside and left the tent as quiet as deepest night.

The clicks of the pistol's hammer cocking shattered the silence like an executioner's drumroll.

"Goodbye, Borbin." She squeezed the trigger with all her strength.

POW!

Gray, acidic smoke filled the tent. It burned her eyes, yet she forced them open. Through the haze and sparks, she watched Borbin's head snap backward.

Every muscle in her body tensed. Her arm remained outstretched, keeping the smoking barrel leveled at him. She waited, unblinkingly, for the smoke to drift up into the tent's ceiling, insistent on seeing the aftermath.

Trails of blood ran down the lines and ridges of Borbin's face from the hole in the center of his forehead. His jaw muscles remained clenched, even in death, keeping his scowl. His eyelids drooped yet couldn't mask the hateful glare he'd died with.

A moment passed, and his right arm slipped from his lap and hung limp at his side. His body deflated in the chairs he was spread out in, but his cursing grimace held.

Still, there was no light in those eyes. He was dead.

Borbin was dead!

And Recha . . . was numb.

There was no excited glee, like witnessing the double envelopment. No righteous fury. She didn't even feel the muggy evening heat. She was merely . . . numb.

She tried to focus on her heartbeat, hoping its pounding would bring her something. Instead, she heard the persistent ringing of the shot, refusing to fade, while her chest felt hollow, as if neither her heart nor lungs were there.

A large, callused hand grabbed her outstretched one. The strength broke through her arm's stiffness, and her grip relinquished her pistol. Her entire body relaxed at once, and she gasped, deeply drawing air into her screaming lungs.

"Recha!"

She heard her name spoken in unison from three different voices. Hiraldo stood in front of her, Sebastian's pistol in his hand. Cornelos stood beside her with a reassuring grip on her shoulder. Sevesco was a couple of steps behind her chair.

"Borbin"—her voice came out soft as a hush—"is dead."

The three men shared a look.

"He is dead," Hiraldo confirmed, looking down at the marqués's body.

"It's all over now," Cornelos assured her, squeezing her shoulder.

Sevesco brought a silver cup of wine and held it out to her. "Your wine, La Dama."

Recha stared at the cup, at the red, rippling liquid. For three years, she hadn't tasted it, just as she'd sworn.

She gingerly reached up. The cup felt incredibly light in her fingers after holding the pistol. She gazed down into her own reflection, her face a pale mask staring back at her.

"To victory, Recha?" Sevesco asked, holding his own cup up.

She shared a look with each of her Companions. Hiraldo stood straight, hands folded behind his back. Cornelos watched on with concern. Sevesco attempted to smile, yet it never touched his eyes.

"To Sebastian," Recha replied, softening all their expressions. Then she threw her head back and drank.

Chapter 37

"Your days of sitting out the Campaigns are over."

Recha eyelids flickered rapidly. She caught faint glints of light from some unknown, distant source. She neither slept nor lay awake. She hung somewhere between, waiting for either her mind to collapse to unconsciousness or some excruciating body pain to force her awake. Alone with curses echoing in the dark.

"May you know nothing but betrayal and paranoia."

Sleep rejected her, and an enveloping numbness separated her from her body. Her head swam in a nauseating void. Every vein felt compressed that it was questionable whether this was the beginning of a serious illness or the worst headache of her life. Her nostrils flared, bringing in the scent of stale, musky air, laced with foul after-traces of blood.

"May the others drag you down and suitably rip you apart like the bloody marquesa you are."

Gruesome images flashed in her mind. Corpses piled in heaps. Men lay in fields, clinging at their horrendous wounds. Surgeons frantic to treat as many as they could, failing, and their patients wailing as they bled. One such patient resembled Baltazar.

Papa!

Her mind's scream sent a groaning grumble reverberating in her ears. It rolled through her mind like a bucket of water being shook from side to side. When she groaned back, she realized she had tried to speak her choppy complaint and it had come out a mumbling, moaning mess from deep in her throat.

"And on that day, on that gloriously justified day, may the Savior himself forsake you, Recha Mandas!"

She saw herself in the middle of that blood-stained field. From head to toe, she was coated in the gore of the dead and bleeding surrounding her. The world began to shake. And as an endless tide of calleroses stormed her from every direction, she wore an enormous, maddening grin on her face and laughed at that tide. Until it swallowed her, and that laugh became a maddening scream.

That scream allowed all her feelings to rush in. She gasped and recoiled. Her back arched. She was laying on something. Something cushioned with fabric that caught her hair with the slightest movement. She lost all control of her body, as every muscle decided to simultaneously stretch.

Her left leg caught on something. A sheet maybe? The fabric draped over her leg, pulling tight without any room to give, and her limb refused to—

Her entire calf muscle balled into a tight, stinging *fist*!

Recha snapped her eyes open. She sprang forward, grabbing the cramping muscle with both hands as tightly as she could. A hiss ripped through her throat.

"Gah!" she cried, squeezing her eyes together until tears dripped through the corners.

She rolled her head into the cushioned mattress of her tent's bed. Instantly, the scent of sweat overwhelmed her nostrils, yet the pain in her leg immobilized her. She squeezed hard. Her fingernails dug through the fabric of her underskirt—not a sheet—with her teeth clenching as the ball of muscle stubbornly refused to loosen.

When it did, everything became *worse*! The cramp began to loosen, the blood began to pump through, beating and tightening. The veins in her head did likewise. Recha let out a deep groan as her head swam, becoming ten times heavier, and forced her face into her lumpy mattress. The pounding heartbeat consumed everything, starting from her head and spreading like fire to her toes. Her body went limp and pulsed with every beat against the mattress fabric.

Her only comfort was being on her stomach. She pressed her head into the cushion to shut out the faint glint of light to the embrace of total darkness. She didn't know what was happening to her, expect that there was no fighting whatever fit her body was having. She accepted her fate. To lay there. Let whatever tantrum she was trapped in run its course.

Bit by bit, the pumping slowed. The pounding softened. As they did, so did her breathing. She avoided the stale smell by breathing through her mouth, and with each slow, deep breath, sleep finally opened its embrace to her. Everything, after all that pain and suffering, became warm, cozy, and comfortable.

The warmth became heat. It spread from her cheeks and forehead until her whole face was set on fire. It raced through her scalp, and sweat followed. It broke out over her body, turning her skin into a sticky paste, clinging to the mattress. The skin on her face itched, her hot breath dried her throat. She gasped, throwing her head back.

"*Why?*" she cried in frustration. "Why? Why? *Why?*"

She kicked her feet into the mattress and smacked her bare heels against the cloth wall of her tent. She slid her arms under her, braced herself, then pushed. Her arms wobbled, and her elbows buckled, crashing her back down on the cot. She punched the mattress, but her meager strength barely pressed the stuffing in.

"*La Dama?*"

The tent flap burst open, flooding it with searing light and a gust of fresh air.

Recha was blinded instantly. Her eyes burned as rainbow splotches blurred her vision. She rolled on her side, throwing her hands before her face.

"Savior forsake *you!*" she screamed. "What are you doing, Cornelos?" She skuttled back into the shadows on her cot, rubbing her eyes. Each rub made the splotches worse.

A shy cough came from the door. "My deepest apologies, La Dama," someone who wasn't Cornelos said, his voice lower in tone, "but Commandant Narvae hasn't reported yet. I was on guard and heard—"

"Where's Commandant Narvae?" she demanded, keeping her hands shielding her face to block the sunlight. "What hour is it? What do you want? What's going—"

"I'll take it from here, guardsman," Hiraldo said. His deep voice made her ears twitch. "Return to your post."

Recha peeked through her fingers. The shadows of two figures blocked out most of the retched morning—at least she thought it was morning—sunlight. She sat up, bringing her legs up and resting her knees against her chest. Her toes wiggled against the cushions. She took advantage of her hands at her face to rub and dig the crusts of sleep from the corners of her eyes.

Hiraldo's heavy footsteps thumped on the rug carpeting the bottom of her tent upon his entrance, blessedly closing the tent flap behind him.

"Hiraldo?" Recha asked, picking the last of the hard crusts from her eyelashes. "What are you . . .? You should have—"

She sniffed sharply, freezing. She sniffed repeatedly to get the scent. Her mouth watered before her mind fully confirmed it.

"*Pork*!" She instantly sat up straight, perking her head up out of her hands. Skillet fried pork! It was impossible to mistake that scent!

Hiraldo walked into sight in full uniform, wisely not wearing armor. He came up to the cot and held out plate. "I commandeered some pork my officers found this morning, along with eggs and bread of all things," he said. "Leave it to officers to be the best scroungers."

Recha made out the slices of ham on top of each other, the outline of a couple of eggs pushed together over to the side, and a husk of bread in the dim light. She seized the plate like a ravenous *mellcresa*, folding her legs to hold it, and viciously attacked the bounty.

She bounced a scalding piece of pork between her fingers to raise it up for a bite. The slice of flesh was perfect—not too thick, not too thin, not overcooked, not undercooked, with the right amount of crisp to have a crunch. The salty, greasy texture urged her to eat faster while the heat burning the roof of her mouth urged her to eat slower. She took a bite of bread as a compromise to cool her mouth but refusing to slow.

A drawn-out creak announced Hiraldo opening the tent ceiling flaps to let in light and air. The light was enough to illuminate her tent without being blinding.

Recha tore off a shred of pork with her teeth and dabbed the bread into the yoke of one of the eggs, breaking it and soaking a mouth full in the gooey, yellow contents. She was still chewing the pork when she bit off the bread, adding it altogether in her mouth.

She moaned and rolled her eyes, her cheeks bulging as she indulged in the salt, grease, yeast, and yoke mix. Her eyelids fluttered back open, and she stopped mid-chew at Hiraldo staring blankly down at her.

"*Waath*?" she mumbled with her mouth full.

Hiraldo straightened his uniform. "Careful not to eat too fast," he advised.

"*I*—" She swallowed. "I'm hungry! I can't remember when I ate last." She scooped up more egg with her bread and ate it. She frowned as she chewed and watched him step away and ease himself down on one of her wardrobe chests. "What are you doing here, Hiraldo? Shouldn't a general have more pressing duties after a battle than bringing me breakfast?"

"Midday meal."

Recha paused, a bite of pork halfway to her mouth. "Huh?"

"It's almost noon."

"Then why did you bring me . . .?" She held out the pork, yet her question got mixed with a mass of others. She shook her head back and forth, attempting to sort them all out at once. "Why hasn't Cornelos . . .?" She gasped, dropping the pork on the plate, her eyebrows shooting up her brow. She tossed the plate aside on her cot and threw her legs over the edge. "*Papa!*" She hazily remembered going to check on him but couldn't remember his condition. "I got to go check on . . . *Oh!*"

Her stomach rolled and gurgled. She wrapped her arms around her belly and doubled over, collapsing on the cot.

"Easy!" Hiraldo warned with his hand out. "Don't push yourself. Sevesco said this might happen."

"Sevesco? *Ah!*" Recha groaned at the rumbling pain inside her belly. She squeezed tightly, closing her eyes and holding her breath—everything she could to hold herself together. Sweat pooled and dripped out of her forehead. For a moment, she feared she was going to burst. Just as suddenly as it'd started, the rumbling stopped, and the pain slowly drained away. She relaxed with an exhausted gasp yet remained bent over with her arms around herself just to be safe.

She slowly raised her head, arching an eyebrow and doing her best to grimace with her mouth open, puffing in air. "*What . . . did . . . he . . . do?*"

Hiraldo kept his chin up and met her eye. He pulled his hand back and sat stiffly straight, as if making a report. "Nothing. You went to the field hospitals after . . . last night, to check on the field marshal," he said. "From what I was told, you walked in the middle of his second surgery, and the sight of the field marshal's condition made you . . . demanding."

Recha had a feeling he was being delicate not to say *hysterical*. Yet, the retelling did refresh the memory of the field hospitals, the wounded men laying in rows, and walking in to see Baltazar on the surgeons' table, pale and sweating while the surgeons frantically stitched.

"Oh," she said, dropping her head.

Every hair on Recha's body stood on end, and a rush of goosebumps spread down her arms. The sweat became so cold on her forehead as images, each far worse and more embarrassing than the other, played in her mind.

"Oh, by the Savior, please don't tell me I did anything stupid," she begged.

"Nothing stupid, embarrassing, or undignified," Hiraldo assured, shaking his head. "The doctors had to give you something to calm you down. You became lightheaded, and then unsteady on your feet. Cornelos caught you before you fell and had you taken to your tent."

That explains why I can't remember how I got here.

"Where's Cornelos?" she asked.

Her heart sank at Hiraldo's blocky face tightening, his lips white from being pressed together, and his chin trembled. "Resting," he replied. "After awkwardly explaining why you need help to undress by two women camp workers, he stepped out to take first guard. When the women came out, they say they found him collapsed on the ground. I had my soldiers stationed to guard you to let him and the rest of your guard rest."

Recha dug her fingernails into her elbows. "Savior help them. I pushed them too hard yesterday. Especially Cornelos."

"They performed their duty," Hiraldo said. "It speaks well of Cornelos to have picked such men and the lengths he'll go to keep you safe."

Recha snickered and hung her head. *At what expense to himself?*

She held that pose for a few moments until the final knots in her stomach unraveled and whatever it was passed. She didn't want to risk it, though, and kept her arms around her. She merely lifted her head, swinging her hair out of her face.

"Well, I—" Her eyebrows leapt again. "No! Papa! How—"

"The field marshal is well!" Hiraldo said. "The surgeons said it was difficult to make sure the artery was closed and sewn up. They had to operate a few times, but luckily, they didn't have to amputate his arm."

A rush of relief swept over her, every muscle in her body relaxed at once. She laid her head back, exhaling loudly and slumping her shoulders. She squeezed her eyelids shut, holding the tears of joy in, although a few slipped through the corners. There was nothing to hold back her broad grin.

"Bless the Savior." She giggled and rolled her up.

Hiraldo, though, had a stiff upper lip, almost a scowl. "Was there something else?"

"Recha"—his voice sounded choked, his chin wobbled—"he's finished. He'll never be fit for duty for the rest of this campaign. The amount of blood he lost . . . He was very pale when I saw him." He drew himself up with a deep breath, restoring his officerly calm. "The surgeons recommend he not be moved for a few days, but after yesterday's battle, that shouldn't be a problem. After that, they recommend he be sent home to rest."

The image of Baltazar laying on a table, pale and sweaty from loss of blood, played in her mind again. His skin clammy to the touch. His breathing labored.

Her heart ached. A great man like him shouldn't be in such a state. Not after the greatest achievement of his life.

"The Half-Conquering Hero of Lazorna," she said, "has commanded his last battle."

"Aye." Hiraldo slapped his knee, sticking out his broad chest. "And what glorious battle it was! I don't think I'll ever see anything that beautifully done again. A double envelopment!" He shook his head with a lopsided smile.

She smiled with him. "A fitting retirement, but will we be able to continue the campaign without him?"

"We'll be able to continue the campaign," Hiraldo said with certainty.

Recha eased up, her legs throbbing, on the verge of going to sleep. Her stomach thankfully seemed to have fully settled. "How's the First Army?"

"Casualties were manageable. The worst came in holding the left against the oblique. That press was"—his fists clenched, turning his knuckles white—"brutal. We paid them back, though."

"Yes, I noticed." Recha crossed her legs and spotted him raising an eyebrow. "When the envelopment came together, the First Army pressed it the hardest. You even charged in with your calleroses at the first opening. I was watching."

"I knew the situation on the field and was given the order to attack. I saw no reason to restrain my men. Besides, I wanted to get to Borbin." If his chest could tighten any more, his uniform would rip open.

Recha smirked. *I can make him a general, but he'll always have a calleros's pride.*

"What about the other armies?"

"The Second is in good order. General Priet reported that controlled withdrawal and stretching his line back allowed him to manage the enemy better and keep casualties low. The Third took the . . . heaviest losses." He frowned and licked his lips. "Recha, General Ross reported this morning that he's looking at possibly a quarter-percent casualties, wounded and killed." His eyes went misty, distant. "He didn't sleep last night. I think he and his staff were too busy figuring out who made it out and . . . who didn't."

"The price for holding the line. I guess they won't be ready to move in a couple of days, either."

"If Marshal Narvae gives them the rest. He's already given Marshal Bisal orders to scout the fastest way out of these hills, and Marshal Olguer has orders to pull available calleroses from all the armies into a strike force to pursue Borbin's army that got away. I think he plans to finish where Vigodt left off and march the armies up the Compuert Road."

Recha frowned at that. "Even with the number of our wounded and prisoners?"

"That I don't know." Hiraldo folded his arms. "I've been busy with my duties, and he's been busy taking over the field marshal's. I'm just surmising off his orders."

That would be the natural course of action. We didn't catch all of Borbin's army in that envelopment, and it could always reform. But . . .

She pushed herself to her feet to think better. Her stomach swam again and made her legs wobble. She stuck her arms out for balance and held her hand to Hiraldo, who brought his up to catch her. Luckily, her stomach settled, and she slowly set to pacing, folding her hands behind her back.

We still have enemies out there. We still have fighting ahead of us. But how do we win? Borbin is dead. His son is dead. But the campaign still goes on. How do—

She stopped suddenly in front of her tiny cupboard used for a writing desk. The memory of Baltazar playing jedraz again making everything clear.

"A query for you, Hiraldo," she said, turning on her heels. "What is the fastest way to declaring victory?"

Hiraldo frowned at her, as if she had asked something obvious. "Defeating the opposing army, of course."

"We've done that"—she held a hand up in a shrug—"but are we able to declare victory?"

He opened his mouth to answer yet paused briefly. "No?"

"No," Recha agreed. "We've defeated the enemy on the field. I . . . executed the enemy marqués." She swallowed from the mental image of Borbin with a hole in his head. "However, the campaign will still go on. What's the fastest way we can declare victory in this situation?" She knew she could come out and say it but felt like showing off.

Hiraldo closed his mouth, folded his arms, and sat back. His eyes bounced back and forth, working his jaw in thought.

Recha put a hand on her hip, about to harmlessly chastise him for taking so long until his eyes lit up.

"The capital!" He snapped around to her. "You want to march on Manosete!"

Recha grinned. "We capture Manosete, we roll up the rest of Orsembar. Even if Borbin's remaining army reforms, how great will their morale hold once they hear they've lost everything." She fished out parchment, ink, and quill then set to scratching in the dim light. Hunched over, she ignored the knot quickly forming in the small of her back to write everything speeding through her head. "You still willing to deliver orders for me?"

"Always." Hiraldo grunted, standing and hunching his head under the tent's ceiling. "Are you sure you want me to deliver them?"

"I don't have time to dress, and these orders need to go out as soon as possible. Marshal Narvae will remain as acting field marshal for the time being, and Bisal's order to find the fastest way out of these hills will remain in effect. I'm countermanding Narvae's orders to Olguer. All calleroses are to remain assigned to their armies and tend to their horses and wounded.

"Send dispatchers with Bisal to Commandant Leyva. He and the Fourth Army are to proceed with the seizure of Puerlato with all haste. Bombard the gates and walls until they have gaping holes and collapse, get the garrison to surrender, convince Puerlato's inhabitants to revolt, which ever he can perform.

"To General Priet, the Second Army is to rest today and be on the march by dawn tomorrow, out of these hills and to Puerlato. They are to support the Fourth Army in taking Puerlato if it has not fallen by the time they arrive."

"You, Hiraldo, will march the First Army out the day after the Second, marching all the prisoners we captured here with you. It'll slow you down, but once you get to the Compuert Junction, turn the prisoners over to whatever holdings Commandant Leyva has built, and then march west to Luente. If Puerlato's taken by then, or when it is, General Priet is to march there, as well, and combine forces with you.

"As for the Third Army, it's to wait until the others have marched and follow a day later with the wounded. If Puerlato's taken, then the wounded are to be given rest and hospital there. The Third Army is to rest and recover until ordered.

"Once Puerlato is taken, the Fourth Army is to march up Compuert Road and take as much as it can. Me and the rest of the general staff will make our way to join you at Luente after leaving the Third Army at Compuert Junction. We'll march on Manosete together."

Recha wrote furiously. She flipped back and forth on different pieces of parchment, making them out to their respective officer.

"If I may add," Hiraldo said.

Recha held her quill in her inkbottle and looked up.

"All of that will take some time to coordinate. Manosete may be well fortified and provisioned. We may not be able to besiege it with only two armies."

"That's the reason I'm giving Sevesco his own set of orders," Recha replied. "Rather, I'm going to let him run loose for a while and spread every rumor he can think of. He should be able to think of plenty. Just so long as they think Borbin is still alive and we're not a threat. Until it's too late, of course." She winked and went back to writing.

It took her several minutes to get everything written out. She glanced up several to times to catch Hiraldo grimacing out through the tent ceiling flap. The corners of his mouth drooped and drew back up repeatedly.

"Is there something else I'm forgetting?" she asked. "Hiraldo?"

Hiraldo rolled his head back, his scowl instantly gone and back to being a placidly waiting officer. "No," he replied.

"You sure?"

Hiraldo's drooping scowl returned, and his brow furled. "I . . . I'd just like to say, what you did last night . . . you did it well."

Recha's quill fluttered. Its fluff's muted-green color wavered. It took a second for her to realize her hand was trembling. She put it back in her ink bottle then went to sorting her pile of orders.

The attempt at distraction failed. The memory of the shot repeated itself over and over in her mind. Her final goodbye rang in place of the powder's ignition. Worst was the coldness afterward. She hadn't felt any joy. No satisfaction from seeing the man who'd taken her beloved from her brought low. Finality, yes, but a cold finality. A sense of an action taken that could never be undone, for good or ill.

"Do . . .?" She licked her lips, holding her stack of orders tight. "Do you think Sebastian would have understood?" She looked up at Hiraldo blinking at her.

"Understood what?" he asked.

"Me . . . executing Borbin," she clarified. "I don't regret what I did. It's three years too late for that. But, to execute a wounded, helpless man with my own hands. Even with all the political, *pragmatic* excuses I could drum up, there's no denying I did it because he hurt someone I loved!" The papers crumpled in her clawing grip. Rogue tears streaked down the lines of her face. "Would . . . Sebastian have understood? Or . . . not see me as a woman who could do such a thing?"

Hiraldo worked his jaw, as if chewing on his words. Recha wasn't sure if he was trying to hold them in or find them. It surprised her when he knelt in front of her, propping his arm against his knee, his wide shoulders brushing into things.

"Sebastian would have understood," he assured her.

Recha shook her head. "I keep telling myself that, but—"

"No, he would have understood." Hiraldo rubbed his chin. "Back in the campaign for the Laz, he kept pushing the men to march faster. He set out orders with schedules, trying to get us to places hours, sometimes a day, before we could realistically manage. Some of the officers reported complaints from their men, which is typically their own concerns worded that the men were complaining, but"—he waved that away—"when they asked him why the brisk pace, he said he would set the fastest pace he could, whether that was attacking any enemy on sight or burning every in our path of march, just to get back to you."

Recha's cheeks warmed. Sebastian had been eager after he'd returned from that campaign. He'd gone to see her a day before reporting to his marshal or her uncle. That togetherness with him had been . . .

She blinked the stray, small tears away and turned her face away.

"Sebastian told me that he just wanted to drive out the Pamolidians twice as fast as my uncle thought he could," she said.

"He did have a few wagers on us being the fastest companies in the campaign," Hiraldo admitted. "But his main reason for speed was getting back to you. And I think, if he ever lost you, he'd have done just what you did. Only"—he snorted—"I don't think he could've waited three years to do it."

The warmth from Recha's cheeks flooded down to the rest of her. It was hard to explain, yet it somehow felt like that was what she'd been wanting to hear. "Thank you," she said softly, "Hiraldo."

Hiraldo hummed and held his hand out. "If I may suggest, why don't you rest for today? I'll relay your orders, as promised, but there shouldn't be anything pressing that needs your attention today. The officers can handle things."

Recha snickered and turned over the orders. "Are you suggesting your marquesa be lazy for today, General?"

"Not at all, La Dama." Hiraldo took the orders, straightening them in his hands as he rose with a grunt. "Even marquesas need a day after action to recover, same as any soldier. Only, unlike soldiers who are eager to take days off, marquesas seem more determined to work themselves to death. Them, field marshals, and the like. Just thought a friendly suggestion was warranted."

Back to being the strict officer then. She smiled.

"Thank you, General. In that case, I will take it under advisement. Probably finish eating and wait for whatever the doctors . . . *gave* me to pass. I'll likely visit the field marshal again later. If you need me, I'll either be here or visiting the camp hospital."

"Yes, La Dama!" Hiraldo snapped his heels together, went straight as he could, and snapped head down, the tent's low ceiling preventing him from performing a proper salute. He then shuffled around and headed for the tent flap.

Despite her eyes having adjusted, Recha still kept her head turned against the Easterly Sun's glare during the brief opening.

Once alone, she eyed the plate on her cot. It had likely gone cold with half remaining. Her belly squeaked, although she wasn't sure if it was still ravenous or upset. She moved the plate to her stool and picked at the pork and bread, tearing off small bites and nibbling on them.

Her stomach didn't revolt, so she decided to take her Companion's advice and let everyone else take care of things while she lazed in her tent. She nibbled on her food, taking the first moment in a long time to relax, and desperately avoid thinking about those cursing voices that had plagued her the night before.

Chapter 38

Eulalia, Bayona—Necrem tightened Malcada's brittle—*I'm coming home today.*

He rarely thought of Manosete, the city, as home. Living in the city of the man and rulers who'd destroyed his family's happiness did build resentment for the city itself, especially with them relegated to living in its outer slums. However, Borbin was dead, those rulers, those calleroses, along with him, and having a chest under his wagon seat with enough deberes to rebuild his and his family's life twice over made him overly anxious to reunite with them.

The army filling the roads and setting up camp several miles north of the city posed the greatest problem with that.

Drums rapped a steady beat, moving streams of soldiers in rows down the main roads. Their forests of pikes, braced on their shoulders, waved in the air. However, Necrem saw through their gaps to gaze at the city beyond by sheer, willful focus.

Maybe I can get between one of these companies, he considered. *They're just moving around. I can show them the marquesa's writ, drive ahead of them, and get Eulalia and Bayona out before anything happens.*

Of course, that was assuming a lot. He could make it a few feet before an officer yelled at him to get off the road or some calleroses forced him into a ditch. Traveling with the Lazornian army had offered him safety and treatment after the battle in Ribera's Way, yet it saw to its needs first, even over a man they hailed a Hero a little over two weeks ago.

His knees spasmed as he knelt, hitching Malcada to the wagon. He kept calm the best he could, resisting against all within him from grimacing. The new stitches were only a few days healed, and he didn't dare to strain one. Not today. Not when he was so *close*.

Still, the waiting was maddening, far worse than at Ribera's Way.

"Sir Oso!"

Necrem winced, clenching his eyelids shut instead of moving his sore, scarred cheeks. He turned stiffly and rose to his feet. His body still ached even after two weeks of being pried out of his dented armor once the battle had been over. His fears were realized when he spotted Doctor Maranon briskly walking toward his wagon, waving his arm in the air.

"Sir Oso!" Doctor Maranon exclaimed, coming alongside the wagon, sweat dotting his forehead, with young Stefan and Oberto trailing behind him. "Sir Oso! What is this I hear of you leaving camp?"

"I'm sorry, Doctor," Necrem replied, his words coming out in a low grumble under his new mask of red cloth. "But you're going to have to find another wagon. I'm going home today."

Doctor Maranon stared up at him, Stefan frowned concernedly, while poor Oberto's face went pale.

"My good man," the doctor said, "there's an entire army between you and there. From what I hear, no one's sure if there's going to be a battle for it or not, but I highly doubt they'll let you through the lines. There's nothing you, or *any* of us, can do but wait."

Necrem sullenly clenched his fists, popping his stiff knuckles. "I've waited long enough."

The Lazornian armies had moved much slower after the battle. Necrem hardly noticed the first few days, being one of the thousands in the camps' hospitals. His armor had taken the brunt of the blows yet had still left his body bruised. The worst, of course, was his face. For five days, he'd lived with his entire head wrapped in bandages to let the new stitches heal.

Then came the marching, following in his wagon behind one army or another. He'd bid farewell to Radon at Luente and taken on Doctor Maranon afterward, changing his wagon from carrying a camp smith to a camp doctor to keep his place in the convoy.

His writ kept his wagon from being taken, and his deeds during the battle had gained him respect, which he begrudgingly accepted with either a grunt or a nod. However, the armies' needs came first. Mere travelers on their way home had to wait to use the roads.

"I'm sorry, Doctor," he repeated, "but I just can't wait anymore! Every time I turn my head, I see my home. Thank you for everything you've done for me"— he stuck his broad hand out—"but I *need* to go."

Doctor Maranon frowned with a mixture of concern, sympathy, and sadness. He took Necrem's hand the best he could in a firm, unshaking grip, and squeezed. "Do you know what you'll do if they don't let you through? That special writ of yours may not be enough."

"I'll manage." Necrem squeezed his hand back, forcing the stiff joints to make a firm shake and refusing to be deterred. Then he walked around the doctor to steps up into the driver's seat. He took hold of the seat, put a foot up on the step, and after a few starts and stops, pulled himself up, grunting repeatedly. His freezing, aching joints spiked, both stinging and relieving as he settled down before turning to the lads, who were both casting saddened frowns up at him.

"You're a good lad, Stefan," Necrem said. "Stay with the doctor. Learning to be a doctor is a better trade than most, especially better than being a soldier."

Stefan's checks wobbled, but he stood straight and put on a brave face. "Yes, sir."

Necrem nodded then turned to Oberto. Likewise, the younger boy's cheeks and chin were wobbling. However, instead of a brave face, small tears ran down. Radon couldn't keep the boy and after reaching Luente, so Oberto had remained with them, being an extra hand to help pitch the hospital tents and look after Malcada. Mostly to look after Malcada.

"Do . . . ?" Oberto weakly asked, sniffling. "*Must* you go?"

Necrem's chest tightened, the ache of seeing a child cry. However, he had his own child who cried when he'd been forced to leave all those months ago. He *needed* to get home.

"Yes," he replied. "I need to go home."

"But . . . we *need* you!" Oberto wailed pleadingly.

Necrem let the boy cry, waiting patiently through the sadness's initial onslaught. "Oberto," he said calmly and firmly, "do you remember what we talked about the morning before the battle?"

Oberto's crying slowed, and he nodded, wiping his runny nose with his sleeve.

"I told you I was doing all this to get back home," Necrem explained. "Well, my home and family are just down there"—he gestured toward Manosete—"and I can't stay away any longer. I know you only have a small memory of where your home is, but it'll come back to you, stronger every day you think on it. Stay with the doctor, and the day your memory returns, he'll be able to get you home better than I ever could."

Oberto continued to softly cry. That was the gentlest way Necrem knew to tell him that he couldn't come. It was harsh, but Necrem couldn't take boy in, and the doctor was the best man he could leave the boy with.

"Oso," Maranon said, grabbing hold of the wagon's footrest, "have you thought about the fighting? The Lazornians could be marching in there today. What's worse, people in Manosete are probably panicking right now."

"All the more reason I need to go," Necrem replied, gathering Malcada's reins.

As he pulled them up, Doctor Maranon seized a hold of them. "You may have to fight again! Are you prepared for *that*?"

Necrem held the doctor's worried gaze. His armor was stowed with the rest of his things in the back of his wagon, scratched, scarred, and dented in more places than he could count. He had considered giving it away after the battle, but it was still good steel. Not only that, but the plate was also his best work in years, especially the gauntlets. After so much punishment, those small, interlocking plates still held their shape.

"I have my gauntlets," he replied, nudging them with his boot under his seat next to his deber chest. While they were the last thing he wanted his family to see him wearing, nothing was going to get between him and them today. *Nothing.*

A rolling, distant crackle thundered overhead. Camp workers in the fields surrounding the road stopped what they were doing, while the soldiers kept marching by.

"Storm's moving in!" a worker shouted.

Necrem straightened in his seat. Dense, gray clouds were briskly rolling over them, coming in from the Desryol Sea, blocking the Easterly Sun, and mocking the crusty dirt with relief.

"You best be off then," Doctor Maranon conceded, holding up the reins. "Get ahead of one storm or another. Savior walk with you, Sir Oso."

Necrem accepted the reins with a nod. "Goodbye, Doctor."

Doctor Maranon stepped away, and without another word, Necrem flicked the reins and Malcada slowly lumbered into motion.

Eulalia, Bayona—he set his sights on Manosete—*I'm coming home.*

***

Manosete, *the* historic capital of all Desryol. Recha was still amazed by its size after two days of observation. The city was four *times* larger than Zoragrin, with half of its population living outside its walls. After grasping the size, she finally understood why it had taken a couple of days longer than she preferred for her general staff, Hiraldo, and General Priet to coordinate the First and Second Armies' approach to the city.

Her sight kept drifting up at the towering Hand of the West lording over the sky, despite her being over a mile away from the city's walls. The obsidian structure rose into the air over a thousand feet, dividing into the five towers that branched off it three-quarters of the way up and providing the architectural illusion of a hand, as its namesake.

"That's going to be . . . a nightmare to manage," Cornelos commented, staring in awe at the tower while they rode into one of the city's outlying eastern boroughs.

Recha snickered. "Already thinking about returning to duties as my secretary instead of Commandant de La Dama, are you?"

"Oh no!" Cornelos replied, jumping in his saddle with a faint blush blooming on his cheeks. "I was just thinking . . . what something of *that* size must take an army maintain."

"And it may take more than two armies to capture," Marshal Narvae grumbled. Rather, her new field marshal grumbled.

That, too, was something Recha was taking time to get accustomed to. With Baltazar now safely recuperating in Puerlato, surrendered over a week ago, she had to officially recognize Narvae with the rank. He did step into Baltazar's shoes well enough and had yet to chaff at her keeping a closer eye on him and his actions.

Yet.

"I must warn again, La Dama," he said, "that this is a risky move. We don't fully know the city's strength or if the city's commander can be trusted. I still suggest we send General Ross a change of orders once he reaches Luente to concentrate with us here in case the enemy holdouts make a siege necessary."

Cautious. Recha shifted in her saddle. *Too cautious.*

She bit the inside of her cheek to both keep the comment in and from frowning. That had been Narvae's approach to things after learning their slow approach had cost them their chance to take advantage of Sevesco's rumor campaign.

A few days out of Luente, outriders from the First Army had run into a force of five hundred calleroses from the city, and the ruse was up. They hounded the force yet never caught them or stopped word of their approach from reaching the city.

Now the city's gates were closed. That left Recha with only one tactic to use before resorting to siege—talk.

"General Ross has his orders," she said. "The Third Army is to march back to retake Crudeas and, from there, support Commandant—I mean *General* Leyva"—she shook her head, frustrated at keeping everyone's changing ranks straight—"if the Fourth Army needs it. As for us, let's see how these talks go. *Then* we can discuss besieging here or not."

With any luck, they'll see reason. If they were the bold type, they'd have led the garrison out for us to beat in the field. Instead, they send one message for my army to withdraw, and then another requesting parley. Either I'm dealing with more than one commander or an erratic one.

She glanced about her at the quiet, empty streets and alleyways. Although surrounded by her guard and two companies of calleroses escorting her, the silence was unnerving. *They better not be the devious type.*

The clomping of their horses' hooves echoed off the red brick and white plaster buildings lining the highway. The closed shutters of each two-story building and drafts of swirling dust, carried on the wind, pulling in a storm from the southwest over the sea, added to the borough's deserted atmosphere. Not a dog bark, chicken cawed, or rowdy child broke the silence.

It's as if the town itself is holding its breath.

Creaks of leather and rattling metal came from the calleroses around her. Each of them looked this way and that, checking every shutter, peeking around every corner, and eyeing down every alleyway they trotted by. Their lances waved in the air, and her banner at their head fluttered in the breeze. Their horses randomly snorted and shook their heads, sharing their riders' anxiety.

"Recha," Cornelos whispered.

Recha jumped, sniffing sharply from tingling spike of ice running up her spine. *"What?"*

Cornelos jerked his head back, eyes wide. "You . . . just look tense," he replied, shooting a glance at her waist and back.

Recha raised an eyebrow then followed his gaze. Her right hand had drifted to her waist. Her fingers unwittingly rested on her pistol's stock in her dress's hidden pocket. She cleared her throat and made a fuss over her dress's violet skirts, straightening them with a brush of her fingers.

"It's the quiet," she replied. "Cities shouldn't be this quiet."

"This is normal," Narvae commented. "The fate of any outlying town outside a city's walls. The people must be willing to abandon their homes or throw themselves to the mercy of anyone who approaches. Don't worry, La Dama; if this is a ruse, Savior be with anyone who jumps out, because we're going run them down first and think later."

"Thank you . . . Field Marshal"—she narrowly caught herself from addressing him wrongly—"that's quite comforting." She also noticed his hand rested near his sword, too.

"There shouldn't be any need to worry of that," Cornelos said. "General Galvez is ahead of us with the advance guard. If there is anything amiss, he would have found it by now."

"That's where you're mistaken, Commandant," Narvae said. "It's an easy thing for outriders or scouts to check a field, look through a grove of trees, or clear a ridgeline. But in a city, every house, store, shed—anything with four walls and a roof—can hide soldiers waiting to jump out. Plenty can be amiss, and General Galvez could've ridden right by it.

"And, if I may add, I still hold my strong conviction against the general of one of our armies putting himself at risk in being allowed to enter an enemy city before it's been cleared, La Dama."

"You can"—Recha shrugged—"but there's no point in it now. Besides, General Galvez did advance into Crudeas with his troops; I saw no reason why he couldn't advance with them here."

"In Crudeas, he faced an open enemy," Narvae pointed out. "And a poorly manned garrison. We best expect Manosete to be better garrisoned and more fervently defended. Which is why I advise it is not too late to withdraw and send a message that these talks can take place outside the city's boroughs entirely and on neutral ground."

"Our current meeting location is neutral enough," Recha retorted.

The street widened into an open oval, with all the buildings turned inward to face an ornamental fountain. Trickles of water ran down a pillar of polished red and white marble twisting around each other.

The town oval was bustling with activity. Recha's soldiers, with swords and muskets, were pounding on the door of every house and building facing the town oval. Each group of soldiers had at least two calleroses mounted behind them, urging them on and watching the upper floor shutters. Those doors that didn't open were kicked in. Those that did were generally followed with a panicked scream of a woman being turned out of the way. Although, the occasional curse did cut through the screams.

Recha pulled her horse to a stop, taking in the situation. The calleroses escorting her peeled off and formed up on the eastern side of the oval, facing westward and keeping themselves ready.

"La Dama!" Hiraldo came trotting up over, with ten calleroses on his heels. "You're early."

"I wanted to arrive before the storm," Recha replied. "That way, if the talks were cancelled, they can't say it was because I didn't show." She smirked. With her being her, it also meant whoever commanded Manosete's garrison had to make an effort of showing. Otherwise, they would have given up parts of the city to her without any opposition.

"Report, General," Narvae demanded. "Did you make contact with any enemy force?"

"None, Field Marshal," Hiraldo replied, straightening in his saddle. "We're securing the area but, so far, no company has reported any resistance. No barricades or street ambushes. The streets are quiet, but I believe"—he gestured over his shoulder as another woman screamed from her home's door being kicked in—"most of the residences are hiding in their homes."

"Don't be too harsh on them, if you can avoid it," Recha said. "It won't do if whoever shows to parley sees us mistreating the residence and turning their homes upside down."

"I've ordered the men to mind their manners," Hiraldo replied. "We are, however, commandeering a few houses on this eastern side, putting a few muskets in the windows"—he pointed at the windows above and behind her, a few of the shutters were being opened by her soldiers as he spoke—"in case this parley turns into an engagement.

"However, I don't think the men need much discipline from me to be on their best behavior." He nodded off toward his right. "We're being watched by a higher power."

A chapel of the Savior dominated the south end of the oval. The three-story structure was built from the same red brick and plaster as the homes surrounding it. Yet, it'd been constructed as a miniature castle, with flanking, domed turrets on either corner and a wide, circular window of stained glass over the arching, bronze door.

A congregation stood before the door—deacons in their wide hats, lantern staffs, and dusty traveling cloaks; deaconesses in their pristine white dresses and shawls; and three madres in their official head dresses, arms folded, each watching the scene transpire in the oval with expressions ranging from frowns to scowls.

Three madres! Recha shoulders rose and fell, and her nostrils flared from her hard breathing. She'd expected the Santa Madre from the Grand Temple, but three other madres, as well, added another layer to these negotiations. *The church might as well openly say they're party in these talks instead of moderating.*

A deacon had delivered the message to parley with the invitation to use this chapel as neutral ground. There was no shutting the church out with the fate of who held the city with the Grand Temple in the balance. But this amount of presence meant one thing.

I need to convince the church to accept me, as well as the city's commander to surrender. If I can't, they'll galvanize the population to resist, even if the commander surrenders. Which means—she took a deep breath—*the parley starts now.*

"Order your men once they've finished their sweep of the houses to beg the peoples' understanding outside so the madres can see them," she ordered to Hiraldo. Then she kicked her feet out of her stirrups and skirts out of the way to dismount.

"La Dama?" Cornelos questioned, holding his hand out for her.

Recha dropped down without taking it and set to straightening her clothes. The dress was proper for both formal meetings and riding. The creamy lace around the cuffs and collar stuck to her skin because of the humidity. She took special care to ensure that the outline of her pistol didn't show through.

"Dismount, gentlemen," she instructed. "We're going to chapel, and we can't ride up and lord ourselves over three madres, no matter how bad we want to."

That got a disgruntled frown out of Cornelos and, surprisingly, an agreeing snort from Narvae.

"Continue securing the area, General Galvez," Narvae instructed while Cornelos and a few members of her guard dismounted. "Once you're certain, check on your other companies and take up positions to wait for the city's delegation."

Recha waited for her party to gather around her then made for the chapel. She folded her hands in front of her, putting on a humble display, as any woman on her way to chapel would. Although, her heels joined the boots of the men around her, stepping in unison, the footfalls clapping on the cobblestones like a marching battalion. She led her party up the chapel's steps and stopped, holding up her hand for them to wait as she took one step up.

"Madres of Manosete," she announced with a modest bend of her knees and lowering her head forward, "I am La Dama Recha Mandas, Marquesa of Lazorna. I was humbled to receive the church's offer to mediate these talks. It is my sincerest wish that they will bring this conflict to a swift close without the need for unnecessary bloodshed." She waited, spying on the delegation through her eyelashes.

The deaconesses coldly watched her. Their judgmental stares shouted their disapproval behind their placid expressions. The deacons kept their eyes on her soldiers with white-knuckled grips around their staffs.

"Welcome to Talezah de Manosete, La Dama," the madre in center replied. She was shorter than the others, stouter, yet not bulging in her dress. A woman of late-middling years with olive skin and dark eyes. "I am Madre Caralino. These are my sister madres of Manosete's surrounding boroughs, and in the Santa Madre's place, I welcome you to my chapel."

"Thank you, Madre." Recha perked her head up. "You said *in the Santa Madre's place*; will she not be joining us?"

"The Santa Madre suffered a heat stroke a couple of weeks ago," the elderly, homely madre to Madre Caralino's left piped up. Her worn, leathery skin set her face into a long, drooping frown. Her folded hands, wrinkled and gnarled, were knotted, more accustomed to labor rather than speaking sermons. "We pray for the Savior's healing in restoring her to health."

"As do we all," Recha agreed, putting on a soft smile the best she could.

Fabulous, she inwardly groaned. *We've marched in on more than one power struggle.*

"We're sure you do," the madre on Madre Caralino right, who was taller and far younger than either of her sister madres, snidely remarked. Her cheeks were rosy with only a hint of wrinkles forming around the corners of her light-gray eyes. The straightness of her poise, and the way she held her chin and small nose in the air, screamed her lineage as nobility. "As sure as you rejoice at the added chaos."

Recha held the woman's stare without flinching. *I'm not going to like this one's sermons.*

"Madre Magdola," Madre Caralino hissed warningly, like a disapproving aunt, "please, this is neither the time or place, nor our time and place, to make such antagonizing comments."

"She didn't mean any disrespect, La Dama," the elderly madre apologized sheepishly.

"Don't make apologies for me, Madre Gara," Madre Magdola snapped. "None of us have anything to apologize for, especially to an invader who has brought her armies to turn our people out before our very eyes!" She gestured around at the oval, presumably at Recha's soldiers.

"They're not being turned out," Recha asserted, taking another step closer to the madres. "General Galvez is a cautious officer who refuses to allow me to go anywhere without sending soldiers to ensure my safety. My Commandant de La Dama, Commandant Narvae"—she gestured behind her, pointing out Cornelos, who snapped to attention and sharply nodded a salute—"likewise does not permit I go anywhere without my guard.

"I admit, I am a marquesa with very protective officers and soldiers." She chuckled and smiled. However, it went unreciprocated. "But, as you can see, the people haven't been turned out. Only their houses checked to make sure of . . . honesty."

Some of her soldiers were leaving the houses on the westerly side, offering understandings as they were ordered yet receiving glares in return, followed swiftly by slamming doors.

Best if we move this along.

"Now"—Recha took another step, coming up to Madre Caralino—"might we retire inside? I know we're in desperate need of the rain, but I'd much rather wait for the Manosete delegation indoors before it comes. And, as we wait, we can speak of . . . pressing issues the church may have with me."

Madre Caralino was watching her soldiers take up positions on the eastern side of the oval and leaned back when Recha stepped closer. A flicker of fear raced across her face, and then it was gone. "Yes, La Dama," she said. "Right this way."

The madres eagerly turned for the chapel, their flock of deaconesses crowding around them.

Two are afraid of me, and one is defiant against me, Recha thought as Cornelos came up beside her, bringing up her guard like a protective shield around her. She allowed it since they hadn't checked the chapel for safety and walked with them after the trail of deaconesses into the chapel. *I guess I can work with that.*

***

"Halt!"

Necrem begrudgingly reined Malcada in. She pulled against her bit, throwing her head back and stomping on the hardpacked road. Its gentle, downward slope must have been a relief for her to leisurely haul the wagon down.

Necrem, however, was more mindful of the approaching soldiers. He had miraculously avoided his worst fears of being driven off the road after joining the soldiers marching toward the city. They'd been more concerned with getting where they were told, and so long as Necrem moved along with them, they'd been content. One after the other, companies would turn off the road, marching across thirsty, dried-out fields, encircling the city, and encamping.

He was beginning to happily believe that he would drive away without anyone saying anything to him.

I should've known better. He groaned and sat back, reaching into his pocket to dig out the marquesa's writ.

"What are you about there?" the soldier, presumably the officer since he walked with his hand on his sword while the others carried pikes, demanded. He and his five soldiers walked around and surrounded Necrem's wagon while twenty other soldiers looked on from their small cookfire on the side of the road.

The officer, a younger man likely in his late twenties, stepped up besides Necrem, warily studying him with his red, sunburned face.

"Heading on my way, sir," Necrem replied, holding out the writ.

"On your way?" The officer cautiously took the parchment by the corners, frowning at the yellow sweat stains, and tenuously unfolded the writ. "And which way is that?"

Necrem glanced around at the surrounding soldiers. A couple placidly watched him. A few eyed the back of his wagon with curiosity.

Best not to lie. Probably best not to tell the whole truth, either.

"Home, sir." He leaned forward, resting his elbows on his knees as casually as he could. "I've been away too long."

"Who hasn't?" a soldier joked, to the snickers and soft chuckles of a few of his comrades.

Their officer, though, was reading the writ with a deepening frown. He shot several looks up at Necrem then went back to reading, as if not believing what he held. "Is this . . . *actually* the La Dama's signature?"

The chuckles instantly ceased, and every soldier stood straight and regarded Necrem much more than they had moments ago.

"Yes, sir," Necrem replied, "it is." He passed Malcada's reins from hand to hand, keeping them busy so as not to clench them. *Now? Of all times someone questions that. Now?*

"And you said you were on your way home." The officer gestured down the road. "But, if I'm not mistaken, the only thing in that direction is . . . well, Manosete." He peered up in a sideward glance. "Are you saying, sir, that your home is . . . in Manosete?"

A strong gust of wind blew up a cloud of dust from the surrounding dried-out fields. The soldiers stood unmoved. Their pikes rested against the ground, yet they didn't lean on them. They fixated on him, ready to pounce.

If I just say yes, that might not be good for me. But if I lie, and they don't believe me . . .

Necrem looked down the road longingly. The gentle fields were both dry and barren. The yellow stalks of previously picked crops, the shriveled fern petals, and brown blades of grasses all turned up to the rolling clouds above, begging for relief.

Beyond them, about ten miles away, he could make out the stockyards. There was less cattle in those yards now, but they marked the outskirts of the city. He was too far away to make out movement below, in the close packed streets and buildings, but he was sure some amount of panic must be gripping the people down there.

And Eulalia and Bayona were right in the middle of it.

"My family is down there," he replied. "For ten years, we've . . . lived in that *slum*. Feels like it's been twice as long since I was dragged away from them." He squeezed Malcada's reins and, for an instant, considered slapping them and setting the mule through the soldiers. But she was no war horse, nor had the strength to gallop, either. "I don't care what you do to the city—take it, live in it, burn it all down, and leave it. Whatever you want to do. But *today*, I'm getting my family"—he turned, setting his jaw and making the sides of his mask bulge while he gave the officer a hard look—"and I'm getting them out of that Savior forsaken hole. So, if don't mind, sir, I'd like to be on my way."

The officer held his gaze, squinting up at him and puffing his sun-reddened cheeks up at the challenge to his authority. Any other time, Necrem would have let it go, or rather not started anything at all. This time, though, he was too close. Home was just in sight. He would be damned if he was going to be held up by some young officer who wanted to question what he obviously could read.

"Pardon, Master Sergeant," one of the soldiers said. The others were passing uneased looks amongst themselves. "I think this man—"

"Search the wagon," the master sergeant ordered.

"Sir?" another soldier questioned.

"You heard me!" the master sergeant snapped. "Sob story or not, don't any of you find it suspicious that a man carrying a writ claiming to have been signed by the La Dama herself is passing right through our lines to an enemy-held city? And him, an admitted Orsembian at that! Search the wagon!"

Necrem kept perfectly still in his seat, the implication not lost to him in the slightest.

He thinks I'm an espi? Any other time, that would have been hilarious, but here . . .

Streams of sweat ran down his back at the first shake of a soldier climbing into the back of his wagon. He listened to him rummage around. His shirt clung to his back.

"Anything?" the master sergeant asked.

"Not much, sir," the soldier replied, his voice muffled from being hunched over and facing down. "Mostly a pile of clothes and . . . *armor?* I'll be . . . Sir! There's a whole suit of plate armor back here!"

Necrem swallowed. *Maybe I should have melted it down.*

"A suit of armor?" The master sergeant briefly frowned then took a cautious step back, his hand resting gingerly on his sword hilt. "And what's a person like you doing with a full suit of armor?"

Necrem's guts tightened. *Now he thinks I'm a calleros.*

"I'm a blacksmith," he replied.

"Are there any tools back there?" the master sergeant demanded to the soldier.

The soldier stomped around, kicking over things. "No, sir."

"I thought not." The young master sergeant smirked, as if he were clever. "That's no smith's wagon. You"—he pointed at Necrem—"whoever you are, get down from that wagon.

"Someone fetch the capitán! We have a—"

"*Sir!*" a soldier demanded, grabbing the back of the master sergeant's arm.

"*What?*" The officer pulled his arm away. A furious snarl darkened his already reddened face.

The soldier winced yet leaned in close and began to cautiously whisper. The growing wind whistled over them and drowned the words out from reaching him. Necrem watched, catching the soldier gesture, look, and nod his way. The officer's expression shifted from a grimace to a crooked frown of disbelief.

A few more soldiers from the cookfire joined the group and added their whispers to the first soldier. One gawked at Necrem as if he were looking at the Savior himself. The master sergeant began shaking his head and waving his hand.

"No, no, no," he said over his soldiers' growing voices.

The soldiers, though, shook their heads.

"Ask him," one excitedly insisted. "Ask him!"

The master sergeant let out a loud, frustrated growl and pointed back at Necrem. "You! State your name!"

Necrem took in the soldiers, watching as if holding their breaths and bracing for something.

They know.

He let out a deep sigh and rolled his shoulders. "Oso," he replied too softly then cleared his throat. "Necrem Oso."

"It's him!" the excited soldier yelled. "It's *him*! Steel Fist!"

Necrem's scars and cheek muscles spasmed and twitched at the name.

"He's an *Orsembian!*" the master sergeant barked at the man. "Get a grip of yourself!"

"But, sir," the first soldier intervened, "it is him! He fought in the center in Ribera's Way."

"I heard he fought just using his hands," another soldier added.

"General Galvez declared him a Hero for capturing Marqués Borbin himself," a soldier with a surprisingly deep voice said. "Did it for what the marqués did to his face. They say that's why he's forced to wear a mask."

"Camp gossip." The master sergeant waved it away. "I'm surprised at all of you. All of you know there're thousands of crazy stories after a battle, each one naming someone a Hero or another. I bet he only wears that mask to keep the dust out."

He turned his nose up at Necrem, and Necrem rolled his shoulders, knowing what he was going to say before the first word left his mouth. "Take off the—"

Necrem reached back and undid his mask's knot. The salve was a few hours fresh and stuck to the mask, making sucking sound as he peeled it away.

These soldiers had been on campaign for months, seen several battles, fought in Ribera's Way, and still several blanched at the sight of his face. Several turned away completely. Others covered and felt their own faces, imagining how stitches, holes in his cheeks, and exposed teeth and gums must feel. The master sergeant's bluster vanished, leaving him standing in shocked silence.

Another gust of warm wind brushed against his scars and swept into the holes in his cheeks, tickling his gums.

"Not the prettiest sight, is it, sirs?" he grunted, making a few of the soldiers jump. "I ripped a few of my scars in the fighting, but nothing too serious." He took his time tying his mask back on and fitting it in line with his cheekbones and jawline. When he was finished, he fixed the master sergeant with another hard look. "May I be on way now?"

The soldiers gave their master sergeant long, sideways looks.

The master sergeant swallowed, nervously turning this way and that. His lips pressed and rippled together. "Get down from there," he ordered the soldier in the back of the wagon.

He stepped closer and held up the writ. "On your way then," he said.

"Thank you." Necrem took the writ with a nod then flicked Malcada's reins.

***

This is . . . an odd gathering.

Recha studied the city's delegation in silence. Each member in turn studied her from across the choir loft. The madres had assigned them both to their respective sides of the loft, with Recha, Field Marshal Narvae, Cornelos, and her guard to the left loft and the city's five-member delegation and their assortment of calleroses arrayed behind them to the right loft.

The delegation surprised her in several ways. One, it was smaller than she'd thought. She'd figured every baron left in city would be clawing for a seat at this. The second, none of the members conversed with each other, except for the baron and baroness front and center of their delegation, who had remained arm-in-arm since walking into the chapel. The rest of the delegation members sat apart with a seat between themselves. Lastly, they all lacked a hint of arrogance.

Not one had strolled in boisterously with pomp. Not one had marched in making demands. Not one of the calleroses had strutted to challenge her soldiers. Not a single man had tried to charmingly introduce himself to her as if this were a feast. They'd all taken their seats and waited with a mixture of scowls, nervous glances, and blank stares.

I suppose Borbin took all the arrogance with him on campaign.

Seeing no reason to prolong this, she sat up and cleared her throat. "Good afternoon," she greeted. "In case any of you were in doubt, I am La Dama Recha Mandas, Marquesa of Lazorna. Thank you all for coming to treat with me. I wish this matter can be brought to a peaceful end. Tell me, which among you speaks for Manosete?"

663

She passed a sliding glance down the five members in front, ultimately landing on the lone, elderly man to the left of the couple. The man sat leaning forward with his back arched. A pair of spectacles clung to bridge of his pointed nose, on the brink of slipping off, as his dark set eyes peered over them. His oval-shaped head reminded Recha of an egg, especially from being bald and having the pasty skin of a man who shunned the suns.

"We all speak for Manosete," the man said in a soft, reserved voice. "Each in our own way while Si Don is away."

The corners of Recha's lips twitched, but she reined them in. *Seems they haven't heard yet.*

"And, in what way do you speak for Manosete?" she asked. "Sir . . .?"

"Sir Fanjul Anes, at your service, La Dama," the man replied, pushing his spectacles higher on the bridge of his nose. "I am Si Don's financer, not just for his person, but also for the city and the marc."

"I see. You're here to offer me a sum to withdraw from the city." She smiled and, in turn, the old money counter smiled back. "I'm afraid you're wasting your time, Sir Anes. No amount of deberes will be enough. I'm here for the city itself."

Their back row of calleroses broke out in grumbles and shared scowling mumbles to each other. Sir Anes deflated in his seat. His spectacles slid back down the bridge of his nose, and droplets of sweat broke out across his forehead.

"If it is a fight you want, then we will meet you in the field!" a calleros in the center of the back row announced, leaping to his feet with a few others around him. They all stood proudly in their polished breastplates, with their fists on their hips, posing together with their elbows sticking out.

"All of you look like traveling performers standing like that." Recha snickered, and Narvae joined in, chuckling.

"Are you impugning our honor, La Dama?" the calleros in the center demanded. "We are Orsembar's finest! Chosen to defend this city with our lives by Si Don Borbin himself. You will regret the day of your unprovoked invasion should we take the field!"

Recha let an uneasy silence draw out. With each passing second, the Manosete delegation slowly turned inward to nervously glance between the standing calleroses and her. The madres sitting off to the left between the lofts, too, watched on. Recha remained calmly sitting, letting the quiet erode those puffed-out chests while she stared placidly back.

"I think—"

Thunder rumbled outside, forcing her to pause. Although, watching several of them jump and the baroness squeak did make her grin.

"I think . . . if you were going to take the field against us, you would have done so to block our approach to the city. But if you want to settle this dispute on the field, I will gladly accept. Or rather, I *would* gladly accept. I promised the madres"—she gestured toward them—"to do my best to seek the least hostile method to settle this conflict. But, if you insist on making this a battle, we'll meet you on the field. Maybe you'll fare better than Baron Toloca did the other day." She grabbed the railing in front of her and made to stand.

"*Wait!*" the baron in the center exclaimed, jumping out of his seat and reaching out to her. "Please, La Dama! We assure you we are just as committed to finding a peaceful solution to this conflict. *All* of us!" He shot a glare over his shoulder.

"Am I to take it then," Recha spoke to the baron, "that you are Si Don Borbin's marcador?"

A marcador was the temporary titleholder of anyone a marqués or marquesa left in charge of the marc's civil duties while they were away on campaign. Esquire Valto was her marcador back in Zoragrin. It seemed Borbin hadn't left his equal to look after Manosete.

"Uh . . ." the baron stuttered then nodded, bouncing his curly brown hair. "Yes, La Dama. I'm Baron Esqava Perti, and this is my wife, Baroness Pilar." He gestured to his wife, who hid half her face behind her wide fan. Her gray eyes nervously shimmered up at her husband. They were both young, possibly near the same age as Recha, and maybe recently married. too. "Si Don granted me the honor of—"

Baroness Pilar pulled on his elbow beckoningly. The curling tips of her short, black hair bounced around her ears and on her shoulders. Esqava bent down, and a furious whispering campaign began.

"Instruct the calleroses to sit," Pilar whispered. "No, ask about Baron Toloca. No! That would come off that we were frightened. Demand that she leaves. *No*! That would come off as insulting! Stall until Si Don arrives. No! We don't know how long that will be . . ." On and on she went, getting out a few sentences every second and instantly reputing them.

"Dear," poor Esqava tried in vain to interject. He remained bent over with a gawking expression and shaking head, desperately attempting to calm her. "Dear . . . *Dear*! I'll try. I'll try."

Unsure, Recha surmised about Esqava and slid her assessment to Pilar, *and indecisive. No wonder Borbin left these two. It would take them twenty years to conceive a plot to undermine him, and twenty more to convince themselves to enact it.*

The others in Manosete's delegation were likewise unimpressed. The calleroses that Esqava had snapped at scowled down at the pair. Sir Anes rubbed his wrinkly forehead and hid his face in embarrassment. The rest of the members ignored them, as if they were bored.

"Enough!" Madre Caralino demanded, putting a stop to their whispering. "Baron, Baroness, our time here is short, and the fate of this city and its inhabitants lay in the balance. We cannot wait while you bicker."

"Forgive us, Madre," Baron Esqava asked, lowering himself down to his seat then instantly springing back up, seeing and remembering Recha was still standing. "Oh, La Dama—"

Recha held out her hand to stop him. "Sit, Baron." She waved. "I'm not storming out just yet."

Esqava nervously sat.

Recha followed, smoothing her skirts under her and crossing her legs. She focused on Esqava afterward. However, the calleroses behind him reminded her they were still standing.

"Honestly, sirs," she said with a sigh, "sit down. You're embarrassing your fellow calleroses."

A few looks around the room at their fellow calleroses, who hadn't stood with them and were frowning up at them, was all the confirmation they needed to retake their seats.

"Now, Baron Esqava—"

"Yes!" Esqava jerked his head up from his wife, who had returned to whispering frantically to him behind her fan.

Recha put on the best understanding smile she could and went on. "Baron Esqava, as Si Don Borbin's marcador, allow me to make my demands plain. To avoid the unnecessary suffering and loss of life that would result from a prolonged siege or battle on the field, I demand Manosete surrender. The city's garrison and *every* armed force in the city are to stand down and lay down their arms. The city's constabulary and other agents that keep public order are to remain and maintain that duty alone until told otherwise. The city's gates are to be opened to me and my armies. Upon my entry into the city, you and all members of the Orsembian barony in the city and all city officials are to attend me with a written declaration surrendering Manosete to me. Afterward, I will instruct you on how this city, and this marc, are to be governed from this day hence."

Rather longwinded, she granted. *I've gotten too comfortable around my Companions and officers again. At least I can be straightforward with them.*

However, such formality was required when addressing the barony, and a straightforward demand that they surrender the city, otherwise she would order an immediate attack or besiege the city, wouldn't have been strategically sound, either. It would have been too strong and put them both in a corner, one she, at present, didn't want to be stuck in. She had another strategy in mind should they not surrender.

From their expressions, it appeared most of them had heard the straightforward demand, regardless. Baron Esqava deflated in his seat, slouching back against it. Baroness Pilar dropped her fan into her lap, revealing her gawking, heart-shaped face. Sir Anes paled under a sheen of cold sweat. For the calleroses, they ranged from infuriated grimaces to hardened, jaw-clenching scowls.

"We can't!" Baroness Pilar exclaimed then clapped her hands over her mouth.

"Si Don never left us with that authority!" Baron Esqava shouted.

"All of Orsembar's finances will be ruined," Sir Fanjul lamented, rubbing his forehead.

"We will never lay down our arms!" the boisterous calleros exclaimed. "We will hold this city and lay down as many lives as necessary to defend it! So long as Si Don is in the field, we'll—"

"Emaximo Borbin is dead." Recha's revelation hit them like a flanking calleros charge. Just like the battlefield, a piece of information could crack the morale and resistance of the other side. If that happened, the best thing to do was to keep hammering on it until they broke. "His son, Givanzo, is also dead. Just over two weeks ago, we routed and captured over half his army and over forty standards from free companies, barony regiments, barons' personal standards, and Borbin's own colors. The rest of the army is still scattered.

"I reclaimed Puerlato over a week ago. I have two armies outside your city, but also another army marching up the Compuert Road, and another marching up to Crudeas. Yesterday, my Second Army, north of the city, reported on a small engagement with a force assembled by a Baron Toloca. It was paltry. Barely a hundred calleroses with less than double that of farmers plucked from the fields and forced to stand in as footmen. They were defeated in less than ten minutes."

The demoralization spread from the baron and his wife to the calleroses behind them. A few defiant scowls remained but, one by one, heads dropped.

"How do we know you're telling the truth?" the boisterous calleros demanded. "This could be a deception to surrender the city while, in reality—"

"I can produce the Borbins' bodies if you desire?" she offered. "I didn't bring them to this meeting because it would have been macabre. And a parade of the captured standards can also be arranged." Thunder rumbled outside. "After this much needed storm, that is.

"Frankly"—she folded her hands in her lap—"I have no need for deception in this. I only want to make it perfectly clear to all of you, and whomever is waiting for your return inside Manosete, that no relief is coming to save you."

The calleros balled his fists on his knees and gritted teeth, the grimace telling he was stubbornly refusing to believe her. However, like a battle line collapsing in front of him, he could only deny reality for so long.

"La . . . La Dama Mandas," Baron Esqava stammered, sitting back up with his wife clutching his elbow again, "we appreciate your honesty. However . . . there are others, other elements in the city, who will want to know . . . what are your intentions for the city . . . if we . . . surrender it?"

And just like that, survival becomes what's most important.

"I intend to merge the marcs of Lazorna and Orsembar into one," she replied. "That includes this city. Local officials will remain the same until their duties are reviewed, and as for these *others*, let them know that any barony who submits to my conditions will retain their titles and lands."

"Conditions?" Baron Esqava asked.

"The baronies will turn their focus on their lands and local authority," Recha explained. "Those who prove themselves competent and loyal in their duties will be elevated to higher authority in managing the marc. This authority will apply to Orsembar and not to Lazorna. Likewise, they can have my assurances that their lands and titles will not be stripped from them and given to Lazornian baronies."

Baron and Baroness Perti sat on the edge of their seats, taking in every word. This topic of discussion was clearly more of interest for them. Sir Anes listened just as intently, the color having returned to his face. The calleroses frowned displeasingly down at the baron, though.

"They will have to relinquish two privileges." Recha held up two fingers. "All barony forces-at-arms are to be disbanded. You may keep personal household guards, but Orsembar's armed forces are to be reformed under my army model."

"*Wait!*" the boisterous calleros roared. "You mean to leave the barons with their lands but strip us calleroses of ours *and* our income? That is unacceptable! You will leave us homeless and destitute!"

"I said *nothing* of the kind!" Recha snapped at him. "Calleroses with title to lands will keep them. Your allegiances, however, will no longer be to your barons but to the marc itself. Barons will be prohibited from going to war or raising personal armies. Instead, under the army model, calleroses will be assigned to troops and companies, to be either officers or follow the orders of officers. No more being assigned duties based on your baron's favor. No more being stuck in backwater posts based on your baron's disfavor. You will be assigned your company and your army and perform your duties on the field as ordered!"

The calleros sat, taken aback.

Recha embraced speaking with a calleros again and returned to the directness of giving orders.

The calleros opened his mouth to speak, yet his fellow beside him took him by the arm, shaking his head with a gleam in his eyes. He and several others were already working out the advantages she had to offer.

"You said we would have to give up two privileges, La Dama," Baron Esqava said, frowning.

"Yes," Recha replied. "All *sioneroses* are to be freed. The practice itself will be abolished under my authority."

Baron Esqava gawked. "But . . . but that's going to be . . ."

"Impossible," Sir Anes interjected. "It would devastate Orsembar's finances to lose such a labor force."

Recha folded her arms. "Some of my barons in Lazorna said the same thing. Some of them are no longer barons. Some lost their heads." She let that comment set for a moment. "But understand, the *sioneroses* will be freed, and no longer will men be traded for others to avoid battle.

"Of course"—she grabbed the choir loft's railing and pulled herself to her feet—"you can deny my proposals. You can keep your gates closed. But if you do, these events will happen. I won't besiege you, not right away. Instead, I will take my armies here, join with my other two, and claim every other less defended city and town we find. Every field we take will mean less food will be brought to you, every force we crush will be one less to support you, and every barony who joins me will be one less ally for you.

"We'll lay claim to everything, recruiting and swelling our numbers as we do. There are only two armies outside your walls now, but when I return, there may be four, or *five*. And you will be here, in the same position, only with less supplies, no allies, and utterly surrounded. As for my proposal then, I guarantee you all it will be far less . . . *generous* than what I offer you today.

"Make no mistake, Manosete and all Orsembar are mine to claim, and I'm claiming them. Take this back to those other elements left in the city. They can either join me, or"—she grinned, and everyone in the Manosete delegation paled—"they can join the Borbins."

***

Malcada snorted and flicked her ears in protest of the random sprinkles landing on them. A stray drop landed here and there across Necrem's shoulders and on his back. They were a far cry from what the land needed, soaking into whatever surface they landed upon instantly, including his shirt.

At least everyone's not in a panic. It was the only bit of solace the empty, quiet streets gave him.

He had expected carts or wheelbarrows to be outside every home and building with men hurrying to fill them with whatever possession they could, and the women to be in a panic of what to bring and crying about what to leave behind. Instead, most doors were shut up tight; window shutters, too. Every now and then, his ears twitched from the faint slam of a door or creak of a shutter, but no voices.

Everyone's hiding, he deduced.

Everything was familiar.

He turned Malcada off the main street after passing three blocks into the city, continued over for five more narrower streets, then turned down a sixth after going by a dead-end alley without thinking. The silence persisted, yet the memories came back stronger and stronger.

If he turned his head fast, he swore he could picture a phantom of himself walking along beside him. The plaguing memory of when he walked up and down these same streets to barter, sell, and . . . beg to anyone to buy his steel for the conscription tax.

How long ago was that? Months? He did the figuring in his head, shoulders slumping forward, refusing to believe it was that long yet so short of a time ago. *Lifetimes.*

He rode past Gael's cobbler store, all boarded up.

He went on campaign! Necrem recalled.

Many of Borbin's camp workers and followers had been caught up in the rout after the battle. Many others had been rounded up to put to work by the Lazornians. Some fled. Others perished from injuries and disease, same as soldiers.

Wherever you are, Gael, I hope the Savior leads you home, too.

As for his home, Necrem faced a choice—either go straight home or to Sanjaro's shop. He had left Bayona with him; however, no matter the promise to look after his wife, there was nothing that could force Eulalia to leave her room. Therefore, he decided to make for home.

I'll stop at the house first, he planned. *Make sure Eulalia's been cared for. Make sure she's there. Once I know everything's well, I'll go to Sanjaro's, pick up Bayona, and then we'll leave this place for—*

He drove Malcada around a corner and jerked her to a halt. His house stood a couple blocks down, lopsided as he remembered with only the left side having a second story while the right was only one. The gray overcast formed a shadow on the second-story's windows, blotting them out and not letting him see through them.

A wagon sat in front of his house with Eulalia's dresser loaded in the back. Two men sat on the steps outside the storefront, quietly talking to each other.

Necrem's teeth ground together. A low growl came from his throat. His face went taut, and each stitch began to pull and burn.

Thieves.

And Eulalia was in there.

He slapped Malcada's reins, making the mule whine from the hard crack to her bum. For such a small distance, he drove her twice as fast as he ever had on the road or into Manosete and reined her into a skidding stop beside the other wagon.

He spotted more than Eulalia's dresser now that he was closer. Her nightstand and their dining table, which he and Bayona had eaten alone at together, were loaded, too, along with a few odds and ends that belonged to him.

The two men, possibly in their late twenties and could pass for laborers by their cloths, leapt to their feet at his sudden arrival. One stared blankly while the other looked at him in stunned surprise.

"What are you two doing in my *home!*" he bellowed, glaring at them. His eyes narrowed at the sight of his house's front door leading into his store standing wide open, as if they were taking a break amid looting.

The men jumped, startled. One shuffled backward and tumbled over the front step of the porch. His fellow reached out to help and stopped, hunched over and arms out as Necrem leapt from his wagon's driver's seat.

He hit the ground flat-footed and with a grunt from the jarring spikes radiating from his knees. He growled at the pain, balling his fists, and swung his arms to limp and walk it off, marching straight for the two intruders.

"What are you two doing in my home?" he repeated, this time in a lower, graveling tone. His shoulders were pulled back, bristling. "What are you two doing with my *wife's* things? What did you do to my *wife?*"

"What?" the young man squawked. He held his trembling hands up defensively. His mouth opened and closed rapidly, as if to speak yet nothing came out, his chin wavered up and down. He lifted his head to grovel, wide-eyed, up at Necrem.

Necrem seized the man's left shoulder. "Did you touch my *wife!*"

"*No!*" the man cried, his shoulder buckling under Necrem's grip. "*Please!*"

"Help!" the other man yelled, scuttering on his hands and knees into the house.

Necrem tossed the man he held aside and rushed after the other. "Get *out* of my—!"

He stopped upon the threshold. There, beside the empty store counter in front of the door that led to the leaving quarters, was Bayona. Her baby-blue eyes blinked rapidly. Her mouth hung ajar.

"Papa?" she questioned softly, uncertainly.

Necrem's anger evaporated instantly. His bristling, his gritted teeth, his clenched fists, all of it released at once upon hearing that sweat, soft voice.

"Little Miracle?" he said out of his own surprise.

Bayona gasped, a sparkling gleam erupted in her eyes, and the corners of her lips curled while keeping her mouth agape. "*Papa!*" she screamed with glee.

She sprinted across the store in three bounds, the skirts of her lemon-colored dress flaring about her. Necrem swooped down, wrapped her up in both arms, and lifted her up into air. Bayona squealed with laughter, throwing her arms around is his neck, her legs kicking in the air.

"Papa!" she cried, a mixture of a laugh and a sob. She buried her face in his neck, flailing her light brown hair around as the smell of bath soap filed his nostrils. "Papa! Papa! *Papa!*"

Necrem squeezed her both as gently and as tightly as he could. She wrapped her arms around his neck. Her slender arms shook, quickly spreading through her entire small body, and like a contagion, he began to shake, too. His arms trembled to the point he feared they might lose their strength, so he took hold of her under her arms and lifted her up in the air, just as he had when she was younger.

Bayona's breath caught and, after a moment of realization, threw her arms up and squealed.

"Bayona," he said warmly, holding her in the air. He finally got a good look at her. Her hair had grown out, her color was good, and she had eaten well. There was something else, though. He blinked, taking a closer look. "Did you get bigger?"

"Huh?" She gave him a blank look then grinned proudly. "Yep! I've outgrown two dresses. Ms. Annette keeps threatening to stop feeding me if I outgrow another one!"

Necrem's face softened, and the coarse edges of his scars stiffly rubbed against each other from his cheeks and lip muscles naturally flexing into smile. He lowered his knees and eased her down on her feet. He confirmed her growth after standing back up. When he'd left her, she had come up to his hip. Now she was an inch higher, proving yet again she was going to be tall when she grew up.

Just like her papa.

"Did you get bigger, too?" she asked, tilting her head up at him. "You look taller."

"Hm?" Necrem rolled his shoulders back and stood straighter to ease his lower back. "Your papa's done all the growing he needs to." He chuckled, patting her head. "Not like you. My little miracle's becoming a big miracle."

Bayona pushed up on her tiptoes and rubbed her head against his hand. While doing so, his brow furled, realizing something.

"But what are you doing here? You're supposed to be Sanjaro and Ms. Annette."

"We came to get Mama," Bayona replied, happily keeping her head pressed against his palm. "Sir Sanjaro says we have to go and take only what we need." She pulled back, beaming up at him. "But now that you're here, we don't have to leave!"

A floorboard creaked. Necrem raised his head to find Sanjaro standing in the doorway to the inner house with one of the laborers crouching behind him.

"Necrem?" Sanjaro asked, his face pale. "Is . . .? Is that really you?"

Necrem stood up straighter. "It's me, Sanjaro."

Sanjaro's cheeks flushed, his eyes went misty, and a wide smile blossomed on his face. "Necrem!" The butcher threw up his arms and rushed toward him.

Necrem reached his hand out, but instead of taking it, Sanjaro stormed in and embraced him, making him grunt from the force.

"You're alive!" His friend laughed. "By the Savior's luck, you're alive!"

Necrem patted the man on the shoulder, unsure of what to do. After an awkward moment, Sanjaro finally released him.

"It's good to have you back," his friend said. "Did you . . . come with the army? Are they seeing the Lazornians off? Lazornians, Necrem! They played cowards for three years and now . . . they're outside the city!" A dozen questions came afterward, each one more desperate and demanding for news than the other.

Necrem threw his hand up out of necessity. "I'm afraid there's no army. The Lazornians are still outside the city. I figure they'll be ready march in tomorrow."

Sanjaro's shoulders fell, his hopes of quick rescue—if one could call it that—dashed. "Then . . . it's still good you're back. We need to hurry and get out of here before it's too late."

"Too late?"

"Before the Lazornians attack!" Sanjaro raised his fists defensively.

Bayona rushed behind Necrem, grabbing his pants leg. Necrem looked down at her worried face.

"Are they really going to attack and take us all away, Papa?" she asked.

Necrem balled his fists. He had made it home, and yet the war was still right outside. While Sanjaro, and probably everyone in Manosete, worried about what they might do, he knew exactly what the Lazornians were capable of and what lengths their marquesa would go. They could attack. They could level all the boroughs outside the walls. And they could do all of that with or without moving the people out.

That's what they could do. But . . .

"Don't worry, Bayona," he said calmingly, patting her on the head again. "Everything's going to be all right." That made her brighten a little.

"Necrem!" Sanjaro hissed.

Necrem gave him a firm look. "Everything's going to be all right." He locked gazes with his old friend and held it.

A wave of expressions flowed over Sanjaro's face, from frustration to panic, and then from shock to deflated surrender.

"Everything's going to be all right." Necrem gave him a reassuring nod then turned down to Bayona, softening his expression. "Let's go see Mama. Is she having a . . . good day?"

"Mama?" Bayona paled and slowly reached the point of tears. "Mama . . ."

Ice ran up Necrem's spine. "Bayona? What's wrong? What's wrong with—"

"She's not doing well," Sanjaro added. He folded his arms, frowning. "After you . . . left, Annette and Bayona came to see her. Annette said she was good for a few days, and then . . ."

"And then what?" Necrem demanded, yet no one answered. He stepped closer, raising his voice. "And then *what*?"

Sanjaro threw up his hands.

"Mama's not talking anymore!" Bayona cried. Small tears poured out of her eyes, and she desperately rubbed each one, quickly turning her face red. "She asked . . . for you . . . and . . . and . . . she stopped talking after I told her!" The tears flooded out, and she wailed just like when she was younger.

Necrem's heart felt like in a vice. His chest tightened, and a lump formed in his throat at hearing her cry and speak.

She must think she hurt Eulalia for telling her.

He knelt on both knees, wrapped his hands around his crying girl's head, and pulled her into another hug. "Don't cry," he said as soothing as he could, his voice a low grumble, and stroked her hair. "You did nothing wrong. Everything's going to be all right now."

Bayona cried for a few more minutes, unable to stop. Finally, the tears slowed, and she sniffed. "Really?"

"Mmhmm." He stroked her hair a few more times then pulled away. The mask prevented him, but he did his best to convey a smile through his raised cheeks and eyes. "Let's go see her."

Bayona sniffed some more, rubbing both snot and tears with the sides of her hands, and nodded.

Necrem took her under her arm and picked her up as he got to his feet. He made sure she wasn't siting too high in the crook of his arm, and then headed for the back of the house and the staircase.

"*Necrem*," Sanjaro called out urgently as he walked by.

Necrem patted the man on his shoulder. "Thanks for watching after them, Sanjaro, but it's going to be all right. I'll come back and help with the wagons." Nothing else to say, he gave his old friend a final pat and headed on his way.

The house was still tidy. Some of the furniture had been moved, likely from Sanjaro and the laborers. However, with Bayona living with him and Necrem away, no one had been around to mess up the lower living quarters.

The stairs creaked with his every heavy step, each one feeling heavier than the last.

Bayona kept quiet, a worried frown on her adorable face. She wrapped an arm around his head, and it grew tighter the closer they got to Eulalia's room.

Necrem paused beside the open door. The tightness in his chest lingered and now felt as if about to burst.

What do I say? He stood there for a moment. *Is there anything I can say?*

Taking a deep breath, he took that final step.

There she was. Right where he had left her.

Eulalia sat in bed. The last piece of furniture was a lone island in the empty room. Her honey-brown hair spilled down her back and reached the bedsheet, needing a trim. She peered toward the window to gaze at the rolling gray clouds, facing away from the door.

Necrem swallowed. His knees weak. She was calm, yet there was no telling if this was one of her bad days.

What if it is? What if she has another fit like when I left? What if—

"Mama!" Bayona yelled. "Papa's home, Mama! Papa's home!"

Necrem held his breath, standing stiff and still.

Eulalia said nothing, her attention remained fixed on the window.

"*Mama!*" Bayona cried.

Necrem patted her on the arm and put her down. He took careful, slow steps into the bedroom, watching Eulalia closely after each one to see if she would react until he stopped at far corner of her bed. She faced the window, yet her eyes were vacant.

"Eulalia?" he called.

Nothing.

Necrem walked around to kneel beside her. "It's me, Eulalia. Necrem. I'm home."

Again, nothing.

His brow furled, and his scars twitched. He dug into his pocket and cautiously took her hand. Her skin was soft, her fingers light and small compared to his.

"I brought you something," he said. He lightly opened her fingers with his thumb and laid a necklace of small steel links, polished over the weeks of travel to shine like silver, with an oval gold nugget hanging in the center, shaped like a locket in her palm. He gently closed her hand around it. "I made it to replace the one you lost. Remember, Eulalia?"

They sat in silence, broken only by the soft, sporadic taps of raindrops splattering against the window. Necrem's hand trembled, wanting to squeeze but not wanting to hurt her. He wanted to scream, to bellow and roar until she heard him. However, that could set her off. What good was it to bring her back to only terrify her?

What can I do? He gnashed his teeth, pulling his scars. He hung his head, squeezing his eyes shut. *What can I do?*

Her finger twitched. Then another. Her hand pulled out of his, and a soft gasp broke the silence.

Necrem jerked his head up to find Eulalia looking down into her hand. The shiny steel chain laid over her hand, and the golden nugget hung nestled in her palm. Yet, in her eyes, he saw it. A spark. A bright crack. A glimmer like the first light of dawn after a cloud-filled, dark night.

She turned her head stiffly toward him, eyes blinking, as if just awakening. Her brow furled and unfurled. Her mouth worked, yet no sound came.

Necrem sat there, waiting.

Please, he begged. *Please, Eulalia.*

"Ne . . . Ne . . . Necrem?" she rasped.

Necrem's cheeks trembled, and he licked his tattered lips under his mask. "I'm home, Eulalia."

They held each other's gazes, him not wanting to break the moment and unsure of what do. Her hand shook, and the chain slipped, forcing her to break eye contact and catch the necklace. She raised it up and awed at the gold nugget spinning in the air.

"I made that for you," he said. "I know it's . . . not exactly like your old one, but—"

"You found it," Eulalia said.

"No, I . . ." Necrem held up a hand to explain, but she was already marveling at it with both hands, her thumbs caressing the chain and the gold nugget. "Do you like it?"

Eulalia smiled at him. Oh, how she smiled. Brighter than any Exchange, and the mere sight made his heart hammer in his chest.

"I love it," she said, leaning forward. She slid around in her bedsheets and planted her head on his left breast.

His heart raced faster. The pounding in his chest felt ready to burst.

"Thank you, Necrem."

A wave of fire spread from his chest where her head lay to engulf his whole body. He couldn't move. He couldn't speak. He could barely breathe. It was the warmest he had ever felt in his life, and he wanted it to last for eternity.

Gently, he reached up and cupped the back of her head with his hand.

Please, oh Savior, don't let this ever end.

His sight slowly grew misty, and his cheeks throbbed. Something warm and wet trickled around their curves and into his mask's cuff, dampening it.

"Papa," Bayona said, standing beside him and looking at him with her bright eyes, "I thought you said steel-working folk didn't cry?"

Necrem's chin wobbled. He cupped the back of her small head and gently pulled her into his chest. He held them both close, stroking their hair with his wide, callused palms. "We do when we come home, Little Miracle," he replied. "We do when we come home."

And he was, *finally*, home.

Chapter 39

12th of Iohan, 1019 N.F (e.y.)

The humidity was stifling.

Recha's dress clung to her entire body. Her fluffy velvet skirts gripped to her legs, her lace cuffs made her neck and wrists itchy, and no manner of shaking her sleeves would loosen their strangle-hold around her arms. The weight of her broach pressed her blouse against her collarbone. Sitting rigid, with her back off the coach seat, kept her corset from strangling her. The brim of her cream-colored hat protected her from the Easterly Sun's glare, yet a ring of sweat already tightly sealed its inner lining around the circumference of her head.

That rain's ruining my entrance parade! Or rather, the humidity it left behind was.

Manosete was muggy and steaming after two days of intermittent rain. The breeze coming off the Desryol Sea stood no chance of drifting through the city's harbor and outer buildings to reach the inner city. Thus, Recha and her armies were forced to march through the hazy cobblestone streets while the city's denizens watched from doorways and second- and third-story balconies.

She peeked out through the coach's window at the closely stacked, brick buildings. The bricks had lost their bright, orange hue centuries ago, leaving the clay a dull patchwork of browns and darker tans.

She picked out a few faces peering over the edges and through their balconies' iron bar railings. Mostly the young, curious faces of children, unable to resist the beating drums and the soldiers' pounding bootheels and had to take a closer look before the cautious hand of a parent dragged them back inside.

Recha smirked at three children hanging on a balcony's railing with their arms over the side. Two boys flanked a girl and competed for her attention by pointing down at the soldiers below. The girl instantly spotted her carriage and pointed excitedly.

At least someone in this city is excited for my arrival.

Although, she was entering as a conqueror of sorts, thus it was a bit much to expect the city masses to spill out on every street corner to cheer and wave. At least, that was what Cornelos, Hiraldo, and all her other officers had remarked when she'd discussed how her entrance into Manosete should go.

The downside of having military-minded officers around her was that they all thought of the best ways of securing the city and ensuring her safety rather than making her entrance the grandest show the people of Manosete had ever seen. Therefore, she was stuck riding in a commandeered carriage, whose origins and original owner she could never get a straight answer for, instead of riding at the front of her escorting column behind all the standards they had taken at Ribera's Way.

She took a deep breath and ran her fingers through her hair laying over her left shoulder.

Sharp, metallic pings of horseshoes against the cobblestones cut through the steady beat of marching feet bouncing off the close-set buildings. The cordon of soldiers marching around her carriage like a moving perimeter opened a gap, allowing Cornelos, in full armor and regalia as her commandant, to pull his horse alongside, matching the carriage's speed.

"La Dama!" he said loudly.

"Commandant," she replied, "is something wrong?"

"No, La Dama. We're a few blocks from the Plaza de Dente, and General Galvez has sent back his initial report. The plaza is secured, and the city's delegation appears to be in place, as agreed."

"Very well."

The rain had provided the perfect lull for Baron Esqava to take her conditions back to the rest of the officials and barony in the city. After the first day of waiting, she'd feared they would stubbornly hold behind their walls and force her to implement her strategy of marching around the city. However, agreeing to relinquish the Borbins' corpses to the church resulted in a swift capitulation several hours later.

679

The sight of their marqués and his heir dead must have been enough. She rubbed her eyebrow with a finger. *I wonder if one of the madres had the same idea?*

It made sense for the church to prevent needless bloodshed, yet it still left the question of which one suggested they make the request. That madre could be a useful future ally, both in the city and the church.

She glanced out the window and saw Cornelos frowning at the buildings. "You certain nothing's wrong?"

"Hmm?" Cornelos snapped around. "No, La Dama. It's"—he glanced back at the buildings—"these close buildings make me uneasy, is all."

Recha sniffed sharply. "Which is why all of you put me in this *box*, need I remind you?"

"It is for your safety," Cornelos reassured her.

She waved her hand dismissively. "Just tell me when I can get out. It's suffocating in here."

The parade continued. The rocking of the coach, the marching footfalls, and drum taps all kept time to remind her she was still moving. Her eyelids drooped, getting lost in their harmonizing cadence.

A seizing chill rocked her shoulders, and she took a deep breath, blinking rapidly to snap herself out of it.

Too bad I'm expected, or this would be the perfect time to nap. Especially since there were no cheering crowds to wave to.

She checked outside the window and brightened.

The closely built dwellings were replaced by large, spacious, two-story buildings of cut, white stone and clay-slated rooves. They each bore an official look about them, with pillars flanking their double doors and curtains visibly hung in each wide window. Spaces wide enough for coaches and carriages separated the buildings with walkways to side doors interconnecting them.

Finally—Recha smiled—*we've reached the plaza.*

The buildings fell away no sooner than she'd thought that. To her right and left, companies of her pikemen from the First Army stood in squares, along with rows of calleroses behind and between them.

"Company!" a distant officer shouted. "Right!"

The company of musketeers escorting her carriage broke away, wheeling as their officer instructed to join the rest of the parade at rest. Ahead of them, she rode upon a company of calleroses, each displaying one of the captured standards taken at Ribera's Way. The standard held in front of them all was Borbin's, held lower than hers, of course.

Her carriage began to turn before she could survey more of the plaza, and she rode under a great shadow, a looming column too tall for a tree yet too straight to be a mountain.

We've arrived.

She prepared herself, straightening her skirts, tugging on her sleeves, fluffing her lace, wiping the traces of sweat off her forehead, and hiding any damp strands of hair she found.

Her carriage slowed, and her cordon of soldiers broke away, quickly rushing ahead. Recha pulled back so the waiting delegation wouldn't see her hanging out the window, gawking like a girl entering society.

The carriage came to a stop and rocked, and she counted the seconds and listened, catching every near and approaching footfall in the expecting quiet.

Cornelos opened the carriage door then stepped aside with his hand out. She took it, more for show and a little added security of not slipping in front of whatever delegation waited to greet her. She stepped out into the freedom of the open plaza and onto a black carpet with gold tassels rolled out from the first steps of the leading to the Hand of the West to her carriage door. Two rows of her soldiers stood at attention down the carpet with their swords raised in the air over it.

A divided crowd filled nearly half the Hand of the West's wide steps, six slabs of carved granite, the weight of each likely unimaginable to compose the foundations of the grand structure they sat upon. The base of the tower was constructed in a large octagon. The Easterly Sun's rays shined in a multitude of sparkles against the obsidian sides of the tower, reaching like the stars twinkling in the night sky, while windowless bottom floors in the sun's shadow were black as pitch.

Half of the crowd blended into that pitch. Five straight columns of soldiers in full, black, ornate plate armor and helms stood at attention. Each of their halberds bore black feathers around their axe heads, and upon each of their breastplates was engraved in silver an outreached hand, its fingers splayed out.

In stark contrast, a delegation from the Church of the Savior made up the other half the crowd. All their clothes were pristine white, from the deacons' suits to the deaconesses' and madres' dresses. On the bottom step, waiting in front of their respective delegation, was Madre Caralino and a helmetless soldier with his fist on his sword, obviously an officer.

Recha took a handful of her skirt to prevent from tripping and marched under her soldier's swords. Cornelos closed the carriage door behind her and followed. The thud reverberated through the open plaza, joining rhythmic pounding of troops from the Second Army marching in from the north. The carpet, meanwhile, muffled her heels and those of Cornelos's and her four guardsmen trailing her.

"Madre Caralino," she greeted warmly, "it's good to see you again. I understand you, or the church itself, aided the barony in the city to come to accept my terms. I'll be forever grateful for that." *But not so grateful to be swayed to rule at your whim.* She restrained the thought and held her hand out, smiling as sincerely as she could.

"The Savior leads all who humbly accepts his guidance," Madre Caralino recited, taking her hand. It was wrinkly and aged yet lacked calluses that evidenced any hard, grueling work.

Recha squeezed back to show she wasn't put off before letting go.

"And I would be remised for not saying so," Madre Caralino added, "however, the church's voice was not raised in blind faith to gain your support, La Dama, but in thought of all the innocent people of this city who you did make clear might suffer should your terms be rejected." She folded her hands and pursed her lips.

Oh? I'm to be scolded now, am I?

"Explaining the harsh realities of war isn't a sin, Madre," Recha retorted. "Neither was explaining the measures my armies and I are willing to take to bring this campaign to a swift end. As for the people of Manosete, they have nothing to fear. Every one of my officers are under the strictest orders that there shall be no looting or sacking of any kind. And if any soldier commits them, or any other heinous crime, they will be *severely* punished."

Madre Caralino's expression softened to a thoughtful frown. Her eyes narrowed judgingly.

Not wanting to drag this out, Recha stepped closer and softly added, "And I've also kept my agreement with the church. Not one member of the Viden de Verda has stepped foot in the city, nor will they put any of the barony, their guards, city officials, or members of the city's garrison to the question. And no enclave of theirs will be allowed be built in this city. Just like Zoragrin, in my home marc, Manosete will be given the same protection and providence to the church."

Madre Caralino's lips tightened with every word until her face was as white as her clothes. That agreement had been between the church and Recha, and likely not something they'd shared with the barony. Recha knew the cult would be a source of great contention and, therefore, offered her terms to the madres on how they would be favored while the cult's influence excluded from the city while they had waited for the city's delegation to arrive a few days ago.

Of course, that won't exclude me from using the Viden entirely. Most of the Orsembian barony may be cowed now, but some will plot. When that happens . .

"Welcome to Manosete, La Dama Mandas," Madre Caralino finally said, dipping her head. "Baron Esqava, along with all the heads of the residing barony and city officials, await you in the tower, as requested. Before that"—she motioned to the officer beside her—"may I present Gualdim Coriel, Grand Commandant of the Last Guard of Desryol."

A sharp clang stung Recha's ears from the Grand Commandant snapping his plated heels together. His dark, arching eyebrows accompanied his deep, brown eyes in giving her a wary, guarded look, never blinking as he gave her a respectful nod. Strands of gray dusted the edges of his black beard around his narrow face, leaving only the suntanned edges of his cheekbones and pointed nose exposed.

Of all the soldiers she had observed since entering Manosete, from the gate garrisons to guards outside a few of the baronies' city houses, he appeared the least defeated and resolved to surrender than any of them, him and the soldiers behind him.

"La Dama," Gualdim said in a surprisingly nasal voice, "the city's garrisons have laid down their arms to you. The church has opened their chapels to you. It is my understanding that the various city officials and barons, once loyal to the Marc de Borbin, have agreed to submit themselves to your rule. But know this!" He stepped forward, head high, jaw and beard jutting forward, and chest proudly puffing his breastplate out.

Recha's guards all reached for their swords and moved to put themselves between her and the Grand Commandant until she raised a hand to stop them.

"We are the Last Guard of Desryol!" His bellow reverberated through the plaza, punctuated by the soldiers behind slamming their halberds' butts into the granite steps. "Our allegiance belongs only to the monarchy of Desryol and only by royal decree will we kneel and obey. The Hand of the West is our charge, the last true symbol of the Desryol monarchy. We do not serve this city. We do not serve, nor have we served, *any* marc that held dominion over it.

"We did not serve the Borbins. We will not serve you. You may have this city, but to peacefully enter this tower, the Last Guard demands that you uphold our terms and creed."

Sweat dripped off Recha's eyelashes. It squeezed through her tightly pressed palms she held together so as not to ball them at her sides.

Is this a joke? Or a scheme? Her jaw ached in protest from her clenching it while she inwardly railed. *This city is mine. One gesture from me, and a whole company of musketeers can put that ceremonial armor to the test! I can shut all of you in there and wait a year to see if you're still—*

She took a deep breath to calm and remind herself that she had just promised Madre Caralino and the church she wouldn't sack the city. If she ordered anything like that here, with more of her troops marching in, her soldiers could interpret it as the city resisting and begin plundering it. There would be no way of putting that fire out.

"Which *are?*" she inquired reluctantly.

"That the Last Guard be allowed to uphold its duty," Gualdim began to list. "That we keep are arms and station here at the Hand of the West. To keep it manned, guarded, and preserved until the monarchy of Desryol is restored. That you do not demand we swear fealty to you, nor demand we serve you in any military fashion."

"All that bluster just to keep your station? A station I find miraculous still exists, considering the line of Desryol is over a hundred-and fifty-years dead." Recha's jaw loosened, and the corners of her lips curled. She would have laughed if it wouldn't have come off as arrogant.

The fall of the Desryol monarchy was a history lesson most nobles learned in an afternoon and then quickly forgot thereafter because it became less and less relevant with each passing year. Chroniclers recorded that the last Desryol king divided the kingdom into four equal parts among his four children—three sons and one daughter—instead of following the law of succession. Not a month after the old king had died, the children were already at war with one another, which eventually claimed not only their lives but the entire Desryol bloodline.

With the royal bloodline ended, the lesser nobles turned to carving up Desryol among themselves, beginning the Era of Campaigns and diminishing any importance to the old monarchy with each campaign season. Save for two things: the city of Manosete and the Hand of the West itself.

If this guard has survived for so long, Recha considered, *maybe they'll have their uses.*

"I'm sure those terms can be agreeable," she said.

"And one more," Gualdim added.

Her lip curl deflated, her patience running out. "What?"

"That you do not proclaim yourself as queen of Desryol simply from holding dominion over the city. It takes more than holding a city to be royalty, as I explained numerously to Si Don Borbin."

And he left you alive, did he? Recha pursed her lips and rubbed the sweat from her brow. The heat and pressing matters made the decision easier to run through in her head.

"I'm not here to proclaim myself queen, Grand Commandant," she retorted. "Only to take charge of this city as further proof of my claim over Orsembar. Nothing more."

They stared at each other for a few minutes. He likely was trying to gage if she was lying through intimidation while she merely sweltered. After all, she found little intimidating on this day.

"Very well," Gualdim said, nodding, "the Last Guard will not defy your possession of the city nor bar you from the Hand of the West. The plaza is yours."

"Thank you," she replied.

She turned to Cornelos. "Carry on, Commandant Narvae."

Cornelos clicked his heels together and raised his hand to signal.

A bugle rang out from the north end of the plaza, and ten drums rapped furiously. Everyone turned to face a twelve-foot-tall flagpole of the same obsidian stone as the tower. The bugle sang out in cadence with the drums changing to keep time to accompany the soldiers raising Recha's standard high into the air. It was the largest banner she had, yet she could tell the pole could hold one double its size.

I'll need to commission a larger banner sewn.

"Now"—Recha smiled at the delegation after the bugle played its last note and the drums fell silent—"shall we get out of this heat?"

~~~

"Presenting!" Cornelos announced, shattering the silence and making her jump. "Her Excellency! La Dama Recha Mandas, Marquesa of Lazorna *and* Marquesa of Orsembar!"

That might have been a little too bold. We haven't taken it all yet.

She smiled, nonetheless, and wore it proudly when two members of the Last Guard pushed open the grand black door open with a teeth-grinding creak.

The inside of the Hand of the West was as luxurious as the outside was marvelous. Recha's gaze climbed higher and higher, taking in its vaulted ceiling that stretched three more floors and could swallow her largest ballroom in Zoragrin twice over. Its floor was covered in lush, red carpet. Rich wooden paneling covered the walls for two stories before giving way to the black stone of the tower. Seven golden chandeliers lit the room in candlelight, yet only a quarter of it was filled by the city's assembled barony and officials, awaiting her behind a long table of cypress wood, its polished red shine matching the carpet. It was also terrifically cooler inside the tower, by nearly twenty degrees, she would wager.

The Last Guard members took positions beside the door, and Cornelos and her guard took it as the signal to enter. Recha calmly followed. Her guard entered more as a show of power and authority than need for protection.

While scattered among the barony were calleroses, she had no fear of them. Her terms required that the officers of their guard attended this surrender and offer lists of those calleroses who would remain under the barony's patronage and those who would be dismissed. None of them held the same resolute stance Gualdim and the Last Guard held.

The city's delegation stood out in their array of fine clothes, hats, armor, and parasols. Their bright and light colors created a mosaic of lace, silk, and cloth against the room's paneled walls.

Anxious faces greeted her as she entered. Peering out from under the brim of her hat, if a smile was returned, it was tight, several trembling, as if on the verge of screaming.

Baron Esqava and Sir Anes stood beside chairs on the other side of the table with stacks of papers, ledger and record books, and bottles of ink and quills laid out in front of them. Baroness Perti stood behind her husband, timidly watching behind her fan like the other day. One item on the table caught Recha's eye—a silver case around the same size as her pistol's cleaning kit.

Verdas's payment. She licked her lips, eyeing the case, and was tempted to demand Cornelos seize it immediately. Begrudgingly, she stomped it down. After all, there was etiquette to follow.

Cornelos led her to the single chair awaiting her and pulled it out for her as her guard took up places behind her. Instead of sitting, she remained standing, letting the silence drag. The city's delegation waited silently, expectingly.

"Thank you all!" she proclaimed. "Not just for presenting yourselves here today, but also for agreeing to my terms. I have already given this pledge to the church; however, I also wish to make before all here, as well.

"As my soldiers claim control of the city's garrisons, it is my pledge that there will be *no* sacking the city afterward! I intend that Lazorna and Orsembar be together as one from this day forward."

She turned to Baron Esqava and Sir Anes and said, "Shall we begin, gentlemen?"

"Of course, La Dama," Sir Anes replied instantly.

"As you command, La Dama," Baron Esqava nervously added.

Recha smoothed out her skirts then sat, allowing Cornelos to push in her chair under her. She waited as the two men sat and noticed the conspicuously empty third chair beside Baron Esqava.

"Are we missing someone?" she asked.

Baron Esqava frowned and lowered his head. "Begging your pardon, La Dama, we intended for Sir Varqos Estvia to join us, but he has resigned his post as Commandant de Guardia Policia, and we didn't feel it fitting that he attend."

"He was due for retirement, La Dama," Sir Anes quickly added, his reassuring tone strenuously forced. "He and many of the others found this change too great for them and accepted your gracious offer to resign from their posts." He patted the stack of parchments next to his ledgers, the stiff paper crinkling under his bony hand. "We hope your terms still stand that, so long as the city is surrendered and peace ensured, there will be no reprisal against them."

Recha pursed her lips at the stack. *That's more than I thought there'd be. Means more replacements to find, more time needed to return Manosete to normal . . . more local administration to take up my time. Can't go back on my terms now, though.*

"Absolutely, my terms still stand, Sir Anes. Those officials who wished to resign during this transition will suffer no reprisals."

Sir Anes physically deflated from relief. His shoulders rose and fell, and he patted the stack of resignations, as if comforting an old friend.

"Thank you, La Dama," he said, sliding the stack to the center of the table. "All other officers are still willing to serve and continue at their posts. These"— he spread the numerous ledger books about him—"are the ledgers for the marc and its holding bankers, all the *city's* accounts and its holding bankers and, as you required, Si Don's private accounts that we could find."

Once he had everything spread out, the old financer began opening the ledgers, revealing page after page of tightly compacted writing and letters that, at first glance, gave Recha a headache. Sir Anes, however, stood from his chair, stooped over them, and pointed at the pages, as if preparing to go line by line through them, much to many of the people in the room's silent, pleading dismay, by their expressions.

"Now"—Anes pressed his finger into one of the books—"this shows the remaining treasury of the marc for—"

"Sir Anes"—Recha raised a hand, the first sign of surrender she had made to any Orsembian since her campaign had started—"with all respect, all appears to be in order. My staff can go over it more thoroughly with you later. I think it best we continue with these proceedings."

"Are you certain, La Dama?" Sir Anes asked with a disappointed, drooping frown.

"Quite certain." She waved him down.

Sir Anes folded his clammy hands together and sat back down with a begrudging nod.

Recha motioned at the ledgers to Cornelos and, a few finger snaps later, a couple of staff officers came to the table to gather up the ledgers.

"And Sir Anes," she said once the officers had slid the ledgers over to the side, "until those resignations are filled, I will expect you to take on more responsibility for the city as the senior remaining city official."

Sir Anes perked up. "Of course! I am honored and at your service for the good of the city, La Dama."

We'll see about that.

"I know it's going to be some time to fill all those offices; however, I will need a list of capable candidates to fill them within a week. And, as for the markets, I expect them reopened in two days."

Sir Anes's face paled. "La Dama, are you sure you can't give me more time? Candidates can be found, I assure you, but . . . some may wish to . . . observe your rule. And as for the markets . . . two days are—"

"Necessary, Sir Anes," Recha said sharply. "New ruler or not, the people must eat, and to eat, they must have food. To have food, the markets must be opened. It's the best way this city can be restored to normal life, and the sooner that happens, the best. Understand?"

Sir Anes's mouth worked, likely searching for a reasonable excuse to buy more time. After a minute of enduring her hard stare, he accepted his fate. "Yes, La Dama."

That done, Recha turned to Baron Esqava. The young man sat back against his chair, facing the table like a child waiting to be scolded.

He really isn't meant for these matters.

She glanced at his fellow barony behind him. Apart from his wife anxiously watching him, the rest appeared bored, like soldiers waiting to be dismissed. *This is all formality to them. It's probably going to be the same as the early days when I took over Lazorna. A lot of watching, waiting, and . . . Savior help them if I have to rely on Harquis and the Viden more than I already do.*

"Baron Esqava," she said, snapping him out of his daze, "as the marcador of the late marqués, is everything in order for the formal surrender?"

Baron Esqava lowered his head, sweat glistening off his forehead. "Yes, La Dama Mandas! We've prepared everything, as stated in your terms and—"

"Begging your pardon, La Dama!"

Recha snapped around. Hiraldo stood at the entrance of the room, accompanying a stout calleros in plate armor. The balding man held the bearing of a seasoned, middle-aged guard rather than a soldier. She couldn't explain it, except that he lacked any hard edges. His eyes were soft, and she caught him swallowing under her gaze.

"My humblest apologies on this intrusion, La Dama," Hiraldo said, "however, an urgent matter has arisen. It is of the utmost importance that you hear of this matter now. May we enter?"

Recha gripped her knee under the table to prevent her calm to crack in front of the city delegation.

No, she groaned internally. *Someone's done it. Someone fought back, or fighting back, or . . .*

She swallowed a curse by squeezing hard enough for her fingernails to dig through the skirt's fabric and leave an impression in her knee.

"You may," she allowed, in as controlled yet slight forced tone.

Hiraldo escorted the other calleros forward, along with a trailing group of staff officers. He brought the man within several feet, pointed out where he should stand, and then took a step forward. "La Dama Mandas, may I present Estev Montez, Commandant of the Guard for Dama Emilia Borbin, formally Dama Emilia Narios of Saran."

The name struck her like a pistol ball. *Givanzo's wife! But if the commandant of her guard is being led here, then where . . .?*

She spun around to Baron Esqava, the man already slumping in his chair and refusing to meet her gaze. "Explain this, Baron Esqava," she ordered.

"Your pardon, La Dama Mandas," Baron Esqava said, flinching. "We understood that one of your terms was for Dama Emilia to present herself to you today, as well, but . . ."

"But *what*?" She arched an eyebrow at him. His lack of courage was becoming tiresome.

"Respectfully, if I might interject," Commandant Montez slurred, "I've come to speak in Dama Emilia's place. It's not for this . . . Orsembian *boy* to make excuses for her, *or* this lot of cowards!"

"How dare you?" a baron in the back demanded.

"You insult our lieges, you Saran *pavaloro*!" a calleros sneered.

"The only *pavaloro* here is you!" Commandant Montez retorted. "You and the rest of you calleroses so eager to remain in your lieges' kitchens while you write out fellow men-at-arms!"

Shouts, insults, curses, and finally challenges rang out. Hands flashed to sword hilts. One incensed glare from Recha to Hiraldo was all the permission he needed.

"*Silence!*" he bellowed, snapping the delegation back to their senses. "You are in the presence of La Dama Recha Mandas! One more challenge to violence in her presence and all of you will be *seized*!"

Soldiers came rushing into the room, joining her guard and the staff officers, all ready to draw their swords, as well. The sight of which, thankfully, quieted everyone down.

"Thank you, General," Recha said. "And, while you are here, perhaps your staff officers can join mine in taking up the calleroses lists that they were asked to procure. That was one of my terms, and I'm sure the barons have had plenty of time to think of their decisions. Right, Baron Esqava?"

Baron Esqava swallowed and emphatically nodded. "Yes, La Dama. Each household has brought a list of those calleroses they wish to retain and those they have decided to dismiss. And for that sudden outburst"—he swallowed again— "I offer our humblest apologies—"

"Please, stop apologizing, Baron Esqava," Recha groaned. "It's becoming tiring, and you're in an impossible position, anyway."

She motioned toward the far end of the table where the staff officers stood. "As for all calleroses here, I will forgive your outbursts if you present yourselves and your liege's lists to my officers now."

The calleroses eagerly accepted that, many stepping away as he instructed without a by-your-leave to their barons. Her staff officers too quickly forgot the disturbance, taking up the lists while also taking down the calleroses' names, their barons' employ, and inquire about those who were to be dismissed and where each was barracked in the city.

Back to something important, Recha thought, leaving the mundane work to the officers, and returned to Commandant Montez.

"Commandant Montez," she said, grabbing his attention, "where is Dama Emilia?"

"Dama Emilia is at the villa of her late husband, La Dama," Commandant Montez replied. "And we of her guard have fortified the grounds until we are certain of her safety."

Recha sat straight against the back of her chair to give him a stern look more easily. "Oh, really? Was my word not good enough for your mistress that I would guarantee her safety?"

"With respect, La Dama"—Commandant Montez's nostrils flared, taking a deep breath—"your guarantee came with only that Dama Emilia agree to your terms, but without any assurances. A simple guarantee *isn't* enough."

The sorting and soft talk among the officers and calleroses stopped. The barons and city officials became stiff in place, as if holding their breaths. A couple of Recha's guards shifted their stances, likely preparing to seize the commandant on her command.

Instead, Recha looked to Hiraldo. "What's the situation, General Galvez?"

Hiraldo snapped his heels together. "La Dama, when a squad approached the villa's gates, they found them barred and the walls of the grounds manned. They have refused to lay down their arms until their mistress's demands are heard, and currently, we have the entire grounds surrounded by now. We *could* take the grounds by force. However—"

"That would mean needless bloodshed." She still had a pit in her stomach. "And Dama Emilia's . . . *demands* are?"

"Upon renouncing all claims to the marc of Orsembar," Commandant Montez began, "Dama Emilia requests immediate safe passage to Saran—"

"No." Recha shook her head. "Finishing this campaign will take priority, and I will not be able to guarantee the safe passage westward until it is over."

Commandant Montez cleared his throat and folded his hands behind his back. "In that case, Dama Emilia requests that she be allowed to safely remain in her current lodgings. It belonged to her former husband, after all. Along with that, she demands her guard, all which she brought from Saran, be exempted from disarming or limiting its strength. She'll make another request for safe passage at the end of the campaign."

Recha listened, expecting something more. They seemed perfectly reasonable requests, considering her position. However, willingness to renounce her claim to rule Orsembar because of her marriage to Givanzo and not attending in person negated the true reason Recha wanted her here.

I might as well blatantly ask.

"Tell me, Commandant Montez, has your mistress had her blood this month?" she asked.

Commandant Montez blanched. His jaw opened and closed to work out his words. "La Dama, I . . . I don't . . ."

Numerous other men joined him in blushing or nervously turning their heads, many of the barons under the sideways glances of their wives.

"Yes, you do." Recha snickered. "And I would expect the commandant of her guard to know. But I suppose I can rephrase." She slid her smile away and replaced it with a hard, unflinching stare. "Is Dama Emilia pregnant?"

Of all the possible future threats to her in Orsembar, the possibility of Dama Emilia birthing Borbin's grandchild was the greatest. Timotio was still at large yet on the run and simply needed to be hunted down. Resistant barons could be met and crushed. It was the watchful, rebellious ones who would be the most dangerous, waiting for a chance and cause to rally behind in the future. If they had the marc of Saran at their back, too, they would be the greatest danger of all.

Recha held her stare for a moment before adding, "This is the most important question you must answer for your mistress's safety, Commandant. Depending on your answer, I can grant Dama Emilia's requests or refuse them and order the grounds stormed this instant."

Commandant Montez swallowed and raised his head. "To my knowledge, Dama Emilia is not with child."

"You're *certain*? It would be ill-advised to *lie* to me. No matter what your duty demands."

"I'm quite certain, La Dama. Dama Emilia only spent a few nights with her late husband . . . in a marital way since they were married. If she were with child, she would have shown signs by now."

Recha let him stand there, sweating, while at the same time allowing the others to watch. "Very well, I will allow her to remain on the grounds and keep her Saran guard if she agrees to my conditions. The first, naturally, she must renounce her claim to the marc of Orsembar in writing. If she is harboring any Orsembian dissident on her grounds, they are to be turned over to my soldiers. She is to raise the Saran banner over her grounds as a sign she has renounced her married name. If she does, I will view her as a Saran ambassador, with all privileges that come with such office. And before this campaign ends, I will need to see her in person. Can you deliver these conditions to her?"

"Of course, La Dama," Commandant Montez replied instantly.

"Excellent!" Recha smiled. "She has two days to make her decision. Until she does, no one will be allowed in or out of the villa. If she still refuses to accept my terms or hasn't decided until then, I will order General Galvez to take the villa by force, disarm all inside, and take your mistress into custody. You're dismissed."

Commandant Montez jerked from the pointed dismissal. However, neither Recha nor Hiraldo gave him leave to speak more.

Recha turned back to Baron Esqava, the matter settled. Hiraldo motioned for him to leave, and after clicking his heels together and a sharp nod in salute, the commandant followed the general out.

Recha took a deep, showy breath, encouraging others in the room to relax. "It can be such a joy to talk to soldiers. They give you a few direct comments, you retort with a few direct ones of your own, and that's that. No beating around the bush." She chuckled, and a few of the barons joined her. All she got from Baron Esqava, though, were a few twitches from the corners of his lips.

"Hopefully, that was the most exciting part of today," she said. "Shall we continue with the transfer, Baron Esqava?"

"At once, La Dama," Baron Esqava replied. He went into a flurry of straightening the long declaration in front of him, a piece of parchment three times as long and twice as wide as a normal parchment sheet, with every word written in a flourish and half of it blank for signatures. "We've prepared the declaration, as you requested. All who sign this today not only surrender Manosete to you, but also acknowledge you as the rightful marquesa of Orsembar, pledging our loyalty to you and your laws.

"And also . . . in accordance with your terms of surrender, we offer you"— he slid across both the declaration and the silver box—"the hieratical artifact to lordship of the Borbin family."

Recha raised her eyebrows and gingerly took the box, ignoring the declaration for now. She set it in her lap, running her thumb over the box's latch.

One more piece toward Elegida's freedom.

Unable to contain herself, she opened the box, and her mouth opened. She was greeted by a violet glow that leaked out of the box to cast its light about her. It came from a jagged shard of metal laying crossways to fit its container. The shard's length equaled her hand and was just as wide.

She studied it, struggling to clearly recall her uncle's heirloom that she had given to Verdas three years ago and had cursed herself ever since for getting mere glimpses of it before giving it to the spirit. This shard had edges running down it, as if a blade of some kind. The violet glow came from a foil running down its center that shimmered like glass or crystal rather than steel.

What . . . is this?

"La Dama?" Baron Esqava called. "Is everything to your liking?"

She snapped the lid closed and snapped back to the importance at hand. "Yes," she replied, placing the box back on the table close to her. "I couldn't be more pleased."

She picked up the declaration and sat back to read it. She heard the voices of Esquire Valto Onofrio and his wife, Golina, both in her head, reminding her to read it slow and twice over. Everything appeared to be order at first glance. Manosete was surrendered, every baron who put their name to the declaration swore fealty to her as the Marquesa of Orsembar, their lands, cities, and towns all coming under her protection. She read it three times just to be sure there wasn't any hidden language, no triggering clause that gave them a way out of their pledge.

"Everything appears to be in order," she finally said, happily, laying the declaration on the table.

Cornelos slid a bottle of ink and quill to her. She readied the quill and, hovering the ink-tipped feather over the parchment, glanced up at all the frowns of the barons and officials watching.

"I know this feels horrible to all of you," she said comfortingly. "You feel like you've lost. As if everything all of you have strived for and worked toward will now amount to nothing. But work with me a few years, and I'll show you what we can do together. Trust me; I may demand a high price for loyalty, but I'm not half as greedy as Borbin was."

She failed to see any comforting smiles or accepting nods. *At least I can say I extended the offer.*

She returned to signing her name, making it as large, grand, and with as many flourishes as she could without being flamboyant. Once satisfied, she blew on it and sprinkled some sand to help it dry.

693

"Who wishes to sign next?" she asked, holding out the quill, wearing the largest grin in her life.

In the year 1109 N.F. (e.y.), La Dama Recha Mandas, Marquesa of Lazorna, conquered and absorbed the Marc of Orsembar; the first time in over fifty years one marc completely conquered another. Later historians would mark the conquest as the end of Desryol's Era of Campaigns and the beginning of the nation's wars of reunification. However, those who lived through them would call them by another name—the Wars of the Bloody Marquesa, the second of three events marking the Year of Upheavals.

Epilogue

27th of Mattaeus, 1019 N.F (e.y.)

Baltazar grunted from a jarring bump in the road that sent their carriage rocking. He white-knuckled his wrist sitting in his lap to keep from pulling his arm against his side, but Recha noticed.

"Does it still hurt, Papa?" she asked for possibly the thousandth time since reuniting with him two weeks ago on her return trip to Zoragrin.

Baltazar had lost weight during his recovery in Puerlato. His uniform sleeves were baggy, and his face was thinner, revealing more of his cheekbones and jawline.

"No," he grumbled, rolling his left shoulder while looking out the carriage window.

Recha pressed her lips tightly together to keep from grinning, only to smirk crookedly. "You better work on that before you see Mama Vigodt; otherwise, she's going to scold you for such an obvious lie."

"Hmm," Baltazar hummed, unfazed by her warning. "I suspect I'm in for a fine scolding either way. Mama Vigodt's likely been expecting this campaign to be over months ago and me home by now."

"Was *that* the reason you always marched your troops so fast? Mama Vigodt always expected you home sooner than your commanding officers?" She giggled.

Baltazar snorted. "All women expect their men to be home sooner than the commanding officers."

"That's rather presumptuous of you to say." She arched an eyebrow at him.

"I don't think so." Baltazar shrugged. "After all, you thought the campaign was over months ago when you took Manosete. But, as I told you, campaigns are more than decisive engagements and seizing a few key cities."

Recha pursed her lips, unable to think of a quick, witty retort. Mostly because he was right, and she wasn't going to admit that. The surrender at Manosete had been her last exciting day of the entire campaign. Her days after that had been mired in administrative and civic duties. Gone were days on the march. The political life of a marquesa had returned the moment she'd signed her name to the declaration, and there had been no going back.

"I believed the death of Borbin and his son, the rout of most of their army, and the capture of their capital would have taken most of the fight out of those who'd remained," she explained, drumming her fingers on lid of the silver box containing the Borbin heirloom.

"Your stratagem was correct," Baltazar said. "At that time, the quickest way toward securing victory over most of Orsembar was marching on Manosete and taking it. You provided the final morale boast to our soldiers that we were going to be completely victorious in this campaign and denied the remnants of Borbin's army a significant place to rally. I couldn't have done it better myself."

Recha's cheeks warmed, and she went to straighten her hair to hide them. "Thanks, Papa."

She caught her reflection in the carriage windowpane. The setting Easterly Sun's rays caught the bags under eyes and the wrinkles at their corners, strands of hair hanging out of place everywhere, despite her relentless amount of combing. To distract her from how ghastly she looked, she instead focused on the setting sun and the reddish hew it cast on the drifting clouds as it descended. The sight was enough to think of something else that was setting.

"This was your last campaign," she said.

"Yes," Baltazar replied, sitting a little straighter. "I'm afraid I've marched my last mile. Although . . . it was a fine one."

"You missed most of it," Recha pointed out.

After Manosete had been taken, small fighting had continued for two months. That remnant of Borbin's army had been found north of Crudeas four weeks after the surrender and had taken two days for the combined force of the Third and Fourth Armies to squash. The Second had arrived for the mop-up and race to secure the northwest corner of the marc. All of which both she *and* Baltazar had missed.

"I upheld my duty at the most important time of the campaign." Baltazar waved it away. "That's all that matters."

There was something finite in his mannerisms, something final in his words, drawing out warm tears to form in the corners of Recha's eyes. "You really are leaving me, aren't you, Papa?"

Baltazar softly smiled back at her. "There comes a time for all old soldiers to go home, for marshals to stop giving orders, for calleroses to rack up their lances, and the weary footman to retire to his trade. It's the best any of us can hope for."

"Is that what you and Fuert Ribera talked about at Puerlato?" she teasingly asked. While he'd recovered in Puerlato, Fuert Ribera had been kept there as an honored guest. Rumor had it the two had become regular jedraz opponents.

Baltazar smiled reflectively out the carriage window. "I'm sure he understands. We can both enjoy our retirement, free of the battlefields and their holds over our families."

"But . . ." Recha clutched the silver box until her trembling fingers turned white. Hearing him talk like that made this carriage ride feel like a final goodbye rather than a simple ride to a crossroads. "But you're my marshal. What happens if something happens and it's too much for Feli or Ross to handle? What if we can't capture Timotio, and he raises a rebellion while we're stretched thin? Then there're the barons. All of them scheming and watching. And the other marcs! What if they all come against me at once? What if they aid Timotio? They'll . . . they'll—"

Rip you apart like the bloody marquesa you are!

Her throat seized up. Borbin's final curse echoed in her head like a chittering *mellcresa*. Her shoulders felt too heavy to keep up. She wanted to double over, to curl up in her carriage seat for a week, alone and undisturbed by anyone.

A strong, callused hand took hers. She lifted her head to see Baltazar leaning forward, biting through whatever traces of pain in his side to squeeze her hand tightly.

"Recha," he said in his low, fatherly tone, "that's just your exhaustion speaking. You've come so far, but you're looking ahead and only seeing the worst consequences all coming at once." He rubbed the back of her hand with his thumb. "Once you finally get some rest, I'm sure you'll see that none of them can happen like you fear."

"I haven't been sleeping well," she admitted, his hand a comfort, as it always had. She snickered. "Does it show?"

"Not when you need to show authority." Baltazar gave her hand one last squeeze then sat back with a stifled grunt. "But if you were to come home with me, I'm afraid Mama Vigodt would lock you away in the ground's cottage for a few days."

That sounds wonderful. Unfortunately, she knew she didn't have the time.

"I can't," she said with a sigh. "This little venture is probably the only place I know no *one* would come after me. If it weren't for that, I would have put this off for another month or so."

That was partially a lie. She *wanted* to see Elegida and had wanted to since returning to Zoragrin. That also meant upholding her bargain to Verdas and the likelihood of speaking to that spirit, too. The mixed mission did ward off any barons or tagalongs, though, which was a positive she happily accepted.

Two months of dealing with Orsembian barons, and then a couple of weeks reacquainting herself with the Lazornian barons had proven two things—at their core, they were all political animals looking out for their own interests, and they were all tiring. She was grateful for this small time alone with Baltazar.

"Are you ever going to tell me what sort of . . . arrangement you have with the Viden?" Baltazar asked.

Recha sat up. "I thought you didn't want to know, so long as they were kept out of your way."

"That's when I had a campaign to marshal and didn't want cultist fomenting religious arguments among my armies." He folded his arms. "Campaign's over now, and before I return to retirement, I want to make sure I don't leave you in worse hands than simple barons who you've spent three years bludgeoning into place."

"I didn't bludgeon anyone." She sniffed sharply at the comment. "I replaced several, sure. Some tested me and had to be made an example of, absolutely. But none were bludgeoned." She chuckled, but Baltazar didn't join in. She bit the inside of her cheek from him not falling for the diversion.

I could tell him. Elegida's alive, and if I gather these artifacts to the spirit possessing her, it might give her back.

She dismissed the thought in an instant. He would react as she knew he would. He would demand Elegida be rescued immediately, probably even go so far as command their escort to storm Cuevo in a daring attempt. But that wouldn't guarantee Elegida would be freed.

It was a question she had struggled for years to discern an answer to: how could she free someone from a being that could instantly possess them, body and mind, in an instant? The answer eluded her because she still didn't understand how Verdas or the Viden cultist got their strange powers, and until she did, she couldn't free Elegida by force. Baltazar wouldn't be able to, either. That left only the old lie.

"It's just a mutual agreement," she said. "The Viden serve me, and I allow them to exist. You needn't worry about them, Papa. I know how to deal with them."

Baltazar leaned his head back against the seat, turning his frown to look down his nose at her. The silent stare almost worked.

"I only wish dealing with the other marcs would be as simple," she said, changing the subject. "Worst situation or not, none of them will ignore what I just did."

Baltazar remained unmoved, sitting there long enough that she feared he would press the Viden issue. Finally, after the carriage hit another bump in the road and sent it shaking, he blinked.

"Your position is still the same, Recha. You had three marcs to face before the campaign; you still have three marcs now. Take every foe one at a time and handle them each in turn."

Recha took deep, measured breaths. Her shoulders rose and fell with the rocking of the carriage. Her head gradually tilted while she lost herself in the silent contemplation, broken every so often by the turning of the carriage's axle beneath them and the wheels crunching the rocks of the road.

"Marqués Dion will be the most difficult to deal with," she finally said.

"Oh?" Baltazar raised his head. "Not Marqués Narios?"

Recha stiffly shook her head. "To casual observers, yes. I just defeated and supplanted his greatest ally, killed his son-in-law, and his daughter is still in Manosete. It's natural to suspect he'd be furious and plan the next several years of campaigns against me."

"You don't suspect he will."

She drifted her head back, gazing up at the varnished wood of the carriage roof. "It may feel natural, but it's not. Narios suffered a humiliating defeat last season, and we still haven't had word on how he fared this year. He wasn't allied with Borbin by choice, nor was Emilia's marriage." She smirked. "Who knows? He may be grateful that I cut that marriage short."

"Is the widow?"

"Hmm?" Recha pulled her head down, frowning.

"Narios's daughter," Baltazar clarified. "Is she grateful to be a widow? Or is she like you?"

Recha *harumphed*. "Emilia is nothing like me. I don't think the poor girl's ever had to think for herself. Her papa spoiled her to want for nothing, and when she was married to Givanzo, the Borbins didn't see a need for her to think either.

She's only sixteen! Oh, and I did discover that it was her own guard, not *her*, who insisted on more protection for her.

"As for being grateful, I'm not sure if she feels one way or another about Givanzo's death. At my departure gala, she kept bouncing between Hiraldo and Luziro Ribera! If she wasn't laughing at one of their jokes, she was laughing and trying to talk to the other."

Baltazar chuckled. "At least she has good tastes when allowed to choose."

"I guess she does." Recha threw her head back against the seat and laughed, adding to Baltazar's chuckles.

The relaxed posture felt too inviting to leave, and after finished laughing, she rolled her shoulders into the seat cushions and bit her lip as the politics came back to mind.

"If I treat Emilia right, work out her return, along with the Saran *sioneroses*, I can try to use them as gestures of good faith to start talks with Narios. If he fared as poorly as he has for the past several years against Dion, then he may welcome talks. Dion, though"—her smile slid away—"if any of them are going to be a problem, he's most likely to be the one."

"Allies usually are the first ones to become enemies," Baltazar agreed. "That's what made your uncle paranoid about me campaigning in Pamolid."

"Well, Dion's already paranoid of me. There's a stack of correspondences *this* thick"—she raised her hand in an exaggerated gesture with her index finger and thumb stretched apart—"from Dion since our campaign season started."

"I don't suppose there was one thanking you for relieving pressure off Compuert?"

Recha lifted her head and shot him a flat look. "Not. A. One," she replied dryly then plopped her head back. "From the start of the campaign, he sent messages that he was gravely mistaken of Borbin's intentions and requested we *reevaluate* our campaign negotiations on the *prospects* of us aiding Quezlo in defense against Borbin. Then, after Borbin marched away to face us, there are a couple of correspondences that he claimed was mistaken, that they drove Borbin away and all was well." She huffed dismissively.

"The worst came after Manosete surrendered. First, he asked if the rumors were true that we defeated Borbin in the field. Then he demanded clarification on the declaration I made the barons at Manosete sign. One went so far as claiming I had no authority to take the city nor keep it. And the last one I read came a few days ago. He is requesting if we can *negotiate* the *providence* of the cities down the Compuert Road." She shook her head. "If he thinks I'm going to return those cities to him, he's sadly *mistaken*."

"And that's what can spark the next campaign," Baltazar said agreeingly.

"With Dion, yes, but with Pamolid, Marqués Hyles could campaign against me next year out of sheer paranoia that I'm going to unleash you on him again. Not to mention making a fool of his nephew for years." She groaned and threw her hands up, cupping and rubbing her eyes in frustration. "Add dealing with the Orsembian barons while changing their laws to match Lazorna's, moving Orsembar into our army system, freeing all the *sioneroses* while also not bankrupting the marc, ruling *two* marcs at once . . ." She gritted her teeth and let out a strangled growl. "Everything was so *simple* when we were campaigning!"

She rubbed her eyes until bright splotches of color blossomed through the pitch black of her closed eyelids. When her eyes started to sting, she dropped her arms, letting them flop onto the seat. Her eyelids fluttered lazily open. The splotches lingered, denying the light for a few more moments before they cleared, and she found Baltazar staring at her.

"I might've pushed too far, haven't I?" she asked.

"Recha, after three years of balancing Lazorna on a dagger's edge, none of these challenges facing you are new," he replied knowingly. "There's something else, isn't there?"

Of course he'd notice. She debated saying anything. Her frown deepened. The wrinkles of her furled brow felt like they were digging into her skull.

"It's something Borbin said before he . . . before I killed him," she admitted. "After all his pragmatism failed, and I made it clear that none of his promises would save him, he had one final curse for me. 'May the others drag you down and suitably rip you apart like the bloody marquesa you are,' he said." She wrapped her arms around herself and leaned forward, ignoring the silver box's edges pressing through her clothes and into her belly and legs. "I didn't care at the time. I had what I wanted—Borbin at my mercy and him realizing he was going to die. I had my revenge.

"But after that . . . I kept thinking about what he said. Hearing it over and over. I tried to shove it away as the last words of an arrogant man. Focused on winning the campaign instead. But after Manosete and dealing with the barons, I can't help but feel like I've done this all before. Just like three years ago, I've turned everything upside down and now have upset barons all around me, disgruntled calleroses with uncertain loyalties, and freed *sioneroses* who don't know where to go."

She bit her trembling lip and raised her head to Baltazar listening with concern. "What truly bothers me, Papa, is that I enjoyed the campaigning. I enjoyed marching with the armies, watching the battles, being involved with them, and the victories afterward. The months in Manosete were . . . *torture* in comparison. A return to the dull politics while *hungry* for every scrap of news from the armies. I was furious I couldn't be at the second battle of Crudeas, to see the last of Borbin's old army broken.

"I fear I might not be able to go back to ruling. I might get too addicted to campaigning. I . . . might become that *bloody marquesa* that Borbin cursed as."

Baltazar's thick eyebrows trembled from his worried frown. "Nothing more dangerous for a calleros than to lose themselves to the thrill of battle and find they cannot live without it."

"I'm a marquesa. That makes it a hundred times more dangerous for me."

Baltazar closed his eyes and exhaled deeply from his nostrils. His worry disappeared, replaced instantly with commanding stoicism. "Then there's only one solution," he said, opening his eyes and leaning forward. He held his hands out to her, and she accepted, reaching out to hold them in the center of the carriage while they held their heads together. "This must be your last campaign, too."

Recha's stared at him in shock. "But Papa—"

"Your duties are to your marcs now." Baltazar squeezed her hands. "That dagger's edge you've balanced yourself on for these last three years, perch yourself upon it and never step off. You hold a position of strength now, Recha, one the other marcs won't easily advance against. Use it. Show the other marcs that it's too deadly a gamble not to be cordial toward you."

She squeezed back. "But what if they see me as a threat that must be brought down no matter what I offer them? What if I must campaign against all of them, season after season?" Her hands trembled. "Trapped following the Rules of Campaign in all but name."

They sat in silence. She could see the other marcs making grand declarations, calling her the Bloody Marquesa. A blood-thirsty monster, killing her way to more power, marc after marc, and all her charity and any good were only in service to that end.

"You could stop," Baltazar suggested. "You swore two oaths—to avenge Sebastian and to bring an end to Rules." His lips trembled. "As a father who lost his son, I will be forever grateful that you upheld your first. Especially that it was *you* who did it.

"But that second oath"—he shook his head—"it's too much. You can give it up. Focus on ruling Lazorna and Orsembar the best you can and be an example for the other marcs that they don't have to follow the Rules of Campaign."

"I've . . . considered it," she admitted. "I've thought about the . . . enormity of it. Stopping all the marcs from campaign against each other year after year"— she snickered—"part of me thought it insane that night after swearing to it.

"But then I started to rule and kept Lazorna out of the campaigns. I saw the good it did. Those years of peace. I was planning for a bigger campaign in the future. However, the people lived well, not burdened by those needless annual campaigns.

"And then there's me. I got my revenge, expanded my power, and then stopped? Everyone will claim I did all of this for my own gain. This will all be for me, and that will tie Lazorna's and Orsembar's peace to me, too. It'll end, and they'll both return to following the Rules of Campaign the moment I'm gone." She shook her head. "I can't leave my people to suffer like that."

Baltazar flashed a comforting smile, his bristly mustache fanning out. "Then my original advice stands. This needs to be your last campaign, too. Be the marquesa who rules from afar, one who seeks diplomacy first, campaign second. Spread the tales of how you freed the *sioneroses* and have armies that can defeat foes three times their size."

She smiled with him. Her vision blurred from the few lone tears that leaked from the corners of her eyes and left warm trails down her cheeks.

"Promise me two things, Recha," Baltazar requested.

"Anything, Papa."

"If ever I saw two people grow up destined to be together, it was Sebastian and you. But now that you've avenged him, don't wed yourself to his memory. If you find someone whom you can love again, don't forsake it. Don't go through life alone. Man or woman, people need more than duty to carry them through life, and Sebastian wouldn't want you to be alone."

Oh, Papa. She blinked more tears away. *I don't . . . I can't . . .*

"I . . . can try." She swallowed her doubt to give him the response he wanted. "What's the second?"

Baltazar looked down at her hands and caressed the back of her knuckles with his thumbs. "Don't let any more blood stain these hands. That's what calleroses are for. Promise me you'll use these hands to build that new world you swore to make. No more killing."

Recha interlaced her fingers with his. "*That* I can promise, Papa."

"Hmm," he hummed approvingly and nodded.

The carriage slowed to a gradual stop. Horses snorted and trotted around the carriage, and moments later, a knock came at the carriage door.

"We're at the crossroads, La Dama," Cornelos called.

Baltazar grunted, amused. "We made good time."

He pulled away, but Recha held on to his hands. She didn't want to let go. She knew he would be gone the moment he stepped out of the carriage. She held on, willing this moment to last just a little longer—seconds, minutes, however much longer she could cling to.

Baltazar noticed, and he smiled broader. "It's all right," he assured her. He pulled his left hand away to wipe the tear trails away from her cheeks. "You'll accomplish more than any ever dreamed. And we'll all be proud of you—me, Mama Vigodt, and your true papa and mama, all of us." He leaned forward and kissed her forehead. His mustache tickled her skin. Then he opened the carriage door, allowing the red, setting sunlight to flood in. She blinked her vision clear to see the outline of three men on horseback around a waiting, saddled horse.

Baltazar grunted and carefully climbed out of the carriage, measuring every step until he stood on solid ground.

"Are you sure you can ride, Papa?" she called.

"I've always promised Mama Vigodt I'd come riding home," he shouted over his shoulder. "I can't break my promise now."

Recha sighed, shoulders deflating at how romantic the sentiment was.

She watched him strain and pull himself up into the saddle, biting her tongue to stop from ordering him back into the carriage or to quit being stubborn and accept Narvae's helping hand.

Baltazar let out a low groan when he finally mounted and sat straight in the saddle, passing a nod to each of his Companions.

"By your leave, La Dama," he said to her. "It was a privilege and honor to serve."

"The honor was mine, Field Marshal," Recha happily replied.

"I'll tell Mama Vigodt to expect you once you're done with the Viden." He wheeled his horse around, kicking up a cloud of dust, his Companions on his heels.

"*Papa!*"

"Don't make a liar out of me!" His teasing reply was echoed by Narvae laughing and Bisal letting out a whooping holler.

Recha watched them as they grew smaller and smaller on the horizon. Four comrades, four Companions, who had ridden off to battle countless times. Now they were each returning home, riding into the setting Easterly Sun, never to ride forth again.

A few more tears ran down her cheeks, as she couldn't imagine anything more fitting and beautiful for men such as they.

"La Dama?"

Recha blinked and turned to Cornelos, who stood by the carriage door.

"Should we follow after them?" he asked. "Postpone your visit to the Viden until later?"

She sniffed and shook her head. "That won't be necessary, Cornelos. Let's be off."

~~~

Recha drummed on the lid of the silver box in her lap. The rhythmic thumping saved her from the nauseating silence of Verdas's sitting room.

How much longer? She'd been waiting for over an hour.

Vastura'd been there to greet her upon her arrival and had ushered her through the estate. She'd denied her from seeing Elegida and had asked her to wait, that the *Master* wasn't ready to see her.

What does a spirit have to get ready for?

She rose from her chair, keeping the silver box in hand. She moved around the chair to the small window, fanning herself. The room was chokingly humid, and the faint smoke from the wicks of the burning oil lamps irritated her nostrils and made her nose run. She checked around the edges of the small window, and as she suspected, there was no way to open them.

This little cottage is no more than a prison. She ran her fingers around the edges of the windowpane. Through her own reflection, she peered into the sheer void of night. The faint glint from the odd window of the surrounding mansion barely cut through, leaving a black sheen across the glass. *How am I going to get her out of here?*

A shriek ripped through the cottage. A door slammed open. The doorknob struck the wooden wall with an earsplitting crack.

"Get out!"

Elegida!

Recha spun on her heels and dashed into a sprint without minding her skirts. She instead furiously kicked them out in front of her. She turned a corner and narrowly missed a cultist fleeing down the hallway with a look of terror on his face.

"Please, Master," Vastura said, her urging voice coming from the bedroom at the end of the hallway, "tell us what is wrong? How can we help?"

"There is no help!" came the shrieking reply. *"None!"*

Recha sped down the hall and shoved her way into the room through two other cultists, both women clutching their hands to their chests in utter shock.

"Elegida!" she cried and stopped two stumbling steps into the room.

Elegida lay on the bed. Her entire body was arching upward toward the ceiling, as if she were trying to fold herself backward. Her feet, shoulders, and head were the only parts of her body touching the mattress. Her hair splayed about the top of bed, and she clutched her head with her hands. Vastura was the only cultist trying to calm her, possibly because she was the only blind Seer present, as well. The two other cultists huddled in a corner, as stunned as those in the doorway at the sight.

She's going to snap her spine!

"What are all of you *doing*?" Recha demanded. She carelessly tossed the silver box on the bed and leapt on Elegida. She knocked her legs out and wrapped her arms protectively around her sister, forcing her down and holding her as she started to convulse, scream, and kick.

"La Dama!" Vastura shouted. "You must unhand the Master!" The Seer's milky-white eyes grew wide, and her face was stricken with aghast concern. The cultist reached for her with an outstretched hand.

Recha easily slapped it away, snarling at the woman. "What have you done to my sister? Get out! All of—"

"That's not your sister!" Vastura cried, shaking her head furiously.

"What?"

Two hands seized the sides of Recha's face. Ten wet, sharp fingernails dug into her skin and wrenched her head to look down. Recha instantly broke out into a cold sweat, goosebumps raced down her body, and her strength failed her.

She stared down into two flesh-pink, glowing eyes and a mirror image of her face twitching and snarling between hysteria and unbridled rage.

Verdas was the one in control. Verdas was the one going insane.

Verdas was *terrified*.

"Do you . . . *feel* it?" the spirit whispered.

"Feel what?" Recha asked back. "*Ah*!"

She hissed from the fingernails digging deeper into her scalp and was forced to let go to grab Elegida's wrists to keep the spirit from clawing her face. Verdas clung to her and, no longer being held down, began to sit up. Recha hissed, tugging on her wrists, but the grip was like iron, bringing their faces close together.

"That *heat*!" Verdas hissed. "That . . . all-consuming heat." It let out a strangled groan. Tears leaked from its eyes in a constant flow. "I thought I felt it . . . flickers . . . flares . . . here and there weeks ago. And I just . . . denied it." Its lips curled and let out a cruel chuckle. "But there's no deny it, that heat belongs to only one. He still exists! He's *back*!" Verdas threw its head back and screamed, sending Recha's ears reeling.

She pulled back and accepted the cuts to her face to free herself from the spirit's grip. She pushed away, rubbing her face to check for blood, finding a cut on the right side of her temple.

"What is it talking about?" she demanded to the other cultists, but they all stared at her, speechless.

Suddenly, Verdas's wail cut off.

Recha watched as it slowly wrapped its arms around Elegida's body, bringing its hands up to grip the shoulders. It lowered its head unnaturally slow. Elegida's face was as pale as her dress. Verdas let the jaw hang agape, eyes bulging, and the pink pupils shrank to pinpricks.

"*Two!*" Verdas gasped. "The atmosphere crackles and boils. They stir. It will all happen *again*! They will all stir! *Kiso-einshin* . . ." The spirit devolved into babbles and slowly tipped downward, folding Elegida's body in on itself and gently started to rock.

It's finally happened. Recha watched, unable to move. *The spirit's finally shown it's insane. How am I supposed to free Elegida from . . . from . . .?*

She angled her head and listened more closely. Everything Verdas sputtered sounded like meaningless nonsense. Crazed gibberish. Yet, there was something . . . in the cadence of its voice. Pauses. Some of the babble sounded like it was repeated, repeated phrases mixed into the nonsense.

Is that . . .? She leaned forward. *Does . . . this spirit have its own language? Do spirits have languages?* Of course, being that Verdas was the only spirit she knew of, that was a question she'd never thought to ask. One glance around the room proved the other cultists were just as clueless as she.

I can't let this go on. Elegida's still in there.

Recha reached down and took hold of Elegida's shoulders, cupping the tightly gripped hands. "Verdas," she called. "Verdas, who are *they*?"

The babble instantly ceased.

Verdas raised its head with unnatural stiffness. Every facial muscle twitched and spasmed. The lips moved, smacking, and the tongue and throat clicked inside, as if the mouth was dry. Pink, dilated pupils bounced back and forth, as if the spirit were searching for a word on the tip of its tongue.

Then the pupils snapped back, growing larger. The facial twitching, lip smacking, and tongue clicking all ceased at once. There came a staggering exhale, making the jaw tremble.

"*Dragon,*" the spirit let out in a hush.

The pink in Elegida's eyes recoiled, fading from the pupils like draining water. The glow from the crystal around her neck grew feverishly bright then winked to a faint distant star in an instant.

Recha stared into those milky, unresponsive orbs that were now her sister's eyes, feeling the tension leave her body from her grip on her shoulders.

"Elegida?" she called gently.

"R . . . R . . . Recha?" Elegida's voice was soft and hoarse. Glistening pools of tears blossomed around Elegida's eyelids. Her chin wobbled, and her cheeks flushed. "*Recha!*" Elegida wailed, throwing herself into Recha's lap and burying her face in her skirts.

Recha threw her arms protectively around her, holding her sister close. "It's all right," she said comfortingly, rubbing her sister's shoulders and back. "I'm here now. Your sister's got you now."

The rustle of movement on the carpet caught her attention. She snapped her head up and glared at Vastura and a couple of the other cultists inching closer to them.

"If *any* of you touch her, I will have you *all* executed," she threatened, snarling and clinging to Elegida. "Every *single* member! Get out! *Out*!"

Elegida wailed louder at Recha's scream, forcing her to gently stroke her fingers through her hair while calmly shushing and rocking her. At the same time, she fixed a sharp glare on each cultist as Vastura gathered them up and left.

Finally alone, she held Elegida in her arms, calming her through the wails and tears until they stopped, her body stopped shaking, and she listened to her sister's soft, steady breaths. Her mind began to crawl with every shush, every gentle rock, and every soft breath. While she got Elegida to sleep, sleep denied her as a repeating question circled inside her head.

What's a dragon?

THE END OF

FOR THE BLOODY MARQUESA!

Almanac of Seasons

This world goes by many names, depending on whom you ask. Many of this world's inhabitants also have a different sense of time. For simplicity, however, we shall remain with the humans.

Humanity's arrival to this world has been long since soaked in myth, legend, and history, but it did not take them long to realize this was a far different world than the one they came from. It was both ancient but new; familiar but alien. It took years of adjusting until they finally calculated the changes in seasons and the passage of time.

This world revolves in an infinite pattern, exchanged between two suns, which humanity have named after the direction they rise—the Easterly Sun rises in the east and the Westerly Sun rises in the west—and this pattern of exchange revolves around a four-year cycle. Upon calculations, humanity also realized that the number of months are different depending on which sun the world revolves around, as are the seasons different. A new calendar was necessary, and a new system to track the year was established. The Easterly Year is marked as e.y., and the Westerly is marked as w.y. The seasons during this cycle are displayed as follows.

Easterly Year

Petrarium	Andril	Iam	Iohan	Filippum
4th - Exchange Ends (Cycle Begins)	13th - Great Easterly Spring Begins			
Summer				

Vartholo	Mattaeus	Alphei	Simem	Iouda
			22nd - False Fall Begins	

Thoma				
18th - Short Summer Begins				
25th - Exchange Begins				

Westerly Year

Reun	Vell	Iuda	Esstonder	Zabulon
4th - Exchange Ends				
17th - Winter Begins				

Dane	Naphtal	Gad	Aster	Benjamine
8th - Short Spring Begins		12th - Great Summer Begins		

Josephus	Ephraim	Manas		
		28th - Exchange Begins		

Easterly Year

Petrarium	Andril	Iam	Iohan	Filippum
4th - Exchange Ends		11th - True Fall Begins		

Vartholo	Mattaeus	Alphei	Simem	Iouda
6th - False Winter Begins				3rd - False Spring Begins

Thoma				
9th - Short Summer Begins				
25th - Exchange Begins				

Westerly Year

Reun	Vell	Iuda	Esstonder	Zabulon
4th - Exchange Ends	13th - True Winter Begins			

Dane	Naphtal	Gad	Aster	Benjamine
		5th - Spring Begins		

Josephus	Ephraim	Manas		
	14th - Summer Begins	28th - Exchange Begins (Cycle Repeats)		

About the Author

ZACHARY T. SELLERS is a licensed attorney in the state of Arkansas and currently works as a practicing attorney, serving clients by day and writing epic fantasy by night. *For the Bloody Marquesa!* is his second published work in his series, *The Conflicts*. He plans for the first three books in the series to center around their own conflicts spanning across the same continent at the same in universe time. Where they will lead, he doesn't know yet, much like the march of real-world history. He is eager to find out though.

Visit Zachary T. Sellers' official Facebook page to keep up to date with all his latest news.

https://www.facebook.com/Zachary-T-Sellers-108414535096643

https://www.zacharytsellers.com/